THE **KINGDOMS** *of* **DAY**

FIRST OF THE HOLY HOUND TRILOGY

M.N.M. Abbott

ACKNOWLEGEMENTS

A special thanks to my family for being there even when they physically couldn't be. Thank you Granny Anne for being my first and biggest fan on this adventure. Every-one out there who read this before it was in print, (you know who you are) thank you for enjoying the story and helping me reach for the stars. In a small way all of you have helped me make this grand fantasy become a reality.

As for new readers, thank you for turning the page and I hope you see this to its end.

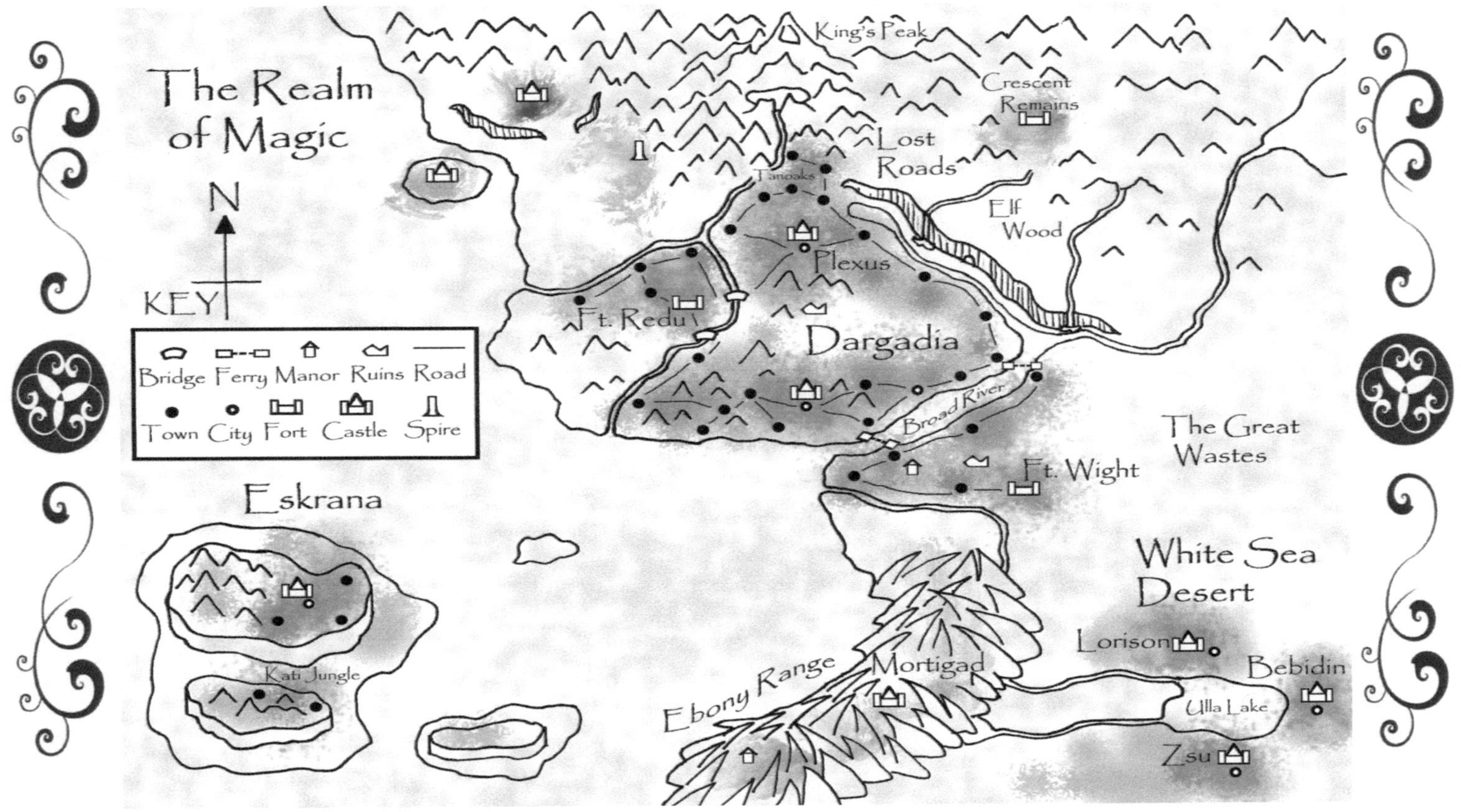

The Realm of Magic
N
KEY
Bridge Ferry Manor Ruins Road
Town City Fort Castle Spire
King's Peak
Crescent Remains
Lost Roads
Elf Wood
Tanoaks
Plexus
Ft. Redu
Dargadia
Broad River
Ft. Wight
The Great Wastes
White Sea Desert
Lorison
Bebidin
Ulla Lake
Zsu
Ebony Range
Mortigad
Eskrana
Kati Jungle

Chapter 1
REMINISCING ON THE RECENT

"Okay, question number seven." Pearl asked, "What's the other name for wolf's bane?"

Shari bit her lower lip, strumming four well-trimmed nails on the table. This was an easy question, but the answer wasn't coming to mind.

Red-haired Judy grew impatient. "Aw, come on! You have to know this."

Lacey's dark hair swung across her shoulder as she turned to shush her. "Let her figure it out. Of course she knows."

Pearl giggled and her feathery blond hair shuddered. Using their personal nickname for Shari, she coaxed her. "Come on, Adwen. Wolf's bane."

Puffing and sliding the spectacles up her nose, the shy brunette pondered. "Is it something like 'hood'? Oh! It's monk's hood!"

Marking down another point, Lacey smiled at Judy. "You know she's going to win this time. You're going to buy us all sodas again."

Judy was dismissive. "She has to get them all right."

Waiting for the next question, Shari smiled. It had been three years since first playing this game. Lacy, Judy and Pearl found her one day crying in library after escaping another bully. As a token for becoming their new friend, they nicknamed her Adwen.

There were twenty minutes left before the buzzer signaled the end of the lunch break. Countless books surrounded them. Like always, the librarian didn't seem to notice or care, busy stamping and organizing paperbacks and sturdy hardcovers.

It was Judy's turn to come up with a question on the topic of werewolves. Clearing her throat and crossing her arms, she rolled her eyes. "Okay. What are the symptoms of someone who has been bitten?"

Shari puffed. "That's easy. Heightened aggression, cravings for human flesh, paranoia, hallucinations, and insomnia and/or night terrors."

"Hah!" Judy laughed. "You forgot split personality!"

Pearl argued, "Not always!"

"She's right. Not all of them have bipolar attributes." Lacy marked down another point.

Shari shrugged innocently as Judy gave a sly smile.

"Last question."

"I'm ready. Show me what you've got."

After thinking it over with the others, Lacy smiled. "What makes werewolves different from shape shifters?"

This was a little tough, but Shari had read up on a lot of folklore and fiction. "First, shape shifters are found worldwide and in a variety of animal types. They can also take the actual shape, while werewolves keep the general form of a man with hands, arms, and torso. Also, shape shifters cannot make a human like them. Most are born with the abilities."

Pearl asked when she paused, "And? What's the biggest difference?"

She almost forgot. "Werewolves are cursed. Until the day they die, everything they love or strive for will be destroyed. They're doomed."

Judy sighed while Lacey and Pearl laughed and applauded. The vivacious redhead rolled her eyes, counting out change. "Does everyone want the usual?"

They nodded.

She was about to find the vending machine, but paused when Lacey asked Shari a question.

"So, Adwen, are you going to the sports banquet tomorrow night?"

Pretending to be calm as her stomach felt light, she answered, "Yeah. I kind of placed at district for the hundred meters. Why wouldn't I show up if I got something?"

Her friends exchanged glances, and Pearl hesitantly asked, "We know that. What we really want to know is who's taking you?"

Giving up, she grimaced. "My dad's taking me. He was my private coach after all."

Lacey and Pearl shook their heads and Judy snapped, clenching a fist around the quarters and dimes. "That's not the point! We know what's going to happen! You can't keep letting him ride you for not being what he expects and wants! You need to stand up to him!"

Shifting in her seat, she didn't want to talk about it anymore.

Judy fumed, stalking away to get the sodas.

The high school sports banquet began later the following evening. By the time the orange sunset died in the distance, everyone gathered in the cafeteria-turned-ceremonial hall. Boring tables students usually crowded around were lined up, disguised with red and gold tablecloths. Shari snuck a few fudge brownies from the spread and quietly devoured them beside her father, Nick, waiting among the rest of the athletes and proud family members.

Her father kept himself in relatively good shape. His black flattop and handlebar mustache convinced most that he was prior military. He was proud of what his daughter had accomplished, but it didn't change the fact of how this final season in varsity track had ended.

Shari checked to see if anyone were watching before sweeping the crumbs off her lap. All eyes and ears were turned to the podium. No one was a witness to her bad manners, and she was content to pretend to listen. At that moment, Eric Spade, the biggest bully in her graduating class, held up his M.V.P. trophy and basked in the applause.

She frowned.

Nick frowned as well, but clapped to acknowledge his skill.

When the head football coach gave his parting words and proceeded to pass the podium to the track team's head coach, Nick leaned over to whisper to his daughter. His tone was full of disappointment. "He doesn't deserve to hand out those awards. He only got the position because he has so much money. We had three years to show him what you could be. If you had taken first there wouldn't have been a question. Look at that smug fake."

A tight knot formed inside and climbed up her throat. If

she had only tried harder in practice and not let the preppy girls bother her, she could have taken first, rather than trail behind in third place.

The thickset balding man smiled while he gave out letters and medals for field event players. One of the first runners he awarded was his own son, who was the only reason he put in for the title of head coach. He hugged him, wept and had his picture taken, same as the rest.

After the long distance runners were given medals and letter awards, it came to Shari's event. Wiping his eyes with a napkin, the track coach cleared his throat and spoke into the podium microphone. "Now for the one-hundred meter dash. This girl came out of nowhere and surprised all of us. She started out at a seventeen flat and reached the thirteen second times in her first season. I'm very glad to be giving away another letter, and a bronze medal for varsity district hundred meters to Shari Gates."

Everyone clapped. Going to claim the tokens, she stood beside the coach, where he held out a hand for her to shake. Her mind was blank, but she made herself grasp it, remembering how he had always ignored her. He had only put Shari in for the race because the other girls had either pulled up lame or quit. Shari blinked and listened as he spoke again, weeping like an emotional mother.

"I'm so very proud of this girl. She really came through for this team." Handing her the letter and placing the medal around her neck, the coach prepared to put an arm around her as his wife stepped forward to get a picture.

She was instantly sickened. Refusing the embrace, she watched him and his wife become confused.

"Don't you want a picture?" the simple woman asked, holding up the camera.

Shari shook her head and politely replied, "No, thank you."

Whispers swept the onlookers and the girl departed to rejoin her father. Sitting beside him, she sighed and realized that her hands were shaking. A moment later the man returned to giving out awards. She alone denied his request for a photo.

Twenty minutes later, the ceremony ended and the attendees did their best to empty the tables covered in sweets.

Afterwards, Shari and her father were in the old worn-out Ford pickup. Headlights on high, they rolled away down the dark backcountry roads.

The beginning of the drive was quiet. Shari was thankful Nick was silent. When he did speak, she braced herself.

"I'm proud of you. You showed him how you felt without being disrespectful. It would have been much better to be wearing a gold medal when you did it, but I think we got the point across."

Not wanting to start an argument, Shari said nothing and studied the heavy bronze coin, depicting a winged shoe. At the final race of her high school year, she had been three yards behind the other two girls. Their finish was close, but there was no question that she had taken third. It felt so far out of reach.

His next question came from nowhere. "Are you still hanging around with those three weird girls?"

She turned her gaze to the window, watching silhouetted trees and mountains rushing past. Not prepared enough to form a lie, she sighed. "Yeah. I still read in the library with them."

There was a long pause before he shook his head. "You know you only get picked on because you hang out with them. You're as high or low as the people you surround yourself with. It's only a few days before you graduate, but things could have been so much better. Why do you spend time with them? Why do you stick with people who act like nobodies?"

Shari clenched the third place pendant tight. Keeping herself from bursting out was hard. Then she reminded herself that she didn't even know what to say. What could she say? No words came to mind so she shrugged, muttering, "I don't know. They're nice to me. They make me laugh."

"They dragged you down. Getting out of that group is going to be good for you. Make friends with winners."

"Like Eric Spade?" she asked without realizing she was going to speak. Her own response surprised her, and she listened as Nick became angry.

"You know what I'm talking about," he glowered warningly. "Surround yourself with people who are go-getters, people who can show you how to be proud and hold yourself well. Eric is a goon. Go for people who have confidence."

Lacey, Judy, and Pearl had been trying to give her those things ever since they first met. Holding tightly onto her medal, she stared out at the woods. Those three girls were her closest friends, and her father would never accept them as a substitute for respect.

Wednesday and Thursday went by quickly and without incident. There were hours of final test taking, seconds between classes, and minutes to spend in the library. She won the next game and was beaten the following day by Lacey. They joked through their questions involving ghosts and teased one another on the topic of zombies. The next category was going to be sea monsters.

Friday began like the others, bullies on the bus ride to school, and boredom in classes she had barely passed in the final exams. Everything was going smoothly, up until before lunch in gym class. Being that it was the last day of school for the two dozen senior students, their instructor chose to let them have a game of dodge ball.

It was not a secret that it was their favorite, like every generation before them. Several rubber balls were set along the half-court line, a whistle was blown, and the violent game commenced. Jocks and even a few scrawny nerds rushed forward in a hurry. Laughs and shouts quickly followed as an echo of nine rubbery pings rang in the broad gymnasium. Naturally, the nerds were small enough to avoid the majority of the attacks, and three players were already out on either team. More red spheres flew back and forth, forcing teens to duck or sidestep, spreading around.

Shari was terrible at throwing, but enjoyed the dodging aspect. In rare instances, she was lucky enough to catch one, returning a player to the game. She laughed and passed off the ball to a more able thrower, face split by a clever grin.

Partway through the class, the teacher went outside to speak with another instructor in private.

As it just so happened, Eric Spade was in this class. A fellow jock passed him a ball, and he noticed the teacher leaving. Then he spotted a prime target, attempting to hide near the sidelines. Kelsey Bellows was a rotund girl who lacked any talent for sports. Seeing this more vulnerable player, he watched the gym door close. Then he put all of his strength into the throw and sent the ball flying through the air like a rocket.

Everyone heard a loud ping and watched her fall. It had connected with her nose, which began to run with trails of red. The blood trickled down Kelsey's chin. She was stunned, eyes watering as she tried not to cry.

The players all froze and Eric laughed with his motley crew crowding around. "That was a good shot, wasn't it? Are you going to cry? You should work out more so you don't fall down so hard. You made us think there was an earthquake!"

Others were laughing and Eric's girlfriend chimed in with a cruel shot, "Oh, don't cry, fatty. You'll make yourself melt, and you'll be uglier!"

No one was making an attempt to stop them and Kelsey failed to hide a sob.

"Leave her alone!"

Everyone stopped to stare as Shari glared at Eric from near-by.

After a second of frowning angrily, the athletic bully laughed. He knew messing with the weird girl with glasses would be much more fun.

"Why? Do you have a problem, freak?" he spat, moving closer until their noses almost touched. "What's wrong, four-eyes? You don't think my jokes are funny?"

She didn't blink. Adrenalin flooded her body and there were no reproachful thoughts. Her sapphire eyes were welded to his as she coolly replied "I just thought you could use a little advice."

Eyebrows raised, he crowed mockingly. "Oh ho, what is it, freak?"

With a response formed, Shari prepared for the consequences.

"Don't you think it's dumb for an inbred redneck to pick on people with weight problems?"

Eric glared back as his friends chuckled and some laughed. His temper broke and he pushed the spectacled girl to the ground.

Shari felt no fear, even as he crouched low, about to beat her to a pulp. She stared defiantly, waiting for flying knuckles to crash into her cheek.

The gym door opened and the instructor returned. "Mister Spade!"

Instantly releasing his fellow student, he rolled his eyes and muttered swears.

"Eric Spade! Come with me! Right now!"

He didn't give Shari a second glance as he was ushered out of the gym.

Then Shari turned her attention to Kelsey, whose nose was still a bloody mess. She extending a hand to help her to her feet

"Are you okay?"

Along with everyone else, Kelsey was stunned. Nodding, she accepted the kind invitation.

"Come on," Shari gently murmured, guiding her past the hushed classmates.

Others moved aside to let them pass, gawking. Shari Gates was one of the most timid girls in school. None of them ever thought that she was capable of standing up to a varsity jock like Eric Spade.

After eating lunch alone, as usual, the teen followed her old routine and made for the school library. Past the withered librarian and her equally ancient stamp set, she strode between tall book cases to find her friends. They clapped and whooped excitedly, making her blush. They always beat her to their table, no matter how early she came in.

Face turning red from embarrassment, she sat among them, "What's going on?"

"Are you kidding?" Judy laughed. "It hasn't been an hour and everyone knows. You have the whole school buzzing!"

"You go, girl!" Pearl added and beamed.

Lacey smiled. "What are you so embarrassed for? You just stood up to Eric Spade! You should be proud of yourself."

"Yeah, well, I didn't really know what I was doing."

Judy chuckled. "That doesn't matter. You're a hero, Adwen!"

She smiled back, turning an even brighter shade of pink.

Lacey seemed intrigued and searched her eyes before asking, "What was it like? When you stepped out in the open and stood up to him, what did you feel?"

The others were silent and listened.

"I don't know," she began, recalling the moment. "When I saw him over her I couldn't help myself. I remembered what it was like. I just couldn't stand there and watch. I didn't care what happened to me so long as he stopped hurting her." Then she smiled and chuckled. "I guess I'd rather him beat me up than watch him treat her that way."

Pleased by the answer, her companions exchanged satisfied smiles.

Eager for a change of subject, she rubbed her hands together in anticipation. "So, how about those sea monsters, huh? I was up all night reading for this one."

Immediately, the mood at the table turned gloomy. Her friends were somber, and Pearl spoke first. "Not today. There's something else we need to talk about."

Forgetting the game completely, she was concerned. "What's wrong?"

Judy folded her arms. "This is the last time we're going to get to meet like this. Tomorrow is the graduation hike and the next day is your ceremony."

"We won't get to see very much of you after this."

Shari was somewhat abashed. "I'll come up to visit every chance I get! When the next school year starts, you'll be seeing a lot of me."

They looked doubtful and Lacey sighed. "We hope so."

Tired of letting the dreary mood hang any longer, Shari smiled toothily.

It was contagious and they were soon smiling as well.

Once everyone was feeling reassured, Pearl cleared her throat and announced, "We were thinking that we should discuss something a little more exciting. What are your plans for summer vacation?"

Puffing and rolling her eyes, she admitted, "I haven't a clue what I'm doing for vacation."

"Sure you do," Judy informed. "You're coming with us to the Lake of the Woods."

"Judy!" the other two exclaimed in unison.

"That was supposed to be a surprise," moaned Pearl.

Meanwhile, Shari was ecstatic, grinning and squealing at the thought. The seat could hardly contain her jubilation. "That place rocks! I can't wait! The last time I was there was years ago!"

Done giving the redhead a dirty look, Lacey tried to gather their friend's undivided attention. "Adwen? Hey, Adwen? There's one thing you need to do before we can let you go."

Calming down, she continued to smile. "What is it?"

"You have to stand up to your dad," Judy replied. "Eric should have been good practice. Tell him to stop harping on you for once."

The condition killed her high and she grimaced. "Seriously?"

Pearl was encouraging. "We know you can do it. At least try."

Judy was much more insistent and added, "Do more than try, Adwen. He's been blaming everyone else for your insecurity when the problem is him! Your own dad is the reason you're so afraid. The bullies were bad, but he didn't help much by feeding you so much bull crap."

"That's enough," Lacey snapped before turning to Shari. "She's right, you know. This has to happen."

Shari bit her lip, thinking of possibilities. "He is picking me up after school today. The thing is, you guys remember how he doesn't let a word in."

"We have all of the confidence in the world that you can do it," the dark haired girl reassured her. "We're behind you a hundred and fifty percent."

Shari fed off of their warm, encouraging looks. They could always help her feel stronger than she thought she was.

A loud buzzer sounded the end of lunch break and the girls gathered their bags. They left the maze of bookshelves, stuffed to the ends with knowledge and separated in the hall. She waved good-bye, and the trio returned the gesture. Shari dashed off to her next class and couldn't help but feel a sense of finality in the moment. Things were never going to be the same between them.

The last hours of school were trouble-free. She used what

remained of the classes to get ready for confronting her father. Unlike dealing with Eric Spade, making him mad would not do any good. Before she knew it, the school day was out, and she hadn't the faintest idea of what to say. Shari followed the rushing tide of students swiftly flooding out every door into the brilliant sunshine.

It was a beautiful day. Racing to their cars and buses, they passed Shari patiently waited on the curb. When the filthy white truck came around the bend, her stomach tightened.

Heart pounding, the girl pushed the pair of glasses farther up her nose. The half-rusted vehicle came to a smooth halt and she struggled to remain calm, climbing inside. Tossing her backpack behind the seat and closing the door, Shari buckled up while they rolled away.

Content to spend more time with his eldest child, Nick beamed and laughed. "How do you feel, High School Grad?"

Lost in thought, she managed to say, "Pretty good."

"So, how was your last day? Did anyone give you a hard time?"

"Not really," she lied, half ignoring him and thinking of how to begin.

Nick sensed she was being distant and reassured her happily, "That doesn't matter. You get to leave all of that behind. Forget the bullies -- and those three weird girls."

His last sentence lit a spark of anger. Beginning to fume, she clenched her jaw and glared out the window.

Nick went on, "Now that you're not going to be around those people, you --"

He was cut short by an outburst from his daughter. "Stop it!"

When he remained silent, her tone was harsh. "Just, stop it. Those are my friends. While everyone else was picking on me or pushing me aside, they stuck with me. They tried to help me be everything you keep saying I should be. I'm different, Dad. No matter who I hang out with, I'm always going to be treated differently. Stop talking about my friends like they're some kind of disease."

Her father wasn't sure of how to respond and kept driving.

They were nearly home and she added coldly, "You have no right to tell me who to hand around. I'm not spending time with druggies and drunks. My friends are good people. I'm eighteen years old. Who I call my friend is my choice, not yours."

Tongue-tied, he parked the truck under the crumbling car port. They got out together, maintaining a silence that lasted the rest of the afternoon and into the evening. Neither mentioned the ride home to the rest of the family.

Morning came, bringing a wash of warm colors from over the mountain tops. The light stretched into Shari's room an hour before her alarm clock sprang to life.

The annoying tones made the girl groan, roll over, and reach lazily for the source. Her hand missed its target on the first try. Forcing bleary eyes open, her blurred vision could just make out the object, beeping and blinking. This time, her fingers came down to hit the snooze button, restoring silence.

She stretched under the soft, fluffy covers, arguing with herself whether to get out of bed or not. Everything was so warm and cozy, but she groaned again, folding away the sheets. It was an hour and a half before the graduation hike and riverside picnic. With even more resistance, the girl found the will to sit up, collect her glasses and leave for the stairs.

Shari yawned, rubbing the sleep from her eyes. The television was on down below as someone was watching the news. As she put on her spectacles at the bottom of the steps, the recliner came into view, holding her depressed father. She paid him no mind and he didn't seem to notice. He was far too distracted by self-pity and the interview with a soldier in the Middle East.

"Staff Sergeant Alexander Greeves sustained only two injuries during his heroic actions and will also be awarded a Purple Heart in his awards ceremony tomorrow when he is presented with the Congressional Medal of Honor." The reporter smiled for the camera beside the photo of a stone-faced man with a clean blond crew cut. "This is Lisa Campbell, reporting on the war on terror."

The moment the woman finished, Nick began to channel surf.

With the distraction gone, finding a suitable breakfast was

much easier. It was Saturday, which meant her two younger siblings were still fast asleep. She served a hefty bowl of cereal and went to sit in the dining room, watching the backyard come to life. She munched away as daylight crossed the pinnacle of their home, touching many Japanese maples. Her mother had done well in turning their once-hideous yard into an earthy haven. She could hear the sounds made by Sarah using the shower. This reminded Shari she still needed to get dressed.

Returning to the kitchen wearing summer hiking clothes, Shari greeted her mother. Sarah was busy filling the now bookless backpack. She peered inside to find it mostly stuffed with snacks and a water bottle.

"You're on a roll, Mom."

Sarah had ice blue eyes and a smile as warm as summer. Her gaze was sharp and clever when she laughed. "Yes, I am, Miss D."

Not all of Shari's grades had been good. "What else will I need to take?"

"Nothing. That's about it."

"What about sunscreen?"

Reaching down into the depths of the pack, Sarah retrieved the bottle with the little girl and the dog tugging at her bathing suit.

Shari shrugged. "Okay, then I guess we can get going." With the pack closed and the car keys in hand, they were on the way out the door.

Sarah had not been fooled the night before. She knew Shari and her father had been in a conflict. She held the door and cleared her throat.

Shari gave a confused look in turn.

Nodding towards the living room and the recliner, she asked without words if she were going to say good-bye.

Nick continued to switch from show to show, ignorant of their looks.

Shaking her head and grimacing, Shari left the house.

The hiking trail was a twenty-minute drive away. Their course took them around another mountainside, following the roadways across rivers and creeks through many more valleys of green. No matter the time of year, deep emerald pines were everywhere, defying the hot and cold months.

Eventually they turned off onto a gravel road. Down the grade of dirt and rock, she saw the students congregating.

She shared a half-hug with Sarah inside the car. As the teen girl got out, Sarah called, "Hey, Shari?"

Ducking her head to see inside, she asked, "Yeah?"

A proud, beaming smile was on her face. "Be careful out there. I love you."

Shari laughed. "I love you too, Mom. I'll see you later."

After she closed the door with a dull thud, small rocks crunched under the tires of the shiny, clean sedan. Sarah pulled away, turned around and disappeared up the way she came.

Suddenly, a horribly familiar voice was behind the girl and she froze. "What's up, freak?" Eric sounded very disappointed, and when she faced him, his expression was the same.

With an equal level of displeasure, she frowned. "What do you want?"

Grimacing as if he had swallowed vinegar, the bully replied, "I wish you would find a hole and go die in it. Somebody put me in the same hiking team as you."

She ignored the shot. There were a lot of other students milling close by and she would have thought he would be less aggressive. "Okay," she grumbled and suddenly added without thinking, "More time with the inbred redneck."

When he was about to lunge there was a loud squealing that made him flinch.

Shari saw her chance to escape and swiftly disappeared into the crowd.

The students grumbled and swore while the megaphone was being adjusted. It whined and whooped until the instructor figured out how to work the settings and quickly apologized, "Sorry about that. These things always act up on me. Welcome to the graduation hike!"

With most of their attention, he continued, "Today we're going to celebrate the completion of your senior year. But we're not doing this in honor of the end of one thing, rather the beginning of another. Twelve years of school are behind you. What lies ahead is a future; a new adventure into the unknown. The world is at your fingertips, and that is what we're going to celebrate today. In a short while everyone will be put into groups and we'll set out down along the river.

"But first," he smiled and gestured for someone close by join him. "We have a very special guest acting as a chaperon. He graduated two years ago and has become an officer of the force. Please give a warm welcome to Police Officer Towers."

As soon as she glimpsed Jack through the throng, a fluttering feeling was in her chest. Shari had tried to talk to her old crush when he was a senior. He had in turn, rewarded her daring with a very cold rejection. Despite his cruelty, she couldn't help but find the strong young man attractive.

Jack Towers stood at a height of five feet and five inches. His strong face was youthful, and his mahogany eyes showed calculation. Even though his short hair was black, a small patch on the middle of his brow grew out white. He died it red to make the defect seem more interesting. Dressed in a casual collared shirt and slacks, the young officer rolled his eyes and waited for the man to finish his deep speech.

"Everyone," the instructor went on. "You are all about to embark on an amazing journey. Welcome to the rest of your lives, and good luck. Now come on over to the side. We've brought bottled water and let out the listings for teams."

Many had already seen who their traveling companions were and made way for those who hadn't. Jostling among them, Shari eventually reached the printed lists of names. The instant that she found her name, she saw Eric's as well. Groaning, her gaze went to the other names. A girl by the name of Ashley Alhouse was there. This girl was very quiet and from the popular crowd.

Not minding her in the team, she spotted the name of their leader. Her stomach did a flip and she clenched her teeth. Another jock was to be their chaperone; Jack Towers. Shari turned away to find her group, hoping that Ashley wouldn't add to her bully troubles.

Sweaty, irritable, and thirsty, Eric complained out loud. "It's too hot out here! Hey! When do you plan on stopping?"

"We'll be back in the shade soon," Jack grumbled for the fifth time.

The four continued up the rocky path. Shari was content to keep her eyes on the rushing river beyond the abrupt drop. Though she tried her best to admire the scenery, it was impossible not to glance at their guide from time to time. Eric caught her looking at least once, but didn't bother to remark.

They reached the trees and the way became shaded. Oaks, pines and beeches stood in close quarters, blocking the mountains and the riverside from view. Even though they were very high up, the earth leveled out into a peaceful, secluded clearing.

Rocks covered by blankets of fluffy moss surrounded a spring, where the water came up out of a fissure in a stone slab. It ran crystal clear from the thin crack like tears. Their chaperon admired the strong shade and the beauty of the place. "We can rest here."

"Finally," Eric huffed and found a stump to sit on.

Ashley knelt down to feel the water. Smiling, she laughed, "It's so cold. This is such a nice spot. I really wish I hadn't left my camera."

"You've got that right," Shari added with a grin. Without thinking, her gaze momentarily went to Jack, and swiftly to someplace else. He had seen her looking again and she began to loathe herself. She could still see him in the corner of her vision.

Shaking his head, he found his own seat and began rummaging through his bag of snacks and things.

Embarrassment made Shari anxious, and being near the men wasn't of much help. It was time for her own break and quietly left her things behind to wander into the forest off of the trail. Not sure if anyone would object, she glanced back and got a surprise.

Jack was taking a knee before Ashley, holding out a ring. Sunlight struck the diamond and it flashed like a star.

She realized now why he had made an appearance and smiled. It made her happy. Entertained, but still stressed and looking for relief, she went farther into the trees, searching for the ledge over the river.

Chapter 2
THE FALL

Shari stood on the edge of a vast canyon overlooking the river below. Warm sunlight shone on her fair skin, her bright blue eyes studying the opposing bank. Along the small sandy beach water lapped lazily. Heaving a sigh, the young girl brushed back wavy brown hair and let her gaze wander. It was the beginning of summer and weeds on the tree dotted slopes were turning gold.

The last few days of high school were exciting by her standards. With the fresh memories of jocks, parents, and the recent glimpse of a marriage proposal, Shari was completely distracted. The sights and sounds seemed to almost disappear.

Shari stood unaware at the edge of the cliff. Wind tossed her wavy hair and she never noticed the birds had gone quiet. Even if she were alert, she never would have heard the figure approaching through the trees.

A stalker approached the spectacled girl. Standing just behind, the figure loomed like a vindictive shadow, watching with fascination. She was completely unaware of his presence. Then a sadistic grin splayed across his face. Swiftly, he gave the small of her back a sharp push.

A sick feeling filled her when she found herself falling through the air. The girl screamed a bloodcurdling cry, plunging into the rough waters. She was poor at swimming and the merciless flow took her to a patch of rapids. Another frantic scream leaped from her throat before being drowned by white water. Under the surface she was flung about in flashes of light and dark. When she stole a gasp of air, her glasses were gone and she never saw two fishermen.

Nevertheless, they saw her fighting for her life and swiftly mounted a rescue. With the gear they wore, diving in would be no use. One pulled out a satellite phone, dialing for help, and the other followed with a long fishing net in hopes of reaching her.

She resurfaced long enough to see him trying to keep up. Her limbs were beginning to wear out and the current gained momentum. She started to cry and fight harder. Rainy Falls, a ten foot waterfall plunged to a depth of near thirty feet.

She could hear the roaring sounds. Too exhausted, it was all she could do to keep her head up. He was a few yards away when the girl screamed one last time before disappearing from sight.

The fall was quick and she sank into the dark depths. Instantly the water around her turned ice cold. Her mind began to work fast. She needed to find the bottom to push herself up for a breath.

Surprisingly, smooth rocks brushed past her toes. Without hesitation, she kicked off the riverbed. A few seconds later her head exploded through the surface and she gasped. All around was an icy river, though the girl was too tired and blinded to see.

Two figures on shore spotted her drifting amid the ice. Dashing over, they tried to call out, but she succumbed to the cold and went under.

One leapt in and dove down, resurfacing with her in his arms. He and his companion pulled her onto land, checking the frozen girl's vitals. She was alive, but would not last if she did not get warm.

Comforting warmth enveloped her where she lay. She thought she must be home as she rested in a large bed covered in blankets and furs. Late afternoon light spilled through a little window and bathed the table loaded with assorted herbs. Here and there were grinding tools while hanging from the ceiling were a rainbow of dried plants that filled the air with relaxing aromas.

Etchings and carved fittings gave the place a master craftsman's beauty. Cherry wood framed the one window and door. Intricate symbols flowed across wood like ivy, glistening with the glow of gold filigree by the light of the dying fire in the hearth.

The girl remained still as the door opened and a tall man

with long black hair entered. His lean frame and face were mostly hidden beneath a black cloak and hood. He had some kindling in the crook of his arm, and for a moment, he stopped to glance at her before turning to close the door.

At the sound of its being shut, she finally opened her eyes and froze. This was not her bed. Paralyzed by shock and without her glasses, she was just able to make out the man approaching the fire. Then, realizing she had been stripped bare, she was on the brink of panic. Terrified and embarrassed, the girl waited and observed the stranger who had revived the little flame.

He stayed knelt for a long while deep in thought. He was troubled. It was no accident that he had found the girl the other day. What troubled him was that something else was to come. It would be far less pleasant and the undetermined gnawed on the back of his mind like a dog on a bone. Foresight was his greatest gift, but he could not see everything. He knew he was to help her in special ways, but honed instincts told him the things he could not foretell were the ones to worry about. As he continued to brood, the sun outside steadily waned and the tangerine dusk turned the room a rich orange.

The girl was just beginning to relax when the door opened yet again and another man stepped inside. He was tall like the first, but lacked the elegant features and movements. His hair was short, curly and as dark brown as his curious eyes. In his thirties, he wore a puffy white undershirt complemented by a leather vest laced up the front with cord. About his waist wrapped a thick black belt to hold the trousers to his strong body. On his feet where calf-high leather boots that looked worn. Closing the door, he addressed the cloaked stranger in a cheery tone.

"My hunt went well. I've caught two more hares for the stew." He looked quizzical when there was no response. "You are always doing that. Why do you stare into nothing as if you might see something? Eh?" When still no answer came, he sighed. "Your deep thinking confuses me." Shaking his head, he turned to gaze at the girl.

The girl was on edge by how strange these men were and strongly considered the chance they were both insane.

"Healer! Our beautiful guest is finally awake."

She tried to sink deeper into the blankets in dismay.

The cloaked man's voice was smooth and clear as crystal. "I know, Hunter. She has been awake since I entered."

The girl's breath caught in her throat.

"Well then, if you don't mind, I'll be the first to welcome her." And the boisterous man strode across the room.

Sitting up, she quickly gripped a blanket close to her naked self and cringed.

He stopped a few feet short of the bedside, pulling over a stool to sit. Very encouraging, he continued to smile. "There is no need to fear, my lady."

Looking very doubtful, she said nothing.

"We're not going to harm you." She didn't reply or look any less frightened, and he became concerned. "Can't you speak, my sweet?"

The hooded stranger gracefully stood, sighing, "Let her be, Hunter. She can speak quite well. The problem lies in the fact that she does not know what to make of you." Turning and gently lowering his hood, he faced them. "Nor of me."

Her eyebrows raised in disbelief. Even without glasses, she could see the man's face was beautiful. Also, curving out from under his onyx black locks were elegantly pointed ears. Strong firelight emanated from behind, giving his form a regal aura.

Frowning in disappointment, the other replied, "I cannot see why she would fear me, but it is shocking for most to see your breed. Are not all of elf-kind gone from these lands?"

Astounded, the girl was convinced that both men were complete lunatics.

"Granted, Hunter, but you must take into account that she has found herself in a stranger's home and awoken with all of her garments missing."

Raising an eyebrow, he asked, "She's not been harmed, so why should she be this melancholy?"

It was time for the elf to raise an eyebrow. "That is a thing you cannot begin to understand. That is modesty."

The girl couldn't help but choke back a giggle. When both looked back again she swiftly took the look from her face.

The hunter smiled and apologized. "Oh, where are my manners? Allow me to introduce myself. My name is Regorian Lancer. As for my elf friend here, well, he's neglected to give me his name. I call him Healer."

And the "elf" took a smooth bow.

"Now, would you be so kind as to grace us with your name, young lady?"

She was going to say Shari, but blurted out, "Adwen." Her own reply surprised her. "My name is Adwen."

Regorian was pleased. Taking one of her hands to give it a little kiss, he cooed, "A perfect name for one such as you. It is mysterious and beautiful, just like those blue eyes of yours. You aren't a relation to the Princess Eyrie, by any chance?"

Nonplused, she stared. "Uh..."

The elf joined them, saying, "I think our Lady Adwen has had her fill of your flattery, Hunter."

He sighed. "Perhaps you're right." Standing to leave, he announced, "I shall return shortly with your meal, my lady."

The elf watched him go and turned to her when they were alone.

Adwen expected him to try and coax her into conversation. Surprisingly, he made no such attempt. He stood and examined her with his exotic eyes. They were a soft brown that seemed abnormally piercing. The last light of day faded until the only light came from the hearth.

At last he sat gracefully onto the stool. "I hope you can forgive Regorian's boldness with women. He is quite fearless."

Unsure of how to respond, she remained silent.

"It was he who saved your life. His lack of fear is why you are alive. You are safe within my walls. Can your eyes see the marks around my door?"

Nodding, she replied, "Yeah."

"No one with an evil heart may enter by that door. Every room in my house bears the same inscriptions. You are safe from the dangers outside."

Her prior thoughts of his insanity were only reinforced. Much calmer than before, she asked, "So, when can I go home?"

The elf studied her sweet, questioning face. "On the morrow we shall talk of how to get you home. For now you must make me a promise, Adwen."

Growing even more suspicious, she listened.

"Outside of my home is great danger. You must promise

not to leave without our company."

The request was too mysterious. She concluded that an escape was called for.

She nodded.

He knew she wasn't being honest. After peering into her mind a moment ago, the elf learned that she thought he was completely mad. There was nothing he could do so he gave a kind smile.

The door opened and the hunter reappeared with a steaming bowl. "Your stew is ready, my lady."

Getting to his feet, the elf gave the hunter the stool to set the serving on.

"I'm sure you'll enjoy it. I pride myself on my recipe for rabbit stew." Presenting a clean wooden spoon as well, he yawned loudly. "And now I bid you both good night." He bowed to Adwen. "My lady." He nodded to the elf. "Healer." Yawning even louder, he left to sleep in his own quarters.

"Peaceful dreams to you, Hunter," called the elf. Alone with her again, he looked into her bright blue eyes. If only she could know what he did, he thought. He respectfully bid her good night, "Peaceful dreams, and let the Light Spirits watch over you, Lady Adwen."

"Good night," she answered apprehensively.

The elf bowed and stepped back before silently turning to leave. He had lived to see the best of times and the very worst for this kingdom. Foresight wasn't needed to see that a new chapter in history had just begun.

Chapter 3
UNDER THE BLUE MOON

It didn't take long for Adwen's appetite to get the best of her hesitation. The stew was even better than Regorian claimed. In a few minutes the bowl was empty and she sat on the side of the bed with a sheet draped about her naked body. Stomach satisfied, the issue of insane captors needed attention.

"These guys are nuts," Adwen muttered aloud.

Her search for clothing was short. A set of garments and shoes lay by the foot of the bed. She put on the long, soft dress that smelled like flowers. The pair of light slippers were a surprisingly perfect fit. Now dressed, Adwen crept to the door and reached to open it, but thought twice and turned to the window. She quietly swung open the pane and gasped as an ice cold gust came through. After snapping it shut again, the sight of strong moonlight on snow made her stare. She was sure that it was supposed to be summertime.

Getting over the initial shock, she rushed to the bed and grabbed the warmest blanket from the pile. Armed against the frigid night, the girl climbed through and into the snowy scene. She closed the window tight to keep the cold from alerting the men of her escape.

White powder crunched pleasantly as she made her way through the trees. She had no idea where she was or where she was heading. Her toes were chilled while the blanket kept the rest of her comfortable. Ducking beneath low branches, she pulled the fur tighter, admiring the beautiful night.

Hours passed in the frigid night. Growing frustrated, she stopped to survey the land. "Where am I?"

As far as her bad eyes could see was dark forest and distant mountain tops. The lay of the land was very different from her home. A colossal mountain in the north stood taller than the rest and was very far away. Finally, she looked up at the full moon. Her eyes widened. It was full and glowing bright blue.

A small noise almost made her leaped out of her skin. Straining to make out faded shapes in the surroundings, her heart pounded. There was nothing. Now very wary, she continued, keeping alert to noises that were not her own.

Adwen wandered through the dense cover in search of an opening. As the forest became sparse, she found a snowy meadow. Glancing back again, she saw only trees and solid shadows on the snow. She didn't trust her bad eyes when they saw nothing out of the ordinary.

Pressing onward, there was movement amid the drifts. Unable to identify the thing, and in spite of fear, Adwen went nearer. Detail steadily became clear. An animal grazed on new green shoots buried beneath the frost. The creature was larger than a deer and as pale as the powder under its four cloven feet. Once she was a few feet away it raised its head and stared.

Jaw dropped, she gasped and a trail of steam followed her words. "No way."

Sprouting from the white creature's forehead was a single spiraling horn. Adwen thought she was either as insane as the men or trapped in a dream. Big glassy eyes watched intently as tears welled up in hers. That's when it slowly dawned on her that the men, the blue moon, and this animal were all very real. She dropped to her knees, overwhelmed.

The unicorn continued to observe, gingerly approaching. When she raised her head it bowed its long, slender neck to inspect her. Smiling weakly, she let the magical creature sniff her face. When a tear rolled down one cheek, the animal drew back with a start. She slowly stood and reached out to touch it.

The animal froze, and as she could almost feel the breath from the unicorn's nose, it bolted, vanishing into the forest like a ghost.

Then she heard the dreaded sounds. Behind her came the crunching of heavy footfalls. A low sound like thunder came and her body quivered as her eyes continued to water. She let out an unintentional whimper. Suddenly there was quiet. For that moment the silence was complete.

Swallowing hard, she mustered what little nerve was left to glance over one shoulder. Once she saw it, the breath became lodged in her throat a tear of terror rolled down and her stomach bottomed out.

The thing was darker than the shadows it had come from and possessed a grotesque, sinuous face. Its jaws were long, merciless, lipless, and full of evil fangs. Both eyes were lidless; nothing more than small red specks drilling into her meek form. The crimson head resembled bloody wolf skull. When the monster snorted, a cloud of steam shot through the air and its ragged tail flicked.

A fresh wave of horror washed over her as the werewolf seemed to grin with its lipless jaws. She sobbed, frightened to move. Then its mouth opened and out came an unearthly roar, shattering the fragile quiet like glass.

Adwen screamed. Control of her fear-wracked body returned and she ran into the thicket. Darting around bushes, she screamed again as she heard the beast's bulk snapping trees like toothpicks. Its heavy breaths were fuel for her fear as it continued to crash through the woods like a runaway bulldozer.

The werewolf lunged and she cried out but it only got a maw full of fur. As the thing flew by, she recovered and kept running for her life.

Once the abomination realized it had missed its prey, it ripped the blanket from his jaws. Tossing it aside angrily, the beast roared in frustration and resumed the chase.

Adwen did not know where to go and it did not matter. Her lungs burned. Thicker trees were up ahead and she made a beeline for them, hoping they would slow the creature down.

The werewolf was strong and her efforts made little difference. Its continued after her and pounded the trunks into splinters. The chase continued longer than she could endure. Her legs grew heavy. She put on another desperate spurt of speed and exploded through the brush into another clearing. Then she realized her fatal mistake too late. Without the cover of the forest the monster was free to pounce. She could hear it gaining.

At the far edge of the clearing, the elf suddenly dashed out with a glistening bow and arrow drawn. The young woman was running towards him with the monster just visible over her shoulder.

Roaring triumphantly, the beast leaped for the kill. Adwen screamed and the elf let his silver-tipped arrow fly.

He watched in horror as the two tumbled together into the snow. A gasp escaped him as a steamy cloud. Fearing the worst, he dashed toward their forms.

The thing had landed on top, crushing her. Straight away, he struggled to roll the carcass off. It took all of his strength to push aside. His arrow had struck it between the eyes which were now dark and empty like sickly caves. The creature was already reverting back to its more human shape.

There the girl lay face down in the snow illuminated by moonlight. He gently turned her so she could breathe while red began to stain the snow. When she was prone he found that he had acted too late. The monsters jaws left deep gouges across her collarbone and half way to her breast. The wound bled profusely while her head had been struck by a rock buried beneath the drifts.

A sick sensation filled his heart. He knew what to do for her now. Hurried and with conviction, he scooped her up and ran for the sanctuary.

Regorian searched high and low for Adwen. The elf had left earlier without a word. Thinking to check on the girl, he found her missing. Outside the entrance of the sanctuary, the hunter called the girl's name.

"Adwen! Adwen!" He waited for an answer and when none came he was ready to yell again.

The sight of someone bounding through the snow like a deer made him pause. When the figure was close moonlight revealed the elf carrying Adwen in his arms. He rushed past and inside.

The hunter started to follow, but noticed something. Light from the open threshold casted onto a dark spot on the snow. To his distress, it was thick red blood.

Regorian found them in Adwen's guest room with the elf knelt at her side holding a hand upon her chest. The bleeding was out of control, turning her skin pale. With his palm on the damaged flesh, the elf sang an ancient prayer.

The hunter couldn't take his eyes from the gouges. The wound was clearly from a werewolf. Hanging his head, he clenched his fists in frustration. "What a horrible thing to happen to such a sweet girl. She should not die in such a terrible manner."

Finishing the first step in the ritual, the elf moved on. He quickly cleaned the blood from his hand, retrieving a piece of neatly folded silk. On the smooth cloth rested a large silver oak leaf. Treating it with various powders, the healer stated firmly, "She shall not die."

Regorian gawked. "What?"

"The girl shall not die. She will endure."

The hunter frowned. Every woman bitten would fall into a fever and perish. The storytellers said a spell was cast at the first appearance of werewolves and the ones who cast it had foolishly thought it would slow their multiplying.

"Stop, Healer. There is no point in prolonging her suffering. The fever will take her if not the wound first. You know as well as I that no woman from this world can survive this."

The elf was almost done preparing the leaf. "There are two secrets that elude you. The first is that she is not from this world."

Regorian could not believe his ears. Then the hunter's surprise faded. If it were true and she could survive the fever, then that meant she was a monster.

Quietly, he pulled the razor-sharp hunting knife from his boot, raised it high to plunge it deep into her fading heart.

The instincts and reflexes of his host were too quick. The healer deftly caught the hasty hunter's wrist without dropping the fragile leaf. The elf glared back with wild, ageless eyes and coolly added, "The second secret is within her." With frightening ease, he disarmed Regorian and stuck the knife into the table. "She is not capable of being cursed. The evil of the werewolf cannot take her."

They glanced at the girl. Her face was very flushed from loss of blood. Holding his other hand over the shinning leaf and closing his eyes, he murmured again in his ancient language.

The hunter was confused. "Do you mean to say this girl is immune to the curse?"

The elf completed the blessing and slowly took his hand from the leaf. There was a single bead of his blood resting on the surface like a drop of dew. In dismay, Regorian watched as the elf overturned the leaf and let it fall.

Adwen was weak and briefly returned to consciousness in time to see the leaf land atop her injury. Then her eyes rolled back. She slipped away into a deep fevered sleep.

Regorian confronted the elf, outraged. "What have you done? Spells with blood! I thought you a healer, not a weaver of dark magic!"

The healer was patient. "You know very little of magic. Blood is the life essence of the living. To mutilate the flesh or take life from another are among the most evil of acts, but the willing sacrificing of one's own life to save an innocent is something different entirely. That is something beyond any magic."

They stared while she lay with the silver leaf upon her mutilated shoulder. Before their eyes the bleeding ceased. For a moment the wound flashed a silver sheen and began to mend until her fair skin was without blemish. It looked as if the damage had never been done, but she remained feverish with sweat across her brow.

Taking back the leaf, the elf examined it to find no smudge of blood or filth upon it. The elf seemed content and folded the mysterious token in the silk to stow it away.

Further astounded, the hunter could not believe his eyes. "How...how did you do it? How did you take away the mark? I thought it impossible for the bite of a werewolf to be healed. I have seen werewolves after they have been slain. The place where they've been bitten either becomes a scar or hardly heals at all."

Concocting more medicines, he replied, "That was not my doing. It was hers. I have only lent the strength she needed."

He stared at the wayward girl in awe. "So she is unchanged by the incident."

The elf glanced sidelong at Adwen. "In a manner."

"Well, is she or isn't she harmed?" he shouted angrily. "Speak more clearly and stop twisting your words, Elf. Now answer my question more thoroughly and be to the point! Is the girl changed or harmed?"

Shaking his head, his long black hair glistened in the light from the fire. "You are asking me to reveal a deep secret indeed." Watching her sleep, the elf thought that if it would keep Regorian from pulling out another knife, he needed to tell. He heaved a heavy sigh. "She is not harmed. If she is changed, that remains to be seen. I may only give the secrets I am allowed, so when I finish telling, please do not ask more of me."

After considering it, the hunter agreed. "Of course. Now explain."

"Evil things cannot change her heart or her soul. These two halves of who she is are not easily tainted or touched by darkness. No evil being or demon may touch Adwen's heart and survive. But the third part of Adwen's being is the part that could be susceptible to change: her body."

Turning back to her, he became worried. "She is a rarity; one of a kind. Adwen is not able to be cursed because a curse upon her turns to blessing. In an old, forgotten tongue there is a phrase for this occurrence: light out of dark. That is the name for what she is."

The hunter found he had little to say. He grew suspicious. "Elf, why did the girl sneak out into the night?"

He was confused by the question. The instant he saw into Regorian's eyes and sensed his thoughts, his own feelings bordered on outrage. "What are you trying to insinuate?"

Raising an eyebrow, he grimaced. "I got the distinct sense she thought we both were mad. I think I shall half-agree and say what she cannot; you must be completely mad."

His patience with the human was stressed. "What I say and what is can be compared after a whole day has passed. Tomorrow night's full moon shall shed light upon who is the fool."

"I stand by my previous statement, Healer. I can promise you something: if that girl turns when the moon rises, I shall perform my sworn duty."

The elf nearly lost his temper. "You know the codes embedded in the walls of this sanctuary! There shall be no taking of innocent life. You will be cast out and unable to ever return."

"That is, if she is innocent then. Good night, Healer." With a final glower, he slammed the door on the way out.

The elf took a deep breath to relax. He returned to making salves for pain and sleep. Adwen was healed, but the loss of blood was great. It would take time for her to regain strength. The small grinding tool ticked against the bottom of the cup as he mixed dried leaves into a powder and stole a glance at the blue moon.

The elf eventually ceased his grinding and shook his head. Everything was happening so quickly. It saddened him to see her half-dead in his home. His heart told more than any premonitions. It said her will to live would eventually be tested. What he wondered was, would she make it or break under the strain? He could not know for sure.

Chapter 4
A DREAM

The herbs were strong. Adwen's head spun like a lazy top. Powerful drugs made each movement awkward. When she did to open her eyes, everything was doubled. After a moment of struggling to tell up from down, she looked around once more. Everything was blurry, but the effects were slowly wearing off.

The fire smoldered in the darkened hearth. Night had come again and light from the full moon poured in through the closed window. It took a while for her to realize she was lying on the floor. Trying to focus made her head ache so she chose to crawl back into bed.

Climbing up made her world spin. She grasped the bed frame for support, clenching teeth, pausing until the dizziness subsided. The room came into focus, but something didn't feel right. Soon every detail was so visible that it was as if she had her glasses back. A small noise drew her attention to the door. It was cracked open and she focused on the dark space. Surprisingly, her sight pierced through the shadows and caught movement.

A small click reached her ears. Then at last she comprehended what was in front of her. Regorian was knelt low, aiming a mahogany crossbow directly at her.

She gasped and froze.

The weapon fired and the arrow hit her middle, passing through to strike into the wall.

Adwen fell backwards, reeling. Laying on the mattress, grabbing at the sting, her heart raced. Her hands shook feverishly while looking to see if she had been shot. There was blood on her palms and oozing from the hole. But that wasn't what terrified her most.

Both her hands were large, black, and armed with sharp claws. Adwen's mind flew into utter panic. And as the hunter reloaded, she reared up and screamed.

But the sound that came out was not a scream. An unearthly wail filled the air, terrifying her even more. Her movements were lightning quick as she scrambled away and dove through the window, shattering it to pieces. After taking a tumble in a snow drift she regained balance, bounding away.

Pain spiked with every move she made. On all fours, she bolted, glancing against trees as the drugs and panic confused her. Whenever she clipped the boughs and trunks she let out a painful yelp, but did not dare stop. She eventually began to trip and stumble until she crashed into a mound of powdery snow.

Panic was finally broken, but not her fright. Staggering in the frosty drift, she stood on all fours, breathing in rapid gasps. Glancing at her stomach where the pain was erupting, her terrified eyes followed the steady trickle of red.

Then she realized again that it wasn't her body and looked back to her hands. Terror swept over her and she tried to scream, but it came as another terrible sound. Out of breath, she hung her head and started to cry. It upset her more to hear animal whimpers instead of human sobs.

Massive clouds swept in. A sudden and powerful gust bowled her over and buried her with flurries. The blizzard came from nowhere quickly strangled the moonlight. With it gone, Adwen's form withered down into the snow. Her naked human skin was no longer shielded from the cold bite of the elements.

Adwen struggled to climb out of the drift. Pain made her cry out as she crawled from the deepening snow. Wind whipped about and she heard her own voice in the swirling air, but it still wasn't completely human. Sobbing and freezing, she fought to keep moving.

Slowly making her miserable way through the blizzard, step by step, she continued in hopes of finding somewhere to hide. Her pathetic, unclothed body resisted the winter. Eventually the frost numbed her pain.

Through the storm she could not see the slope ahead and tumbled far down. Colder than ever and growing weak, she found enough drive to forced herself up. Teeth chattered, limbs shivered uncontrollably. Then she spied something past the wind and snow. Smells of dust, straw, and a hundred other scents met her nose. Having grown up in the country she knew the smell of a barn.

Adwen tugged at the swinging door and squeezed through, closing out the wild weather. Involuntary shivers and shakes racked her as she felt her way around. The dark was blinding, but her ears caught the sounds of animals. Bumping into a rail, she reached out, found a horse blanket and didn't hesitate to wrap herself up.

She soon began to sway as she wandered and finally collapsed into a pile of straw. Not bothering to stand, she curled up with the blanket around her. Seconds passed and Adwen fell into a deep sleep while the last blizzard of winter howled throughout the night.

Chapter 5
A REALITY

The following morning was cloudless. Sunlight shone on the whitened landscape as two young boys in woolen coats trudged through the snow. The eldest opened the barn door revealing everything within. A gray stallion occupied the far corner stall, in the sty lay two pigs while a goat and several chickens nestled in the loose straw. Later they would collect the eggs and then try again to reach the high loft, which they had been told so many times not to visit. They didn't know why and curiosity drove them to misbehave.

The eldest barked out orders. "You get more straw for the pigs. I'm feeding the chickens and the horse."

"No! I took care of the pigs yesterday," the little boy protested. "It's your turn!"

Rolling his brown eyes, he sighed. "Fine. Do it today and I'll do all of the chores tomorrow."

A broad smile spread across his face as he immediately dashed for the tools.

The older followed to get the animal feed, smiling as he muttered, "What a gullible git."

Retrieving the pitchfork, the small child awkwardly carried it to the pile of loose straw. He didn't think twice about the horse blanket as he took aim with the pitchfork. Then he stopped, certain he had seen it move. When the blanket moved again something underneath growled.

Terrified, he dropped the handle and darting to the older boy tapping his shoulder anxiously.

The chickens clucked happily as the eldest was tossing feed. Annoyed by the rough poking, he snapped, "What do you want? You haven't finished your chore yet!"

The younger boy's face was blanched as he couldn't utter a word, pointing to the blanket.

Growing curious, the eldest followed to investigate.

They stood together, watching the blanket. It was simply lying on the straw. The eldest was about to clobber the younger, but finally heard the growl and almost jumped out of his boots. There was a stick on the ground, so he picked it up and inched closer to give a prod. Nothing happened, but when he poked harder they heard a girl's voice grumble, "Five more minutes, please."

They exchanged looks and the little boy took a fist-sized rock from his pocket, glancing to ask if he should use it.

Pleased that he was finally using his brain, the elder boy nodded.

Sizing up the talking blanket, the little boy lobbed it and struck Adwen on the back of the head.

She cried out, "Ah! Ouch!"

Frozen by shock, the two watched as a blue-eyed girl sat upright with the blanket wrapped around her and yelled, "Hey! What was that for?"

They screamed in unison and made a mad dash for the exit.

As they ran, she leapt after them, wrapped in the thick wool. In the blink of an eye, she cut off their only escape.

Skidding to a halt, the boys screamed again. They backed away in terror and their ankles caught on a stray rake, causing them to fall backward into the straw.

She stopped, still groggy and a little less irritated. Why were they so scared of her?

Trembling, the boys stared at her bright blue eyes.

"Please, miss, we're real sorry!" the older begged. "Don't eat us. We taste horrible."

Then the other whined and pointed. "Yes, I taste gross. Eat him!"

She gave a perplexed look.

The older froze with surprise and mounting wrath, slowly turning to echo, "Eat me? Why, you little..."

The little boy winced as he was about to be pounded, but Adwen spoke out, "Hold on a second!"

They screamed again and clung to each other, cringing.

She was taken aback. Her head still hurt, but the deathly fear in the boys made Adwen reevaluate the situation. Then again, she could not recall how she got to this place. Sighing, she stalked off and sat heavily on a bale of straw near the scavenging chickens. Adwen felt disoriented and hugged the blanket tighter vainly trying to remember.

The boys watched as she gazed at the ground. There was little doubt in their minds that this naked girl wasn't human, but she did not appear to be dangerous either.

Then the boys watched as their favorite hen went to inspect the stranger. It cooed loudly. Then they gasped when it suddenly jumped up and perched on her knee.

She turned to the ginger hen. It was so funny clucking to her. An amused smile curled her lips and she scratched its head. The bird clucked in appreciation and settled down, ruffling its feathers contentedly.

When she didn't harm the hen the boys got to their feet. The eldest was bolder and approached. With the door open, sunlight lit up Adwen's fair skin in a pleasant way. Now that she didn't seem so intimidating, he cleared his throat, thinking of what to say. Embarrassment washed over him that the girl was only wearing a blanket.

Adwen glanced over wondering if he would scream and run away if she uttered a word.

He went rigid at the blueness of her gaze. The color and brightness shocked him.

"Uh, what's your name, miss?"

She thought about the answer. Should she use Shari? It didn't feel right to use it now.

"I'm Adwen," she murmured, watching the smaller boy come to join them.

The older introduced himself. "My name's Collin."

His counterpart hid behind him and mumbled, "My name's Remy."

She gave a half-cocked smile. "Hello."

"Why are you here in our barn?"

Adwen was troubled. "Would you believe me if I said I don't know?"

Remy blurted out, "She's a werewolf!"

Collin panicked and quickly covered Remy's mouth, smiling in hopes she wouldn't take offence.

She raised an eyebrow. "I think someone has been watching too many movies."

"What are movies?"

She scoffed in amazement. "Wow. Look, I'm no were-wolf. There's no such thing."

Collin reassured her, "Of course they're real. I've seen one."

She rolled her eyes. "You probably saw something that only looked like a werewolf."

Her denial confused them, and they exchanged glances.

"What makes you so sure I'm a werewolf?"

Remy took the hand away from his mouth to be heard. "You were growling in your sleep!"

"Are you sure I wasn't snoring?"

"He's right. You were growling."

Giving up on the argument, she sighed. Suddenly, her stomach grumbled and they jumped. Exasperated, she groaned, "Aw, come on! I'm not a werewolf and I'm not going to eat anyone, all right?"

"Right, Miss Adwen." Collin gulped. Neither appeared convinced.

"Would you like to have some bread and cheese?"

Before she could reply, Collin steered him away to have a private word. The boys were very quiet, but her enhanced hearing caught the conversation. She thought they were simply poor at whispering.

"Are you dense? She wouldn't want to eat bread. She would want meat. Besides, we don't know if we can trust her yet."

"But she's nice and she is hungry. Clucky thinks she's nice, too."

Collin was losing patience. "Are you listening to me? She wouldn't want to eat our bread and cheese."

Then she interrupted them, "If it's not too much trouble, I would like some bread."

The little boy's face lit up with joy. "See, you don't know everything." He giggled and went racing out.

Irritated, the remaining boy shrugged. "Well, I better go and make sure he doesn't ruin the job, Miss Adwen." He gave a nod and ran after his overexcited companion.

She was left alone with the animals and troubled thoughts.

None of this was making sense. How did she get here? She huffed and stared up at the ceiling, mentally retracing her steps. The last clear memory she had was of eating rabbit stew. Next, she escaped out the window, but what had happened in the woods?

Leaning against the pig pen, tired and frustrated, she closed her eyes. Sunlight warmed her skin. Slowly, a memory formed. Regorian was looking at her through a gap in the doorway with a crossbow. He pulled the trigger, she felt the arrow hit, and she snapped her thoughts back to the present. It seemed so real. Could it have been? If it were real, then there would still be a wound on her body.

Fearing the worst, she looked at where she recalled the arrow running through. There was nothing. Not a mark could be seen so she covered up again and let out a sigh of relief. It was a just a dream. She scorned herself for ever thinking it could have been real. Never the less, it being a dream still didn't explain this situation.

Collin and Remy came striding back with a clay cup and a bundle of bread and cheese. Smiling, Remy happily handed over the drink, looking proud of his resourcefulness.

"Thank you! Thank you very much!"

He beamed when Adwen downed the water. Then she gladly exchanged the pottery for the bread. She bit into the loaf to find it was fresh and swallowed before quickly taking another bite.

They watched her eat it all, forgetting the crumbs that fell. The hen was glad to gobble them up as they tumbled down.

Just when she was about to devour the cheese, Collin asked, "Miss Adwen, where did you come from?"

She paused to say, "Not from here, I can tell you that much. I'm from a place really far away where it's summer already." The cheese was all that remained and it tasted dry and sweet.

"Right, but where before here?"

She had a mouth full at the moment, but gulped it down, giving a troubled look. "I've been trying to remember, but I just can't. All I can remember are dreams."

"What did you dream of?"

An image of a red-skulled monster flashed before her eyes

and she turned a little pale. Suddenly she wasn't so hungry and put the cheese aside. Studying the boys closely, she muttered, "I don't really know. One dream was of something out in the woods. The other..." She trailed off, unable to finish. Maybe it did happen? Adwen shook her head to empty her mind of monsters and crazed hunters.

"You can stay here tonight if you want!" Remy crowed.

The others looked at him.

"When the moon comes we can come and play!"

Collin's gaze shifted to Adwen for her reaction.

Wearing a frown, she shook her head. "Nothing will happen when the moon comes up. You need to stay in your room and get some sleep. I wouldn't want you to get in trouble with your parents because of me."

Then Collin looked troubled. "My parents passed away last winter. I'm living with my cousin Remy and Uncle Domus. He's the head of the whole village."

She was instantly apologetic. "I'm sorry!"

He appreciated her sympathy. "No, I'm fine now. Uncle Domus takes good care of us and the maid, Miss Cottonpot."

A fresh smile found its way back to her face. They were so kind, and best of all, they didn't seem scared anymore. "The food was delicious, thank you. And next time, could you try to bring something for me to wear, please?"

Remy giggled uncontrollably.

"We'll bring the stuff tonight when we come see you," Collin chuckled. He saw her become disappointed and quickly added, "We wouldn't get in trouble, honest!"

She shook her head. "Nothing is going to happen when the moon comes up you know."

He smiled and admired the pretty blue of her eyes. "We'll see." Turning to Remy, he commanded, "Come on, you. We still need to finish the chores."

They went about their business and she visited the other animals. The goat followed her begging for the lump of leftover cheese while Remy moved straw to the pig pen. She eventually joined Collin in feeding the horse.

The beast poked his head out and gave a little whinny, raptly staring at Adwen. He was strong, ash gray and unbelievably dirty. It seemed as if his coat had been bathed in soot. She let him smell her hand and his whiskers tickled her palm.

"His name is Auburn," announced her small guide. "My Uncle Domus says he used to be a very powerful creature from legends. I don't know if he's telling stories, but no matter what, he's always covered in soot." He gave Auburn's neck a hardy pat and a cloud exploded into his face. Rapidly fanning the air, he coughed and sputtered.

The boy's antics cheered her up and she giggled.

Once the tasks were finished, it was time to leave.

Collin gave a warning before they departed. "It would be safer to stay in the barn, Miss Adwen."

"Why?"

Remy answered for him. "The woar dogs that protect the village from monsters might try to hurt you. They don't like strangers."

She greatly appreciated the warning. "Don't worry about me. I don't want any trouble."

"Well, we'll see you after moonrise then."

With another grimace, she huffed, "I guess I will."

Again, they left her alone and closed the door. Still tired, she returned to the mountain of straw for rest, and hopefully, much more pleasant dreams.

Adwen had a quiet sleep, even though the hen had taken a liking to her. The friendly bird chose to bed down beside her. When the girl awoke, the sun had almost set, splashing a vivid splay of colors onto the sky.

Bleary eyed, she went to close the shutter window and was in awe of the incredible sunset. A seemingly endless spread of gold and orange scrolled across the clouds, casting the earth in a fiery glow. A long moment passed and the last light became evanescent on the horizon until darkness was complete. With nothing left to see, she closed the shutters for the night.

It was probably going to be chilly, she thought, retrieving the hen to return her to where the others roosted. Setting down the small bird, Adwen found her way back to the bales to wait for the boys.

Minutes went by and her mind wandered. She missed home. She missed her mother and siblings, but was still frustrated with her father. Then she decided maybe she missed him, too. Along with her family, she missed the warmth of summer.

Missing home was someone's fault. She was sure the one who pushed her had been Eric Spade. This was all his doing. No longer groggy, she fumed at the nerve of the bully. She could have drowned. Everyone knew he was a jerk, but even she hadn't thought he was capable of murder. The fervent venting seemed to give her a splitting headache.

Hot sweat beaded and pressure in her head steadily worsened. Before long she could hear her heartbeat in her ears. Confused and afraid, eyes watered while she cradled her throbbing head, begging it to stop. She lay down on the bale, whimpering from the ever-building pressure under her skin.

When Adwen opened her eyes again they were no longer blue. They glowed violet in the dark like lantern flames. Her sight penetrated the shadows in absolute detail. How could she see through the dark so well?

That was the final thought that crossed her mind before the pressure piqued, and it felt like her heart might burst. The real agony began.

A gasp dragged out of her as a searing sensation shot up her spine, causing her whole body to arch back involuntarily. She cried out at even more pain while her spine crunched. Then the rest of her anatomy began to grind and shift. She screamed and her voice mingled with a feral animal cry. Horrified, miserable wailing continued as her skull, hands and legs crackled, expanded, and elongated. Skin blackened and bristled as a dark wave swept across her. Brown hair on her head darkened and shortened to match the rest of the black coat.

The strain caused Adwen to tumble from the bale onto the floor. It held her in a paralysis as muscles grew, molded, and hardened. Every breath was ragged and shallow from the intense pain as ribs split and stretched. It felt as if she were exploding in slow motion. Eventually, the torturous sensations faded, but the pain held her still and quivering for what felt like forever.

Then everything abruptly ceased and she slackened and slumped. Vast new lungs drew a deep breath and exhaled, making dust and bits of straw fly. Adwen's mind was numb from the shock. Cool air was soothing and shaky breaths were the only sounds in the dark. After a few minutes she got the courage to open her eyes. Her mind became more lucid and she hesitantly tried to move.

Sidling over to sit against the bales, she was terrified, but had to know what had happened. She bravely looked down and the sight slowly dawned on her pain battered mind, making violet eyes dilate. Her hands had become large, covered in black fur, and armed with large claws. The same fur was everywhere else and her chest had flattened and become broad. Both feet were stretched into four-toed paws, while ankles served as secondary knees. Lastly, she saw something long and dark move. Once she realized it was a tail, she couldn't bear to look any longer. Shaking, she started to cry, but could not sob. After letting out a few whines, she heard someone call out.

A masculine voice asked, "Why do you cry?"

Startled, she scrambled onto all fours, scanning the barn frantically. There was no one except her and the animals, but she knew someone had spoken. When she tried to reply a low growl escaped her throat.

The sooty horse leaned out of the stall to neigh. As he spoke again, she was stunned.

"Do not bother trying to speak like a human. The body you have isn't made for that." His chuckle was a funny neigh and a snort.

Adwen allowed her new vocal cords to work the way they could best. Frightened, she asked, "Are you talking to me?"

Auburn tossed his mane. "You're speaking back, aren't you?"

She whined in reply, "I guess so."

"So why do you cry, little one?"

She looked up balefully. "I've become a monster."

He gave a hearty laugh, tossing his mane. "Don't be silly! Of course you're no monster."

"What's the difference?" she growled.

The horse stared and snorted, "There is a big difference, indeed. For one, you look nothing like a monster."

"But look at me. I'm a werewolf!"

"No." He stomped.

She flinched in surprise.

"You couldn't possibly be that. Those despicable abominations have a red face and burning lights for eyes. No, you are anything but a werewolf, young one."

She puffed and sat, looking sullen. "What am I, then?"

"You are obviously not human, but you are no monster." The sooty horse thought to himself for a moment. She looked back hopefully and he nickered. "I would have to say you are something new. You shall have to learn and understand what you've become for yourself."

Thoroughly disappointed, she could hardly call that an answer.

Then Adwen and Auburn's ears perked at noises from outside.

"Looks like you have visitors."

"No, not now," she whined, getting up and backing closer to the stall.

"What's the matter?"

Head down low, she whimpered, "I don't want anyone seeing me like this! Tell them to go away."

"Sure I could, if I could speak a word of human."

Whining and whimpering, she hid behind the bales. Her tail tucked as she hoped they would leave. Ears low, she peered over the straw to see the door ease open.

Two pairs of wandering eyes appeared with a lantern bobbing over their heads. The boys inched inside and Collin held the lantern as Remy carried a satchel. They stood in the pool of light, scanning the shadows for their strange visitor.

"Miss Adwen?" Remy called, "Are you there?"

When she didn't answer, his cousin steered him to the door.

Auburn suddenly whinnied, "She's over here!"

The hair on the back of her neck bristled in dismay. "What, are you crazy?" Then she saw Remy running towards them and growled indignantly at the stallion.

The beast of burden cocked his head, amused.

Both boys came running and stopped cold when the light splashed over her pitch-black body. It dazzled her momentarily while they gasped. She blinked until her sight adjusted and they continued to ogle.

Remy slowly approached.

Head and ears low, she backed away until meeting the barn wall. Her tail wrapped around her leg and the little boy kept inching closer.

Collin reached to stop him, but he shrugged him off. Setting the satchel aside.

She flattened to the ground, trying to disappear and the little boy joined her. She whined, "Please, just go away. Please go."

All he heard was hound whimpers. He couldn't understand and reached out to stroke her shaggy coat. "It is all right, Miss Adwen. I'm not going to hurt you."

She whined again, "Please, go away."

The little boy wasn't going to stop. Distressed and ashamed, she yelled at him. "Just go away!" The outburst came as a vicious bark and a snarl.

Collin quickly snatched up his cousin. Horrified, they recoiled.

She was surprised as well and completely mortified at what she had done.

"Don't go near her," Collin warned. "She's a wild animal."

It felt like she had been shot. She stared wide eyed and whimpered, "I didn't mean to. I mean..."

They continued their cautious retreat with the lantern in hand.

The situation was too much and she couldn't bear to stay any longer. She cried loudly and darted past, heading for the window.

Remy broke from his cousin's grip, rushing after her. "Wait, Miss Adwen, wait!"

"No, Remy. Let her go!"

Nosing the shutters open, she was prepared to leap through when he caught up. The little boy latched a hug around her thigh and wouldn't let go. She remained leaning over the sill, frozen while his arms squeezed tight.

He buried his face into her fur. "Please stay, Miss Adwen."

She was too confused and ashamed to face him.

"Please, Miss Adwen. I'm not scared."

The words caught her attention and she turned her muzzle

to glance with one big, mournful violet eye.

His face was undeniably sweet. "Please stay."

Quickly averting her gaze, she stared out the window.

"I want to be your friend," he sniffled.

Adwen whined to herself. She didn't want to stay, but he was so accepting that she simply couldn't leave yet. Letting out a huff, she dropped down, sulking.

Without warning, he hugged her around the neck, catching her throat hard and making her choke.

He let go and giggled. "Come on, Miss Adwen. We brought presents!" Dashing back to the satchel, the little boy sat in the straw. Hesitantly, she made her way over to lie on the dusty floorboards beside the fearless little boy.

Collin kept his distance, unsure what to think of the situation. When he saw the huge animal -- who was somehow the girl from before -- settle by his cousin he began to relax. Remy was rummaging for something as Collin joined them at last.

Still maintaining a short distance between himself and the creature, he studied her. Not nearly as large as a werewolf, and quite unlike them, she possessed the face of a lean, black dog. Her eyes were a wild shade of violet and her fur coat wasn't ragged or mangy. It looked well-groomed and parts glistened in the lantern's glow. Her body, much like a werewolf, had retained a very human shape. She was lean and showed little to hint that she was a girl during the daytime.

Adwen looked over and he froze. She had felt his gaze and dipped her ears in a timid expression. While Collin did his best to smile, she let the corners of her own mouth pull back a little, worried her toothy maw might frighten them.

Eventually Remy found what he was searching for and pulled out a ratty piece of parchment. Holding it up, he brandished a doodle done by a child's hand, depicting a girl with a chicken in her arms. "There you are. And there's Clucky."

She was amused.

He started laughing. Then Collin let out a giggle and she looked between them, wondering what was so funny.

Remy laughed, "She likes it! Look! Her tail's waging!"

Sure enough, her long bushy tail was flopping as she lay on her side. The older cousin smiled while she looked back at herself in astonishment. The disobedient tail continued to flop, embarrassing her further.

While she was distracted, Remy gave her fluffy neck another big hug and proceeded to climb onto her back. Once he was aboard, she turned to look at the excited child.

"Can we go for a ride, Miss Adwen?"

She tossed Collin an exasperated look, hoping he might remove his cousin. He merely watched so she chose to take matters into her own hands.

"All right, kid. Here's your ride." Getting up on all fours, her rider laughed. Then she approached the pile of straw. Remy was unprepared as her front end dropped and he was dumped headlong into the mound.

He reappeared with bits all over and protested, "Hey! What was that for?"

Colin laughed while he clambered out of the mess. Then both boys raced to the satchel. Collin picked it up first and held it out of reach while Remy squealed, "I want to give it to her!"

"I picked it out so I get to give it to her." When the small boy fell quiet, Collin pulled out a leather collar with a metal latch.

Adwen was apprehensive, hoping he would not try to make her a pet.

He smiled and explained, "This collar used to belong to a dog I had. She saved me from a monster once when I was still with my parents. She was very special, but I think you should have it. Hopefully it will bring you luck."

The gesture was a comfort and she lowered her head to receive the token.

After a few seconds it was clasped shut and he stepped back to admire it on her.

It felt uncomfortable so she shook her head until it sat just right.

"She's a pretty thing, isn't she?"

Collin nodded and agreed, "Yes."

If she were in her human form she would have gone red in the face.

Remy yawned, rubbing his eyes, and Collin noticed. "Well, we best be leaving now."

The little boy handed over the satchel and Collin pulled out a dress. It was light blue and looked like a close enough fit for her smaller figure.

"It used to be my mother's," Remy explained, "but you need it more than she does."

Collin neatly laid the dress out on a bale and smoothed the wrinkles the best he could. Gathering their things, they said their goodnights.

In response, she waged her tail and cocked her head. "Good night, boys."

The barn door finally closed and Auburn snorted, "They are good children, aren't they?"

"Yeah." Then she panted, "That's straight from the horse's mouth."

He snorted, "I can't help but think you've made another jest."

"You'd be right," she grumbled as she settled in the straw for more rest.

"Do you still think yourself a monster?"

Her ears drooped. "I don't know."

The horse thrashed his mane and bits of ash fell. "Well, it shall always be your decision."

Many fears were quelled for the time being. Prior beliefs of magic were gone along with her hopes of a normal summer vacation. Her tail curled in distress. For now there was only one way to escape this world. She would return to sleep.

Chapter 6
AN HONEST MEAL

A chill permeated the air while mist hung low across the crisp open field. Just as the sun peeked over the tops of the leafless trees, Adwen began to rouse. At first she opened her eyes lazily, but then quickly sat up to see if she were normal. Her heart leapt with excitement at the sight of her human body. For the first time, she wasn't unsettled by being completely bare. She wasted no time in putting on the dress.

There was a snort and the horse stuck his head out, looking at the young girl in her new garments. She turned about, admiring the gown. Smiling, she asked, "Well, what do you think?"

He whinnied and shook his mane.

"Well, I think it looks all right." While clothing herself she removed the collar and left it lying on the bales. She didn't need it now that she was human again. Finished admiring the outfit, she greeted the horse.

Preoccupied with petting the filthy stallion, she allowed her mind to wander. No more memories surfaced like before, but thoughts of home were strong. How far had she gone? Just as she wondered when the boys might come, the barn doors opened. The suddenness made her jump. Adwen latched onto the horse's muzzle, arms wrapped around him, frozen on the spot as a large man entered.

A strong, middle-aged man strolled in wearing a thick jacket and scarf. Her improved sight discerned his black hair, thick jaw, and clean-shaven face. His sharp brown eyes were complacent, settled upon the sty as he toted a bucket full of smelly slop. Casually dumping the contents in the trough, he listened to the hogs snort, gobbling it down.

He set the bucket aside to pat one and the rail groaned under his weight. After a while of watching them feed, he felt a pair of eyes on him. Soon he spied a young girl, anxiously hugging Auburn's head. He had suspected the other day that his boys were hiding something in the barn, but he wasn't expecting to find a woman.

She wet her lips and squeezed the horse tighter.

An amused look came over him and he left the pigs to investigate. With every step he took, her expression of fear grew until her eyes were wide as saucers. Once he was close enough, he noticed their blue color and restrained a gasp. Captivated, he greeted her with his deep, gentle voice. "Good morning, young lady."

She was anxious and caught off guard, but forced out a reply. "Good morning."

"What are you doing in my barn?"

Reminding herself that lying was not one of her talents, she chose to stick to half-truths. "I needed a place to stay."

Taken aback, he replied, "Well, this barn is hardly a place to stay the night. You could catch your death of cold in here."

She shifted a little. By now Adwen was aware that her body was impervious to freezing temperatures. A small breeze brought the man's scent under her sensitive nose and she realized this must be Remy's father. Then she remembered she was wearing Remy's mother's dress and struggled to remain calm.

"I didn't want to bother you."

"That's hardly a reason to stay in a cold barn," he scoffed. "Why don't you come to the house and warm yourself?"

She hesitated.

In response, Auburn pulled himself from her grip and nosed her forward roughly, nearly knocking her to the ground. She stumbled until she was before the big man.

Embarrassed, she turned and gave the horse a dirty look.

Domus smiled. The animal usually didn't take a liking to strangers.

As Domus watched with growing curiosity, she faced him and gave a shy answer, "I guess I'll go inside."

As they crossed the snowy field the mist dissipated. Crunching along toward the lodging, Domus couldn't help but see the girl didn't have any shoes. This roused his suspicions and he began to wonder why the boys had not brought her to the house. He stole a glance to see if the cold were bothering her, but she didn't seem the least bit hindered. More suspicious than before, he asked, "Whatever became of your shoes?"

She was aware that he was on to her. It was expected. "I lost them while I was in the woods."

He arched an eyebrow. "The woods are dangerous. What were you doing there?"

In a matter-of-fact way, she answered, "I was running away from two men and I got lost in the snow."

The answer seemed valid, but that would mean she had gone through the blizzard. This girl didn't look prepared for a trek through a storm. A smile parted his lips. "Then you must be the luckiest young lady I've ever met."

She gave a smile of her own. "Thanks." The suspicious look he wore did nothing to put her at ease. They continued up the porch and into the cozy cabin.

Inside was well kept. When the door closed her nose picked up the scent of a strange woman. She could only assume it was the housekeeper the boys mentioned.

Domus pulled out a chair from the oak table. "Sit. Make yourself at home."

Wary, she took the offer. "Thank you."

He left to hang his coat. "My maid, Miss Cottonpot, shall be down shortly. I'll have her make some breakfast. What do you like?"

She shook her head. "I'm not picky. I'll have anything."

While the girl waited, her host pondered on how to uproot her secrets. Auburn seemed approving, but he was not truly convinced of her honesty. The cold snow hadn't bothered her so she was not completely human. Was she a winter nymph of some sort or perhaps a spirit? He couldn't tell from looking, but he had ways of finding out.

A weathered woman silently crept into the room.

Domus gave the maid a warm welcome, "Good morning, Miss Cottonpot. We have a guest."

The thin, haggard woman with the temperament of an old goat replied with a grouchy, dismissive, "Eh." Then without being asked, went about cooking breakfast.

Adwen restrained a chortle, finding the maid's attitude

entertaining.

Eggs and ham sizzled and crackling over the fire. When the maid reached for a plate and utensils Domus stopped her and she tossed a stern glare.

He looked over to be sure the girl wasn't watching and passed a different set.

The plate was made of fine porcelain with flowing etchings around the edge, complete with matching silverware. Her expression became questioning as she looked between him and the girl.

He reassured her with a nod and she accepted the items.

Their odd guest was unaware that these things were enchanted. Wicked people who ate from the plate would taste refuse or rotten things. But a good person would greatly enjoy the meal . The fork and spoon were made from pure silver, and when the holder told a lie, they would leap from their hand. Miss Cottonpot had seen Domus use this set before. As the maid served breakfast, he seated himself across from the girl. Then the maid returned to cooking.

Adwen couldn't help but sense some tension, but nodded and was gracious. "Thank you very much." Looking more closely at the set before her, she stared. She could tell that the utensils were silver. If she were burned, she would be exposed as monster. But what if they didn't burn her, she wondered?

Domus watched her gaze at the silverware.

There was little time to stall. Bravely, she picked up the silver spoon and braced for a burn. Nothing happened. The silver didn't harm her. There was a great feeling of relief while the man continued to observe and Miss Cottonpot listened as she cooked.

To cover up the odd hesitation, she pretended to examine the utensil. "This is beautiful silverware. Where did you get it?"

"They've been in my family for generations. I'm glad you like them."

Feeling more confident, she picked up the fork and decided to try some eggs.

Miss Cottonpot heard the sound of metal touching porcelain and paused. Domus kept his appearance relaxed.

She was starving. The only thing she had eaten in the last

day was some bread and cheese. When the eggs touched her tongue her eyes widened.

Domus smiled and the maid waited anxiously.

"These have to be the best eggs I've ever tasted in my whole life." Then she proceeded to dig in.

Relief swept over the old woman and the man was glad to know what kind of stranger he had in his home. Judging from how the girl feasted, she was an exceptionally sweet soul. Now was the time to test her honesty.

She scooped up more eggs and savored the taste before wolfing them down.

"To properly introduce myself, I am Domus Aralias Falkner. What is your name, young lady?"

While holding the spoon and fork, she swallowed and replied, "My name's Adwen." She took another mouthful of the eggs.

"Are you from around here?"

"No, I'm not. I'm actually pretty lost." She gave an embarrassed laugh. The spoon and fork remained in her grip.

Then Domus thought of a good question. The dress she had on seemed familiar. If he weren't mistaken, it once belonged to his wife. He rubbed his chin with a finger before asking, "That dress you're wearing, it's very pretty on you. Where did you get it?"

"It was a gift." The silverware stayed in her hands.

"How kind of them." He raised a curious eyebrow. "From whom, if I may ask?"

She blurted out, "My mom." As the words left her, the fork and spoon flew out of her grasp and landed on either side of the plate. Blinking and confounded by the incident, she thought she had been strangely clumsy.

Domus smiled. The boys must have given the dress to her. He didn't mind. It suited her rather well and Miss Cottonpot was certainly not going to be wearing it.

Still hungry, she picked up the fork and continued to feast.

"Where is your home?"

Swallowing again, she replied, "I doubt you've heard of where I'm from. It's a little town and things are very different there."

"Really? How did you get to be here then?"

"The river." She was so distracted by the meal that she failed to see the growing look of curiosity on his face.

"Then you are from a town up the river?"

"Yes," she said and the fork jumped from her hand again.

No one traveled by river this time of year. That was far too dangerous. This town was the last along the west mountain river before the sea. This was a very strange girl.

Adwen studied her hand, wondered if it were something she had done. She was now thoroughly suspicious and began to pay closer attention.

Domus decided to take a direct approach. "Have you ever met my two boys?"

Just as she picked up the fork and spoon she answered, "No."

The silverware leaped for a third time.

She froze and her face slackened. As the two locked eyes, she saw his clever grin and knew what was happening. This wasn't a breakfast; this was an interrogation. Silent and cautious, she picked up the fork and spoon, waiting for his next question.

He thought his lovely guest must be very daring to pick up the silverware knowing they were telltales to her lies. "Young lady, are you dangerous?"

Staring back with determination in her voice, she muttered, "Sometimes."

The answer concerned him. "Would you ever harm anyone?"

The question struck a nerve and she was insulted. She grimaced and pushed the plate away. "No." The silverware stayed obediently in her hands.

"Aren't you going to finish your meal?"

Adwen frowned. "I'm not hungry. Do you have any more questions?"

Studying her cold expression, he thought of a better one. "Just one more: are you human?"

She blinked. She wasn't sure, but now she would know. And so would the other two people in the room. Maintaining a defiant stare with her interrogator, she gently held the silverware in her fingertips and answered, "Yes."

Her heart fluttered and a sick feeling settled in the pit of her stomach as the silverware jump and landed by the plate. For a while she stared at the table as the sensations of disbelief weighed down on her shoulders. Eventually she got the courage to look at Domus. With no questions left, what did he plan to do?

As they stared each other down, the frightened maid had stopped cooking altogether. Then the tense air was broken by the sound of little feet coming down the stairs. They chattered, discussing their chores.

Their parental figure maintained eye contact with Adwen and called to them. "Don't worry about the morning chores, you two. I've already taken care of them. Come have your breakfast. We have a guest."

When they rounded the corner, they failed to hide looks of shock.

"Boys, this is Adwen. Adwen, these are my two boys. This is my son Remy and my nephew Collin."

The two gawked.

"Say good morning, boys," the sly man instructed.

Both blurted out, "Good morning."

"Good morning," Adwen muttered, maintaining her stare.

"I found this pretty young lady in the barn."

Collin could only utter, "Oh."

The boys sat at the table and the maid returned with two more plates. For the first time, Miss Cottonpot saw the guest's face and did a double-take. Her eyes were so blue.

Adwen stared back not knowing why the woman was surprised.

Quickly, she averted her gaze and went to fetch Domus'.

Adwen waited, anticipating an attack of some kind from this big man sitting across the table. If she had to, she would make a run for the door. He would never catch her after that.

The boys quickly ate, nervous that Domus might know their new friend's secret.

When his own plate was on the table, he laced his fingers and leaned forward thoughtfully, trying to come to a decision. Finally, he nodded. "Boys, I was just thinking. Miss Adwen may need a place to stay the night."

They stopped eating to look up.

He smiled. "I think the guest room upstairs shall do well, don't you?"

They began to grin and nod.

Adwen was confounded. Was this some kind of trick, or was he actually giving her a place to stay? He seemed honest enough, but his crafty eyes made her uncomfortable.

Domus chuckled at her expression. "Well, Miss Adwen, what do you think? Would you be willing to stay the night?"

"I'd like that. Thank you."

Off in the corner, the maid dropped the cooking things in dismay.

"It's settled then." He called to the maid, "Miss Cottonpot?"

Looking ill, she turned to answer, "Yes, sir?"

"I'd like you to take this young lady and show her the guest room."

Pale in the face, she nodded and Domus graciously signaled with a hand to follow.

As they went along the hall, Adwen detected a strange odor in the air. Once the maid stole another glance she realized it was the poor woman's fear. Together they went to the second floor. Miss Cottonpot was wary of their guest and refused to enter with her. Eager to leave, the maid opened the door and used it as a shield between them.

Adwen was about to go inside, but stopped to give an apologetic look. "Thank you, ma'am."

The old woman attempted a smile and it made her lips twitch pitifully. Scrounging up a little courage, she answered, "You're welcome, miss."

Adwen smiled kindly and entered.

Chapter 7
NO TEARS

Adwen ran her hand over clean blankets covering the bed, meandering to the window. From what she had seen of the house there was no electric power or plumbing. Through the single glass pane, she glimpsed the barn as well as a picturesque view of snow-covered forests. It was breathtaking, but she would rather be home.

Knocking at the door yanked her attention back to the room. Upon answering, she was greeted by Collin and Remy.

"Hello, Adwen!"

"Hey, guys."

"We want you to come do the rest of the chores with us." Collin smiled while his cousin nodded rigorously in the folds of his scarf.

She could not say no to them. "Okay."

They grinned and Remy led her by the hand as they swept her through the kitchen. They passed the adults and firmly closed the door on the way out.

The man and his maid returned to their prior conversation.

"If you recall, the silverware showed she was speaking the truth. She said she wouldn't harm anyone."

The maid's distress remained unsmoothed. "You're relying on forks and spoons to tell you that! Domus, do you have any idea what she could be? No, you don't, and that leaves to question what she can do. She could be fooling us!"

"No one can fool the enchantment on the dinnerware, and I can tell she has only good intentions. I don't need magical plates to tell me that."

"Well then, I hope for your children's sakes that you're not wrong," she huffed. They watched from the window as the boys took the strange girl to the barn.

Adwen opened the door and the explosion of farmland smells made her even more homesick. They fed the chickens, the goat and Auburn in his stall. She couldn't understand what the stallion was saying anymore, but thought he might be chuckling in amusement. When they finished, Collin picked up the large collar and stuffed it into his coat before departing.

Closing the barn door for the boys, she looked over and saw a small village down the hillside. Little chimneys smoked everywhere as people went through the muddy streets.

Without warning, a clump of snow struck Adwen squarely in the back. The chill in the air didn't bother her and her feet were resilient, but the snowball was quite cold.

Both boys laughed hysterically, but when she turned and glared they stopped and gulped. Then she grinned toothily and knelt down to make a snowball of her own. Collin giggled and Remy squealed, darting out into the field.

The three laughed and lobbed snowballs for hours. She soon discovered that she could dodge them very easily. By the time they finished playing, Adwen was performing a variety of acrobatic flips and twirls. Both boys tired out long before she ever broke a sweat.

Collin panted. "All right, so we can't get you with our snow. It's getting late. How about we go inside?"

A giddy thrill filled her at this newfound agility, but she could see the boys were ready for rest. "That sounds like a good idea."

Going inside, they walked her to the room. Adwen intended to turn in early.

"Well, good night, boys. See you in the morning."

"Wait." Collin stopped her as he pulled the collar from his jacket.

He held it out for her and she shook her head. "It is okay, Collin. I won't need it tonight."

"Why not?"

"Well, there was a full moon last night right?"

Remy nodded, and Collin said, "Yes. But..."

"That means there isn't going to be a full moon tonight. It would be better if you kept it for me."

Little Remy tilted his head and his cousin looked at her quizzically. "You really aren't from around here, are you?"

She gave a shrug. "I thought you already knew that. Why?"

Trying not to laugh, he replied, "There are four moons and at least one is full at any time. There is a full moon every night."

"That's very funny. I remember seeing just one moon and it was blue."

"The blue moon only happens once in a hundred years when the four moons eclipse. That lasts for three nights. You're lucky to have seen it."

"Okay, Collin, your jokes need some work. I'm going to sleep now."

When she was closing them out, Remy spoke up, "He's not joking, Miss Adwen! There are four moons and they're going to be out tonight."

Gradually she began to believe. They had been right the night before when she had not listened. She opened the door again, growing nauseous. "You're serious? Every night there's a full moon?"

They nodded.

The concept set in. Recalling the transformation caused her to flush. She felt sick and her legs turned to rubber. Using the doorway for support as her skin blanched, she repeated aloud, "Every night?"

The boys watched her expression of horror grow. They hadn't thought it would upset her this badly. Collin felt sorry for frightening her while Remy gave her a gentle hug around the middle.

Distracted, she hardly noticed Remy attempting to comfort her. "Everything's going to be all right, Miss Adwen. We'll take care of you."

His affection brought her back. It was difficult to think, but she was able to respond, "Thank you, Remy."

Collin looked sullen. "Miss Adwen, does it hurt to..?"

No sooner did he ask than she looked at him and did not need to say a word.

"We thought it'd be best for you to hide in the barn from Uncle Domus," he added. "We'll be waiting there before the moon rises."

She nodded weakly, still dazed. "Yeah. Okay." Collin

handed her the collar and Remy followed him down the hall. When they were gone, she eased the door shut.

Adwen felt trapped as she went and slumped onto the edge of the bed. She looked at the large collar in her hand. It was at least twelve or fourteen inches in diameter and had fit perfectly the other night. Nausea curdled in her stomach like she had swallowed worms. Unable to look at the collar anymore, she set it aside, flopped back and gazed at the ceiling.

Warm sunset colors eventually faded from the window. Lost in thought, she relived the moment the utensils jumped as she said she was human. Adwen closed her eyes as tears rolled down her cheeks to the clean linens.

Periodically her gaze fell on the window. When darkness set in, she sat up and heaved a sigh. The dim lighting made things hard to see, but she could just make out the tough leather ring on the bed beside her. As acceptance of her fate, she picked up the collar and put it over her head, letting it rest neatly on her shoulders.

Alone and thinking of nothing in particular, a funny feeling came over her. It was a gnawing and uneasy feeling tickled on the back of her neck. Eventually it began to run up and down her spine. The sensation urged her to her feet and she nervously started to pace. Inside she knew one thing and she muttered it aloud: "Something's wrong."

Anxiety continued to rise. Adwen stopped and turned to the window. Instincts screamed that it was something outside. Going to look, it was pointless. Her eyes couldn't see through the dark.

Behind the house, one of the four moons began to rise. Adwen felt pressure under her skin. Then her eyes turned to violet and she could see perfectly. She spied the boys slipping into the barn. At last, she saw it along the tree line. A dark manlike figure crept across the snow like an animal, making a beeline for the barn.

The breath caught in her throat as she started to fight the window open. In her haste, she almost forgot the latch. Flipping it, she swung the frame open and climbing onto the sill. It was a long way down. Glancing across the field again, she saw the fiend prowl closer to the door. There was no time for fear of heights so she mustered her courage and jumped.

Adwen landed with ease in the snow and sprinted. Heart pounding like mad, horror filled her when she saw the figure enter and she cried out, "No!"

Adwen was almost there when the full moon emerged and stumbled. She fell, sliding through the half-melted snow, hugging expanding ribs with throbbing arms. Partially blinded by tears, she felt herself changing, tearing and ripping the dress to shreds.

A terrible roar came from within the barn along with the boys' screams. Out of desperation, Adwen forced herself to keep moving and the tattered dress fell from her shiny black coat. Crawling, her changes completed just as she reached a clawed hand to fling open the barn.

The boys huddled by the sty while the hogs squealed, the chickens hid in the straw and the goat bleated as it rushed past her. In the midst of the chaos the werewolf stood snarling before them.

On all fours, she bounded between the boys and the beast as it finished its own transformation.

The werewolf stood glaring down at her.

Hoping to intimidate the abomination, Adwen roared as loud as she could.

The diabolical thing stared. Adwen was very large, but a mountain of muscle, black fur and rage glared back. Huge fangs hung before her black-furred muzzle and the evil jaws opened wide, letting loose a deafening, blood-curdling roar.

She whimpered nervously to herself. "Oh, no."

Its eyes glowed bright and it swung at her with a huge fistful of claws.

The boys screamed as she collapsed, but adrenalin was surging through her. Adwen rebounded almost as soon as she went down. Snarling, she lunged and clamped jaws onto the monster's throat. It roared in surprise and the boys cheered as she thrashed.

Then she felt five claws sink into the back of her head. The werewolf gripped and proceeded to pull her off like a tick. When it ripped her away, strips of flesh and fur were in her fangs as she dangled in his powerful grasp. The monster bled in torrents and didn't seem to care. It roared again and squeezed, driving claws into her skull, making her howl writhe desperately to get free.

A rock suddenly struck the werewolf in the muzzle and it swiftly glared at the culprit.

"Leave her alone!" Remy hollered. He was ready to lob another while Collin tugged at him, attempting to make a getaway.

While the dumb monster was distracted, she gave a powerful kick to the side of the werewolf's face.

It staggered and shook its mangy head. Then it growled and roared, smashing Adwen face-first into the ground, dazing her. The boys called out as she was barely conscious. A few croaking guffaws came from the werewolf as he lobbed her limp body up into the loft.

Her head spun, but she came to when the boys screamed again. As everything returned to focus, she stared around in surprise. Domus had a large stash of weaponry in his loft. Beside her were a bundle of spears.

The boys tried to run for the door, but were quickly cut off. Cornering them by the wall, the werewolf stalked the children. It savored the moment, but then Adwen leaped down, spear in hand, landing on two feet beside the boys.

When the brute roared, she roared back and thrust the spearhead into its gut. He howled and she drove him back until there was a terrible crunch when the spear went through and penetrated the oak siding. Chickens screeched, leaping and scattering away from the werewolf mounted on the wall.

It slumped over on the shaft, seemingly dead while its muscular body was bathed in moonlight. Certain the fight was over, she breathed a sigh and turned to see if the boys were unharmed.

Collin smiled, but Remy screamed, "Look out!"

To her horror and surprise, the monster's crimson head lifted up, eyes burning. Slow croaking laughter grew louder and only she understood when he growled, "You cannot defeat me with steel, stupid dog!" It laughed louder and pulled itself along the spear.

Disturbed, she let go and recoiled, dropping to all fours. The three stared in horror while the werewolf laughed louder as it neared the end.

There was a loud snap. The werewolf froze and was silent.

Then it collapsed and the weight broke the spear as it fell. A large silver-tipped arrow was buried into its side up to the feathers, piercing the beast's heart.

Domus notched another and entered the barn as the dead thing started withering away into the man it once was.

Adwen cowered when he stepped inside. Then as he saw her violet eyes in the dark and took aim. She froze and stared.

The boys called out to stop him. "No!"

Remy ran and hugged her around the neck so his father wouldn't have a clear shot while Collin retrieved his lantern and the horse blanket. Draping it over her, he stood between his uncle and the black hound.

"No, Uncle Domus. Don't shoot, don't shoot!"

Maintaining his aim he ordered, "Step aside, boys!"

"No, Father. I won't."

"We're not going to move, Uncle Domus."

He was furious. "That's enough! Now step aside!"

As they continued to defend her, clouds rolled in and covered the full moon. Her body steadily shrank, fur retracting as her skin lightened. The last thing to change was the color of her eyes.

The boys fell silent, standing their ground.

Domus nearly gasped when he saw the blue eyes flash in the dim light.

Adwen timidly stared back.

His jaw dropped. "You? So this is what you were hiding."

She ducked her head.

Lowering his bow with the arrow still notched, he calmly addressed the boys again, "Step aside."

The two exchanged looks and hesitantly moved.

He watched her cringe and commanded, "Stand up."

She was terrified, shaking like a leaf, but obeyed, keeping her eyes down out of fright and shame.

There was no trace left of the black hound from moments ago, with the exception of the collar around her neck and the smear of blood on her lower lip. Gently, he reached out and placed his fingers below her chin to lift her gaze up to meet his. Her brown hair fell away to reveal wild blue eyes.

Domus spoke even more gently. "You saved my boys. Thank you."

Her frightened expression disappeared.

Taking back his hand, he added, "Miss Cottonpot is on her way to bring the villagers. They will have weapons and woar dogs. It is not safe for you to stay."

Auburn whinnied loudly in the corner. Then he leaped from the stall, startling the onlookers. He pranced out into the open, shaking off the soot. Then he whinnied again and the soot burst into bright white flames. Ashes were gone and he was snow white with gold fire rippling over his body. They watched in awe as the magical creature approached and bowed low before Adwen.

"He shall take you to some place safe." Domus gestured to the fiery stallion.

She was still stunned by everything. "But he belongs to..."

Holding up a hand to silence her, he stated, "He was never my horse." He lifted her onto Auburn's back and the flames were warm, but did not burn her or the blanket.

He gave the magical beast's flank a hefty smack to send them on their way. While they trotted off, the boys called out, "Goodbye, Adwen! We won't forget you!"

The dark was held at bay by Auburn's flames as he trotted deeper into the woods. She clung to the blanket and the base of his mane, unsure where they were going. The blazing white stallion seemed confident with the direction.

Overwhelmed and tired, she listened to the horse's hooves and let the rippling glow of his flames put her into a light trance. They soothed her mind, restoring recent lost memories. The rush of intense emotions made her quiver and she laid her weary head on Auburn's warm neck.

After the short rest, she looked into the distance to see lights looming. Then Adwen realized what she was seeing and gasped. Auburn bore her toward a colossal oak tree. The great leaf-crowned column reached high into the night sky with many lit windows above its roots. She could make out an open door from a distance. A figure was there to greet them when Auburn slowed and came to a stop.

She dropped from his back, eyeing the hooded stranger. Going closer, he lowered his hood and she froze. The instant she recognized the elf, she was on full alert, scanning the shadows for the hunter.

"He is no longer here." The healer smiled and assured her, "Regorian shall not be back." Holding out a hand, he invited her in.

Wary none the less, Adwen studied his face before finally entering the sanctuary. Then the elf closed the door.

Her host's cozy study was packed full of books and scrolls on shelves and enough chairs for a small party, though none were from a matching set. The fireplace warmed the room, easing some of the tension in her shoulders as he directed her to a soft chair. Holding the blanket closer, she sat and felt confounded.

Before leaving her side, the elf touched a finger to the collar and sounded pleased.

"It seems you have friends." Taking his seat across from her, he spoke with his smooth, gentle tone. "I'm sure you have many questions."

"How do I get home?"

The elf expected this and admitted solemnly, "I cannot tell everything that you ask, but I may tell you it can be done." The elf went on. "You stumbled into this world and only you are capable of finding the way. To do so, you must begin a journey through these lands."

"You've got to tell me something! Please, tell me, why do I have to go on some journey?"

He frowned and repeated, "Your fall into this world was caused by a mistake, but you were meant to come here. I have waited in this sanctuary for that purpose. I have been waiting to help you and to share with you my gifts. I am meant to help you begin this journey."

"A journey to what?" she cried, tears swelling in her eyes.

The elf gave her a pitying expression. "Part of your journey is to search for something. Beyond that, there is little I could tell you, child."

"Why?" she sobbed. "Why can't you tell me anything?"

He placed a comforting hand on her quivering shoulder. "I can only tell you what you need to hear."

Taking a deep breath to control sobs, she asked, "What can you tell me?"

"Everything is going to be all right."

She began to weep again.

"Look at me, Child," he soothed, lifting her chin. Her eyes changed from blue to violet in an instant, but he was not concerned. With a thumb, he gently wiped some of the tears away. "No tears," he whispered. "No more tears, Adwen. I promise to you, one day, you shall know peace. You will find home, but first you must begin your journey."

Blood pressure rising caused her to sob harder.

He took his hand away, and before the changes came, she hung her head and heard him say, "Until we meet again, Lady Adwen."

Absolute anguish forced her to double over. She swiftly turned jet black and screams turned to miserable howls. After the crunching and painful stretching sensations released her, she let the blanket fall away and looked up to find the elf.

He was gone. The entire oak sanctuary had vanished and she was alone with the white fire horse in a vacant meadow.

Adwen heard the stallion trot past as he was about to leave. Alarmed, she whined in dismay, "Wait!"

He paused and glanced back.

"Please," she whimpered. "Don't go."

Auburn snorted and came plodding over to nuzzle her behind one ear. "I cannot stay," he gently informed.

Her ears drooped. Sitting, she whimpered more, desperately wishing not to be left alone.

"You shall see me again one day," he reassured her. Then he swished his tail and nickered, "Here. I will show you the proper path."

The luminous stallion turned and broke into a brisk gallop. Adwen gasped as there was a burst of flames and he disappeared in an explosion of gold embers. Where he vanished, a strip of snow melted, revealing green grass and blooming sweet blossoms. She stared at the magical marker he had left behind, pointing north to the mountains.

Chapter 8
FEDIUS TOTH

The four moons shed their glow upon the earth. Trees cast odd shadows and stars winked. The heavens were peaceful while creatures contended with the cold. The black hound with violet eyes sulked on her lonely path.

Pushing past another shrub, she grumbled, "So, I'm the only one who can get me home." She let out a sigh. Frustrated and depressed, Adwen stopped to glare up at the sky, growling, "It would be nice if I had some place to go!"

There was no answer from the stars as expected, but off to the side through the forest came a sound. Someone was running and they were coming closer. Then she heard barking and ducked behind a bush just as a man sprinted past with huge canines on his heels. Driven by fear and desperation, he nimbly climbed a beech tree and the pack circled, barking out jeers and threats.

Adwen was curious as to what was happening.

The blond young man in the leafless boughs panted, winded from running for his life. Seven beasts snapped and barked endlessly. Once Adwen was close enough, she could hear the dogs laughing. They were each one hundred and fifty pounds and covered in messy brown fur. Their tails were docked, leaving short, fuzzy stubs. Their tails looked funny to Adwen, whereas their vicious front ends did not. Metallic armor strapped onto their heads served as face guards, equipped with a silver spike protruding from the forehead.

One of her claws landed unexpectedly on a stick. It snapped, alerting the largest of the pack. He saw her hunkered at the edge of the clearing and bayed, calling two others to his side. Together, the three fearlessly approached.

The leader growled. "Who are you, monster?"

"I'm Adwen."

He growled louder. "You have no business here."

One of his companions snarled. "You'll leave if you know what's good for you!"

Turning her attention to the man in the tree, she saw he wore nice peasant garments and a blue traveling cloak. His blond hair was short with a small rattail just above his neck. He looked no older than twenty. The stranger's face was young and his soft brown eyes stared at them.

"What do you want with him?"

The leader rumbled threateningly. "He's not for you! Turn back, now!"

Having faced a werewolf earlier, she didn't find the dogs very frightening. "What did he do?"

The dogs were losing patience. "It's none of your business! We're not interested in you, monster. Don't interfere and you won't get hurt."

Other dogs stopped to watch and the man saw his chance to escape. But as he lowered a foot down, one dog looked and snarled to make him think twice.

Eyeing the leader, she crept closer to the tree, careful to keep her distance from the pack members. "Tell me what you want with him and I'll think about it. He doesn't seem all that bad to me."

Another growled. "This is our business and not food for the likes of you, monster!"

She paused and glared, not pleased at being called a monster again. This time she growled as well. "Just tell me what he did wrong."

While Adwen was distracted, the leader swooped in, ramming her side. The silver spike punched deep into her ribs, bowling her over in the slush and mud. She snarled, grabbing at the bloody wound as the pack hemmed her in and their leader rumbled.

"This is business. It's not personal and it has nothing to do with you. Now leave and stay out of this, monster!"

She greatly disliked pain. Hot blood stained the snow red and the injury spurred her anger. Violet eyes aglow, she gnashed glistening fangs. "Stop calling me that!"

The rumbled. "Don't you know who we are? We are woar dogs! Born for the hunt, we live to fight and kill monsters such as you.”

Her upper lip quivered dangerously.

“You are a strange monster. That wound should have killed you by now. It’s odd. You look rather weak for a were-wolf.”

She snapped salivating jaws. “Maybe that’s because I’m not one, fleabag!”

One of the dogs lunged for insulting his leader, but was ordered to stay back. “This kill is mine!”

Adwen roared and he lunged, snapping his fangs in her face and caused her to stand upright like a great bear. The dog leaped, ramming Adwen’s stomach, knocking her to the ground. As she rolled over he pounced, sinking teeth into the side of her neck. While she roared, thrashing to shake him off the dog bit harder, digging in his claws. The pack laughed and cheered.

Infuriated, Adwen reached for the dog. Her long digets wrapped around his armored muzzle then sharp claws pried back. While she pulled the jaws from her flesh, her own claws pierced tender gums. Their leader snarled with droplets of their blood trickling out his maw. Swiftly, she stood and slammed him to the ground.

Pinned on his side, he struggled and barked in a fit of rage. “I’ll kill you, monster. I’ll take you down!”

Without thinking, instincts drove Adwen to fit her jaws around the dog’s throat.

He wasn’t threatened by the gesture, gnashing his teeth. “I’ll tear you apart! Then I’ll have that man’s heart for dessert!”

“No!” Adwen’s jaws clenched.

He fell silent and so did the pack.

Surprised by what she had done, Adwen felt strange.

The young man and the remaining woar dogs watched her fangs leave his bloody throat.

Vigor coursed through her. There was no pleasure in what she did. The dogs intended to harm the man and instincts said he was innocent. She was determined to help him and confidence came from realizing she could do precisely that.

The woar dogs growled and some stepped forward.

Light from the four moons masked her in solid shadows,

and her violet eyes burned. Baring bloody fangs, she snarled. "Who's next?"

The challenge was answered by the entire pack. They attacked in a frenzy of fangs and growls. Some rammed with spikes and others pounced. She reared, tearing them off and throwing them into trees. Then a dog paired with another in biting her feet, pulling them out from under her. As she fell another leaped for her throat, but she caught him and his jaws snapped before her nose.

Five others tore at her as she howled in anger. Punching the dog she held, she gave a fierce kick to send another through the air. Its back broke against a pine. The four remaining dogs were not intimidated by dwindling numbers.

Rolling over, she lunged and her teeth came down on a neck. He yelped before she chomped and threw his limp body aside. One rammed her ribs and she cried out, snatching him up and casting him into the beech tree. He fell to the ground, staggered and rejoined the fight.

Adwen bled in torrents. One of the last three sunk its fangs into her wrist, making her roar. Then the others latched onto her thighs, thrashing with all their might. Howling louder than ever, she grabbed the brute on her wrist. He snarled and yelped as she used him to swat one of the others away. Both got to their feet, staggering and horribly injured.

The last of them was the smallest and let go to jump back, barking. He was practically a pup and she loomed over him, bleeding and glaring.

Her battered ribs expanded as she took a deep breath and released a long and angry roar.

It forced the dog to be quiet and he give a hesitant look.

Baring wrinkled, bloody jaws, she seethed.

Then the pup's courage broke and he turned tail. The remaining injured following suit. She watched as they disappeared through the trees. A moment later, the dog she had knocked out came round and joined in the retreat.

The young man in the boughs stared while the black creature tried to take a step and staggered. It swayed then fell like a ton of bricks in the bloody snow.

He quickly climbed down and approached. At first he thought it might be dead, but saw the steady rise and fall of its sides. The black creature was injured, but very much alive.

A dull pain and stiffness brought Adwen back to consciousness. The more awake she became, the more painful it was to breath. It was still night when she opened her eyes. Sitting across a small fire was the young man, warming his hands. She watched him poke the burning pieces with a sturdy stick, sending embers flying. The light reflected in his childish eyes as more glowing particles drifted off.

Uncomfortable, Adwen tried to readjust herself. Doing so caused the pain to spike and she cried.

The young man heard her whimper and stopped to give a pitying look.

To avoid more discomfort, she held still. Then she saw him coming closer. Unsure what he had in mind, she waited, feeling very vulnerable.

He knelt alongside, staring unflinchingly into Adwen's violet eyes. Once she was visibly calmer, he reached into a small buttoned pouch for a dark green leaf. He held it out for her to take.

She stared, wondering what it was for.

He finally spoke and his voice sounded young and kind. It was also sincere. "Go on. Take it."

Gently, she accepted the bitter herb into her jaws, but hesitated to bite.

"Go on. I promise it will help. Eat it."

Carefully crunching it to bits, she swallowed and the effort hurt. A few moments passed and the stinging and soreness started to die down. She breathed a heavy sigh of satisfaction at the numbing effect.

The young man took off his blue traveling cloak and covered her with it for warmth.

Adwen continued to stare, wondering why he wasn't afraid. But then an additional trait of the herb took effect. She blinked blearily as he took his place on the other side of the fire. In seconds, she was fast asleep once more.

The air grew colder as the night wore on until just before

daybreak. The full moon still hung overhead as the young man slept.

The hound began to wake. She could move without hurting and opened her maw in a fearsome yawn. Catching sight of the full moon, she saw the new day about to arrive. The young man stirred and she knew he would awake shortly. Sitting upright, holding the cloak about her, she watched the sky brighten.

The fire had smoldered out hours before and the cold made the young man shiver on the frozen earth. Turning over and sitting up lazily, he rubbed his eyes and yawned. "Ah, what a night." When he took his hands away, he saw the black hound gazing at the sunrise, holding his traveling cloak about its shoulders.

Dawn came. The first light gleamed and the black hound's form melted. His surprise grew as the creature steadily vanished and a young girl materialized in its place. Her violet eyes became a deep blue while wavy, brown hair draped over her shoulders, veiling a smooth face and soft pink lips. The sun climbed higher, casting warm light over the girl's pale complexion. When she turned to look at him, he was stunned and completely speechless.

She muttered warily. "Hi."

The man continued to stare. "Hello."

"...You look surprised."

Closing his gaping mouth at last, he answered, "I am."

"What were you expecting?"

He rubbed the back of his neck. "Well, not a lady."

She blinked. "You were expecting a man?"

"Well, yes. I've never heard of a woman being a..."

Her expression saddened. "A monster?"

"I was meaning to say hound."

She stood and the cape draped down to her ankles.

At last, he set his surprise aside and quickly joined her. "Thank you for saving my life, miss."

Gazing at her feet, she replied, "You're welcome."

"What is your name?"

"Adwen."

"My name is Fedius Toth, but you can call me Toth." He smiled and added, "Again, thank you for last night. Is there anything I could do to repay you?"

Feeling even more awkward, she asked, "You don't have a change of clothes, do you?"

Toth blushed and chuckled. "No, but I do have a few coins left. There should be a town not far from here where we could remedy that. It would be a pleasure to be of service if you're willing to accompany me."

A smile flickered on her face. "I'd like that. Then you can have your cloak back."

Toth laughed. "Until then feel free to keep it. I'm not the type to deprive you of your dignity." He laughed again and scoffed, "Well then, come along. The closest town is this way." And he started off with a modest Adwen in tow. They hiked north in silence. As they continued, the air warmed unlike Adwen, whom Toth could tell was depressed.

"That collar you have. I'm curious as to how you came by it."

Glancing furtively, she muttered, "It was a gift."

"It's a nice collar. Whoever gave it up must really have taken to you."

All of the while she kept her gaze low. "Yeah, they were nice people."

"Where do you intend to travel?"

"I don't know."

"Are you lost?"

"Very."

Her shyness concerned him a little. They continued on and he didn't ask anything more. Soon the village was sighted from atop a hill. Once they reached the dwellings, Toth cautioned her, "It may be best to wait here while I buy your garments."

"Okay."

It was a short wait before his return with a proper dress. It was brown and not nearly as nice as the previous one, but it would do. Now clothed, she joined him as he returned for more supplies.

A heavily worn street stretched through the village, tattooed with impressions of cart wheels, horse hooves and many boots. Sleepy villagers made their way from place to place, going on about their business, none paying any mind to the strangers visiting. Adwen wore the cloak with the hood drawn and the collar tucked out of sight. Her guide apologized for not finding shoes, but she reassured him that there was no need.

The two studied the shops as they walked. Eventually they came across a shop called the Sturdy Mule and decided this was their best bet for traveling goods. A tiny copper bell chimed as they entered and again as the door closed. Inside was warm, dry and a wide selection of supplies lined the shelves. Behind the counter stood a middle-aged woman with a strong, friendly face and dark brown hair, streaked with gray.

The shopkeeper greeted them. "Good morning to you!"

Adwen kept her hood up and nodded while Toth returned the greeting, "Good morning to you, ma'am!"

"Welcome and what might I do for you?"

He approached to do business, but Adwen felt more comfortable waiting by the door. Being in the village and knowing what she had become made her uneasy. Her companion bartered and she allowed her gaze to wander. A few saddles sat on stands and burlap bags were piled waist-high beside the counter. Her blond counterpart bought a dark green cloak from the rainbow assortment. As lovely as the shop seemed at first glance, her sixth sense warned that something was amiss.

Then she saw a stranger she had not noticed before, standing near the counter. A tall, gaunt man glared sourly at the cheery shop woman.

Adwen continued to stare. Something about him didn't seem right. Once he spotted her, his expression became one of surprise and great outrage. She froze when the angry man took brisk strides to stand over her and sneer, "You can see me?"

She was very confused and shrunk back in fear.

"You can see me, can't you, little beast?" the man barked, putting his face up to hers as it twisted into a nasty grimace.

It was only once he was so close that Adwen realized this man had no scent. Toth and the woman didn't even seem to notice or hear as he began to yell, "You listen here, beast! Tell that hag to shut down my shop and burn it to the ground! Do you hear me? Tell her to leave and never return! Tell her she should go back to the hole I found her in!"

Ducking down, she huddled against the wall.

He grew angrier. "Are you listening to me, you little monster?"

Finally she began to cry and Toth and the shop woman paused to see her cringing, tears rolling down her cheeks. Her distress gave them cause for concern, but he passed the coins, closing the deal. "I think these will do. Thank you very much, ma'am." Gathering up his purchases, he loaded them into one of the free knapsacks.

She was still crying as he approached and the ghost stepped aside. His familiar scent reached her and she felt his hand touch her shoulder.

"Are you all right?"

Glancing up, she took a breath and nodded. Then she watched the angry specter stalk behind the counter. Pausing beside the knapsacks, he bellowed, kicking them over.

The shopkeeper jumped and Toth turned in time to see.

Heaving a sigh, the woman started cleaning with the ghost standing over her, arms folded.

"We should be on our way," her companion stated, shouldering the bag. The brass bell chimed lightly as they departed.

They made no more stops and left town for the muddy roads through the forest. While she dried the last of the tears, he asked, "What happened in the shop, Adwen?"

"There was somebody else in there. It was a man and he was yelling at me."

He eventually made an educated guess. "You saw a ghost?"

Not knowing what else it could have been, she nodded. "Yeah. I guess it was."

Then he shrugged. "Well, I suppose it's only natural that you would be able to see them."

He noted Adwen's questioning glance and elaborated, "Humans normally cannot see ghosts, but animals and inhuman creatures have heightened senses. Being able to see spirits and sense things around you can be rather helpful!"

Adwen couldn't help but smile. He was being very kind and trying hard to make her feel better. Outside of the village she felt comfortable enough to put down her hood. The sun rose higher and the light warmed her pale skin, soothing her.

Wild birds sang in the evergreens, a sure indicator of an approaching spring. Snow melted quickly, leaving mud, rocks, and grit in its place. The soles of her feet were tough and the muck felt good mashing up between her toes.

"It has been helpful."

He was surprised to hear her speak without prompting. "What has?"

"My sixth sense. It has helped me before."

Toth smiled. "How?"

"To tell when there's danger. It told me when the two boys who gave me this collar were in trouble." She pulled the gift out from under the cloak to admire it.

"See what I mean?" He laughed. "You have much of which to be proud."

She smiled at his beaming face as they went deeper into the forest. The day was bright and she was beginning to enjoy her stronger senses. Then a strange scent passed by and she stopped smiling. The same warning itch at the back of her neck had returned, but this time it didn't come soon enough.

A muscular man leaped out from a bush, snatching her up from behind.

Adwen screamed and Toth dropped his sack, prepared to fend off the assailant. But he was bashed over the head by another vagabond. She watched him fall unconscious and five more bandits gathered around. The burliest of the thieves held her fast while she struggled and they laughed at their lucky catch.

Her sensitive nose got a whiff of his body odor. She thought she might be sick from the stink. "Let me go!"

All of them laughed and her captor guffawed. "Go ahead and struggle all you want! I like it that way."

Mortified, frustration and fear made her scream and flex, whipping her head back into the villain's face. He staggered from the hit and stumbled, blood oozing out his demolished nose. The strike would have killed him if had it been any harder and his comrades were shocked.

She broke free from his weakened grasp only to be grabbed by two more and screamed again. Her inhuman strength made her difficult to hold. Thrashing around, she managed to throw one off, but before she could lose the second, was struck on the head with a club. Staggering, she wasn't finished fighting and attempted to recover. Once the second strike was dealt, however, she collapsed.

The punishment Adwen took was much harsher than what was given to Toth. She didn't come to until much later. Both were bound to the base of a broad tree while the bandits rummaged through their supplies and other loot. Gathered around a fire, they drank deeply from stolen flasks of mead and gin.

At nightfall, Adwen's nocturnal sense of time drew her back to consciousness, along with the feeling of callused fingers handling her face. The bandit's horrible stench burned while his manhandling confused and annoyed her. Once the sun was out of sight, she was fully aware of the dirty man fondling her by the chin and pulled away.

His hand snatched her up again and squeezed till it hurt. As she stared back, he smiled, exposing a corroded, yellow grin. "You're going to pay for what you did to my friend's face." He chuckled. "We've been waiting for you to wake up so you may enjoy it! My friends and I are going to have some fun with you tonight!"

A patch of blood was dried on the side of Toth's head, but he felt well enough to speak up in her defense. "Leave her alone, you filthy wretch!"

The wicked man let go to give him a swift backhand. "Quiet, you! You get to watch!" Hearing his companions calling, he concluded tormenting the captives to join them.

Toth recovered and turned to her. "Are you all right?" The sounds of her soft sobs reached him. "It's going to be fine," he whispered and smiled slyly. "In a little while you can teach these vagabonds a lesson they'll never forget."

Her shoulders shook with sobs and her eyes turned violet, glowing brighter.

"They won't be able to harm you," he encouraged with a chuckle. "You'll be able to break these ropes and we can escape. You'll get your fangs and claws and --"

Suddenly she cried out at the top of her lungs.

"No! I don't want to. I don't want to be that thing again!" Coughing, tearing and choking on words, she shouted, "I want

to go home! I want to go home where none of this is real! There's no such thing as monsters! There's no such thing as magic! *None of this is real! None of this is real!"*

Toth stared, dumbstruck at her words.

A full moon appeared at last and the pressure reached its peak. Crying out louder, she tried to fight the change. As a result, it came on much slower and more painfully. The more she resisted, the more excruciating it became and her unearthly shriek filled the air.

The bandits cupped their ears and saw her thrashing against the ropes, but could not see the bonds stretching. In a hurry to silence her and end the terrible sounds, one took out a knife and buried it in her side.

This was a mistake. The sharp addition of pain freed her from torment, turning it to wrath in an instant. In a flash, glowing eyes snapped up to lock with his and he recoiled. The bandit let go of the blade, leaving it sticking out of her shifting form.

No longer fighting the transformation, aggression fueled it like gasoline on a flame. The ropes snapped like kite string as she expanded, became black as coal and reared, pulling the knife out with sharpening claws. Casting the weapon aside, she gave a punishing backhand and sent the man flying into the campfire. His comrades grabbed their weapons while Adwen's jaws twisted into a terrible snarl. She leaped between them in a flurry of claws and roars, knocking the men aside as easily as ragdolls. Whatever strikes they managed to land only doubled her anger as she went on a rampage.

"Run for it!" one cried. "She's a monster!"

The wicked band scattered, not bothering to take their loot with them.

Toth tossed aside the remaining ropes and turned to where she was crouched, breathing in heavy gasps. As he was joining her, she snarled and bolted into the dark.

Running after her, he called out, "Adwen! Adwen, wait!"

Unable to think past misery, it was several minutes before she could hear his voice. Getting a hold on herself, she came to a stop. Once he came close she whirled around, snarling and gnashing jaws. *"Get away from me!"*

Toth kept his distance, but was not afraid of the display.

Fangs bared, her upper lip quivered threateningly. "Just leave me alone."

He sighed, shaking his head. "Before you go, could you hear what I have to say?"

She kept growling, but stopped baring her fangs as a consent to the request.

"You're not alone. We both have something to hide." He covered his ears. When he put his hands down, both ears were long and pointed.

She ceased growling to stare.

"I'm not an elf. I am only half. I lack the powers and longevity. My mother was an elf and passed away while I was young, leaving me to live with her friend's family." Becoming somber, he continued, "We both have to hide what we are to survive. You hide because of misunderstandings, and I because of very much the same. Elves that are still in this kingdom are better off hiding from humans. People are simple and most believe elves can create miracles. Sometimes they demand miracles."

His face turned even more sullen. "And sometimes they think you can save someone with a miracle that you cannot do. And when you don't, because you can't, they blame you for the death of that loved one." Giving a wry smile he added, "Then with an accusation of murder, they put a bounty out on your head."

Both her ears went up as Adwen cocked her head.

"You're really not from this world, are you?"

Hanging her head, she gave a whine.

Then he became serious. "You've saved my life twice in two nights. There are powers that would demand I repay the debt in full, but I very much doubt I could. So I have a request to ask." After taking a deep breath, he announced, "I would be honored if you would have me as your guide to help you find your way home. I'm sure there are writings of doorways to other worlds. So what do you say? May I join you in your travels at least as a friend?" Extending a hand, he added, "Well? Odd ones must band together, right?"

Her luminous gaze searched him until she whimpered and gave his hand a lick.

Toth was very pleased. "Thank you! And also, I understand a little of the dog language. I can interpret most of your words and phrases and I can improve." Together they started back for the empty camp and he chuckled. "Come, Adwen. What do you say we see what our scummy friends have left?"

Returning to settle by the fire, they searched through the bandits' treasures. Toth hesitated to toss the drink aside and kept only what food and gold they could carry, along with a dress they discovered among the collection. It was lightly soiled, but a good fit for Adwen. She would need it since her last dress had been destroyed the same way as the others.

She was content to watch him finish eating and bed down for the night. His ears were disguised once more and he used a bag of loot for a pillow. While sifting through the stolen items he came across a sturdy satchel, perfect for carrying their belongings. After bidding goodnight, he lay down to sleep.

Toth made her feel better somehow. She was a powerful beast with claws that could easily tear him to shreds, but he wasn't the least bit afraid. Her senses could detect fear and there was none in Toth whatsoever. The way he treated her made her feel normal.

With the blue cloak draped over pitch-black fur, she rested and gazed at the crackling flames. Her long tail gave a small flick. It was comforting to know she had at least one friend in this world.

Chapter 9
NOT A MONSTER

Adwen thought she smelled a deer. She wasn't sure, since she had not seen and smelled the difference before. The pair found their way back to the road and set out early for the next town. Spirits were high and they were hopeful this venture into society would be better than the last.

"Fort Redu has everything! They have a market, horse stables, street-side entertainers and all kinds of food and things to buy. You'll love it!"

She was skeptical. "If it's a fort, doesn't that mean there are guards?"

He batted a hand at the worry. "They won't stop either of us from venturing inside. Fort Redu is a trading town and the guards only stop those who seem like trouble."

The half-elf's assuredness did not boost her confidence. Changing the subject, she asked, "Last night you said you don't have any powers. How can you hide your ears?"

"Well, I don't have the same powers as elves." He shrugged. "They are at one with nature and a half-elf is not a common mix. I have only a fraction of the powers a full elf would possess and those are weaker still. They could conceal their entire appearance if they pleased, but I can only disguise my ears. Then again, the fact that my ears are so elf-like is odd in itself."

She raised an eyebrow. "Why?"

"Half-elves appear completely human and have no powers. Their instincts are keen, but beyond that they are completely mortal. I'm not truly a mortal human, yet I am not an elf. I'm rather stuck in the middle of things."

"Okay, and you also said you have a hit out on you?"

"I have a what?"

"I'm meant the bounty put out on you. Sorry."

"Oh! The man who called on the bounty hunters was not aware I could alter my appearance. So long as I can disguise my lineage for a time I shall be safe." Then he was curious. "May I ask a question of you?"

"Sure."

"Why don't you have a need for shoes?"

"I'm not entirely sure, but there was this elf I met in the forest. He saved my life and said he gave me some gifts. That might be why I don't need them."

He was aghast. "An elf shared his gifts with you? That hasn't been done in...I don't know. It's been hundreds of years. You must be very special. Do you want to know the secret of the elves?"

"What secret?"

"My mother told me when I was young. The elves have sailed across the sea, but a very small number remain. All of them hide in wait and do not reveal themselves unless to play their role. Don't you see? You are going to impact the unfolding of history!"

"That's kind of cool."

He laughed harder. "You have a strange manner of speaking. Tell me more of your home world. If it isn't a bother, I would like to hear how you came to be in Dargadia."

"Well, to start with, we have no magic so we use something called technology. We use electricity and metal to make machines that do things for us."

"That sounds like a strange world indeed!"

"You've got that right."

"Then tell me how you found this world?"

"I went on a hike that my school set up. We were put into teams and there was this bully. While I was standing on a ledge over a river, he shoved me in."

"Stars above!"

"I went over a waterfall, and when I came up again I was here. The elf and a hunter saved me, and that night I tried to escape. I was convinced they were crazy! That's when I was attacked by a werewolf. It bit me here." She gestured to her shoulder. "You can't see anything there anymore. It didn't even leave a scar."

"Extraordinary!"

"The first night I changed the hunter tried to kill me. I ran and that was how I met the boys who gave me this collar. I saved them from another werewolf and a white horse with gold fire carried me back to the elf again. That's when he sent me on this journey. Then I bumped into you."

"That is an incredible tale."

Adwen scoffed. "If I told that story in my world they would think I was totally nuts."

"Then you shall have to beware with whom you share your tale when you return."

Thoughts turned toward her family. In a somber tone, she confessed, "I had the chance to say goodbye to my dad and I didn't. I didn't even tell him that I still cared."

Seeing her become sad, he made an effort to lighten the mood. "Come now, I promised I'd find a way to get you home. We could try the city of Deleon below Castle Gailari-en. There is a grand library that might have tombs or scrolls to help find what we seek." She still seemed put out. "Think on the good things. Remember those horrible bandits? It looked as if they were going to need more than better weapons. Judging from their faces, they needed a clean change of trousers!"

Recalling the utterly terrified and stupid expressions, she started to giggle. It turned to contagious laughter that infected her merry companion.

He gasped through fits of laughing, "When we reach town you should try not to smile too broadly."

Her cheeks were bright pink. "Is it against the law to have a sense of humor?"

"No. You must be inconspicuous and your smile would bring unwanted attention."

She stopped laughing to inspect her smile with fingertips. Both incisors were pointed and the start of small fangs. Horrified at the discovery, she quickly covered her mouth.

"Do not worry on it. You're still yourself," he reassured. "It is a sign that you're gaining in strength. It is a good thing!"

Thoroughly disturbed, Adwen didn't find this appealing.

Toth put a hand on her shoulder. "Come now. Town is around the way and I'll be sure to get you some sweets. That should cheer you up!"

The fact that she was still changing worried her. If she kept getting stronger, how much more of her would be altered?

Sighing, she lowered her hands as Fort Redu was in sight. A tall timber gate allowed passage beyond the forty-foot walls of stone. Archers and armed guards in shining armor wearing red and gold capes paced the ramparts.

He saw her expression and chided, "Don't worry so much."

She drew the hood far over her head anyway. "What makes you so sure they'll let me pass?"

"If they get a good look at your eyes they might even bow. In this kingdom, blue eyes are rare. The only people who have them are part of the royal family. Folk might even mistake you for the Princess Eyrie."

A smile flickered on her face at the idea of being mistaken for a princess. "I would feel tons better if they just ignored me."

"Suit yourself. Once we reach the gate, shall I speak for you?"

"Please do."

The west gate was open wide enough for a horse to pass through. A single sentry stood watch, suited in armor forged from silvery steel and armed with a long spear. When the travelers approached he challenged them in a drone tone, thoroughly bored. "State your business."

Toth answered smartly, "Trading goods and food, sir."

The sentry staved off a yawn and dismissed them with a lazy wave. "Move along."

Adwen breathed a sigh of relief, but did so too soon.

The sentry suddenly called, "Hold!"

Toth stopped and she froze. As he pointed the butt of the spear at her bare feet covered in mud, she thought they were caught for sure.

He chastised Toth, "Her feet, boy. If you plan to pass by this gate again you ought to take better care of your woman. Buy her something proper for her feet."

"Yes, sir. I will, sir."

The sentry eyed him closely. "Move along now."

When they were out of earshot, she chuckled nervously, giddy with relief.

"That was fun!" Toth laughed, "I told you they wouldn't

stop us. You worry too much."

She grumbled, "I'm just going to have to worry for the both of us."

"I have little doubt that you can. Now, to the market and town square!"

"How do you know this place so well?" she asked as they weaved through a series of narrow alleys.

"Here was where I stayed before the bounty hunters caught up with me."

The homes and buildings were cramped and their height blocked out most of the light. Main streets feeding into the cobbled stone market were cluttered with people hustling and bustling. Dozens of stands stood and hundreds of smells bombarded her. The scent of humans was overwhelming along with that of their delicacies. If a dog could find Toth in this throng, it would be a miracle.

As she massaged aching sinuses, he pointed. "Come this way. I think I see the food traders!"

After wading through the masses, he quickly bought goods for their journey. Confident in the safety of the crowd, they wordlessly agreed to enjoy themselves for a time. While eating fruit they watched street-side performers. An old, bearded vagabond played a flute while a stocky mutt at his side bayed.

She giggled and Toth tossed a few coins into the hat.

The man thanked them kindly and went on playing. As they were leaving, Adwen thought she heard the mongrel say something flirtatious, but wasn't sure.

Toth was leading her to where he last saw the candies, but she became side-tracked by a menagerie of caged song birds. They were beautiful and their sounds exotic. All of her attention was captured by a bright green bird smaller than the palm of her hand. Its song fluttered like the high notes of a piccolo. The bird had her transfixed until it paused. Before it continued singing, she thought she saw a familiar figure walk past the cage amid the milling crowd.

Regorian glanced at her and did a double-take.

Adwen's insides summersaulted and she darted into an alley. Heart banged against her ribs, she leaned against the wall and tried to catch her breath.

Toth soon found her. "I couldn't find the sweet stand.

What's wrong, Adwen? You look as if you've seen another ghost."

"Do you remember the hunter I told you about?"

Nodding, he replied, "You mean the one who tried to kill you? What of him?"

She gave a frightened look. "I saw him."

Toth was astonished. "Where is he?"

She gestured back across the street, but didn't dare look herself. "He's the tall guy with short curly hair. He has a big green cloak and a fancy crossbow."

He peered around the corner a moment. "I think I see him." Then he exclaimed, "That is Regorian Lancer!"

"You know him?"

"Everyone this side of Broad River has heard of him," he explained, but thought again. "Well, at least the women have heard of him. They never stop babbling about him."

Her friend's apparent lack of concern disturbed her. "Toth!"

At last he focused on the matter at hand. "Right. Well, has he seen you?"

She uttered breathlessly, "I don't know for sure, but I think he did."

Then he shrugged and stated matter-of-factly, "Then we should leave. There are many people near the east gate to hide amongst and it's the nearest exit."

They ran through the streets at her friend's fastest pace. Before long, the flowing crowd and the vast gateway were in sight. As they realized the gates were closing her heart sunk. Peasants booed and jeered at the guards angrily for locking them inside.

A sentry on the wall blew his horn and it was echoed by many others from around the structure. Every sentry atop Fort Redu sounded the call. The signal meant something terrible to the people who lived within, who darted for their homes, bolting doors and windows shut.

Visitors were left in the open and they gathered closer as Regorian stood on a barrel to speak.

Recognizing him, Adwen sank into the alley. The people fell silent while a few women sighed and the hunter's voice rolled over the crowd.

"Listen well. Both gates into Fort Redu are now closed."

Everyone gasped and murmured as a man bellowed, "What for?"

"There is a creature. A very dangerous creature lurks among us." The news aggravated them and he was reassuring. "Remain calm and by the gates for safety. The archers shall protect you and their aim is good. I trained some of them myself. This beast is in disguise and I do not wish for panic. I shall seek out the monster and not rest until I have rid this town of its presence."

Adwen gritted her teeth. As Toth joined her in the shadows, she thrust her back against the stone wall. "Damn it!"

He scratched the side of his head. "Oh dear. This is a bit of a problem."

"What are we going to do now?"

"Hide, of course."

Being the prey of a skilled hunter was wearing her patience thin. "No duh! Where do I hide?"

Counting off of his fingers, he replied, "Night shall fall in three hours so it must be devoid of humans, yet close by. There must be other tracks to disguise your own and an easy escape." He rolled the thoughts around until he came to a conclusion: "The stables!"

The crowd settled as she and Toth backtracked. Regorian was somewhere among the buildings playing a deadly game of hide and seek. Adwen wasn't in the mood to play, but she had little choice. Without a word, they skirted along shady alleys.

Fort Redu's stables were large, but few horses occupied the stalls when they entered. A short way down the aisle they decided to hide with a big mare in her stall so that any rustling might go overlooked. She didn't mind as they joined her, climbing over and landing in the mixed straw and hay.

Looking up at the beast of burden and panting from running, Adwen smiled. "Hello there."

The horse neighed and Adwen's jaw dropped as she understood: "Greetings!"

Toth saw that she could communicate and instructed, "Adwen, ask them for assistance if they can give it."

She nodded and turned to the mare. "Sorry to bother you, but we need a place to hide. There's a crazy hunter after me."

Shaking her mane, she replied, "Of course you may stay."

"When the moon comes up, something's going to happen to me and I need you and the rest to not freak out. Can you do that?"

She was cordial and curious. "How strange. Yes, dear. I shall do my best."

An adolescent male heard and leaned over to see the intruders. Very opposed to the decision, he snorted and stomped around. "You're not a human! You can't stay here! Get out! Get out now!"

"You will mind your tongue and show some courtesy," she brayed and tried to bite his neck. "I say they can stay and they ask that you be quiet!"

The stud snorted and backed away grumbling.

"How did you fare?" Toth asked.

"This one will give us a chance, but this male next door might not be helpful. Now, if only I could keep myself quiet through the change."

He began to rifle through his satchel until he pulled out a green leaf. "This isn't a sweet, but it should help."

Recognizing the bitter herb, she frowned. "Won't that put me to sleep?"

He shook his head and handed it over. "This leaf is of a different quality. Before moonrise put it on your tongue, and when you feel pain, bite. That should last long enough for your transformation."

The next few hours were quiet. For Adwen they were tense. The only sounds were those from the horses and the half-elf napping. Another snore came and she shook her head. How could he sleep at a time like this? He was so relaxed.

Inside the stables grew darker as she saw the sun setting through the gaps in the walls. Feeling herself becoming more energized, she knew night was moments away. Moonrise wouldn't be long after.

She prodded Toth to wake him and he mumbled unintelligibly. Yawning and stretching awake from the cat nap, he turned and sighed. "That was a good rest. Is it night already?"

Giving a nod, she didn't dare speak for fear the hunter might hear. The itch on her neck had returned.

"You look worried. What is it?"

"I think he's close. I've got that bad feeling."

"If he's getting near then we should move."

"No. The moon is too close. I'll be all right, but you should leave. Maybe I can keep away from him until sunup or something." She grimaced. "Either way, this stall is going to be cramped."

Studying the confines, he nodded. "You are right about that."

The mare was very large and there would be just enough room to share. Toth clambered out with the satchel and was quickly passed Adwen's traveling cloak and dress.

Peering over the stall door, Adwen's eyes turned violet while she stood wearing only the dog collar. She spoke and her voice was mingled with a growl, "Hurry up and leave. I've got his scent." Her eyes suddenly grew wide and she stared out along the street.

A lone armed figure moved in the shadows between the homes.

"It's him. Hide!"

Toth stutter-stepped, frantically searching for a place. He then spied a pile of straw and buried himself in it.

Adwen crouched low and put the herb on her tongue as instructed. A few minutes passed and she could still smell Regorian. Once the changes began she winced, biting into the herb. The pain didn't disappear, but it was dulled to the point that she could keep from screaming. Her transformation disturbed the mare, but she kept quiet, as did the few others in the stables.

Meanwhile, the stallion did no such thing. As soon as he realized what was happening he went into a panic, braying and stomping around in terror.

When the change was complete, Adwen quickly leaped and climbed into the darker reaches of the rafters. Darkness concealed her as she watched hunter enter.

He coolly stalked the stables, studying every detail. Crossbow at the ready, he approached the panicked animal. Deciding that perhaps the beast was witless, he searched his surroundings again. Soon his sights fell on the lonely pile of straw. Eyeing the stack suspiciously, he crept closer, prepared to squeeze the trigger at the first sign of movement.

With her friend in danger, Adwen acted quickly. She dropped out of the dark, landing in the aisle and roared as loud as she could.

Regorian instantly whirled around and fired.

She turned aside just in time to feel the arrow pass by, disturbing the thick fur across her chest. With a loud snarl, she retreated into the rafters again before he could reload.

Once he had another ready he aimed upward, searching and listening for his quarry. The stallion had finally stopped panicking and the stables were silent.

Adwen moved soundlessly for the nearest exit, but stopped cold when there was a loud snap as an arrow struck the crossbeam by her nose. She stole a glance as he reloaded and realized the moonlight outside revealed her through the gaps in the shingles.

Snarling, she darted among the crossbeams and supports as he tried to get a clear shot. Once he pulled the trigger and missed again, she dropped to ground level. While he drew another she rush for the street. Her shoulder clipped the hunter, knocking him to the ground.

Regorian was unharmed and recovered in time to see her bound to the rooftops. Cursing himself for being outwitted, he took to the streets. Four moons were visible, illuminating buildings and deepening the gloom.

With the hunter gone at last, Toth escaped out the opposite side of the stables. Everything was dark, but Toth was not lost. On his way to the town square, he stopped by a corner, huffing and puffing with hands on his knees.

Something large landed beside him, startling him. He jumped away and backed against the adjacent wall. But as he recognized the violet eyes glowing in the dark, he calmed and chuckled.

She towered over her friend, cocking her head. "Where to from here?"

It took a moment for him to make out what she'd said. "You'd be safer remaining on the roof tops. It will make you impossible to track."

She whined. "Where will you go?"

"I'll be well enough. You must hide."

A window across from them cracked opened and candlelight light fell on Adwen in the alleyway. The woman inside shrieked at the sight of the lycanthrope monster, abruptly snapping it shut.

Adwen's thick hair bristled as she felt the itch creeping up her neck. She spied Regorian rounding a corner and snatched Toth around the middle, leaping to safety. With the friend under one arm, she made sharp claws gouge wood and clay shingles on rooftops. When they came to an especially dark spot overlooking the town square, she set him down. The stands were closed, giving the once lively place an air of foreboding.

Leaning back beside her, he sighed. "That was close. Thank you."

Her tail swung, but then they gave a start when the hunter's voice echoed to them.

"I'm here, monster! Come and get me!"

With so many alleys, it was impossible to tell where he was calling from.

A cloud covered part of the full green moon and Adwen gradually shrank. When she could speak, she hollered out with a raspy voice, "Stop hunting me!"

"End this hiding, Adwen," he called back. "Come out and face me! You must be destroyed!"

She snarled and yelled, "You're wrong!"

"You were made what you are because of a monster! I have made an oath; a promise to defend this land and destroy all monsters and their creations. You must be slain!"

"No! You're wrong. I'm not a monster," she screamed through shrinking jaws. "You're making a mistake!"

Toth gasped, "Adwen!"

The hunter aimed from a corner below.

Clouds unmasked the moon and she quickly regained hound shape in time to leap away with the half-elf clinging to her back.

Scrambling and bounding to escape, she leaped from one building to the next. But as she strayed too close to the fort wall, archers loosed a volley of arrows. She yelped, evading the assault and soon found another secluded place to rest. While she panted, Toth dismounted down to look around. He became hopeful and smiled.

"Not to worry! See the building to the south? It is not far from the wall." He pointed to a structure with two bell towers on either end. It was the tallest building along the southern districts.

She nodded her fanged muzzle.

"You jump higher and move faster than anything I've ever seen. If anything can escape from this place, you can."

Adwen studied the town hall. Ears back, she knew staying here too long was certain death. After Toth climbed onto her back she bounded away.

Racing over buildings felt like flying. As they approached the large plaza before the town hall, Adwen prepared herself and took a deep breath. With all her might, she leaped. Toth squeezed as she sailed through the air and their weight came down on the shingles of the grand structure. Adwen worked hard to run up the steep angle. But when she reached the peak, she came to a stop.

Toth clung to her collar as fell off and nearly tumbled to his death. Regaining his balance beside her, he exclaimed, "Why have you stopped?"

She did not answer.

He followed her gaze to the base of the second tower.

Regorian Lancer stepped into the moonlight with cross-bow loaded. Holding it at this side, he studied the black creature, pondering what to do now that she was before him.

Together they stared each other down under the brilliant moons. The hunter watched the violet-eyed hound glare as she dipped her shoulder to allow Toth on.

She growled softly, "Don't do this, Regorian."

Frowning, he shook his head and raised his weapon. "I must honor my oath."

Snarling, she bolted straight for him.

He fired, but she leaped and it missed, striking the shingles with a loud snap.

She passed far overhead and kicked off of the tower, re-bounding towards the ramparts. Archers gasped and yelled as she came down among them and quickly leaped over the side. The armed men craned their heads and aimed bows, but saw nothing. There was only dark forest below and beyond.

Adwen ran as fast and far as she could until finally becoming tired. Letting her friend down to walk, she prowled on all fours, panting happily at the excitement of the escape.

Toth smiled proudly and laughed.

"He's going to follow my tracks, you know."

"That can't be helped. For now we have no choice but to continue afoot."

Wagging her tail, she panted, "That was so awesome! I didn't know I could do all of that stuff!"

"You did well."

As the misfits passed an open meadow, a musky scent reached her and she paused to look. A herd of wild animals were lying and standing in the moonlight.

"Wild roans," Toth whispered.

Grass on the hillside had already sprouted and the young shoots were what the horses liked best.

Her friend sighed longingly. "It would be nice if they could be ridden."

Adwen already had the same thought and started trotting towards them.

He whispered after her in warning, "Adwen, no! They're too wild. They'll attack if you get too close!"

She heard, but wasn't listening. While he remained at a distance, she went closer to the proud beasts.

A breeze came from behind and the roans spooked. Then a powerful, battle-scarred stallion charged, ears back and nostrils flared. Huge muscles rippled beneath scarred hide. The horse's neck arched aggressively and his mane flapped as he ran at the intruder.

Halting before her, he brayed fiercely, "Don't come any closer or you will meet your end with me, beast!"

She could tell the horse was serious, but did not want a fight. Careful not to provoke the animal, she replied, "My name is Adwen. Who are you?"

"I am the king of this hill, hound! You have no place here. Leave before I'm forced to make you!"

Adwen quickly decided to play to the stallion's overinflated pride. "My friend and I need your help, sire."

"Why would I help a lowly creature like yourself?"

Not sure of how to answer, she cocked her head. "I don't know. I had to ask because you are the only one who has the power to help us. We really do need your help, sire."

He was amused enough to cease stomping and snorted, "What do you want, beast?"

"We need to be carried as far from here as possible."

Tossing his mane, he laughed. "What a foolish creature you are! Why should I help you?"

"You would be getting rid of us," she pointed out. "You would know we were out of your territory."

The hound had a point. "How do I know you won't harm those I would send?"

"I still have the scent of a mare that helped me earlier. I didn't harm her and I promise I won't hurt anyone from your herd."

He cautiously sniffed her and backed away. His pinned ears became erect in astonishment at the honesty. After a brief moment of pondering, he snorted. "Very well. I shall grant your wish. I shall send two, but they shall only take you so far as the next human town. If they are harmed or do not return, I will kill you when you next cross my path. Am I understood, hound?"

She panted gratefully. "Completely, and thank you very much for your help, sire!"

The stallion called two young males forward and Toth watched in astonishment as she led them along.

He rode and she ran alongside. Once the moons set she changed and dressed, then the second horse carried her as well. They could only hope Regorian would have difficulty following now that they possessed mounts.

Chapter 10
THE BLOODY BROTHERS

The horses trotted at their own pace. Neither Adwen or Toth dared to spur them on. If they did not approve of their treatment, they would simply throw them off and leave. The day was warm as the earth awoke to the start of spring.

Adwen managed to get a small nap in while riding. When she awoke again feeling refreshed, she was disappointed to find the day coming to an end. Yawning, she addressed the roan beneath her, "How much farther is it?"

"A few miles and across a river. We shall take you as far as the man bridge."

Toth rode ahead of her cast in gold and pink by the sunset with the surrounding forest. Smells from the river drifted in over the treetops.

"We should stop soon," he warned as she came alongside. "Once the full moon rises we may continue." When she did not reply he was curious. "Adwen?"

A disturbed expression came over her. The horses both snorted and shifted nervously. "They smell something," she explained. Closing her eyes, she took a big whiff and grimaced. "They don't like it and neither do I."

The scream of a woman came from the thick of the forest and Adwen yelled at the horses, "Stop! Please stop!"

The roans hesitated and grumbled, but came to a gentle halt.

Leaping down, she went to the side of the road and waited, listening. Toth joined her, staring into the darkening wood.

One of the roans whinnied, "We must continue. It is not safe."

Giving him a determined glance, she replied, "We have to go in there."

The beasts snorted and stomped defiantly. "We will not! We are not man-servants!"

"We are going in there." Then she remembered how overly proud the creatures were. "This is no time to be afraid."

The adolescent males pawed the ground. "We are not afraid!" Then they approached, ready to follow.

Toth nudged her with an elbow. "You seem to have a way with horses."

She shrugged, smiling.

Her nose was their guide. The scent was strange and made her spine tingle. They all heard the scream again closer than before. Another breeze blew by, delivering the scent of a young woman. Wicked laughter and two harsh voices made Adwen's skin crawl.

Through the trees two men tormented a very frightened woman. The lovely young blond in a lavish velvet gown cried and shrieked. Her ruby cloak and dress had rips and tears as the attackers harassed the woman ceaselessly.

It was the men who gave off the terrible scent that disturbed Adwen and the horses. Though the odor seemed familiar, she could not place it. Either way, these men were vile.

The younger was lanky with long, dirty blond hair that reached past his shoulders. His face was youthful and might have been attractive if it weren't twisted into such a horrible smile. The older companion was far more powerfully built. While the top of his head was bald, his dense beard was dark and short as it grew around a blocky, grinning jaw.

The horrid twosome wore ragged clothes which reminded Adwen of biker thugs. They taunted the frightened woman. One ripped her cloak again as she screamed and they laughed, tossing her about, taking turns toying with her.

Adwen's eyes flashed bright blue in the shadows. "We've got to do something. I have an idea."

The brutes continued passing the woman back and forth until she collapsed on her knees in tears, crying for help. They laughed louder and the long-haired man picked her up, breathing down her neck. Holding golden strands to his nostrils, he sniffed and scoffed with a raspy voice, "It still smells like daisy pollen!"

The girl attempted to fight back, but he was too strong.

His cohort came close, deep voice booming, "Does it really? What do you say we find out what the flower looks like after we pluck her petals off?" Both laughed, but suddenly stopped when they heard a voice. Their eyes fell on a hooded young woman at the edge of the clearing.

Adwen curtsied and called to them, "Excuse me. I'm very lost. Can you give me some directions back to the road?"

They exchanged smiles and the lanky man chuckled, "Looks like this is our lucky day, eh, Brother?"

"It sure is. Now we have two toys with instead of one."

The big, bearded one strolled casually toward the woman without fear or the slightest suspicion.

Adwen waited until he was close then leaped and knocked the brute to the ground. The other villain was so stunned by the sight that he was unprepared when she darted straight for him as well. As his grip on the blonde girl slackened he was tackled into a tree, freeing the frightened stranger from his grasp.

Toth rode through on horseback, whisking the woman out of danger. When the second roan came by, Adwen quickly dashed from the stunned villains and vaulted onto its back.

The horses ran with their passengers and Adwen whooped, laughing triumphantly. Her plan had worked and they were escaping into the night while the roans whinnied in an enthusiastic reply.

Toth and the strange woman were ahead as she rode a short ways behind. She could make out the girl's long pale hair flowing in the wind. Strong moonlight was making it shine like ripples on a pond.

Giving a start, she quickly turned her attention to the glowing horizon. A full moon was rising. Amidst the excitement she hadn't noticed. Her eyes were already glowing violet.

About to call her friend, the moon rose full. Breath was ripped from her lungs by the jolt of cramping muscles in her back. Her body involuntarily flexed and she fell, tumbling through dry leaves as the changes gripped her insides.

A loud whinny reached Toth's ears and the second roan passed him without a rider. His own steed skidded to a halt and turned back to collect the fallen companion.

Adwen saw him coming and cried out, "No, Toth!"

The horse stopped dead.

Gritting sharpening fangs, she cried, "Keep going! I'll catch up!" The agony made her double over in the leaf litter and she screamed, "Go!"

Toth and the remaining roan fled. The horse ran fast between the trees and through the brush like a nighthawk until they had no choice but to stop in a clearing for rest. After sliding off of the winded roan he helped the woman down and was surprised to receive a swift slap to the face. Confused, he felt his cheek, wondering why she would do such a thing.

The pale woman glared and shouted, "Coward! How could you leave that brave girl behind! How dare you?"

Taken aback, he explained, "She said she would catch up with us, ma'am."

Still outraged, she shouted "That's no excuse. No man should ever leave a woman behind to die!"

"You don't understand, ma'am. Adwen can take care of herself and she did say she would catch up."

"She fell from her horse! You saw how much pain she was in. She was clearly injured, you spineless worm!"

Her rage was beginning to distress him. "Please, ma'am. Calm yourself. Adwen will be fine, even if those terrible men manage to find her."

The woman paused and shook her head in dismay. "It is you who does not understand! Those weren't just men." Suddenly her expression turned to terror and she shrieked.

Toth turned to see the black hound bounding towards them, eyes glowing bright like fireflies. He was glad to see her.

The woman was not and screamed a second time, clinging to the roan in hopes of riding away. The horse was far too tired and wasn't afraid as Adwen came closer. He wouldn't let her on no matter how much she urged.

Joining him, Adwen growled, "Well so much for that dress. Now we have to go into the next town to buy a new one."

Shaking his head he added, "You certainly do go through them regularly."

The woman yelled at him, *"What is that thing?"*

Adwen whined and flattened her ears at the young woman.

"There's nothing to be afraid of, ma'am." Toth put a hand on the creature's furry neck to demonstrate. "This is my friend, Adwen."

"Your friend is this monster?"

More insulted than before, Adwen padded a short distance away, grumbling. "Same old story, huh, Toth?" Then she huffed loudly. "And you're very welcome too!"

Clearly unable to understand animal speech, the woman found it difficult to believe this was the girl from before.

The half-elf went to her side to translate. "Adwen said you are welcome for her help."

"This truly is your friend? How?"

Toth chuckled. "It's quite a story, ma'am."

Adwen suddenly snarled and leaped past their heads to collide with a huge werewolf. The beasts rolled around in the leaves, snapping and slashing.

The woman screamed and Toth helped her onto the horse. As he lifted himself after her, a second monster came at them.

The roan whinnied, and before it could reach them, Adwen intercepted the large set of open jaws. She gave a loud yelp as incisors ensnared her shoulder. They went rolling across the ground. They watched in horror at the fighting creatures and the horse bolted, disappearing with them into the forest.

Adwen slashed and kicked desperately until it lobbed her into an old pine. Bleeding profusely, she snarled and stood upright to face them. The vile things began to stalk closer and she roared, "You want a fight? Come on!"

The werewolves both froze. Then they glanced at one another and started to laugh. Their croaking guffaws continued as they stood and shrank down into the two men who had been tormenting the woman. They even regained their grubby garments as they changed into their more human forms.

Astounded, she looked between the werewolves and the full moon in confusion.

The bearded one clapped clawed hands and laughed at her surprise. With his deep, ominous voice, he praised her. "That was very good coming up from downwind before. I have to admit, you had us fooled. We were very surprised, weren't we, brother?"

His counterpart grinned. A bit of drool fell from his lips.

"Yes, we were." Even in his more human form, his teeth were jagged fangs.

"You interrupted our game, so now we think we'll play one with you. The rules are simple."

She gnashed her jaws, growling. "What rules?"

The pupils of his eyes glowed red. "We win and you die. It's funny that you would ask us to play. No one does that anymore. You aren't even powerful enough to change your form when you choose. How pathetic."

Balling her clawed hands into fists, she snarled.

"I am Korig and this is my little brother, Kotig. You are about to learn why the Kingdom of Dargadia calls us the Bloody Brothers."

Rapidly and horrifically, they began their transformations. The skin on their faces blistered and bled as if they were held over a blaze. Both cried out and laughed hysterically throughout the hideous process. Bones twisted and snapped while their skulls elongated under bloody, melting faces. Enormous razor-sharp fangs grew and they became much larger than the first werewolf she fought.

Though frightened, her courage held.

Both werewolves laughed and roared, charging with jaws open wide. Adwen was swift enough to evade Kotig, but Korig was right there waiting. As the first brother missed and ran headlong into an oak, Korig snatched her up by the leg. He quickly lobbed her over one shoulder into another tree where she crumpled up in a heap.

She struggled to get up and he sank long fangs into her neck. As she yelped, he thrashed, shaking her like a rag doll. The monster smashed Adwen against the ground mercilessly until his brother could join in. Kotig bit one of her legs and pulled, laughing with sadistic croaking guffaws.

In a desperate attempt to escape, she gave a hard kick to Kotig's nose.

He lost his grip and the force bowled Korig over backwards. Out of surprise, he let go and Adwen swiftly got to her feet.

In a rage, Kotig rushed her and she slashed his face. Huge bleeding gashes were left and he fell back, reeling and howling. Then Korig came out of nowhere and swung at her chest with a dinner plate-sized hand. Claws sliced her and she made a high-pitch yelp. Then the monster followed through with a powerful back hand, dealing an oozing gash to her muzzle.

Korig was ready to take another swing just as she leaped into the trees above. Just as he left the ground Kotig pounced, but plowed straight into his brother. Together they piled up, snarling.

Wounded and weak, Adwen found the strength to run from sheer desperation. She bounded from tree to tree, landing on bigger limbs, but the Bloody Brothers caught up.

Korig ripped across the ground below as Kotig bounded through the tree limbs at her heels. She heard them and tried to move faster, but Kotig gained in the chase. Then Adwen landed on an older limb in a dead tree. It made an unsettling crunch as she bounded off to another.

Kotig was so obsessed with catching his prey that he hadn't noticed. Once his bulk came down, it gave way. He landed onto his brother, causing a catastrophic crash that sent them tumbling. Korig was the first to pick himself up and scan the trees, but she was already gone. He roared in outrage and punched his foolish brother in the jaw for his idiocy.

Adwen continued on, growing delirious. Eventually the forest came to an end and the ground abruptly dropped off. Before she knew it, she was freefalling into a river. The shock from the rush of cold water cleared her head. When she resurfaced and gasped for breath, she saw little lights.

A town rested by the bank and a street beyond was brightly lit with many torches and lamps. The flames were beacons for her bleary eyes. Water lapping greeted her by the time her claws gripped soil and she limped onto dry land. Streams of water and blood trickled from matted fur and torn flesh.

Reaching the homes, she stood upright, using the side of a house to stand. Pierced muscles screamed from the effort. Sidling along the surface, blood smeared the planks until she limped into the light. It was quiet and her sensitive nose detected people nearby.

Shuddering, she staggered about, searching for Toth and the young woman. They would have made it this far with the lead she had given them. All was still and she howled balefully at the far end of the street, "Toth?"

There was no answer. Adwen limped a few steps farther into the open. Her bleeding slowed, but she grew weak. Red droplets trailed at her paw feet. A breeze went past and she caught his scent.

"Toth?"

An arrow whistled through the air and struck her stomach.

Letting out a yelp, she staggered back into the side of a home as five archers with silver-tipped arrows dashed out of hiding. Helpless, she yelped and heard a voice call out to halt the archers.

"No, stop!" Toth came and she whimpered as he shielded her from them.

"Move aside, boy!" One yelled, but Toth refused.

Then another voice spoke. "Hold your fire! Listen to the man! The creature is not to be harmed!"

They lowered their aim and stepped aside to make way for the young blond woman. Moving closer, she commanded, "This creature is under my protection."

Everyone stared, awestruck by the sight of her.

An archer muttered warily, "Are you..?"

"Princess Eyrie. I am your princess and daughter to King Lorvan. Do not slay this creature. She has just saved my life."

They were taken aback and stared at the strange beast. She had oozing battle wounds everywhere while her gaze was fixed on the princess.

Pain was crippling, but Adwen could not hide her surprise. Then her vision blurred and swam.

Toth saw her sway and tried to catch her. "Adwen!" The weight was too much for him and she collapsed.

Eyrie ordered the men closest to her. "You two! Find a way to bring her to the healer's quarters."

After giving a start, they quickly obeyed.

The town healer was an old man and not a night owl. He was sound asleep when persistent knocking sounded at the door. "I'm on my way, blast you! Give a man a chance to take a step. Patience is a valued thing!"

When he answered at last, he found the princess, Toth, and two men.

"By the light spirits, what's all this?"

The men worked together to carry Adwen's unconscious body inside and laid her prone so as not to disturb the arrow. She completely covered the healer's table and her hound feet hung just past the bottom end.

He loudly protested, "I am a distinguished healer of men, not a tender to beasts from the forest!"

The princess glared. "You will do what your title implies. You shall heal this creature we've brought to you. If you do not, I shall see that you answer to my father."

He grumbled and went about gathering powders from shelves and cupboards.

Toth remained by Adwen's side, frowning at the gaping wounds. He stroked her neck. The soft coat shined in the candlelight while the gashes on her chest glistened with fresh blood. The bleeding had almost stopped and her long head and muzzle lay beside him.

The healer applied brown paste around the base of the arrow as he mused. "It's strange, amazing even, that a werewolf would survive being struck with silver."

"She's not a werewolf," Toth corrected him.

He gave a surprised glance and his bushy eyebrows went up. "Well, then your creature is strange." Setting the remaining paste aside, he gripped the arrow and firmly pulled it out. He blinked and was even more bemused. "This is a very strange creature indeed! The other wounds still bleed, but the arrow wound looks well on the way to healing. Your animal is strong!"

As the healer returned to work, Toth looked outside at the night sky before quickly removed his cloak and casting it over Adwen's body.

The old man rounded on him. "What do you think you're doing? I have a job to do, boy!"

A moment later everyone watched in amazement as the creature began to shrink, turn pale and become an unconscious young woman. When Adwen's appearance was completely human again, the old man continued to stare.

"Well?" the princess snapped. "Are you going to heal her or not?"

The healer swiftly went back to the task.

Light poured into the room, warming Adwen's cheeks, bringing her out of a deep sleep. She found herself in a room with the sun shining through a glass window. The soft bed linens made it feel as if she were home, though she knew it was not so. The thought depressed her until she realized she was not alone.

A young woman with chestnut hair saw she was awake and said with a curtsy, "Good morning, my lady."

Again, she was without clothes. Covering up as she sat, Adwen agreed that waking in a bed was a very good morning. Rubbing away a bit of sleep, she replied, "Good morning." The gashes on her face and chest were almost gone, nothing more than tiny cuts.

"The princess waits for you in the other room, my lady."

Surprised, she stopped rubbing her eye. "What?"

"Her Highness wishes to speak with you privately, my lady. There are garments beside you." She curtsied a second time and quietly departed.

The feeling of grogginess was gone and excitement made her jump out of bed and dress herself with fervor. A princess wanted to talk to her and she was not about to pass up the opportunity. The dress left for her was dark blue silk with gold embroidery along the hems.

Admiring the gift in a mirror, she frowned and shook her head. "There's no way this dress is going to last."

As she had been told, the princess sat waiting in the next room by a window where the sun shone on her golden hair. She turned and approached, smiling kindly, wearing a crimson dress that made her look like the royalty she was.

Adwen smiled and thought to say hello, but caught herself forgetting who this was and quickly bowed, embarrassed.

Eyrie's smile made her aquamarine eyes glint and she gestured to the plush seats. "Come. Sit with me."

The chairs were not those of a commoner. All of the furniture and décor was lavish and didn't suit the dark wood cabin. Adwen sighed as she sat, thankful for the comfort. Then Eyrie's voice brought her attention back.

"I want to thank you properly for what you've done."

Her cheeks turned bright red. "Well, I didn't really know what I was getting into, Your Highness."

The princess shook her head. "You were very brave. You may not have known the danger, but you acted nobly when you were made aware of it. Thank you from the bottom of my heart, Adwen."

She blushed harder. "Uh, you're welcome, princess."

"Your friend had said your eyes were like mine. I would have to disagree. They are much bluer. You are a stranger to this land, are you not?"

"Yeah, kind of."

"My father and I are all that remain of the royal family. There is no other explanation for a blue-eyed traveler. Toth also tells me you are trying to find your way home. Before you do, I would like to make a request."

She gave a shrug. "Sure, anything."

The princess turned hesitant as if she thought the request was too great. "If you decline, I shall understand, and you just may. In a week's time there is going to be a masquerade ball. It is my twenty-first birthday celebration in Castle Gailarien. I would very much like for you to attend and allow me to bring you and your brave companion before my father, King Lorvan."

Adwen's eyes went wide.

Eyrie saw her expression and repeated with a sad tone, "As I said, you would more than likely decline. I cannot supply an escort. You would have to find your own way, but I can arrange for your attire and..."

Adwen grinned and giggled.

A pleased expression suddenly grew on the princess' doll face. "Will you attend?"

"Of course I will! I've always wanted to go to a masquerade!"

Eyrie clasped her hands together and stood. "It's settled then! I shall give you a piece from my other dress, a written invitation, and the name of the royal dresser in the city beneath the castle gates! The piece from my dress shall serve as proof of identity for the dresser once you arrive."

"But what will I do to pay?"

"It shall be taken care of. The dresser is a bit of a snoot. If you do not arrive in the best of his work, I shall give him less than desirable commendation. Now come! We have a feast to attend."

"An early birthday dinner?"

"No." The princess shook her head. "This feast is in your honor."

"Huh?"

Adwen learned that the princess had been making secret visits to the village for years. She would be sent to attend lectures and then make for her private getaway in Breed Town. In the feasting hall they held celebrations upon her every visit. All of the villagers were present and seated at long tables covered with platters from last year's harvest. The spread was not lavish, but it was delicious and there was plenty to go around. Naturally, the princess was given the head of the largest table where Adwen and Toth sat at either side. The two reveled in their good fortune. Princess Eyrie stood and raised a hand for silence.

When the clamor died away, she spoke. "Thank you, good people who once again welcome me here. Most of you know this feast almost did not take place."

A few people showed shock.

"I had been abducted by none other than the Bloody Brothers."

Whispers and murmurs buzzed until she continued and they were quiet.

"But they were stopped. Two brave individuals took it upon themselves to step into harm's way and stand up for a helpless stranger. They did not know who I was, but they acted." Glancing over at Adwen's modest expression, she lifted her cup and announced, "I raise a toast to the one who deserves my thanks and yours."

Eyes wide, Adwen was speechless as everyone raised their drinks.

The princess cried, "To Adwen, the Tame One!"

The entire village repeated, "The Tame One!"

Everyone toasted and drank heavily. The two guests of honor stared at one another and Toth chuckled at her astounded expression.

"This feast is for you, Tame One." Eyrie smiled. "Eat what you may."

They ate their fill and the people of Breed Town gave her

countless beaming smiles. Once some of the men ingested more mead, they continued in toasting to the title the princess had given her. She couldn't help but laugh, unafraid to reveal her small fangs. None of yesterday's worries bothered her and she intended to enjoy the moment while it lasted.

When the feast ended it was past noon and time to say farewell. Before leaving on horseback to rejoin her father, the princess gave them what they needed to attend her celebration. Toth accepted the piece of the princess' torn dress and invitation, keeping them safe in his satchel.

Replacing the collar around her neck, Adwen couldn't stop grinning. She was not ashamed of it anymore and wore the token proudly. Soon they were off and on their way to Castle Gailarien. Walking past the next bend in the road, Adwen laughed. "Well, it sure has been one thing after another."

"Yes, it has. This road should be much safer than the other on our way to the castle."

"How do you guess that?"

"You know very well that this land holds many dangers, and even more dangerous fiends than one can count. For a being such as you, it would be far too great a risk to take the road that strays north." He had a tone of warning. "In that direction lies the grand Hall of the Master Knights."

Chapter 11
A MASTER KNIGHT

The Master Knights was a prestigious order of highly skilled warriors. It was established hundreds of years ago when a warrior, whom the people called the Master Knight, mysteriously appeared and saved the Kingdoms of Day from the forces of darkness.

When the order began, an enormous glistening fortress was constructed for both the housing and instruction of brave warriors. The Master Knight resided in his fortress for many years. No one knew where he had come from, or where he went, but it was well known that he accomplished many amazing feats.

Inside the marble halls the names of each knight were etched shortly after their passing. Behind each tablet, a scroll containing all the knight's accomplishments is stored. The dream of every knight was to be remembered into eternity. Disgrace was the only fear they knew. If a knight were to ever become what he destroyed and not take his own life, his name would be scratched from the records. If this were to happen, his family name would be cursed and spat upon by all who heard it said. No knight would dare to let this occur under any circumstances.

The knights trained under four professions. They had to choose wisely whether to be a slayer of dragons, witches, vampires, or werewolves. Each branch possessed three special suits of armor for only the worthiest to adorn. They were lavish and the extravagant helms resembled the creature the knights specialized in destroying.

One cool evening, four knights were on their way to answer a summons. Their leader was an owner of one such set of armor; it was of the werewolf slayer. The silvery surface glistened like a polished mirror in the painted sunset. His powerful warhorse was large and bold, its muscular neck held high as the others galloped alongside in the dying light. Dark capes furled and flew from the knights flags. They rode on into the wilds, far from any sanctuary.

Night joined them as they came across a shadowy glen. Upon entering darker shadows the horses became nervous and slowed.

Their leader held up a gloved fist. As the others stopped, he pressed on confidently towards what disturbed their mounts. The three who stayed back watched with bated breath. There was a new warrior with them on their quest and a more experienced knight leaned over to whisper to him.

"Watch closely. You have the opportunity to see how he earned his slayer's armor."

Their leader moved his chocolate Clydesdale slowly along the tiny brook. Horse and rider kept an attentive eye on the prowling things. He left his sword sheathed. A red crescent moon and a quarter of gold hung in the sky, awaiting the third and fourth to come. Tonight the full moon would be green and it could be seen rising out of the distance. It gave off a powerful glow that restricted the dark farther under the trees and rocks. When the lime glow splashed across the slayer's armor his wolf-faced visor shined. It seemed almost to come alive upon its master's head with silent wrath, frozen in a steely snarl. The knight fit a calm grip on the sword hilt, waiting.

Naked man-like creatures sulked, salivating in eager antici-pation for a feed. They smelled him through the silver-steel armor. The knight knew all too well what they were and was not afraid. This was what he had trained for since the age of ten. This was his specialty.

At last, the green moon rose. Instantly, the man-creatures howled and began their hideous transformations into were-wolves. Haunting screams from eight monsters echoed through the trees and the knight drew his sword.

The warhorse did not need to be spurred to charge at the changing creatures. Light lanced across the blade as he swung over the shoulders of a monster, cleaving the head from its twisted body. The first was followed by two more brutes, send-ing hot blood pouring into the stream, turning it shades of black and bubbling crimson.

One of the foes was fully transformed. It leaped from a boulder and roared, but made a fatal mistake by doing so.

In an instant, the silver-steel weapon was pointed at the monster's open jaws and it came crashing down, knocking him from the saddle. The point of the sword erupted out of the top of its blood-red skull as they hit the ground with a thud.

The knight stood as the last three advanced to meet him amid the carnage. They growled and snarled at the man in silver-steel armor. To touch it would burn them and their evil fangs and claws could not scratch the surface, let alone pierce it. It protected him well, but there were plenty of gaps to take advantage of. Through training and experience, he knew a werewolf's nature was to attack rather than wait. All he needed was patience for them to meet his blade.

They attacked at once and he swept his sword up in a wide arc, cutting air and evil flesh. Even more red gushed out to soil the earth by his feet while another leaped and he stepped aside only far enough to avoid it. While the third was running past, the knight pierced its heart, putting an end to the raging horror. When its mangy form collapsed and became still, he turned to deal with the final beast.

It was distracted, attacking the horse. His steed reared, swinging shod hooves as it slashed and snapped in a blind frenzy. The knight briskly approached and took off its head in a single sweeping stroke, slinging blood and fur. It collapsed and the horse calmly joined his master while he bathed the blade in the clean side of the stream.

Once the filth were washed away, he sheathed it in a smooth, disciplined motion. Greeting the loyal steed with a pat to the nose, the knight climbed into the saddle.

The leader rejoined the company and an experienced knight chuckled, "Now that you've had your fun, we should return to our task."

The three subordinates chuckled in their helms as their ranking officer quietly turned his horse.

The four knights reached the village the following afternoon. One removed his helm and read the note aloud as they rode through the street. Brack was thirty-seven years of age, had a neatly trimmed beard and held up the letter in his big hands.

"Knights, you are needed," he read. "The village of Vanguard desperately require your services. To the north by the river is a home that once belonged to a man who has since passed. Now every man who stays there meets his end at the hands of werewolves. They hide in the day, but attack the cabin the night. We have tried to stop them, but to no avail. They are sure to be in great numbers. Please send your best. The Mayor of Vanguard."

Finished, Brack rolled the parchment and tucked it away, smiling broadly. "It looks as if they've gotten their answer, sir."

Their leader remained silent. Unlike his men, he continued to wear his helm and Brack was not bothered by the lack of a reply. They knew each other well and his merry smile only grew.

Darek, the other experienced knight was also a close friend of the slayer. He was twenty-nine and kept his face clean-shaven with black hair short and neatly combed.

The novice knight had never been on a quest and was twenty-four years of age. Knights were only allowed to join the ranks after completing special training within the castle walls, usually around the age of twenty-seven. Some completed earlier and were allowed to take up quests. He was nervous, but tried to hide the fact. It was no secret that the average life expectancy for a werewolf slayer was short. A knight was considered either skilled or very lucky to last a year in the field. Only the best survived and he was in the company of the best. Darek had been slaying werewolves for nearly three years, while Brack had four years of experience.

When they attempted to purchase food on the street, the people were so overjoyed that they gave the goods free of charge. A few villagers saw the leader wearing his slayer armor and gasped. They knew this knight. None had met him or seen his face, but his name and reputation were renowned throughout the kingdom. He was their hero and his presence brought hope.

They soon started for the house described in the summons. The slayer was focused and quiet as ever as he took them through the trees up a barren path. From around the next rise in the earth they spied the cabin. Every window was shattered on both floors and the front door hung from one feeble hinge. They dismounted and turned their horses away to a creek, intending to collect them after the task was complete.

The signs of many bloody encounters were evident from the threshold. Blood stains and claw marks were underfoot and marred the walls. After a thorough search of the place it was noted that no bodies or physical remains could be found. Together the men cleared the largest space of mangled furniture, stacking debris in corners out of the way for the eventual battle. Once the room was staged it was time to wait.

As the last of the candles were lit and strategically placed, Brack sat in a flimsy chair, adjusting his helm and addressed the fresh knight.

"You notice how there were no bodies or bones left behind?"

He nodded as he put on his own helm.

"That is an indication of two things that could be occurring. First, and most likely, these werewolves are killing for food and taking flesh to a den." His gaze became darker. "Or it could mean something worse: that the beasts are banning together and adding to their numbers. If they were killing for pleasure they would have simply left a mess and moved on."

Darek sat on a badly clawed dresser. His gruff voice was muffled by the helm. "Perhaps and perhaps not. Werewolves and other monsters have been doing strange things of late. Until we discover why we'll simply continue our duty and put them in their place."

The young knight shifted nervously.

Brack chuckled. "You'll do well. Remember your training and Darien's Breath for better focus. Look at our superior. He's been performing the breathing ritual for the past hour since sundown."

Their leader was in a chair directly across from the cabin door, which was set back in its frame with an overturned cabinet. The slayer breathed in a steady rhythmic pattern, gazing out his helm. For seven years he had been the best that the order had to offer.

A harsh chill coursed through him and he jumped to his

feet, kicking the chair aside while staring raptly at the door. The others saw him move and quickly took their positions, drawing swords. Back to back, the four stood vigilantly on guard. Nighttime insects went quiet. All they could hear was the breath inside their helms and heartbeats in their chests.

Their leader was calm and did not hear those things. Because of the meditation-induced trance, he only heard silence and would only hear the sounds made by his enemies. The silence dragged on and the others shifted to be more ready for the imminent attack. He was stone-still with silver-steel sword at the ready. Dim light illuminated the slayer's blade, glinting off two smooth red gems set into the blade above the hilt. His dark cape draped down to touch the ground, meeting the other three of his companions.

Without warning, the front door exploded as a monstrous werewolf came ripping through. It lunged and roared, swiftly joined by many more coming through the windows. One by one, the knights slashed and cut them down. Fresh coats of red blood painted the timbers a hairy, muscular bodies quickly piled up, slowly changing back into fanged men where they fell.

Their leader never lost his footing or his ground. Masterfully, he slaughtered each one that came within the reach. His sword slit their throats before greeting the next wave of attackers in kind.

Brack continuously broke the creature's bones while Darek disemboweled a few. The inexperienced warrior held his own, relentlessly slicing and killing monsters as they appeared. Crimson splattered their armor. Fluids soaked and stained their capes, yet even more lunged forward to their deaths. Thirty lay dead once quiet was restored. When no more came, the commander turned to face his companions, inspecting their conditions.

He found Brack and Darek by the young knight, who was holding his wounded hand and watching thick blood flow. He had been bitten during the battle. Removing his helm, he looked to the experienced knights, frightened.

Darek set a firm, bloody glove on his shoulder. "You know what must be done."

"Don't worry, boy," Brack assured him. "Your name shall

be set into the hall forever. We will see that it is done."

Tears formed in the young man's eyes and he smiled weakly. They watched him remove his chest plate and set it aside. Then he took out a six inch, silver-steel blade. Every knight kept one in just such a case as this.

The slayer stood over him and the young man looked up proudly, smiling as he saw him nod his wolf-like helm, candle-light rippling on the snarling visor.

He beamed at his superior and announced, "I am glad to have had the opportunity to call you brother." And he plunged the blade in deep.

There he knelt, dying as their leader gently lined up the edge of his sword with the young man's neck. It was his final act of mercy and a reward for the knight's courage and honor. To end his suffering, he lifted the blade and swiftly brought it back down.

It was time to return to the Hall of the Master Knights. They drove the horses hard. Their mounts were well bred and as well conditioned as their masters. On the second day, they arrived. Across the rolling hills they raced towards the city gates. Watchmen let them pass into the beautiful city of Plexus.

Though the horses were tired, they were glad to be home in the white stone streets, headed for the grand fortress. The Hall of the Master Knights dwarfed the great city and the entrance onto the grounds was always open, but well defended by guards and magical wards. No evil magical being could set foot past the threshold. As they rode inside the paddock squires waited to take the horses to the stables.

Dismounting, the slayer approached the fourth horse baring their fallen companion. He moved his fingers in a blessing over the body and placed a hand upon him as a final farewell. Finished, he led the way to the armory. It served as a locker where the knights kept their armor in personal storage along with a few other possessions. When they entered, those who were stowing and adorning armor and weaponry gave warm greetings.

"Ah, the masters of slaying return!"

Their leader passed them by while Brack and Darek returned the small salutes, tapping fists to their chest plates.

Another asked, "Where is the lad? I want to hear his story of his first kill."

They exchanged somber glances and Darek replied, "His passing ritual is to be held tomorrow at dawn."

While they conversed, the slayer went across the room to retire his armor. His fingers were like lightning pressing the correct combination of enchanted panels to unlock his personal compartment. Then at long last, he removed his helm and gently placed it inside the proper cubby. Running a hand through sweaty brown hair, he let out a heavy sigh before ceremoniously removing the rest. One by one, he snapped off the latches of his arm guards.

A few of the newer knights entered, laughing and talking about their morning's spar. They carried on as they went to the lockers nearby. One had done well in the ring and laughed. "So who else wishes to have a drink before facing your mortality once more?"

They laughed and sincerely declined.

Twenty-eight years of age, the bragging knight had medium-length black hair and dark brown eyes. While removing his cape, he discovered how filthy it had gotten. Then his attention fell on the brown-haired man not too far away. Smiling to himself, he could see how young the man was and assumed this was a novice.

He approached and chuckled. "Here, squire. Take my cape and have it cleaned, will you?"

Some of his friends laughed, but one was not amused and made an attempt to stop him. He knew who the knight was and desperately reached for his friend in hopes of pulling him back.

Shrugging him off, the man continued, "I'm speaking to you, novice!"

The companions of the slayer heard the noise and turned to watch.

Darek chuckled. "Shall we go closer to protect the stranger?"

The slayer acted as if he had not noticed and kept removing armor.

Quickly losing his temper, the man cried, "Are you deaf or a fool? Answer me, dog!" He threw the cape at him and started to draw his sword. But when he looked up again the slayer already had his own out and the tip was touching his throat.

He stared in shock at the man who stood at a height of six-foot-two. His body was lean, toned and his hair was short with long bangs that hung down just past his beardless cheekbones, framing bright, emerald green eyes. Cold and calculating, the slayer glared back at the ignorant knight with a murderous intensity. The foolish knight did not dare speak for fear of provoking his hand into flinching. The razor-sharp edge balanced on his rapidly pulsating jugular.

Brack and Darek calmly went to the frozen knight's side and Darek announced, "Well done. You have just insulted your ranking officer and the captain of the entire order."

His dark eyes widened in horror and astonishment. This man who was perhaps no older than twenty-one was his commanding officer. The green-eyed knight was by far the youngest in the room. Everyone had said he was young, but not this young. This was Sir Oryn Reynard Conrad, their captain and the soon-to-be General of the Master Knights.

Oryn glared unblinkingly and glanced down at this knight's drawn sword. Scowling, he sneered in a low and deadly tone, "You have enough pride to draw your sword at me." His green glare narrowed even more. "Then let us see if you have enough 'honor' to back your challenge."

The man blanched. Being a master of the blade was one of the many reasons Sir Oryn was their captain. Chances of beating him were slim to none, but this was his ranking officer. He had enough pride to not throw away his honor before him.

The captain took a few paces back and slowly lowered his sword as the tone in his masculine voice turned even colder. "What is your answer?"

He swallowed hard. Taking the fighting stance that served him best, he held the sword tight, prepared to dual Sir Oryn.

Onlookers moved aside as the slayer took his own stance. After a moment of sizing each other up the dual commenced. The knights swung through a series of vicious volleys. Ringing of silver-steel echoed off the walls and in the ears silent bystanders. Before long Sir Oryn's blows came more rapidly, wearing down the challenger. Any attempt to reclaim ground resulted in losing more as the captain drove him into a corner. When the man had no place to go Oryn deftly smacked the man's cheek with the flat of the blade. With the opponent distracted, Oryn kicked the man's sword out of his hand then snatched it out of the air. Straight away the blades were held in a scissor to the rude knight's throat. It was over.

Everyone clapped at the display of swordsmanship as the defeated knight was still in shock.

Oryn returned the weapon, but the cold expression on his face never thawed. "What is your name?"

The black haired man panted. "Jacques, sir."

"I shall remember. I recall every man who has dared to call me a dog."

A small squire suddenly burst into the room, panting from running. "Sir Oryn! I have a message for you." The boy bent down with hands on his knees, gasping.

"What is it?"

"The king, sir. He is here to see you. He awaits you in the higher study."

"Thank you." He waved a hand to dismiss him. "You may take your leave."

The squire departed and Oryn sheathed his sword. Storing it away, he locked the compartment and departed with Brack and Darek, never giving Jacques another glance.

If he had, he would have seen him glaring vengefully.

Their footfalls echoed along the marble corridor and Brack chuckled. "You remember every man who has called you a dog? How many have been that daring, sir?"

"The count is three."

Darek added, "Well, I can't blame them too much. With your long face you have to see a resemblance."

Oryn stopped dead in his tracks to give his icy glare.

Instantly, Darek was taken aback. "Forgive me, sir. I was too bold!"

They continued and Brack shook his head.

Records and other historical texts were kept in the higher study. Each was priceless and irreplaceable. Only the king, the elders of the order and the commanding officers were allowed to visit freely.

Brack and Darek halted beside the carved oak door as he approached and knocked. Then the response came from inside, "Enter."

As the two were left alone to wait, smiles spread across their faces. They knew Sir Oryn like a true brother and it was no secret that King Lorvan treated him like the son he never had. But Sir Oryn, because of his loyalty and respect was not able to respond in kind. Brack and Darek thought the relationship was hysterical at their captain's expense.

He was at the window overlooking the city. With the sun still high, it illuminated the study and exposed the king's strong elderly form. His neat beard was mostly white and flecked with blond. King Lorvan turned his weathered face and his soft blue eyes sparkled in the light. The crow's feet showed even more when he smiled at the knight who stood at attention in a white linen shirt and black dragon skin trousers.

"You summoned me, Your Highness?"

"I did, lad. I have come for a short visit. I felt the need to go abroad and see how my favorite knight was getting on." Then he ruefully shook his head. "I heard a whisper of your recent quest and what happened to that poor boy."

Oryn held his bearing. "He was a knight, my king. He died well and with true honor. He fared better than the past few I had taken on in training."

The king studied him sympathetically. It was difficult to tell if Oryn were either hiding remorse or was simply out of touch with emotions on the matter. Giving a sly smile, the king stated, "Oryn, I want you to make a promise to me."

"Yes, my king?"

"I want you to accompany me back to Castle Gailarien with the rest of the knights who are to be awarded soon. I want you to escort me, and when you have done that, I want you to have a holiday."

"My king?"

"You have done your people and my kingdom a great service many times over and it is long overdue that you had time to serve yourself for a change. Take your men to the streets of Deleon and my castle. Enjoy the things of which you deprive yourself regularly. You have seen enough blood for a thousand lifetimes." The twinkle in his eye grew. "I don't think you have seen enough of the beauties that live and breathe the free air, my boy!"

Caught off guard, Oryn cleared his throat. "I have known women before, my king. They all lack the... quality I would ask of them."

The king chuckled and rapped him on the shoulder. "You are a handsome young man! You could have the pick of any woman you choose!"

Embarrassed, he managed to say, "Thank you, my king."

Outside, Brack and Darek suppressed a dire need to laugh out loud.

With a hand still on his shoulder, he asked, "But will you promise me, lad? Will you come and at the least allow me the honor of presenting you your new rank?"

"Yes, my king," he answered without hesitation.

Shaking his gray head, he smiled even more kindly. If the young knight dropped his strict manners he would not mind in the slightest. It would have flattered him.

"Good," he chuckled, giving his shoulder another hard rap. Folding his hands behind his back, he returned to the window. "I intend to leave at dawn. Be sure the men are ready. Do not forget to inform them they are to take time for themselves."

The slayer bowed low with his fist across his chest and responded, "Yes, my king." Taking his nonverbal dismissal, he swept out of the room without another word.

King Lorvan chuckled and stared out at the view. "What a silly young man."

Chapter 12
RAIN, MUD AND BLOOD

Fore the next two days Adwen and Toth found no troubles on the road. They saw many travelers on horseback from. A few from Breed Town even tipped their hats. Daytime was safer for rest so they slept during daylight hours. Adwen spent the most time on watch. She needed the least amount of sleep and observed the passersby. The clothes they wore reminded her of Europe just before the Renaissance period.

The one night was uneventful and they enjoyed the peaceful walk by moonlight. After enduring another painful yet shorter transformation, she admired the sea of stars over them. The second day was clear until thunderheads began to drift in from the coast. By noon the day became dreary. Then as evening arrived a storm blotted out the sky.

"Finally," Adwen crowed. "No full moon!"

Thunder rumbled overhead and Toth added, "Yes, there will definitely not be a moon tonight, but I can tell you what there will be." He pulled the hood over his head as the first drops struck.

They ran through the trees looking shelter while it poured. Wind howled relentlessly at their backs. When they reached a rocky wall Adwen discovered a cave concealed by vines. Checking for danger she found it empty and they climbed inside. It had been devoid of animal life for some time and they huddled in the little alcove.

"How far are we from town," Adwen asked, lounging beside the entrance.

"It's just down the hill. I saw lights from over the trees."

"Good."

At their current pace they would reach Castle Gailarien just in time for the celebration. Toth couldn't see very well in the shadows, but Adwen's sapphire eyes had developed a soft glow to them. Even in human form she could see in the dark.

"Would you like something to eat?" he asked, rummaging through the satchel.

"No, thanks." She watched the storm. "I'm not that hungry."

"Is something wrong?"

"I don't know. I've just got a funny feeling." Then she spied movement on the road and her heart skipped a beat. "I see something!"

"What is it?"

The storm hindered her sense of smell and obscured detail. Lightning flashed and illuminated two burly figures prowling through the night. Their eyes glinted red.

"We've got double trouble."

Korig and Kotig tried to track them in the storm, but the footprints had been obscured and their scents washed away.

"Stars above, it is a blessing the rain came when it did!" Toth laughed as he sat.

She kept a wary eye out and saw Kotig unwittingly look directly at their hiding place. Korig slugged his shoulder and pointed to the town. Forgetting suspicions, Kotig followed down the hill. The two vanished along the road and Adwen clenched her fists.

"Those poor people."

The lightning let him see what was happening and Toth shook his head. "There's nothing you can do. I'm sorry."

Then the wind blew a faint scent past the rain causing her stomach to flip over. "The hunter's here!"

They both peered back the way they had come and could see him slowly moving along. Regorian tracked them by the slightest signs of bent grass and broken twigs.

Watching the hunter coming closer, Toth frowned. "My stars, this is a tight spot."

"Where I come from its called being between a rock and a hard place." Turning to her friend, she gave hurried instructions. "I'll distract him. You go to town and find a place to hide where the brothers won't smell you. I'll lose Regorian and catch up."

Glancing at the houses ahead, he asked, "You will be careful, won't you?"

She watched the hunter eyeing their camouflaged hideaway aiming his crossbow at the entrance.

"I've got this," she added with more determination. "Get ready to run when I lead him off." Then she tore the side of her dress so she could move freely. Her nails had become hard and sharp, making it a simple chore.

Regorian could see the blades of grass bent over in places. There were faint footprints that seemed to lead to a small cave. Vines grew along the rocky mountainside making it difficult to spot. Crossbow drawn and aimed, he prepared for the unexpected.

Something flew out of the darkness so swiftly that he had no time to react. It cut his feet out from under him. The next thing he knew he was on his back in the mud. Coughing and sputtering, he rolled over to see a figure betwixt the trees. The lightning struck again, silhouetting the strange young girl. Her blue eyes flashed and she glared before darting off.

Regaining footing in the slick soil, he followed through the brush. More thunder rumbled as he searched amid the undergrowth without success. Then he spotted movement a few yards away and went to investigate. When he reached the place there was nothing. Then he realized her tracks were in the mud all around. The rain quickly washed them away as the hunter realized she could be anywhere. He studied the budding trees for any sign of the agile creature.

He could not see her watching from the bushes close by. Lightning streaked overhead, illuminating the man with the loaded crossbow. She waited patiently for the roar of thunder to mask her footfalls. When his back was turned, the deep rumbling rolled and she dashed out. Diving for his feet, she flipped him high into the air. By the time his body reached the ground, she was gone again. His head struck the ground hard and he was stunned. More rain splattered onto his face as he struggled to get back on his feet.

Meanwhile, Adwen was in the trees leaping from limb to limb on her way to the village. She knew Regorian had a good eye for tracks, but if his quarry didn't leave any it would be impossible to follow.

Upon reaching the outer wall, Toth took a moment to catch his breath. The satchel was not as light as before their visit to Breed Town. Completely drenched, he allowed himself to recover then skirted the stone defenses to the main gate. When he reached it, he made an unfortunate discovery. The gates into the village were high enough to keep out wild animals, but not strong enough deter the Bloody Brothers. Both timber barriers were destroyed and the only guard was dead, his throat torn out.

Alarmed, Toth searched past the entrance for the villains. Adwen murmured beside him. "This is not good."

The sudden appearance made the half-elf all but leap out of his skin. Putting a hand over his hammering heart, he watched her study the morbid scene. Much calmer, he replied, "No, indeed it is not. Not good at all." Then he rubbed his throat, disturbed.

"We need to go inside," she stated, not happy at the prospect.

"Are you sure we should do that?"

"We can't stay out here. If that hunter is as good as I think he is, he'll find us. The Bloody Brothers are still in there somewhere, but we stand a better chance hiding in the streets than out in the rain with Regorian." Swallowing hard, she led the way.

The dark was blinding and she served as Toth's eyes. Between the buildings they found an open barn. It was dry, and the straw was soft and warm. Her friend was pleased.

"This will do. Is it possible for you to tell where the monsters are? It would make sleep easier knowing if they are far away."

Adwen did not reply and stood at the corner, staring across the main street wearing a look of sheer horror. After she gave a small glance, he joined her.

The Bloody Brothers were inside an inn called the Sleeping Dragon. They could see frightened village people through the windows. A bartender cringed behind the counter and Kotig came into view, cornering a young woman up against the bar. He sniffed her, drooling all over, making her squirm and cry.

Adwen glared. Teeth clenched, her hands balled into tight fists until the sharp nails cut her palms.

Her friend saw the look in her eye. "Don't! Please don't, Adwen. They'll kill you!"

"Those people will die if I don't do something!"

Toth paused.

"I can't just stand here or run knowing I'm letting it happen. I'm faster than they are. I think I stand a chance."

Nodding somberly, he agreed, "If you must, then I cannot stop you." He held out a hand and shook hers. "If anything happens, it has been an honor to have known you, my friend."

Handing over the collar for safe keeping, she gave a wry smile and turned to go. When she reached the open street, she broke into a sprint.

Inside the inn, Kotig smelled the sweet scent of the terrified woman, laughing at her fear.

A man behind him suddenly stepped forward. "Let her alone!"

The salivating fiend whipped around to pick him up by the front of his shirt. The man gasped at the werewolf's speed as he was lifted up, staring at two rows of pointed teeth.

"What do you think you're goin' ta' do about it, weakling?"

Korig leaned back against the door, watching him play with the humans.

As Kotig was about to bite his challenger's throat, the window shattered and glass flew in every direction. Adwen collided with the werewolf, causing him drop the man and roll over into the tables at the far side of the room. The people stared as she stood by the counter.

The man on the ground looked up in awe. Her blue dress was soaking wet and her matted hair hung about her shoulders. When she turned, her bright eyes startled him.

"Are you hurt?"

He gawked.

To snap him out of it she shouted. *"Are you all right?"*

He recovered from the shock and nodded vigorously as

the woman led him to the rest of the huddled villagers.

Korig began to chuckle and clap in amusement. "Ah, Adwen! What a wonderful entrance. For a while I didn't think I would find you here! We saw the town and I just knew I would find you hiding among these petty humans."

"Leave them alone, Korig," she sneered. "You want me, let's take this outside!"

With a finger to the side of his beard in mock thoughtfulness, he rolled his eyes. "Hum? I don't think so." Then he grinned and displayed sharp yellow fangs. "You have to understand it's so much more fun with all of these people."

The villagers cringed and huddled closer as Kotig got back to his feet in a rage. He roared and charged.

Adwen stood her ground, clenching her teeth.

Korig held up a hand and ordered him, "Be calm, Brother! We don't want to finish her off too quickly. We want to enjoy this!"

Kotig hesitated and Adwen darted up into the crossbeams. Laughing sadistically, he leaped after her. Not one moment later, she swung around a support, firmly planting both heels into his face.

The Bloody Brother was stunned and fell to the tables with a loud crash.

His muscular companion was outraged. "You fool! How could you let the girl insult you yet again? Get up!"

He was far too busy telling his sibling off to prepare for Adwen's assault. Dropping suddenly from above, she tackled Korig and sent him rolling out into the muddy street.

She managed not to send herself along with him and gave a start when the people screamed. Turning around, she found Kotig roaring and transforming into his true form, glaring at her. She dove under one of the many cluttered tables before he lunged. Tossing furniture aside, the werewolf rummaged for his prey. When he came to one of the remaining tables he crouched to look beneath it. There was nothing, but he could smell her. When he moved to stand, he found her on top.

She delivered a kick to the bottom of his muzzle, rocking his head back, but he continued to glare, unfazed. As she leaped in an attempt to hit harder, a set of claws slapped her. The force sent her rolling across the floorboards. Digging her short nails into the wood, she regained control. The fibers squealed as she scratched the planks and slid to a stop.

Kotig noticed a bit of her blood on his claws. Excited, he tasted it and found it to be delicious. Croaking with laughter, he and the frightened villagers looked to Adwen.

She watched as drops of her blood speckled the floor. The pain was irritating as she slowly stood and looked up, rage building. Four gashes ran down the side of her face as she seethed, blue eyes glowing like balls of flame.

The eager monster put up his claws and laughed, egging her on.

Bellowing in rage, she ran and leaped. They collided and went careening through the open door. As she tumbled down the steps of the inn, the werewolf rolled even farther and exploded into a neighboring house, vanishing from sight.

Adwen found her footing again as the rain was coming down in sheets and heard a scream. Whipping around, her eyes grew wide at the sight of Korig holding the woman from before, pressing her to his hip. A surreal feeling of panic filled her and she screamed, "Let go of her!"

He laughed as raindrop's collected in his beard and streaked his bald head. "This game is over, Adwen. You lose! Now it's time for you to come here."

She looked between him and the helpless woman. "After you let her go!"

The grizzly man put up a hand and wagged a finger. "No, no! Did you think you could defeat my brother and me with the form you have now?" His laugh was merciless.

Adwen stared back defiantly.

"Have you not noticed? You have not been able to do us any harm! With the form you possess you cannot hope to beat us!"

She was beginning to feel sick to her stomach.

Once he saw the look of frightened understanding, he chuckled. "Now, how is this going to end? Shall you step up and take this lovely woman's place or am I going to taste her flesh as an appetizer?"

Her stomach flipped at the thought, but she was too scared to go to him.

The woman pinned to his side sobbed as he sniffed her

and sighed. "This woman does smell good. I wonder if she'll taste the same way."

Panic threatened to overwhelm Adwen as her fists shook.

"Now come here, Adwen, like a good little dog," he chided. When she did not move he started to transform and said with a terrible voice, "I said come *here!*" He roared and the woman screamed.

Adwen shook like a leaf, staring at the monster and the woman in his grip.

"Fine then. I'll have a small bite before I finish you!" He opened his lipless jaws, slowly moving to bite the woman as she screamed louder.

It was too much for Adwen to resist and she lunged. "No!"

When she leaped, the werewolf quickly released the woman to swat Adwen out of the air like a fly. The hit knocked the wind out of her. Falling on her back in the mud, she turned over and tried to stand. She barely had her face out of the muck when Korig planted a beastly padded foot into her back, crushing her with his immense weight.

A less than human scream dragged out her throat as she clawed the ground, desperate to escape the pain. Another monstrous growl rumbled down to her, "Ah, it is a good night for rain, mud and a little bit of blood, isn't it, Adwen?" He stepped off then gave a punishing kick, sending her tumbling across the street.

Her violent rolling stopped once her head struck a house's foundation. For a moment she was almost unconscious, but the sound of the werewolf's laughter brought her back. Stunned, she couldn't move and her eyes watched him stalk closer.

The rain came down harder. Light from the inn silhouetted his wicked form. Korig's eyes were bright and he laughed. "You are pathetic! Did you really think you could defeat me? Did you think you could save these humans? What were you going to do?"

He suddenly roared and staggered, dropping to his knees, grabbing at an arrow in his shoulder. Wisps of steam issued from where the silver seared his flesh and his roar became a howl. Another arrow whistled through the rain, but Kotig came from nowhere to tackle his brother out of harm's way. As Korig pulled the sting from his shoulder they both turned to look down the street at the attacker. They were on all fours, snarling when a third arrow flew and they fled from Adwen's line of vision.

She was still stunned and waited to see who had chased them off. After a while of lying in the downpour, she saw Regorian. Adwen blanched and tried to force her body to work. Both feet slipped and slid in the mud as he took brisk strides. By the time he reached her, she had only managed to sit upright. Clenching teeth and eyes shut tight, she waited for the arrow that would surely be coming. Panting heavily, she waited a long, agonizing moment.

The shot never came and she slowly opened her eyes. He stood over her extending an open hand. The gesture was confounding at first. Giving a questioning look, she hesitantly let him help her up. Once back on her feet, she took a few wobbly steps back. Toth came out to stand behind her. Adwen knew he was there, but didn't take her eyes off of the hunter.

Finally, as she turned to leave Regorian asked, "Where do you intend to go?"

They stared in surprise.

"Are you going out into the wilderness with the two of them?"

Her gaze lowered to the flooded street. She didn't know where else to go.

"How would you like to stay at an inn for the night?"

They both blinked in disbelief. She glanced at the brightly lit windows where a few people peered out. Uncertainty built up inside the more she studied the curious human faces.

Adwen murmured, "I don't think they would want me to."

"I think you may be pleasantly surprised. What do you say?" As she gave the half-elf a glance, Regorian added, "He would be welcome as well, I'm sure."

They cautiously allowed the hunter to lead them up the steps to the Sleeping Dragon. But once her muddy feet were before the threshold anxiety of how she would be received froze her in place. Standing at the open door, Adwen's heart raced and she could not muster the courage to enter.

"It's all right, Adwen," Toth reassured. "I'm sure it's safe."

She muttered, "That's what you said the last time."

Meekly glancing around at the silent villagers, Adwen gingerly stepped inside. The hunter gestured for her hand and she took it, letting him coax her farther. She gave a start and gasped when a soft blanket was wrapped about her shoulders. The woman from before and her husband had brought it.

The couple smiled. "Thank you for helping us."

Far too nervous to speak, she smiled weakly. The blanket was warm and she wrapped herself in it, unconcerned with being filthy.

The hunter brought her to the bar where she and Toth took a seat and he called on the barkeep. "Sir, would you kindly serve these two good people?"

The bearded bartender nodded happily. "Of course, anything!"

Thoroughly confounded, she turned to Regorian and demanded, "Why are you doing this? I thought you were hunting me."

"I *was* hunting you. As to your first question..."

He turned to address the guests and keepers of the inn. "Everyone, the identity of the young lady who has rescued you tonight is none other than the Tame One!"

At the announcement, the people began to smile and chatter.

One called out, "Is it true that you saved the princess?"

Another retorted, "Of course she did, you dolt! Did you not hear the Bloody Brothers say she gave them trouble beforehand? Thank you, Tame One! Thank you!" They began to clamor and crowd around the counter and the two friends shared stunned looks.

Toth asked with a scoff, "Does word travel this quickly where you're from?"

Amid the excitement she was far too distracted.

The barkeep approached. "What will you be having?"

She was still stunned. "We don't have much money."

He laughed merrily. "It's all free to you and your friend! Help yourself!"

They glanced at one another and she replied, "I'll have a glass of water, please."

A broad smile was on Toth's face. "I'll start with your ale!"

Regorian sat beside her and began to explain himself. "When I followed your trail to Breed Town I received less than friendly treatment once I told that I was hunting you." Then he scoffed and went on, "One was forgiving enough to inform me on what had happened involving you and the princess. They also warned that the Bloody Brothers were stalking these parts. Forgive me for the confusion in the woods. The dreary weather made telling your tracks from theirs rather difficult."

She smiled at the thought of how angry the villagers might have been with him.

He gently took her hand and cooed, "Could you find the will to forgive me for my misunderstandings?"

Regorian's flirtatious manner made Adwen raise an eyebrow. "Sure. I forgive you."

The hunter lightly kissed her fingers. "I shall pay your way tonight and see to it that you are given everything you could want."

She breathed a dry laugh and asked doubtfully, "They wouldn't have a way for me to bathe, would they?"

"But of course, my lady!" the barkeeper boomed.

At first she thought he was making a joke. "You've got to be kidding. Really?"

After passing their drinks, he chuckled. "This is the Sleeping Dragon, ma'am! This is one of the finest inns outside the two great cities. The Sleeping Dragon is one of the last inns with enchanted accommodations. When people were not afraid to show off magical qualities, they would work in simple places such as this and leave behind wondrous things. There is a room in the upstairs with a bucket that never empties. When you tip it, warm water will forever pour out." Then he added as a friendly caution, "We almost flooded out once when we had an especially clumsy customer. They had stopped up the pipe that empties to the outside."

Not a moment later, Regorian cried, "She shall have it!"

Upstairs, the bed was made with expensive linens and Adwen could see the magical bucket and bathing area as soon as she was let inside. When the maid showed her the room, Adwen stood in awe at the wonderful features.

The little maid explained, "There are plenty of things for you. The vanity contains anything a lady could want, and also, one of the guests has requested I offer you a change of clothes."

She watched her place the clean garments on the bed and replied, "Thank you so much."

"You're very welcome, my lady!" The plump maid curtsied and showed herself out.

Adwen enjoyed the shower very much after going so long without. The grit and grime washed away from her skin, spiraling down the drain. While bathing, she realized for the first time how much leaner and more toned her body had become. There were plenty of soaps for her hair, and she didn't wait to test them all. Once she was clean, she put on a nightgown that had been left.

Opening the vanity, she found a brush and started tending to the knots and rats built up from the recent confrontation. Noticing the mirror, she paused. Her eyes were brighter and her cheekbones were set a little higher. The changes were a little alarming. When her hair was combed, she looked much tamer and wasn't concerned with the claw marks. Heaving a sigh, she knew they would be gone by morning and flopped back onto the soft mattress and pillows, smiling to herself.

Sighing aloud, she asked herself, "Well, what next?"

Early the next morning, Adwen and Toth were outside waiting for Regorian, who had decided to escort them the rest of the way. Assistance with fending off the Bloody Brothers was not something they were willing to turn down.

"He seems like a good man," Toth noted. "I don't understand why you don't take to him like the other women do."

Adwen wore the traveling dress donated by the villagers. It was deep green with wide, gold-etched borders and a belt. It had more than enough leg room for running if the occasion called for it. The collar was around her neck again and resting on her chest above folded arms. Giving a skeptical look, she grumbled, "I'm not that easy. And most of all, he's a pretty boy who acts like a man-whore."

"I don't understand your odd words. Do you mean to say

that Regorian is a lecher?"

She rolled her eyes. "That's exactly what I'm saying."

"No, he seems respectable. I think he is quite honorable."

The door to the inn opened wide, revealing Regorian with a pretty young lady at his side. She smiled dreamily up at him as they strolled down the steps, yawning and looking content.

He called down, "The two of you appear ready for travel."

Adwen and Toth exchanged looks and she laughed wryly. "There's another thing they say in my world when this kind of situation comes up: I told you so."

They stared as the hunter stroked the young lady's face with a finger.

The half-elf chuckled and admitted, "Well, I should think you did tell me so."

Regorian crooned, "I shall return one day. Do not worry, my sweet." Then he gave her hand a kiss. "Farewell."

All three started walking along the eastbound road and entered the forest. The silence was eventually broken by their new companion.

"Lady Adwen. Were the magical accommodations to your liking?"

Uncomfortable with his suave manner, she avoided eye contact. "Yes, thank you."

"It pleases me to hear you were pleased."

Adwen rolled her eyes. "My nose tells me you were 'pleased' just before you left the inn."

Laughing in merry guffaws, he replied, "Your nose is an honest one indeed!"

Once she and Toth exchanged another stunned glance, she was ready for a change in conversation. She recalled the previous night and what the bartender had mentioned. "Regorian, the barkeeper said people with magical powers are too scared to show themselves anymore. Why?"

With a dark chuckle, he answered, "The Order of the Master Knights, of course!"

Chapter 13
A FORTUNE OF DESTINY

A horse and cart went rushing past while the driver brandished a whip and shouted. One wheel struck a large puddle left over from the recent storm and nearly splashed Brack and Oryn on the cobbled sidewalk.

"Hey! Watch where you're going, you oaf," Brack raged, waving a fist.

The royal city of Deleon rested below Castle Gailarien. It was framed by a network of streets and ancient buildings. Poor districts lay near the main gates while more elegant upper-class rested by the castle grounds. After the worst of the traffic had passed they continued down the street. Both were out of their armor and sported a fresh set of silk garments.

"I would prefer to go this day without being badgered, Brack. Do not draw attention to ourselves. Why do you think I never remove my helm while performing my duties?"

"I'm sorry, sir. Some city folk are outrageously rude!"

They crossed another street and passed boutiques selling expensive goods. Oryn was doing as promised; attempting to enjoy himself. He would succeed so long as commoners didn't recognize him or know his name.

"It has been years since I last saw these streets," Brack exclaimed. "I recall there being magical entertainers on nearly every corner. Do you think they don't exist anymore or are they in hiding, sir?"

"They are hiding. Beings of magic do not die out. The magic in the earth spreads and finds new beings to influence. They are among us."

His companion sighed. "That man in training who threw his cloak at you a few days ago: I've been seeing more of his sort coming into the order. The Master Knights have become not much more than glorified bounty hunters."

"Be that as it may, we have sworn to serve the kingdom. We are to control the beings and creatures with powerful potential. We do not simply slay monster. As the Master Knights, it is our obligation to judge inhuman beings. If they are dangerous, unable to be controlled, or will not serve us they are to be destroyed. If they are cowards then let them hide. They shall be found."

Brack nodded in acknowledgment. "Yes, sir."

As the men continued on their way three richly dressed women spied them. They approached with smiles and batting lashes. A blond with large curls stroked a finger down Brack's chest. "You look like a big strong man. How would you like me to show you around?"

A doll-faced redhead played with Oryn's bangs and cooed, "My name's Lorene. What is your name?"

Brack enjoyed the attention, but the captain was far from interested. Without a word, he shot the girl a cold look and stepped past. She acted hurt, but soon joined her friends who were busy swooning over the other stranger.

Stopping a few yards away, Oryn called out, "Are you going to continue with me or have you found your company for the night?"

The older knight was torn. He looked between his friend and the three young women fawning over him. Clearing his throat, he held them at bay. "I'm very sorry, but I must be going, ladies." They all sighed and groaned in disappointment before letting him pass and rejoin his superior. "What was wrong with those women, sir? I was under the assumption that you were looking to have a good time?"

Glaring straight ahead, he stated, "I am here to enjoy myself, not to catch a disease from a prostitute."

Brack gave his shoulder a tap. "Uh, sir? Those women weren't prostitutes. The ladies of the night are across the way." He pointed to several voluptuous women with dirt on their cheeks and yellow teeth. Oryn looked in time to see one wink and another wave.

Completely disgusted, he grumbled, "I don't have any interest in those creatures. If a woman with some dignity or honor were to speak to me I just may answer in turn. I have no interest in a woman who cannot follow the codes I abide by."

"Are you referring to the slaying of large monsters, sir?" he chuckled.

"No," Oryn glowered. "The moral codes that separate man from beast: being respectable and having dignity enough to not bow before another man for nothing; to have honor."

"Yes, sir."

As they neared the next block, Brack spotted a familiar shop with silk curtains. Many candles were lit filling the mysterious shop with flickering amber twilight. "Sir, there's a shop just over there we should visit. It is amazing! I recall the same fortune teller being here as a boy."

Deciding to humor his companion, Oryn followed.

The space was dark with little flames glowing in the shadows and a shriveled woman seated at a small table on the floor. There were no trinkets or cards in view, only the small woman and another burning candle.

When she spoke, her voice was as frail as her body. "Welcome, welcome, children. If you are seeking knowledge or advice, this is the place to be. Come closer, if you please." Her old eyes were faded to the point that their original color could not be discerned.

Brack approached and took a seat on a cushion while Oryn stood by to observe.

The woman gently took his hand, running fingers over every line and miniscule crease. After a few minutes, she sighed and spoke soothingly, "You have a hard road to walk, child. I see a close companion disappearing for a time, leaving you and one other to stand alone. You must stay strong, child. Hold on to hope, never surrender your faith and you shall prevail in the end." She gently closed his hand. "That is all you need know."

Taking it back, he gave a kind smile. "Thank you, ma'am."

As he was getting to his feet, the fortuneteller finally noticed Oryn and gawked.

Suspicious of her, he stared back at the growing look of astonishment. He turned away as she called out, "Wait! I must speak with your friend in private!"

Oryn kept walking and firmly declined. "I have no interest in palm reading."

Her tone turned to dangerous warning. "Maybe not, but

you have no idea of the repercussions in store for you, Sir Oryn Reynard Conrad!"

They both stopped dead. The captain of the order questioned his companion, "Did you ever tell her of me?" He slowly turned his head to scowl at the elderly woman.

"No, not a word. I'll wait outside, sir." Brack exited the shop and closed the door, cutting off Oryn and the old woman from the rest of the world.

Turning to face her, he demanded, "How do you know me?"

When she spoke again her voice was changed, gaining strength and youth. "Step forward and I shall show you, young knight."

Curiosity got the better and he approached.

A tassel hung beside her and she tugged at it sharply, opening a hatch high overhead. Blinding sunlight spilled down, illuminating them against the complete darkness. The candles were blown out and the curtains snapped shut. When he looked at her again, she was no longer small and wrinkled.

Before him stood a tall, beautiful elf woman in blue and gold regal dress. Her pointed ears curved out from beneath the long pale hair that draped past her waist. The elf's eyes were an incredible hazel that seemed to burn into him. She gestured to the cushion. "Please, sit."

They sat and she stated, "I have been waiting a very long time for you, Sir Oryn, last of the house of Conrad."

"Do you have something of importance to tell me, *elf?*"

His tone put a sour taste in her mouth, making her frowned. "I do indeed. You would do well to heed my warnings. If you do, I can promise you shall receive what you currently desire most."

"What might that be?"

"Revenge. If you heed my words, you shall receive all you need to accomplish it."

The wild promise did not impress him. "Then speak and be done with it."

She glared. "You shall meet a young woman. She is the key. She will give you everything you could ever want and more."

He highly doubted that.

"You shall know her because you shall attempt to kill her." She raised a finger. "But you will fail. Follow her and keep her close. Let no harm befall her and you shall receive the power and the chance to exact your revenge. That, I promise you."

He stood. "I've had enough tickling of the ears for one day, woman." Then he turned to leave for the darkened door.

"Sir Oryn," she snapped. "There is one last thing you should know."

He halted to listen.

"You will pay a price most dear for living with hate so long."

His green eyes flashed.

"The price shall be your life." She waved a hand. "Farewell, son of Conrad."

Turning to search for the door, Oryn discovered he was already outside. He whipped around to see her, but found just an empty alley. The elf and the entire shop had vanished.

Brack turned and found the shop missing as well. His jaw dropped. Stunned, he managed to ask, "Would I be mistaken in assuming we've found a magical being in hiding, sir?"

A LOOSE END

Korig and Kotig arrived in a dark place, taking brisk strides down a grand hall. Invisible eyes in the walls watched as they went. Every stone seemed to breathe. They felt no fear of the darkness or of the evil-bleeding stones. This was their master's home. When they reached the heart of the hall they halted and took a knee, bowing low to the throne. No torches were lit to show the flushed color of their skin. Floating green lights faded in and out all around, giving their eyes a little light for nocturnal sight.

The bored voice of what sounded to be a young man echoed. "What took the two of you so long to return? I was beginning to worry. So, did you enjoy dispatching the Princess Eyrie? Don't spare me the details."

The two glanced sheepishly at one another until Korig hesitantly answered. "She still lives, my lord. We were interrupted in the act and... she escaped."

The voice chuckled. "You two are comically incompetent. How did my two best get 'bested' by the young princess? Do tell."

Korig's deep voice sounded ashamed and disgraced. "There was a strange girl, my lord. She distracted us so her companion could aid the princess in escaping. She also managed to elude us, twice."

The voice was entertained. "Twice! By a girl?" His cruel chuckle reverberated off the walls. "I thought that, at the least, you would have trouble from the miserable knights. They have been very bothersome. But a weak, helpless woman! This is too much for me to believe!"

"She was not a human, my lord," Kotig blurted out and slobbered. "She changes when a full moon rises. She is a black hound with eyes violet like... like lightning. She is more like a hound than a wolf, my lord."

The voice became curious. "Tell me this lady dog's name. My interest is piqued."

Korig grunted, "Her name is Adwen, my lord."

"What?"

The two werewolf brothers quickly dropped their gaze to the floor.

Cold with malice, the voice spat, "What was that name?"

Head hung low, Korig replied, "Adwen, my lord. Her name is Adwen."

The voice asked with threatening menace, "When she is not a hound are her eyes blue?"

"Yes, my lord; an even brighter blue than the Princess Eyrie's."

The voice had fallen quiet and the brothers were bold enough to look up at their master. He was slouched in the dark throne, cradling his head in his hands. Frustration emanated from where he sat. Eventually he murmured to himself, "So, she survived."

The brothers asked in unison, "My lord?"

"This is a loose end. She is a very large loose end who could ruin and destroy everything we have worked so hard for. Adwen must be taken care of and quickly. Her power grows, and with every rising of the sun she grows stronger still. Where is she? Where is she going? Tell me now!"

"She travels for Castle Gailarien, my lord. We overheard this news. The princess has invited her personally and made arrangements for her to attend her birthday celebration."

After thinking it over, their master spoke again and sounded pleased. "Well, I have a plan. It seems your letting the princess live shall work to our advantage. Perhaps we can have a little fun while we're at it." The voice laughed maniacally. "I'm going to teach the two of you how to combine business with pleasure."

The dark halls rang with his gales of wicked laughter.

Chapter 14
BY WAY OF APOLOGY

"No, don't shoot!" Adwen cried as Regorian aimed his crossbow.

The hunter attempted to reassure her. "My lady, fox is a decent meal. Rabbit grows boring after so long."

The day of the celebration had arrived and Castle Gailari-en was only a few miles away. Four stone towers could be seen reaching over the forest. No sooner had they spied the fabled place than a wild red fox crossed their path carrying a pixy on its back. As Adwen was making conversation with them, Rego-rian drew his aim.

"When I'm talking to one I'd be happier if you didn't try to kill him. Four days of eating your rabbit stew isn't so bad. I kind of like it."

The hunter blinked and mused, "You can speak with ani-mals? You are a wonder, my lady!" Lowering his weapon, he bowed apologetically.

Toth chuckled as his flirtatious mannerisms annoyed her.

The fox chided, "You travel with a vicious human, miss. How do you get by?"

"Just fine, thanks. Can you tell me if you've seen two were-wolves called Korig and Kotig? They gave us trouble a few days ago and I thought maybe --"

The pixie suddenly interrupted. "You thought we might tell you something?" She laughed sadistically.

Toth and Regorian couldn't understand the fox, but the pixie was easy to interpret with its high-pitched voice.

"You ungrateful little fly!" Regorian snapped. "How could you be so rude to a beautiful lady?"

The pixie blew a raspberry and laughed. While the fox rolled his eyes the creature used the pixie's moment of silence as an opportunity to answer. "I could tell you, miss. They haven't been seen for the last two days in these parts. I heard the crows say they went far north and northeast. For the now these woods are safe to travel, friend."

Stamping furiously up and down on the animal's shoulders, the pixie squealed, "Not friends! Not friends to us! She is friends with big stupid hunter and humans!"

Regorian restrained himself from firing an arrow at the sprite and Toth sniggered.

Adwen nodded. "Thank you very much and happy hunting."

The fox chirped as he left, "Happy hunting, miss." While the small beast trotted off, the pixie could still be heard pitching a fit at the fox for ruining her fun.

When they were gone she translated. "He says the Bloody Brothers went far north and northeast."

Continuing onward, the hunter fiddled with his goatee, deep in thought. "Why would they end the hunt? So strange that a werewolf would simply give up on its chosen prey."

Adwen glowered, "So long as they are far away I couldn't care less what they're doing. I just want to go to this masquerade and go home. That's all I want."

A hurt look came over the hunter. "Lady Adwen, why is it that I bother you so? I thought you had forgiven me. What have I done to make you so cross?"

She seethed, but found the will to hold her tongue.

Toth shook his head and put a hand on his shoulder. "Flattery does not flatter her, my friend. Speak to her the way you speak to me."

"Lady Adwen, am I being flattering to you?"

Exasperated, she slumped her shoulders dramatically. "Yeah! Flattering is an understatement. It's annoying. I don't like it when guys talk to me like I want them." She realized that he couldn't understand a word and shook her head. "Never mind. Just listen to Toth. He's got the right idea."

Soon after, they arrived at the royal city. The gate was very busy due to the ball preparations. Carriages from around the kingdom rolled past. Adwen lent her collar to Toth so as to be less noticeable, but she stood out despite the precaution. Most took notice of the strange young girl who wore no shoes. Paying no mind to curious stares and whispers, she found many shops and carts with shiny trinkets distracting.

Regorian didn't think much of the city, but his younger companions were impressed. The princess' directions led them a few blocks from the gates onto the castle grounds. Tall structures made of white stone housed small gargoyle statues, their tongues pointed to the sky in a silent roar.

"According to these directions, we are searching for the Peacock's Graces," the half-elf read aloud.

Adwen had looked at the note and the characters the princess used were similar to her own alphabet. While she was content to let him decipher the parchment, Regorian was not literate at all. To find hunts, he let scribes read posted bounties in exchange for coin.

Adwen was naturally the first to spot the image of a proud peacock and a shop name beneath it in curly letters. Her eyes had become much sharper, but not as sharp as her sense of smell. The streets towards the outer wall made her reel, but as they got closer to the castle the odors became more tolerable. During their stroll, horses pulling carts greeted her warmly. But once the trio rapped on the door of the shop, they were not made to feel welcome at all. The princess had warned that the man was snooty and he did not disappoint.

A pompous man with a large nose and thin mustache answered. His clothes were as colorful as the bird on the sign while his curled fingers were covered in gold rings. Snout in the air, he waved a hand. "Be gone, filthy peasants. I have no coins for you to leach from me. This is a shop for fine, respectable people."

The hunter kindly corrected, "We are no beggars and there is business to be made."

After raising a plucked eyebrow, he huffed, "I doubt that you would have the means to pay for my services even if you served me for the rest of your little life."

Regorian gestured to Adwen. "Your services would be for this young lady, sir."

He sniffed dismissively. Once he saw the blue of her eyes the snooty man gasped. His upper lip twitched in surprise and distress.

Toth pulled out the piece of silk and showed it to the man.

He stared at the cloth then at her again and muttered

through a pained smile, "Will you please excuse me a moment?" Snapping the door shut, he disappeared. Outside on the street was busy and loud, but Adwen could still hear the man raving, yelling obscenities at apprentices. It sounded as if the princess had told him she would be coming and that he would rather serve a sewer-rat than a commoner.

Finished venting, he opened the door again and was very contrite. "Thank you so much for coming. My name is Nadler. I have been expecting you! Come in so that we may begin the fitting for the royal ball. Please come in!" He gave another agonized smile as they entered.

The hunter declined with a sweeping bow. "I have other business to attend to, my lady." Then he was off and disappeared around the block.

"Hey, where are you going?" she hollered after him.

"Regorian is arranging things in the case of a certain emergency," Toth explained. "The night should stay clouded, but it is a good precaution, I think."

Once inside, Nadler looked over his two customers with a critical eye. Then he clapped to call the servants. "First we shall have you bathed. You are attending the royal ball, for goodness sake! After cleaning, the fitting shall begin."

A few servants rushed them to the back and behind pairs of screens. They were briskly stripped and bathed. The humans never said a word and Adwen was far too surprised to speak. Dressed in clean undergarments, Toth had the servants stow their traveling clothes in his satchel.

They were taken back to Nadler, who told them, "The first step has already been taken care of by the princess. The garments have been selected and the cost taken care of." At the mention of money he sucked on his lower lip as if it were a dreadful thought. "Here are the garments."

He clapped his gaudy hands again and the servants opened a cabinet to reveal a brass buttoned outfit for Toth. Beside it was an elegant dress covered with tawny owl feathers. The white silk glistened in the light while the seams and hems were stitched and sown with spun gold. A matching mask depicting an owl face was also covered in gold and crowned by plumes.

Together they stared at the display.

Nadler asked curiously, "Do you not like them?"

Toth couldn't speak, but she gasped, "They're beautiful!"

He was flattered. The strange woman was much more acceptable now that she was clean. Clapping proudly, he announced, "Let us begin."

The fitting took hours, but Nadler worked efficiently. Once finished, he judged them again with an artist's eye.

"Now for the hairdressing and makeup."

He clapped and Adwen was whisked off by three ladies. The women gossiped while they worked, combing her long hair, curling it, attaching fine jewel-encrusted fittings that resembled holly leaves. One woman began tending to her nails and didn't know what to think of how hard and sharp they were. Those who applied her makeup were surprised to see her small fangs while adding lipstick. Soon the task was done and the ball was due to start in an hour.

With small slippers on her feet, she came back out to see Toth and Nadler. Her companion stared and the royal dresser was pleased.

"How do I look?" she asked, blushing.

Nadler smiled proudly. "Like you belong in the castle, young lady."

They left at last and Regorian awaited them beside a coach. The driver tipped his feathered hat and the hunter was in shock. In awe, he dropped to his knees on the sidewalk and took her hand, staring into her eyes. "Angels and every princess to live in the castle surely envy your splendid beauty, Lady Adwen." He breathlessly kissed her hand and got back to his feet, continuing to admire her.

She could not help but smile this time. "Uh, thanks."

Toth pocketed the royal invitation from his satchel as he passed the hunter their things and climbed aboard. Once Regorian sat beside the driver, they were off.

Tension and excitement inside the coach was high. Adwen's heart fluttered as she admired the long glossy gloves on her arms. As fiddling with the fine mask, she could hardly contain herself.

"This is crazy! I'm going to a masquerade ball. This is so awesome!"

"This is quite exciting," Toth agreed. "There will be music

and dancing in the grand hall. It's going to be wonderful." His eyes twinkled happily at the thought.

The coachman reached the gate and showed the guards their royal invitation. Then they passed through the grounds to the castle itself. Everything was green with flowery vines, trimmed hedges and a wonderful spouting fountain before the stairs. Sunset was upon them with the sky completely clouded over. Bright torchlight poured out the castle windows.

They climbed out of the coach as Regorian dashed up the steps to a maid and back. Going to Adwen, he presented a small bottle of perfume. "Here is your safeguard in the case of a full moon. I have an acquaintance within the castle. I gave her this to mark the way to the safest quarters. The door shall be unlocked and the maid just inside has taken your belongings there."

Accepting the vial and carefully smelled it she found she had underestimated her senses. When the stinging subsided, she took her hand away and choked out, "Thank you, Regorian. You didn't have to do this."

He shook his head. The short black curls swayed. "Of course I had to, my lady. It's my way of apology for my flaws." Lightly touching her cheek with a finger, he sighed. "It is my weakness for lovely ladies, I'm afraid."

Turning away, he climbed up to rejoin the driver. "For now, I bid you adieu. Farewell, my lady. I have plenty of hunting to return to." The driver reined his horse. As they rode away Regorian blew a goodbye kiss.

She shook her head and smiled. "What a flirt."

At last, Toth asked, "Well, shall we go inside?"

They turned to face the stone steps awash in warm light.

Adwen's eyes flashed with excitement and she grinned. "Oh, yeah. Let's do this!"

Together, the two entered the halls of Castle Gailarien.

Chapter 15
MASQUERADE AT THE MASQUERADE

Their footsteps echoed along the stone corridor. Countless tapestries hung from the walls and statues stood proudly. An escort brought them to a curtain over a high stone arch. Merry music and conversation were dulled to a whisper by the thick veil as Adwen and Toth's excitement mounted higher.

The half-elf readjusted his mask and whispered, "I hope they have food."

Her heart was fluttery with anticipation. "I'm pretty sure they do, but I can't wait for the live music!"

"I feel the same!"

She stifled a giddy squeal when the portly escort spoke to someone on the other side. A moment later a man announced, "Presenting Lady Adwen and Fedius Toth."

She stepped inside and the sight took her breath away. Golden ribbons and glass ornaments hung everywhere in the cavernous grand hall. A single round window set high in the dome ceiling. White walls glittered golden fixtures and fittings. Across the sea of strange masks ascended the stair to the king's vacant throne. On either side of the steps to the gaudy chair stretched twin red carpet halls. Guests wore expensive dresses, suits, fluttery capes and pale party masks.

Adwen was so stunned that Toth had to remind her to keep going. As she followed, a few women stared, jealous that their gowns weren't nearly as grand. She failed to notice and joined the throng.

Toth pointed out the spread beside the musicians' stand. Together they made straight for the plates while trying not to look desperate. While she eyed a bowl of saucy meats a man came alongside and bowed.

"Lady Adwen, you're looking quite lovely tonight."

She heard him, but hardly gave a glance. "Thank you."

The young gentleman's eyes sparkled through the holes in his mask. "Would you care to dance?" he asked, holding out a gloved hand.

She could not tear her gaze from the sweet smelling meats and was on the verge of salivating. With her attention glued to the platter, she murmured, "Uh, maybe later, but thank you."

Disappointed, he bowed and walked away.

Just when Adwen was about to try something, the party fell silent and Toth tapped her on the shoulder. Afraid something might be wrong she whipped around, half-expecting others to be staring at her. Relief washed over her as she realized they were watching the throne. The king had arrived and everyone gathered in close. Toth tugged at her arm and they merged with the humans before old King Lorvan.

The party hushed when he spoke. "Welcome. Many of you have traveled far to take part in this celebration. Before the princess arrives, I have a surprise. I have invited some of the most prestigious knights in our land and I shall be presenting them with rewards for bravery and unwavering loyalty. Among them is a man you all have heard of. My dear guests, I present to you, the Master Knights."

The grand curtain folded back behind them to make way for a line of royal guards. Marching toward the throne, they parted the crowd forming two ranks to make a path through the guests. They drew broad swords, ready to salute as an orderly assembly of knights entered.

Each wore a formal uniform of black cloth with high collars, trimmed and threaded with spiraling golden designs. Small dark capes hung from their shoulders and trusty swords were on their hips. Hair was combed back and beards perfectly trimmed. Leading the way was a young knight with brown hair and emerald green eyes.

Adwen watched him closely. His gaze was deep and focused.

"He looks kind of hot." She asked her companion, "Who is that?"

There was no answer and she looked around. Toth was nowhere in sight. She quietly searched and could not even catch his scent. Countless perfumes and strong colognes bombarded her, making the feat impossible. Realizing he must be on the other side of the formation, she forced herself to relax. She would find him once the party continued and the guards were gone.

The knights formed ranks beside the throne and King Lorvan waited till they were at attention to continue, "Leading our knights tonight is the Captain of the Order. Most of you have never looked upon his face, but know his name. This is none other than Sir Oryn Reynard Conrad."

The crowd murmured excitedly and the disciplined young knight did not move a muscle. His bearing held like stone.

The king informed them, "Every knight you see has earned a medal for bravery and another rank." He moved to stand beside Sir Oryn. "This day Sir Oryn has accomplished something that has not been done in centuries. He has attained the rank of general."

A squire presented a jeweled piece on a cushion.

King Lorvan held up the gold medal decorated with three red gems. Everyone cheered as he hung the symbol by the two points that held his cape and it glistened at his neck. The people continued to applaud as the king stepped back and the knights bowed low before the crowd.

When they were standing again, the crowd fell silent and the king announced, "Until the princess joins us, we shall continue with music and dance." He clapped and the royal guards proceeded to leave the way they came. The knights remained in their positions as the king sat back in his throne.

One or two grumbled impatiently. They would be at attention until the princess arrived.

Meanwhile, in the shifting crowd of guests, Adwen desperately searched for her friend.

"Toth? Toth, where *are* you?"

The musicians played a sweet song. People began to dance, making her efforts more difficult. With their whirling and twirling, senses were overwhelmed and she could not see the blond half-elf anywhere. A soft melody rang in her ears as human smells blurred with that of flowers and musk. Growing anxious, she stood and craned her head, peering between dancers. Frustrated and about to look elsewhere, her eyes fell on a dark stranger.

There he stood watching like a shadowy hawk. Dressed in

wine red, his pitch-black cape came almost to the ground. Features were concealed behind a sinister white mask of a grinning cat, crowned by a red jewel and a flourish of long purple feathers.

The ominous figure captivated Adwen. Power from the mask hypnotized, cutting her off from the dire need to flee. As he led her to dance, she stared raptly, transfixed. Amid the throng and before the steps of the throne, the pair danced to and fro. His touch was subtle as he took the lead. After a few minutes, he gently removed the owl mask, revealing her young face. Lost in the trance, her distant stare locked onto the wicked, smiling plaster.

Beside the throne, the knights watched everyone dance. Sir Oryn spotted a beautiful young girl. He had never seen her before. The breath caught in his throat. Stunned and without air, he stared.

One of the knights saw him sway forward an inch, gawking at the girl. He grinned and leaned in to whisper, "Good choice, sir. I wish the best of luck in catching that beauty."

Calmly regaining his composure, he glared and warned in a deadly tone, "Rothay, you shall stand at attention or I shall personally see to it that you do not stand for the next month."

A few chuckled as the knight smoothly corrected his stature, smiling. "Yes, sir."

Oryn was also at attention once again, but found it impossible to avert his eyes from the young woman dancing with the dark garbed man.

Adwen didn't know how long she danced. There was no sense of time. All of the sudden, the trance fell away. As she came to and was fully conscious, she noticed a familiar feeling in her veins. She had little more than five minutes before a full moon emerged. Turning away from the figure, she darted for one of the castle halls. She desperately sniffed for the perfume trail. Only after escaping the crowd did the aroma finally cross her nose and she ran, following the scent to the safe room.

Sir Oryn observed the young woman leaving the masquerade and found himself doing something strange. He murmured to King Lorvan, "My king, I request that I may depart temporarily. There is a matter that needs my attention."

"You may go." He waved a hand to dismiss him, smiling.

The men chuckled and suppressed laughter as they watched their leader go and pursue the girl. Leaving the formation, he wandered to the large tapestries behind the throne. Where the works of art hung to the ground, he discreetly slipped behind and down a secret passage. This way would surely help to head off the girl before she wandered too far.

Adwen panted, moving as fast as she could without tripping on the dress. Fear spurred her precarious pace. Violet eyes scanned for witnesses as she moved with inhuman speed. Just when she thought it wouldn't end, it brought her to a door. Dashing inside with moments left, she searched for the satchel. One of the herbal leaves would help to keep quiet through the excruciating change.

A moment later, Oryn stepped out into the hall from behind a statue of a duchess. Hearing a door close let him know the girl was close. The knight listened while he strolled coolly in search of young woman. The passage was long with many doors.

Then the quiet was shattered by a bloodcurdling shriek. His pace quickened and he followed the sound. Screams soon ceased, replaced with fearsome growls and snarls. His concern quickly became rage as he reached for his sword. When he came to the door, he gently eased it open to glimpse inside.

Moonlight filled the dark side of the room, illuminating the shredded remains of the woman's dress. Tattered pieces trailed behind a long table into the dim glow. Finally he spotted the beast crouched low on the other side of the table. The knight scowled. This monster would pay dearly.

Adwen hunkered low and continued wiping the makeup from her muzzle with the last of the dress. Toth was likely to show up soon and she was not in the mood for horsing around. White and pink powders would look very silly on her hound face. She growled in frustration at the misfortune of a full moon rising. Confident her fur was clean, she stood and examined the surroundings. Turning around, she was surprised to find the knight from the celebration. His sword was moving through the air, swinging straight for her throat.

A surprised yelp jumped out of her and she pulled back.

The razor-sharp tip left a shallow scratch on her neck and would have cleaved her head clean off if she hadn't moved. Falling backward, she flipped over onto all fours.

The knight honed in on her and lunged again.

She barely leaped out of harms way and onto the long table, but he was still in hot pursuit. Oryn stepped off a chair and sliced for the black creature.

Barking in dismay, she jumped and Oryn's sword struck oak planks, gouging deeply into the smooth surface.

She moved for the door, but thought twice about leaving. If she went out the other knights might add to her troubles. By the time she changed her mind, he was coming again, apparently irritated she wasn't fighting back.

The knight jabbed for her middle and she stumbled backed into a towering bookcase. It wobbled when her weight struck it and she gasped. He was charging, and without thinking, she leaped over the knight and kicked off of his shoulder.

As she landed gracefully, he was thrust hard into the bookcase, causing it to wobble more precariously. When she whipped round, the rage in the knight's face was frightening. His long bangs fell down, framing burning green eyes. A murderous glint was in them. He hardly moved another step when a vase came down to meet his head with a crash. The knight collapsed in an unconscious heap.

Adwen put a clawed hand over her chest, breathing deep sighs of relief. She crept towards the fallen assailant and quickly kicked the sword away. With one padded foot, she turned him over onto his back. He was still alive. A small trail of blood was down past his hairline. There was no telling when he would come to. Not about to waste time, she set him in a chair beside the table and used a rope from the curtains to go about binding him.

Oryn's head ached horribly. There was pressure over his chest and arms, restricting movement. Slowly opening his eyes, he found a pair of large claws tying him up. Even more slowly, he raised his head and saw the face of the black hound. He was unafraid and glared.

She was about to form a knot when she realized the knight was awake. For a long moment they stared at one another and she let out a soft growl. "It isn't tight enough, is it? Here, let me fix that." She sharply pulled the ends, constricting the bonds.

Oryn winced a little and glared with even more malice.

Cocking a furry eyebrow, she grumbled, "Good."

The door opened as Toth entered, panting and then quickly closed it. Removing his mask, he laughed. "I sure wish I had your nose. It would have made finding you easier." Then he spotted Oryn. "Oh! I see you found yourself some trouble again."

Finished making a double knot, she grumbled, "If you don't remember, trouble always finds me." Folded long arms over her chest, Adwen glared at the disgruntled knight.

Seeing the spot of blood on his scalp, he sighed. "Oh stars above. You bashed him on the head!"

In protest, she panted, "No, he did that himself. I just watched." Her tail waged happily.

"I'm sorry about this, Oryn. She didn't mean for things to get out of hand."

"Hello, Toth," he replied with a calculating look. "I hadn't thought that the next we met you would be with this sort of company."

Adwen was taken aback. "Whoa, hold on! You know this guy?"

"Yes. I knew Oryn when he stayed in my village as a boy." To his old friend, he added, "Really, Oryn, this isn't what you might think."

"How did the two of you get in here?" He watching the hound closely all the while. The violet-eyed creature ripped a curtain from the wall and draped it over itself like a cloak.

Toth noticed him staring and turned to watch as well. He enjoyed this change.

As the clouds drifted in her form began shift and shrink gently down. The black fur melted away and her body came to a height of five-foot-six. Wavy brown hair fell about her shoulders along with the thick, dark curtain. Her skin turned pale and her eyes a deep, luminous blue. When the change was complete, she faced them both.

The knight wasn't glaring anymore. His face showed utter shock. This was the last thing he was prepared to see.

Her eyes glowed like blue fire as she glared. "What were

you expecting?" she asked with a harsh tone as she slowly approached. "Were you expecting some hairy Neanderthal of a man? Tell me if I'm far off."

He could only stare in silent amazement.

She went on, "I have just one thing I want to say to you. In the past two weeks a lot of people have tried to kill me." Putting her face up to his, she sneered, "But you, by far, are the craziest."

The shock finally faded and he returned the angry gaze.

Pulling away, she added in a matter-of-fact tone, "And by the way, to answer your question, we were invited."

Confused, he turned to Toth for a confirmation and he nodded. "It is true. We were invited by Princess Eyrie."

"I believe that you could be invited by the princess," he replied and scowled at his feminine companion. "But I cannot see why she would invite an animal."

A twinge of anger flared in her. "Excuse me. What did you just say?"

His answer was an icy stare.

"Oh, so I'm the animal here. Who came barging in swinging his sword like a -- wait." The anger disappeared and curiosity took its place. "What are you doing here anyway? The last I saw, you were standing by the king. What were you looking for?"

Calm and collected, he replied, "I was mistaken. I was looking for a woman."

"Ah, man. I walked right into that one. Toth, your friend has a way with words." Returning to the window, she studied the far drop to the ground and the dark woods beyond.

"I'm sorry. I've never seen her get this disgruntled before. Let me help you out of these ropes."

As he was about to reach for the knot, she dashed over in the blink of an eye to stop him. "Hey! He is staying tied up! What's the matter with you?"

"Why? He isn't going to do any harm."

Totally aghast, she shook her head. "Are you kidding me? I know you're not this dense. Look at the room!"

For the first time he looked at the slice in the table, the battered bookshelves and the broken vase.

"The dress on the floor was my doing, but I didn't make

that mess." Retrieving the knight's sword while clinging to her heavy wrappings, she brandished it in front of him. "He almost cut my head off! He tried to kill me!"

"You're still alive. It looks to me like he failed."

The words rang in Oryn's ears as he recalled the elf woman's words. Doubtful and suspicious, he stared at the strange girl. What could be so powerful about this beastly woman?

She noticed his almost dazed expression. "What?"

He saw her holding his sword and noticed the cut on her neck was healed.

Eyeing him closely, she touched a finger to the flat of the blade.

When she wasn't burned, the knight was confounded.

"This is silver-steel, isn't it?" she asked and then quickly dismissed him. "Never mind. The look on your face is a dead giveaway." Slamming the sword on the table, she turned to Toth. "He stays tied up and that's all there is to it." Fuming at the nerve of the knight, she returned to the window.

The half-elf smiled, shaking his head. Then he looked around and asked, "Adwen, where is the satchel?"

Without turning, she sighed. "When I was on the ground, I saw it at the end of the table on a chair."

He found it and returned the collar. She placed it around her neck as he went to show the princess' invitation to Oryn. Holding it up for him to read, he insisted, "The princess did invite Adwen and me. She was going to arrange an audience with King Lorvan."

Adwen suddenly shouted, "Toth! Quick, come look at this!" Once he was at her side she instructed him, "Look at the windows near the top of the tower over there."

Oryn stared as their faces displayed looks of shock and horror.

They couldn't hear the commotion in the tower, but they saw wild movements and shadows pass. Thick blood splattered across the window before the body of a guard crashed through and fell to the gradient slope, hundreds of feet down. A moment later a giant dark creature climbed out from the shattered frame carrying a frantic woman in a white dress. It leaped and made for the forest, headed eastward towards the half-red moon.

Adwen put a hand to her mouth and Toth was speechless.

Watching their expressions made the knight impatient. "What has happened?"

She gasped, "The princess has been kidnapped!"

His temper flared and he snapped, "Did you have a hand in this?"

Outraged, she stomped over to put her nose up to his. "Calling me an animal is one thing, but calling me a criminal? Now you're pushing it!"

He remained silent, observing and studying her eyes as they turned to violet.

Loud shouting could be heard along the hall from agitated guards. "The princess has been taken! Rally the guard! Go to the king! Protect the king!"

The two companions exchanged worried looks, but then she smiled and her eyes twinkled. "Are you thinking what I'm thinking?"

Her friend was confused at first, but soon caught on and added, "I'm thinking someone must save the princess again."

As her smile became a childish grin, she added, "And?"

Now he was smiling. "And I'm also thinking, you have an exceptional nose!"

"Exactly," she replied. Then her attention went to the door as the guards were coming closer. "And I'm thinking that we need to leave." Adwen gasped and buckled over in pain. The full moon was revealed forcing her to change so rapidly that the transition left her reeling.

"That sucked! I'm never going to get used to this."

While the black creature growled and grumbled, Oryn glared. This beast was obviously no werewolf, but far too similar for his liking. Her true form repulsed him the same way the sight of those monsters did. The fact he had been attracted to its human disguise sickened him.

Toth gathered up the satchel, slinging it across his back while Adwen waited before the windowsill. A cool breeze ruffled the thick coat on her neck as he climbed on.

When she was about to jump, he stopped her. "Adwen?"

"What?"

He sighed. "We can't leave him this way."

She glanced sidelong at the knight tethered to the chair.

The strong young man appeared calm, but she wasn't fooled. She could see the horrible glimmer in his eye. He wanted her dead. Giving a long huff, she left the sill to stand over the angry knight. After sizing him up, she used a hand full of sharp claws and slashed the ropes.

The instant he was free, he leaped from under the restraints and clutched his sword, ready to reprimand the creature. By the time he turned to confront her she had gone. A chilly breeze rustled the curtain and he dashed to the opening. He watched her land on the rocks and race off. She bore Toth into the woods and he was careful to note where to find her trail later. Once the animal was out of sight, he was off running down the hall with a determined gleam in his cold stare.

Chapter 16
OTHER PLANS

The halls of the castle were chaotic. Yelling of royal guards and rattling armor all but drown the frantic chatter of party guests. Word quickly spread that there had been or still was an intruder.

Sir Oryn dashed through the secret passage. When he burst into the throne room the guests had been evacuated and guards took positions. He went to the nearest one and asked, "Solider, where is the king? I have urgent news."

Surprised that the general was addressing him directly, he sputtered, "He -- the king has been escorted to his private study, sir!"

"As you were," he dismissed and took off again. Dozens of men lined the walls ready to deal with any threat. He found ten more with partisans standing outside of the doors to the study and they parted at his approach. Taking brisk strides towards the king, he swiftly dropped to one knee with a fist across his chest, bowing his head low. "My king."

King Lorvan was stern. "Rise, Sir Oryn. What is the matter? Do you know what has happened?"

Standing at attention, he stated, "My king, I bring news of the princess. She has been taken."

He was horrified. "Did you see the assailant?"

"No. I did not, my king."

Spying the small trail of blood on his scalp, the king asked, "Was it the same who attacked you?"

"No, my king. I encountered two guests with less than human qualities. It was they who witnessed the attack on Princess Eyrie."

The king slumped in his chair and solemnly commanded, "Tell me all that you know."

"The assailant is extremely dangerous. It is a dark being. From the library in the east wing the guests witnessed the act. It escaped from the tower to the forests farther east."

"Who were the guests you speak of?"

"They were a half-elf and a beast, my king. They too have fled. They were not involved and merely witnesses."

The king arched an eyebrow. "If they were, then why were you harmed?"

Oryn momentarily dropped his gaze. "Clumsiness caused my wound." He would have been more than happy to lay the blame on the beast, but he wanted all attention directed away from her and towards the kidnapper. If what the elf woman said were true and he had to tolerate the company of an animal, then so be it. It was crucial that no one knew she existed. They would kill the creature on sight and deny him his revenge.

The king pondered and then commanded, "I hereby order you to find the Princess Eyrie, Sir Oryn. Bring back my daughter at any cost and kill the monster that has dared to lay a hand on her."

"Yes, my king." He bowed and was about to leave.

Then the king stopped him, "Sir Oryn, I also order you to take every able knight with you on this quest."

Oryn was not pleased, but did not protest. He could not openly deny a direct order so instead forced himself to nod his head again. "Yes, my king."

"Now go!" he ordered. "Prepare and set out immediately!"

Bowing deeply, he took his leave out the solid oak doors.

The others could not know his intentions. He needed to elude them and find the creature with the bright blue eyes. Not the king, not the order and especially not the prospect of losing his life would stand in his way.

He would follow the first of the king's orders; the creature would track the princess, and when she was recovered, both the monster and it would die. So long as the other knights did not interfere, his plan would succeed. It would be far too easy.

Chapter 17
A NEW QUEST

Dark treetops swayed in the wind as Adwen carried Toth. Trotting on all fours, she followed the heavy-footed trail of the giant fiend. Most of the forest bore green leaves and blocked out the moonlight, but she hardly noticed a difference with her hound eyes. Adwen moved with snout to the ground. Toth clung on tight, listening as she growled in her dog language.

"That was such a nice friend. He was so polite and courteous."

"He is a good friend, but I thought you detested him?"

She growled, "It was a joke. It's hard to make a sarcastic tone when I'm like this. I was trying to say he was a complete jerk! I hope he has something better to do than come after us. I haven't been able to pick up the scent of the princess. Whoever has her tore the guards to pieces. All I can smell is blood."

"Is any of it from the princess?"

"No and that's at least one good thing. Whatever we're following doesn't even seem to be wounded." She whimpered, "I don't know about you, but that makes me nervous."

A steam cloud was on his breath and he shivered. "Just keep going. We need to help the princess."

The night had grown cold and was getting colder. The chill didn't bother her, but looking back at her friend, she knew he would freeze. Adwen caught the scent of humans and saw a stream of chimney smoke over the trees. For his sake, she quickly found the home with firelight spilling through the windows onto the porch. It looked safe though she could smell a dog tethered near the door.

Toth kept shivering, but looked and saw the dwelling. She crouched atop a steep grade eroded by the seasons. He shivered again as he realized what she was up to. "What are you doing? I'm all right. Keep going."

Making up her mind, she skidded down the slope and struggled to maintain balance. As predicted, the mutt began to bark and she growled, "I don't believe that for a second. You won't last the night in this. I'm taking you to stay someplace warm." When they were closer she let him off. "I'll wait out here. I'll be fine."

He gave an appreciative nod and shuddered.

She wagged her long tail. "Go on. If that dog gives you any trouble, I'll teach him to play dead."

Making for the house, he chuckled through chattering teeth. "I haven't forgotten the last time you taught that trick."

The door opened and she darted back up the slope. From behind a tree, she watched as a kind woman let him in and closed the door.

Adwen breathed a sigh of contentment as she curled up in the dirt. The ground was hard, but it would do with the raised roots cradling her. The thick fur would keep out the chill until moon set. Resting her long muzzle on a root, her violet eyes shifted as she wondered about how her family. Did they know she was even gone? Had as much time in her home world elapsed since the fall? Her mother would be worried out of her mind. Her siblings would be traumatized. She didn't quite know what her father would do. She missed them.

As she was about to fall asleep, her ears pricked at the sound of Toth's voice.

"Adwen? Adwen?"

She peered around the wide trunk and saw three figures standing outside. Among them was her companion. He hollered again, "Adwen! Adwen! If you can hear me, say something."

After hesitating, she barked and frightened the dog into silence. "I'm over here!"

"Come down. There are two good people I want you to meet."

The three heard something disturb the embankment. They watched as she came out of the dark and stopped a few yards away. He smiled while the mother and her teen son looked nervous.

More hesitant than before, she whimpered loudly. "Are

you sure this is a good idea?"

"I asked if you could come inside and they said to bring you in before the night worsened. It's all right, Adwen. You can come in!"

She studied the frightened humans and slowly padded to his side. The two watched in amazement as she didn't harm him and whimpered, "I'm going to take your word for it again, but please don't make me say I told you so."

Chuckling, he ruffled the long fur on her neck.

It was strangely reassuring. Holding head and tail low, she moved slowly so as not to startle the humans. They stepped aside as at her approach. Stealing a glance at their faces, she was sure Toth hadn't told them what she was, but crept inside anyway.

The cozy two-room home was full of warmth from a hearth and she could tell they lived very modestly off the land. They had a large dinner table and shelves of plates and personal valuables. Joining her, they closed the door and Adwen instinctively sniffed, taking in a snout full of dust that induced a violent sneeze.

The explosive sound caused the boy's mother to stymie a scream. The boy had jumped, but smiled at his own surprise when he realized what happened. Toth hadn't noticed them give a start, but laughed at Adwen's funny sound.

Giving an awkward glance, she wagged her tail and hung her ears apologetically. "Sorry."

She began to realize how much she was adapted to her new body. The need to use her sense of smell was difficult to resist. Claiming an empty corner, she lay with her back to the wall and folded claws beneath her head.

Toth draped his cloak over her and she lifted her head to whine, "Just to tell you again, I really don't like this idea."

Her accusing look made him chuckle.

The woman left for sleep while her son stayed behind. He looked sixteen years of age and his medium-length rusty hair was a mess. The young man looked fit and healthy as well as excited at the sight of Adwen. Then he asked as Toth sat across from him at the table, "Is this really the Tame One?"

Rolling her eyes, she grumbled. "Oh, so that's how you got them to let me in. Ah well. I guess that's good enough." Flopping down again, she tried to fall asleep.

"Yes, the very same. Some of the rumors you have heard are true."

He described their endeavors late into the night. The sounds of their conversing didn't bother her. She was too tired and far too hungry to care. Sleep was all that sounded good to her now, except for Regorian's rabbit stew.

Early in the morning, Adwen was first to wake. The full moon had set and she was in human form. She found the green garments lying beside her, quickly dressing herself. Toth and the boy fell asleep at the table. Her friend used the leather satchel to rest his head.

Smiling, she went to watch the sunrise. Outside was a rolling landscape of forest and hills. Farther to the east the earth sloped gently downward. That was the way the tracks had gone. The sun climbed higher, brushing the night aside. Dawn's first light seemed to dance in the chilled morning air.

Behind her the boy stirred and awoke with a yawn. She heard the sleepy sound and spoke to him without turning around, "Good morning."

Surprised, he replied, "Oh, good morning." Wondering why there was a girl standing at the window, he looked into the corner for the hound, but it had vanished. As he turned back to the girl, she faced him and he recognized the large collar hanging from her neck. Her blue eyes caught him by surprise, making him stare.

Paying no mind to the familiar response, she smiled as she went to her snoozing companion. A dragging snore suddenly escaped him and she couldn't help but giggle. He drooled on the leather bag in his sleep.

She greeted the boy, "What's your name?"

He blinked dark brown eyes, trying not to stare. "My name is Tamis, my lady."

"Thank you, Tamis, for letting Toth stay the night here. He would have frozen out there last night. The cold caught us both by surprise."

"It was no trouble at all. It was a pleasure to meet the Tame One. You are the Tame One, aren't you?"

A little embarrassed, she answered, "Yeah. The princess gave me the title."

"Is it really true? The princess has been kidnapped by some kind of evil being?"

"It looks that way. We'll have to leave soon, but I'd like to let Toth sleep for a few more minutes. He needs it."

The half-elf snored loudly beside her again.

"Would you like something to eat?" Tamis offered, "We have dried meat!"

"Yes, please!"

Going to a small chest, he took out a bundle. The food was wrapped in a thin cloth and she thanked him before biting into preserved flesh. When it was mostly gone, Toth started to wake. While he was stretching, she asked, "I'm not about to eat all of the food you have, am I?"

Tamis shook his head. "No, my lady. There is plenty from the deer I hunted. We won't starve even if you have more!"

She was content and ate all but the final piece. When Toth was alert enough, she offered it to him.

He shook his head, "No, thank you, Adwen. Tamis has filled the satchel with bread and cheese. It's made a wonderful pillow."

She giggled at his mild humor.

"So, we should be moving on then?"

"Yes. We will, after you put on your traveling clothes."

Rubbing his eyes, he replied, "What's wrong with these?"

Folding her arms, she grimaced. Still dressed in his silk suit, he looked like a rich fop. "I'm sure we'll be traveling past other towns and that means there could be bandits. Dressed like that, you'll be sure to get us mugged. We don't need any more pitfalls."

He laughed. "I thought you enjoyed trouncing bandits?"

She shook her head and chuckled. "I'll be waiting outside."

As she shut the door the air felt crisp. Wild birds sang in the trees and fluttered around. The scruffy dog was still tethered to the porch, looking up hesitantly with head held low.

"What are you so shy for?" she teased. "You were acting pretty tough last night."

The dog whined, "I'm sorry. I didn't know who was there

in the dark. I thought you were a bandit. You're not cross with me are you, miss?"

He was not nearly as large as a woar dog and would not have stood a chance against her in a fight. "I'm not going to hurt you. My friend and I are just passing through. We'll be leaving soon."

The dog sniffed and his tail wagged. "Is that food you have there?" He could smell the dried meat in her hand.

She tossed it to him and he snapped it up. When it was gone he cocked his head and wagged his tail. "Got any more?"

"No, I don't." She shrugged. "Sorry."

A moment later Toth joined her, dressed in his traveling clothes. The mother and son came to see them off.

The old woman stared at Adwen curiously, but never said a word. She was still afraid and did not know what to think.

"Thank you again for letting us stay the night. We really appreciate everything you've done for us."

Tamis smiled. "You're welcome, my lady. Come back anytime!"

They exchanged farewells and were on their way through the forest once more. After relocating the tracks, they followed them for hours on end. The smell of blood was gone and now she could catch the scent of the kidnapper. The spine-tingling odor was familiar somehow. But later in the day, something else began to bother her.

The afternoon was warm and the trail took them through an open clearing. Then Adwen froze.

"What is the matter?" Toth asked. "Is something wrong?"

She was nervous. The nagging feeling in the back of her mind had returned. "I can't smell who, but..." She glanced over her shoulder at the dense tree line. "I'm pretty sure we're being watched."

Toth looked between her and the forest in confusion.

"We're being followed," she murmured.

Chapter 18
AN UNINVITED ALLY

Broad River was in sight. Two towns rested along its west bank where travelers and traders crossed. It was too deep to build a stable bridge and the current too strong for any boat, so ferries were used instead. Sunset was upon them, so Toth built a small fire and they felt rested in the forest, but Adwen could not shake the feeling of unseen eyes upon her.

As when Regorian traveled with them, she departed for solitude before the full moon. She was determined to not destroy her clothes by transforming in them. That meant removing them beforehand. Once she was a hound again, she rejoined her carefree companion by the flames.

He was unsure of her paranoia. Her nose constantly tested the air and her violet eyes wandered as he chided, "There's no point in worrying. If someone were there they would have attacked. There is the chance you're simply imagining this feeling. You worry too much."

"And you don't worry enough," she growled. "Every other time I've felt like this there was something there. It's not my imagination. If we're being followed by Korig and Kotig, we can't afford to fall asleep at the same time."

Toth yawned and laid his head on the satchel full of bread and a little less cheese. "Then you won't mind standing the first watch. Wake me for my time."

"I won't be able to sleep anyway. I'll just stay up."

When she looked her friend was already asleep, softly snoring.

Again, she sniffed in the direction of the stalker. No matter what she never caught the scent. It was frustrating. They were never close enough to be seen, never made a sound and never caught upwind. Were there multiple watchers or just one? She couldn't be sure and not knowing was most disturbing.

The hours of the night dragged on. Once the full moon disappeared, she shrank into human form and dressed herself long before sunrise. In the dim twilight of dawn, she thought she saw something, but it turned out to be a foraging animal.

Toth suddenly rolled over and yawned, causing her to jump and almost scream. Calming down, she sat on an old log to watch her drowsy friend stretch awake.

Opening his eyes, he saw sunlight reaching from the east and yawned again. "Well, it would be best to set off soon. We best get going."

She nodded and smothered out what was left of the campfire. Only a few embers remained, but it gave her something to do while he prepared.

Exhausted yet alert, she watched their backs on their way into town. Adwen's powerful senses were tingling, listening for anything lurking in their wake.

The half-elf paid no attention.

The muscles in her back were rigid, but she kept her hands relaxed. The tracks of the fiend had become large boot prints left by a heavy man. It seemed to Adwen that the fiend could change its shape. Now very sure that the monster could pass as a human, she knew it could easily fool the villagers into granting a ferry ride.

"It could be carrying the princess along," Toth offered. "We should ask the people if they saw any odd strangers passing through."

"Yeah, but what if your asking questions gets them into asking questions about us?" Adwen pointed at her dog collar. All of her nails were short and sharp, while her small fangs could easily be concealed. As for her blue glowing eyes, they would pose a problem in keeping a low profile.

"First we should buy you a cloak for easy concealment. And are you sure you don't need shoes?"

She rolled her eyes. "Yeah, I'm sure. I haven't been whining about that, have I?"

He laughed at her grouchy demeanor. "You are exhausted aren't you? Why did you not wake me so you could rest?"

"You know why! There's no way I could fall asleep with the feeling of someone watching me. It makes my skin crawl." She shuddered at the thought.

Laughing again at her silly worries, he reached into the satchel for more bread and cheese. When he offered some she turned him down. Adwen was far too nervous to have an appetite.

The riverside town was a hub for trading uncommon goods from eastern Dargadia. Townspeople flitted through the streets of Nereid, passing between trading posts on the docks. The duo visited a shop to acquire another traveling cloak and discovered their coins were running low, but it was a necessary expense. Now much more inconspicuous, they went around interviewing locals.

They asked many traders if they had seen a stranger and a young girl passing through, but no one saw a thing. After a few hours they asked nearly everyone. Eventually they found the stables and Toth asked a short, stocky man with a bushy mustache.

He studied them and thought it over before saying gruffly, "Of course I've seen two odd strangers. You fit the description nicely. Besides you, I haven't noticed anything out of the ordinary."

Disappointed again, they turned away.

Then he suddenly called them back, "Hold on a minute! I think I did see a strange fellow and a young woman in white. They came through just the other day."

Adwen and Toth quickly went back to listen to the details.

"The girl was strangely quiet. I thought she could be a mute. She had on a dark cloak and seemed almost asleep on her feet. Anyway, the dark stranger asked to buy a horse." He shook his head. "What struck me as odd was that he specifically asked for my slowest. I did as he asked and gave him the slowest beast I had."

Exchanging looks, they silently agreed it was very strange.

He went on, "I don't recall his face for some reason and the girl's face was hidden beneath a hood. They crossed the river at noon yesterday. I'm sorry I can't tell you more."

"Not to worry," Toth assured him. "That was better than we could have asked for."

"Why would you be following them? Does he owe money?"

Adwen's sight was hindered by the hood that concealed

her glowing eyes, but other senses more than compensated. Only her lips could be seen moving as she replied, "That man took our friend. We plan to catch him and bring her back."

"Oh!"

Then she had an idea. "Could you please show me the stall where you used to keep the horse?"

"That would be fine by me, my lady. Looking around is free of charge." He chuckled and led them in past many strong horses. Most were curious about her and whispered amongst themselves.

While the man spoke to Toth, she stopped and informed the horses, "You know it's rude to talk about someone when they can hear you, right?"

Caught by surprise, their ears went straight up and their eyes widened. Entertained by her own shenanigans, she thought what she'd said was clever.

The mustached man took good care of his horses. He presented a clean stall, cleared out and prepared for any other beast of burden that might fill it later. Being as casual as possible, she stepped inside and began to sniff.

The man scratched his hairy neck and thought aloud, "I don't know why you'd want to see an empty stall, but this is it. The beast was not only fat and slow, but it had a smelly hide to boot. It was a stinky animal, and to be honest, I'm glad to be rid of it."

She quietly agreed as she cupped a hand to her nose, sickened by the powerful stench. The man had cleaned the space well, but even then she quickly found the scent left by the putrid creature. This was all good news for their search.

Having what she wanted, she turned to go. "Thank you very much. You've been more help than you think."

He showed them out and bowed, smiling. "It was a pleasure to help a young lady. I hope the two of you catch the brute. May the sun spirits always guide your feet."

After thanking him again, they made for the ferry. As they went, Toth turned and smiled. "You got the scent of the horse, didn't you?"

She showed him a big toothy grin. "Yup!"

Then he noted her change of mood. "Do you still feel that you're being watched?"

"Of course not. I'm in a town full of people who have eyes too. Out in the woods was different; there weren't any distractions for my senses. They could be following us right now and I wouldn't know the difference."

Once again they were in luck. The ferry was not in use and currently on their side of the river. As soon as they paid the toll, they would be free to set out. When they came to the pier, Toth started business with the few coins they had left.

She took her chance to look out at the river and was surprised at the distance to go. If she hadn't known any better, she would have thought it was a small lake. Broad River flowed south to empty into the sea. Its rippling waters were clear in the morning light. The ferry itself was simpler than expected. It was a platform large enough to accommodate two carts with room to spare, near twenty feet wide and thirty across. On either side were benches with high railings to lean against or for tethering horses.

She was eager to go aboard, but the ferryman blocked their way. They were short by two coins and the worker was hesitant to let them pay that cheaply. After studying him she could tell he was kind. With the hood masking her face, she approached.

The muscular man stopped listening to Toth and addressed her, "I'm sorry, miss, but your friend doesn't have enough for me to let you on."

"Please," she asked sweetly, "we have to cross. What's two coins worth?"

The man sighed. "That's one loaf of bread on the table for my family. I'm sorry, but I cannot let that slip by. Times are hard enough."

"Are two coins worth a life?"

The man was taken aback. "Wait a minute, are you threatening me?"

"No. Our friend is in danger. A dark man took her across yesterday at noon. We need to catch him, and if you don't let us cross she could be dead before we find her."

"Well, I...uh..."

"Please," she said in her gentlest tone. "Please help her if you can't help us. We have to cross."

With a pained look, he massaged the back of his head and

grappled with the prospect. She cocked her head, and at last, he heaved a sigh. "All right. I'll take what you have. Get aboard."

Toth quickly thanked him and they hopped past as he called to his friends, who were playing cards nearby.

Four muscular workers quickly rushed through their short game where one came out victorious. The winner laughed heartily while his companions tossed down hands in defeat, leaving the table to earn their keep.

He whispered to the two trekkers, "Do me one favor and don't breathe a word. If the others found out, they would skin me alive."

She shook her head and Toth replied, "We promise not to tell."

Their ferry began to move. Down below the water was so clear they could see fat fish swimming far beneath the surface. The floating platform was raised high to keep pesky river creatures at bay as well as to withstand the weight of whatever might be on board. They were moving so very slowly. Inch by inch and foot by foot, they drifted away from shore.

Toth turned to her as they looked out across the water. "There isn't much sense in standing and watching our progress. Now would be the most opportune time for you to rest." They settled down on a bench to wait out the lazy ride and he pulled the hood farther down to shade his eyes.

She pulled her own back, content to see the pier float away. The lapping sounds made by the water were calming. Adwen's gaze followed the hustle and bustle of the commoners, buying and trading goods. The more she stared at the busy streets, the more she felt something was amiss. She studied the crowd a little longer. Hardly a moment passed before she saw what didn't belong.

A massive warhorse was up the street and aligned with the pier, pawing the ground. An armored rider sat atop its back. The shining swordsman wore a helm with the image of a wolf. His suit glistened like a star as the silver-steel helm appeared to snarl. The ferry was not too far from shore.

Tapping Toth's shoulder roughly, she gasped, "Toth, I see him."

"What?" He had been half-asleep. "You see whom?"

The knight's war horse snorted.

Toth pulled back the hood of his cloak. Once he spotted him, he muttered, "Oh, my stars. It's one of the Master Knights."

She slugged his shoulder and grumbled, "I told you we were being followed."

Upon the hill the knight's steed shook its mane, braying with anticipation. It was eager to get into action, but his master was steady.

"Hey, Toth? He can't reach us out here, can he?"

He didn't answer and watched nervously.

"Toth?"

The half-elf murmured, "Oh, no."

The warhorse reared and brayed and the busy street cleared to make way as they charged at a reckless pace. The knight made for the pier and the stud's nostrils flared.

In shock, Toth sat quietly and Adwen climbed up onto the bench to avoid the chance of being trodden over. Horrified, she cried out at the top of her lungs.

The ferryman was startled as the rider went leaping past, landing on the floating platform. Adwen screamed in surprise when the huge animal rocked the wooden island. She heard the horse slew out a stream of swears as he barely stopped before the edge. Stamping and snorting, the creature spat, "They must make these damn things longer!"

The rider coolly dismounted and went about tethering the vulgar-tongued steed to the nearest rail.

Too outraged to be afraid, Adwen hopped down from the bench and approached the knight. "Hey! Get your own ride across the river. You can't just..."

Her sentence was cut short when he swiftly brought the tip of his sword to her neck. Stopped dead in her tracks, she had second thoughts. Then the wind blew his scent directly into her face.

"You!"

Sheathing his weapon, Oryn turned back to his chore.

Toth joined her and watched apprehensively. "Are you all right?"

"I'm fine," she grumpily replied. "It's your friend."

Oryn finished lacing the reins and removed his helm,

stowing it and paying the two no mind.

Unlike her, Toth was thrilled. "Oryn! I'm glad you could join us!"

Adwen protested vehemently. "Hold up one second! He's not coming with us! Did you totally forget he tried to kill me?"

Undeterred, he replied with a smile and a shrug, "Of course, I haven't."

Seeing that she could not talk any sense into him, she rounded on the green-eyed man. He was sifting through many saddlebags, counting supplies.

"And what do you want?" she glowered. "Why are you following us?" He didn't acknowledge her. Very tired and even hungrier, she thought she might explode with outrage.

Toth stepped closer. "Why have you come, Oryn?"

To her annoyance, he answered right away, "You are following the trail of the princess' kidnapper. That is the same path I intend to follow." Turning to face Toth, he continued, "If my guess is correct, this assailant could be a powerful demon. I do not suffer such fiends in my kingdom."

Toth was satisfied while she was even more outraged. Arms crossed, she called him out, "Oh, I get it. You'll talk to him, but you won't talk to me!" Her glare intensified.

Without glancing at her even once, he added, "Toth, keep your pet quiet. It is quickly becoming an annoyance."

Adwen fumed, *"Oh!"* She stomped off to the farthest corner away from the terrible intruder. Exasperated, she sat and leaned forward, resting her tired head in her hands. Long hair hung about her face like a thick curtain.

A moment passed before Toth quietly sat alongside. "He didn't mean what he said, Adwen. He doesn't understand."

Face buried in her hands, she grunted, "Whatever."

"If you're hungry, I still have some bread and cheese."

"I'm not that hungry," she lied. Realizing she was taking out some of her frustration on her only friend, she sat up and sighed. "No, thank you. I'd rather get some sleep."

He gave a kind smile. "I think that would be best. You've earned it."

She watched him go and saw that the knight had been staring the entire time. He was studying her. Judging from the cold expression, she concluded he was sizing her up.

Fed up with being stared at, she lay down, covering her face with the hood. The sun was high, warming and relaxing sore muscles until she fell into a deep sleep.

Oryn watched the odd creature closely. This strange beast of Toth's was unlike any he had encountered. It could be dangerous. She had many striking similarities to werewolves, but the differences were what concerned him. This beast was not weakened by silver. He wanted to know why.

Toth noticed his childhood friend staring raptly at Adwen. "She's usually much more pleasant company. After she has some sleep and food in her belly, I'm sure you'll like her much better."

He doubted the creature being in a friendlier mood would do anything to change his opinions. "Where did you find this pet?"

"She is most definitely not my pet. It's more likely I'd be hers."

The statement disturbed the knight and he gave a questioning look.

"I didn't find her. She found me in a bit of trouble. I was being attacked by seven woar dogs near the North Brother River. Adwen saved my life."

"That is an obvious stretch of the truth," he replied with a sneer.

Smiling, he shook his head. "You don't believe me?"

"You are saying this pitiable beast defeated seven woar dogs on its own. I find that story difficult to swallow. Also, it has a strange way of speaking. Where did it come from?"

After taking a glance at her, he shook his head. "That is Adwen's secret to tell. If you really wish to know, you could ask her."

He grimaced at the thought of making conversation with the animal. Instead he asked, "Is there anything you are willing tell about this creature companion of yours?"

"Adwen is actually quite brave. On our travels together we managed to save Princess Eyrie's life."

His skeptical expression increased. "I find that far more difficult to believe than your first tale."

"Believe it or not, you saw the invitation. It was a gift in return for her bravery. At any rate, you wouldn't believe much else. I admit, the rest is rather farfetched."

Oryn watched her sleep and thought to ask a more important question, "Has she ever harmed a human? And does she require human flesh to survive?"

"Of course not!" Toth scoffed, batting a hand through the air. "She eats just about everything else. The only men she's harmed have tried to kill us or were intending to do worse. I don't know what Adwen is, but she is most definitely not a werewolf."

Knowing it did not crave human flesh brought some assurance. He could, with less worry, take this creature among humans. He thought that perhaps this animal could prove useful to the order after this quest was compete. If he could control her, then she would not necessarily have to be destroyed.

From his studies, he knew no werewolf could sleep soundly. They had incurable insomnia, and when they did sleep, had horrible night terrors. This female hound was sleeping peacefully. What could the animal's weakness be? Where did it come from? What was it?

Adwen dreamt of being home. Both Toth and Oryn let her sleep, knowing they would be relying on her strength to find Princess Eyrie. The more she rested, the better off they would be once they resumed the hunt.

The sun started to sink into the mountain-dotted horizon. A hand suddenly nudged Adwen's shoulder. Refreshed, she brushed back the hood to see Toth. Before saying a word, she checked to see if the knight were watching. He was and with the same unreadable poker player expression. She groaned.

"I'm sorry I had to end your rest, Adwen. I thought it best. The sun is near setting and there are two full moons out."

Glancing around, she saw the orange and gold moons were full. Cloud cover would not come until after the sun had gone. She could only hope both would be hidden before the barge reached shore.

"Well, that's just great." She sighed and shook her head. "So I'm going to start my night early, huh?"

"Yes. Not only that, but I thought you should know you shall need to prepare yourself. The fever you have before a change shall begin once the sun touches the horizon. And because of the two full moons your body will want to change much sooner. Your fever will be quite unpleasant, I fear."

This news was disappointing, but she was surprised at how knowledgeable he had become. Giving a sideways look, she asked, "Thanks, but how do you suddenly know so much?"

"Oryn told me these things. He knows quite a lot."

The stony knight was still watching. His emotionless stare made Adwen shiver.

She groaned, "Do we have to bring him with us?"

"I believe we do. We shall need his skills. It is far more dangerous on the other side of the kingdom."

"I've gotten tougher, you know. Name one reason why we would need him."

Holding up two fingers, he replied, "I could name two and they are Korig and Kotig. You may be stronger, but both of them together still outmatch you. With Oryn we won't have so much to fear. He is the greatest werewolf slayer since the first Master Knights. The Bloody Brothers wouldn't dare to hunt you now."

She recalled her own confrontation with the knight. "So long as there aren't any more shelves with pottery to fall on his head, that is." Her face split into a smile at the recollection.

He was glad to see her happy. "You'll be fine. I wish you well, my friend."

As he left she felt relief. If the knight were correct about the effect of two full moons, then this fever would last until the sun disappeared. She hoped he was mistaken.

Adwen's stomach growled pitifully. She was very hungry, but Toth was talking to the knight again. So long as they were conversing, he wasn't staring. The sun drew closer to the distance and she sat up. She saw the bright sphere connect with the mountain tops and her skin instantly felt hot. Blue eyes turned neon violet and glowed in the dusk.

When Oryn saw the sun, he stole a glance at her. Just as suspected, she was affected by the double moon. She did not seem mentally unstable as werewolves would be. This creature was relatively calm despite growing discomfort. He could make out the pained expression and beads of sweat.

The pressure was more than she had felt since her first experience changing. The headache was splitting and her body felt tender. Sitting as still as possible, she didn't dare move too much. Every sinew felt as if it could burst into transformation at any second and the sun was not even half set.

Toth paused as he noticed Oryn staring. She was in obvious agony, buckled over. Whenever the pains flared, she let out a quiet gasp and shuddered.

The pain came in waves. Her insides felt as if they slithered like a ball of agitated snakes. It hurt so horribly when internal organs tried to shift that it took her breath away. The pressure in her right hand was the worst. Once again, her friend's scent reached her and she carefully looked up. He was beside her, rummaging through the satchel. Relief swept over her as he retrieved one of the medicinal leaves.

Before he could hand it over, the knight stopped him. "Is that the leaf of a healer's aid plant?"

"Yes, it is. She needs this for the pain."

"If you do not have an adequate supply, it would be best to not waste them. That herb is rare east of the river. It would be wise to save it for a real injury and not for your pet's harmless aches."

Adwen's hand shifted and crunched. She gasped, tears streamed down cheeks as it took all of her willpower to not scream. Her hand was larger, resembling what it would be once the sun departed. A few agonizing moments later, the claws disappeared and her hand appeared normal, but the same pressure remained.

Her companion felt horrible. "I'm sorry." He put the herb away. "I only have a few left. If anything were to happen, we would be in dire need of these leaves. Can you forgive me?"

Taking a shaky breath, she replied in a betrayed tone, "Yeah, I get it. You're going to listen to everything he says now."

Saddened, he shook his head. "I'm your friend, Adwen. I'm trying to help the best I can. There is very little I can do."

She appreciated that he wished to help. "I know you're my friend, Toth," she murmured and shuddered again. "I'm just not happy with your knight friend." Her watery eyes glared past his shoulder.

Oryn was watching closely.

"Toth," she uttered through a wave of pain. "I could use a little privacy so I don't change in these clothes. Do you think you could tell him to stop staring for a few minutes, please?" She winced at another wave.

Right away, he left to relay the message.

With no place to hide, she would be forced to remove her garments in the open. She hated the idea of being without clothes and it had happened too many times already. Gingerly getting to her feet, she stood on rubbery legs, waiting to see if the knight would grant her this little.

Her friend finished speaking and she saw the knight scowl. A moment later they both turned their backs to face the slowly approaching shore. Tiny lights from distant widows blinked in the shadows.

Once their gazes were elsewhere, she felt brave enough to remove the dress. The cloak and collar could be worn during the change, but the removing of the rest was made difficult by straining muscles continuously fighting her every movement.

Oryn stared vacantly across the water at nothing in particular until a thought occurred to him. What if this creature were a new and more dangerous brand of werewolf? If she had once been a human girl capable of surviving a marking, then there would be a scar left by the menace.

She was distracted by agony when he coolly glanced over one shoulder. He silently studied her and then looked away. Her skin was pale and completely without scars or markings. She looked much stronger than any woman he had ever seen and was intrigued.

The knight quickly caught himself admiring what he had seen and swept the idea from his mind. He was thoroughly disgusted with himself for forgetting for a second what she really was; just an animal.

Fluctuating blood pressure made her unsteady as she set the clothes aside and sat with the black cloak wrapped about her. Falling would not be pleasant.

"Thank you," she said in exchange for their courtesy.

The warhorse snorted indignantly, "What an indecent wench, undressing in my master's presence."

Hearing his comment, she retorted, "Ah, shut up, you mule!"

The horse stared in utter surprise and Oryn sneered, "What did you say to me, mongrel?"

"I wasn't talking to you," she glowered. "I was talking to your horse." Another shudder wracked her.

He was mildly surprised, but kept it hidden. "You will mind your tongue, dog, if you possess any sense at all."

"Yeah, sure, but you should talk to your horse. He swears worse than a drunken sailor."

Oryn turned to Toth.

Shrugging, the half-elf smiled. "She can converse fluently with animals. It has come in rather handy."

Before the knight could reply, the sun set at last and Adwen let out a terrible roaring cry. Her back arched as her spine elongated beneath dark fabric. It was disturbing, but the two observers could not look away as her head stretched and fangs sprouted in lengthening jaws. No longer clinging to the cloak, she dropped from the bench and rapidly turned a shiny jet black. It ended soon after and she breathed in heavy gasps, glad the experience was over.

With a loud whinny, the horse broke free from his restraints and charged before Oryn could stop him. "I'll kill you, beast!"

She yelped and flew out from beneath the cloak, flinging herself over the edge. While she dangled by two sets of claws, the horse attacked. Gigantic hooves came down and she barely kept from being stomped upon. There was another yelp when the horse barely missed her claw tips.

Then a whistle came from the knight and he paused, glaring with ears pinned back. They both heard him call out, "Ranger, stand down!"

Ranger snorted, "You only live because my master wishes it so." Then he called her a stream of swears and curses before obeying.

With her own ears back, she hauled herself up and snarled, "Stupid horse."

"Are you all right?" Toth asked as he went to her. Then before she could respond, he was scratching behind her head.

She grumbled, "What are you doing?" Losing her train of thought, she was content to sit. Once he stopped, she came to and was embarrassed. "Thanks, I guess. How did you know that it would do anything?"

"I didn't," he chuckled. "I thought of what would usually

calm dogs and it just happened to work on you as well."

She grumbled in reply, "Please don't do that again." Her dog-like tendencies were beginning to disturb her. As Toth went to collect her garments, she glanced at the knight.

Oryn's eyes sparkled dangerously. From the expression he wore, she could tell he liked her much less this way.

She barked, "What are you looking at?"

With frightening speed, his hand flicked to his sword and he glared. He squeezed the grip in a threatening manner. If she tried to approach it would come unsheathed.

Adwen's muzzle wrinkled into a quiet snarl.

Then Toth exclaimed, "This is not good."

All eyes fell on him as he pointed to the pier that was approaching. Clouds were moving in, but would not cover the two moons soon enough.

"Toth, instruct your pet to leave."

They both stared back at Oryn, flabbergasted.

"Tell the dog to swim downstream. It would be unwise to have it stay aboard once we come within the reach of their lanterns. Direct it to leave."

Heaving a sigh, he turned to her. "Well, Adwen, you know he's right."

Angry and betrayed, she stood upright and stepped onto the bench to examine the current. Then a smell drifted in on the wind from shore, causing her hair to stand on end. Toth wondered what could make her freeze so suddenly, but Oryn was not so patient.

Drawing his sword, he stormed over to where the lanky form leaned on the rail, staring at the river's edge. Pointing his weapon at the water, he warned with an even deadlier tone, "You will jump now or you shall swim to shore with a trail of your own blood. The creatures of the river will not make pleasant company."

Her ears drooped and she whimpered, "Please don't do this. They're waiting for me! They're here!"

All he could hear were hound whimpers and whines.

Toth tried to stop him, but acted one second too late.

Oryn swung the blade, forcing her to leap and the two heard a splash before seeing her bobbing in the current.

"Oh, stars above!" Toth gasped and shook his head.

"Oryn, you should have waited! She is in danger if she goes to shore alone!"

Surprised, he asked, "What danger?"

The cold river soaked Adwen's fur. Outraged, she could hardly contain herself. "What a jerk! He's nothing but a big, ego-tripping bully!"

Swimming was easier for her as a hound and she allowed the river to sweep her past town. Once on solid ground, she shook water rigorously from her coat. The last droplets dribbled from her jaws as she froze, listening for danger. She did not see either of the brothers, but grew nervous. All of the insects were either silent or none existed.

Standing on shore staring was not going to get her to safety so forced herself to continue. The extreme silence added to the dread her sixth sense instilled. She crept through the trees and undergrowth, keeping ears and eyes open. Eventually she found the empty highway. The forest was still and every hair on her body bristled. She went out into the open. No attack came. Not wanting to move, but unwilling to wait, she made for the village where her companions would surely be landing any moment.

A breeze brought the first smells from the village and then a fully transformed Kotig leaped from between the trees with a roar of delight. She heard him soon enough to save herself from his jaws and their bodies collided. The two were a tumbling mess of snarls, slashing and snapping as they wrestled in the dusty road, grappling and clawing for control.

Korig came storming out, roaring at Kotig as he also transformed, "Fool! Now is not the time!" Angry, he kicked Kotig and caught him in the jaw.

With Kotig stunned, Adwen slipped out from beneath him to lunge for Korig's throat.

His reflexes were too quick and his monstrous claws gripped her by the front. The razor-sharp points drove into her torso like meat hooks and suspended her up high and in immense pain. When she let out an earsplitting cry, he chuckled and squeezed harder before casting her aside.

Croaking guffaws made Adwen's blood run cold. She tried

to gather herself up as Kotig returned, slashing her muzzle, leaving bloody gashes.

The sudden sting brought her to and she rolled away to safety. As he attacked again, she repaid him with her own claws, raking across his skinless face.

Both of the bloody beasts snapped and swung at one another as Korig continued to struggle for control over his ravenous sibling. For the first time, she was holding her own against the brute, but Korig was growing more impatient by the second. When his temper reached the breaking point, he threw a fist at Kotig's jaws and another for Adwen. The werewolves worked themselves into a blind rage. Then she was on the receiving end from both monsters.

A moment later Oryn came charging down the road with Ranger. Wearing the slayer's helm, he drew his silver-steel sword and prepared for the onslaught.

Korig saw him charging. When Oryn swung for the unsuspecting Kotig, he snatched his dumb brother by the scruff and threw him out harm's way. Then he lunged and lowered his shoulder into the knight's steed.

Many times had Oryn and Ranger fought and slain werewolves, but never once had they met the Bloody Brothers. The usual werewolf was all rage and little sense. Knocked off balance, knight and horse toppled to the ground.

Even though Oryn was surprised, he was quick enough to not be trapped beneath his mount. The knight landed on his feet and side-stepped the fallen companion.

Ranger was stunned and whinnied in shock and surprise. On his side in the dirt, he was vulnerable whiel Korig stood over him, ready to swing a set of claws for tender underside. His skilled master would not be able to save him this time.

Adwen pounced onto the werewolf's gargantuan shoulders, sinking fangs into his upper jaw, snapping his head back from the frightened horse.

Ranger quickly took his chance to find his footing and bolted.

While Adwen had the monster preoccupied, Oryn moved in to finish him. His throat was exposed and the knight felt the undeniable urge to cut it.

There was little warning as Kotig threw a heavy tree limb at the knight's head. The helm hindered the Oryn's peripheral vision, but he was fortunate enough to notice. He ducked down as a branch caught his helm and tore it off. Unfazed, he watched the monster charge and prepared to strike him down with a single swing.

Korig finally got a hold of Adwen. Ripping her from his shoulders, he snarled and threw her into his brother. They tumbled into the bushes.

Kotig was busy dealing with Adwen again and the knight turned his attention back to the towering Korig. This werewolf was visibly more powerful than any he had faced. Oryn had read and studied such monsters for years and knew this was what the writings referred to as an alpha werewolf. Oryn smiled while the monster stepped forward in the moonlight. This would be a true test of his abilities. His eyes glinted at the thought.

Korig roared and slashed, careful to avoid the silver-steel weapon. As the knight jabbed and swung again, the werewolf snarled, slowly backing away.

Becoming bolder, the knight backed the monster into a tree and attacked again, sure he had won.

Korig allowed the greedy warrior to corner him. When he swung for the final time, Korig did something the knight had never seen in his seven years of slaying. The alpha caught his sword in his jagged maw, grabbed Oryn's other hand as well as the front of his body armor, immobilizing him on the spot. Silver burned the monster's mouth and hands, but he laughed at the pain. The touch alone was not fatal.

Scowling at the vile creature, Oryn cursed under his breath. There was another snarl and it caught Oryn's attention. Breath lodged in his throat at seeing Kotig bounding towards him. In a last-ditch effort to free himself, he vainly struggled. With nothing else to do, the knight glared defiantly as Kotig leaped. There was only dread and hate for the monsters that were about to be his end.

Adwen came out of nowhere. Her jaws clamped down around Kotig's and they both went rolling through the dirt. The sight infuriated his sibling so much that his own jaws slipped around the sword.

Feeling the telltale movement in his hand, Oryn swiftly

wrenched it free, giving an additional twist. The double-edged blade flayed the insides of Korig's mouth, causing blood to pour from fresh wounds like water.

Howling madly as he bled, the beast retreated while the knight drove him away.

Adwen was proving to be more than Kotig could handle. Growing more confident, she roared and forced her enemy to recoil. Together, they both forced the brothers back. She snapped and slashed and the werewolves stood their ground. Finally they roared in anger before fleeing, going southbound. They disappeared, leaving with weeping wounds and damaged pride.

On all fours panting, she watching them retreat and howled with excitement.

Toth finally caught up and made straight for her, laughing. "That was a good show, Adwen! But I think you ought to cease your howling."

She panted, "Yeah, sure!" Though Adwen was covered in bloody gashes, but didn't care. Her long bushy tail swung happily while Toth draped the dark cloak over her. Clouds blotted out the moons and she reverted to human form.

She stood and held the cloak close with the collar resting about her neck. Smiling past a few misplaced strands of wavy hair, she was proud of herself.

"Dog!" the knight suddenly yelled as he stormed over. Pointing his sword, he sneered, "You interrupted my battle with the alpha werewolf. If you ever interfere again, I shall not hesitate to share my father's sword with you. Am I clear?"

Affronted, her blue eyes flashed and their glow intensified with her loathing.

The defiant expression made him more agitated and he snapped, *"Am I clear, dog?"*

"Yeah, I got the picture." Then she added at his puzzled frown, "I understand."

Angry, but satisfied with the reply, he sheathed the weapon and went to Ranger.

Toth shook his head, frowning as he stomped off.

She couldn't believe the nerve of the knight. She muttered to herself as she watched him go, "Next time I'll let them rip your face off."

Chapter 19
COINS AND KISSES

In the riverside town of Poplin there was only one place for travelers to stay the night. The Fat Fish Inn stood across from the pier, profiting well off those who had crossed the river too late. For obvious reasons, most avoided the highways after dark. Staying at the Fat Fish was a much wiser decision.

As Oryn led Ranger away to the stables, the steed snorted at Adwen gruffly. "I doubt your wit is any sharper than your fighting tact, you pestilent cur. Mind your tongue in my absence." Then he nickered and added, "Keep a watch over my master all the same."

She shook her head, realizing he was trying to thank her for saving their lives. Adwen and Toth leaned against the wall by a torch lamp on the street. Small insects fluttered close to the flame. Oryn's maltreatment distracted her from the sting of battle wounds.

"Toth? Is there any explanation for why he's treating me like this?"

"What do you mean?"

"You know what I mean." Adwen sighed, too tired to be angry.

"Well, you could ask him why he dislikes you."

"Do you know why he hates me?"

"That's part of his past, Adwen. I have kept your secrets. He is my friend as well. I will not tell the past of someone who may not wish it shared."

She shrugged and stared absentmindedly at the hovering moths. "Fair enough."

At last Oryn arrived and they entered.

Inside was much like the Sleeping Dragon. The first floor served food and the counter steadily dispersed room keys and mugs of ale. Here was the center of entertainment and socializing for townspeople and travelers. But unlike the Sleeping Dragon, this downstairs was very busy.

The innkeeper had his hands full tending the crowd. Maids were not only paid to wait on customers, but also entertained. Each dressed somewhat scantily, and once they received what Adwen first mistaken for a tip, they engaged in flirtatious behavior.

Adwen was uneasy. In her home world she would have avoided places like this. After squeezing through to reach the counter, she stayed close to her male companions. Being only clothed by a cloak in the midst of many drunken men made her anxious.

The innkeeper looked young to be running the inn himself. Once he spotted Oryn in armor, he dropped everything to see what this guest wanted. Interrupted customers swore profusely, but he ignored the inebriates and greeted the knight.

"Good evening, sir."

"Good evening, innkeeper."

Adwen didn't pay attention to the rest of the conversation. An exceptionally drunken man attempted to make small talk with her. She ignored him the best she could, but he continued to ramble about how his week had been. Her anxiety grew, fearing he might try to touch her or pull her hood down to reveal her blue eyes.

Oryn soon received the key and a maid escorted them upstairs. When they reached the room the knight gave a few coins. As she tried to entertain him he stopped her. "The coins were for your good service, not for your services."

Bowing her head in appreciation for the gift, she left for other duties below.

The room was tidy, but dust and other less pleasant smells wafted to Adwen's nose. Some of the stranger odors came from the sheets. These rooms had obviously been used many times before.

That was when she realized there were just two beds.

Oryn proceeded to settle in. Kneeling at a bedside, he proceeded to remove and stow his armor underneath. Toth set the satchel on the foot of his own mattress, careful not to forget her garments, laying out them on the dresser.

Glaring at the knight, she folded her arms and frowned. After a while of watching, she cleared her throat for his attention. "Can I ask a question?"

He was silent as he removed one of the last pieces, thinking it over. Eventually, without facing her, he answered, "What is it that you want?"

She carefully asked, "Why did you -- I mean, where am I supposed to sleep? There're only two beds and there is no way I'm sharing with either of you. So, what's up with that?"

There was a long silence as he finished stowing his armor. She kept in mind that the sword was still on his hip. When he finally stood to face her, she looked determined to get an answer.

With a harsh glare, he sneered, "You are an inhuman creature in my charge and I say animals and inhuman creatures such as you shall sleep where they are meant to: on the ground."

Disappointed, but not surprised, she turned and went to gaze out the window. She heaved a loud sigh, strumming fingers impatiently along her arm.

Oryn decided to test her. "Do you wish to challenge my decision?"

"No, I don't. I just think there's something wrong with the fact that, even after I saved you and your horse, you still treat smalltime hotel whores better than me."

He scowled. "Is there anything else you wish to say while you possess a tongue?"

Cocking her head, she thought for a moment and added, "Actually, yes, there is." She turned and smiled. "How do you plan to explain me to the rest of the people downstairs?" Her eyes changed to violet.

Recognizing the sign, he was neither pleased nor willing to lose the room. "Can you not keep yourself quiet?"

Still smiling, she raised an eyebrow and shook her head. "I could, if you'd let me use one of the herb leaves, but we both know that's not going to happen."

Growing impatient, he snapped at the half-elf, "Toth! Do you know the silencing enchantment?"

He was reproachful and rubbed his head. "I know it, but I doubt I have the power required to use it. I've never tried before."

Pointing a finger at her, he warned. "Your pet has only a few moments before her howls give us away. If you have the power to disguise your ears, then you should have little trouble with the task. Act now or we shall be spending the night in the wilds with the wolves."

Adwen assumed he would use the enchantment on her, but instead, he let the illusion around his ears go. Using what little power he possessed, Toth began a blessing upon the room. He was anxious, but focused in his work recanting a spell in old Elvish. Just as Toth finished, the full moons were revealed.

Collapsing, she screamed and rapidly changed. The two covered their ears while she howled at stretching bones and muscles. When it was over, she growled miserably, "That sucked."

There was a small knock at the door.

Her ears went flat as she tucking her tail and scurried behind the beds.

Glancing at one another apprehensively, the men wondered if the spell had worked or if trouble were waiting in the hall. Keeping cool, the knight took a breath and opened it.

The maid smiled and curtsied. "Sir, I've been sent to inform you that all other services are free of charge for you and your guests."

"Very well. Have you heard anything odd?"

"What do you mean?"

Obviously she hadn't heard the loud howling when the whole of the town should have taken notice. Toth's spell had worked.

"It does not matter. Thank you."

Before he could close the door, Toth all but leaped forward to speak. "Wait a moment, miss." He leaned against Oryn's outstretched arm. "Do you mean to say the drinks downstairs are free of charge as well?"

"Of course," she said smiling, but became intrigued. "Where did your hooded friend go? And I don't recall you looking that way."

He had forgotten to hide his ears.

As the knight pulled him back, Oryn dismissed the maid.

"We are thankful for your employer's generosity. Good night to you." Shutting the door and restoring privacy, he rounded on Toth. "I believe it's time you explained yourself. Why do you hide your ears?"

The half-elf was not paying attention. He giddily restored his magical disguise. "Did you hear that? Free ale! We can speak later. If you need me, you shall find me with a pint in each fist!"

Adwen came out in time to join the abashed knight in watching their friend dart downstairs. The two were left to themselves. Leaving the bedside, Adwen's claws tapped the floor on her way to close the curtains. Both ears twitched when she heard Oryn settle on the linens. She glanced and saw the silver-steel sword resting across his chest while he continued to watch her. Determined to ignore the knight's gaze, she studied the room. A large mirror on the backboard of the dresser caught her attention and she became curious. She had never seen herself as the hound before.

She expected to see something resembling the werewolves, but was surprised to find her reflection was strikingly similar to a lanky black dog. Her muzzle was long and solid. Incisors protruded ever so slightly. The fur was soft, shiny and clean where she didn't have fresh cuts. Her eyes were eerie. She appeared the way she felt: strong yet half-starved.

After adjusting to the sight. she eventually noticed the knight's reflection. His sharp green eyes were still studying her. Sleep suddenly became more desirable than staring at cruel mirror images. Worn out, she moved to borrow Toth's pillow. She knew he wouldn't mind, but stopped short of the footboard. Oryn's hand was on his sword, ready to swing if she reached for it.

Disappointed again, she huffed and went to settle in the far corner, scooping up her cloak as she went. Curling up in the corner with the black garment over herself, she quickly sank into a dreamless sleep.

The curtains were thrown open wide and sunlight came blazing through onto Adwen's face where she lay. She snoozed in human form with the cloak still over her. The collar set at an odd angle around her small neck. The bright light from the window did not wake her, but then she felt something sharp prick the end of her small nose. "Uh! Ouch, what the..?"

Oryn stood over her with the sword in her face, already suited in armor.

Annoyed, she grumbled, "What do you want?"

Knowing she was fully awake, he put the weapon away. "Toth never returned. Dress yourself and seek him out."

Her eyes followed as he left for the door and she laughed dryly. "And without even saying please. Why don't you go find him?"

Stopping in the doorway, he replied flatly, "Because I have other business to attend to. He is likely at the bar. Have him ready to depart before I return. Am I clear?"

"Yeah, I understand." Once the door closed she rolled her eyes and took advantage of the empty room to dress herself.

Downstairs the bar was quiet with a few drinkers lingering from the night before. Three men sat together in the middle of the room and Toth was passed out at the counter. She shook her head when she spotted him slouched over. When she reached him the scent of alcohol was intense.

The bartender came close and chuckled. "Your friend sure can hold his ale. He took part in a drinking game in the late hours. After he won he sat himself here and hasn't moved." Then he noticed her blue eyes and did a double take. Bowing his head, he whispered, "My apologies, Princess Eyrie."

She blushed. "Don't worry. I'm not the princess."

He dipped his head again, clearly not convinced. "Of course you're not, miss."

Forgetting about the man behind the counter, she tried nudging her friend into waking. "Come on, buddy. It's time to get up."

Toth groaned as he slowly came to.

The other men in the room noticed and started to discuss her, smiling.

She continued trying to wake him with little success. And when she heard the men talking, the attempt became motivated by distress. They were getting out of their chairs and approaching. Shaking his shoulder roughly, the sixth sense made her aware of their intentions. They were not going to be pleasant company. Adwen guessed that their muscular leader must be one of the ferry workers from this side of the river. Both his friends were strong as well, but lacked the same large frame.

"Hey there, sweetie," he called.

A worried look came over her as she paused to give a glance.

"Those are pretty eyes you got there. How about letting your friend sleep it off and coming to a room with me? I'll make it worth your while." He brandished a pouch full of coins.

Disgusted, Adwen turned away and replied, "No, thank you. I'm not interested." She quickly went back to shaking her friend's shoulder. Leaning in close to his ear, she whispered, "Please wake up, Toth!"

"Ah, come now, little thing. What if I promise to give you a big kiss?"

His friends chuckled.

Without turning, she refused. "No. I'm not interested."

Losing patience, he roughly grabbed her by the arm. "No woman talks to me like that! You're coming with me!"

Toth finally managed to come around just as the man lost his temper. Fighting the hangover, he slurred to the stranger, "Hey, you let her alone, you big dolt."

"Stay out of it." Before the hung-over half-elf could form another sentence, he was shoved to the floor.

The blatant attack spurred Adwen into action. In the blink of an eye she pulled out of the man's grip and slammed her shoulder into his chest. He was thrown halfway across the room, bowling over furniture with a loud crash. Drinking cups and bread platters spilled everywhere.

Shaking with rage, she stared at what she had done. Her eyes were alight with a fiery glow as she glared at the remaining goons. Breathing in deep, rattling breaths, she waited to see if they would retaliate.

At first they gawked, but once the shock was gone they were angry. They came at her. One tried to grab her arm, but she dodged and dealt a swift backhand across the face. The strike nearly spun him around before she delivered a kick to his side, rolling him up and sending him into the far wall.

Then the other grabbed her around the middle from behind, pinning both arms to her sides. She squirmed and he laughed, "Gotcha!"

Adwen disagreed. He smelled of sweat, ale and a variety of other odors. She flexed her body backward into a powerful reverse head-butt. It struck the center of his forehead and he was stunned. Instinct took over as she drove her elbows into his bloated gut, forcing him to let go. Free once again, she turned to plant a foot in his chest, bowling him over. Her heart raced and her eyes were wild. The two friends were out of the fight, but the leader of the motley crew was awake, crawling away beneath the tables to the door.

He was scrambling out from under the last when two startlingly strong hands snagged him from overhead. Adwen held him dangling by the front of his worker's garments as she stood on the table. The brute stared, dumbstruck as she put her face close to his and sneered.

"I'm not a barmaid or a whore you can buy with coins or kisses." Adwen wondered what to do with him.

Then she gave a small gasp and froze as cold metal touched her throat. Oryn's scent wafted to her and she rolled her eyes. "Good morning. You missed the fun part."

"Drop him," he directed while the edge of his sword balanced on her neck.

Studying the man's dumb face, she gave a wry smile. She let go and he dropped to the floor with a dull thud.

He recovered in a flash and vanished out the door.

When she faced him, he gestured with the blade and ordered, "Down."

Adwen dropped from the table, but then he put the sword tip to her chest. Moving backward with hands up, she was forced to the bar. When she could go no farther, the knight commanded, "Sit."

A grimace made her lips purse and her brow furrow. She grimaced before hopping up to take a seat on a stool.

His poker face firmly set, Oryn asked, "Why did you attack these men?"

She folded her arms smartly. "Let me put it to you this way: you can get away with those dog commands, but don't ever tell me to roll over. These guys tried that, if you get my drift."

The bartender finally spoke up, "Sir?" Oryn turned, and he continued, "She is innocent, sir. These men tried to pay her to share a bed. When she denied them, they attacked. She was defending herself."

Toth appeared from behind an overturned table. Struggling to his feet, he confirmed the story. "It's true. These blubber heads were bothering her."

The knight did not look pleased with Toth's state.

Adwen suppressed a giggle.

After giving the bartender a few coins for his troubles, Oryn turned to his company. "Toth, fetch your provisions from the room and wait outside."

He nodded and moved for the stairs.

Then he glared at Adwen. "You, come with me."

The two exited the inn, and once the door closed, he rounded on her. "From this time on, you shall do exactly as I say! Whatever I say, you will answer to without question. Do you understand?"

"Yeah, sure."

"Do you know who I am, dog? I am Captain of the Order. And as such, I have the authority of the elder council. You shall call me 'sir' when you speak to me."

She glared back in silence.

Angrier than before, he snapped, "Am I clear?"

"Yes, sir."

"In the future you shall not attack a human under any circumstance without my consent. I should kill you now for your insolence, but you are far too useful for the moment. If you outlive your usefulness, I shall not hesitate to end your life. You will mind your tongue!"

Pulling a six-inch silver-steel knife from his boot, he held it up for her to see. "More than once a man has allowed his tongue to flap freely like a flag. Those men no longer speak. Watch your tongue closely or I shall watch it for you." Stowing it away, he commanded, "You are not to move from this place until I return. Am I understood?"

She grimaced and eventually answered, "Yes...sir."

Oryn's green eyes flashed and he left her standing outside

the Fat Fish.

She shuddered from the intensity of the confrontation.

Toth eventually joined her. An open barrel held clean water nearby and he set the satchel down to revive himself, splashing handfuls onto his face.

"I never thought I'd miss Regorian's antics," she murmured.

He heard and looked over, wiping away droplets. "Sorry, what was that?"

"Nothing. How's your head?"

"It is better, but not nearly as well as yours." He tried to smile.

"Has he always been like this?"

"The last I saw of Oryn before the masquerade was when he was about to depart for the Hall of the Master Knights. He was ten years of age and I was a few months younger. That was the first time I saw the look he has now."

"You mean the empty stare?"

"That's the one." He took a few drinks from the barrel. Then he looked up the street and was pleased. "Ah, Oryn's returned with the horses!"

For a moment there was relief at the thought of riding, but then she saw him and was disappointed. He was astride Ranger toting a cream-colored mare for Toth. Oryn lent him the reins and looked at Adwen.

Arms crossed, she wore a skeptical expression.

After a moment of glaring, the knight asked, "Is there something you wish to say?"

When she answered she was animated and sarcastic, "No, not a thing. I'm excited to get going while you guys ride and I walk who knows how many miles." Then she added with an even more sarcastic emphasis, "I'm thrilled."

He raised an eyebrow, somewhat astounded. "This horse was a gift from the town. It was all they could spare. Not only that, but you shall have to be on foot to track. I am certain you cannot follow the scent of the fiend from horseback."

"Okay, granted. But the monster's tracks ended back on the other side of the river. We're following the tracks of his horse."

"The fiend has bought a horse?"

Astride the mare, the half-elf answered, "Yes, and it was the slowest and smelliest in all of Dargadia."

Oryn sat quietly contemplating. It had to be wrong. Did this fiend know that he was being followed? The knight hoped very much they were simply tracking a stingy villain.

Toth saw his thoughtful expression and was curious. "What is the matter?"

"It is nothing. We must continue."

The trail led down the highway and out of Poplin, following the river. Where the road prepared to veer into dense forest, the travelers rested and refilled flasks.

Ranger entered the shallows to drink and Adwen went out until the water was just below the hem of her dress. There the dirt was swept away from her feet along with a little frustration. Between the coolness of the water and the warmth of the sun, it was difficult not to relax.

As the horse drank his fill, Oryn knelt down to gather water. Once the flask was recapped and stowed in a saddle bag, he looked to see what the creature was up to. She was staring out over the river at the far off mountains. King's Peak towered over the rest of the surrounding range. Her thoughts were elsewhere and her eyes distant and unfocussed.

"Dog, you should keep your thoughts and your head where it is," he warned. "If you cannot pay attention, you could find yourself crossing to the world after." When she didn't acknowledge him he glowered. "Answer me, dog."

"My name is Adwen, and I heard you... knight."

"I thought I gave you the proper instruction of how to address me."

With a tone of aggression, she replied, "I'm sorry, sir. This is the first time in a long while that I've had a peaceful moment. Could you please at least let me have this?"

He was outraged by the insolence, but would allow it for now. When the time came he would put her in her place.

Wind blew over the river, rustling her hair as she continued to stare into the distance. Bright sunlight lit up her pale skin, and where it struck wavy strands, golden highlights glistened. The light seemed almost to dance while her eyes glowed softly in the shade.

Blinking hard, Oryn realized once more that he was admiring the creature's human disguise. Clearing his head, he regained composure. Angrier with himself than with Adwen he returned to the road.

Toth was devouring a ripe fruit the bartender had given as an apology and Oryn instructed as he passed, "After you've finished that, collect the dog so we may return to the task at hand."

Due to a mouth full of sweet fruit, Toth nodded in answer.

They went south until they reached a fork in the road. The well-worn highway led farther south, whereas the tracks took a detour. The other road had not been used for some time. Fallen branches lay everywhere as the forest attempted to reclaim it with patches of grass and weeds. Hoof prints from the fiend's horse were the only impressions along the forgotten path.

After the main road was far behind, Toth turned to the knight. "Why do you suppose this road hasn't been used?"

"It's possibly nothing more than a path to an abandoned village. It can be difficult to survive if there is no source of fresh water. Few knights are familiar with towns and roads east of the river. The people living here have had to pay bounty hunters in the place of the Master Knight's services. Knights would only venture this far if there were an exceptionally dangerous threat."

Toth's reply was a nervous murmur, "Bounty hunters?"

The day was ending and they had gone deep into the forest on the abandoned road when something foul blew in on the wind. Adwen and the horses smelled it and Ranger snorted, stomping and swearing angry curses. The mare whinnied and fought against Toth's efforts to continue. The travelers had no choice but to stop. Calming his horse, Oryn watched Adwen as she froze, staring into the sickly breeze.

The smell was disturbingly familiar to her and brought back unpleasant memories of an experience in the countryside.

After waiting a while the knight snapped, "What is happening, dog?"

"There's a bad smell coming from down the road."

"What is the smell, Adwen?" Toth asked.

"It smells like death."

She had discovered a rotting deer carcass once while exploring the woods of her home world. It was horrible, but this was far worse and not because of sharpened senses. This smell of decay made her spine tingle and her hair stand on end.

His senses weren't as sharp, but Oryn knew well the smell of death. What he also knew was that on this side of the river, one could easily mistake the smell of death with another odor altogether.

After pondering a moment, he commanded, "Seek out the source of the stench. Return to report what you find."

She gave a nervous glance, but obeyed, following the road out of sight.

Toth watched her go. "What do you suppose she will find?"

"At the best she will find the dead, but I suspect the undead is what the beasts smell."

Toth was shocked. "But why did you not warn her of the danger?"

Oryn frowned. "You forget the dog's strengths. She has very little to fear. I find it strange that you treat the beast as if it were human. That could prove unwise."

Smiling, he commented, "You don't seem to see what I see in her."

The statement bothered Oryn, but he decided not to ask.

Adwen burst out of the bushes startling the mare. Calming down, the horse shook her main and snorted.

Adwen's expression was disturbed.

"What have you found?" the knight asked.

Glancing between them, she gulped. "I think you better come and see this."

Chapter 20
THE DUKE OF SIGMUND MANOR

From a distance the three-story manor seemed to watch them. It was practically a castle having many ominous facets. Two gigantic windows on the highest floor were all that was visible from over the wall onto the grounds. The tall gate was open wide enough for a rider to enter.

Their horses stopped fighting the reins and took them closer. Once they could see the tracks leading through the gate, they halted. Adwen and Toth could do little more than gawk. The old place seemed to be surrounded by a haze. For a long time the three studied the place with unease and hesitation. Strolling in would not be wise.

She gulped, wondering why the tracks could not simply go around.

Oryn announced, "The manor must be searched. The princess is likely to be found within."

Adwen shook her head. "No, she's not. The princess isn't here."

"What do you base this assumption on?"

"My instincts! I know she isn't here."

He glared. "Your instincts? How can you be sure?" When she didn't have a reply he sneered, "Even if the princess is not to be found, the manor must still be searched. There could be clues as to the kidnapper's identity or even a hint as to where they may be heading. You shall enter alone to search."

Horror played across her face. Finding her voice again, she protested, "You're sending me inside of that by myself? I don't think so."

She and Toth watched as he dismounted and coolly approached. Wearing his poker face, the knight asked, "Why not?"

Adwen folded her arms firmly. "If I go inside by myself

there's no telling what will happen. I just know that it wouldn't be good."

"You wouldn't do this even for the princess?"

Fear was slowly turned to panic and she snapped, "That's not fair! Why don't you go inside? Are you scared?"

Oryn's movements were smooth and quick. Adwen was unprepared as he pulled the knife from his boot. In the blink of an eye the tip pierced deep into flesh below her collarbone. It was intentionally nonfatal.

She screamed and withdrew, dropping into a crouch. Holding a hand to the fresh wound, she stared in shock as his cold eyes bored into hers without remorse.

"You are the best equipped to enter this den of undead," he sneered. "Toth and I are not. My training has been for werewolves. For dealing with undead and vampires, I am ill-equipped and undertrained. If Toth or I were bitten, we would be finished."

Pointing the weapon, he continued, "But you are better suited for the task than anyone. You are immune to the undead affliction. You may fight the things that lurk and have little more than your usual battle injuries. I thought you would have entered at the very least for the princess' sake."

The cut stopped bleeding and was almost gone, but she held a hand to it all the same.

Then he spat, "You are a coward."

Toth watched helplessly as his friends conflicted.

"The day is late," the knight went on. "Prepare yourself. When a full moon appears you shall enter. Do not disappoint me." He stowed the knife and turned to lead Ranger away.

Adwen gradually stood, staring reproachfully at the dreary place. The higher levels of the manor seemed to peer over the outer wall, like a creep eyeing his next victim. She could not shake the feeling of being watched.

She did not notice Toth approaching. He touched her shoulder, and she quickly recoiled out of fright. Once she realized it was only him, she relaxed.

He tried to come close. "Let me take a look at that."

Pulling away again, she restrained a sob. "I'm fine."

He frowned. "You don't look fine. You look exhausted. Is there anything I can do to help?"

She was beyond exhausted and far from admitting it. Her nerves were under control, but she continued to shudder. "No," she replied before sneering at Oryn. "Just keep him away from me." Stealing a glance at the setting sun, she prowled into the forest for solitude.

Toth glanced at his other friend who was busy double-checking supplies. Finally taking the reins of his mare, Ulna, he joined the knight. She stood obediently as her new master tethered the reins to an old elm. The knight finished his inventory as he came alongside.

With concern in his voice, the half-elf asked, "Was that necessary? Adwen did not do you any harm."

"What does it matter?"

Frowning, he shook his head. "Had you only explained the situation, I'm positive she would have agreed to your plans. There was no need to harm her."

The knight knew Toth well and was not perturbed by his questioning. The half-elf was as harmless as a moth. "What I have done was necessary. By now the mark I gave your pet is healed and her hate towards me deepened. In a short time, you shall see that rage can be a substitute for courage when used correctly."

He sadly shook his head. "Hate? Hate and anger are what has made your eyes so dead, friend."

Becoming stern, he stated, "Maybe, but they have given me strength and kept me alive."

Sighing, Toth shook his head again. There would be no point in continuing the subject. He was not a condoner of Oryn's views and not foolish enough to try to sway him.

Light from the setting sun cast gold and orange shades across the cloudless sky. Shadows became solid, stretching as darkness fell. While the green half-moon and the crescent gold climbed ever higher, they lit up the night until the full orange and red moons could appear.

When they did rise, Adwen's howls echoed to them through the blackened trees. Shortly after her cries ceased, both men watched her return walking upright with garments rolled under one arm. She did not make a sound lending them to Toth.

Ulna snorted nervously before recognizing her scent.

"What manner of werewolf are you?"

Her mood had not improved in the last hour spent alone. After the transformation, she had rolled up the clothes and caught herself using her jaws to carry them. The creature-like tendencies were an added worry. Where they getting worse?

"Don't worry, Adwen," Toth reassured. "Oryn says if you can hold your own against Kotig, then a few undead should be easy. You'll do well."

Both ears flicked back. "Yeah, sure." Leaving him, she started along the road that led to the gate. Oryn was astride Ranger, wearing his slayer helm in case she flushed out the kidnapper or an accomplice. If anything left the manor grounds it would not get far.

As she was passing by, Ranger snorted, "You're a poor excuse for a fighter compared to my master, but if you do as before, then you should fare well."

Knowing it was the warhorse's best attempt at encouragement, she was thankful. "If you say so."

Ranger snorted, "I did say so, you hairy cur."

"Thanks," Adwen panted and suddenly paused as an impulse came over her. "Just don't hold any grudges for your master." With one clawed hand, she knocked the knight out of his saddle. He hit the ground with a resounding thud.

Swiftly dropping to all fours, she raced away knowing he was furious, but that he wouldn't follow. She could hear Ranger calling out a variety of colorful slanders. Unable to laugh as a hound, she let loose a loud howl. "Ha! Oh yeah, serves you right!"

By the time she finished celebrating, she arrived at the gate. Merriment dissipated, leaving behind uncertainty. She agreed with Oryn's hunch that undead were here. How could there be anything else in a place that smelled of varying kinds of decay? Nothing moved on the other side and she sensed no danger so she crept inside.

Past the wall was empty. Scanning surroundings, she sniffed. The tracks led across the courtyard to the stone stoop. It was likely that the horse was led away while the fiend continued up and inside.

Sensing movement, she glanced back. There was nothing. Nevertheless, she knew something had been there. Adwen grew nervous and wracked her memory for the things she knew about undead. Her school friends had covered this topic thoroughly. Zombies could be slow or fast and were attracted by loud noises. Armed with that knowledge, she carefully eased the entrance open. A hinge squealed and she bared her fangs at the shrillness. After slipping inside, she closed it shut.

The main hall caused her to reminisce on videogames with zombie mansions. A domed ceiling was high overhead as twin staircases arced around to the second floor. Before her were double doors to another room. Everything was dark, dusty, musty and decayed. Wary, she forced herself forward and decided to search the first floor.

She discovered the library. It has once been a bastion of knowledge, harboring a massive collection of writings and scrolls. Every wall was lined with book spines and racks of rolled parchment. Three towering cases stood in the center below the second-floor balcony overlooking the space. With banisters all around, she thought it looked like the inside of a zoo exhibit.

Then there was a noise. Whirling around to confront the threat, her fangs were bared.

It moaned in the corner and took a shuddering step. Then it took another.

She stood upright and found she could not move. The idea of dead rising from the grave frightened her the most.

The zombie moaned again and started to reach for her. Out of fright and disgust, she snarled and slashed the corpse's head. It was easily crushed by the force then crumpled to the floor and did not move. Panting hard and shuddering, she smelled the horrible pungent odor of rotting flesh and examined her claws. They were covered in brain matter and squirmy maggots. Frantically, she yelped and tried to shake off the muck as fast as she could.

Another set of doors eased open as a mob of the disgusting undead wandered in, moaning and groaning. A second wave was coming through the doors and she snarled, "You have got to be kidding!"

Before the swarm could get close, she leaped onto the nearest of the bookcases, eyeing the second floor. Seeing more zombies arriving there as well she hesitated. Then the sound of books falling off shelves got her attention. The maggoty things were starting to climb.

"No way!"

Adwen gripped her wooden perch, beginning to rock the bookcase back and forth. She shifted her weight, swaying the case as the zombies held fast. Eventually the case swayed hard once more and tipped far over the mob. She rode the top to the ground, crushing most of the moving corpses under the shelves and masses of books.

Proud of her small accomplishment, she panted, "Well I guess I was overreacting."

Then the books moved in places and mangled hands reached out.

No longer pleased, she growled. "This sucks."

She jumped over waving arms onto one of the remaining cases. Leaping to the second floor walkway, there were only a few ghouls. They posed little threat so she darted past and to the next room. There was a metal coat rack and she used it to jam the way shut behind. The zombies were stalled for the time being.

Thick dust on the floor was disturbed where the kidnapper and princess had passed. The lounge ran the length of the manor. Shadows engulfed the left wall and empty fireplace, surrounded by high-backed chairs. The other side was illuminated by moonlight through many high windows between long, moth-eaten curtains.

She sniffed at the tracks through the sprawling lounge. Adwen stalked with nose to the floor, shadows cast by the curtains rolling across her soft coat. Soon she paused when a silhouette was far too short and narrow. First she turned an ear to the figure. When there was no sound, she slowly glanced. At first sight it was a beautiful woman, but Adwen knew better. There was the smell of human blood on the breath of the lady vampire as she hissed.

Adwen's sixth sense started to warn of danger. She wrinkled her jaws into an intimidating snarl. But Adwen did not see two others coming from the shadows behind.

They pounced and bit into the sides of her neck.

The attack surprised Adwen and she roared, thrashing and rolling madly. She panicked and attempted to brush them off, but they had a death grip with sharp nails and fangs. Adwen could feel them sucking the blood out of her and roared, thrashing harder. Flipping and tumbling in a frantic fit, small tables were bowled over as chairs were broken and tossed about.

During Adwen's thrashing, one vampire was run through by a wooden table leg. The shrieking female let go at last, crying out before turning to ash. Regaining control of herself, the hound ripped the second vampire from her neck, toss it away. After glancing briefly at the pile of vampire remains, Adwen growled.

The pair of vampires quietly stood under the wall of glass and moonlight.

"Okay, you bloodsucking skanks," she snarled. "I'm ready when you are."

The vampire she had thrown attacked again, hungry for more. The other stood by to watch. She was in no hurry.

When the undead flew at her face, Adwen leapt aside, slashing with her own claws. She missed, but barely. The vampire rebounded rapidly, scrambling across the wall over the hearth like a crazed gecko before leaping at the black hound. And again, Adwen avoided being pounced upon by the thirsty creature.

As the lady vampire came for another pass, Adwen backed up to the hearth. Over the mantle were two crossed epées. Just as the undead woman swooped in, Adwen snatched one up and took aim. To her complete surprise, the vampire fell for the trick and ran directly into the point, shrieking angrily. The body dissipated into nothing and the hound glared at the final undead sister. She hissed as Adwen growled, "Come on."

The vampire flew in fast.

Adwen tried to catch the fanged woman with the sword, but failed. It dodged her blade and clawed her across the eyes with razor-sharp nails. Yelping in pain and surprise, Adwen tripped backward over a fallen chair. The cuts bled, but her eyes were unharmed. She saw the vampire come in for a second pass, but still wasn't quick enough to fend off the assault. She was slashed on the nose and eyes again before being bitten on the neck.

Clinging tightly to the hound's back, the undead took a

deep draw.

Alarmed, Adwen tore the vampire off with great difficulty and tossed her aside.

The bloodthirsty woman landed on her feet and charged once more.

Adwen swiftly and purposefully fell backward over a broken chair as the vampire lunged. As she fell, she struck out with the sword. The blind attack proved lucky, resulting in plunging the epée through the vampire's still heart.

Clawing vainly, the sister turned to dust, screaming, "You'll pay! You'll pay!"

Picking herself up in the now overturned lounge, no more undead broke the silence. Wary yet glad for the quiet, she continued and kept the sword. It proved too useful to discard.

The tracks wandered through the next door and into an empty drawing room. There was very little to be found there; more dusty books stuffed on shelves, forgotten by the living and untouched by the undead.

More faded footprints led up another flight of stairs. Once on the third story, she cautiously approached the door to the topmost room. Ears twitched and nose tested the air while she reached for the handle. Taking a firm hold with long fingers, she gripped the sword tight and gave a gentle turn. Old hinges groaned when the door moved.

From the threshold she could see this was a private study. Huge tomes occupied lofty shelves surrounding a wooden desk and a high-backed chair. Moonlight splashed through huge windows into the room while the dark ceiling remained empty save for cobwebs and spiders.

Not sensing danger, she entered. For a moment she ignored the tracks in the dust and briefly searched for hidden enemies. Everything seemed safe. Then the princess' scent came to her and she began sniffing. Her trusty senses led to a small chair beside the desk. It was empty now, but she was sure Princess Eyrie had sat in it barely a day before.

"She is no longer here," cooed a voice.

Her head whipped round to look in a corner. When the man stepped out into the pale glow, she snarled and gripped the sword.

With a young face and neat attire, his long gray hair was

tied back in a ponytail. The vampire's eyes were black like coals. He stopped and informed with a smile, "They departed early yester morning." Cocking an eyebrow, he invited with a hand. "Speak to me. I can understand you."

Ears pinned back, she snarled, "Where is she?"

"She is with my friend. He had brought her here for a short stay before continuing on. He's told me a few things about you, Adwen." A broad smile exposed a pair of fangs.

Gnashing jaws, she rumbled, "Who is he? What does he want?"

The vampire shook his head. "I'm not telling; not just yet." He laughed softly like a haughty aristocrat.

Her eyes glowed brighter and she showed her own fangs, backing away from the desk as he stepped behind it. Moonlight shone upon her back and the vampire remained intrigued by the lack of terror.

"I can see my lovely ladies welcomed you warmly. It is high time I introduce myself properly. I am Edmund Fredrik Dillinger, the Duke of Sigmund Manor."

His face shifted into that of a hideous, pale demon and he shrieked. A force in the air struck Adwen like a wall of wind, picking her up and sending her backward through the glass. She lost her grip on the weapon and swiftly fell down out of sight. Dozens of shining shards tumbled after her from the window as razor-sharp rain.

The duke's face reverted to its more pleasant form and he smirked. Leaving the desk, he strolled casually to the shattered scene where she vanished. He stood by the ledge and scoffed, "That was easier than he had said it would be. What a stupid dog." With the tip of his boot, he brushed a sliver of glass over, admiring the mess he created.

Adwen sprung up over the brink from nowhere. Her jaws clamped down onto the vampire's head like a steel trap and the force pushed the duke back. They landed on his desk where she snarled, mauling the vampire viciously. Their combined weight crushed the wood into jagged shards.

The duke felt no pain. As she tore at him, he laughed. "Now that's a good sport!"

Something stabbed deep into her and twisted, making her roar and leap away. After pulling the duke's dagger out, blood poured forth. She held a hand over it to stymie the flow. Enraged by pain, she glared at where she last saw the ancient vampire.

He was gone, but his voice echoed from no discernable location, "This was fun. I only wish we could have met sooner. They say the first dogs came from wolves. I shall not allow the same to be said of you."

The sixth sense could not warn her in time. Long fangs sank into the already bitten flesh of Adwen's neck. She roared and reached to pull him off when he took a deep draw. The leaching of her blood was so much that she crumpled to the floor. With little effort, he took another deep drink and her instincts took over.

She yowled, staggering to the shattered desk. Falling to her knees, she gripped his shoulders. Once she had a hold, she ripped him off and brought him down onto jutting splinters.

He gasped at his horribly gored stomach in amazement. The duke tried to free himself, but she held him down with one padded foot, snarling. Confusion played across his face. "You... you were supposed to be... easy."

She broke a shard from the demolished desk, taking aim at his heart. In one strong motion, she drove it down.

The duke's head rolled back and he slowly withered away on the floor.

When the last of him was gone, her vision swam and she fought to stay conscious. Too much blood had been lost. Steadying herself, she waited for her head to clear then immediately returned to the search.

Examining the chair yielded only a little information. The abductor had carried her out somehow, but there were no other doors. Tracks led away from the seat to disappear before a wall of books. Where they vanished, Adwen stopped. Standing upright, she eyed the bookcase and noticed a suspicious-looking candlestick bracket. The dust on it had been disturbed and she rolled her eyes.

"What a cliché," she growled. She tugged the hidden switch and waited to be shown a flight of stairs.

A trapdoor dropped out beneath her. She let loose a surprised yelp as she went sliding down a shoot. It went far down, turned and then spat her out into the withered garden on the far side of the manor.

Adwen tumbled and landed in a heap. Much weaker, she shook off the dizziness. The tracks met with those of the horse and led out a hidden exit through the outer wall. Wild plants and stones on the other side disguised the gap perfectly. Mustering her strength, she limped along on all fours. She had seen enough of this place.

Both men spied her leaving the grounds. When they joined her they could see the new collection of wounds.

While the half-elf was concerned, Oryn was not. Still wearing his helm, he asked, "What did you find, dog?"

Glaring up at him, she spoke in a series of barks and whimpers.

"She said Princess Eyrie is not here," the half-elf relayed. "They left this morning."

Not happy at the news, he glowered. "Did you learn nothing of interest concerning the kidnapper?"

She snarled and growled in response.

Toth looked disturbed. "What is it?"

"The vampires were waiting for her. The kidnapper warned them that Adwen was coming."

"What? Are you sure you understand what the beast says?"

"Yes, I'm sure I'm translating right. The kidnapper warned the vampires that Adwen was on her way here."

This was even worse news. Their quest was going to be more treacherous than he thought.

"Oryn?"

"What is it now?"

"Adwen is in need of rest. She will need to stop soon."

They looked down from their horses. Even without the wounds, she looked far worse than when she entered. Her ears and tail drooped and her eyes were dim. Panting in exhaustion, she appeared pitiably weak.

Oryn firmly stated, "We cannot stay. The longer we linger, the more danger we are in. Rest for your pet can wait. We must move."

Toth sighed. Ranger and Ulna galloped and Adwen tried to keep up. They followed the trail farther down the abandoned road.

Chapter 21
ANOTHER REALITY TO ACCEPT

Oryn pressed them hard. He didn't know whom they were following or to where, but the knowledge that they were expected made him wary. As they continued, he kept a vigilant watch along the roadside and even the skies.

The half-elf observed from atop his mare. Ulna was becoming fatigued, but the knight and his steed seemed undaunted. His childhood friend was beside him and they were on another adventure.

The horses galloped with Adwen between them. The others were oblivious to the toll their pace was taking on her. She occasionally leapt over fallen trees and the effort steadily wore her down. Her tongue lolled and breathing was labored. Every muscle worked hard and long past their limit, until they became numb.

Another mile passed and Adwen's strength finally failed. One of her arms gave out and she collapsed, tumbling a few yards along the road.

They heard a pitiful yelp and looked back in time to see her roll to a stop.

Dazed, she could hear the horses approaching. As they came alongside she tried to get up. Limbs were numb and lungs burned. At first she couldn't even raise her head, but she fought and grappled with a disobedient body.

Toth swiftly dismounted while Oryn observed.

Another minute of struggling later, she found her feet and staggered onto all fours. Adwen stood shaking like a leaf with head hung low. When she mustered the will to start again Toth stopped her.

He held her back with arms around her shaggy neck. Stroking, he gently whispered. "Take it easy, Adwen. Stop a moment and rest." Looking up at the knight, he protested,

"She must stop. Adwen can't take much more of this."

Oryn studied her and shook his head. "The beast shall get rest, but we must move."

"She is too tired. Can't you see something is wrong?"

Oryn was patient. Looking at the setting moons, he replied, "She has the strength to go on until the moon sets. Then we shall stop. Let her go. Return to your horse."

Toth studied the horizon as well. Against his own conscience, he released his hold. She was still panting and shaking, but to his sad astonishment, found the power to continue. At a trot, she went past and he frowned as he got into the saddle. They both caught up and followed at her speed, as she could clearly not go at theirs.

The knight was sourly disappointed with the hound. If they were to catch the kidnapper they would have to rest for only a few hours. The trail was still warm, but getting colder than he liked. He could afford to let the hound sleep for five hours. True to his word, they halted shortly before the moon had gone. Oryn chose a cozy meadow beside a deer trail that lead to a clear running brook.

Adwen did not look any better, but Toth quietly supplied her clothing and left her to go change and dress herself. He was deeply concerned.

The moon set, she changed and returned to where her fellow travelers set up camp. Finding a tree with soft green moss at its base, it was time to lie down at last. The night had been long. With ease she fell into a deep sleep before sunrise.

"Wake up," she heard Oryn sneer. "Wake up and get up, dog. It is time to move. We go now and we catch our intended prey before the day is out."

The sky was overcast. Somewhere above the clouds rested the noon day sun. A cool breeze rustled new leaves in the surrounding boughs.

She could hardly move and felt the knight's chilled sword tapping her leg, prompting her to action. The pleasant sleep had done very little to restore strength. Opening her eyes, she stared blankly.

He frowned and waited.

Tired and sluggish, she slowly got to her bare feet before the knight.

Satisfied that she was ready, he turned to go.

Adwen took two steps then blacked out. She toppled to the ground and the sound of the impact surprised Oryn into whipping around.

"Adwen!" Toth cried out as he dashed to her side.

Once she started to come to, she found herself propped against the tree. Her friend was knelt beside her while Oryn stood behind him, glaring. They were losing precious time.

Confused, she spoke in a weak voice, "Hey...Toth? I don't feel so good." Then she scoffed at her own dry humor.

He smiled. "You don't look very good either."

"Thanks," she replied. Her vision blurred and they watched as she was about to pass out.

Toth franticly patted the side of her face. "Adwen. Adwen, you must to stay awake. Adwen?"

She blinked hard and forced her heavy lids open.

The knight studied her symptoms. Wounds were healed and she showed no sign of any undead curse. Whatever the problem, it had little or nothing to do with the scuffle in the manor. She was fatigued. Then a thought crossed his mind.

"Toth," he asked suspiciously. "When did your pet have its last feeding?"

After thinking it over, he woke her enough to speak, "Adwen? When did you last eat something?"

It took a few moments to understand the question and retrieve the answer. Eventually she groggily replied, "Uh, just before we left Tamis' house."

"That was four days ago! Adwen, why did you not take some bread and cheese from me? You're starving!"

"I...I don't know. It just...didn't..." she managed to say before passing out.

He didn't try to keep her awake this time and turned to Oryn. "What is wrong with her?"

Disappointed, he answered, "The dog is experiencing a form of starvation."

He looked horrified by the reply. "But why would she not

eat the food from my satchel? There was plenty to share."

"Because bread and cheese would do nothing for the dog. It would only make her ill to eat it at this stage. She may consume them on occasion, but the nature of what she is demands she have raw flesh. I'm sure the battle with the undead resulted in the loss of much of her blood. Your dumb animal would have lasted a few more days before reaching this severe a state if not for the incompetency. When was her last feeding?"

"What do you mean?"

"When did the dog have its last full sitting of raw flesh?"

"Never. She's never had a meal of nothing but that."

"That's impossible. How has she survived this long without starving?"

"We spent time traveling with Regorian Lancer. There was fresh rabbit stew every night. He left us shortly before the masquerade to return to hunting. Apart from stew, Adwen has not had a meat diet."

Oryn heard of Regorian Lancer. He did not think highly of his reputation among common folk, but his prowess and skill were commendable. Regorian the Hunter had not only allowed this female hound to live; he had shared food with it.

"Has she never hunted for herself?"

Without a second thought, Toth responded, "Not ever."

He found the information difficult to swallow, but believed him. If she had never hunted it would explain many questions. If she had never hunted, that meant one of two things: either she had been well taken care of all her life before finding Toth, or this creature had once been human. The two theories were both absurd so he quickly dismissed them. No matter the past, the present was what needed attention.

"Your pet is allowing the trail to get colder by the hour and my patience is wearing thin." He scowled at her. "But there is only one solution for this."

An hour passed and Adwen had not moved. As she started to wake it was to a smell. It was so appetizing that her mouth watered. The scent was strong, pulling her out of the starvation-induced stupor. When her eyes opened she was confused. Then she was surprised and disgusted. A dead rabbit dangled from Oryn's hand in her face. The bloody matted fur was brushing her nose, but that was not what upset her most. It smelled positively delectable. She wanted to eat the thing on the spot.

Turning her nose away, she batted the fresh kill, knocking it from his hand. The sudden exertion left her drained and she slumped, short of breath.

Outraged, he snapped, "Stupid dog! I go through the trouble of catching you a meal and you throw it aside like nothing. Why?"

Straining for the strength to speak, she panted, "I'm not going...to give you an excuse... to call me ...an animal anymore."

For a moment he stared in surprise before storming over to retrieve the rabbit. When he returned, he held the limp body before her and scowled. "Look at this. Do you see this? Whether you choose it or not, this is what you are. This is what you require to live. You are a creature that needs this and only this to survive."

Oryn glared and his voice was ice cold. "You are not a human. You cannot be human, no matter how hard you try. The sooner you accept this fact, the better off we all shall be and the sooner the princess will be found." Finished, he dropped the carcass in her lap and trudged off to tend to his horse.

Tears swelled in her eyes trailing down her cheeks. A few seconds passed and she was asleep again.

Toth witnessed the confrontation from a distance. He cared for both friends and wished they could get along. Quietly taking the rabbit, he found a place to clean it.

Oryn took notice. "Do you intend to cook or to clean it?"

"Regorian taught me his recipe for rabbit stew. If I cook this, I have little doubt she will eat it." He found a small knife hidden at the bottom of his satchel and started the skinning. "Do you have anything to cook it in?"

"Cooking it would take away much of the nourishment. For energy and strength, raw flesh is more suitable. You'll boil out half the nourishment."

"If I cook it, she will have at least the one half. Yet if it remains raw, she will not touch it." He wore a look that made it clear he would not be swayed. "She needs this."

Grimacing, Oryn sighed and reached into the saddle bags for a cooking pot and spoon. He explained as he handed them over, "Once she has eaten the stew she will still not have strength enough for a long journey. She must hunt. A freshly killed rabbit would give her strength enough to last two days. But after eating a bit of stew, she shall have no choice but to catch something tonight. If not, she will be no better off tomorrow than she is now."

Accepting the things, Toth nodded.

After sleeping the entire day, she could sleep no more once a delicious aroma filled her nose. She almost gasped when she opened her eyes and saw Toth holding out a bowl of rabbit stew. At first she thought it must be a dream, but found it was real when she took it and quickly started gulping.

When she finished devouring the serving, she breathed deep sighs of satisfaction. "Thank you, Toth. Thank you."

"You're welcome."

Her blue eyes become bright in the twilight as the food restored some strength.

Thinking about Oryn's warnings, he knew he must say what to do with the short-lived energy. He also knew she wouldn't be pleased. "Oryn's right, you know."

She could not look him in the eye. Regardless, his caring tone drove her to pay attention.

"The stew can only grant you strength for tonight. Tomorrow will be the same as this morning if you cannot get something more." He frowned. "Cooked food is not enough for you now. You must hunt tonight for yourself."

The last statement rang in Adwen's ears like a death sentence. She didn't want to believe it. She couldn't.

"It's nearly sunset. The skies are already clear. Oryn found an abundance of things living in the woods." He saw tears welling in her eyes and put a hand on her shoulder. "Please do not cry. You have all of my confidence you will do well. You always do well."

She was silent as a few more tears fell.

Taking the empty bowl, Toth returned to the small fire the

knight had started. They camped a few yards away through the trees and the horses stood close watching their masters. The flames snapped and cracked. Embers flew as Oryn stoked the kindling with a sturdy branch.

Toth took a seat nearby and Oryn looked up. "Is your dog still being stubborn or is she coming to her senses?"

"She will do it. Adwen can be stubborn, but she is no fool."

Looking skeptical, he replied, "Your pet has yet to prove your statement." Giving a final prod, he sat back to enjoy the glow. For a moment he contemplated destroying the animal in the morning if she failed to catch a meal, but thought twice. The very reason he had evaded his own men and lost them at the first opportunity was to catch this female hound alive. He still wanted to get his revenge. The elf woman had been clear Adwen must be living.

A long silence passed between them before someone eventually spoke. The sun set at last and Toth asked, "Why don't you have any confidence in her?"

Not understanding, he asked, "Do you mean to imply something?"

"No. I just want to know if you have any confidence in her."

Thinking contemplating the answer, he replied, "I am certain in the dog's strength, but none in her character. She is a mangy beast and you can always have confidence that a beast will be simply that. You cannot trust such animals to be civilized or noble."

For a time they fell silent and then heard the sounds made by Adwen and her transformation. The full moon had appeared and they patiently waited for the horrible cries to cease.

After many nights and full moon risings, the changes took less time. Even with the briefness, it was never any less excruciating. They watched her with ears were back and her tail drooped. She looked sullen as she quietly dropped folded garments beside the horses.

Ulna sniffed curiously, but never made a sound.

Without a word, she sulked off in search of prey.

They watched her go, both hoping for her success for separate reasons: Toth, for the sake of her health, and Oryn, for the sake of their quest. He knew disobeying an order from the king and evading his men would reap heavy repercussions. The only way he could return was if he didn't come back empty-handed.

Everywhere were earthy scents. Nearly every tree was home to a number of creatures. None were large or easy to catch, but birds and vermin were not the only things to be found. Adwen spent hours stalking the animal she was looking for. The deer was close according to her sense of smell. She had discovered its favorite grazing spot. Settling into a hiding place, she sniffed at the enticing smell brought downwind.

Tiptoeing into the moonlight, the lone doe sniffed for danger. As the deer came closer, Adwen felt strong instincts attempt to take over. Her whole body felt a powerful urge to spring and take the doe now that it was in sight. She fought the wild instincts and stayed were she was. The urge to lunge was so intense that muscles in her hands twitched and haunches quivered.

She didn't know how to feel. Over the last few weeks her mind remained the same while her body became something entirely different. Human instincts were replaced by feral drives. She recalled how angry she had been when Oryn called her an animal. It was like everything else he had ever said to her: harsh, cruel and absolutely right. No matter what she tried to do to prove him wrong, she was still becoming this.

In the moment when the deer first came into view and again when it stepped within reach, she came to a hard decision. She knew it was pointless to deny what she was. The only way she could move on was if she let go of what she was hanging onto. Adwen was clinging desperately to the memory of Shari Gates, the human girl and high school graduate. She had become Adwen, the Tame One, the violet-eyed hound. She could not afford to lie to herself any longer.

The deer's nose tested a patch of sweet blossoms that sprouted from the base of a tree. As it was about to take a nibble of the soft pink petals, the doe spooked. Quick as lightning, it looked straight up into the boughs. Hidden animals and bugs in the clearing fell dead silent.

Adwen crouched low on a branch, locking eyes with the doe. It turned and tried to bolt, but she was quicker. Dropping onto the frightened thing, she pinned it to the ground. Feeling it struggling nearly sent her into a wild frenzy, but she resisted. Once she had full control of herself, her long jaws fit over the frantic creature's throat. If she were going to kill her, she was going to be merciful with as little suffering as possible.

Beside the campfire Oryn and Toth finished off the last of the rabbit stew. The knight thought it was delicious, but kept the thoughts private. His old friend dipped a piece of bread into the broth and ate it while it was still warm. The rabbit had been small. It would not have revitalized Adwen fully, but was enough for them. Once finished with his half, Oryn confronted Toth.

"Do you understand why your pet allowed itself to starve?"

He swallowed a mouthful. "She didn't understand her needs. If I had known, I would have tried to help sooner. We simply didn't know."

"That is only a part of the problem," he scolded. "You allowed the dog to view itself as a human. Because of the illusion you helped her believe, she did not pay heed to the cravings for meat I'm sure she was experiencing. Part of the blame for the dog's starving falls on you."

Toth paused and pondered, then a smile appeared and he went back to eating.

"What's so amusing?"

Swallowing the last of his meal, the half-elf chuckled. "I find it amusing that even though I know Adwen's secrets, you still can't see what every other good soul and I have noticed."

"What might that be?"

"Adwen is special. As piercing as your green eyes are, you can't seem to see past the surface of things." He looked up at the starry sky. "Oryn, I hope I am there the moment you see what we all have."

He was skeptical, but curious. "See what?"

Toth shook his head. "She is beautiful."

A blood-curdling roar broke the calm and the horses stomped nervously.

In a flash, they were up and off toward the sound of Adwen's roar. Oryn was hoping to get another chance at slaying Korig. But when they found her they realized there was no real danger.

Jaws dripping with blood, she crouched over a doe she had killed.

A small pack of wolves attempted to take her catch while she held them back with deadly swipes. The pack was four strong and none foolish enough to get close. Toth and Oryn were some distance away where they could go unnoticed. Her gentle friend had never seen her so fierce; not even pitted against the Bloody Brothers. She had turned feral, staking a claim over the carcass.

Adwen snarled in warning at the hungry wolves, *"It's mine! This is my kill! Stay back!"*

"This is our territory and our prey," one barked. "Hunt elsewhere!"

She snarled louder, gnashing bloody fangs. *"Not on your life! You can have whatever is left when I've finished. If you want to fight for it, be my guest!"*

The wolves had been trying to scare her off and did not want a fight they could not win. Hungry and unhappy, they were willing to wait for scraps.

"Now get back and stay back!"

Adhering to her conditions, they slowly backed off.

Toth was glad, but could not bring himself to watch her feed. He turned back for camp having seen enough.

Oryn had not. He now knew she was capable of following her animal side. Out of curiosity, he remained to learn more about her nature. So far, she was acting like the beast he had known her to be all along.

Once the wolves were at a comfortable distance, she was able to regain control. The tight snarl faded and she looked down at the dead thing. Its eyes were open and faded. Moonlight made the blood shine like silver.

Between the trees the knight continued to watch as she stroked the doe. Though he could not understand her speech like Toth could, knew she spoke to it.

Stroking, she softly growled, "I'm sorry. I had to." She glanced sidelong at the flowers. "All you wanted was your blos-

soms. I'll let you have what you want."

Oryn watched with building curiosity as she slashed open the belly.

The sight did not unsettle her creature mind as she reached inside. A moment later, she held the heart in her claws. Adwen looked balefully at the glistening mass with flattened ears. "I promise you won't go to waste."

The wolves were watching and listening with no less curiosity than Oryn. At first he was confused, but when he saw her make a small grave beside a patch of blossoms, his jaw nearly dropped.

Once the heart was covered by a blanket of soil, Adwen was content. She eyed the carcass, saliva pooling in her jaws. Addressing the pack, she growled, "I'll try not to make you wait long."

Without regret, fear, or human instincts to hold her back, she consumed most of the kill. As promised, the scraps went to the wolves. Neither she, the knight, nor anyone else noticed what happened where she buried the heart. The blossoms were in bloom, bigger and sweeter smelling than ever.

Chapter 22
RAINY WEATHER

Dawn shone while the earth was still cool and Oryn was first to awaken. As bleary eyes opened he found a smoldering campfire. Streams of smoke curdled over charred kindling and twinkling cinders. A moment later he was fully alert. Adwen's folded clothes were gone yet she was no where in sight, feeding growing suspicions. While Toth still slept he got up and silently strolled away from camp, following a faint trail.

She had gone along a deer run. Events from last night put him on edge though Oryn was intent on seeking her out. So when the tracks took him down a hill toward a brook he quickly spotted her and stopped.

A black cloaked figure sat on a log with back turned. Brilliant sunshine glinted off wild ripples to dance about the solid silhouette. Certain it was her, the knight pressed onward with great stealth. Conditions were perfect to avoid detection. She would not see, hear or smell him near.

Adwen wiped more tears with dry palms, steadying her breathing. She shuddered from the effort of subduing more sobs. Then she grew stark still. A moment later an angry growl accompanied the gurgle of the stream. She spoke aloud without moving, anger and bereavement cracking her voice.

"What do you want?"

Oryn froze in place. He had not made a sound and the wind was blowing the wrong way for her to catch his scent.

She snapped, "I know it's you. It's always you."

The knight could not help but notice her voice was different somehow aside from the coupling of animal sounds. After a while of staring, he stated, "You've changed."

The callous response did not shock Adwen. It was a cold jab that threatened to provoke more tears. "It makes me sick to know you are always watching me, studying me. That's why you're here, isn't it? Want to get a good look at the freak?"

The hostile tone made him grip the hilt of his sword.

Adwen's razor-sharp senses heard the leather groan as he squeezed. Recognizing the sound, she replied angrily, "I'm sorry. I'm ruining your fun? Fine then."

When she stood and dropped the black cloak from her shoulders he braced himself for anything. Anticipating either an attack or a pitiably hideous sight, Oryn was ill prepared.

Adwen did not attack. A few inches taller than the day before, the green traveling dress fit looser. Sunlight made parts of her hair shine amber as it flowed down like a caramel tide to the middle of her back. When she turned, he didn't move. His expression remained stony. Only his eyes showed a reaction as they dilated from the shock.

The creature before him was hardly recognizable, but ghastly she was not. Childish features were gone. With the frame and form Adwen possessed she resembled an elf woman of the wilds. Her strong, svelte body stood firm in defiance of the threat she saw in him. Sharp fangs were pearly white behind soft, trembling lips.

Of her altered guise, one thing was unmistakable; her eyes. They were sharp, powerful, and pained with a telltale glisten of tears. Oryn had been to the sea once. Those eyes shone a brilliant sapphire blue like the pure waters of the Dargadian coast at high tide.

She stared long and hard, but the knight was unreadable. A moment passed then she held both hands out, inviting him to get a good look. When she spoke again the pain and frustration put stress on her voice.

"Happy now? Does it make you happy to see more of what gives me pain?"

Oryn remained speechless.

Affronted by the lack of an answer, hands dropped to her sides in defeat. "Well? You hate me so much, why don't you say something? Say something else to put me in my place. Are you enjoying yourself?" Adwen growled, more tears swelling.

The knight's mind was blank. There was nothing to say.

Angrier, she snapped while a vicious growl followed her words. *"Say something!"*

His gaze shifted as he finally muttered, "We shall be waiting with the horses. Do not take too long."

She saw his hand leave the sword as he turned back to camp. The abrupt and empty statement left her outraged. Along the ridge of her nose small snarl wrinkles formed. A deep growl rumbled in her throat as she swiftly punched a tree, imbedding a fist in the bark. Taking her hand from the indentation, knuckles were bloody with large slivers.

The power Adwen possessed was great. She watched as bleeding ceased and new flesh appeared. Splinters were forced out, dropping to her feet. Dog whimpers came as more tears swelled.

Oryn reached camp and felt relief. At last he could breathe. While under her stare the air was trapped in his chest until it hurt. The whole experience was awesome and very unsettling. He was unsure if the discomfort were from a magical force she exuded or if the issue was within himself. Confounded, the knight pondered, trying to recollect his faculties.

Light from the sun finally reached where Toth slept and he started to come round. He stretched, yawned and spied the knight standing beside Ranger. Scratching the back of his head, he greeted, "Good morning." He looked around. "Where is Adwen?"

The knight remained lost in thought. "The dog is by the brook."

Thinking nothing of it, Toth got up to prepare for travel. He noticed the knight beginning to recount supplies then decided to do the same. The half-elf was nearly finished with the brief inventory when he saw Adwen walking back.

Wearing the cloak with hood drawn, she wore the collar around her neck. From beneath the brim he could only see the leather band and half of her face. The frown she wore was very telling. Straight away, he darted to Adwen's side.

She tried to avoid him as he forced her to stop. "Adwen? Are you all right?" She didn't answer. Then he realized she was taller. "Adwen? What is the matter?"

She made a failed attempt to pull away as he reached for the hood. Black cloth fell away and he saw her face, though she tried to turn aside.

He was astonished. "By the stars above. Adwen... you're beautiful."

"Don't, Toth." The snarl marks flared while she tried not to break down. "I thought you'd know me better. I just want my face back."

Oryn heard and paused before continuing. Too many witless wenches he encountered would sell their soul at the drop of a coin to be beautiful. Then what Toth said in rebuttal surprised him more.

Putting a hand on her shoulder, he turned her so as to get a better look. After a while, he said with the utmost sincerity, "This *is* your face. This is who you are on the inside, Adwen, but now on the outside as well."

Adwen finally returned his gaze. For a moment she was speechless, but shook her head and donned the hood again. "It doesn't matter. This still isn't the face I used to have."

Finished counting supplies, the knight joined in watching her storm off towards the road, shouting angrily.

"Hurry up! We're wasting daylight, aren't we? Let's get going already."

Oryn grimaced and Toth frowned.

It was the horses that struggled to keep up. Her senses were so much sharper she never needed to stop to find the tracks. With keener sight, every mark was easy to spot on the barren road. She ran and the long cloak furled behind her like raven wings.

Hours passed until the forgotten road took them back to the main highway. Tracks from the kidnapper's horse blended with countless others. She still had the scent and bolted. Many miles later, dark clouds moved in. Drops fell in a fine mist that first dulled and then snuffed out the scent completely. Once it was gone, she came to a stop and snarled, panting angrily at the road.

The riders came alongside and Toth called to her, "What's wrong?"

"The scent is gone. I can't smell anything in this stupid rain!" She growled at the storm.

"Keep moving. The trail has led down the beaten path thus far," Oryn directed. "We shall go until the nearest town and see what is to be found."

She darted off again. Her drive to find the kidnapper was a perfect distraction and she knew they had to be close. Five more miles along the road, though only for a moment, she caught the scent of the horse. Dashing around the bend, she suddenly skidded to a halt.

Ranger and Ulna almost ran her over. The war horse snorted and swore, but soon froze as well. Even the Clydesdale was nervous at the sight of the horse up ahead, lying in the mud and pouring rain. Oryn, Toth and the mounts waited quietly as she went to investigate.

Going closer, Adwen saw a dark pool around the body. Then she paused and searched in the trees for what might have been the cause. When the sixth sense did not forewarn her, she went closer. From where she approached she could not see the state of it. But as she circled around, her eyes went wide. Cupping hands to her mouth, she thought she might be sick.

The horse was clearly dead. Massive bite and claw marks gored where its belly had once been. No feast had occurred here. The parts were present as though something huge had slaughtered it. A monster mutilated the horse while it was still living.

Coaxing their hesitant mounts to go near, the men came to see why she was so horrified. Toth all but vomited and Ulna moved a few steps back from the scene.

Oryn quickly studied the evidence. The fact that nothing had been eaten suggested a werewolf. They could not consume a horse, but they would not hesitate to kill for entertainment. One fact that made him doubt his own theory was the bite marks. They were like a werewolf's, but more than double the size of any he had seen. This monster could have bitten off the pony's head with a single bite.

Adwen was transfixed by the size of the wounds. She could not smell it, but sensed something evil had been here. The most evil presence she could imagine had been where she stood and it was running loose. She highly doubted she would feel safe enough to fall asleep later.

Oryn moved Ranger away from the carcass to speak with Toth and her incredible ears caught every word.

"This is a waste. Toth, ask your pet if it could use what's left."

In a fit of rage, she lunged and he turned just in time as

she tackled him from the saddle. They landed and went tumbling through the mud, each trying to get control of the other.

She was fast and much stronger, but the knight had skill and years of experience. The struggle was brief and ended with Oryn on top. He managed to get his knife out and pin her down. Sitting on her middle restraining her arms with both knees, he gripped her collar in one hand, pressing the flat of his knife to her throat.

Outraged, she growled and tried to wriggle free. "Get off of me, you son of a..." But she stopped in mid-sentence and coughed.

He pressed the blade against her esophagus, pulling on the collar for leverage. Small beads of blood appeared along the side of the knife, but the cut healed seconds after he eased off. Anger made her pure blue eyes shine. This time Adwen's appearance did hinder his actions. He glared back with just as much rage.

Rain fell harder and Toth merely watched in shock.

Her vicious growls were involuntary. When she had enough breath, she spoke slowly and clearly, "Let go and... get...off."

Oryn quickly applied pressure again. When she fell silent, he ordered, "Answer my questions. Why did you attack me?"

"I don't know," she replied with a soft growl. "Why did you mock me?"

Surprised, he paused before answering, "I was not intending to mock. Judging from what was done to the animal, we shall need you at the peak of your strength. There is no point in passing up the opportunity when it presents itself. The flesh from this horse would be no exception. Do you disagree?"

Her growl was louder. "Yes. I shouldn't have to tell you, I don't eat horse; especially when it's been touched by something evil to the core."

After thinking over her words, in quick fluid movements, he stowed the knife and stood. Using his grip on the collar, he hoisted Adwen to her feet.

Adwen clenched her teeth and backed away, snarling with wrinkles on her nose flaring.

"If something evil had not touched this dead creature, would you eat of it?"

"After what happened the first time?" she retorted. "After what eating that deer did to me? No! No, no, and no! It's your fault that this happened to me!"

He snapped back. "You stupid dog. You are the only one to blame, not I! Only you are responsible for the changes you've made of late. Now, tell me, who taught you the blessing you performed and do not lie!"

Confused and frustrated, she shook her head and screamed, *"I don't know what you're talking about! What blessing?"*

"Don't play coy with me. Who taught you the Hunter's Promise?"

"Pretend for a moment that I don't know what you're talking about!"

Oryn scowled through the downpour. "I saw what you did to the deer."

Seeing her look of outrage and confusion, he explained, "The Hunter's Promise is a blessing and tradition nearly forgotten by all. The tradition originated from a blessing. The first to perform and teach it was able to speak to any soul they chose in the flesh or the ethereal. When they performed the Hunter's Promise, if the soul were pleased with their sincerity, among other things, they could bestow a gift." Oryn's eyes seemed to search her for an answer to a question he had not asked. "And only if the soul heard them, could the gifts be granted."

She was still confused and cried, "But what does that... why is this still my fault? I don't understand!"

He was losing patience. "You performed the blessing and the soul of the doe heard you! The soul of the animal saw fit to grant you with not one gift, but two! It bestowed upon you both power and beauty. You still have yet to answer me! Who taught you the blessing?"

Adwen was dumbstruck. The changes to her more human body had been because of one thing. One act of pure-hearted kindness for a fallen creature had caused her all of this pain. She felt numb.

After standing in the rain with everyone looking to her for the answer, she shook her head and murmured, "No one did. I was being myself. If I had known this was going to happen, I would have done things differently."

The knight practically shook with anger as he stormed over and glared into her face. He searched her eyes and sneered, "This is your one and only warning. If you ever lie to me again, I'll cut out your tongue. After all, it's your nose we need." He looked her up and down before returning to his horse. Back in Ranger's saddle, he issued orders: "Before we venture into town, search for anything of interest. Be quick about it before we catch our death out in this weather."

Stalking off to investigate, she snapped, "Someday I'm going to make you sorry!"

He made a wry smile, highly doubtful. "I welcome it, dog."

There was nothing. There was no sign of the princess, the kidnapper, or the monster that butchered the horse. Rain poured onto their heads in sheets by the time they reached an inn. The Merry Monarch's rundown exterior did not give credit to whomever owned the establishment. Oryn dropped them off on the doorstep and took the horses to the stables. Dark rainclouds poured torrents onto the little town and the two stood under the porch eaves, waiting patiently for the knight's return.

Her hood was drawn under the shelter of the dusty porch. Adwen watched runoff roll down, splashing onto the stoop.

After a while, Toth put a hand on her shoulder. Though he could not make out her expression, he knew she was as dismal as the weather.

"We'll find them. We shall find them and send you home. I have not forgotten my promise."

She whispered mournfully. "So what if I go home? What would I do? Go see my family? Yeah, right. I don't see that happening."

He frowned and allowed her to talk.

"With the way I am now, I'm not so sure I should go home. And if anyone found out what I am... I don't see that going well."

Raindrops trickled from her cloak. Toth saw a tear fall among them to land on the dirty porch. The sky blackened as night began and the storm worsened.

Adwen sensed the knight approaching. She could sense him from yards away, and once again, she was disappointed to know he was right; she was a dog. She even growled when he came close to led them into the Merry Monarch.

The interior was almost as filthy as the porch. It was much like the Fat Fish except for the drastic difference in attendance. There were nine customers in all; two of which were women who were not even drinking. Five men sat together playing a quiet game of cards. Even in passing, she could easily tell these were bad men.

One glanced at the new arrivals and quietly returned to the game.

The old, decrepit innkeeper at the counter was irritable, but gave Oryn due respect for being a knight and greeted him lazily, "Good evening, sir. What may I serve you tonight, ale, ale, or perhaps ale?"

"None of the drink. We are in need of a room." He took out a large pouch of coins to show he could pay.

"A room for three, good sir?" The man eyed Adwen suspiciously.

Shaking his head, he corrected, "No, two will do." And he shelled the coins out onto the dusty countertop.

The old man's eyes studied the coins and he was satisfied. "Very well, sir. My nephew shall show you the way."

A little boy no older than twelve suddenly leaped out from behind the counter to greet them in a cheery tone. "Right this way, travelers!"

He was small, quick and very polite as he brought them to a room on the third floor. Opening the door and holding up a hand, he presented the spaces. "As you asked, good sir, two beds to do with as you please. Sleep well and enjoy your stay in the Merry Monarch." Then he bowed and was gone.

Right away, Toth set his satchel on the foot of his bed and headed for the door with a gleam in his eye. "I'm going to mingle and see if I can get into a game of cards. I haven't played in ages!"

"After the first game is finished you are to return here," Oryn advised. "We don't need to search for you at the start of the morning."

He nodded and was on his way, but heard Adwen and stopped.

"Toth?" She pushed back her hood and wore a worried

expression.

"Yes, Adwen?"

"Be careful down there, okay?"

He gave a big smile. "Of course." And he vanished.

Not liking the feeling as he left, she stood and whined at the closed door.

"Stop your mongrel sounds," the knight grumbled. "They don't match your size and appearance. It is irritating." He had already removed his armor and lay down with the sword over his chest, eyes closed as he tried to sleep.

She could not help it. Her growls and whining were unintentional. Growling, she turned away from the door to stop herself.

Crossing the room, a mirror caught her eye and she felt paralyzed as she saw herself. The eyes looking back at her through the reflection were an unbelievable blue with a strong glow. She watched as they became glassy and finally looked away. Moving to the empty corner, she lay on the hard wood floor.

She could not return home, she thought. She could hardly recognize her own reflection. Adwen looked nothing like Shari Gates. She was gone. Choking back more tears, she curled up, wrapping arms about herself for the semblance of comfort it might bring.

The knight was near sleep when there was a sound. He realized it was her humming. Though he thought to tell her off, instead he listened. The docile, somber tones stirred something within his heart. In that moment, he felt pity. Adwen's sad song dwindled away as they both drifted off into sleep.

She dreamed.

Adwen found herself in a silent crowd. An assembly of men and women stood in a hazy fog dressed in the darkest of colors. None spoke near by, but a faint voice could be heard at the head of the masses. Unable to make out the words, curiosity urged her to seek out the source.

Everything was gray and ominous. Some of the faces seemed familiar. The closer she got to the speaker, the more difficult it became to squeeze past. Gently working through the thicket of gloomy attendants, she reached the front and froze.

A preacher perched beside a grave.

She reached the scene as the casket began its final descent. The black coffin lowered into the pit until an inscription beneath the tombstone was unveiled.. It read: *The angel with a heart of gold.* And as the dark box vanished, the name of the fallen was inscribed: Shari Adolfa Gates.

Chapter 23
BOUNTY HUNTERS

Adwen's eyes snapped open as she sat upright. Her heart still raced. Even after recovering from the fright of the very lucid dream she remained uneasy. Something was not right.

It was a few hours past dawn. Getting to her feet, she saw Oryn was close to waking, but she couldn't tell if Toth were awake or not. His bed was empty. He had not returned.

Padding to the vacant mattress, she gripped the footboard with sharp claws, scratching nervously. There was a sick sensation in the pit of her stomach. Sensing eyes on her, she looked at the knight.

Finally awake, he took a moment to glare before glancing at Toth's bed. The satchel lay on the unwrinkled sheets. He could tell by her expression that this was not a good omen.

They headed for the door as Adwen put on her cloak.

With the hood drawn, she was first to reach the main floor. Dashing down the final steps, she startled the innkeeper's nephew.

He had been cleaning a mess from the night before. Shards of glass were scattered with spilled ale. The boy stepped aside as she rushed for the table. Startled, he watched her touch the surface with soft hands and heard sniffing beneath the hood. He noted the clean, sharp claws, gasped then ran to his uncle behind the counter.

By the time Oryn caught up she found Toth's scent. The strong odor of alcohol made finding difficult. She soon spotted a dark splotch and quickly put her nose to it. A bit of her friend's blood was on the table. Stepping back and starting to cry, dog whimpers escaped her throat.

The knight's hand clamped tight around her arm and she fell silent. He whispered angrily, "Control your sounds. We do not need any more attention."

Adwen wrenched free of his grip and moved away. Taking a breath, she tried be calm and listened as he went to speak with the innkeeper.

On the other side of the bar the old man loaded his crossbow and the boy stood by, watching the dark-hooded figure. With the weapon cocked and aimed, he rested it on the counter for support.

"What happened here?"

The determined old man was less than cooperative. "What does it look like? There was a bar fight."

Intent on getting information, he tried to be patient. "What happened to the man who checked in me? I know you know what became of him." Normally not one to resort to bribery, Oryn wanted to find Toth fast. Showing the innkeeper his bag of gold, he attempted to coax the truth out.

Gritting his teeth, the old man's face turned beat red. "You truly are a fool! Keep your coins, knight! I won't be dealing with you. Take your dark creature with you and be gone!"

The man's daring outraged him. "You are too bold, old man. Mind yourself more carefully."

His nephew tugged at his arm and they both looked at Adwen.

She slowly approached. The weapon didn't frighten her.

They saw her smooth, clawed hands come up and the man readied to fire, but she was only putting her hood down. When they saw her for the first time her exotic face was still damp from crying and she pleaded softly.

"Please. What happened to my friend? Please tell me. Please."

The old man froze and blinked. His grip on the crossbow loosened. Both were stunned and instantly lost fear.

Oryn saw her words crack through the old man's mental armor. "We must know what happened."

Right away, the innkeeper returned to being angry and snapped, "You must know you have little influence in this region of Dargadia. To assume we will aid the knights of your order without question is too much. You will get no help from me, Sir Fool!"

"How dare you!"

"No, how dare you! The Order of the Master Knights has

abandoned this side of the river! I know your type, knight. Whoever you catch you judge. And whoever you judge is condemned to death or worse. It won't be long before you start --"

"Please!" Adwen called out to end the argument. "Please, can't you at least tell us what happened?"

Again, Oryn saw her get through and the elderly man softened.

He sighed. "The lot playing cards were bounty hunters. They had at one time been tracking your friend and all but given up when they lost most of their woar dogs to a beast."

Adwen thought this sounded familiar.

"You're the Tame One, aren't you, miss?" the boy asked.

The old man looked from his young nephew and back while she stared in silence.

Oryn eyed her with suspicion as the innkeeper continued, "They started buying your friend a round of drinks. After a few pints were down his throat, he was easily coaxed into removing the magical disguise for his ears. Then they knew for sure that your elfish friend was their missing target." Disarming the crossbow, he handed it over to his nephew. "They roughed up your friend. They gave him quite a beating."

"But why? Toth's not a bar brawler. Why did they do that?"

"It was a penance for the loss of their dogs. Only three made it back alive. Two were so badly injured that they were put down." Seeing her frightened look, he added, "Your friend seemed like a kind soul and far too innocent to deserve the beating. I tried to stop them, but..."

The knight was irritated by how cooperative the innkeeper was with her questions. She must be using magic with her voice, he thought. He attempted once more to talk to the old man. "Can you tell us what we need to know?"

To his disappointment and surprise, the innkeeper wasn't through telling him off yet. "I can tell you what you need to know! What this kingdom needs is more of the magical beings you kill for petty complaints from normal folk. The people need creatures like this Tame One!"

When he continued, it was all Oryn could do to keep from uttering a word.

"As for knights like that captain of yours, Sir Oryn -- yes, his name has reached even here. You force into hiding magical beings with the power to save the land. It's because of knights such as him that the kingdom is falling to pieces! When you return to that castle of yours, find Sir Oryn and tell him the innkeeper at the Merry Monarch says he can eat fodder!"

Stunned, Adwen's eyebrows raised and she stole a glance at the knight. She would have laughed if the situation was less serious.

Oryn looked as if he were about to explode. The knight fumed and his pupils were the size of pinpricks, but he didn't dare reveal his name. The others would search everywhere and eventually come here. He could not afford to give himself away out of pride.

"Do you know where they took Toth?" she asked.

He hesitated. "Would you let them live, Tame One?"

"If Toth is still alive, I will only do as much as needed to stop them. I just want my friend back."

The old man frowned. "They take up shelter in the old temple ruins to the north in the forest. If they are not there, they would be making for one of the river towns. The bounty was for your friend to be delivered alive. If you hurry, you can catch them."

She was relieved. "Thank you so much, sir."

His nephew answered for him, "It is a privilege to meet the Tame One, miss."

With the information they needed, Oryn had had enough of being insulted. "All right, dog," he sneered and gave a rough push. "Get moving."

She snarled and the boy frowned, crossing his arms.

The innkeeper shook his head. "Best be careful, young knight. A creature can only be tame as long as you allow."

Both travelers returned to their room. Adwen gathered up the satchel and waited as the knight donned his armor. Once fully suited, he led the down and out the front door.

Once they departed, neither Oryn nor Adwen spoke for a long time. Oryn remembered a map of the old kingdom territories in the order library. An old temple ruin lay somewhere north of Kimble Town.

The temple had mysteriously fallen into rubble more than

six hundred years ago. Over the centuries, roads to it were engulfed by the forest. They needed to find the tracks of the bounty hunters to reach it in time.

The task was easier said than done. The storm effectively covered the trail. There was hardly a scent to go by and the faint tracks she found were their only hope.

Oryn was astride Ranger, toting Ulna along. They followed the tracks for hours. As the day wore on, she grew anxious. Dusk eventual fell and the last of the sun's rays filled the forest with an eerie glow. Uncertainties tortured her as the minutes dragged painfully by.

Oryn was first to break the long silence. "Why did the old man listen to your word and rebuke mine? What spell did you cast to take control of him?"

She continued to work, mildly amused. "I don't know any spells. I remembered how you said I had spoken to the soul of the deer and thought I'd see if it worked like you described. Whatever I said got through and he knew I wasn't lying. I think he just didn't like you very much."

He scowled. "There hasn't been one like him since. It simply is not possible."

Heaving a heavy sigh, she continued tracking.

"Why did the innkeeper's boy call you the Tame One?"

She didn't answer, focusing solely on the trail.

He was more curious than angry and found patience. "Why won't you tell me?"

"There's no point in telling you anything. You only hear what you want to hear. You'll never listen to a word I say."

He coolly replied, "Well then, pretend I'm listening."

Surprised, she stopped and looked back at the clever knight. His face was blank, but she could sense he was, in fact, listening for a change.

"When Toth and I saved the princess she convinced a town to have a feast in my honor. She dubbed me the Tame One. I guess a lot of people know me by that name now." Finished, she went back to tracking.

The two horses exchanged glances. It seemed outlandish, but not unbelievable.

Oryn took it in and asked, "What did you save the princess from?"

"The Bloody Brothers."

The sun set at last when he gave his next question. "How did you survive the encounter?"

Adwen stopped and stood as he came alongside. Anticipating a negative reaction, she took a breath. "If you really want to know, I had to run. They almost tore me apart."

"No one must run from anything. You fled because you are cowardly. Knights have courage in the face of battle."

She had anticipated he would say something to that effect. "You don't have courage."

He dropped from Ranger's back and her heart leaped, but she did not flinch. Not even when he pulled his knife and held it to her throat, cornering her up against a tree. He glared with cold green eyes, but she returned the stare without any sign of timidity. She had not backed down in front of Eric Spade, and to her, Oryn was no different. He was just another bully.

Leaning in close, she could hear the leather of his gauntlet groan while he gripped the knife tight and whispered, "Say I'm a coward... now that I have my blade to your throat. I dare you."

With the edge scraping tender skin, she said, "I did not call you a coward. I said you don't have courage. There is a difference. A coward has fear and runs. To have courage, you need to have fear, and I have plenty of that. The thing is, I have enough courage to stand and face it. You don't have courage because you're not afraid. You have no fear. Every time I look at your eyes, all I see is hate."

Oryn blinked. The stone cold expression melted and uncertain curiosity replaced it. He had one question left that had to be answered.

"Who are you? Tell me the truth."

For a while she stared. Anguish resurfaced. Dropping her gaze, she didn't know what to say or if she could say it without breaking down. Glancing back, she wondered if he were serious.

The determined and curious expression remained.

Adwen hung her head. "I used to be Shari Gates. I'm not from your world." She looked up again. "But you probably already guessed that."

He was shocked, but let her continue.

"I didn't come here by choice. My first night in this world I was bitten by a werewolf. I was not marked or cursed. An elf saved my life. I've never tasted human flesh and I've never hurt anyone unless I had to protect myself."

Her eyes watered. "Toth has been so kind to me. He's my only friend in this world. I would sooner have you cut my throat now than let him be thrown to the dogs." Glaring back, she waited to see what he would do now that he knew the truth.

That she had once been a human after all was his first thought. He understood she was waiting to see if he would end her life. His mind was reeling from the sudden revelations. Then he realized his knife was still to her throat and his body was practically pressing hers against the tree. Slowly, he removed the knife and took a step back. Her glowing eyes were still locked with his.

"Why do you take the name Adwen?"

A tear rolled down her cheek. "Friends from my home world gave it to me. For some reason, it seemed appropriate to use it. After all, I'm not Shari anymore." A chill went down her spine like ice water. It was the first time she had spoken the dreaded words aloud.

He watched Adwen drop her gaze again. Everything she had said was unbelievable, but he believed anyway. As her eyes turn violet and glowed brighter, he asked, "Have you picked up the scent?"

Staring off at nothing, she nodded. "Yeah. It's faint, but it's them."

For a brief moment of silence the two stared at the ground, stunned.

He murmured, "You may have your privacy."

"Thank you."

Ranger stood by patiently, waiting for his master. When Oryn was seated with reins in his hands, he pondered Adwen's story. But all ponderings ceased when roars came rolling through the forest. The orange moon rose full and she made baleful howls. He waited for the sounds to stop, but for once, he did not hate her for it. A few moments passed and the forest hushed. By the time she arrived, the knight already donned his slayer helm.

Adwen returned and was unmasked by the shadows. As her human form was changed so was her true shape. She was sleek. Her jet black coat was abyssal silk over a streamline figure fitted with rock hard flesh beneath. The knight watched her stow the clothes in Ulna's saddlebags. Readjusting the collar on top of a new glossy coat, she stood beside the horses. She smelled traces of the humans on the breeze and growled.

"Forward," Oryn commanded.

Off on a bound, her nose led the way around the darkened forest. Weaving between trees and bushes, the knight knew they were close as her pace began to quicken. She eventually stopped and crouched as the horses came up behind. The knight came alongside and she gestured with her jaws. Moonlight illuminated a small whisper of smoke from a fire.

"Go quietly. Observe and return to inform me of their numbers."

Adwen growled in acknowledgement and dashed ahead.

Beneath the trees was dark and she blended perfectly, following voices from downwind. The ruins were mostly leveled by time while an old tower still stood. Flooring inside had gone and the roof was out on one side. It made a perfect cave and kept most of the weather at bay. Looking for a view into their hideaway, Adwen found a section of rubble that formed a perfect stair up to the gaping hole where smoke escaped. Her black nose tested the air before she peered down inside.

Seven men in sat around a fire. A few played cards again while others sharpened hunting knives. Their woar dog lay beside the horses, keeping a watchful eye on Toth. They had put a sack over his head and restraints on wrists and ankles.

She bristled all over at the scent of fresh blood and realized it was her friend's.

One of the captors was passing by and gave him a hard kick in the ribs.

An angry snarl jumped out of her in response.

The bounty hunters were oblivious, but the woar dog raised his head. Gazing up through the gap, he saw nothing.

The knight saw Adwen returning. Since her translator was unavailable, he kept questions simple: "How many did you count?"

Adwen stood and held up seven long, clawed digits.

"Is he with them?"

Growling, she nodded.

Pondering, he asked, "Are they inside a structure?"

She nodded again.

"Is the dog with them?" When she gave another nod, he asked, "Did you go unnoticed?"

Adwen folded her arms and cocking her head. Rolling her eyes, she emphasized that she was sure.

Something burst from the bushes and pounced. The woar dog caught Adwen by surprise and they both fell, snarling and barking. In a few seconds he was pinned. The dog snarled and snapped while she gave the knight an apologetic glance.

"I thought you said you went unnoticed," his muffled voice glowered through the helm. "Kill it before it can call its masters and give us away."

Meanwhile, the dog continued to spew threats. "I'll get you this time, monster! Let me go!"

Gripping his faceguard, she growled a warning, "Aren't you paying attention? He just told me to kill you."

The dog silenced and whimpered pitifully.

Growing impatient, the knight commanded, "Hurry and be done with it. I shall have to form another plan."

She cocked her head wonderingly.

The knight explained. "You were to alert the dog then lead them all into the forest. If they saw you they would not hesitate to give chase. There is a reward out for any dangerous creatures. They cannot resist the chance to earn more gold."

She panted happily at the dog, "Would you help us if I let you go?"

"What? Betray my masters? They are my pack!"

She growled softly, "All I want is to get my friend back."

The dog growled, "I lost the rest of my pack trying to catch that man!"

"I'm trying to save your life. If you won't cooperate, he will have you killed and I will probably have to hurt your masters. If you help, I promise to let them live. You remember what I'm capable of, don't you?"

He whimpered in affirmation.

"So will you help us?"

The dog thought long and hard, glancing between Adwen

and Oryn on his horse. Finally, he answered, "For the survival of my masters, I... I will help you."

Her tail wagged and she released him.

The knight was confounded. "What are you doing?"

Ignoring him, she instructed, "Go back and when you see me, don't warn your masters right away. I'll give you a signal to start barking, okay?"

The woar dog growled, "Just keep your promise."

Oryn watched her stroke his coat, consoling him. He knew she had swayed the animal of something.

"Has the dog agreed to aid with your distraction?"

Her head cocked and her tail swung from side to side.

The dog felt guilty for agreeing to foil his masters. He growled at the prisoner and lay down to wait beside him.

One of the men tossed a scrap of meat. "Good boy. Keep a watch on that slippery one."

He snatched it up and chewed happily. When the morsel was gone, he turned to Toth and growled, "You are more trouble than you're worth. When you're gone, I hope my masters never look for you again."

Not knowing what to make of the dog's words, Toth kept quiet. He was in no hurry for more beatings.

A few minutes passed until the woar dog saw Adwen's glowing eyes looming by the entrance. Her form hunkered by the opening in the wall. The bounty hunters were too wrapped up in their tasks to notice her stepping inside. Then she nodded and the dog leaped forward, barking.

At first the hunters were startled, but then Adwen roared. The thunderous sound echoed in the chamber endlessly. Some hunters stumbled while others jumped to their feet, grabbing weapons. Firelight danced across her black coat and her violet eyes shined so brightly they appeared to burn.

A hunter fired an arrow and she leaped back, loping away. Getting to frightened horses in a hurry, they raced off through the shadows and sparse moonlight, their dog leading them on a wild goose chase.

Toth was left completely alone. All was quiet, until he heard footsteps as someone entered the tower. Expecting one of the men about to give him a thrashing, he braced himself. Instead of a beating, the sack was removed from his head. His young face was bruised and cut all over, but he looked up with happy relief. Oryn began to untie him and the half-elf couldn't wait to see Adwen again. He had something very important to tell her.

The woar dog lead his over-ambitious masters along a false trail.

Adwen doubled back. Coming from the side, she silently lunged for the rider bringing up the rear. She swatted him from the saddle. And as he fell, Adwen landed on top of the animal, sending it into a terrified fit. In the horse's panic, it stumbled and crashed while she leaped for the next.

She landed on the backside of the second horse, grabbed the hunter and lobbed him into his neighbor. Both cried out in surprise and were quickly left behind. Her tongue lolled while she enjoyed the sight immensely.

The horse beneath her brayed in anger and she looked in time to see the remaining hunters taking aim with bows. Her ears dropped in distress and they loosed their volley.

Thinking fast, she reached up and snagged a strong, low-hanging branch. Arrows flew harmlessly past as she disappeared amid the leafy branches.

Turning their mounts, they returned and encircled her tree while the dog barked up at the boughs. They scanned the branches for movement with weapons drawn, but it was too dark.

After leaping to another tree without their noticing, she dropped down behind and tugged a hunter out of his saddle. Before the others could stop her, she took his weapons and hung him on a branch by his belt.

Once there was a clear shot, they fired and missed again.

Moving across the ground like lightning, she went for another bounty hunter. Their arrows struck the ground as she passed under the belly of a horse, sending it into a panic. It reared, swinging its hooves in terror as his rider fell. He was knocked unconscious while his steed bolted and fled.

Two enemies remained. Swooping in for an attack, this

time she wasn't evasive enough. As she leaped through the air, his companion launched an arrow and it struck deeply into her neck.

Snarling at the sting, she connected with her target and they landed with a loud thud. He remained alert and tried to fight her off until she hit his jaw, careful not to kill him.

The remaining hunter and his tree-bound friend watched her turn and face them. The arrow should have killed her. The shaft protruded out from behind a long pointed ear. He had only made her angry.

Violet eyes burned and he was not as eager to shoot again. Holding his quivering aim, the man stared in fear. The dog had disappeared and he faced Adwen alone. She gnashed jaws loudly as his hands shook. He began to sweat.

On all fours, hair standing on end, she snapped and snarled.

"I dare you. Shoot. See what good that will do."

Though he didn't understand her animal language, the sounds had clear meaning. The hunter gulped, too terrified to move. But then his horse finally lost its nerve. Adwen snapped viciously and the mount whinnied and bolted. He barely held on as the frightened animal bore him away.

Satisfied, Adwen stood, yanking the arrow out. The wound healed rapidly. Then she glanced at the hunter hanging in the tree and walked toward him.

Panic made the man shiver and shake. Big beads of sweat ran down on his face. Terrified, he closed his eyes tight, waiting to be ripped to pieces. Then there was a loud snap and the bounty hunter gave a start. The tall, black creature had only broken the arrow in half. Frozen in disbelief, he watched her drop the pieced and go down onto all fours, leaving him alive, dangling pathetically from the limb.

The four moons were high. She was eager to know if Toth were safe with the knight. Adwen hoped he was not too hurt and felt satisfaction at giving the bounty hunters a little justice.

But as she reached a small clearing all senses alerted her to something strange. Night insects hushed, wind brought in strange scents. The weight of eyes were upon her in the patches of moonlight.

The thick hair on her back stood as she became wary, wondering if it were Korig and Kotig. Then she recognized the smell of horses and metal. A small flash of light from a knife nearby made her stare and growl.

"I know you're there. Come out."

Rhythmic beats growing louder made her turn about and stand upright. Stunned by the appearance of knights on horseback, she was caught off guard. They both came charging in caring long poles with rope which Adwen mistook for whips.

The ropes were tied to the saddles of the horses. A coil fed from a bag along the pole shaft and ended in a small noose. Their movements were smooth and accurate as they slipped the nooses around both her wrists, tightened them and dropped the poles as they flew past.

Adwen gasped, eyes wide in horror. The cords simultaneously became taut, sweeping Adwen backward off of her feet. The horses raced past either side of a broad tree until Adwen smashed into the trunk. The ropes snapped tight, forcing the horses to halt.

Her left shoulder crunched. She let out a horrible crying howl and continued to yelp, fighting to keep both appendages. The tension was tremendous. Pressure across her chest made it difficult to breathe.

After a few seconds of letting her writhe the knights came out of hiding. Three gathered close along with a scruffy teenage boy, congratulating each other. Once they finished laughing, the leader turned his attention back to her.

She kicked at the ground, sliding farther up the tree. With her back flush with rough bark, she had a better angle to fight the ropes. She tried to snap them, but it was no use. The knight was before her ceremoniously unsheathing his sword. Adwen watched wide-eyed, helpless as he pointed it and spoke.

"Beast, you have been judged. As a Knight of the Order, I find you guilty of crimes against human kind. For the murder of a human, I now forgive you."

Raising the blade high, he prepared to slice her in half. Moonlight lanced off of the blade while it arched through the air and Adwen closed her eyes and yelped.

A loud clang of metal on metal made her eyes snap open wide. Oryn arrived in the nick of time and used his own sword as a shield against the blow.

The knight got one good look at his wolf visor and gasped behind his own, "A slayer! Sir, please stand aside. I must finish my task."

Oryn pushed back a little and his angry voice was muffled by the helm. "And you are impeding mine. Stand down or risk challenging me to a duel."

Quickly backing off, the knight allowed Oryn to stand.

"Sir, we have been hunting this monster for weeks. Why do you stay my hand?"

"This is not the beast you're searching for. Return to your hunt."

But the knight was tired and hadn't slept in a week. He bravely took a stance and held his blade at the ready. "Sir, this black wolf is what we've been hunting for and I shall finish my quest only by slaying it."

Without warning, Oryn batted the sword out of his hand with such force that it was impaled in a nearby tree.

Now armed only with a knife, the knight was greatly outmatched. The others watched the slayer step forward and warn, "This creature is with me. It is not and cannot be the beast you are searching for. Do not try me again if you'd like to keep your hands."

The knight had a sudden realization. "Sir Oryn? My humblest apologies, I had no idea you were questing in this region. What can my knights and --"

"Silence! Do you not recall there are currently two officers with wolf slayer's armor? You are addressing Lieutenant Peregrine!"

Adwen stared, dumbstruck at the lie.

The knight was confused. Lieutenant Peregrine was supposed to be questing farther west. "Sir, may I request that you remove your helm?"

Outraged, Oryn bellowed, "Are you questioning me? Mind yourself more carefully when you dare to call me a liar!" The knight's armor was not as protective as Oryn's and left his throat exposed where the tip of his sword now rested.

The knight held perfectly still and spoke softly, "Sir, I

apologize. I was far too bold to question you. I am at your mercy."

Oryn let a moment pass before taking the point away.

Then the knight asked, "Sir, the creature, why do you not slay it? My knights witnessed it attacking men in the woods not far from here."

He coolly replied, "Step back and you shall see."

Adwen panted in frightened gasps. She held her breath and winced as her ropes were cut.

The others drew swords as she was released and dropped to her knees, crying. Clinging to her arm, she heard him command, "Stand." She gave a baleful look and slowly obeyed. Keeping quiet through the pain, and to the astonishment of the knights, she did as ordered.

While she cradled the injury, he spoke with the knights. "As you can see, this creature is well within my control. It has been aiding in my quest and is the key to its success." Putting away his sword, he added, "I have judged this beast and have found it noble."

Adwen did a double-take.

"It has displayed honor, courage and unquestionable loyalty to the kingdom. The disposing of it would be foolish considering its willingness to take orders and its uncanny ability to make wise decisions. If any of you choose to question my judgment, speak now. You shall in turn deal with me."

He meant it and Adwen was stunned.

None were willing to speak against him openly.

With the matter settled, he was curious. "Now, tell me of this black wolf you search for."

Their leader called the boy forward and explained, "This young man was witness to a murder. His father was killed by a powerful werewolf. It attempted to feed on him in front of the boy."

"But I got him good," the teen boy added. "I cut his side with my silver dagger."

The knight continued. "It was not felled. The beast can change at will and in its more human form dons a blood-red leather jacket. Have you seen any by this description, sir?"

He was intrigued and very tempted to join, but his current quest was too important. Reassuring himself that this hunt could come later, he replied, "No, I have not. As you can see, this creature cannot change at will."

The boy added, "And the werewolf was three times that size with red eyes."

He found it even more difficult to resist the temptation. "I wish to each of you the best and may the light spirits watch over you."

The knights saluted and their leader answered his farewell. "And may the sun spirits guide your feet. Farewell... Sir Peregrine." With that, they gathered their things and went on their way, leaving in search of the wounded werewolf.

Pain shot through Adwen's arm again as her body attempted to heal itself. Something was going awry and making it more difficult. Falling to her knees, the agony made her moan and lick at it, not knowing what else to do.

Looking down, the knight shook his head. "That won't help you."

Adwen stopped licking. She knew that, but it was an instinctive habit.

"It is likely dislocated. Let me see." He reached out to feel her shoulder.

Not trusting him, she whimpered and pulled away.

He asked flatly, "Do you wish for the pain to stop? Let me see."

Still apprehensive, she let him and watched as he felt the joint. When fingertips found it, she yelped.

"It is dislocated. Relax and allow me to set it," he instructed before gripping the arm and bracing her shoulder. "This will be painful." In one motion, he gave a hard twist.

A loud crunch followed as bone reentered the socket and she cried out.

Letting go, he asked, "Has the pain gone?"

Adwen gingerly moved it around. Then she gave a nod.

Without another word, he turned to collect the horses.

Adwen would have said thanks if she could. What the knight had done astonished her. He had been kind.

Returning astride Ranger, he led Ulna by her reins carrying Toth in her saddle.

He smiled through bruises and swelling.

"You're still alive!" she barked and ran up to meet him.

Long arms gently encased the half-elf. He gave her neck a hug while she grumbled and her tail wagged.

"I thought I wasn't going to see you again."

He scratched behind her ear and replied, "You always worry too much."

"We've spent too much time here," Oryn grumbled. "We may very well have lost the princess. We must return to town and --"

"Wait a moment!" Toth interjected and they paused. "There is no need! I heard an interesting story from the bounty hunters. The morning before we arrived a pair of strangers appeared. When they came through town everyone avoided the tall, dark character. They said he had an evil presence that could make a whole room turn cold. And not only that, but the man had mentioned their intended destination."

They asked in unison, "Where?"

"Fort Wight." He smiled. "The town down the road is where we may find the princess and her kidnapper."

Chapter 24
END OF THE ROAD

Fort Wight was ancient. It stood as an outpost long ago to combat the terrors which leaked from Mortigad on the south-eastern border. Living in a land known for sightings of wandering corpses made the people tough and wary.

The three of them set out and traveled through the night. It was noon when the trekkers reached the well protected town. Guards at the gates were thorough in their inspection of visitors. Adwen rode with Toth and when the guards attempted to inspect her for evil qualities, Oryn gave them reason to let them pass. He got their attention with a gesture and flashed his sword, daring them to touch his companions. They made it inside with no other problems.

Their blond friend was sore and very tired. He yawned and winced when at seizing aches and groaned. "I hope we find somewhere to sleep soon. I feel as if I've been rolled down a mountain side."

Adwen was unaffected by remaining awake so long. After spending so much time out in the wilds, she almost forgot the overwhelming nature of towns. Her senses were irritated by a barrage of quick movements and nasty smells that she thought might make her nose bleed.

Farther into crowded streets, they made for the market. The street was jam-packed with traders and haggling buyers. Moving was slow with the horses, but it provided a high vantage point for searching. The knight came to a stand selling food, handing Ranger's reins to Toth. As Oryn went to barter the half-elf looked uncertain holding the reins of the warhorse. The massive creature smelled his hands and snorted.

Adwen was content to sit with him while the people milled past. Loud conversations and other sounds of Fort Wight irritated her ears. And no sooner did the sounds start to get to her, than the hair on the back of her neck stood on end. An ice cold chill ran up and down her spine. Fingertips fidgeted and she no longer took notice of the crowd. On full alert, she looked to and fro as the black hood concealed searching eyes.

Toth heard her growl dangerously. "What is the matter?"

She growled louder and warned, "He's here. He's here somewhere. I can feel that thing's evil presence in the air!" Adwen's head whipped this way and that, looking for the source.

While she kept her head on a swivel, Toth desperately tried for the knight's attention. The noises of the street drowned him out and Oryn continued to barter.

Then Adwen saw. Her stomach seemed to disappear as she glimpsed the fearful face of Princess Eyrie at the far end of the market. She saw her scream just as a dark gloved hand took her around the corner.

The sudden sighting and disappearance were more than she could resist. Snarling angrily, Adwen leaped from Ulna's back and into the busy street.

Toth saw her darting off. He became desperate for Oryn's attention and swore under his breath. Using a piece of stale bread, he threw the leftover loaf.

It struck the knight in the head and he whipped around in anger, but soon saw Adwen gone. The frantic look of Toth made it clear what the matter was. Dashing from the trading stand, he climbed onto Ranger as fast as he could.

Adwen struggled to move amongst the crowd. Her rapid actions made a scene, upsetting people with inhuman swiftness. Getting nowhere, she paused in the street and bystanders gave a wide berth, fearing she might attack. Fed up with trying to blend in, she growled and leaped onto a stack of barrels. Then she bounded to the rooftops, making the crowd cry out in terror. Once free of the clamor and stink of the humans all senses became clear.

She felt the evil presence as it was moving to the east gate. Baring sharp fangs, she dashed to the edge and leapt across to another. Traveling by rooftop in broad daylight drew the attention of archers on the wall. They sounded the alarm and fired dozens of arrows in an attempt to bring her down. All missed and went whizzing past. She was too quick.

Just as the east gate was beginning to close she dropped from a nearby roof and darted through the narrow gap.

Both guards stared dumbstruck as she left. The creatures usually came towards them instead of running away.

One turned to his partner and asked, "Should we keep closing the gate?"

Outside the town, she caught the kidnapper's scent. It still seemed familiar. Adwen sprinted down the trail towards sickly trees. The cloak slowed her down so she released the clasp and let it fall behind.

Ahead the ground beneath turned steep. In her haste, a foot caught on a rock and she tumbled down the hillside. She rolled and the collar fell away, landing not far from where she finally stopped. The spill made her dizzy. After shaking it off, she righted herself and was gone again.

At the fort, the guards finished pushing open the gate and reclaimed their posts when Oryn and Toth rode up.

The knight demanded, "Which way did she go?"

They pointed in unison. As the two left, they watched with curiosity. Glancing at each other, they shrugged. Neither knew what to make of the odd excitement.

Both riders left the road where they saw her footprints in the mud. Upon entering the forest, Toth yelled, "Where do you think they are going?"

Oryn yelled back, "I'm unsure, but they are headed for Dead River."

Dead River remained dry for centuries as a deep trench strew with stones and sun bleached wood debris. The scent brought Adwen to the old remnants of a crumbling bridge. She was ready to cross, but heard rumbling. It grew louder. The ground trembled and a wall of water roared down, refilling the trench. Her jaw dropped at the muddy flow while it ripped at dry clay riverbanks, forcing her to step back.

A faint scream came amid the sound of rushing water.

Adwen saw something bobbing in the raging current. To her complete horror, Princess Eyrie was quickly being swept away.

The princess saw her chasing alongside and tried to scream something, but water choked her words.

Running as fast as she could, Adwen tried to think. She had become very swift and strong, but was not able to keep up with the rushing flood; she could not save the princes while in human form. It was high noon and the moons would be unable to aid her. The princess began to lose to the current and sank below the frothy surface.

"No!" Adwen cried out in desperation.

An abrupt edge was fast approaching, perfect for leaping off into the monstrous rapids. The gap between her and the ledge steadily closed as she focused, trying to change. Nothing happened, but she didn't give up. Making her final approach, she prepared to leap.

Heart racing, she took two more driving steps and a deep breath. Sailing through the air, she drifted towards the violent, creamy flood. As she fell, without effort or pain, she changed. The shredded remains of the dress trailed on turbulent gusts and the seamless transition was complete before she hit the surface. Plunging down deep, she fought her way back up. Jaws and head exploded into the open air.

She was gasping when the princess reappeared close by then quickly sank. Adwen swam hard to keep her own head raised. Not willing to wait, she dove under. It was impossible to see as she reached out with large claws, found something and resurfaced with the princess.

Eyrie coughed violently and held tight to Adwen's neck.

Now that she had her, Adwen struggled against the current for dry land. The princess' gown made progress difficult. Adwen relentlessly slashed and kicked to safety. The rush of the flood ripped at the edges of the riverbed, creating a wall of crumbling earth. They reached it and she clung to loose mud and rock. The princess was exhausted, but didn't let go as she began to climb. Adwen grasped each hold deliberately. Slowly the two rose up out of the water.

A patch of earth she grabbed suddenly gave way, causing the princess to gasp and squeeze her neck. After finding a more solid patch.

At last, she reached the ledge and hoisted both of them over. The princess was soaking wet and tired as she finally let go. Climbing down, the pale girl tried to get enough breath to speak, spitting out water.

Standing upright, Adwen observed for a moment and knew she would be all right. Curious as to how far she had climbed, she approached the ledge. It appeared much more treacherous from the top.

Then Princess Eyrie screamed, *"Adwen, no!"*

She turned and looked.

CLIMBING THE WHITE OAK

All was dark and Adwen fell for the longest time. It felt like floating on a breeze. No thoughts. No worries. There was nothing to think about. She was freefalling with no way to tell how much farther to go or a reason to care.

She felt nothing as the world around her took shape. Upon reaching the bottom, everything seemed like a dream made of faded shadows. Beneath her was darkness veiled by mist while a black, twisted forest materialized. The contorted trees showed no signs of life.

There was a single light in the utter darkness of the eerie dreamscape. Way out in the distance she could see a glistening tower made of a billion stars. A bright light winked from the top as if it were calling out. It urged her to hurry.

Only then did she notice creeping forms. Things flowed amongst the twisted trees as if they were one. Red, glowing eyes circled and glared from many faces. They came in every size and shape imaginable. The endless horde was coming for her.

She started for the glistening tower. She did not run, fly or swim, but drifted through the forest like a comet in the nothingness of space. She moved swiftly with the fiends in hot pursuit. They did not want her to reach the light.

As she neared her destination the shining tower was revealed to be a tree. The colossal white oak stretched up forever. The luminous monolith stood alone to push back the dark and its steady, cleansing light reached Adwen. It filled her with power. Steadily, she began to pull away from the wicked swarms. No sooner had she reached the trunk of the oak than the demons ended the chase.

Adwen's form became defined by the pure light that filled her like an empty glass. Now resembling her human self, she was like a strange ghost. A smile came to her as she watched them retreat. Turning back to the tree, its branches flashed, flowed and glowed with many white lights in the place of leaves. They beckoned.

Heeding the call, she leaped to the lowest bough. Some lights briefly took the form of living beings. She could see their smiles. Suddenly, a wonderful urge struck her to reach the top of the white oak. So her ascent began. Adwen jumped, leaped and climbed for ages. The tree was impossibly tall and didn't seem to end, but she wasn't deterred. Going ever higher, she was filled with more white light.

The little beacon flashed brighter overhead, signaling the end of the long journey. The single light was many times more brilliant than those of the spirits. As she climbed along the final bough, Adwen discovered the source. This great white oak had a single leaf on the very end of the highest branch. The surface glistened like polished silver. She was about to touch it, but stopped. An incredibly bright glow spilled down from overhead, shining with the intensity of a sun. Lifting her gaze to the pure energy, she felt a force gently raising her higher.

Adwen drifted into the great light high over the land filled with dark and shadow.

Chapter 25
IT'S WHERE THE HEART IS

Nothing could be brighter than or as resplendent as the light over her. It was noon and the sun shone down through fresh green summer leaves, filled with the buzzing of insects and wild birdsong. The air was pleasantly warm and a soft breeze drifted across the lake to caress Adwen's face where she lay on the richly pebbled shore. The warm draft passed over her. When it touched skin and rustled hair, she took another breath at last.

Her lungs quickly filled and Adwen gasped, coughing out what had settled within her for so long. Every muscle was stiff as she struggled to turn over and purge the last of the water. It felt as if fingers of sharp glass danced across flesh. The sensation of blood flowing back to veins was a great discomfort as she lay on her side, coughing.

After a time, breathing became relaxed. She could hear the rhythmic sloshing of water on rocks and feel it breaking across her skin. No longer in hound form, she realized she had somehow fallen back into the river and been washed down to who knows where. Taking another deep breath, she opened her eyes.

From where she lay, a dense forest and a stone-strewn shore filled her view. Forcing her bare body to stand, she peered through the trees. Then there was a dull roaring and she leaped into a thicket. The sound had come from out across the lake. She spied something red skimming across the choppy water in the distance and gasped.

It was a bright red jet boat. The docks and the lodge on the other side were the same as she remembered. This was the lake where her three friends were going to take her for summer.

Jaw dropped, she covered her mouth in shock and

laughed, "I'm home!"

Adwen paused to examine her hands. They had sharp pearly claws. Her sense of smell was still heightened as she could detect the gasses from the boat on the next strong breeze. Using her tongue, she checked to see if the fangs were gone. To her disappointment, they remained quite long. She was still not human.

Heaving a sigh, she began a cautious search for clothes. She did not dare to change shape now. She would much rather be seen in a naked near-human body. Her nose served her well once again and she found a cozy log cabin. Not seeing movement, she crept closer, smiling at the sight of a satellite dish on the slanted roof. Since there were no clothes on a line, there was no alternative but to open the unlocked sliding glass door.

The idea of stealing put her on edge, but if she were caught there was little they could do to stop her. What were they going to do? Chase her down and catch her? Not likely, she thought. Testing the air, she smelled a human female, various chemicals and food. The human scent was faint. Confident that the house was empty, she carefully slipped inside and closed the door.

It was a single story home with high rafters. She had come in by way of the living room. A broad smile curled her lips as she passed the widescreen television set. In the stranger's bedroom she approached the dresser, but stopped dead when she spied the shower. A happy glint lit in her eyes as she darted for it without a second thought.

Hot water was soon running down her head and along her sloping back. Adwen began to laugh. She had missed hot showers. Clean and happy, she dried herself with the softest towel from the cabinet and got into some clothes. She found an orange high school sweater and a pair of stretchy jeans. As she was enjoying the soft clothes, the sound of a truck motor caught her ear. Frozen, she listened to the engine stop. There were footsteps on gravel and the front door opened. When it slammed shut, she almost jumped. The owner of the home had returned.

There was the clatter of keys placed on a tile counter along with two paper bags of groceries. She could smell vegetables, laundry detergent and sugar cookies among the contents. Stealthily, she peered out the doorway. When the person turned to put something away, Adwen quickly ducked back into hiding.

For the first time since entering, Adwen took notice of the photographs in frames. Then there was a picture in a smaller frame and she felt stupid for not noticing sooner. The photo had been taken years ago while she was still shy little Shari Gates. The tan girl with an arm around her was the same one putting away groceries; it was her best friend Kayla. She was trespassing and stealing in her best friend's house. Caught in the dilemma of wearing pilfered clothes, Adwen thought perhaps Kayla might be forgiving.

Kayla had long black hair and dark tan skin. Dressed in her favorite green tank top and jeans, she closed the refrigerator and was nearly finished putting everything away. A small sound came from the bedroom window and her hazel eyes darted to the clear glass pane. Huffing aloud, she returned to the chore, not giving it another thought. Odd birds in the area always flew into it leaving a feathery mess.

"Stupid birds."

There was a sudden knock at the door and she frowned. A local deputy from the lake campsite was always dropping by to say hello and ask her out to dinner. Rolling her eyes and clenching hands, she prepared to resist his petty attempts. Taking a deep breath, she opened it wide. Douglas the deputy was not at the door. Instead Kayla found an exotic-looking young woman. Her eyes were a perfect shade of violet and she wore an orange high school sweater. Everything about her appearance was unusual, but then she smiled. Kayla's eyes became wide with shock.

Adwen was careful not to reveal sharp fangs. "Hi, Kayla. Long time no see."

Kayla's look of shock quickly changed to horror as she screamed before slamming the door.

Stunned by the reaction, Adwen looked herself over to see if she had changed without noticing. She had not. Heaving a sigh, she thought this could have gone better. Though Kayla had closed the door, she hadn't the mind to lock it.

Opening it a crack, she called inside, "Kayla? Come on.

I've had a really rough trip and I need somebody to talk to. Can I come in or not?"

There was no answer, but Adwen entered anyway. Her friend had vanished, but the smell of fear was strong and sounds of shaky breathing were close. Going to check the bedroom, she was met with a surprise.

Screaming frantically, Kayla leaped out to attack with an aluminum baseball bat.

Adwen ducked as it whooshed past. "Whoa! What are you doing?" Then she moved aside just in time to escape more frantic swats.

Chasing after her into the living room between the sofas, Kayla swung the bat again for her face. But once Adwen caught the swinging bat in midair, she froze.

Adwen felt sheepish and chuckled. "Some friend you are. I don't need any more enemies with you around."

Abandoning her only means of defense, Kayla stumbled back only to land on the plush sofa. Her skin was clammy as she watched Adwen set the bat aside, sitting across from her in the other chair.

Adwen ran a set of sharp claws through her long, soft hair and sighed. "I thought at least you'd be glad to see me."

Finally finding the nerve to speak, Kayla asked, "Shari?"

She blinked. "Yeah, it's Shari."

Though calmer, Kayla still looked frightened. "Why -- how did you get here?"

Her smile was accompanied by a wry laugh. "It's a very long and very weird story. How about you tell me why you tried to kill me after I said hello?"

Kayla stammered, "You -- you're dead. You drowned in the river. Everyone saw you go over the falls. You never came back up."

"I went... somewhere else. The river took me far away and I've been trying to get back this whole time." She paused then became serious. "When was my funeral?"

Kayla didn't answer.

Knowing the vision in her dream was somehow true, Adwen grew frustrated. "How long did you all look for me? Three weeks is all you waited? You didn't even have a body to bury! How long has it been since my funeral, Kayla? Tell me and tell me honestly."

Stunned, Kayla murmured, "How did you..? The funeral...Your family had your funeral after three weeks of looking for you, Shari. Everyone who knew you was searching the river day and night. Half of the town was looking. All they ever found were your glasses. Your dad kept searching the longest. Even after the funeral, he went hiking for miles trying to find you."

Hearing word of her father smothered the anger. Becoming worried instead, she hesitated to ask, "How long ago was my funeral, Kayla?" Something strange had happened after saving the princess and before arriving in her home world.

"Shari, three days ago was the anniversary of your funeral. It's been more than a year. How did you know when they had the funeral?"

The news left her numb. It was the moment she had turned around to look; she had died. Her death was so quick she had not felt a thing. She had been dead for an entire year.

"Shari, what's making your eyes that purple? Are they contacts?"

Snapping out of the daze, she replied, "What?" Getting up, she went to a mirror. They were violet, but she was not about to transform and wondered why. "Yeah, contacts. They're cool, huh?"

The rumble of another vehicle came from outside and Kayla leaped from the sofa. Past the window curtains she could see the colors of the deputy ranger's truck.

"Shari, you need to hide. Go in the..." By the time Kayla turned she had already disappeared and Douglas was knocking at the door.

Answering it, she sighed and grimaced. "Douglas. What are you doing here?"

Douglas wore thick glasses and a rather bushy mustache for his age. Clearing his throat, he adjusted the belt needlessly and smiled. "Just checkin' up on yah. A lot of vandals have been trashing the camp and making a ruckus. Thought I ought to let you know. You can't be too careful nowadays."

Adwen watched from a prime vantage point in the rafters. She smiled at her flustered friend as she attempted to shoo the dorky deputy from the doorstep. She made up excuse after excuse to make him leave, but he would not get the hint. At last, Kayla lost her temper, slamming the door shut and that was the end of it.

With the confrontation over, she turned to search for her unexpected guest. Kayla didn't see her and thought she was gone then turned around.

Adwen dropped down a few feet away.

Stifling another scream, she stammered in disbelief, glancing at the rafters. The lowest beam was fifteen feet straight up.

"How did you do that?"

Adwen wore a hesitant expression. "How about I tell you later in the truck? I think we should go somewhere else. We don't need Dudley Do-Right bugging us."

Kayla agreed.

The two rode in Kayla's green Ford Ranger, zooming over twisting country roads, headed for the highway. From the passenger seat she stared out at the rolling country hills between the Rocky Mountains. Tears threatened to swell. Her old home was still as beautiful as she remembered. A few minutes into the ride, she convinced her driver to play the radio and a power ballad completed the state of bliss. Among the little things she missed, music was the thing she missed most of all.

They were close to town and Kayla restarted the conversation. "So, how did you do it? There's no way you jumped that high. How did you get up there?"

Avoiding the subject, she asked, "How's your mom? Does she still work at the bank?"

Kayla's temper had always been short and she snapped, "Shari! You go missing for over a year, turn up out of nowhere at my door and -- are those my clothes?"

"Uh, what happens if I say yes?"

Kayla's rant continued. "You snuck into my new house! You stole my clothes!"

"And I took a shower." Adwen cut off the mounting tirade. "I'm sorry. I'm a little frustrated, too. I woke up this afternoon and found out that I've been dead for a year. Then my best friend tried to kill me with her pee wee league baseball bat. You think you've got it rough? I've been through some things you wouldn't believe."

"Did someone kill you?"

That was the one explanation for how fast she had died. Someone did and Adwen had a wild guess. Clenching fists until claws almost drew blood from palms, she replied, "I've got a pretty good idea who."

"Who?"

"It was this guy. He's a complete jerk and he treated me like an animal. He's six-foot-two with brown hair and green eyes. I think he's almost twenty-two years old by now."

"Why would he kill you? You look... different since the last time I saw you."

Adwen thought about teaching the knight a hard lesson if she ever got her hands on him. A soft deadly growl came from her.

"Is that your stomach, Shari? You sound hungry."

Adwen cleared her throat. "Yeah, sure. I'm starved."

Kayla grew more impatient. "When we stop for food are you going to start telling me the truth?"

Shaking her head, Adwen replied, "I'm not so sure you'll believe me. I'm warning you, it's going to sound crazy."

Pulling into a fast food restaurant, Kayla parked and stated, "My dead best friend is sitting in my truck and bumming cheeseburgers. I don't think things get much crazier than this."

Climbing out of the seat, Adwen murmured, "You'd be surprised."

Once they ordered and received the greasy food, they brought the tray to a table with a window. There wasn't a cloud in the sky. The sun made everything glow and Adwen had a sip of soda, savoring the carbonation. The bite on her tongue brought on a smile and she took another swig.

Sitting across from her, Kayla frowned and cleared her throat.

"What do you want to know first?" Her friend gave a sardonic look. "There's a lot to tell. We have to start somewhere. Fire away."

Glaring, she asked, "How did you make it up into my rafters?"

She shrugged. "I jumped. I jumped up and climbed into your rafters."

Kayla snapped, "That's impossible! Explain how you could jump that high. Olympians can't jump that high without a pole or something"

"All right. All right, just calm down and I'll tell you." She shook her head and looked apprehensive. "I'm warning you: it's weird."

Crossing her arms, Kayla strummed fingers and waited.

Looking her dead in the eye, Adwen answered, "I'm not human anymore." Taking another long sip from her ice cold soda, she tried to wash the bitter taste down.

Kayla raised an eyebrow. "Are you okay, Shari? All right, let's just say you aren't human. What do you mean by that? What proof do you have?"

Thinking it over, she replied, "There is one really convincing thing I could do, but it's not appropriate for here. But, uh, I can smell things."

"Smell things?" she repeated flatly.

After taking a deep breath through her nose, she exhaled slowly. "The big guy behind you ate blueberry pie for breakfast, the old lady way over there is wearing a lavender perfume, and..." She took another whiff when she wasn't convinced. "You haven't put on any deodorant today, and you drank beer with your scrambled eggs." She smiled as a look of shock appeared on Kayla's face.

Becoming disturbed, she asked, "Why won't you smile?"

After carefully checking that no one was looking, Adwen flashed a toothy grin, complete with sharp, inch-long fangs.

Her hands rested on the table and Kayla noted how strong the nails looked. After years of having her own done, she knew no salon could do this work. They were the same white and pink coloration as human nails, but looked like dangerous animal claws.

Worried, she asked, "You're not wearing contacts, are you?"

Adwen stopped smiling and nodded. "I think you've got the idea." Her eyes glowed brighter.

Kayla was shaken. "Why? How did you...?"

"I went to another world. A place where magic and..." As she trailed off, her eyes grew wide. A familiar face just entered the restaurant.

Kotig wore street punk clothing and a small, two-way radio on his hip. Approaching the counter to heckle workers, he failed to notice her sitting a few tables away.

Kayla followed her stare and groaned. "Oh, this guy is bad news."

"You have no idea." Adwen put up the hood to disguise her face. It was only a matter of time before he would smell her. "How do you know Kotig?"

"Kotig?" Kayla asked. "This guy is Kevin Dozer. Him and his big bad brother showed up a few months ago and have been wreaking havoc everywhere. The stupid cops never do a thing about it. How do you know them? Shari, are you all right?"

She was sweating. Her vision swam and everything felt strange. "I...I don't know. I'll be back. Don't go anywhere without me."

Keeping out of the werewolf's line of sight, she darted to the restroom. It was empty and private. A sensation of warm energy coursed through her as she clung to the edge of the sink. Eventually, her vision cleared and the changes began.

Pail skin took on a copper tone. Ears came to graceful curving points. Hair on her head became feathery white with a silver shine while rich golden bangs swept off to one side. As her eyes glowed brighter, her lips turned from pink to a glossy black.

The clothes on her body flowed. Cloth swam and settled across her, changing into a set of gray fighting garments. On her hands manifested black fingerless gloves. A strip of white wrapped around her torso in a weave until her waist.

Before she could marvel, her sixth sense warned of something horrible happening. Trying to dash to the door, movements were uncoordinated and clumsy. Her body felt fluid in motion, but she managed to open the door as Kotig approached Kayla, grinning broadly. His clawed hand suddenly snared her throat.

An explosion of feelings caused Adwen to sprint in an attempt to stop him. Urgency gave stability to her new body and she lunged.

Hearing someone coming, Kotig swung a fist. It caught her in the jaw, throwing her into the decorative glass column filled with water. She fell unconscious as a flood from the shattered tank gushed out onto the tiles.

"Shari!" Kayla screamed and spat at him. "You son of a..." She was quiet as he squeezed.

Kotig studied the strange elf-like creature on the floor and sniffed. Then he laughed. "That's not Shari, you stupid girl. This is Adwen! Oh, this is going to be fun. First, you're my appetizer." The fiend was ready to bite, but stopped. He sensed a strange energy.

A force pulsed from Adwen and the water around her was pushed away. Methodically picking herself up, she opened her eyes. They shone pure gold and locked onto Kotig, staring blankly.

The brute dropped her friend and smiled. "On second thought, I've missed all of the fun we used to have. What do you say? Do you want to play, Adwen?" He roared and everyone screamed as he quickly transformed into a hulking werewolf.

Adwen's body transformed as well. There was a bright shimmer and a white coat of fur spread over brass skin. Her height shot up to seven feet as she became an elegant, snow-white hound. Upon her forehead glinted a golden blaze that streaked down to her black nose. In silence, she waited.

The anticipation for the werewolf was unbearable and he lunged.

Then her snow-white body finally moved. In a fluent and graceful spin, she delivered a punishing kick. He was sent flying, shattered through the windows and rolled into the sunny parking lot.

Her blank gaze followed.

Kayla stared in confusion and other onlookers who were too scared to flee froze in place.

The white hound took a graceful step. There was a bright flash as she performed a blink, becoming pure light to reappear outside in an instant. Adwen began to slowly pace around the monster.

Kotig looked up and snarled. Where her foot had struck his head was burned. Turning over, he roared and charged again.

Stepping aside, she swiftly brought an elbow down into his back, slamming him to the pavement.

A new burn smoked on his mangy hide. The monster got

up and slashed continuously in a blind rage. She was too fast and the attempts counted for nothing. Outraged, he lunged to grab her around the middle and she avoided him, jumping back a couple of yards. The white hound's stare never wavered.

His black bulk leaped with jaws open wide. As he was over her, one of Adwen's clawed hands knifed through the air. Long fingers pierced his chest. There the werewolf was suspended and frozen, suddenly weightless. Then she roared and pure light filled him, blasting out of open jaws and lidless eyes. When the rays of gold vanished, Kotig was reduced to a cloud of ash. The werewolf dissipated, consumed by the next passing breeze.

Finished purging of the monster, she took back her hand and glanced at the restaurant.

Kayla could not move as the white creature reverted back into the copper-skinned woman from before. This was Shari? Speechless, she watched her go to the truck.

With the back of a clawed hand, she gently stroked the glass on the driver side door. The engine suddenly roared into life and it opened as if to invite her inside.

Kayla's jaw dropped.

Two golden eyes gestured for her to join in the passenger seat. She was terrified, but found herself obeying. Racing out and getting in, the pickup backed out of the lot and drove off long before the police arrived.

The truck was parked on the shoulder of a country road outside of town when Adwen came to. She woke slowly at first, but then with a start, ready to fight. Whipping her head around, she found herself in the driver seat. Kotig was nowhere to be seen.

Completely confused, she found Kayla beside her. She looked afraid, but unharmed. Calming down, Adwen asked, "Where's Kotig? What happened back there and how did we --"

"He's gone," Kayla told her urgently. "You need to go see your family."

A few brief images passed through her mind. She didn't

recall everything that happened after being knocked out, but remembered killing Kotig. Why couldn't she remember everything? She had been knocked out, hadn't she?

"Shari, you need to see your family. Did you hear me?"

Catching a glimpse of herself in the rearview mirror, Adwen felt sick at the thought. She shook her head. "I can't. They can't see me like this."

"Shari, please!"

"Look at me!" Adwen yelled and growled. After taking a breath, she stopped growling. "Why do you want me to go see them? My name is Adwen now. Shari is dead. My parents and my brother and sister don't want to see Adwen. They want Shari Gates. I can't give them that."

Tears swelled in Kayla's eyes as she was shaken by the outburst.

Turning away to look out the window, she sighed. A moment of silence went by until Adwen conceded, "If you still think I should go... then we better get moving."

Very relieved, she dried her eyes.

Adwen paused. Staring perplexed at the steering wheel and clutch, she blinked and asked, "Uh, could we trade seats?"

"Why? What's wrong?"

"I can't drive stick."

Uncertainty was agony. A few more miles down the road was the old farm house Shari spent her whole life in. Certain they would not recognize her, she was resigned to doing as Kayla asked. If worst came to worst they could both get back in the truck and leave. However, the fear of being rejected gnawed at Adwen's insides.

Pulling into the driveway at last, Kayla turned off the ignition. "What are you afraid of? You jumped at that monster and killed it without flinching. Why are you so scared to see your family?"

Adwen shifted uncomfortably. "Yeah, well, Kotig was predictable. Plus, if he hated me, I wouldn't care."

"Come on. I'll knock." They left the truck and went to the porch, shaded by a star-leafed maple.

The family Doberman came over, growling, "Who are you, stranger?" Then the dog sniffed and became excited, panting and wriggling. "You're back! I missed you so much! Pat me! Pat my head for old time's sake!"

"I missed you too." Adwen smiled and humored the loyal pet.

The dog paused and stared after understanding what she had said.

Adwen followed her friend closely with the dog licking her hand. Then as Kayla knocked, Adwen lost her nerve, darting around the corner of the house. Listening from the hiding place, there came the sound of the door opening.

"Kayla! What are you doing here? I was just thinking about you. Do you want to come in for a little while?"

Recognizing her mother's voice, she peered out from the corner.

"In a moment." Kayla smiled. "But first, I've brought someone to see you."

Adwen knew that was her cue. Each step closer to the doorstep felt like walking on thin ice. Sarah looked older. There were lines from worry on her face and more coloring in her hair to mask gray.

She saw Adwen and didn't know what was happening, confused as to who this strange barefooted girl could be.

Her heart pounded. When her own mother still didn't recognize her, she dropped her gaze. "Sorry if I'm bothering you, but..."

Sarah gasped.

Looking up, Adwen watched her hand cover her mouth.

Tears filled her eyes as she whispered. "Shari!" She leaped forward and wrapped her arms around her, sobbing.

Holding her, she soothed. "It is okay, Mom. It's all right. I made it back."

They went inside and both siblings were playing video games upstairs. As they came down, Maria recognized her instantly and raced over to hug her tight.

Tony was skeptical. "Who are you and why are you doing this to my mom? You're not my sister."

Letting go, Adwen smiled. "Has anyone ever found out about the time you broke one of Mom's favorite CDs and hid the pieces under Dad's truck tire to make it look like an accident?"

They all watched his jaw drop. "That is you, isn't it?"

"I guess it is." She laughed as he came over to hug her as well. "Where's Dad?"

"He's at the river," her cheerful sister replied. "He's been going to shoot guns a lot lately, but he'll be back soon."

"Where have you been?" her mother asked. "What happened to you?"

Adwen could hardly believe this. They all knew who she was despite the changes. She was back with her family, safe and sound. Smiling happily, she slumped into the recliner and shook her head.

"I don't know how to start. It all sounds too crazy, but..."

A sense of great danger suddenly tingled in the back of her mind. She felt sick. No, she thought, not now that I'm home.

The expression of horror confused them all and Kayla asked, "What's wrong?"

A window shattered and Adwen was struck in the head by a high caliber round.

Her mother screamed as she was bowled over, landing face-down on the floor. Before anyone could move, five armed men dressed in black Kevlar and masks burst into the room. The intruders held them at gunpoint while others searched every room. Once they were sure no one else was inside their leader spoke gruffly into a radio.

"We found the family, sir, but there was someone else here. The individual has already been neutralized. It looks like a female."

A deep voice replied, "Move the family out in ten minutes. Keep them quiet. I'll be taking care of Daddy. Have your men confirm the hit and bring the body out last."

"Yes, sir."

Adwen was alive, having healed in seconds. Playing possum, she laid still and waited. A gun muzzle began to prod her head as her mother and sister sobbed on the sofa.

The man knew she had been shot, but saw no blood. He took a firm hold of white hair, lifting her head off the carpet.

Adwen swiftly planted one foot on the floor and kicked the intruder into a wall. There was a small gasp as he dropped dead and the other gunmen yelled, quickly opening fire. The shots that hit her did nothing. Once wounds healed, silver glistening fluid shined and dissipated without touching the ground.

In the blink of an eye she snarled and punched a man through the broken window, kicked another up into the ceiling then tackled the next, crushing him against a wall of river rocks and concrete. None of the fallen moved. Those who still lived breathed laboriously.

One remained. He shouted, holding a gun to Sarah's head, backing away into the kitchen.

Frightened and quivering, her mother didn't resist. Large tears streaked makeup beneath light blue eyes.

Adwen glared and snarled, showing pearly fangs. "Let go of my mother."

Falling silent, the man hid farther behind Sarah like a shield.

Adwen's eyes flashed gold and she let out a thundering growl.

Startled, the man panicked and pointed the weapon at the eerie woman instead.

There was a bright flash. Adwen was suddenly standing with her face in his. The intruder's gun arm extended over her shoulder.

Sarah pulled free from the loosened hold, darting to safety.

Adwen's smooth black lips curled into a sneer. Gripping the stunned man's throat, she lifted him and threw him headlong into the side of the kitchen, knocking down photos, shattering glass.

Then Maria cried out, "Shari! It's Dad! He's outside!"

Giving a nod, she bolted for the backyard.

Nick aimed the .44 revolver with Korig in his sights, face set in a hard grimace.

The thug casually stalked closer wearing a jagged grin.

Whoever was threatening him had no fear of the gun pointed at him and that smile made Nick's skin crawl. If they came too close he would shoot to kill.

Both gave a start as Adwen slid between them, staring down the bearded fiend with a vengeance.

Surprised and intrigued, the werewolf chuckled. "Well, well! Who might you be, pretty little elf?"

Nick bellowed a warning. "Get out of the way!"

"Stay back, Dad," she yelled with a growl. "He's mine!"

Maintaining his aim, Nick felt his heart skip a beat.

The werewolf was surprised and very pleased. "Adwen! I was told you were dead!" He laughed. "Well, it seems my master's attempt has failed."

"Tell me who your boss is!"

"I don't think so." Giving a sly smirk, he spoke into the radio. "Hey, Brother. I've found an old friend of ours back from beyond the shallow grave." There was no answer. "Brother? Kotig? Damn you, answer!"

"He's not going to pick up."

His irritation mounted at the insinuation. "Impossible!"

"Then how about I prove it?" she replied, growling.

Enraged, he transformed and roared, making Nick back away. Then the man stumbled in shock when Adwen changed. She became a snow-white hound being and the light in her violet eyes burned.

Korig rushed her and she threw a swift punch that struck the monster's jaw. The werewolf staggered and stumbled from the force. Shaking off the momentary daze, he felt the burn from her touch and stared, hungry but hesitant.

When Korig found his footing they circled one another. Both growled as Korig was uncertain and she waited for his patience to wear thin.

Adwen's eyes suddenly flashed gold. An epiphany came to her. She stopped circling to cock her head, contemplating the idea. Holding out open arm in an inviting display, she growled, "How about a free bite? On the house."

He was suspicious and growled, "What are you doing?"

Confidently, she replied, "Consider it payment for the death of your brother."

For a moment the werewolf gaged Adwen's uncharacteristic confidence, but he could not resist. *"Don't mind if I do!"*

Like a steel trap, his maw came down onto her strong elegant neck.

Baring her own jaws at the pain, she allowed him sink his fangs deeper. At any moment, he would be very sorry.

Korig soon paused and quickly let go. He fell back, reeling and howling in agony. Silver blood filled his red jaws, trickling down his throat. Every place the shining liquid touched sizzled and smoked. The monstrous werewolf writhed on the ground, flailing and burning.

For as evil as he was, she found herself pitying him. Korig's frantic spasms diminished before Adwen took him by the throat as if he weighed nothing. Her wounds gradually healed as she recalled destroying Kotig and felt energy building in her free hand, making it glow. Prepared to knife her claws for his heart, she snarled, "This is for threatening my family!"

Adwen plunged them into his chest. The released energy burst out through frozen eyes and jaws as bright white light. The blast of power dissipated and then the beast met the same fate as his brother, fading into dark dust and ash.

She growled as the last remnants drifted out of sight.

The sound of her father's amazement caught her ear and she turned to look. He was shuddering with the magnum held high.

When she took a step toward him, he bellowed and his voice cracked. "Stay back!"

She paused, but inched slowly closer. The gun could not harm her.

There was an explosive crack and she yelped, buckling over and cradling her stomach. When the gunshot wound healed, silver blood shimmered into nothing and she stood with ears down and whined. "Dad, it is okay. It's me."

He was unable to understand. Nick fired again as she kept coming. The confounded man pulled the trigger again and again, making her cry out repeatedly. Soon the bullets were spent and she stood over him.

Throwing the empty pistol at her, he began to sob and punch her solid body with all his might. His efforts were wasted and he yelled between sobs. "Die, die, you monster! I want my daughter back! Give me my daughter!"

Adwen wrapped long arms around him as he cried. He sobbed and eventually stopped fighting, tears soaking feather-soft fur.

Her animal voice whimpered back. "I missed you, too. I'm so sorry I didn't say goodbye."

He couldn't understand, but it made no difference.

The loud beeping of a car horn got their attention.

Kayla sat in her truck and everyone else waited in the van, calling to them.

When Adwen saw their faces, her eyes flashed with gold. A powerful urge took over, making her shoulders sag and ears droop miserably. Ruefully, she gave her father a gentle push.

He turned around, shaking his head. "I'm not leaving without you."

She wanted to go with them so badly, but a powerful feeling tugged her in a different direction. Somehow she knew staying would put them all in greater danger. Adwen's heart ached at seeing them calling. Adwen's family kept calling, even when she bolted to the open fields, headed to the nearby forest.

Chapter 26
JUSTICE, PEACE AND LAW

The creek twisted and wound through rocky wooded terrain, riddled with countless deer trails. Making her way down natural granite shelves, she approached the water's edge. A hot summer strangled the flow and she knelt low, gazing into the mirror surface, shifting into her elf-like form.

Overwhelmed, she murmured to herself, "Why is this happening?"

A woman's voice answered, "Because you are Adwen."

Startled, she stood and backed away from three women who stood side by side in white robes. Their eyes fixed upon her intently.

The appearance of the strangers was without warning, leaving Adwen alarmed and off guard. "Who are you? What do you want?"

The blond woman's chortle was sweet and sincere. "We are here to help."

"We are friends, after all." The redhead nodded.

A moment passed and their guises changes within the snowy linens. Each became less like a reflection of one another. The statuesque women became a trio of very familiar faces.

Lacey smiled. "Don't look too surprised. You should have guessed we were not just playing games in the library for all those years. We are the Spirits of Order, dedicated to the survival of light and life. We are your mentors."

The declaration astonished then frustrated her. "Why didn't you tell me who you were?"

Judy shook her head. "You were not ready. We had to watch and see who you were as a simple human girl. The three of us have judged you for the length of our friendship."

"For what?" she asked reproachfully.

"To know if you would be the warrior you were meant to

be," Pearl soothed. "To see if you would selflessly defend simple humans of any race or creed, or even those who have tainted hearts. Here is where your true journey begins."

She was shaken. "Did one of you push me into the river?"

Frowning, they shook their heads and Lacey answered. "That was not our doing. We armed you with knowledge so that when the day came you would not be without a defense. There are two realms of the living, Adwen. You were born into the one ruled by logic. To let you be thrown into the opposite one without aid would have been far too cruel. We have come to care for you."

Not knowing what else to ask, she sighed. "Then what do I do now?"

Pearl replied, "We have gifts before sending you on the right path. Come closer."

Hesitantly, she forded the stream and approached.

Judy spoke with cool distinction. "As you travel there shall be more terrifying foes than you ever thought possible. My gift is small, but shall be of great use." Holding out a hand, she offered a glowing wisp of light.

Adwen reached for it and the glint leaped to meld with her gloves. Armor pieces materialized with golden studs on the knuckles.

Judy proudly folded her arms. "The Hands of Justice are my gift. I trust that you will use them well."

Adwen admired the weapons as Pearl came forward.

"My gift is not of force or strength. I have always been your peaceful friend and that shall never change." She lent her own piece of light and it drifted down to became a pure white cloth, draping around her neck.

"Sometimes the best choice in times of danger is to hide. In the absence of true sunlight, don this hood. You will be invisible to the most perceptive of eyes, even those who belong to the darkness. Wherever sunlight touches you while wearing this hood you will be revealed."

When Adwen finished feeling the soft cloth, Lacey stepped closer.

"My gift for you is knowledge. You have the power to travel between the two realms of logic and magic. Though you may bring others through these gateways, only you may open the corridors. Find the passages and apply their many benefits to your ultimate goal."

"And what is that?"

"Answers to questions you've had since the beginning shall come to you soon. Patience."

"Will they tell me why you call me Adwen?"

Lacey shook her head, amused. "We did not name you. You have been Adwen since before you were born."

Feeling weary, she sighed. "I'm tired of being confused. Please, just tell me what is going on. What if I go the wrong way or make a stupid mistake?"

The three spirits changed back into their pristine, eerie forms. "The journey for you is as important as the destination. You shall never go astray, Adwen. Have faith. You only have to continue what you have always done."

Disappointed, Adwen frowned. "And what have I been doing?"

Pearl beamed. "Following your heart."

Her words melted Adwen's mounting anxiety, like always. It was clear that these entities truly were her friends.

In unison, the three Spirits of Order bowed their heads.

As they did she sensed a strange energy from behind. Light rippled as a large orb manifested, suspended in mid air. Waves of translucent colors coursed from the center like a newborn star.

Turning back, she asked, "Is this one of the gates?"

There was no one; the spirits had gone.

Mustering up some determination, she prepared for whatever lay beyond the mystic portal. Adwen clenched teeth that swiftly became jaws as she became the snow white hound. She growled and leaped headlong into the swirling light. When she vanished, it too was gone without a trace.

Chapter 27
MURDERER

An enormous waterfall roared into the earth and rocks. The endless torrent created a vast pool where the sun was high and tall trees were a lush leafy green. A soft breeze blew as the gate opened by the top of the falls and Adwen plummeted into the water with a great splash.

Quickly resurfacing, she swam to the sloshing shoreline. She eventually reached the rocky shallows then stood on all fours, rigorously shaking water from her coat. Droplets flew everywhere in a sparkling spray. Standing upright, she looked around. The sight filled her with awe as sunlight shone over the cascade, illuminating rising mist. Closing her eyes, she took a deep breath, feeling the warmth of the sun. She could smell the sweetness of magic in the air.

"I'm back."

Then her sixth sense warned of an impending attack. She whipped round, ready for the figure charging through the shallows; a knight without a helm. Her sharp eyesight saw his shoulder-length brown hair, long features and harsh green eyes.

Oryn drew his sword and prepared to strike.

Instantly in a rage, she roared, *"Murderer!"* Anger twisted her jaws into a fierce snarl as she leaped through the air.

Focused and alert, the knight saw the golden stripe on the creature's face between violet eyes. For a moment, the eyes flashed gold and the mark briefly took the shape of a golden symbol that he knew well.

The sight of the mark broke his concentration. Aggressive abated into dumbstruck awe, swiftly ending his charge while the creature loomed. The symbol was soon gone and the eyes returned to violet. Jaw dropped, he watched as the white beast landed in the shallows before him. With lightning speed, it slashed his chest armor, sending him flying.

Flexing claws, she roared far louder. *"Murderer!"*

The knight was vulnerable and Adwen lunged again. Leaping through the air, her jaws opened wide to rip flesh from bone.

As her jaws were inches from the knight, a thick tree root snatched her out of the air. Adwen roared and went into a wild frenzy, snapping and tearing at wood while it coiled around her arms and middle. Fangs ripped off chunks and tossed them aside, but it did not release her.

The root twisted back on itself, holding her over dry land. The man who commanded the muddy tendril made it hold her just out of reach. He looked her over while she continued to fight. Of average height with medium length blond hair, most of his locks were held back by a red cloth that served as an patch for his left eye. The one-eyed attacker had long elf ears and wore simple traveling clothes.

Once she noticed him, she let the root alone to snap and snarl voraciously. *"Let me go!"*

He was unafraid and tilted his head. "Adwen? Is that you?"

Ceasing her snarling, ears became erect with surprise. "Toth?" Her body shifted within the restricting root into woman form.

Toth looked as if he could laugh out loud. "Adwen! It really is you!"

As he stammered and attempted to converse, she cleared her throat. "Uh, Toth? Could you, uh, let me down first?"

Taken aback, he chuckled. "Oh! My apologies. I hardly recognized you." Sweeping a hand through the air, he dismissed the root and it retracted into the earth.

Raising an eyebrow, she gave her friend a disturbed look. "That's pretty creepy, Toth. I take it some weird stuff happened after I left."

"So much has happened. We searched everywhere for you!"

While he continued spewing out his excitement, Oryn staggered to his feet. Slick rocks made it difficult, but once he gained balance, he stood with sword in hand. The knight gazed at the eerie woman. He knew immediately who she was;

somehow, it was her. He gawked as Adwen's violet eyes glanced his way.

Toth rambled on, not realizing she did not hear a word, until she held up a finger and excused herself. "Could you hold that thought for a minute? I'll be right back."

"Oh, sure."

Entranced by her, Oryn stood like a flabbergasted statue.

She could see he was surprised. Cool and collected, she gracefully stepped through the rippling shore to stop before him. They gazed at one another for a long moment of silence.

He remained captivated and stared into her brilliant eyes. When he blinked at last, he failed to see her fist fly for his jaw. He was rendered unconscious and collapsed into the water.

Toth gave a start and dashed after them.

Grabbing his chest plate with both hands, she lifted him up and screamed in his face.

"Did you think you would get away with it? Did you seriously think you could do that to me?"

His head lulled pathetically.

The half-elf reached her side and pleaded. "What are you doing?"

Growling, she asked in a deadly tone, "Haven't you been listening? Your friend killed me! Right after I saved the princess from the river, he snuck up behind and murdered me!"

He was abashed. "What are you talking about? The day Dead River flooded Oryn was with me. He never left my sight. How could he have killed you?"

Snarling, she snapped, "That's easy. He..."

The moment suddenly returned to her. She had been looking over the ledge at the muddy water. Then the princess screamed and she turned around. There had been someone standing by Eyrie, pointing a weapon.

It was a handgun. Just before he fired, she saw he was wearing a mask. Crested with long purple feathers, it resembled a wicked grinning cat.

The memory of her death subsided, leaving an empty sensation. Her killer had been the masquerader from the party. How did he get a gun? There were no guns in the realm of magic.

She felt the weight of Toth's hand on her shoulder and she

came to. Oryn was hanging by her grip, groaning as he began to reawaken.

Toth reassured her. "He didn't do it, Adwen. What are you talking about?"

Once the moment of revelation was over, she let him drop face-first into the shallows and walked away. Reaching dry land, she stopped, clenched her fists and screamed out all of her rage. The deafening roar echoed through the surrounding forest, frightening birds from trees. Finally dropping to her knees, she swore quietly. "The whole time... the whole time it was him. He was right underneath my nose!"

The water spurred Oryn's recovery. He coughed violently as Toth helped him up. Angrily shrugging him off, he felt his sore jaw and glared at Adwen. He was enraged by the sucker punch and took his sword back from where he dropped it among the stones. Prepared for a fight, he called to her.

"Dog! How dare you? You hide away for a year's time and return only to insult me! Turn and face me!"

Lost in contemplation, she ignored him.

"Face me, dog! I challenge you! Turn and face me!"

Adwen's magical voice could be heard over the roaring of the falls. "Leave me alone, knight. I'm not in the mood for games."

Then he sneered. "You're even more of a coward than I recall."

Her eyes flashed and she slowly stood. Turning around, she glared. "All right, I accept your challenge."

Aware of the coming fight, Toth backed away to dry land.

As Oryn found a strong stance on smooth rocks, a gleam of excitement appeared on his face.

Staring him down, she cocked her head glowered. "I'm going to take your sword and I'm going to beat you with it."

He thought the threat was quaint.

Silently, they sized each other up. She flexed powerful hands and knuckles crackled.

She made the first move. Breaking into a charge, she leapt into the air, headed straight for him.

The knight smiled and brought back his sword, ready to bat her down with the flat of the blade. His weapon arced for her side.

But then she did something strange. Just before the sword could connect, her body shimmered and there was a flash.

Adwen vanished from blade's reach and reappeared between his arms. Adwen's back brushed against his chest plate. His eyes widened and she was too swift. The breath caught in his throat as her knee came up, knocking the sword from his hand. She snatched it out of the air, and before he could flinch, her elbows came back into his chest.

They dented his armor and bowled him backward in the shallows. Oryn attempted to sit up, staring in disbelief as she turned, feathery hair tossed about by the wind. Violet eyes burned in the shade of her brow. In a single leap, she went up high and pounced. Bare feet landed on his chest armor and she brought the sword driving down.

Oryn's heart raced. The sword entered the water between rocks inches from his cheek. The side of his face reflected in the flat of the silver-steel.

She knelt low, leaning in close and growled before speaking.

"You lose."

She threw a fist for his other cheek, rendering him unconscious yet again. Satisfied, she felt no more rage and was calm.

Toth called out. "Please bring him out of the water. If you hadn't knocked him out, I could have helped him back to camp myself."

Adwen did not mind at all. "Sure. No problem."

The knight's sword in one hand, she grasped Oryn by his armor with the other. She followed after the half-elf, dragging him along rough terrain, smiling to herself.

Fanger and Ulna were tethered in a clearing and both stared dumbstruck as she brought Oryn along.

Ranger snorted. "So, the cur returns."

Ulna whinnied nervously. "Don't pester her, Ranger. She's obviously stronger than before. Mind your manners."

Smiling as she passed, she set Oryn against a tree and took a seat on the opposite side of the fire by Toth. They both glanced when he groaned, but he was still unconscious.

"You've changed a lot." Toth beamed happily. "You look well."

"You've changed too. You look different. I hardly recognized you back there."

He glanced down and gently touched the cloth covering his eye. "Some things in my appearance have changed."

"It's not that. You seem so much more confident. You seem... strong."

Taking his hand away, he gave a modest smile.

"But the longer haircut and the eye patch didn't make it easy, either. Not hiding your ears anymore?"

He chuckled. "We missed you."

"You and maybe the horses, but you don't mean that *he* missed me, do you?"

"He was frantic when we lost your trail. He had an absolute fit that you'd disappeared, acting as if the world was going to end. Where did you go?"

"Yes, dog. Do tell?" Oryn grumbled. He had awoken and sneered. "Where did you run off to hide for all of this time?"

"Glad to see you haven't changed one bit."

Feeling uncomfortable, the knight examined his chest plate. There was a massive scratch and two concave dents. Had he not been in armor he would be dead, but he was more disappointed with the state of the armor.

Adwen was curious. "Where's your helm? I'm surprised you weren't wearing it."

"It was destroyed," Toth answered.

"What? How?"

"Where your trail ended we followed the river. Farther down were three sets of tracks. There were large boot prints from a man, smaller human prints and close to the ledge were giant dog prints."

She grinned toothily and chuckled. "Those were me."

"So you managed to change at will?" After admiring her, he continued, "Your tracks and the smaller human ones never left the river while those of the booted man wondered off. Could you make sense of that?"

"The smaller person was Princess Eyrie. The kidnapper took her after he killed me."

Toth's eyes went wide and Oryn stopped fussing over his armor to stare.

Her friend was aghast. "Did you see who it was?"

"It was someone from the masquerade ball. He was tall

with a mask that can hypnotize and confuse, shaped like a grinning cat."

"I remember seeing you dance with him," Oryn mused.

"That was the guy. That was the kidnapper."

"I've seen a drawing of the mask before. It's the Mask of Deceit; a perfect disguise for the wicked and powerful to elude suspicion. Very few can ever recall sightings."

"Well, we saw it."

"We followed the river for a few days," Toth continued. "We couldn't give up searching for the princess and turned back and follow the tracks east. We hunted for months on end through the woods and towns until the wastelands. It is a dangerous place without proper supplies. When we were fully prepared and could no longer wait for you, we set out.

"After two weeks of trekking we found a tree. An old oak grows out there. By my reckoning, it was the better part a thousand years old. When we went too close, we were attacked. It is odd venturing into the plains only to find a very angry mountain golem. He was twenty feet tall and had buried himself among the roots. It knocked Ulna and me over, trying to quash Oryn and Ranger. When it couldn't catch him, it turned and came for me. They blocked its way and it shattered Oryn's helm. When it came for me again it swung one of its arms and a stray rock flew, hitting my eye."

He touched his fingertips to the cloth thoughtfully. "Something came over me. I called out to the ancient oak and the roots ripped the thing to pieces. We made our way back to the woods with the little food left in our bags. The tracks of the villain ended a mile before we found the tree. They simply vanished."

"I'm sorry I wasn't there to help, Toth."

"If you had been present, we might have caught the kidnapper." Oryn glowered. "If you hadn't run off to hide for a year."

Perturbed, she scowled. "I had been dead up until a few hours ago when I woke up in my world. At least, I'm pretty sure I was dead. I remember seeing spirits and being chased by thousands of demons."

Hardly paying any mind, he took out his knife and pointed it at her. "I know you are lying. Only one has ever ventured from the land of the dead."

Folding arms smartly, she rolled her eyes. "Well, it's true."

She watched him ignore her and start cutting off lox of hair in brisk, frustrated swipes. He gradually cut it back to its shorter length, keeping cheek-length bangs.

She shook her head and chuckled. "What are you doing?"

"Correcting an oversight. It hindered my vision."

Adwen began to laugh. "You're going to blame what happened back there on your haircut? Seriously?"

Glaring threateningly, he sawed off another lock.

"Do you know where the princess might be?" Toth asked.

"I don't know. Whoever took her had been trying to get me killed. He wanted me to follow. I don't know why, but I'm sure the princess is still alive somewhere." Her eyes flashed gold and she added, "I think we should start by going back to that tree in the wastes."

"We can begin at dawn." Toth turned to the knight. "What do you say to that?"

Oryn continued sawing at hair and grumbled. "High time."

Four moons were high late in the night. The campfire crackled as Oryn was roused from his sleep. His jaw hurt terribly. Once realizing Adwen was missing, he glowered, thinking she might be trying to disappear again.

Her trail led back to the falls. As the natural wonder came into view, he spotted her. She perched on a rock out by the deep end with back turned. He was about to yell and chastise, but realized she had no clothes on.

His eyes went wide and he ducked behind a broad tree. As his heart raced he heard a splash. Looking out from the hiding place, Oryn saw Adwen had dove into the water. The knight watched her surface, treading water under the pale moonlight. Surprise grew when she was joined by two creatures. Sirens met her and she looked nervous, but that passed once they started tending to her hair. The spirits laughed and sounded like burbling brooks as Adwen's eyes sparkled.

Oryn was breathless. No knight had sighted a nymph of any kind in centuries. He thought he must be dreaming and lingered, knowing the enchanting scene would never leave him for as long as he lived.

Chapter 28
WITCH OR WARLOCK

Oryn awoke in the cool morning to find he was alone. His body was sore, but not so much as his jaw. He massaged it gingerly after getting up and searched for the others. It eased his frustration when Toth was not difficult to find.

He stood with the horses beneath a towering beech tree. All three gazed upward as he approached. "What are you all staring at?"

To answer, the half-elf pointed.

An object was high in the tree bathed in dawn's first light, brilliant rays flowing across the surface like a firestorm. It was Adwen. Sunlight that touched her skin swirled and wove across her body in streams of gold.

As the sun cleared the horizon the light stopped dancing at last. Adwen smiled and sighed in contentment.

Oryn murmured before turning back to the clearing. "Retrieve the dog. We must depart."

"Adwen! We're setting out shortly."

She hadn't noticed her audience. A clever grin parted her lips. "Just a second!"

To his horror, Adwen jump and plummet for the ground. As she landed nimbly before them, the horses gave a start. She laughed as the startled half-elf held a hand to his heart.

"Forewarn me when you intend to do things like that. You had me worried."

She raised an eyebrow. "Well, it's about time you worried about something."

Both of the horses neighed in amusement and he shook his head.

The forest around them was rich with birdsong and the

scent of pine. Toth was in good spirits, Adwen was content strolling along between them and Oryn was as disgruntled as ever. His sore jaw hurt even more and the pain compelled him to use it regardless. Because the princess hadn't been found, he had been unable to return to the order. Missing his personal captain's quarters and clean bed linens, the knight was looking for a head to lay the blame upon.

"If you hadn't run after the fiend without my company, all of this could have been avoided. Because of your foolishness, the fiend is gone along with the princess. We may never find them now, dog."

Unperturbed, Adwen smiled. "She's alive somewhere and we are going to find her. And if your jaw hurts so much, why don't you be smart and shut up?"

Her smart-aleck response further aggravated him. "And now that you've returned we shall need to be on our guard. I have little doubt the Bloody Brothers will show themselves. I learned from Toth that you attract them like bees to pollen."

A clever grin split her face. "You sound so sure."

"What is so amusing?"

"To put it bluntly, they are both dust. They no longer exist."

"You destroyed the Bloody Brothers unassisted? Impossible."

Toth was quite pleased and silently celebrated in Ulna's saddle.

"You don't have to take my word for it. Keep a look out for them all you like. They are never coming back."

They traveled all day and stopped for the night. She caught a deer for their dinner and finished what they could not. While they feasted, the half-elf and she shared stories of misadventures by the fire, laughing as Oryn sat quietly and brooded. The knight allowed Adwen to stand watch, considering the chance that she may be telling the truth regarding the Bloody Brother's demise.

The following morning they pushed the horses hard, reaching the forest's edge by noon where the wastelands began. Deceptively pleasant looking plains were a gentle shade of green due to spring rain storms. Relentless winds rippled the vast waves like a verdant sea. Strong gusts were harsh, pulling at their hair and garments.

Toth pointed off into the distance. "It is several days ride if you know where to search. We have enough supplies so we may begin immediately. You should be able to catch food enough for us to survive."

Adwen hardly heard a word. Her eyes flashed gold and a sudden realization came to her. She could not understand where the idea came from, but did not care. It was helpful.

Musing at the strange idea, she asked, "What if we could get there today?"

The men exchanged looks and the knight shook his head. "Unless you intend to fly us there, find patience."

Saying nothing, she smiled to herself. Adwen transformed and followed the horses over the first hill, bounding in white hound form. Without the knowledge of the knight and the half-elf, she spoke with the horses.

"Want to go a little faster?"

Ranger snorted. "We must pace ourselves, mutt. It is a long way."

"Not that far, if you do as I say."

The horses paid close attention as she gave instructions.

Oryn soon noticed her communicating with the beasts. He was about to reprimand her until something strange happened. Adwen howled and the other beasts brayed proudly in answer. Their bodies shone a pale gold, invigorated with power. Suddenly, they took off like shooting stars. The riders clung to their shimmering mounts for dear life. Wind pressed like a hurricane, threatening to rip them from the saddles. When the knight and half-elf were beginning to tire and barely held on, their horses started to slow. Gradually, the glow left their now clean coats and they trotted along.

The men were braver and raised their heads. Before them stood the ancient oak of the wastes. They had arrived.

Coming to a stop beside the tree's great girth, Adwen reverted to woman form and whooped loudly. "We've gotta do that again sometime!"

Toth was exhausted. "I might have enjoyed it more if it hadn't lasted so long. I thought you agreed to warn me when you next tried something odd."

"Sorry, Toth. I was talking to the horses."

The animals neighed with delight. They were not the least bit tired, having borrowed her energy for the journey.

Ranger shook his mane. "You should have acted sooner, mutt."

Giggling to herself, she went to inspect the peculiar tree.

Climbing down was difficult for both men. Saddle-sore, Toth touched solid ground to find his legs were rubbery and gave out. Struggling back to his feet, he heard her laugh.

"Are you all right?"

"I'm fine." He winced at the stiffness. "I just need to stretch myself a moment."

She continued to inspect the thick, rough bark. Her senses detected old magic. The others followed until she came across an indentation. It was shallow, oval and very smooth.

Frowning, the knight stated, "I don't recall that being there."

The groove was the size of a dinner plate with a faint symbol in the center. Brushing away at bits of dirt to see it better, she didn't recognize it.

Perplexed, she asked, "What is that?"

Becoming suspicious, he replied wonderingly, "I know this mark well. It is the symbol of the Order. It was the mark of Darien Andredan, the Master Knight. The symbol stands for his five virtues: faith, courage, compassion, mercy and hope. Let it alone. It is likely that the last to touch it was Darien himself."

"It looks like it's there naturally. Was Darien an elf?"

"No one knows of his origin, save for one elf. He vanished as well. Now stop touching the Mark of Andredan. You do not have the right."

While she paid no attention to the knight's shortening temper, her eyes flashed gold again. "That looks almost perfect for a big hand, doesn't it?" Against the knight's wishes, she transformed and gently pressed a hand into the shallow shape.

For a moment nothing happened, but then her hand began to glow with white light and it pulsed outward, running through every crack and bend, making the tree shudder. When the oak began to twist, groan and contort before their widening eyes, they backed away.

"What have you done?!"

The oak continued to shift and move until it created a giant living arch with a weaving stairway up to its center. A rippling, glowing light gate materialized. The shimmering, transparent orb sat at the center of the arch, waiting for Adwen and her company to enter.

After changing back, she announced, "We're going through that."

Stunned by the sight, the knight shook his head. "No. There's no knowing what awaits on the other side."

"I know where this goes. This is a gate to my world, the place where I was born. Take only what we can carry. The horses will have to stay behind."

Toth nodded and went to gather a few supplies from Ulna's saddle.

Outraged, Oryn stepped up to her and sneered. "You are not in the position to be giving orders, dog. We are not entering the portal."

Not intimidated, she placed a hand on her hip. "I'm going to count to ten, and whatever you can get from your horse, you can bring."

He glared as she started the countdown.

"Ten... nine... eight... seven ..."

He watched her finish counting then let loose a series of barks and growls to the horses. Then they whinnied and bolted away. Toth only just finished gathering the essentials into his old satchel. Wide-eyed, the men watched their steeds shimmer with a dose of Adwen's power for protection and speed, disappearing amid the rolling hills.

Oryn bellowed, "How dare you! You are not leading this quest! Summon the horses before I cut off your head!"

Folding her arms, she cooed, "Oh, I'm shaking in my boots. In case you haven't noticed, you don't have control. You are just going to have to deal with it."

Furious, he held a finger in her face. "I'm warning you. We are not to enter that gate and you are to call the horses."

"What are you going to do to me? Fight me? You're only going to lose."

He grabbed her roughly by the wrist, twisting her around in a disabling maneuver.

She was far too strong and fast. Reversing his hold, she

twirled and held him in the same position, with an arm behind his back.

In response, Oryn reached down and snatched up one of her ankles.

As he pulled hard, she used her immense strength to escape by flipping out of his grip up into the air. In a split second, she landed on her feet over and behind. Before he could react, she snatched both his wrists and pressed his face down into the grassy turf.

Unable to free himself, he grunted, tasting the earth.

Folding his arms gently behind him, she leaned in close.

The knight was unable to look back and see her eyes shining a brilliant gold. What he did notice was a distinct change in the nature of her voice and choice in words. It was calm and collected like a teacher to an unruly pupil.

"This is pointless. If you wish to get what you want, you must stop these attempts at assertion over me. You have never changed and change is what you need. Stop fighting me, start listening, and most of all, open your eyes, knight."

She released him and by the time he faced her Adwen's eyes returned to normal along with her nature. It left Oryn confounded.

"We are going in whether you like it or not, even if I have to throw you. So how is this going to be?"

Starting up the steps, she turned her back and was soon joined by the curious and eager half-elf.

Oryn stared after her in confusion. Something in Adwen was clearly beyond him and the fact was disturbing. When he saw them waiting, he swallowed injured pride and followed.

Passing through the shimmering portal, they were instantly enveloped by the shadows of a small cave. Oryn could see her leading Toth to the exit by a riverside. Once he caught up sunlight dazzled his eyes.

Cocking an eyebrow at the water, he huffed. "This looks no different from where we were." Then he saw them gazing back over the cave and she was grinning.

The sounds of the river were almost equal to that of the bridge traffic. Oryn's jaw dropped like Toth's as they gawked at cars driving past.

Laughing at the dumbfounded looks, she beckoned,

"Welcome to my home, boys! Let's get going. There's a lot more to see."

The knight continued to stare. "More?"

She led the way up the embankment to a sidewalk. As they went along the bridge, she anticipated their lack of attention to traffic. The two were ogling absentmindedly and Toth was about to step off of the curb. When she caught his arm, pulling him out of the way of a speeding SUV, the driver honked his horn angrily.

Rattled, Toth was short of breath. "This world is treacherous."

The knight replied, "There are as many distractions as there are dangers."

They continued on and passing drivers stared at their medieval attire. Adwen explained as much as she could while they walked to ensure her companions avoided more trouble.

"To where are you leading us?" Toth asked as they waited at another traffic light.

The knight caught on much quicker to rules of traveling. He thought some of the streets of Plexus could utilize traffic signals as well. Perhaps men with colored flags, he pondered.

When it was time to cross, she answered, "I don't know exactly where we're going. Something's telling me to go this way." She shrugged. "Not sure why, though."

Before long, they found themselves in a large parking lot, surrounding a gargantuan structure. Oryn couldn't help but stare at the wide variety of colorful cars and trucks with a hand on his sword. He failed to notice the scabbard about to brush a green Cadillac. It barely tapped the surface when the alarm whooped and squealed, startling him. Whirling around, he drew the weapon, staring wide-eyed at the shrill alarm.

Suddenly, it chirped twice and fell quiet. He saw Adwen's hand on the side and knew she had silenced it.

"Are these things living?"

"No, but they can be temperamental. Don't touch if you can help it. We don't need any more attention."

He finally noticed two elderly women murmuring about his odd looks and armor. They moved on and he stowed his sword. It was clear that their attire made them stand out like a bonfire on a clear night.

"How did you come by these new powers?" Toth asked as they passed a few motorbikes. "I discovered mine through endangerment. How did yours awaken?"

"My new powers started to work in this world when Kotig showed up."

For a moment the knight was silent and soaked in the disturbing news. He added his own perspective with a dark tone. "If you speak the truth and did see Kotig in this realm, then there may be a much greater threat than even the Bloody Brothers could have posed."

"Really?"

"The only way an alpha werewolf could pass between worlds is through dark gates. There have been rare sightings where fiends were witnessed disappearing into wicked portals. The worst of what you have revealed is that these greater gates may only be opened by more powerful demons. These activities are a bad omen. Small gates were left open for weaker creatures of chaos, but this could mean one or more of the greater are free."

The half-elf soon lost focus on the conversation, staring up at the huge building that cast them in its shadow. He pointed hesitantly and murmured, "Are we venturing inside this place? What is it?"

"It must be a fortress; or perhaps a temple."

Adwen giggled and shook her head. "It's called a mall. Think of it as a giant market place. What are you two waiting for? Let's go in!"

Very wary, the knight and half-elf followed to the glass doors. When they reached the threshold of the motion sensor, the entrance opened wide and the men jumped back. Adwen remained calm and they knew there wasn't a threat. She was busy studying a vivid poster.

"What does it read, dog?"

The skin on her sun-kissed face beamed with amusement. "This is too perfect to be coincidence. This says today there's a comic book convention. We're going to blend right in!"

Everywhere was busy in the cavernous main lobby. While many of the passing people were dressed normal, here and there were colorfully clothed characters. Spying a teen boy dressed as Superman, the knight grimaced and thought they

looked ridiculous. While he glowered, the half-elf was intrigued.

Adwen paid the shoppers no mind as instincts guided her.
The three walked abreast down the tiled floor. Toth turned
his head this way and that, attempting to soak in all the sights
at once.

Oryn kept a close eye on their wayward guide. Since their
conflict at the portal, he was certain she had changed in many
unseen ways. She was unpredictable and yet seemed confident
in spontaneous choices. Now that he found himself in her
strange and hazardous world, he concluded there was no alternative but to rely on her experience. She was right. He was not
in control. That fact was not a comfort.

Four young men sat together in the food court, sharing
burgers and pizza. They had spent a few hours in the mall and
all but one looked content. Eric Spade sat quietly, listening as
his friends gibbered and laughed at costumes.

"Look at those nerds!" They rolled with laughter. "Even
look at the girl! What a bunch of losers!" They all laughed
hard and Eric was curious enough to glance at the spectacle.
Staring long and hard at the girl, he was certain he recognized
her. When he was sure, he ran after her with anger burning
inside.

Casually strolling along, Adwen heard a voice yell, "Shari!
Shari Gates!"

Stopping dead, she turned to see who was calling out.
Oryn and Toth halted as well and watched curiously as the
man stood a few paces away. His face was red with rage.

Recognizing him at once, she stared in silence.

Eric glowered. "I knew it was you as soon as I saw you,
you smug whore!"

The knight raised an eyebrow at the blatant slander,
amused that it did not provoked her.

Adwen remained collected and calm with a note of pity in
her voice. "What do you want, Eric?"

His friends joined him as he began to rant. "The day you
jumped off that cliff you ruined my life! I was investigated by
the police for weeks! The evidence in court proved I didn't do
it, but my family still thinks I did, you stupid slut!"

Adwen was surprised to learn he was not the culprit. "You

didn't do it? Eric, I didn't jump. Take your friends and go back to lunch. I have somewhere to be."

His temple vein pulsed as he headed her off when she turned away. "No, you don't! I don't care about mall cops. I'm going to make you pay." Eric threw a right hook for her stomach.

Adwen effortlessly swung out of the way in a dancing side-step. She stared raptly as he stumbled past.

Oryn observed her new movements. They were fluid while she turned, leaned and twirled with ease. She let Eric stumble past again and he bellowed, spinning around for a punch to her cheek. The knight was not surprised when she ducked down low, subtly striking his chest with an open palm. The touch was enough to knock him back across the tiles, sliding fifteen feet into a table. A few chairs were bowled over and he made no effort to rise.

His companions saw that Adwen had a challenging look in her eye. They weren't as foolish as Eric and kept their distance. Two lifted him by his arms as he glared at her.

"You're different, Shari. You're an even bigger freak that I remember."

Oryn observed her expression closely.

There was no malice or anger. She looked disappointed. "And you haven't changed at all. You're still nothing more than a bully." She never looked back and walked.

The encounter sent her mind into whirlwind of thought. If Eric Spade hadn't pushed her, then who had and why?

"Who was that urchin, dog?" Oryn demanded.

Interrupted, she was perturbed that he refused to call her by name. "That was the person I closely compare you to."

"You compare me to that street trash? I have nothing in common with sewer vermin."

"Yes, you do. You both like to push people around, have issues, and most of all you love getting into a fight."

He wasn't going to deny that he loved battle, but took issue with being set alongside scum.

At last, the three merged with the comic convention. Books and colorful comic booths stood all around. Not every-one attending was in costume, but most wore a happy smile. Fans of various fictions clumped together by setups and talked excitedly about favorite stories.

Adwen, Oryn, and Toth passed a few, and when some stared, she smiled. Her senses still led through the thick of the crowd when a girl dressed as an anime character stopped them.

Excited, she squealed. "Oh wow! What cos-plays are you guys? Your gear is so awesome!" Then she turned to the knight. "That looks like real metal! Can I hold the sword?"

Oryn gave a look that was an obvious decline.

Smiling, Adwen said to the disappointed girl, "That's okay. He's just acting in character. He's Oryn, the jerk of the team." Then she gave an innocent look while he fumed.

Ecstatic, the girl clapped and squealed again, remaining in character. "That's so cool! I've got to go! I'll be late for some autographs!" Right away, she darted off.

Adwen shook her head smiling. "The people in my world have no idea that people like us exist. To them, magic is imaginary. These people are fiction addicts and story lovers."

Oryn stared back blankly.

"What?"

"Toth's left us."

"What? Where'd he go?"

He looked toward a particular group of fans dressed as elves. Some of the outfits looked very convincing as others did not. Toth was carrying on with them merrily.

Her cheeks and sides hurt as she laughed uncontrollably.

The knight continued to stare. "He believes them to be true elves."

Oblivious, the half-elf enjoyed the company until she tapped his shoulder. Adwen remained unable to speak from combating the need to burst out giggling.

Oryn approached and cleared his throat. "These are not elves."

Toth was confused. "Of course they are. Look at them!"

The knight had looked and very carefully. Several of the "elves" wore cheap rags and one had dark skin and pale ears. He could tell they were far from genuine and shook his head. Then to prove his point, he plucked an ear from the dark-skinned boy.

Toth's jaw dropped as the young man protested.

"Hey! That took more than an hour to fit on! Give it back!"

Oryn handed over the false appendage and Toth grimaced. Realizing his mistake, he sheepishly turned to Adwen as she giggled. "May we please explore elsewhere?"

"Yes, buddy. We're going this way."

The convention rested near the south exit around a large fountain. Tan marble carved in the shape of two robed boys poured a bronze pitcher from a pedestal. A man with dark eyes and a pale complexion sat back against the side chewing bubble gum, looking bored. Mildly alert, he wore deep crimson clothes and a black cloak. In one gloved hand he fondled a cruel staff. He observed the crowd, thumbing the dark red jewel on the one end, chewing impatiently. With the other hand, he brushed back greasy black hair as he blew a large bubble. Popping it with a finger, he pushed it back into his mouth to begin another. Then his gaze fell on Adwen, who stared past the throng. He blinked as his chewing slowed.

She had been watching the entire time and eyed him carefully. This man was not like the others. There was the scent of magic, but not the kind she knew. It made her hair stand on end. The skin on the ridge of her nose wrinkled and her violet eyes glowed. Oryn and Toth only just noticed the man by the fountain as he looked their way.

Then the stranger's eyes went wide and he swallowed the gum. He saw her snarling and got to his feet, raising the staff.

Acting quickly, she grabbed her friend's garments and pulled, yelling, "Get down!"

No sooner did they drop flat than a green ball of lightning shot from the staff, striking a pillar behind them. People screamed, startled by the explosion of concrete pebbles. Some darted for cover and others were curious enough to go closer and investigate. Others panicked and left the mall in a hurry.

The three looked up and Toth exclaimed, "I thought your world was devoid of magic! That is a warlock!"

"A witch? Keep the people back." She jumped up to confront the startled villain.

Getting to his own feet, Oryn grumbled. "It is a *warlock.*" Together, they worked to give her room and protect helpless bystanders. They didn't understand what was happening and some thought it might be a stunt.

Eyes alight, she snarled and asked, "What is your name and why are you here?"

"Not that it matters, but it's really none of your business." He swung the staff again and another green bolt shot for her.

It was easily dodged and ricocheted off of the floor, blasting a comic stand into flames. Growling dangerously, she stared with clenched fists.

"You have no more right to be here than I." Throwing another bolt, he spat, "but I'm quite sure only one of us is leaving here."

When Adwen moved to dodge, the bolt separated into three. One caught her shoulder. She yelped as she was knocked down and a black scorch mark fizzed and smoked. Swiftly leaping to her feet, she went on the offensive before the warlock could launch his next volley.

Some bystanders started cheering as she leaped around, avoiding searing strikes. Minutes into the battle, people were whooping and applauding, convinced everything was a show.

The warlock was losing patience wasting dark spells. To end the fight, he charged her and put all his remaining power into the staff, making it glow red hot. He hoped one well-placed blow would slow her down.

Realizing the danger, Adwen held her ground. Then her eyes suddenly flashed gold and instinct took over.

They all watched the warlock swing his staff for her head and a bright white flash burst from her body. Once the light was gone, everyone's eyes recovered and they gasped. The magical girl had vanished and a white hound creature stood in her place. She held the head of the evil weapon in her glowing hands and the light repelled the wicked spell.

The warlock gasped. "No! Not you!"

Adwen snarled. "Who?"

Wrenching the staff from his grasp, she kicked him away. He skidded into a burning pile of comics and stared in terror. She lobbed the spent tool into the fountain, snarling, "Tell me what you know! Who are you and why are you in my world?"

The warlock stumbled to his feet, shaking his head. "Not in this life! Ne-never!"

"Then I'll make this quick."

There was a brief flash. She was instantly before him and staring down. Fear held him in place and he watched her large claws drive into him. There was no blood or pain and he was frozen and empty. Then there was only white hot light as she destroyed him from the inside. The warlock turned to dust, every particle parting into nothingness.

As Adwen changed back, her companions joined her and watched the silent crowd. Then there was a loud whistling and all erupted into cheer.

"Dog? Are these people aware that this was a battle?"

She shook her head. "They haven't got a clue. It's time we got moving before somebody stops us. Let's use the escalator."

The applause continued as they moved to leave. She was halfway up the moving stair when she looked back and saw the two at the bottom, hesitant to step on.

"What are you waiting for? Let's go! They won't bite!"

Oryn and Toth didn't trust the contraption, but wished to leave even more. The first to brave it was the knight and he quickly learned the handrail was not keeping time with the steps. He let go, whereas his friend did not.

Toth clung tightly to the banister and was soon sprawled out on the moving steps. Adwen shook her head and the on-lookers laughed at his expense.

The winded half-elf was overwhelmed by this strange world. "Your technology is not as convenient as you de-scribed."

She laughed, leading the way through the closest exit. The day was still bright and a glowing portal appeared just off the sidewalk at her approach. It shimmered out of thin air, rip-pling with blue light.

The half-elf asked hopefully, "Are we returning to our own world?"

"Yes, but I've got a feeling we're about to find something new." She brushed away the crumbling remains of a black scab on her arm, completely healed by the daylight.

Oryn grimaced while Toth showed relief.

She asked, "How about we see what's next?"

After the three walked through the portal it vanished with them. A few seconds afterwards, police cruisers came whirling into the lot, prepared to deal with a disturbance.

Chapter 29
REFLECTIONS OF TRUTH

Everywhere was green. Humidity moistened rich, dark soil underfoot in the tropical rainforest. Hundreds of animals whooped and others screeched at the strange trespassers. It was warm and Adwen drew a deep breath, taking in foreign of smells.

"Where have we gone?" Toth asked.

A small monkey inspected the knight as he stared back. "Have we left your world?" He raised an eyebrow when it stuck out its tongue.

They walked through thick undergrowth. Brushing past a large fern, Adwen finally answered. "We're somewhere in your world."

Disappointed not to be in Dargadia, Oryn took brisk strides to catch up and scowled. "What makes you so sure of that?"

Stopping, she smiled and pointed at a branch high overhead. "We don't have snakes with wings where I'm from."

Both men spotted the coiled serpent with a pair of vibrant rainbow wings. It stretched them lazily and yawned, working its toothy mouth.

"Also, if this jungle is anything like the ones in my world, make sure you don't touch the plants, try not to touch the trees and definitely don't touch the snakes and frogs. Then again, don't touch anything. Most of the plants and animals here are very poisonous."

As her back was turned, Toth hadn't heard and reached for a bright red fruit. The knight spotted him about to take a bite and swiftly batted it from his hand.

They quietly argued until Adwen paused and murmured, "Keep it down. I think we're being watched."

All was quiet and they waited.

Feeling wary, the half-elf leaned in close. "By what?"

Oryn replied. "Something big."

They both saw him gazing off through the trees. Their hearts skipped a beat and they held their breath. Indeed, it was something very big.

A gigantic bear on all fours stared. Its head was the size of a school bus and its lower lip hung low, drool pouring from colossal jaws. Taking another step, it was incredibly stealthy.

She whispered to her anxious companions. "In a moment, I'm going to change. When I do, as quickly as you can, get on my back."

Oryn was not thrilled with the idea. "You intend to carry us both and elude this animal?"

The giant bear grunted, apparently hungry.

"How about we find out?"

She quickly transformed. As soon as they grabbed a hold of her shoulders and neck, the bear grunted and charged. Though she could not run as fast, she was able to keep ahead of the giant predator. It chased them wildly through the jungle, snapping trees and making the ground shake. She burst into a clearing before a cliff face and they were out of time to go any-where but up.

They bear roared an she dashed to the rocky wall. As it burst into view she was out of reach, continuing to climb with her friends holding on tight. The brute grunted and began throwing its bulk against the plateau, causing rocks to rain down.

The knight's hold tightened, Toth yelled and she let loose a long howl. The melodious sound echoed and irritated the bear. It pounded the cliff harder to get its meal. Adwen began to lose her hold when something flew at the bear.

Crying out, the creature backed away with a spear protrud-ing from its nose. It roared, scratching at the small sting.

There was the sound of loud wing beats before three grif-fons with dark-skinned riders appeared. The proud creatures hovered as the warriors fired a volley of arrows. After a few more stings, the bear became frustrated and lumbered away. It would find easier prey elsewhere.

The beast left and a griffon hovered closer, reaching out a talon. Toth was first to accept and happily held on as a second collected Oryn. With the load gone, Adwen could grip the rocks much better.

The strangers and their flying mounts stared at her clinging to the cliff and one prepared to fire.

Toth yelled at him, "Wait! Aren't you going to help her as well?"

All three protested angrily in a language they couldn't understand and when they looked again, fell silent. She had changed into her woman form and was now having difficulty holding onto the sheer cliff. Wind whipped silver and gold hair wildly with her garments.

Adwen wore an uncomfortable smile. "A little help would be great right about now."

They were carried away from the north side of the mesa and over miles of jungle to the outskirts of a city. Adobe structures and cobbled streets weaved and wound about like the strands of a crazed spider's web. As the griffons flew over houses Adwen could see there were accommodations on the rooftops. These people lived alongside the griffons.

A large palace rested atop a hill overlooking the plateau dwellers, surrounded by watchtowers manned by men and griffons. Riders sounded horns and the beasts displayed wings at their approach. While Oryn and Toth were carried to the ground before the gate, she was taken around the backside overlooking a cliff then into a cavern.

She prepared herself, expecting anything but a warm welcome. When she was let down inside a torch-lit tunnel, she realized this was a dungeon. A few guards approached and grabbed her roughly by the arms. Adwen quickly threw them off.

They backed away pointing spears, yelling in their language.

Her eyes glowed. "I don't understand you."

The griffons silently observed as the guards continued to threaten.

"What are you going to do with my friends?" she growled, and the men yelled louder.

A voice called out, bringing silence to the dungeon. Entering the room, a well-dressed man came to stand before her. Completely unafraid, he spoke with a thick accent.

"Your friends are unharmed. They will remain unharmed

so long as you cooperate with our laws."

She raised an eyebrow. "Well, what are your laws?"

"First, you must come with me." He instructed the guards. They did not yell or utter a sound as they led her to a cell, placing her inside. Once she was locked behind steel bars, he answered. "The first law to be honored is that all 'contagious creatures' are forbidden. To break this law, the punishment is death."

Adwen's eyes flickered. "So, what happens now?"

"You will be tested. Can you mark a human being?"

She paused and thought hard. "I've never tried."

Bemused, the man replied, "Then you shall, now." He clapped and the guards brought forward a filthy man in rags. "Bite this man. When a full moon rises, we will know the truth."

Staring apprehensively at the frightened human, she wondered if she could mark. Even if she could, she did not want to.

She glared and growled. "No. No one deserves that. I won't do it."

He smiled. "This man does. He is to be executed at dawn for the murder of his neighbor." Becoming serious, he added, "But if you refuse, your friends will be the first to die."

A chill went up her spine at the thought.

"Choose wisely." He commanded the guards, gesturing to take the captive close, forcing one arm through the bars.

She watched as he cried and fought back. There was nothing Adwen could do to save this man. He was going to die. Toth's and even Oryn's life were not worth refusing.

Closing her eyes, she hung her head. It was hard to muster the will, but she forced herself to change into her creature form. The astonished guards almost stepped back at her approach. Acting quickly, she lunged and snapped at the filthy man's arm. He screamed out loud and she let go as soon as she bit into him. Feeling ashamed, she spat dark, bitter blood onto the dirt.

The guards tossed him into the neighboring cell, where he cowered and wailed.

"Your friends will be thankful for your choice."

Reverting to woman form, she spat out more blood. Some

had gone down her throat, making her nauseous. She gave an accusing sidelong look.

Then he asked, "Is there anything the guards may bring to you while we wait?"

Confused by this courtesy, Adwen studied the nobleman. "You wouldn't happen to have any milk to wash this taste out of my mouth, would you?"

Snapping his fingers, he ordered one of the guards to the task. Amused by her manner, he introduced himself. "My name is Isla. What is your name?"

A moment later she was passed a clay cup. "Thank you." She washed away the horrible taste, and when the cup was empty, licked her lips. "My name is Adwen. What kind of milk is this?"

"That is griffon milk. I will return when the moon appears. Afterwards, we will see what is to be done with you and your friends." Nodding, he strode out of the dungeons.

Guards posted along the wall across from her stood in silence. Each dressed in colorful clothes with decorative beads of bone about their necks, wrists and ankles. She could smell fear in the air and wondered if it came from the guards or the murderer beside her. The man sat cradling his bleeding arm, giving furtive glances.

Adwen was nervous, pacing in her cage. Suspense bred anxiety as the minutes passed. Was he going to change? If he did, what would he become? She hoped he wouldn't change for many reasons beside the fact that Oryn and Toth's lives depended on it. She did not want the burden of knowing she could cause that kind of pain. Minutes went by like hours and sunset came as slowly as a thought in a weary mind. No longer pacing, she sat at the back of her prison. The murderer had not changed yet and there were no windows in this dungeon.

An hour past sunset, Isla returned. He appeared calm, but she detected he was ether secretly excited or nervous. Not giving the murderer a second look, he entered, clapped his hands and issued an order to the guards.

They hesitated and stared.

He repeated the order in a much sterner tone and one brought forward the key. Opening her cell, he stood before the bars and bowed his head low. "I am to collect you. If you wish to see your friends, come with me."

Adwen was suspicious. "What?"

He politely replied, "Your friends are unharmed and await you. We mustn't keep them. The king is waiting as well."

"What are you talking about?" she exclaimed, a little outraged. "First I'm an intruder and now I'm suddenly a guest?"

Isla bowed his head lower still. "The king is awaiting your arrival so he may apologize personally. If you would, please, come with me."

The situation felt strange, but she did not want to stay in the dank prison. She followed upward to the rest of the palace.

White and blue stones covered every surface. Each corridor held archways with fine pottery and torch light. They passed a small garden where griffons preened beside a fountain. The creatures stared as they passed.

Isla spoke again. "I have been instructed to find you suitable clothing for the feast. We have something prepared."

Stopping dead in her tracks, she shook her head. "There's something weird going on and I want to know what. Where is the king?"

Apologetic, he reassured her, showing anxiousness now that there were no other witnesses. "My king is regretful for the misunderstanding, Lady Adwen. He awaits you in the feasting hall."

The reaction surprised her. Her eyes flashed gold as a thought came to her. "Well, you don't need to give me a dress. I have my own." She focused on her garments and they shifted into a casual evening gown, retaining the same color assortment of gray, white and gold. He was surprised and she kindly asked, "Will the king mind if I come like this?"

Shaking his head, he answered, "That will do."

Two guards opened the doors when they came close, revealing the grand dining hall. Mirrors framed with gold and jade decorated the walls around the long and lavish table. Platters of rich-smelling food stretched before the twenty dinner guests with the king at the end. In the bright space she could see her friends seated at the head of the table.

As she entered, the king stood and the others fell silent before following suit. They stared in awe as Isla led her to the last vacant seat beside him. He was a few inches taller than

Oryn until he bowed his bald head deeply, smiling.

As confused as ever, Adwen sat across from the knight and alongside Toth, both of whom wore clean robes and looked just as confounded.

Once everyone was seated again, the powerful host turned to address her kindly. "Has Isla told you that I wish to make amends?"

"Yes and I wanted to ask you something." She became sheepish. "What is all of this for?"

Seeming embarrassed himself, the king gestured to the spread. "This is a part of my amends. We knew you would arrive, but were unsure of what would please you. I am King Zulo Lebam. I welcome you to Eskrana, Lady Adwen." And he dipped his head.

The knight had been suspicious leading up to this impromptu dinner party. But now he resisted the need to demand answers. A king from a foreign land had bowed his head to Adwen twice in an evening.

Adwen also wanted to ask more questions. Instead she waited to see where the evening would take them. Throughout the feast, if she made eye contact with other guests, they would ether quickly look away or anxiously whisper to a neighbor. After the dinner was concluded, the three guests were escorted by the king and Isla to a more private chamber.

There was hardly a word between the travelers. On pins and needles, they waited for an explanation for the welcome. While Adwen eyed the king apprehensively, Oryn never took his eyes off of her. The knight wondered if she created a lie to gain their trust.

Isla and King Zulo invited them into a lounge. Soft moonlight shone onto a white stone floor through an open marble sill. The king's advisor dipped a torch into a trough of oil. In moments, the walls were lined with lapping flames, filling the bleach-white room with warm light.

Silken chairs stuffed with down feathers sat in wait for them. The end of the room was elevated with three broad stairs. A short distance past the final step stood a towering narrow frame veiled in a large red cloth. What was beneath stood near nine feet in height and seemed even taller atop the stairs.

Once two guards closed them in, the king smiled. "Now

that we have met, it is time to discuss business. Have you been faring well, Lady Adwen?"

Staring quizzically, she shrugged. "I've been doing okay, but what business?"

Now he was befuddled. "You do know why you are here?"

Slowly, she shook her head. "I jumped through a portal with these two and ended up here. I didn't know where I was going."

Thinking it over, he asked, "The treaties?" After seeing her confusion grow, he understood. "Ah, I see. I must explain this to you?"

She nodded, thoroughly dumbfounded.

King Zulo began, "Long ago, there was a dark army. The only one who saved this world from the darkness was Darien Andredan. The Order of the Master Knights in Dargadia train in the many deadly arts he taught to his men hundreds of years ago. The Kingdoms of Day are separated from one another by both sea and desert. The only way they could unite was by his efforts. He found the kings and formed the Alliance of Day. Without him and his many powers, the kingdoms never would have united and mustered their armies. Together with Darien the Master Knight, all fought to defend the green lands of Dargadia, the heart of this world. If either he or Dargadia had fallen, all would have fallen."

When he finished there was an uncertain quiet about the room. Toth was mildly familiar with the Dark War, but Oryn was very knowledgeable. He had studied it for years and used sword skills began by the Master Knight himself.

Adwen stared for a moment. "Okay. So, what do the old war and this Darien have to do with me?"

The king gave her an astonished look. "Adwen, you are Adwen Andredan, Darien's one and only rightful heir. His powers and treasures are your birthright. You are the true descendant of Darien Andredan, the Master Knight."

The half-elf's jaw dropped, hardly believing his pointed ears. His eerie friend was from the true bloodline of the fabled hero of light.

Oryn couldn't breathe as he stared, stunned. Why couldn't he have seen it before? With all of the knowledge he possessed, he should have known it from the start. He continued to stare, wide-eyed and in complete shock and awe. Then his shock slowly developed into swelling disgrace.

After a few seconds of surprise, Adwen let the information soak in then laughed. "No. That can't be right. I was born in a different world. I can't be who you think I am."

The smile in the king's eyes spread to his face. "The world without magic? His bloodline was hidden and thought lost, save for the royal family of Dargadia. All of the royal family are born with blue eyes because of their heritage, but Darien had known a true love before the princess of the green lands. His great love vanished. No one knew what became of her, but the child she bore was the greatest kept secret of the centuries. Their child was left to live in the world without magic, safe from the searching darkness. That was how you were able to be born and how Darien's legacy could continue. You are meant to finish what he began."

"Stop! Just wait one minute." She slumped heavily into a lounge chair, overwhelmed and in a state of disbelief. "This can't be right."

Sitting across from her, the king gently said, "You climbed the Great White Oak and returned from the land of ever-peaceful rest."

Her gaze met his and she was frightened. "How do you know that?"

"Every detail of you was foretold. The visions of an elf king were written and preserved. To keep Andredan's enemies from obtaining every secret, the written works were separated among the kingdoms. I am one of the keepers. My documents told that the descendent would inherit his attributes and earn more powers through many trials of the heart. His true heir would hold a sun blossom in each hand and bear the golden mark upon their brow."

Hanging her head she stared at her feet, feeling numb.

Getting up, he set a big hand on her shoulder. "I would very much like to see your true face."

The request surprised her. Rising from her seat, she studied the king closely and closed her eyes, allowing her hound self to emerge. Her transition was smooth and gentle. Fully transformed, Adwen stood a foot taller than he. Her black nose was level with the man's steely eyes and a tear of awe rolled down his cheek. Ever so gently, he touched the golden mark on her head.

After she reverted back, he dried his face. "Thank you, Lady Adwen. You have made me truly proud to be the ruler of my people. My ancestor was among Darien's four sworn warriors. Now is the time for my family to aid your cause once more."

"So, what do I do now?"

King Zulo could see she was already weary. "Now is time for rest. I will have more to tell once the sun returns to the skies. Before you are shown to your rooms, there is a custom for visitors and special guests I must offer."

Isla left their side and went up the steps, sharply pulling the cloth from the tall object; a lavish mirror in a frame of silver and gold. Swirling designs wove about the frame and clawed legs of the artifact.

"When Darien came, two strange mirrors were discovered. The twin mirrors of Truth and Lies. This is the Mirror of Truth. Its other half was hidden far from here and lost. It was very dangerous, tempting beings close with images of the one thing they wished for most, but could never have. If they touched the glass, they were swallowed into a false world, where they slowly wasted away, distracted by their own bliss.

"This Mirror of Truth is different. It shows the looker their true self. Whoever you may be inside will reflect as an image, revealing nothing more and nothing less than the truth. You may choose not to look, if you wish. Some have lost their minds because of what was shown. For some, seeing their reflection is too much to bear. So beware, Lady Adwen. The same goes for your company. Who among you wishes to look?"

"Will everyone be able to see what my reflection is?"

He shook his bald head. "Only the looker may see their reflection. We will only know if you chose to speak of it."

Taking a breath, she was feeling daring. "I'll look."

Ascending the three steps, she reached the top and stared deep into the spotless, polished surface. After watching her reflection a moment, it blurred and changed. She became confused and a curious look came over her.

"Do you wish to share what you see?" the king asked.

"It's me, but... I'm in half. One half has a violet eye, but the other side looks a little different." Leaving the mirror, she came back. "What does that mean? Am I broken or something?"

"I'm sure it means something far less serious. Violet is the color of incompletion. Do not worry. It is a guarantee that when you next look upon my mirror, the reflection will be changed." Then Zulo turned to Toth, asking, "Do you wish to look?"

Holding up a hand, he declined, "No, but thank you, Sky King. I will pass."

Turning to Oryn, he asked, "What of you, General?"

He was still lost in shock over the discovery of Adwen's identity. Memories off all he had done circled through his head like carrion birds. The entire time he had treated Darien's heir like a beast. There must be a terrible punishment for such a crime, he thought. Distracted, he hadn't heard King Zulo the first time, but when he asked again, looked up at the mirror. Did he dare look?

He hesitated, but curiosity got the better. They watched as he ascended the steps to stand before the candid glass. The knight eyed the head atop the frame. A lion's face with two red gems for eyes glared down. Oryn pondered, if a man were to stand bare and unarmed before such a beast, he truly would know what sort of man he was.

Lowering his gaze, he looked into the mirror. At first he glimpsed his physical reflection, before the surface quickly faded to black. A moment passed and an image took shape, slowly and in full detail.

Everyone watched his face in the surface. They only saw his outward appearance and waited. At the start, he was mildly intrigued, waiting for the illusion to take form. Then his expression became confused. Then he blanched and started to shudder. Eyes watering, his legs turned weak and everyone was shocked as he stumbled backward down the steps. Fleeing from the mirror, he dashed to lean out the window, panting and shaking, attempting to regain control and not vomit.

The room fell quiet while the others stared at him quivering. He did not turn to face them.

Adwen was the most surprised. This was the first time she

had seen the knight show fear. Not even the Bloody Brothers could make him feel this way and it puzzled her.

King Zulo was first to break the silence. "Lady Adwen, Isla will escort you and your other friend to your rooms. I wish to speak with Sir Oryn alone."

"Okay." Adwen cocked her head at the knight. He was no longer shivering, but still gave off the aroma of terror. Allowing herself to be ushered out, she couldn't help but wonder what could possibly frighten him so badly.

Oryn slowed his heart rate further with the breathing ritual, refocusing his mind. He hadn't thought he would see anything grand or regal. What the mirror held was something he could not have begun to prepare for. Even if armed with fore-knowledge, he would have recoiled from the sight.

"Sir Oryn." The king asked in his thunderous voice, "What did you see in my mirror?"

He took his time hiding the look of fear deep down before facing the king at last. Still very pale and unsteady, he used the marble sill for support.

But he did not answer and the king asked again, "What did you see?"

Oryn remained silent and looked ill again at the thought.

Becoming impatient, King Zulo warned, "You have seen something in the mirror that you wish to keep secret, but know this: I will not rest until I know what it is. If I allowed a man to continue traveling with the Heir of Andredan after seeing him flee in fear from the mirror, I would be a fool. So I ask, what did you see?"

His stern words had effect, but Oryn hesitated for a long while. At last he swallowed, and uttered, "I saw a child; a young boy."

King Zulo glared. "I know there is more."

To steady himself further, Oryn took a deep breath. "It was an image of me, as I was, but a boy ten years of age. It was the day my father returned home from his work as a Knight of the Order. That evening, I awoke...."

He could recall every second and each horrible sound.

"...to screams," he murmured, lost in the memory. "I heard my mother and father in the other room; a creature rip-ping them to shreds. When everything fell quiet, I went to have a look. They were in pieces."

Oryn remembered the blood-streaked timber walls, dazed by the scene. "My father's sword was still in the sheath. He hadn't taken it out. In a rage, I took it up and went to find the wretched thing. I found the werewolf in the trees, licking the blood on its hands."

He remembered when it had run at him and how much bigger it was than he.

"I cut off the head with one full swing."

It all felt as if it were yesterday: the body dropping onto him, blood drenching his hair and clothes. He had to fight to climb out from beneath it.

"I found where the head had fallen. It was looking at me. I stood and waited. I wanted to know who had destroyed my family."

Then he became empty and devoid of emotion. "It was my twin; my brother."

The memory of his brother's betrayed expression haunted him. Those frightened amber-gold eyes seemed almost pleading as they dimmed and emptied of life. Oryn had screamed then, but not with fear or sorrow. A blinding rage and heart-wrenching pain forced the cry out of him.

"In the mirror, I saw myself holding my father's sword, bathed in my brother's blood and standing over his head." Forcing the image out of his mind, he locked eyes with the king, uncertain. "What does that mean for me?"

"I suppose, it means you are unchanged since then." He answered, intrigued by the gory story. "You are the same now as you were at that moment in your past."

He had told no one before; but found the topic easier to discuss as he went on. "My brother and I had played on a hill near our home earlier in the day. There was a steep slope with thick ferns and underbrush. He had tripped and fallen. When he reached the bottom of the ravine, he had many cuts and the largest of them would not bleed."

Oryn shook his head regretfully. He could still remember going to him and his brother's saying, "It's just a scratch. I'm not going to cry."

"There had been a werewolf in the brush. We never saw him, but he had marked my brother as he tumbled past."

The king nodded, convinced that the knight could be trusted after all. "Then you would be seeking revenge for your parents?"

"No." The knight's harsh look returned and it was ice cold. "I have avenged my mother and father. The werewolf who slaughtered them is dead. My vengeance is for my brother. My mother's brother fought alongside my father as a knight. He is the only other family I possess. It was he who found and bore me to the Order where I became the apprentice to the captain, Sir Vigo Odette. He trained me. It was he who taught me everything.

"It was at the order that I learned of werewolves. I learned all werewolves are a demon occupying the cursed body of a man. That is why the human cannot recall their nocturnal activities. In some cases, the demon grows bored of tormenting the soul and devours it whole. Then the fiend is in full control, capable of changing at will day or night. I also learned the curse and suffering for the human soul does not end at death."

Wearing a most unreadable look, anger burned red hot inside and he became steady. Green eyes burned into King Zulo. "Upon death, the demon is banished back to the void from whence it came, and along with it, the cursed human soul. At the order I learned, I had sent my brother's soul to the void that night."

Chapter 30
GUESTS AND INTRUDERS

Early in the morning, a gentle knocking came at Adwen's guest room door. When she answered Isla was waiting in the hall.

"If you please, Lady Adwen, the king requests you and your company meet with him."

Yawning, she followed through the cool archways. Soon the king's advisor stopped to knock at another door.

Oryn opened up and frowned. "What is it?"

"The king wishes to meet with Lady Adwen and her companions."

His frown disappeared and he joined them.

Along the way, Adwen took casual discreet glances at the knight. After the revealing of her status, among other things, it occurred to her that his behavior might change. Thus far his demeanor remained rigid and without tells.

He did not fail to notice her observing. He was aware of that and other things perhaps she did not even know. With the powers of the Master Knight, she could already possess the ability see into the hearts of others. Oryn preferred not to be examined. Personal matters were better kept private.

Adwen pondered on when he fled from the mirror. Asking about it directly did not seem appropriate. Either way, the mystery of what could scare him was confounding.

Reaching Toth's room, their guide knocked. No answer came so he knocked again. Not having time to waste, Isla took the liberty of retrieving him manually.

When Isla disappeared behind the closed door, the knight rolled his eyes. Left alone to wait, an awkward silence permeated the hall.

Tension mounted when Adwen cleared her throat, waiting and watching Oryn as he casually readjusted his posture.

Oryn waited as well. The knight prepared to passively accept any harsh words of condemnation. Adwen had every right to punish him, and he secretly wished she would. He hid his shame, refusing to meet her gaze and risk revealing it.

Musing, she rocked back on her heels and came up with a way to kill the quiet. "How is your jaw?"

Not anticipating the question, he answered, "Better." While the knight was lost in thought, she spoke again.

"Thank you."

The suddenness caught him off guard. It took conscious effort not to make eye contact. Oryn's brow furrowed. "What for, may I ask?"

There was a long pause. "For not being a suck-up."

Aghast, his head snapped around to stare. Despite the terminology, he understood and was nearly slack jawed by the modesty and utter lack of contempt.

The awkward feeling lifted just as Isla returned with a very groggy Toth. He had forgotten the cloth for his eye and the scar was obvious. Rubbing the sleep from his good one, the foggy left eye blinked in time with the other.

She restrained a gasp. So much of her friend was changed.

He saw her staring and smiled. "What do you think? Does it make me look rugged?"

Adwen returned a wry smile. "Yeah. It does make you look rugged."

Pulling out the cloth from a pocket, he covered the scar once more.

The dark skin on the king's scalp glinted in the sunlight from the open windows. His steely gaze brightened and he stood to bow low at her approach.

She and her friends returned it.

A large golden griffon lounged beside his desk. The honey colored creature shuffled powerful wings and screeched. "Welcome, Adwen Andredan!"

"Good morning, travelers of worlds. We have much to discuss."

He waited till they were seated and sat back in his carved jungle wood chair. "Now, to business. The task ahead of you,

Adwen, is first to reunite the Kingdoms of Day. To do this you must collect treaties from each land neighboring Dargadia. When you seek out the rulers of the desert, be ready. Each will test you to see that you are the true heir."

"What kind of tests will they have?"

"I'm sure they will involve your capabilities. Each ruler, including myself, will have conditions for such an alliance. My treaty is already written and I have but to sign. After obtaining all four, you must take them to the presiding King of Dargadia for his seal of approval."

"Well, why haven't you signed it yet? Is something wrong?"

"No, there is not. I will sign before you depart. I meant to meet with you to provide further guidance." Then he saw that the knight had a question and raised an eyebrow. "What do you wish to ask, sir Oryn?"

"What is the condition for your alliance?"

Shaking his head, he replied, "I am sorry, but only Lady Adwen and the King of Dargadia may know. If they wish to tell after the task is complete, then they may. Do you understand?"

The knight respectfully replied, "I did not intend to overstep my bounds."

Wanting to alleviate the tension, Adwen quickly asked, "I do have some questions."

The king's eyes sparkled. He nodded and turned to Isla. "If you could, please escort Sir Oryn and Fedius Toth out to wait. Our conversation should not be long."

As they were taken to the hall, the knight gave her a sidelong glance. At last the door closed, cutting off his view.

King Zulo laced his thick fingers. "What would you ask of me, Lady Adwen?"

She thought hard to phrase the question. It felt awkward. "You said the kings were going to test me. Was your test for me to bite the murderer?" He looked unsettled and she was alarmed. "Did he change? He didn't, did he?"

"No, of course not. I suspect you were bitten by a werewolf in your first life." Her silence confirmed the assumption. "Darien's blood is unlike any other. If his flesh were harmed by a curse, he would become more powerful and gain attributes to better defend him later. If you could mark a man, it would not be as simple as a bite. Feel free to use your fangs as you like. The men you use them against will not change."

She gave a sigh of relief.

Out in the hall, Oryn stared vacantly over the city. Griffons flitted from roof to roof while citizens wandered down streets. It was an image of prosperity. While observing the lively scene, the shame he bore weighed on his mind.

The half-elf stood beside him and firmly asked, "Have you told her yet?"

The knight grimaced at the view. "Told what to her?"

"Have you apologized?"

His grimace deepened. "No, I haven't yet."

Folding arms firmly, Toth was not pleased. "Do you intend to? Or are you are waiting till you mean what is said?"

With a glance, the knight showed a disgruntled frown.

"I doubt she has forgotten your maltreatment, as surely as I have not. Still now, I regretted not taking a stand against your actions." Then a rueful smile appeared. "But now that I've waited, I see there is little to regret. Do you feel any shame at the things you did, now that you know her for who she is?"

The knight was already frustrated and being called out as a fool did not improve his mood. Maintaining a calm composure, he replied, "I intend to make amends. Do not press me where there is no need. I will apologize when the proper moment arrives. As for punishment for my trespasses, whether she knows it or not, it is her obligation to reprimand and make me to pay. She will do so in time and I will accept without question or retaliation."

Listening to the knight, Toth grew angry. "Whether she punishes you or not is nothing to be concerned with. She is uncommonly forgiving. The damage to your armor and your face is surely an adequate punishment to her. The wrath that you need fear is from the great magic. Adwen serves those powers as Darien once did. The wrath of the Light Spirits is what you need fear. I am sure in time you will feel their hand of judgment over your head. I will pity you then."

Isla stayed out of the heated conversation. When near the knight he had the same sense the half-elf did. The air about Oryn was like the hush before a storm; the silence before the whistle of a lash. He was in store for suffering. Isla already felt pity for what the future might hold.

After Toth's proclamation, Oryn had little to reply. The fortune he was given so long ago had warned him. There would be many repercussions for living with hate. A chill climbed up his spine at the memory of the elf woman's words. "The price will be your life."

He glowered. "So be it."

Adwen was nervous and anxious to set out, but had one final question. After hesitating, she became too curious.

"Last night, did Oryn tell you what he saw in the mirror?" The king's eyes hinted that a sensitive topic had been touched on. "Well, what I mean to ask is, can he be trusted?"

The king sighed. "He told me what he saw, and yes, Sir Oryn may be trusted. The general is a good man who has many demons to face. In the mirror, he saw pain. I suggest that you let him keep his secrets until he deems them worth telling. He should serve you well."

Though skeptical, the tone in King Zulo's voice persuaded her. "Well, I can't think of anything else to ask."

"Are you certain? You have nothing more to ask of me?"

Then an idea came to her. Adwen smiled toothily, quickly becoming excited. "Can I see more of the griffons before we leave?"

Immediately, he burst into deep, merry guffaws. "Yes, Lady Adwen! It would be an honor and my pleasure!"

With the treaty signed and sealed, it was stowed in Toth's satchel. The king and Isla then began their grand tour of the surrounding city of Meier. Griffons rested atop homes under personal shelters watching her pass. Some clicked beaks in greeting.

"Every child who reaches the age of ten receives a griffon egg." Isla explained, "If it breaks, they will not get another. Once it hatches, the griffon is their life partner. The breed of the hatchling decides their future profession. Sea griffons are catchers of fish, crested griffons are great monkey hunters and so on. Together, they learn to make their kingdom great."

"What happens if they don't have a griffon?" Toth asked.

"Then they must take up a task that does not require a griffon. Those without are sometimes looked down upon, but that is not common. It is difficult for a griffon hatchling to grow close to an adult human. Many children have broken their eggs and are not without work. Some of our best citizens do not have one. As a child, I carried my egg in a bag on my back like the others. The strap broke. I regret not having such a partner, but I am living a comfortable life on the ground."

Their tour took them past fountains and wells in town squares.

Adwen eventually asked, "Where are we heading?"

The king smiled. "It is a surprise."

The next griffon they saw was the size of a Clydesdale. Its beak was thick, black and serrated. It screeched shrilly in the field among the others as the king presented the breed that was twice the size of the rest. One spread its bared wings, displaying a cherry and black wingspan more than thirty feet wide. Armored trainers and keepers tended to them and taught simple commands.

King Zulo saw her smiling. "These are the ones we have been breeding since Darien's disappearance. These are the Kaluka."

"Cool. What does it mean?"

He pointed at a Kaluka as the rider on its back issued a brief command. The griffon opened its beak and a short, shrill sound came out. A resulting blast of air struck a boulder, fracturing the stone like glass. The creature's trainer rewarded the action with a piece of meat.

"It means *to crush*. What do you think of my part in your army, Lady Adwen?"

She was very impressed. Giddy from the show of force, she fought the need to laugh out loud. "That is so awesome!"

For a while they watched the training until the tour came to an abrupt end. She sensed danger and the griffons did as well, ignoring their masters, displaying wings and screeching at the distance.

King Zulo became harsh and glared at where the Kaluka screamed. "The harpies are coming."

Birdlike creatures with a man's torso and bright orange eyes loomed. Their feathers were long and brown and talons were in the place of both hands and feet. A flock of two dozen swooped low for frightened citizens, brandishing bone knives and long wooden spears. People screamed while griffon friends flew in to fend them off.

A harpy was about to cut a woman, but Adwen was fully transformed and swatted the avian warrior aside. She bounded for another, retaliating as the Kaluka provided air support.

Toth commanded a tree root to snatch an enemy out of the air. The whip-like tendril ensnared it and retracted beneath the rocks, leaving a plume of feathers and a smear of blood.

Atop a bridge, Oryn battled two spear-wielding harpies at once. They were a poor match. The knight could not help but think they were like children. Their height was close to that of a teen and their battle experience was comparable. He easily slew them and watched the remaining survivors take wing. The short battle ended and the people cheered while the Kaluka chased the creatures away.

Toth beamed as Adwen joined him, reverting to woman form. Putting a hand on her hip, she laughed. "When did you get the stomach to do something like that? You're starting to scare me!"

"What do you mean?"

She raised an eyebrow. "You used a tree to pull another living thing the size of a man through an opening the size of a saucer. Job well done, but I just had to let you know that you're scary."

They both chuckled as the others arrived.

King Zulo was pleased. "Thank you, Lady Adwen. The harpies attack often and are difficult to chase away. They rarely kill, but we take no chances. Now, are you and your friends ready to travel?

People in the streets repeatedly thanked them on their way to a lower district. A large shelter for griffons that lost their human companions came into sight. Many brought offerings of food and children played with them when chores were few. The king described the location of an old gate created by Darien. It was on a small island and he assured it would be much safer than the alternative.

"The air over Mortigad is thick with danger. It would be foolish to fly over the great black nightmare. Some of Darien's gates reach between kingdoms, while hidden gates span from this world to the other. Hidden gates could be anywhere and can only be seen at your approach. The kingdom gates are over altars and you will find one on a small isle out to sea."

Upon reaching the griffin shelter, King Zulo announced, "Here is where I leave you. I wish you fair winds and clear skies." He lowered his head to Adwen and she bowed back.

Astride his golden griffon, the king gave Oryn a stern nod. It was returned just as the creature thrust itself into the sky. The sudden gust blew dust and pebbles in all directions.

The sheltered griffons spotted Adwen and came trotting close, clicking beaks and cooing praises in hopes of being her ride. Some started snapping at one another, but she ignored them, spying a falcon griffon in the back by itself. While her friends picked their mounts, she escaped the crowding creatures.

The one in the back got nervously to his feet when she came and fluffed himself.

She smiled. "You look good enough to fly. Are you up to it?"

He burbled. "Me?"

"What's your name?"

"Low Feather, Lady Adwen. Am I flying for you?"

"If you feel like carrying me!"

The others looked thoroughly envious when they left for the street. While the knight picked a sturdy black griffon, Toth sat atop a fishing mount. She came out riding Low Feather and he fanned his wings, eager to fly. Two guards with bald eagle griffons arrived and Isla gave further directions.

When he finished, the guards nodded and he bid Adwen farewell. "Take care and fair winds to you all. We look forward to your return, Adwen Andredan."

He bowed low and the guards issued commands to their feathered companions. They shrieked and took off all together, climbing ever higher.

The king's advisor waved until they were out of sight.

Adwen enjoyed herself, darting through clouds. Sharing power with the creature, they flew tight circles around the rest. Both escorts marveled while Toth laughed at the acrobatic maneuvers.

The griffon glowed gold while sharing invigorating power. Flying far from the formation, the two drifted close to the choppy sea. They skimmed the surface and salty spray made her whoop. Adwen couldn't recall ever feeling this alive. She still did not know the extent of her powers and did not care for the moment.

The team reached the island sooner than expected. Adwen was naturally first onto solid ground and danced about excitedly. Then she laughed to the escorts as they joined her, taking a bow.

"Thanks bringing us here safe. It was fun!"

They hadn't understood, but their griffons exchanged looks.

Low Feather squawked. "I hope to be your ride again soon!"

Toth was glad to be on the ground and Oryn was beside himself. The foolhardy wasting of power was frustrating. They were meant for a greater purpose than self-entertainment.

She bid the guides and the griffons goodbye. While they turned back for the flight home, the adventurers entered the ruined shrine. Weather had worn away the spiraling columns almost beyond recognition. Inside was dark and Adwen led the way, acting as their eyes. A damp stone passage took them down deep. Where the tunnel ended, they stopped to gasp in awe.

Reflecting off of a vast shallow pool were sparkling lights from countless blue crystals embedded in the walls. The glow illuminated the way to the stone altar that presented yet another rippling portal of light.

Approaching the threshold, she turned to her wary company. "Are you guys ready for this?"

The half-elf swallowed hard and the knight grimaced.

Sensing Oryn's disapproval, she giggled and they went through to the other side.

Chapter 31
THE ARENA

They thought they might be standing on the sun. The vast White Sea Desert's natural brilliance strained their eyes, heat percolated from the dunes. Having arrived instantly, the knight stood with the others staring at the desolate landscape. At first he was in awe, but in a flash he was angry.

"We won't survive more than three days in this retched pit! What are we to do for water now that we cannot go back?"

Adwen said nothing and strolled up the slope behind. Toth struggled to follow in the hot, shifting ground.

"Dog, what are your plans?" the knight demanded, squinting after them under the oppressive sun.

Neither companions answered. As both friends reached the top they stopped. When Toth appeared pleased, she folded her arms in satisfaction.

Curious, Oryn hiked to the crest of the dune as well. Only once there did he spy a lush oasis. For a moment he thought it might be a trick, but it seemed real enough when the travelers reached the shade of the unusual grove. A crystal clear spring awaited in the island of green. Palm fronds acted as leafy eaves, sheltering them from the boiling heat.

Toth dashed to the spring to fill his flask and she called teasingly, "Watch out for snakes and scorpions. Their poisons could get in the water."

Toth abruptly paused to look back in alarm.

Laughing, she waved a hand. "I don't smell anything, buddy! Fill it up and let me check it before you drink."

At her side, the knight was intrigued by the hardiness of the foreign flora. These trees produced what appeared to be gigantic husked fruit. When his gaze fell on Adwen, her arms were folded and she smiled with a raised eyebrow.

"Well? You wanted water, right?"

Keeping his expression blank, he looked to the spring. "It is adequate." Becoming uncomfortable, he strode over to join Toth. He suddenly felt flush and attributed it to the heat..

Left alone, Adwen sniffed the air deeply. A sly smile crept over her. Going to a place where the brush was most dense, she lay down to rest. She folded arms behind her head, closing her eyes.

A long moment of quiet passed. Then a stealthy hand brought out a knife, holding it to her throat as a second grasped her by the arm. An armored man crouched over her and she looked up, still smiling.

Loud enough for her friends to hear, she greeted the stranger. "You sure took your time."

Toth and Oryn whipped around to see the assailant. Before either could move, many more emerged from the brush. An armored man with a bushy black beard called out in a strange language far different from the last kingdoms'. Adwen noted their garments bore a striking resemblance to the Greeks or Romans of antiquity.

Oryn was silent, tightly squeezing his drawn sword.

The man over Adwen shouted at him again, but spoke their language instead. "Put down the weapon or your woman dies!"

The knight scowled at the threat before stealing a glance at her.

Adwen gave a reassuring nod.

His expression hardened until it was a distasteful grimace. Bitterly, he handed over his father's sword and a knife.

Camels and a horse-drawn prison cart were hidden in the thick of the oasis. Bound at the wrists, three were locked inside and towed away.

Adwen's pleasant smile never faded as she reclined against steel bars, enjoying the sun's warmth. Her new body absorbed the energy. It felt as if there were many indistinguishable hands caressing and soothing her skin.

After getting over the disappointment of capture, Toth was busy observing the odd humpback animals. He could not help but stare.

Not having a care for the camels, the knight was preoccupied studying Adwen. These men were no match for her so why be taken prisoner? He thought it through and finally stated, "You were aware they intended to take us captive."

Lost in a state of euphoria, she gave the knight a lazy glance. She wore a careless smile and answered softly. "Yes, I did."

"Do you mean to use their ignorance to reach civilization?"

"Maybe I have a plan and maybe I'm just going with the flow. What do you think?"

He did not enjoy being teased, but accepted the treatment. She had yet to give his warranted punishment, so any annoyance she caused was welcome. If the punishment were left to the Order Council, he would surely already be missing strips of flesh from his back. Was this her way of giving justice?

"I think you are playing the fool, luring them into thinking you are the lesser, when, in fact, you are a master in the game." Glaring, he added, "You're leading on and testing the adversary."

Her violet eyes glowed as she looked amused. "Are you talking about these guys or about yourself?"

Before Oryn could respond, Toth asked, "Adwen? What are these beasts? They do not seem magical."

"Those are camels. They travel and live in the desert. If they drink enough water they can last for weeks before needing another drop."

"Stars above!"

Adwen thought of something and frowned. "Hey, Toth. Can I ask you something?"

"Of course. What about?"

"When I first came back from the dead, I looked almost the same. Then I got this new look after an hour or so. Why the delay?"

"Magic is energy that behaves like a living thing. It flows and changes and can sometimes be unpredictable. I'm sure your change was linked with your death and revival, but the delay could have been because of something around you. Not all magical changes are instant. Other times, obtained powers only emerge once the proper moment arises."

Adwen nodded and answered her own question. "Kotig showed up. It makes sense. Why aren't my changes painful anymore? They're smooth and short."

Oryn answered instead, wearing a grim expression. "Any forced transformation that is against the will of the body will be very painful. Now that you are free to choose and control your form, there is no pain. One exception to the rule is the transformation of a werewolf, such as Korig or Kotig. They possessed bodies that did not belong to them. Their changes would always have pain. They stole the bodies they occupied."

"Are you telling me that those guys were demon-possessed?"

"Yes. All werewolves are cursed human bodies, harboring a demon. It is the mark from a werewolf that summons and seals it there. It cannot be exorcised. Only death can banish a demon from a werewolf. When facing one of the accursed things, before you is neither man or beast; it is a demon wrapped in a fleshy shell. They know no pity or fear. A werewolf is a true abomination."

Adwen almost shuddered. "It's no wonder you hate them so much. They sound sad and disgusting."

Turning his gaze to the arid landscape that steadily became dry fields of wheat, he thought it was a great understatement.

Hours passed. An enormous fortified wall came into view. Their mobile prison took them through a fortified gate, and as they passed the guards, many busy people stared and a few children ran alongside to see the new captives. Giggling excitedly, they came close until they saw her violet eyes flash. She smiled to herself as they gasped and darted out of sight.

Moving along the dusty street, they saw the greatest structure of the city. Countless arches and pillars supported the crouching coliseum. Entering through a broad tunnel, they went down past many patrons and lit torches.

The knight grew concerned. "Dog?"

Ever since leaving Eskrana, Oryn spoke the term without venom or authority. As the tone had changed, Adwen found she did not mind it so much.

"Yes, knight?"

"These are dungeons, are they not?" He had the sense that something dangerous awaited at the end.

She happily answered. "These guys are a lot like a people who once lived in my world. It is most remembered for their architecture and Coliseum. People attended to watch hundreds of men and animals fight to the death." Giving the knight a sly smile, she added, "If this coliseum is anything like the one from my world, then you just might enjoy it."

"Why would I take to such a wretched pot of death?"

"Whoever is the last man standing is given supreme glory." He was surprised and she raised an eyebrow. "I thought you liked battle?"

He did, but fighting to the death for another's entertainment was not to his taste. Breathing in a slow steady rhythm, he focused thoughts and slowed his heart beat. In moments, he was centered.

Observing, she became confused. "What are you doing?"

"I'm readying myself for battle."

Chuckling, she shook her head. "Don't bother. If I get my way, you won't set foot in the arena. Whatever they have in it, I'm sure you would be dead in seconds."

Finally arriving in a dimly lit corridor, they stopped before two massive doors. Light seeped through the gaps and she could smell stale blood. Many inhuman smells reached her as well. Raw energy in her chest made her eyes shine like stars in the gloom.

Twelve armed guards in red arrived and one let them out. A royal guard among them took Adwen by the arm, cutting her bonds while both friends were dragged to the doors. As he turned with her to leave, she broke free and headed them off before the arena gates.

Surprised by Adwen's sudden appearance, the troops halted and stared.

"Let them go! Send me in to fight!"

After exchanging looks, they all laughed.

"Step aside, delicate desert flower! By order of King of Loggias, only men may enter."

The royal guard caught up with her and tried to drag her away.

Not willing to be brushed aside, Adwen got their attention by kicking the royal guard's chest plate, sending him into the far wall. While they were stunned, she quickly snatched the nearest spear and used the shaft to sweep out five pairs of feet. They fell with a loud crash and she stuck the weapon into the earth, demanding more firmly.

"Let them go and put me in the arena! You'll get a much better show that way!"

Provoked and taking her seriously, they were about to attack when a booming voice stopped them dead in their tracks. The royal guard, while keeping his distance from Adwen, answered in English.

"The woman, my lord. She wishes to enter." When she glared, he stammered, "And she wishes for the others to be spared."

A tall, toned, robed man with a beard emerged from a side tunnel. "I would prefer she be at my side. Why is she still here rather than by my seat?"

Taken aback, he answered, "She is deceivingly strong and refuses to leave or allow them passage."

The man – evidently the king -- nodded and almost laughed. He looked her over while politely explaining. "My dear, the arena is no place for you. No man has survived. Come join me. I promise it will be a spectacular sight."

Growing angry, her eyes glowed even brighter. "First of all, these two men are my friends. I would not enjoy watching them die. Second, perhaps if you send in a woman, you might see a difference in the survival statistics."

Entertained, the king laughed in booming guffaws. "If that is your wish then you may enter along with your friends and fight together. You may live with their help."

"No! I'm going alone. If I die, then you can put them in. Let them stand by you and watch. I'm taking their place."

Her eyes shined and the guards looked to their king. The people would not be pleased to see a woman entering the arena.

Playing with his beard, the king thought long and hard. "This woman may enter. At her request, the men shall join me in my booth. If she fails to survive the first battle, they will replace her."

Her stare twinkled in the dark. "You won't be disappointed."

With a sympathetic tone, he replied, "I am already."

A pair of guards opened the gates to allow Adwen through into the bright sunshine and roaring crowd. When the entrance was shut and locked, the king turned to the guards.

He murmured, "For the first battle, put in Garcon."

They exchanged mischievous looks and some scoffed.

Under the shaded king's compartment, Oryn and Toth stood beside the throne. King Loggias approached the ledge overlooking the arena. Raising his arms, he waited for the murmuring stands to hush.

Adwen stood patiently in the center of the dusty ring, breathing in the smells. Disliking the scent of human blood as much as the taste, she glared up at the booth in anticipation.

Beside the king, two young men blew horns. Other horn blowers encircling the arena blew the same tone together and a gate on the far side lifted.

Excitement came over Adwen as she prepared to face whatever was released. Out of the dark came a roar and a loud grunt as a beast lumbered into the light, strings of drool weeping from its jaws.

Adwen became perplexed. Standing with head tilted, confusion played across her face.

An elderly bear grunted again, swatting the dirt aggressively. "You come to challenge me?"

She restrained a scoff.

He charged while she stood smiling. The animal came upon her, reared and was ready to swing a paw full of claws for her head.

Many gasped and cheered, while some were outraged and booed at the king. Then, suddenly, everyone fell silent. The only sound was the echo of the bear's groan.

Adwen had flipped the beast over and pinned him, careful not to harm him.

Garcon grunted in surprise. "How? How could you defeat me?"

"Stay down and don't get up until I say. I don't want to kill you if I don't have to."

He grunted obediently.

King Loggias was in shock while Oryn and Toth exchanged smiles. The king was right. This would be entertaining.

Standing over the brute, magical power magnified her voice until it could be heard by the entire crowd. "An old hungry bear? If that is your idea of a challenge, then you must have very feminine men fighting here!"

The people muttered as the king gave a dry laugh.

She chuckled and called out, "Send something bigger."

Very intrigued, he instructed the horn blowers. "Magill!"

They blew a different tone and it was answered by the others. Another gate opened into the arena and Adwen warned the bear. "Now would be a good time to leave."

Garcon scrambled to the safety of his cage before it could close.

When the new creature roared out from the shadows, she was sure the king was taking her seriously. Ten feet tall and brown like the bloodstained dirt, the Minotaur displayed long, black, raking bull horns. His loincloth was ragged and the axe in his stumpy hands was sharp. Twirling the heavy weapon menacingly, he stopped forward to roar in Adwen's face. The deafening sound rang and the crowd hushed.

Not intimidated by the show of force, her eyes glowed and she bowed deeply.

As she did, he snorted. Silently, he raised the axe and swung.

In the blink of an eye, she stepped aside and jumped, twirling through the air. While the weapon struck dirt and dust, her foot came up and struck the underside of his muzzle.

The creature stumbled backward.

Adwen nimbly landed upright, ready to continue. Her silver and gold hair settled about her shoulders and the people began to cheer. The Minotaur recovered from the blow and glared. Bellowing in anger, he charged with axe swinging from side to side.

Dodging every blow, she ducked under another swing, punching his stomach and the beast-man stumbled backward.

Worked into a blind rage, he attacked as she dashed and twirled in close to deliver a fierce kick. When he was buckled over gasping for air, she punched his jaw, bowling him over.

The crowd got to their feet. Struggling back onto cloven hooves, the minotaur roared in defiance.

While the creature bellowed, she lunged, snagging one

pointed horn. Building up incredible momentum, she swung around hard and fast.

Shocked, the Minotaur cried out just before the stress was too much for his neck. There was loud snap as she let go, landing on her feet. The bloodthirsty creature fell with a heavy thud, great girth flinging up a cloud of dust.

More cheers erupted before the king laughed, raising a hand for quiet. "That was most impressive, my dear! You owe me a new Minotaur. I must know what sort of woman must you be to kill it with your bare hands?"

Smiling impishly, she answered, "Send in something big and you might find out."

Mirthful laughter filled the air and the crowd returned to clapping and calling. After the arena guards dragged away the corpse, the choir of horns sounded for the next battle to begin.

A giant desert scorpion the size of a car rushed out of a dark gate. It hissed, whipping its stinger rigorously. No matter how many times it tried, the strikes always missed.

Sidestepping another blow, she snatched and ripped its stinger off. It shrieked in pain and snapped pincers, missing as she flipped up high to thrust the sting deep into its abdomen. While it squirmed and curled up into a fetal ball, she coolly stepped away. As it stopped twitching, she smiled and gave the king an innocent shrug.

In reply, he laughed and called to his horn blowers, "Angoras!"

A fire drake was released. The flightless fire worm scratched and slashed for her with blinding quickness. When all else failed, it used a whip-like tail to snatch her up by the ankle. With Adwen immobile, it prepared to breath fire.

Before he could exhale, she turned and smashed its tail with a balled fist.

Crying out, it spewed flames from its mouth and completely missed. The creature tried to recoil, but hardly got the chance before Adwen was too close. Her sharp claws slashed at the fire lizard's tender throat.

In the king's booth, Loggias pondered aloud. "Her manner of fighting is strange. It is so much like..."

"An animal," Oryn finished for him.

The king glanced at the knight who hadn't taken his eyes

off her.

Adwen's motions reminded Oryn of dancing. Like water, Adwen seeped through and penetrated the opponent's defenses effortlessly.

Nearly gutted, the crimson reptile slunk back to its cage in tatters. Nugent, a giant three-headed dog entered next. But before she could do any harm to the king's personal pet, Loggias stood and signaled that the battles halt. Nugent was obedient and retreated at his command.

She watched him leave then looked up curiously.

He whispered into the ear of a horn blower, causing him to blanch.

Growing more curious, she watched the servant nod and run off. Then the king told the remaining boy to make a very different sound with his horn. He nervously obeyed and blew a deep tone. The ominous call rounded the stands.

People began to scramble away from the arena. Women screamed as many tripped and stumbled in urgency to get clear. The first servant reappeared presenting a small chest. Out of the now-open box, the king took a black horn with swirling etchings inlaid with gold. It glinted in the sun and he took a deep breath before blowing the guttural instrument. While the sound echoed in the air, he hurled the artifact into the arena. The fragile thing arced for the ground and every frightened eye followed it.

Adwen's thoughts halted as her sixth sense filled her with dread. Something sealed inside the fine shell made Adwen's skin crawl. It shattered on the ground and a deep black fog erupted from the shards. A thick cloud swelled to over a hundred feet high like a thunderhead. Rumbling sounds came out from the pitch black as something solidified within and a breeze lifted the haze, sending the crowd into cries of horror.

A giant beast with two heads and a monstrous fanged serpent tail stared around at the humans. The monster's heads were of a wicked lion and a goat. Dark smoke curdled from both mouths and nostrils as the vile thing spotted her. The chimera had found its first victim after centuries of confinement.

This was not what she had expected. Adwen's spirit friends from school had taught her about this horror. In legends it was defeated by a warrior riding on the back of Pegasus. She didn't have a winged horse and this monster made the descriptions in stories pale in comparison.

A green tongue of flame shot from the lion's jaws, narrowly missing as she darted away and between its four clawed feet. When the fire struck ground, it scorched the earth black. The chimera was swift for its immense size.

Oryn and Toth were now staring down anxiously. The knight's heart leaped to his throat as she was snatched up by the serpentine tail.

It coiled around her and she screamed in frustration and fear. Trapped, she stared back at the rearing reptilian head. The blood-red eyes dilated and it hissed, showing long fangs that looked like glass spikes. It yawned wide with an even louder hiss, prepared to swallow her whole.

Suddenly, she let out a ringing cry. The sonorous note hung as there was an explosion of white light from her body within the coils. Pale flames burst forth and her claws tore the serpent tail to bits, making the other heads cry in agony.

Pieces of the tail rained down along with the white hound that appeared out of the fire. Gracefully, she landed on all fours and muscles rippled in her back beneath a glossy white coat. Dark flesh fell around her and she shook the long fur on the arch of her neck. She roared angrily at the writhing chimera.

Gasping, the king leaned heavily upon the rail and his bearded jaw dropped.

Fangs bared, she raced around the four towering legs as they stomped and swatted. The more she evaded, the angrier the creature became. It stomped again with one of its forefeet, trying to crush her.

Not flinching, Adwen darted up the leg and leaped for the goat's head. Once she landed, claws dug in deep while she ripped into an eye with voracious jaws. Purple blood spilled out, vaporizing on contact with Adwen's body while the giant horned head swung wildly. But her claws held fast and fangs continued to rip at tender tissues.

Then she heard the lion head roar and paused. The goat's fearsome neighbor was opening its maw and about to breathe black tongues of flame. With no time to think, she let go and leaped for the arena floor.

The goat head was engulfed in fire, but it was unharmed. The horned head turned to find the white hound still sailing toward the ground and belched forth a massive column of evil fire. Green tongues engulfed her and the watchers in the stands cried out while she fell. The goat continued to scorch her and when it finally stopped, the ground was charred and a sooty body lay quivering.

Adwen's burns were severe, but she fought through the pain to stand. Once on all fours, she rigorously shook her coat, tossing away most of the ash. Silver blood shone in patches while the stinging from the injuries infuriated her. Eyes flashing gold at the chimera, she let loose a defiant roar.

It replied with a roar of its own, along with two more columns of fire. Avoiding the devastating blasts, she circled the arena, using the time to plan. The blood of the chimera was purple and it seemed to her that it could be a demon. She dodged the continuous attacks until it was time to try a new and rather risky plan.

Darting for the far side of the arena, she skidded hard, kicking up a cloud of dust that hid her from view. A second later she came flying out, making straight for the chimera. It blew flames as she charged and she narrowly weaved around the blasts. Finding a gap between the rivers of flame, she leaped for the beast's broad chest. Both Adwen's clawed hands filling with white light. She snarled and prepared to plunge them into evil flesh.

The heads moved to snap her up. But then the chimera began to roar and screech. White light shone out the mouths, nostrils and eyes. It soon fell quiet and burned from the inside, falling as a giant heap of ashes, slowly being blown away.

Adwen struggled to climb out of the pile and stumbled until she found her balance on level ground. She panted and shuddered; the energy she spent to kill the monster nearly wiped her out. The light in her half-cast eyes was dim.

Armed guards rushed out with a net and she did not resist. As they proceeded to drag her away, she was content with the chance to rest.

Guards brought Oryn and Toth into the bowels of the coliseum with King Loggias. Walking in brisk strides, the king questioned them.

"What -- who is she? Where is she from?"

They did not answer.

"What game are you playing at? I was told you were discovered in an oasis without camels and no proper supplies. Who are you?"

"We are traveling on business," Oryn replied. "If you wish for more knowledge, speak with the dog."

They came to a tunnel near a lift system. A moment passed and the groaning sounds made by the lift grew until the platform arrived. The gate was thrown back and more guards dragged out the net with Adwen before the king.

The way she had been brought angered the knight. If his hands were not bound he would grab the throat of the closest guard and squeeze.

After the folds of the net were pulled back, she lay there for a while, staring and panting. She mustered the strength to stand. The silvery wounds glistened by the torch light. Taking a gentle bow, she changed into woman form. The burns remained and garments were singed around them.

King Loggias studied her carefully. "Who are you, hound?"

She took a deep breath and answered. "I am Adwen. I'm here to make a deal with you and the other leaders of the White Sea Desert." She paused before continuing. "I am the Heir of Darien the Master Knight."

The guards were stunned and the king cocked an eyebrow. "Then, if you are, I have a more personal test. The chimera was left by Darien, but I have one of my own." He gestured towards the tunnel. "Just ahead is a cavern and a narrow stretch of ground, leading to a chest. Only the true heir may reach it alive."

Her eyes wandered to the faces of her companions. Toth was reassuring as always and Oryn sported a poker face. Try as she might to read his feelings, he was talented at hiding them. She felt uncertain. When there was no guidance to be found, she turned to the tunnel.

In the dark she picked up the scent of a living thing. The

air was moist and her vision cut through the shadows. Taking a breath, she carefully strode along a narrow stretch of earth deeper into the dark. Everything was quiet, save for the soft dripping of water in the depths. Adwen's sixth sense warned of a presence just before the still air began to swirl in strong gusts. Wings were beating closer and she finally saw it coming.

At the cavern entrance, the others saw it glow steadily brighter. The feathers across the giant owl shimmered with every color. Moth markings flowed across the animal's broad wings as the luminous bird hovered.

It stared and screeched. "Who dares approach this chest of destiny?" Giving an aggressive thrust with its wings, it threatened to blow her off her feet into the deep. The glowing owl went low and gripped the path like a perch with huge talons and screeched again, displaying eye-marked wings. "Speak! Tell me your name and why you have come!"

Her eyes adjusted to the light it gave off and she hesitantly answered, "I am Adwen. Who are you?"

"I am a guardian; summoned and appointed to guarding one of the treasures of Andredan! Are you Adwen, descended from Darien?"

"I was hoping you could tell me that. Everyone keeps saying I am. Do you know?"

Her answer surprised the guardian. The great owl tucked its wings and turned its head upside-down, perplexed. Big mother-of-pearl eyes blinked back and it hooted. "You would ask another as to who you are?" It turned its head upright, ruffled its feathers and shrieked, bobbing its head. "What a strange question to ask of me."

The owl crept along the path to lean down close, examining her. She could see her reflection in the richly colored face. It blinked and clicked its beak, "Of course you are. You could be no one else." It jumped back with a great thrust to land on a gilded stand beside an isle of stone. The glow from the guardian filled the cavern.

With no further trouble, Adwen reached the platform of stone where the golden chest rested. Gold inscriptions covered the seamless chest. She was about to open it when the owl screeched at her.

"Heir of Darien! Now is not the time."

Startled at first, she asked, "Why can't I open it?"

The bird cooed. "Because this treasure serves a purpose. When you next visit this hallowed place, you shall see."

The king smiled as he witnessed the guardian bowing and started to laugh. "What a marvelous day! The heir has come, and now we can prepare our army for the great battle!"

Her friends were in awe as well. Oryn was more certain than ever that she was the heir. He had known real nightmares, but each moment spent in her company was like living a different life. It was a wondrous dream.

The Past (Part 1)
THE WAKING NIGHTMARE

A red dawn stained the sky the morning Malkum Buskin went to see his sister and twin nephews. He had served alongside his brother-in-law, Sedro Conrad, for years in the order and hadn't seen his sister and nephews for many months. As he rode over the grassy hills on the outskirts of Tanoaks, the mountains wore their snowy caps like always, but the air was not as sweet. From atop the final hill he could see the broken door and windows and his heart felt sick. Malkum urged his horse into a gallop, fearing that a waking nightmare awaited him there.

Reaching the lodging he saw the remains of Sedro's horse, Ranger, a few yards away. Now his heart hammered as he dismounted and simultaneously took out his sword. He crept to the bloody doorway. Upon entering, the knight found pools of blood across the floorboards and Sedro's severed arm at the threshold. Dismembered remains were strewn everywhere. After a few moments of shock, he noticed the boy sitting on the table. The child was so motionless he seemed like a statue. There he sat, bathed in half-dried blood, his feet dangling as he silently hung his head.

Malkum couldn't tell which of his nephews was holding Sedro's sword. They looked so alike that the only way to tell was to see their eyes. Before Malkum could utter a word, the boy looked up. It was Oryn. His gaze was no longer bright like he remembered. Those amazing eyes were like snuffed candles. He resembled an angry walking dead the way he stared.

Malkum struggled at first to think of any words. "Are you hurt?"

Oryn slowly shook his head. He hadn't blinked yet and continued to glare.

Relieved, Malkum took another step. Spying the remains

of his sister made him turn white as a ghost. Tearing his eyes from the grisly sight, he focused on his disturbingly calm nephew. "Where is your brother?"

The question caused his gaze to drop to the floor and young hands clenched his father's sword. Shaking all over, he did not cry.

"Oryn?" he asked, frightened to hear the answer. "Where is he?"

His face quickly turned back up and he sneered. "Gone. He's gone, Uncle." His hands shook horribly and face turned red with rage.

Malkum saw blood and black hairs caked to the side of the blade. There were claw marks all about the home. A werewolf had been here.

"Show me where your brother is. Please, Oryn. Where is he?" Not knowing was torture.

Sliding down with the sword in hand, he glared even more fiercely. Stepping over the pieces of a shattered childhood, the young boy brought Malkum away from the home and into the woods. Amid the trees and brush was where they found him.

Malkum all but vomited. "You... you did this? Why?"

Oryn stared at the small, nude, decapitated corpse and answered without emotion, "I killed the werewolf, Uncle. It was him." He pointed the filthy weapon at the leg of the naked body. "See? He was bitten. See the scratch? My brother was the werewolf, Uncle and I killed him."

Malkum could see the boy was right. It was not a normal injury. Drawing his living nephew close, he led him away. A dull pain filled his heart as they went to the horse. He did not know whether to weep for the dead or for the boy who survived. His strong, brave nephew was stained by this evil event. It was evident in his beautiful green eyes. He would never be the same.

Malkum bore him to Tanoaks and to their friend's home, the Red Lily Inn. Mabel and his wife kept Toth as their adoptive son. The knight knew Toth and Oryn were close friends. The innkeepers had three children, one of whom was sickly, but Toth, the half-elf boy was treated like one of their own. Once there, the blood was cleaned away. By the time the Mabel's children awoke, Oryn was clothed and sitting in a room

to himself.

When Toth neared the downstairs, he overheard the adults talking about Oryn and his brother. He couldn't believe his pointed ears. It couldn't be true. This was all some terrible trick. The door to his friend's room was ajar and he peered through, but before he could go inside, Malkum stopped him.

Tears forming in his soft brown eyes, he asked, "Is it true, Master Malkum? Are Master and Missus Conrad gone? And what about... is he gone, too?"

He nodded and steered Toth away, closing the door with a click.

Later their good-byes were said and Malkum and Oryn departed for the Order of the Master Knights a few hours' ride away. The grand city and the enormous fortress did nothing to move the boy's emotions. He had been silent the entire journey and never said a word when they entered the gates.

They were greeted by an older knight in a shining set of slayer's armor. Much older than the rest, he kept his white beard short and well-trimmed. The rest of his hair was tied back and he spoke in a strong, demanding tone.

"Malkum Buskin, you have returned early. Was there no better reason for you to stay at your sister's home? Her food is far better than anything offered here."

Malkum climbed down and lifted his nephew after him.

The strong old knight asked firmly, "Who is the boy?"

Malkum hesitated, thinking of something brief for an explanation. This knight was not one for long stories. "This is the last of the Conrad family, sir. He is my nephew, Oryn."

The news rattled the old knight and he gestured at the sheathed sword on the child's back. "That is Sedro's sword, is it not?"

He nodded promptly.

The knight judged the child with a scrutinizing eye. When Oryn looked up, he nearly flinched. In those green eyes was a look he had only seen in battle-worn men. This child had been witness to great evil.

"What happened?"

"His twin brother was marked. With his fallen father's sword, he ended the beast's rampage in a single swing."

Impressed, he locked eyes with Oryn once again. After a

while of pondering, he nodded. "He shall stay in the order. I will take the liberty of training him myself."

Malkum hoped Oryn would get a chance at an easier life. "But, sir, my nephew is in need of rest. I'm already searching for a proper place to stay in the city."

Becoming stern, the elder knight glared. "I have a place ready for him now! I shall train Sedro Conrad's son starting at dawn tomorrow. The Conrad family has always advanced well among the ranks." The look in the old knight's hazel eyes was like a fearsome fire and he assured Malkum. "Rest is only good for the body, my brother in arms. What this boy needs is a mending of the mind. In time, a balm for his soul will be found. For now, he shall learn of his father's work and make the decisions for his future, just as any other man may upon joining the order."

Young Oryn listened as his uncle bit his tongue. The only place for boys his age in the order was as a squire or a page. To the elder council, someone as young as he being trained was unheard of and unacceptable.

This knight was not like the rest. He had deferred his seat as an elder in the counsel for his love of defending the kingdom. On equal footing with any elder of the order, he was twice as harsh. To go against his command was to risk much indeed.

Unhappy, Malkum nodded respectfully. "Yes, Sir Vigo Odette."

Chapter 32
THE RACE

"Ah, my head is aching something awful. Uh! And my stomach has turned evil." Toth groaned atop his camel on their ride through the desert in search of the Bebidin people. Ahead of them rode two more escorts on camels while she was on a white stallion and Oryn on a black stud.

After the king wrote his treaty, enthusiastically signed and handed it over, they were whisked off to a large feast. A variety of drinks were offered and Toth had drunk them all. Oryn was not amazed, but Adwen was baffled that the half-elf hadn't drowned in the powerful smelling stuff. His hangover was irritating for everyone on the hot sands.

"Maybe if you didn't get so over excited, you would be less miserable. I'm no mother, but you shouldn't drink so much. It's bad for you."

She winced as he suddenly vomited off to the side and the knight rolled his eyes. The humped animal moaned disdainfully at his rider's sickness.

"See what I mean?"

Wiping the sick from his face, he took a deep drink of water from a flask. "I'm sorry, Adwen. I wanted to be the first from Dargadia to taste every drink in the neighboring kingdoms. It's something I've been curious to try and it makes for good conversation later. Perhaps I had too much. I'm well-adjusted to the drink from Dargadia, but not this wicked strong stuff."

"Your problem was that you were overexcited and overconfident."

He chuckled and his head ached. "You're going to lecture me on overconfidence? Who was confident enough to enter the arena alone? You've feared nothing since your return to the living worlds. Where has your fear gone, my friend?"

Oryn was pretending not to listen, but his ears pricked as the conversation turned to the topic of her recklessness.

"I'm not that confident. Death isn't so scary anymore. It's easy to die."

"Is that why you're so unafraid?"

"I still get scared. In my past life I didn't try to do enough. What would you do different if you got a second life?"

Her question got both of her friends to thinking.

Toth replied, "I suppose I would be doing the same sort of thing."

"I'm still unsure about stuff."

"Second life or no," Oryn added, "caution is a part of living."

Adwen laughed and her eyes sparkled. "What's the point of being alive if you're not going to live?"

Oryn stared as she suddenly raced away, sharing some power with the white horse. They could hear her cries of excitement across the dunes. The mount raced around with her, kicking up sand, feeling the stroke of the breeze.

They rode south with the Ulla Lake to their right. It was nestled in the heart of the barren region, fed by two rivers out of the Ebony Range. The water was safe to drink and the undead could not get far enough through the open desert to be a nuisance. Wild growth surrounding the shoreline was enticing in the heat. Eventually the travelers grew thirsty.

While resting, an escort cried out, "Lady Adwen! Three riders approach!"

They wore tan robes and headdresses. Their dark horses looked like Arabian stallions. None spoke as Adwen's company and the strangers studied each other, the slender-legged creatures danced anxiously, snorting.

A rider suddenly looked at the knight. After studying his armor he pointed a riding crop, speaking in a different language.

An escort translated for them, "He said to state your name, warrior. Why have you come into our lands uninvited?"

Adwen stepped forward to answer. "We've come to see your king."

The strange riders stared in silence and one pulled back the cloth over his face to spit on the ground. Then he said in strained English, "Someone please tell this woman to be silent. This is a man's conversation and not her place." He turned back to Oryn. "What is your name and what do you want with our king?"

A dangerous glint was in Oryn's eyes as he slowly replied. "We are here for business that concerns the woman. Make better choices with your words."

The rider sniffed. "What good is this woman to our king?"

Adwen's eyebrows went up and her mouth pursed as she immediately detected the rage wafting off of the knight. In silence, she wondered what he was about to do to this man.

The three eyed him warily as he presented a closed hand as if to show one of the riders something. When curiosity made the man lean over, he instantly regretted it. In a flash the rider was wrenched from his saddle and slammed to the ground. The knight put a knife to the stranger's throat in the midst of everyone yelling and drawing weapons.

Adwen's powerful voice put a stop to the chaos. "Enough! Everyone settle down!"

As the shouting ceased, Oryn remained crouched over the rider and sneered. "I warned you to mind your tongue! You're in the presence of the Heir of Darien!"

The man was confounded and stole a glance at Adwen. Calling to his companions, he made them put their sabers away.

Even after their weapons were sheathed, Oryn toyed with the thought of cutting him for his disrespect. Then he heard her nervously command, "Help him up, knight."

Without hesitation, he put the dagger back in his boot and brought the frightened man to his feet. Oryn stepped back and continued to glare.

The stranger checked for blood and found none. "Thank you. If you are..." He glanced furtively at the knight. "...the heir of Darien, we are to test your skills."

"So what'll it be? A fight?"

Seeing her pleased expression calmed him. "It is a race. You will race us with a steed of your choosing to the watchtower outside our city." He pointed south at a distant structure. He continued to keep a watchful eye on the disgruntled knight. "Do you accept this test to identify yourself?"

A broad smile spread across her face. "Oh, I accept. Let's do it!"

The race was between her and the three riders. Her white horse was small and the three scoffed to one another from atop purebreds.

Adwen whispered to her mount. "They'll have to think a little differently when this is over."

Her horse whinnied.

"Are you ready to begin?"

She gave a sly smile. "I'll be waiting inside your city walls."

They laughed and urged their horses into an all-out gallop.

A dust cloud immediately enveloped Adwen's company. When it settled, Toth stopped coughing and saw Adwen hadn't gone anywhere. She watched the others pull farther away.

Toth and Oryn exchanged looks as she yawned and her horse snorted. A thoughtful smile came over her and she asked the stallion, "Are they far enough away, do you think?"

He nickered. "Not enough to win."

She laughed and her horse brayed. In a flash of gold and sand, they disappeared.

Toth coughed again in the second cloud of dust. "Will she ever take this seriously?"

The knight shook his head. "Doubtfully."

The riders were halfway to the finish and still hadn't seen her yet. One looked over his shoulder, saw nothing and laughed. "Her tiny animal can't keep up!"

They all laughed, until a cloud closed in from behind. As it settled, they stared while she rode beside them.

Adwen giggled at their stunned looks. "Your horses are pretty fast." Hers whinnied with delight and she was off again like lightning.

A rider swore aloud while his friends choked on sand.

Horns were sounded in the watchtower when the Bebidin saw her coming. They tried to assemble the guards at the gates, blocking her with sabers.

She saw them and smiled, urging her horse on. Charging at full speed, she laughed out loud, her horse sailing over their heads. They stared in shock as she landed behind, riding into the city plaza. Her appearance frightened the commoners in the streets and her horse reared, braying. Everyone kept their distance when she jumped from his back and said breathlessly, "I'm sorry! I got a little carried away."

Seven spears were instantly at her throat.

A sheepish look came over her. "Uh, sorry?"

Then the three riders arrived and called out. She couldn't understand what they said, but the guards removed their spears and backed away. They rode up, dismounted and quickly took a knee. Soon they were joined by everyone in the plaza, bowing.

The sight left her overwhelmed and uneasy. Turning to a rider, she cleared her throat. "Excuse me. Please stand up. And could you tell everyone else to stand up too?"

Out of the silence a voice exploded, ranting. A man in expensive silks came stomping into view, long black beard flapping. His face turned the same shade of purple as his garments. Waving both hands around at the people, he hollered as tassels danced about his waist. Then he saw who they were bowing to and turned a deeper shade. He bellowed in outrage to the riders, pointing with a shaking arm.

Adwen was taken aback by this harangue and watched in mild amusement as a rider answered, causing the rotund man to blanch. When his thick eyebrows twitched, she murmured to the rider. "Who is this guy and how did you get him to stop screaming?"

The rider stood and replied, "His name is Shish Safa, the king's advisor. I told him who you are. What is your name, golden child of Andredan?"

Compliments were still awkward to her, but she hesitantly answered. "Call me Adwen. I'm curious, how can you speak English? Everywhere I've been there are people who can speak it."

The onlookers began to whisper and the riders smiled. Each got to their feet. "Because of Darien's ancient instruction. Before he departed, he visited each land, teaching our people many languages. It is law in any Kingdom of Day that scouts and advisors know three languages besides their own."

One of his companions suddenly smiled. "Si, señorita!"

Another chuckled. "Oui, mademoiselle!"

They all started to laugh. "But why?"

He shrugged. "We did not know what language you would

speak! Darien wanted you to be -- what is the word? Ah, well accommodated!" The others patted his shoulders encouragingly, being that he was the best among them at English.

The others rode in and smiled, but the knight was far too preoccupied with studying the structures, wearing a stony expression. Adobe homes were all around with silvery wind chimes in the windows. For the time being, the shining ornaments were silent.

Shish Safa came forward, greeting her. "Heir of Darien, it is good you have come." He bowed his head in a respectful display.

Even though he acted contrite, Adwen couldn't help but notice his tone. This fat man obviously did not approve of her.

"Is there something wrong?"

He babbled in his own language for a moment and then said, "Nothing is the matter. Come, we shall have you properly dressed before seeking an audience with his highness."

She gave a quizzical look, cocking her head. Then she noticed the women here wore conservative robes and veils. After studying her own attire, she realized that she looked like a floozy to them with so much skin showing. At a whim, her wild garments shifted into beautiful gray and gold robes with a transparent white veil. A string of gold pieces hung about her forehead and her violet eyes sparkled beneath them at his surprise.

"I hope this will do. I like to wear my own clothes."

Statues filled every niche of the towering palace, standing as silent sentries. The enchanted figures' heads turned to watch their ascent. They were ageless guardians, forever clutching spears of brass and sabers of jade. Adwen couldn't decide if the place reminded her more of India or Saudi Arabia as they went up the steps.

Inside, spans of blue silk draped along the halls over dozens more of the golden statues with eyes that followed. They smiled as she passed and saluted with weapons. One gave a nod and a wink, making her blush. She was glad the statues were on their side. In the event that any intruder entered, they would be at the mercy of the magic within. This was the Palace of One Thousand Guards.

At last, Shish brought them to a lavish throne room. Red carpets and cushions were everywhere, while a dozen beautiful women lounged about. A teenage boy stood looking out a veranda wearing a white turban with a jade pendant ringed in gold. His dark eyes looked soft and kind when the group entered and Shish announced them, taking a bow.

"King Isban Leshano. You have a very important guest today."

The king studied her and approached. He struggled with English, but found his words well enough. "You are Darien's hair?"

She smiled and didn't correct his pronunciation. "Yes, Your Highness. I've come to make a treaty with you. Is now a good time to talk?"

He dipped his head a little. "Now is a good time. Shish, bring papers to write a treaty." The man bowed low, backing away as the king asked, "Would you come to window to talk?"

She smiled sweetly. "I would love to."

Before they could go, Toth cleared his throat sheepishly. "Adwen? If you could, ask if there is any drink while we wait."

The young king heard. "Drink? We have only water. No wine, no sour water. So sorry."

He was aghast as Oryn glowered and slowly shook his head. Toth began to stammer and the tall knight covered his mouth, dragging him from the room.

Some of the king's wives were entertained by the antics.

Out on the open veranda, the king was thoughtful and concerned. Wind rustled her white veil as she asked, "What's bothering you?"

He wet his lips. "War; it troubles me. Many will die. Fodders, sons, many will fight. Not all will return. Death bothers me, Andredan."

Together they looked out at the busy city where the people were bartering. There was no fighting and no beggars in the streets. His city was peaceful and happy. Not turning away from the view, she replied, "We all die, King. No law and no measure of peace can stop that. If this battle is coming, then we should be happy with what we know."

He nodded and she continued, "I have seen the afterlife.

Where good souls go is peaceful and there is no pain. In the worlds of the living, the price for peace is war. For every bit of good, there is an ounce of evil that tries to take it away. If we are to survive and live free, then we can only fight for it. This city is beautiful. To be afraid of war is right, but not to fight for this would be a crime. Courage for your people is all you need. You will do what is right for them. I know it."

Feeling reassured, he nodded. "Thank you, but I still afraid."

Adwen chuckled. "I'll let you in on a secret, Your Highness. I'm scared, too."

He gave a meek smile in reply.

A different wind crossed their veranda, bringing the sound of many chimes. King Isban pointed out into the desert at a haze. "Sandstorm coming. When gate is closed, storm will not touch here."

Together they turned to leave, but a scent flew in on the breeze. It passed under her nose and she dashed back to the railing, staring out beyond the city wall. The king joined her and she said with a feral snarl, "I smell minotaur!"

Out of the dunes rushed a large war band of the creatures, charging with the storm at their backs. By the time the watch sounded their horns, the beasts were already upon them. Swinging axes and other looted weapons, they stampeded through the gate.

Adwen, Oryn and Toth arrived in the plaza where the battle was going badly. Enemies were everywhere, cutting down guards. Only a fraction of the creatures had been slain. Leaping into the mess of them, she transformed and fought alongside overwhelmed humans.

The knight skirted through the battle to reach the turnstile upon the wall overlooking the scene. After quickly slaughtering the Minotaur in his way, he struggled to close the gate, but the mechanism was too heavy. Down below, the monsters were holding strong and the sandstorm loomed.

As Adwen ripped out another beasts throats, the blood and filth landed on white fur to fall as dust. Dodging another attacker, she slashed his neck with sharp claws.

That was when she saw a Minotaur larger than the rest, swinging a monstrous axe and bellowing. He issued commands near the gate. She was about to go after him, but heard Oryn shout over the clashing sounds.

"Dog!"

Adwen saw him on the ledge, struggling to close the gate. Avoiding an advancing enemy, she leapt up to join him. She skirted around the fallen bodies and changed into her woman form.

She took his place at the heavy mechanism. "I've got this! I saw the leader. He's bigger with little fox tails for tassels on his loincloth. If we stop him, we can stop this attack."

She expected a comment or question. Instead, he dashed off without hesitation.

"As you command."

Running to the ledge, he wrapped a cloth about his head and mouth. Properly guarded against the elements, he took out his sword and dropped down ten feet onto an unsuspecting Minotaur.

Adwen stared after him, completely speechless. He had taken a direct order before she could even get it out. Shaking her head to break free from the shock, she transformed again and snarled at the turnstile. Slamming a snow-white shoulder into a rung, she went to work. It would take four men to close the gate, but it moved with her efforts alone.

Oryn landed on the creature, knifing his weapon down and severing its spine. Balancing on its shoulders, he rode to the ground and heard the Minotaur chief bellow. Glaring at the beast, he ran, avoiding individual battles and maiming enemies as he went.

The chief saw and snorted out ringed nostrils. Waving a giant battle-axe, he backed away to fight in the worsening conditions. Powerful winds picked up streams of sand, flinging grit and lashing anything that was not under cover. It made seeing farther than a few yards difficult. For the creatures, battle in the desert was child's play. When the knight came out to meet him head on, the chief was overconfident. He had never faced an officer from the order.

When the axe swung for him, Oryn ducked in close and the Minotaur roared as a large wound on his leg erupted with red. Kicking at the human, he missed again. In a rage he swung the weapon and received two more slashes, one for either arm. Far too angry to be intimidated by a petty human, he roared and tried once more.

Adwen was slowly closing the gates as the king's men fought the invaders.

Meanwhile, Toth kept the beasts hemmed into the square. Controlling the few trees within the walls, he commanded strong ropy roots. Some Minotaur noticed their leader gone and the gate closing. Many retreated while there was time, leaving behind a meager few to fight to the bitter end.

Having seen Oryn go into the storm, the half-elf muttered aloud. "Don't be too much longer, you crazy fool."

The Minotaur chief's collections of wounds grew. Sand caked bloody fur as he refused to submit. Snorting with frustration, he swung the axe once more.

Oryn avoided it, and this time turned to sever the limb with a powerful downward stroke. The chief's appendage fell and he roared a horrible cry. In a blind rage, he made a final attempt to crush the knight, raking horns down to run him through.

The act of rage and desperation failed as Oryn nimbly stepped aside. With all the experience avoiding werewolf jaws, the horns of a Minotaur were of little difference. He sliced a heartbeat later and the head of the chief went tumbling away, lost to the swirling storm.

Finally the knight turned to find the city, but could not. Then he heard Adwen howl.

Desperate, he sheathed the sword and made for the sound on a dead sprint. The storm was blinding and he and the fleeing Minotaur were oblivious to one another as they passed. Adwen howled again and he could tell the city was close. His eyes were shut tight with sand in them, making tears stream down his face while he gritted teeth at the stinging.

Adwen howled again, urging the knight to return before it was too late. There came a loud boom and the wind and sand stopped flying. The gates were closed and at the threshold was a high mound of white sand.

Toth dismissed the tree roots back to the earth and Adwen bounded down to join in searching for their foolhardy friend. They hoped he was somewhere under the dune and not outside. While the half-elf was digging, she sniffed for any sign of him.

Finding a faint trace, she swept large masses away as fast as she could. There was movement and she reached inside. The knight emerged in her claws, coughing violently as she held him by the back of his armor. With the cloth gone from his face, he had breathed in some of the sand. Before she could think to ask for help, a man and a few women came to take him. Adwen changed to woman form as they quickly whisked him off to another part of the city.

A surviving scout came to her side and she asked, "Where are they taking him? Will he be all right?"

The scout was in awe now that he knew what she was and answered confidently. "He will be well. They are the best medicine workers alive. You will have your warrior back to do your bidding soon. Come and bring your tree-controlling friend."

The scout led the way and witnesses of the battle gave thanks in the form of nods and smiles. Guards who were not tending the wounded or dead bowed deeply. Though the gestures made her uneasy, she did not try to stop them. Something besides gracious courtesies was bothering her.

Oryn was acting in a way she did not anticipate. She didn't know what to make of it. It was the look in his eyes when he answered before leaping into action. Could it have possibly been admiration? She recalled his words, feeling even more confused.

"As you command?"

The Past (Part 2)
MASTER'S FIRST LESSON

Sir Vigo Odette backhanded the young boy. He fell, his father's sword hitting the dirt beside him with a clang. When he tried to stand the old knight planted a boot in his back. Oryn cried out from the pain at first but fell silent, gritting his teeth as his master bellowed.

"You have no right to use those words, boy! That right is earned. Until that day, I shall not hear you say, As you command. Do you understand?"

The boy grunted from the pressure.

"Do you understand me, boy?"

"Yes, sir!" he yelled in answer. The boot came off and he retrieved the blade from the ground of the training ring.

Sir Vigo was unreadable. "To accept a command from me or any other you shall only reply, 'Yes, sir.' Do you understand?"

Oryn's eyes burned with a vengeance. "Yes, sir."

Sir Vigo grimaced. "Mind your rage, boy. Any other master would strike a second time for that look; instead I have a different method of discipline. Did your father teach you anything of the sword?"

"Yes, sir."

"Show me."

The sword of his forefathers was heavy. He obediently extended an arm, pointing the blade at an imagined opponent. It shook and he controlled the tip through a small sidelong figure eight.

"Very good."

Oryn became tired and rested the tip on the ground. The effort brought on a deep sign to recover.

Sir Vigo was satisfied. "For your discipline you shall perform the technique repeatedly. You will only stop on my word. Begin!"

Clenching teeth and hands, he performed it again, again, and again. His arm shook violently until he suddenly let it fall.

"No! Keep that arm up! When you are incapable of holding it any longer, trade hands. Do you understand?"

"Yes, sir."

Sir Vigo observed, knowing he would not last long. After pondering what might motivate the child, the old knight barked, "Boy." Oryn looked up from his work to listen. "If you fail, you will not be failing me, but yourself. I shall return to collect you later."

Oryn's face was blank, but his heart skipped a beat. Failure? He refused to fail himself, and most of all, he could not accept failing his brother. He could not and would not let it happen.

A fire set in his eyes and red hot in his stomach. The sword was not as heavy and the fire became an inferno. All the while Oryn imagined carving out the heart of the monster responsible for this rage.

Hours passed. Rain tapped at stained glass in the tower library where Sir Vigo searched for books and scrolls of history and battle techniques. Then he came across one he had been trying to find. "Ah, perfect. These should suit him nicely." Going to the water spattered window, he looked over the training ring. It was empty, save for one.

Alone in the downpour, Oryn continued his punishment. Droplets pounded the flat of the jeweled blade. A clap of thunder rolled and lightning illuminated him and the razor-sharp edge. His right arm lost feeling long ago and he now forced the less coordinated left to go on. Muscles burned. By sheer force of will, he made the arm do almost as well.

As the arm started to sink, he fought to bring it up. Defiance shone in his emerald eyes, but a gloved hand suddenly grasped his wrist. He looked back into his master's eyes, angry at being interrupted.

Using a soft tone of compassion, Sir Vigo commanded. "Stop. The heart may go on much longer than the body can withstand. To do so now would injure you and delay further training. Do you understand, boy?"

Sir Vigo watched the blank expression reappear on his

young face and the rage retreat.

"Yes, sir."

Leading him out of the rain, the old knight spoke. "Tonight and every night until you pass the trials, you shall study writings for three hours' time. Can you read?"

"Yes, sir."

"Sir?" Oryn grimaced.

"Do you wish to ask a question of me, boy?"

"Yes, sir." He thought out the words carefully. "If we are killers of werewolves, why learn to fight men?"

The question was worded well enough that it did not show too much insolence.

"Because, young apprentice, you shall find yourself facing many more battles with men than beasts. Knights of the Order may be brothers in arms, but to hold tightly to your rank one must put others below you in their place. If you lose to them even once or show an ounce of weakness, they will skin you alive. You must be ready to best them at any hour and in every way. Do you understand?"

His answer was a determined, "Yes, sir." If he had to best the others first, then so be it. A small smile came to him. His wise master would teach him to best them all.

"Before you study tonight, I have something for you to see. It is very difficult to find and catch an alpha werewolf. They are dangerous and unusually intelligent. Using this alpha, I shall teach you what you are facing and who really destroyed your family."

Captured creatures were thrown down stone chutes from the main floor into dungeon cells with thick bars. The only sunlight came through small, barred skylights for whenever a vampire was imprisoned. They would have no choice but to cower at the back in the daytime. One could expect an execution at any time. Few lived past a day in this prison.

Sir Vigo led his apprentice past many empty cells. Five archers came into view, each notching differently tipped arrows: silver, gold, petrified oak, blessed bone and crystal. A few other knights stopped questioning the cell's occupant and turned to welcome Sir Vigo. They saluted laterally with a fist across the chest and greeted in unison.

"Sir!"

"As you were. Has the accused been cooperative with questioning?"

"Not as hoped, Captain," a lieutenant answered. "We know there are two more alphas to hunt by the name of Korig and Kotig. The people are calling them the Bloody Brother's. They share the same leader. We suspect a witch, but..."

"But what, Lieutenant Peregrine?"

"I have suspicions, sir. I think they take orders from an enemy of more evil design and character." The knight resisted the need to shudder. He meant a demon.

A course, crackling voice chuckled quietly in the shadows. The ragged and very muscular man sat on the stone floor leaning in the corner. He turned his head and looked at them, staring. Crackled lips split into a smile and wolfish teeth were as visible in the dark as the red glow of his pupils. He softly clapped clawed hands.

"Are you psychic, sir? How amusing. If not, then how impressive your instincts are." Long, brown, unkempt hair rustled as he shook his head.

Oryn's eyes bored into the caged beast while his master explained.

"This is an alpha werewolf. The common werewolf is stupid. In human form it is a man driven to madness by an undeniable hunger for human flesh. Within each werewolf hides a demon. When a man is marked, it enters and cannot be removed except by the hand of death. Silver weapons are the key to their undoing."

The werewolf sneered. "Silver, bah! It's an irony. What harms us immortal kings on your plane are shiny trinkets and jewelry! Existence makes me sick."

Sir Vigo continued to instruct his student despite the creature's ramblings.

"The difference from the others and this breed is that the demon has consumed the human's soul and stolen the body for its own. If he wished, he could transform before us. What you see, boy, is a demon encased in flesh. Any woman he bites will suffer and die and any man he maims with his teeth will suffer an even worse destiny."

"That's quite right, human, because the man's soul is therein cursed." He looked Sir Vigo in the eye and added, "Whether we consume him or the body dies, their fate is the same. You know very well what becomes of the soul then, don't you?"

He then gave a hideous laugh at the curiosity and disgust on Oryn's face. "Their soul goes straight down." With a clawed thumb, he gestured to the ground. "Right into the black lake of the void."

"No!" Oryn hollered and drew his sword. His arms ached, but he couldn't feel it past the emotional anguish and rage. The burst of energy renewed him as he wished to kill the beast who was laughing.

"Oh ho!" The werewolf clapped and spoke to his sickened master. "Have you seen it yet, old man? The look in this boy. He has a hate that rivals even my master's! How magnificent." The pupils of his eyes glowed bright red at the child who wanted to cut his throat so badly.

"Boy! Stand down! To allow a beast to infect you with words is to show weakness! Put your sword away!"

Hands shaking, Oryn quickly obeyed, never taking his eyes away from the monster. It was still smiling at him. His hands were balled fists as he stepped back. He knew now that his brother was not at rest with his parents in the great white oak of the afterlife. The need for vengeance was tenfold.

The five archers stood at the ready and Lieutenant Peregrine asked the evil menace, "Does the accused have any last words?"

"Yes." He grinned. "Keep this boy alive for as long as possible. I hope that one day my master could meet him. He would enjoy him very much indeed!" Finished, he began to laugh uncontrollably.

"Ready! Aim! Fire!"

Every arrow met its mark, bringing deathly silence. The silver and gold arrows struck both lungs, the petrified oak and blessed bone pierced both sides of the abdomen and crystal went through the sternum. As the abomination slumped, the evil light left its now foggy eyes. The demon was banished back to the void, never to return.

When Oryn was taken to study in the library, he did so

with enthusiasm. His master allowed him to read long past three hours that night.

It was a quiet gift from Sir Vigo. He had not anticipated the demon's revealing the truth. It was not the time for that knowledge and he silently scorned himself for not taking the chance into consideration. He watched the boy soak in every page. It was amazing and tragic that a child was living the life of a man so early. Oryn should be playing with other children in open fields and cobbled streets.

This boy who had not shed a tear for himself or for his family was going to be Sir Vigo's greatest student. He had been waiting and knew in his heart of hearts that this last of the Conrad family was going to be the greatest knight the order had ever seen. It was only a matter of time before Oryn would see the trials and become the youngest ever to be knighted. That is, if rage did not get the better of him first.

Chapter 33
THE GAUNTLET

King Isban warned that the Zsu had been feuding with the rest of the desert peoples. Thus, Adwen and the others had no choice but to trek alone. For ten years there were no dealings with the Zsu. Their people were fierce, skilled in combat, and in addition to their fighting prowess used a very different kind of creature for battle: untold numbers of giant moths with toxic wings. The queen herself had a very deadly pet that no one knew the name of. They had not been seen for the past few years and no one dared to seek them out.

Waves of heat rose up, making everything sway. Adwen had an uncanny resilience to the heat, but her friends were left drained.

Oryn was mostly recovered from the day before, but his eyes needed time. He was forced to wear a blindfold. Toth carried his ointment and administered it every few hours. By nightfall, he would be healed.

"Warn me if there is a threat. I don't need sight for combat."

The half-elf shook his head and laughed. "I'll be the first to let you know and point you in the direction to swing."

Adwen still hadn't forgotten the look she'd seen in Oryn. Though she didn't ask or plan to, the memory of the moment would not leave. Maybe it was due to her position as leader and heir of the order. That explained the look, but she couldn't help but feel there was more.

She grilled him, "Why did you run off into the storm after the minotaur chief? You almost got lost out there."

With the band across his eyes, his feelings were even more disguised. "I was following an order, nothing more."

Flabbergasted, Adwen shook her head. "Did I say, hey, Oryn? Go run out in that sandstorm and pick a fight with the giant Minotaur with the axe? I didn't get the chance to finish saying the plan. All I wanted was for you to get him out of the city and to keep him back until I closed the gate. What made you think I was going to say to kill him at any cost?"

Oryn glowered behind the blindfold. He didn't even know why he failed to think it through. Clearing his throat, he answered, "It was done on a whim. I shall listen further in the future. It shall not happen again."

Pulling alongside, she turned and gave him a very suspicious look. He heard her sniff the air about him and say, "I'll have to take your word for it."

They continued onward. For the longest time all they heard were their camels and the wind. Then a new sound came and it was so distant that only Adwen heard it at first.

"Stop," she called, holding up a hand.

Toth was curious. "What is it?"

She closed her eyes to focus on the sounds. "Someone's in trouble."

A tan, black-haired boy in white robes stood alone holding a shining spear, trying to fight a pair of giant scorpions. Their tails snapped like spiked bullwhips, striking and narrowly missing. Nearby lay the dead camel with an oozing wound on its neck. A stinger struck the ground by his feet and he cried out again. He lost his footing and tripped. There was no time to stand as he scrambled back, having dropped the spear.

From behind a dune sprung a white beast, pouncing on the back of the closest scorpion. The dog creature bit and slashed angrily, the long hairs on its neck and tail bristled. Beneath her, the scorpion tried to strike and she bit the tail, ready to rip off the sting. Preoccupied, she had forgotten the second.

Quick as lightning, its fist-sized stinger punched deep into her muscular back. The young man gasped as she swiftly destroyed the tail in her jaws and roared in pain and surprised. After Adwen came free from the curved stinger, she landed on all fours, silver blood coating her back and the scorpion's tail.

She began to cough violently. Her body arched as she disgorged an oozy mass into the sand. Adwen stared at the glob of poison and snarled. "I hate arachnids."

He marveled as she ripped the tail from the second and slashed at them until they retreated. The wound where she had been struck was almost healed as she stood and turned to approach. Startled by her height, he couldn't help but notice how sharp her teeth were while she panted.

Adwen cocked her head and flicked ears back. She'd forgotten for a moment that she was too intimidating in her true form. Changing into woman shape, a smile appeared on her sweet face. "What are you doing out here?"

The young man could not understand and became distracted as both friends rode over on camels, toting a third.

"We won't hurt you. We're looking for the Zsu."

The young man recognized the name of his people and understood. "Zsu!" He smiled and pointed southwest.

Several miles away, they found a large city. The other civilizations used underground rivers for wells and growing crops, while the Zsu used fresh water from the lake in networks of long canals. Running water was everywhere in the complex system.

Adwen let the young man ride her camel and walked alongside through the street. People stared and whispered, watching her and the boy who smiled and waved. Some would smile back and then become straight faced upon seeing the strangers.

Even the blindfolded knight could sense unease. Toth filled him in and he replied, "Don't be surprised by an attack."

Almost as soon as he finished, a small group of soldiers with spears came at them, yelling.

The young man spoke and the soldiers swiftly took a knee. He told them something and two ran off to the palace while the rest stayed as escorts.

Adwen gave a glance and he smiled back.

"You're not just some kid, are you?"

Though it was not as vast as the others, the palace to which they were led had beautiful walls inlaid with the purest gold. High, broad stone steps led into the grand throne room from which the entire city was visible. Green dotted the streets filled with milling crowds, while in the fields many more tended crops or repaired irrigation. Led by the boy and a few soldiers, the trio approached the throne of the Zsu leader, bowing.

In a regal dress of red silk and spun gold sat the beautiful and sharp-eyed queen. Her long black hair was in a braid. Dozens of gold bracelets hung along her forearms and about her neck. She looked down from and called the young man to her side. They spoke for a moment and the queen made a gesture with a gold-clad wrist for them to stand. She quietly looked from Oryn, to Toth, and at last to Adwen.

She raised her hand and said with a commanding tone, "Speak! Why have you dared to enter my people's land? Where do you come from and why are you here?"

"We are here to talk, Your Highness."

Her gaze narrowed and she stood. "How did you come by my son?"

As his mother questioned the visitors, the prince smiled at Adwen.

"We found him in the desert with two scorpions."

One of her eyebrows went up high. "How far from the city was he?" She shot her son a deadly glance and his smile faded.

She answered honestly. "About three or four miles."

The queen glared and spoke harshly as the prince dipped his head in shame. Turning back to them, she announced, "I am Queen Xenorithia of the Zsu. You have saved my son and I thank you. Who are you and how did you rescue him, when the only one among you who possesses a weapon cannot see?" Her face was blank and her deep gaze glistened with a roiling anger, waiting to emerge if she thought the answer was false.

"I am Adwen Andredan."

For a moment, the queen looked surprised and then she resumed her stern expression. "I suspect you wish for more than talk. Am I wrong, Heir of Darien?"

"You're not wrong. I'm here to help."

"No, you are not," hissed the queen. "You are here to try to coax me into your little upcoming battle. You want me to write a treaty and sign that I will join forces in the Kingdoms of Day."

Locking eyes with her, Adwen was unafraid. The Queen

of the Zsu stalked down to stand before her. She was as tall as
Oryn and her eyes were twice as fierce. Both women remained calm and composed while they studied one another.

Adwen finally spoke. "If you aren't going to, then I would
be wasting my time. All I want to know is if you are willing to
discuss it with me."

Her words reached the fierce queen and she glared suspiciously. "We will talk, but you have yet to pass the test left to
my people by Darien." Seeing the look of excitement in
Adwen's face gave the queen a spark of amusement.

The gauntlet was different from others Adwen knew. A
usual gauntlet was a narrow passage riddled with deadly traps
and obstacles. This was an entire underground maze that
spanned a mile in any direction. Nevertheless, Adwen hadn't
stopped smiling.

For many generations of the Zsu, convicted criminals
were given weapons and dropped through different tunnels to
seek each other out and fight to the death. If one could kill the
others and find the way back, they would be released. No one
had survived and return.

The queen led them into an oval chamber with five trap
doors in a ring on the floor. She clapped her hands, jingling
the collection of thin golden bangles.

Another door opened. Guards entered with four men.
Dirt masked their faces and ragged clothes. They were forced
to take a knee and the queen turned to Adwen.

"These criminals will be an addition to your test. You will
face them among the creatures of the maze. Why do you
smile at this?"

"I'm sorry. The tests haven't really been that hard.
They've been kind of easy."

The queen replied sternly. "They are tests of identity, not
skill. Some men have been foolish, claiming to be the heir.
They are swiftly proven liars. In the scrolls it was written that
the heir would have the guiding hand of the Light Spirits at all
times. Only the one with their blessing could hope to find the
center of this maze and escape."

Adwen nodded, pensively glancing down in thought. "So

how will you know if I've passed or not?"

The queen took a cloth from a nearby pedestal, tossing up a cloud of dust. A giant crystal with dozens of edges slowly turned in midair like a disco ball.

"This is a sight crystal. It can show the entire maze and everyone inside. Your companions may watch while you enter."

"Where did it come from?"

"It was the last crystal to leave what is now known as the Ebony Range. The dark stones once shone, but turned black long ago. This is a relic of the power the range once possessed before its corruption and transformation. This one was brought by Darien and his four sworn warriors."

While they talked, Oryn became more curious by the second. Not seeing was irritating and it was all he could do to not tear off the bandages.

"Are you ready to begin?"

Adwen cracked a smile. "Yes, I am, Your Highness."

In response, the queen clapped. The four murderers were given sabers and pushed into trapdoors as a guard opened the fifth for her, offering a weapon.

Without taking the saber, she leaped down through the dark. Landing nimbly in the ancient dusty tunnel, Adwen's sly smile melted away. Standing still as a statue, eyes alight, she kept her pointed ears pricked. All around was danger in the silence. Though her eyes saw nothing, her sixth sense went wild.

The others stood around the crystal and Toth asked, "Where is she?"

"There." The queen touched a surface on the crystal. It sluggishly rotated to show Adwen creeping through the shadows between flickering torches.

The knight had enough of merely listening. Roughly removing the bandages, Oryn was hungry to get a look and angrily fought the wrappings.

Toth protested. "Wait, what are you doing? Your eyes won't be fully healed till later. I doubt you would take well to blindness. I've half the experience already."

Oryn snapped firmly. "I shall witness this!"

The queen and Toth watched him toss the bandages

aside and carefully open his eyes. They were still irritated and red, but he forced them to open and stare at the crystal.

"How is your sight?"

"It is well. My eyes are nearly healed." All of his attention was on the images.

"What happened?" the queen asked out of curiosity.

Toth answered in a matter-of-fact way, shaking his head. "He fought a minotaur in the sandstorm yesterday." Soon his attention was on the crystal as well.

The queen studied the knight and quietly asked, "Is he mad?"

"I'm only beginning to think so."

Oryn's gaze was glued to the image of the girl and the more the queen studied him, the more she became convinced; if this man were mad, it was from a very simple cause. A sly look crossed her lean face and she murmured, "I believe him to be quite mad."

The knight had not heard and would not have caught onto the insinuation. Everything Adwen did was remarkable and in the likeness of legends told by the fire. He wanted to see it all with his own eyes.

The air was still. Adwen almost giggled, thinking of Indiana Jones. Then her sixth sense warned not to take another step. Swallowing hard, Adwen glanced where her bare foot hovered. She carefully jumped over the seemingly ordinary patch of rocks. Without seeing or smelling it, she knew there was something deadly. Adwen continued following her cautiously through the gloom.

In the sight chamber, the queen smiled.

"Where are the traps?" Toth asked. "I thought this was a gauntlet?"

"Have patience. All it takes is the tripping of a single switch and the gauntlet will come to life."

He stared while Oryn was still consumed with watching Adwen's progress.

All remained deathly still as she reached the first turn.
Then her ears caught a faint shuffling. Adwen glanced back to
find a murderer stared hungrily from afar. The wicked man
laughed and ran for her, waving the saber over his head.

"No! Stop!"

He couldn't understand and did not care. As his filthy
foot came down where hers hadn't dared, her stomach
flipped. There was a loud click and a thud as the trap door
opened under him. His eyes went wide, he fell out of sight and
she flinched when she heard the crunch of bones. The doors
closed themselves and there was silence.

She gave a sigh of relief and turned to leave, but there was
another click, followed by dozens more. Her sixth sense was
screaming inside as her eyes widened. There was no time to
wonder, only to bolt for the end of the corridor.

Giant serrated spikes knifed down from the ceiling
through hundreds of gaps. A large set began to drop over her.
Adwen gained more momentum to escape and blinked as far
as her light powers would allow. All thirty feet worth of spikes
hit the ground at her heels and she kept going. They continued to fall as she neared a wall with a three-foot opening.
Quick as lightning, she leaped through and evaded the last of
the spikes.

Dust from the last corridors' catastrophe settled and
Adwen found herself in a hall lined with statues resembling
the Egyptian god Anubis. The jackal men made of granite
stood tall and proud with shields and axes. Nine feet in height,
their pointed ears almost touched the ceiling.

Adwen was wary and knew at least one would move. She
took a deep breath and pressed forward in brisk strides. Eyes
were following her. The tension in the air continued to rise.
There was no warning when an axe suddenly dropped with a
loud clang just before her toes.

The statue snarled and she instantly reacted. Grabbing
the back of the axe head with one hand, she transformed and
delivered a swift kick to the sentry's snout. It exploded into
bits and pebbles and the body collapsed. There were many
more snarls as the others came to.

Adwen was in no mood for a brawl and changed back.

Axes came down while she sprinted along the hall. She tucked and rolled, sidestepped and dodged each attempt to cut her down. This time there were three escape routes low to the ground, guarded by two statues. Dropping back, she did a homerun slide. She skidded just past as the battleaxes struck, disappearing through the left opening.

The other end of the short tunnel stank like a musty storage room. Crawling out and gathering herself up, she found she could barely see in the intense darkness. Listening to her instincts, she wandered in search of another exit. Her nose detected a wisp of fresher air. Following the hint, she whipped around as there was movement from behind.

Something was running at her in the dark; a mummy preparing to swing a sickle. Before it could strike, she crushed the corpse's head. Her fist exploded it in a cloud of dust and wrappings. Powdery decay got into her mouth as it flew everywhere and she coughed and gagged. Sputtering and waving a hand, she disliked the flavor.

"Ah! I swallowed some! Ah! I hate walking dead things!"

Dozens more were alerted by her and she realized a moment later when they swarmed, raising weapons.

"This is going to suck."

They watched her go through many more tunnels fraught with danger. Every time there was a close call, the queen would look at the knight and see the sick look of worry in his eyes. Then there would be relaxing relief as she escaped untouched and the queen would smile.

Adwen destroyed many residents made of stone or wrappings. Entering a much brighter chamber, she found a raised platform covered in gold coins. High upon a ten-foot column sat a seamless golden treasure box. A narrow beam of sunlight illuminated the treasure. She crept closer, wondering if she dared to leap up and take it. Would there be a giant boulders rolling after her? She wasn't sure what would happen.

The quiet was suddenly broken by the sound of a man's breath. There was a whooshing sound and she sidestepped a flying saber thrown by a surviving murderer. His left arm was a bloody mess as he came to throttle her, but she kicked him in the head in the blink of an eye. There was a snap when his neck broke and he fell down dead.

One other survivor entered the chamber. He was angry and became excited once he saw her. Saber swinging, he ran at her in a wild frenzy.

Adwen ran up to meet him.

When she was within reach, he yelled again and swung the edge for her neck.

In the sight chamber, they watched them collide.

A smile flickered on Oryn's face when Adwen grabbed his wrist, held on tight, twirling over it.

As she rolled over the man's extended arm, her trailing foot caught his jaw. He fell and she stood over him, clutching the curved blade.

Cowering, he tried scrambled backward. Her violet eyes burned in the shadows. Out of fear, he didn't watch the wall behind.

Adwen gasped as his sweaty body touched the odd block and it disappeared with a stomach-wrenching click. She swallowed hard and the man realized what happened. First staring back in horror at his mistake, he then glanced up at the ceiling, screaming.

Down out of the dark fell a large slab.

Dust and pebbles started to fall all around. Everything was collapsing and two more slabs landed beside her.

Discarding the saber, she deduced it was time to leave. All exits were blocked by falling stones. Adwen turned to the column and the treasure. Leaping past falling rubble, she searched for her only means of escape.

The sight crystal turned cloudy, then clear and empty. Toth was disturbed as the queen smiled and started to leave for the stairs. They hadn't seen where she'd gone when the rocks started to fall.

Oryn was already in a rage and rounded on the departing queen. "What has happened? How is she to escape and return now? You let her into a death trap with no exit! How is the heir to return now that --?"

"Be silent!" she snapped and gave him a sly look. "Be calm, Knight from Dargadia. Do you truly believe the heir could not escape the gauntlet? Do you think her some simple woman?" Finished, she waited and closely studied his response.

He was cut to the quick. Why was he worried? Of course the heir could escape. She would be unharmed. How could he be so foolish to think for a second that she was thwarted by a crumbling room? It would take much more than that to stop her. He calmed himself and felt surprised at his own outburst.

Clearing his throat, he replied, "My apologies, Your Highness. My reactions were inappropriate."

Though the knight failed to hide his feeling, the queen hid her amusement well. Together, they left the sight room and made for the grand hall.

All along the way Oryn scolded himself. What was wrong with him? He was losing his wits and making rash decisions. Was he ill?

In the city between taller structures, children played. One had a gold coin and wanted to put it in the empty well while his friends wished to buy sweets at the market. All were chasing him and laughed, racing around under high water troughs from the lake. Droplets trickled down onto their heads as they whooped and shouted.

The boy won the race and reached the well. With a smile, he tossed it in and started to chuckle at the disappointed companions. They moved to walk away when a large gust of air and dirt suddenly shot out of the well. All froze and watched the coin fly up and fall at his feet.

Loud coughing followed the end of the geyser of dust and the children went closer, far too curious to turn and run. Their jaws dropped as a tan girl with black lips, violet eyes and silver and gold hair climbed out. She clung to the edge, coughed for a moment and set a golden box out on solid ground.

Smiling, she said breathlessly, "Hey, what's up?"

Speechless, they watched the odd woman climb out and sit on the rim of the dry well, looking around. Nothing seemed familiar and she cleared her throat, chuckling to herself. "Wow, what a rush." Then she turned to the confused children. "Do you know how to find the palace?"

They didn't understand a word.

She raked a set of sharp nails through her hair and dusted off her clothes. Then she had an idea. They all took a step back as her clothes shifted and turned into a high-collared dress while dozens of gold bracelets appeared on her wrists. She jingled them in a questioning way and asked, "The queen?"

They gasped and stammered, quickly pointing their small arms down the way they'd come.

Her clothes changed back and she giggled. "I thought so." A breeze blew the last of the dust away as she picked up her prize and strolled down the street.

Palace guards stood along the hall to the throne where the queen and the two guests waited. Together they watched the steps.

While they stared, Oryn's eyes were unfocused as he brooded, wracking his brain. He had already come to the conclusion that his thoughts were stuck on something. His attention was not on his work. With that decided, he wondered what could be distracting him. Then something moved at the end of the open hall and he looked.

When he saw her in her true form, glistening in the sun like silver treasure, he knew. All of his distracted actions were because of her. He simply couldn't look away as the white hound came closer. On all fours, carrying a box handle in her jaws, she was gentle and graceful. She set it down to stand upright before them.

As hard as it was to avert his eyes, it was impossible to breathe when she changed into her woman form. A smile sweet as honey curled her black, rose petal lips and his heart skipped a beat. He did everything within his power to hide his weakness, maintaining a stony expression. He would rather die than expose his strange intrigue. It would be an embarrassment and an even greater shame. It was not right to feel this way, whatever it was.

Adwen greeted the firm queen. "Well, what comes next, Your Highness?"

A smile threatened to emerge on the queen's painted face. "Now, first, you shall open your gift." When Adwen looked confused she added, "The treasure of the gauntlet was left for the heir. Open it."

Adwen smiled happily, looking for a way to get inside the glittering box. The only way to open the container was with her strong hands. Nails pierced metal and she carefully peeled away the sides to pull out a smooth stone covered in pitch. Cradling it in her hands, she wondered why Darien would leave a dirty rock.

Then it smoked and crackled. Tiny fractures spider webbed over and it caught fire before exploding into a fireball. The heat and flames began to tame, taking a solid form on her outstretched arm. Flames shrank and turned into the feathers of a beautiful orange and crimson bird. Ice-blue eyes blinked at her from the small crested head and its peacock tail swept the ground like the hem of a gown. The phoenix crowed and bowed.

"Greetings, child and how may I serve you?"

Everyone stared and she smiled. "Wow!"

The bird became disgruntled and ruffled his feathers. "Is that all you can think to say? I've waited centuries to offer assistance and you can only gawk and drivel?" He squawked irritably. "My name is Malik and you will do well to remember it, young Andredan!"

Taken aback and surprised by the animal's fiery personality, she quickly apologized. "Sorry, I just didn't expect a phoenix. I'm Adwen and it's nice to meet you."

Malik's demeanor cooled. "The pleasure is mine, child."

The queen clapped her hands and a guard brought forward an empty scroll. "Now if you will, I believe it's time we talked. Please come with me, Andredan."

Through a pair of doors lay the private study. They entered alone and sat on small chairs as the queen quickly wrote out a long stretch of words. She did not sign the document, but set it aside, turning to Adwen with a hardened glare. "I refuse to sign until you understand my people's terms." Her dark eyes were sharp as glass and drove into Adwen. "We will not fight for the other desert kings. If my people rally together for battle, they will fight under their own banner at your side."

"Why are you angry with them?"

"They stole something precious." In the privacy of the chamber, the queen let anger and remorse crack her voice, but no tears fell. "My father and my husband discovered a sun crystal in the desert beneath the sand. They sent a scout back to say they were bringing it as a gift for the birth of my son. They never returned and the precious gem was gone. All had been slaughtered to the last man and stripped of weapons and belongings. Both kings became more powerful later and we knew they had taken the gem. The crystal we possess is only for sighting. What my husband had found could have made all the desert peoples powerful, but was stolen and no power was offered us.

"I had planned to give the crystal to the Ulla Lake, making food plentiful with more fish to catch from cleaner water. The barbarian king has his grand arena and the fool king of the Bebidin has the palace with a thousand guards. They did not need the crystal so much as my people."

"I will look into this as soon as I can."

"What would you do?" the queen asked angrily. "They would lie. They have it."

A glint appeared in Adwen's gaze. "They can't lie to me. I'll know it when they do. I will find out what happened to your crystal. If I can, I will bring it back. That is a promise."

Her smile calmed the queen. "Somehow I know you tell me truths. I like your voice." Again, she took up the scroll and asked, "Are you prepared for what is to come, now that you are solely responsible for the uniting of five kingdoms? It is a heavy burden. Are you sure you wish for my name on this page?"

A moment passed as she thought about it. Locking eyes with the queen, she was firm. "We can't hope to win this without your help. We need everyone, for better or for worse."

Without another word, the queen signed, rolled the scroll

and put it securely into Adwen's able hands.

The task at hand completed, the phoenix departed in a flash of orange flames, vowing to appear whenever Adwen called. Once Malik had gone, everyone left for the lower chambers of the palace. Secret passages took them to a damp cavern and another glowing kingdom gate. Without being told, Adwen knew it would transport them back to Dargadia.

Along the stone steps, a strange smell met her nose. When she looked up she saw hundreds of swaying moth wings. Countless deadly and colorful creatures clung to the stones and fed off of the minerals brought to them by the seeping moisture.

A bright effervescent light pooled down the steps as the queen bid her good-bye. However, she stopped Oryn for a final word.

"Knight. If you did fight a Minotaur in a desert storm, did you succeed in killing him?"

He nodded. "There were golden rings on his horns."

"I must know." She smiled. "How did you defeat the chief of the wild beasts?"

A proud glint was in his eyes. "I knew my enemy. He did not."

The Past (Part 3)
THE TRIALS

High noon beamed over the training arena in the order fortress. Two knights sat, quietly sharing rumors.

The scruffier whispered to the more experienced. "I heard the strangest story today, sir."

The knight watched others spar and replied. "What about?"

"I heard Sir Vigo has gone before the elders, requesting that his student be tested for the right to join the ranks."

Finally looking at him in surprise, he exclaimed, "Sir Vigo the Vicious is looking to advance Hot Head Conrad? What was the council's answer?"

The knight was disappointed. "I do not know, but the lad has a challenger today."

"Who?"

The younger knight grinned. "Sir Peregrine Gallegos."

The experienced knight was aghast. "Sir Peregrine? He is a slayer, a master of the blade second to only Sir Vigo. The boy will be torn to shreds! When do they dual?"

"It won't be much longer." He pointed to the other side of the grounds. "Sir Vigo is preparing the boy now."

Vigo spoke to the teenager, quietly instructing what to do when his challenger arrived. It had been almost five years since the night Oryn began training. At fourteen years of age, he was almost six feet tall and his eyes were as sharp as ever. His arms were strong, his back tough and his legs steady. Staring out at nothing, he listened carefully to his master.

"Knowing your enemy is one of the deepest traditions of the order. When any challenger comes at you, observe and learn his movements. If he insults you, do not insult him back until you have beaten him. It is a sign of foolishness to insult an opponent before a dual. After they have lost, their actions will show if they have honor."

Oryn's voice was no longer young, but deep and strong. "Yes, sir."

"You have mastered the art of the breathing ritual. A state of calm will aid in the accuracy of your strike. Do not forget your training, lest you lose your arm in this dual."

His green eyes flashed. "Yes, sir."

"The elders do not believe in your skill. They have struck a deal; if you defeat Sir Peregrine, you shall be admitted into the trials for werewolf slaying. If you fail and survive, you shall have no choice but to train for another ten years. You cannot afford to fail and we both know you will not." Vigo paused as they saw the slayer enter the grounds.

Other knights stepped out of his way and all began to make room for the dual.

Sir Vigo murmured to his fierce student. "You have mastered the harnessing of your rage, so know this now. Sir Peregrine uses pride against his opponents. He will insult you before the dual to provoke you. Do not respond. He is looking to falter your skill with the blade. Show him focus. Show him what you can do."

Oryn answered firmly. "Yes, sir."

Sir Peregrine approached, toying with the well-trimmed beard on his chin. He looked around and then laughed. "Sir Vigo! Where is the man who dares to stand before my blade? All I see is a boy. If he is a man he is not a whole one. He has yet to even grow a beard!" He laughed mirthfully at his own joke.

Oryn said nothing as instructed. Even though his face was calm and his eyes showed no feeling, Sir Vigo felt his student become angry.

Sir Peregrine sighed with a mock shrug. "Well, let's get on with it, boy! I only have a little time to play before my lunch. I don't want it getting too cold. Once I've won, my sword will need sharpening."

A clearing had been made as others watched the two sizing each other up. Off to one side, Oryn's master smiled. Sir Peregrine had been off on so many quests there was little time to learn much regarding this student.

Many knights placed bets. Neither combatant had armor,

making the situation even more dangerous if a false move occurred. They would both have to be well honed to not kill the other accidentally.

Sir Peregrine swiftly drew his sword and waved it about, making the metal slice the air in an aggressive display.

Oryn stared unblinking. Gently and ceremoniously, he drew his sword and took an angled stance. His form was smooth and perfect, with the hilt up behind his head and the edge angled down, lined up with his other hand before him. The edge of the metal caught the light, reflecting onto Sir Peregrine's face.

The slayer could make out those empty green eyes, staring back from either side of Sedro Conrad's sword. They held no telltale of skill, intent or even confidence. Sir Vigo's student was like ice that chilled him to the core.

Sir Peregrine smiled and lunged to strike his chest.

With lightning speed, Sedro's sword swept forward and beat it aside. Then Sir Peregrine barely recovered in time to stave off a slice to his own torso. He fended off another attack to his feet, but it was a trick. The false swipe went harmlessly past his legs and then swung around to build up momentum and came in an arch for his neck.

Once again, Sir Peregrine was surprised and caught the blow just in time. To push back, he swung for the boy's neck, but Oryn only leaned away to avoid the hit. His back flexed as he leaned, and when the threat was gone, rebounded to force the knight even farther to the side of the ring.

The sound of metal on metal rang in the shushed arena and not a soul uttered a word. A few coins hit the ground. One man's jaw dropped at the student who was outmatching the second best swordsman in the kingdom.

Sir Peregrine became desperate while his attempts to take ground failed. He made a strike at the boy's head and watched in dismay as he ducked.

The sword passed Oryn by and he stood. There was a strain in the older knight's eyes. Oryn allowed him to swing again, but caught the attack with his sword and delivered more force than before.

With a loud clang, the weapon flew and struck into a bench between two sitting knights, making them leap.

Sir Peregrine pulled out a knife to resist, and when he turned, it was batted away harmlessly. The knight froze as the sword rested against his neck, brushing a throbbing jugular vein. He stared into the young man's eyes and finally saw it; raw hate stared back. The slayer didn't dare breathe.

"Stand down, boy," called his master's voice.

Instantly, the cold swordsman lowered his weapon and replied, "Yes, sir." He sheathed it sharply and maintained an unblinking, reptilian stare.

Approaching, Sir Vigo commanded, "Shake his hand, boy. Show proper courtesy to those who outrank you, even if they do not match you in skill."

Oryn did so, oblivious to Sir Vigo's sly smile at the shock on the lieutenant's face.

The defeated knight found his words at last, "You are well trained. I retract my previous proposal. I would be honored to clean your sword as payment for my insults."

Oryn's voice was cold and harsh. "No one touches my father's blade save for my master and I. Go sharpen your own."

His master dismissed him, "You may take your leave, boy. Go ready your armor for tonight. Prepare to look like a knight for the council elders."

"Yes, sir." Oryn left the arena in as icy a demeanor as he held throughout the battle. No one dared to cross his path and the crowd parted to make way. Once he was gone, everyone began to chatter and laugh as bets were paid.

Sir Vigo's smile grew broader. "Well? What are your thoughts on my student?"

"Have you seen the look in his eyes, sir?" the lieutenant asked, nervously recalling it.

"I am aware. He is in control of his hate, my friend. When he is angered, his strikes become more accurate and deadly."

Sir Peregrine laughed weakly. "Then by insulting him I ensured my defeat. I heard rumor of his anger."

"He has had but a single incident. I first trained him in hand-to-hand combat. Within a year he mastered it and..." Sir Vigo smiled. "...then I taught him the knife. A squire his age had tried to goad him to a fight. Oryn ignored him, at first.

The squire was trying to show the others that my student's blank face was a ruse. Eventually, after a few weeks of it, the squire made the mistake of bringing a knife. As soon as he brandished it at Oryn, he learned that provoking the boy was no more intelligent that setting foot into a den of rabid wolves."

Vigo continued. "He disarmed the squire and carved out his tongue. When he tossed it at the feet of the other squires, a carrion bird flew off with it. No one has dared to try him since. He is quite disciplined, possibly too much so."

Sir Peregrine shook his head. "The elders won't make him a knight, even if he passes the trials. He is so young." A sly spark lit in his eye. "For the old crippled fools to admit him, they must see how far along he is compared to what they are accustomed to."

Sir Vigo was intrigued, but quickly became dismissive. "If you are proposing we make a show of it, then you must consider the risks. Do you recall the last time a man was foolish enough to try such a thing? He was torn apart and eaten alive before the panel. Everyone involved was dismissed from the order."

"But if the boy is as good as I perceive he should have little trouble. If he makes a show of it the elders would have no choice. It would get their attention at last and you know better than I the way the old codgers think."

"Yes, I do. It is the very reasons I refused to join the council. I would rather die fighting for my people than watch younger men do the same while I wait to pass of bowel sickness or something far more embarrassing."

"Yes, sir." The lieutenant nodded while trying not to laugh. Sir Vigo was quite serious on the matter. "Does your student have a sense of humor? Or is he how he seems?"

"I have never seen him jest, nor heard his laugh, if he does have one. The only one who has seen ether is Malkum. He told that when his family was killed he hadn't shed a tear. I asked Oryn if he mourned his losses."

"What did the boy say?"

"He says training was his way of mourning his mother and father. But only once vengeance for his brother is done shall he truly be free to mourn." Vigo added sadly, "I do not know if he shall have it, but I hope for something more for him. I hope one day he will learn to cast aside the rage. I fear that it may consume him."

"If I may, sir, I feel there is yet a little goodness in him. Perhaps if he learns of something outside of his life of vengeance?"

"Perhaps," Vigo shrugged. "But I cannot give him that. These are dark times and the people are looking for a hero. Oryn could be just what they need, but it will not come to pass if he allows himself to be destroyed."

Sir Peregrine became furtive and grinned. "Sir, everyone knows my intuitions are rather accurate. I feel that there is still hope." He laughed and his eyes sparkled. "Perhaps if he met a woman?"

While the lieutenant laughed, Sir Vigo shook his head. "I can't imagine a woman willing to sit close to him, let alone touch him. He frightens them even more than his youthful body attracts them. I have seen some stalking and turn tail once he looks."

"Would joining quests with his uncle make a difference, sir?"

Sir Vigo thought for a while. He had heard something of Malkum from the elders. "I doubt that would be possible. Sir Malkum's latest quest did not end well."

Hours after the fall of dusk, Oryn stood ready. In the moonlight he waited by the gate into the Ring of Trials. Most knights called it the Pit of Doom.

He had sharpened his sword and polished his armor until it shone like stars. On the other side would be his test to become a knight. His thoughts were suddenly interrupted when he heard movement and turned to look back unblinkingly at his uncle.

Stepping into the light, Malkum smiled. It had been months since they'd seen each other and Malkum studied his nephew proudly. While wearing his best commoner clothing, a smile lifted his bearded face.

"If only Sedro could see you now. You look like a knight." When Oryn showed no reaction and gave no response, the smile faded. "I wanted to see you before you entered. It'd only be right to send you off with a bit of encouragement from family."

Oryn scowled and quietly replied, "But you're here for more than just kind words, aren't you, Uncle?" The look he wore was unforgiving and angry.

Malkum shook his head and sighed. "So, you've already heard?"

His nephew did not move or make a sound.

After a moment, he took a breath and announced, "I'm leaving the order for good reason, Oryn. I have served my people, but there are some orders worth refusing. Two men tried to do things to a woman. When she used magic to defend herself, they died." He shook his head. "I was ordered to kill her! I cannot continue to be a part of the order if it has come to this. I cannot kill beings simply for having power and not adhering to everything we think they should be. I have to know." Malkum hesitated and then asked, "Will you come with me? Join me in the mountain villages and help me start a new life away from all of this death."

Malkum watched Oryn's eyes dilate and the cold voice of a man replied, "You are a coward. And if you think I would share a roof with one such as you, then you are an even greater fool."

He felt sick.

"Leave my sight. I never wish to see your face again." Turning away, he placed the shining helm upon his head, ready to face the opening gates into the ring. Steady in his anger, he entered, leaving his sorrowful uncle alone.

When the doors closed, he pleaded, "Please, Oryn. See the darkness around you. See the snakes for what they are before they bite. I hope you learn and understand why I can no longer stay. Good luck to you, my nephew."

Giving the gates a baleful last glance, he went to fetch the rest of his belongings and departed from the blessed halls for the final time. The fortress built by Darien the Master Knight was good, but many in its halls were deceiving themselves and each other. Good knights still remained, but they were surrounded by vipers and hypocrites. There had to be a better way for Malkum to serve his people and king.

With every breath he took in the ancient rhythm, he was further focused. Soon all fifty elders' eyes were upon him and he performed a flawless bow. While holding the respectful pose, he prepared to perform as instructed.

High upon the edge perched twelve archers with silver-tipped arrows. Oryn would be pitted against a single werewolf with no restraints or assistance. In full armor, a man had to destroy the fiend and prove his worth. But tonight the trials would be different. Sir Vigo and two of his most loyal comrades had a surprise in store.

The old knight smiled, standing over the ring.

Surrounding Oryn were twelve portcullises with bars to hold back the deadly beasts. As he went deeper into focus via the breathing ritual, he could hear the snarls over every other sound. Past the wind and clinking of armor and chains, he heard movement and the gnashing of fangs. Everything else was transparent.

Before Oryn stood, he did something no other dared to do for the trials. He removed his helm, placing it neatly before him. Only then did he stand and face the disapproving elders, seated high in the stands. Drawing out his sword, he waited.

Oryn knew they thought he was a fool, but his master was wiser than any of them. If his master bid him, he would remove every last piece of armor for this. Discipline and loyalty were his most prized qualities.

Sir Vigo raised and then sharply dropped his hand.

Everyone watched intently as a gate opened and the three hundred-pound brute prowled out into the pale light, drooling and snarling. Its eyes shined like red stars and Oryn returned its unblinking stare. His heart was steady as he took his stance and the monster lunged. It roared, leaping for him with jaws open wide.

At the last moment, Oryn dodged the fangs and flicked his sharp sword. Blood flew and spattered across his face and short hair. He hardly moved a half-step and managed to slit the thing's throat in midair. It tumbled to the ground in a bloody heap behind him, already shrinking into a naked man.

The elders murmured, preparing to leave and discuss

things elsewhere. Just as the first few stood, Sir Vigo gave a second signal. All eyes were back on the ring as two more portcullis gates opened wide on the young man's either side. The audience held their breath as the beasts raced out for the kill. In the blink of an eye, they reached him.

Oryn didn't move until they leaped. Now that they could not change their path of travel, he took a single step to avoid the first. Then he swung his sword for the throat of the second, spilling more crimson as it died at his feet.

The last came back to try again, swinging a set of claws for his face. With one slice, the young man took its arm. It roared in anger, and as it was distracted, he arched the blade in an upward stroke, splitting the monster from navel to jaw.

It gasped and came crashing down, bathing in a pool of its own blood. Standing over the mess, Oryn flipped his grip on the hilt and pierced the werewolf through the heart.

With silence restored, he took back his sword, wiped it clean with the fur on the monster's back and sheathed it. Every eye followed as he took up his helm, fit it neatly on his head and knelt to the elders.

In the first light of the new day, Oryn would be made a Knight of the Order. In a few days he would be taken by his master to meet King Lorvan. There he would win the attention of the king and be dubbed Sir Oryn. Within a fortnight, he would gain an even more infamous title among the men. Because of his past and his fateful first quest, Sir Oryn would be silently known as the Tragic Knight.

Chapter 34
THE ROSE THORNE

A bubbling spring welled up in a meadow where the travelers reappeared. Bright light shone down and they knew they had returned to Dargadia at last. They were west of Broad River and a few miles south of the high cliffs. Adwen heaved a content sigh. By far, she liked Dargadia the best.

All of the sudden, there was a familiar smell and she sniffed again. When she was sure, she smiled, cupped both hands about her mouth and howled to the trees.

A moment later the horses came galloping out and Ranger whinnied. "Master! The mutt has brought you home!"

Ulna was just behind and neighed to Toth.

While Oryn stroked his nose, Ranger snorted. "I knew the mutt would keep her promise and return you alive."

The knight smiled at his thrilled steed, but Adwen was the only one who knew what was said. The horse waited while his master inspected his condition and nickered to Adwen, "I trust my master was in no danger, mutt? You kept him safe?"

She scratched his ear. "Does he look fine to you?"

The Clydesdale snorted. "Well enough."

She laughed and turned to her friends. "I smell chimney smoke coming from west of here. We've only got a few hours before sunset. My magic kept the horses in good condition, but they are tired and need rest. We still have to get these treaties to the king and we need to get moving."

Astride Ulna, Toth asked, "Can we not spend the night at an inn?"

Slowly she turned to stare unhappily at him. "After every other time we've stayed at an inn? We can't, because you'll get into drinking and that means trouble."

He batted a hand at the air. "Bah! The drink doesn't cause trouble. Other folk cause trouble. Please, may we stay the night where I can drink with others who speak my own tongue? I enjoyed the culturing, but being among people and not knowing a word they say is tiresome."

Oryn hoisted himself into Ranger's saddle and spoke up. "Your habit with the drink is tiresome. The dog is right. You and your mead always bring disaster. Let us continue on and pass the inns by. We do not need any delays with buffoonery."

"Please, I beg of you. One night and one drink. Afterward, I will not bother for more until the treaties are delivered."

Half-tempted, Adwen scratched behind her ear in frustration. A growl rumbled in her throat as she started to consider letting him have what he wanted.

"Please, Adwen?" he begged. "If anything goes wrong I'll... I'll give up the drink for good and find a way to make it up. Please?"

By offering to lose the habit, he tipped the scales in his favor. She groaned and then blurted, "It's a deal, but if anything happens you have to give it up and I get to say I told you so!"

He whooped and laughed out loud. "Do you not always say it?" Reining Ulna, he started for town.

She shook her head and Oryn groaned, "Why did you do it?"

Giving a pained whimper, she replied, "Please don't ask, because I really don't know. Let's just try to keep him out of trouble."

Bellow the cliffs and waterfalls on Dargadia's northern border, small towns thrived off of the rivers and streams they filled. Selkirk was moderately busy with many visitors running about, giving little thought to strangers.

The Mute Mockingbird Inn sat on the outskirts and looked luxurious with clean windows and bright blue curtains. Two caged mockingbirds were inside upon the bar counter. Two men ordered drinks and everything felt peaceful. Where the cages sat, a man approached to sell his services.

One bird cried, "Hello!"

The other bobbed its head, crowing, "Stay the night! Stay the night!"

The bearded innkeeper grumbled. "That's enough of that

now!" Turning his attention to the new customers, he eyed Adwen carefully. "What may I offer you, strangers?"

Oryn laid down a few gold coins. "Two beds. We intend to stay for a night."

The innkeeper took up a coin and bit down. Satisfied, he smiled. "Here's the key. First room up the stairs and to the left. If there's anything else I can do, just let me know, sir."

Another coin was left as a tip and the man continued to study Adwen closely. When they turned away, he resisted the need to protest bringing in such a strange thing. After they were out of earshot, he gave a sigh and grumbled. "What is this world coming to?"

Sunset colors spilled inside and shined through the open window, turning the white bed linens a soft shade of gold. Thin lace curtains floated on a breeze and Adwen rested against the smooth open frame.

"This place sure has grown on me." She laughed a little. "Now I fit in this world better than where I was born."

Both men heard a hint of regret in her soft voice and looked. They knew she was missing something they couldn't begin to understand. As much as her heart ached, she had hidden it well the past few days.

Finally smiling at the brilliant sunset, she let the light to soothe the hurt of not being free to return home. There was still too much to do. Perhaps one day.

A throat cleared just behind and she looked back in surprise. Finding Oryn, she gave a wry smile. "Don't worry. I've actually lost my need to sleep in beds. The floor is more comfortable now."

His face showed discomfort. "Pardon me. I intend to reach past."

She hadn't noticed the chair in the corner.

"Oh! Sorry, go ahead."

Without another glance or word, he took up the chair and started for the far corner facing the door.

She was confused. "I just said I'm sleeping on the floor. You can have the bed, so what do you need that for?"

He paused without looking back. "It would be best if I stood watch."

Shaking her head in disbelief, she watched as he placed it

in the corner. As he was just becoming comfortable, Toth went to beg him for coins. The half-elf was out the door in a flash once he had them.

When it closed, Adwen was still not convinced by the knight's excuse. "You know, I have yet to sleep in a bed since I came back?"

At the time his eyes gazed at the closed door, but shifted to her, showing a mixture of confusion and surprise. "You slept on the floor as a guest of the foreign kings?"

She nodded. "Yeah. I've gotten used to a solid floor, and wide window sills are pretty nice." She shrugged and added, "Beds aren't very comfortable anymore."

Guilt washed over him and he looked back at the door. He couldn't help but think her aversion to the comfort of a warm bed was partly his doing. Then he remembered why he had been so cold and felt sick. He had been using her. At that time, she was only a tool for glory and revenge. More than ever, he felt shame.

His face was blank, but she could tell he was thinking. Calculating eyes shifting as he stared at nothing. When he was silent, she thought the conversation was over. Shrugging, she turned to close the window.

It shut with a light click and Oryn heard her sigh. Out the corner of his vision, he watched her lay down with her head on the hard wood floor. He had not intended to take the chair to stand watch. It was a ploy to let her claim a bed. Now that his plan failed, he felt foolish.

All was quiet except for the comings and goings of other customers in the hall. A few minutes passed and Adwen suddenly heard him speak. She hadn't understood and looked up. "Sorry, what?"

"That young man..." He was staring raptly at the door. "The one who attacked you in your world; how did he know you?"

"He was the school bully. He pushed people around for fun."

"But he knew you. How did he know you?"

She thought about it. "When I was still Shari Gates, I was really shy and timid and he enjoyed picking on me. I never did anything to stop him, but I think he recognized me so easi-

ly because of the one time before I fell into this world."

He listened intently.

"We were playing a game at school. He threw a ball and hurt a girl. When she fell, he wouldn't stop laughing. I believe he remembers me because I was the only one who stood up to him. I got between him and the girl and wouldn't back down."

For a moment he was silent, but then asked, "Why did you protect the girl?"

A somber look came into her violet eyes. "Because I can take it. I can handle abuse and a lot of horrible stuff without fighting back. People used to throw trash from the bus at me while I walked home. What I can't take is seeing someone else taking it. I can't stand seeing others go through the pain I felt every day. I just can't do it."

"Is that why you never attempted to bite before? Because of the chance that you could mark them?"

She thought it over. "Yeah, I guess. No one deserves to go through that every night. I wouldn't even do that to you. That was even before I knew I could not mark people." She smiled and lay back down again.

Oryn's face was blank while his insides squirmed. Perhaps if she knew what he intended to use her for, and what he planned for afterward, she would think differently.

Out of nowhere he heard her chortle. "All you deserved was a good thrashing. I consider us even."

Oryn frowned and pondered. He deserved much worse.

Sunlight left the window, turning the room dark while they slept. Adwen dozed in the corner and the knight in his chair. After a few hours of night slunk by, something made her eyes open wide. An uneasy sensation came over her and a strange bitter scent reached her sensitive nose; dark magic.

She quickly got up to look out the window. Four horsemen in dark red robes like the warlock from the mall were outside. Two more dragged a struggling man from the inn's steps to hand him over. Bound and gagged, Toth disappeared with them off into the forest.

Adwen wore a grim frown then she turned to the knight and barked to wake him.

Oryn instantly drew his sword and was on his feet, wide awake. Calming down once he saw nothing, he looked at her and instantly knew. Lowering his weapon, he sighed and grumbled, "Toth?"

"A bunch of witches have him. I'm going to call the horses. Meet you outside." Her eyes glowed brighter as she opened the sliding pane. "At least he was smart enough leave us the treaties. Don't forget to take them with you!" She cupped her hands to her mouth and howled while the knight grabbed the satchel and dashed out of the room and down the stairs.

In the stables, Ranger broke out of his stall with one well-placed kick and freed Ulna by pulling the lock pin on her gate. The panicking stable boy was powerless to stop them.

Adwen leaped from the window and landed beside Oryn at the steps. Not surprised by her sudden appearance, the knight went up to meet his horse and climbed into the saddle.

"I knew this was going to happen! Why didn't he use the trees?" With the horses galloping after her, she followed the fresh trail.

Oryn glowered, "He cannot while drunk. I'm quite certain he had more than a pint from the counter."

She snarled and picked up the pace. Horse tracks and the smell of dark magic led deep into the trees and far from town. They raced over hills and around rocky formations in the dark. The smell thickened and she slowed when they saw a bright encampment.

"Toth's somewhere in there." She growled to herself. "I think it's safe to say that barging in would be a bad plan. Not many of them can cast spells, but it smells like there are at least forty witches in there right now."

Oryn surveyed the scene and agreed. "Riding into a camp of witches unprepared is a poor plan." He watched wandering troops and noticed that only one of the tents was guarded. "There must be a distraction."

She laughed sarcastically. "Yeah, sure. It'd have to be a pretty big distraction to..."

He was looking directly at her. The hint of a sly expression was on his face and he nearly smiled.

"Oh, no. No! There's no way I'm doing the distraction thing again."

"I'm merely suggesting you have a talent for this sort of thing. I'm confident it would be much easier for you to draw them out than for I." He raised an eyebrow at her aghast expression. "Toth would be appreciative, I'm sure."

Pointing a sharp nail, she glowered. "That's not fair." Then she threw up her hands and stomped off, ranting. "That's not right! If anything goes wrong, I'm blaming you! Got it?" With that she trudged off in a mortified fit.

When he could no longer hear her aggravated mutterings, he smiled to himself and Ranger snorted beneath him. He knew she was more than trustworthy for the part. The red-cloaked clouts wouldn't know what hit them.

Two robed men stood their posts, listening to the sounds from within the tent. Their leader questioned the long-eared guest. In town he told wild stories of adventures in foreign kingdoms and even another world. This camp was not their true base of operations, but a temporary home until the search for an ancient treasure was over.

They were bored and the only source of entertainment was the sounds from the interrogation. One chuckled as they heard an open hand striking a face. His partner smiled and was about to comment, but stopped short and pointed off into the trees.

A ghostly glowing figure strolled through the forest. A woman with golden skin wore a long, snow-white gown. The wind ruffled the hem like a gentle mist over her bare feet. They were captivated as she stopped to smile at them. They stared hungrily and thought she was a nymph of some kind. She looked away and continued on through the dark and out of sight.

One started after her and then the other, not wanting to be left out, quickly followed.

Underbrush made following the figure difficult as thorns and branches snagged their cloaks. Soon they stumbled across a large ravine to a creek below, but the woman was not there. She had vanished. They turned to go back and a white creature leaped from the trees to land before them. A set of sharp claws swung at them and they fell to their deaths.

Adwen growled. "I hate witches."

Then her eyes glowed brighter, briefly flashing gold. Her ears went up and she looked back. Adwen was off like a shot on all fours, ripping through the trees. Something very bad was going to happen if she didn't hurry.

When the guards wandered off, Oryn was waiting in the thicket, but didn't make his move. He could see a silhouette in the tent of someone striking another who was bound to a chair. Eventually, the interrogator grew tired and made to leave. Oryn waited a few moments longer and crept past several tents without being noticed. At the backside of the tent, he searched for any witnesses and slipped under the cloth barrier.

Bound tight and blindfolded with his own eye patch, Toth waited quietly.

The knight listened for more danger. He was no match for a witch, let alone forty. Seeing nothing of any concern, he moved to untie Toth. His face was badly bruised and his lip split.

The half-elf flinched, but once the bonds were cut and blindfold readjusted, he was relieved. He swallowing a drunken belch. "You know, I believe it's time to give up the drink."

Oryn glowered. "We're going to hold you to your word." Carefully helping him to his feet, he found that Toth was too drunk to walk. The knight could see this task was going to be far more difficult than planned.

Toth began to ramble, "I'm sorry. I should not have had so much. Blasted witches! They have no sense of humor, you know?" They crawled out the back and Oryn fought to hold him up. "Well, maybe if they had a little sun on their skin they would feel lighter." He did a sluggish double-take and pointed between the tents. "And that hag, Nadeen. She's got no sense of humor at all."

The knight looked where he pointed and froze as they both realized the witch was staring directly at them.

Nadeen was a voluptuous witch dressed in a gown of black and deep blood red. With eyes as black as her ebony hair, the witch's pale skin had not a single wrinkle or blemish. With the face of a porcelain doll, she had the body of a dark, vengeful goddess.

Her eyes narrowed and Oryn quickly let Toth go stagger behind him. Drawing his sword, he glared while the witch walked in brisk strides, magically summoning a long black rod with a jagged blade on either end.

Taking a deep breath as she moved to strike, the knight brought up his father's sword to block the evil weapon. Metal collided and there was a flash of red. A magical force knocked him back and threw both men into the nearest tent. Quickly, he recovered and got to his feet to face her again. Then he saw his sword.

It was shattered. His mind went blank as he stared dumbstruck at the hilt and the remaining shard. The two gems set into the base were all that remained intact, shining in the dim light. The rest of the camp became aware of their presence and started rallying around their leader. Nadeen twirled her wicked weapon, preparing to destroy them. She smiled at the angry knight.

Suddenly, a deafening roar cut through the night. There were screams and yelling at the back and Nadeen paused to listen to her men being killed. A white beast downed three more with her jaws before leaping high overhead. Adwen landed on all fours before the witch, muzzle twisted into a vicious snarl. The wicked woman watched in shock as the blood of her followers turned to dust on her fur. Fearful, she took a step back and saw the gold mark on her forehead suddenly flash in the form of the Andredan symbol.

She gasped. "Impossible!"

While the witch was distracted by Adwen's snapping and gnashing, Ranger and Ulna raced in to retrieve their riders. Toth and Oryn climbed on without delay and Adwen roared, frightening the witch farther back before leaping after her friends.

Nadeen stood frozen in shock.

The horses were very tired and beginning to slow while they raced along the bottom of the cliffs. Crossing the river into the concealment of its shadow, smells from a deep cave reached Adwen's senses. When the dark of the cavern enveloped her, the horses didn't want to follow.

She barked back at Ranger. "Are you scared? This is a lot better than the witches chasing after us!"

Finding the will to enter, the horses nickered at the unfamiliar smells of fungus and wet limestone. Soon they were having trouble finding level ground among the stalagmites. Ranger whinnied and Ulna snorted as they nearly tripped on rock formations. Then to their surprise, a dim glow illuminated the ground around them.

Adwen had discovered how to release light through her skin when she distracted the warlocks. In her woman form to using her body as a light, she led the friends to safety.

Ranger snorted. "Why didn't you think of that sooner, mutt?"

"Sorry. I only just learned how to do this. Let's go before they catch up. I can feel them getting closer."

The way was long and spacious with sounds of water everywhere in the dark. Adwen hoped their pursuers had not been able to follow, but her hope was pitted against the feeling that they were gaining. Struggling to keep nerves steady, she grew anxious at the slow pace. Her light for the horses could only reveal so much and if one were injured, it could be a disaster.

Up ahead the sides of the cave changed. The light from her skin soon revealed a marbled path underfoot and she stopped to look around. The discovery of a secret temple-like hall confused her and she scanned for danger, sensing old magic hidden farther down.

Upon the Clydesdale, Oryn was lost in raging grief. His father's sword had been destroyed. As the thought flew around his head, he clenched the hilt tight. The sword with which he had vowed to destroy his brother's marker with was shattered. The weapon had belonged to his family since the founding of the order. It had defended the kingdom for hundreds of years and through more than fifty generations of the Conrad family.

Anger swelled and his hand started to shake. His prized possession was shattered. The thought hit him once more and he lost his temper. In a momentary fit of rage, he threw the hilt and everyone froze as the metal bounced, making a loud clanging racket. If anyone else were inside the cave they would hear it as well.

Angry, Adwen whipped around and snapped. "What's wrong with you? Why did you throw..? Was that your sword?"

"Every oath I've ever made was on this blade. Even if re-forged, I've shamed my family. It's broken, nothing more than a hunk of metal."

Adwen was about to reply, but sensed strong magic. A light rose up from the broken sword and vanished into the walls. Many hidden torches burst alight in small stone alcoves. Two by two, they began to burn and show the way.

Jaws dropped, they stared until Adwen blurted, "What did you do?" Then there was the sound of voices from behind. "Keep going. I'm staying back to deal with these guys!" Pulling the white hood over her head, she vanished and the men heard a deep menacing growl.

The witches carried torches, jagged edged weapons and bows made with human bones. Each heard the sound of metal on stone and their pace quickened. The armed troop wore looks of eager anticipation once they knew their goal was close.

There was a snarl in the dark and they halted. Everyone with a sword or dagger drew it out and those with bows notched an arrow. They heard another snarl and flinched. It was close, but they saw nothing no matter how high they held the red glowing torches.

One blurted out nervously, "Where is it?"

Something invisible suddenly struck a man in the face and he went down. The archers fired a few arrows, but missed and there was another snarl before a large rock flew at them. Five warlocks were maimed or killed when the thing came smashing past. They grouped together, facing out in all directions. Terror made eyes twitch and hands quiver.

Adwen transformed into the hound and was instantly revealed by the torches. Her invisibility could not last in this form and she did not care. What was there to fear?

Ripping into the mess of them, she voraciously attacked with sharp claws and teeth, letting herself go into a mad frenzy. She leaped away after culling many and prepared to make a second pass.

They had not been able to cut her with their weapons. The last few archers fired and missed, save for one. A single arrow passed straight through her right bicep. A horrible pain hit her arm like an electric bolt. She roared, slashing at a few more before swiftly retreating into the shadows.

The horses carried Toth and Oryn at a trot and the half-elf asked his companion, "What do you make of all this? Did you know your sword held power?"

Shaking his head, Oryn continued to marvel at the vast passage. "I had never heard such a thing. Where do you suppose it leads?"

"I haven't the faintest idea." Toth laughed and added, "My drunkenness is beginning to fade. Perhaps I could call down the roots from above and aid our escape?"

"That would be a very bad idea, Toth." Adwen suddenly chuckled dryly beside them as she reappeared. They hadn't noticed her approach, holding a hand over her arm. "You'd be more likely to cause a collapse."

Toth chuckled. "Ah, good. The nasty lot learned their lesson?"

A skeptical look came over her. "I'm not so sure about that." The way she stood they couldn't see her arm and she showed her hand, drenched in silver. It was not vanishing like the other times. The smooth substance continued to dribble from the wound.

Looks of alarm were on their faces.

"I thought you were impervious to weapons. Not even desert scorpion venom could harm you!"

She winced at the pain and attempted to stop the bleeding. "Well, I guess they have something a little worse."

"Let me get a look at that!" Toth offered. "I'm sure I could it heal in no time!"

Adwen could tell he was still drunk and snapped. "Stay on the horse! Those guys are right behind me. We have to keep moving."

Loud voices echoed from behind and torch light came creeping around the bend.

Giving a start, they urged the horses to gallop. Then a few

arrows were fired. The companions fled farther down the passage until it grew broad and even higher ending at a cavern. The space was brightened by glowing rubies set in stone far overhead. Beneath the ring of giant gems a vast pool caught the water that poured out of underground streams. A wide stairway led up to the pool and a pedestal pierced by a rod.

Upon reaching the stairs to the giant pool, they saw there was no way out.

Adwen muttered bitterly, "A dead end."

Their pursuers were nearly upon them and Oryn dropped from Ranger's back, pulling his knife. "Toth! Keep the horses close and stay back."

Adwen glared at the mob. "I guess we'll have to do this here."

"So it seems," Oryn replied.

Snarling, she rushed the gaggle and leaped through the air. None of the surviving assailants could cast spells, but some shot arrows. She blinked past them to begin the attack and her fists flew, nails slashing like razors, forcing some into retreat. But others stepped up to take their place. Some managed to cut her with black swords, leaving more oozing wounds. She roared and yelled, enraged by pain.

Out of the slew of attackers, three went for the knight by the stair. He only had a knife and they thought it would be an easy victory.

He twirled the blade as they came upon him with swords. The first swung for his head, but Oryn ducked and disemboweled him with two swift swipes. As the villain fell, the second was more cautious, pairing up with a remaining comrade. They worked hard to push the knight along the stairs to the pedestal. He was at a great disadvantage against their longer weapons, but held the warlocks at bay.

As Oryn's heels touched the edge before the pool, one warlock made a weak stab and an even more pathetic defense. In the instant that the warlock faltered, Oryn sliced him across the arm and then the throat.

The last standing enemy joined Oryn on level ground and they faced off. The knight played with his sharp knife in a menacing display, thoroughly enjoying the fight. Before they could collide, something erupted out of the pool.

Watery spray flew and a giant dragon with white skin and golden scales rose up from the seemingly shallow basin. Along its flanks and down its tail tender white skin was tinted pink by the gems above. Golden scales swept along its belly and down its back through the narrow space between its veined wings. Two long whiskers waved in the air before its crimson eyes as it reared its head, crowned by a mantle of golden spikes. The dragon towered over them, bathed in ruby light and clutching the stony edge of his pool.

The men froze and stared in fright at the guardian.

Adwen paused to see what was happening, but did not have long to stare. Fighting so many assailants was a struggle, especially since the last of them had long black blades. New wounds on her back and arms continued to shed silver everywhere.

A set of dragon jaws came down level with the men's eyes and the whiskers waved around them. The dragon glared and snorted, turning his attention to the warlock. Then the great creature spoke in a deep booming voice.

"Man who dares to enter my den, answer my riddle or you shall not breathe again."

Both combatants stared. The warlock gulped and answered. "Riddle me, Dragon."

The massive beast rumbled. "Trespasser who enters the blessed treasure hold of Andredan of old, what says the true master to claim this weapon I keep in its first master's name? Answer my riddle to live and go, or of my hungry belly you shall know."

For the first time, Oryn and the warlock noticed the rod protruding from the stone. The beginnings of the edges were exposed just above the pedestal. They had found one of the demon-slaying weapons forged by the Master Knight. Oryn had read of the sword that belonged to Darien's second in command. This was the Rose Thorne.

The warlock wet his lips and thought hard before blurting out, "Grant me my sword, dragon!" At first he was excited and greedy, thinking he might get to take the treasure. Only Oryn remembered the guardian said nothing about taking it if he answered correctly.

Regardless, the answer was wrong. The fearsome beast

roared, snapping up the warlock in a single bite. He chewed once to break the screaming man's bones then swallowed him whole. The dragon licked his jaws before turning to Oryn.

The knight took a step back as the giant snout came down to sniff him and the two long whiskers swayed. The dragon looked surprised. White smoke rolled out of his nostrils as it asked in a cool, rumbling tone, "Knight who travels with Darien's heir into the darkening time, to claim this weapon shall you answer my riddling rhyme?"

The question startled Oryn. Without thinking, his mouth moved. "Riddle me, dragon."

This pleased the dragon. "Noble warrior of the sword, what says he who honors this mighty reward?" More smoke rolled around his feet from the dragon's nostrils.

It confounded him. Oryn was no good at riddles and looked more closely at the two-handed great sword. On the gold bracer was an indentation. The guardian let him step closer to see that it was Darien's mark, representing the virtues. What could the odd riddle mean?

Then it hit him. He thought of his oath when he was accepted as a Knight of the Order. He had vowed to uphold all five virtues. Glancing back, he saw Adwen fighting the warlocks. Then he looked again at the symbol and felt crippling regret. Overwhelmed, he dropped to his knees and let the feeling take hold.

Shaking his head, he whispered, "I am not worthy."

"Claim your sword now, and keep your good vow."

He looked up in surprise. Stunned, he put the knife away. With shaking hands, gripped the red hilt. When he had a firm hold, he lifted. The Rose Thorne was heavy. Oryn's hands were level with his brow when the end came free at last. Six feet of silver and gold was in his grasp and he stood in awe at the sight.

The dragon reared to look at the vile intruders and bellowed to Adwen. "Come close to me, child of Darien and company! It is time for you to flee! Flee this place by my secret way and do not return! All of these foul worms shall burn!"

His mighty roar echoed and the ceiling of the cavern looked as if it were collapsing. Where the red gems were set into rock a spiraling path lowered. Not hesitating, Toth brought the horses and Oryn set the heavy weapon across his back by the strong strap below the hilt. Evading the warlocks, Adwen transformed and bounded along the exit with the horses hot on her heals.

When they were gone, the path returned to the cavern ceiling. The dragon roared at the wicked men. They screamed as gold flames poured from out of his mouth, consuming them. Bright tongues of fire devoured all.

The Past (Part 4)
MASTER'S FINAL LESSON

Sir Vigo, Sir Oryn and two others stood in fine commoner garments in the backstreets of Plexus. They were far from the market streets in a much quieter district. Sir Vigo led the way into an establishment decorated with velvet curtains and lace. Women sauntered around in scarcely any clothes, smiling. The madam wore a black evening robe on her svelte body that curved like a wine glass. Her eyes were sharp as she addressed the knights.

"Welcome, gentlemen. Welcome to the House of Desires. How may we please you today, Sir Vigo?" She puffed on her long smoking utensil.

"We are soon to depart for a quest." He took a furtive glance at his student. "One of my knights has just turned the age of a man."

Behind him Oryn was silent, becoming disgusted with the scene.

She released the smoke in a long stream as her eyebrows went up. A smile of intrigue made her soft cheeks lift and her eyes sparkle. "Is that so?" The prostitute studied the young knight. "Fifteen! I'm sure we can give him a many happy returns."

When she clapped her hands several girls came to form a line. They were beautiful and each had a different attraction for the knights, except for Oryn.

The young knight overheard others many times sharing their escapades from the whorehouse. None of the stories held any appeal. He was far too focused on his goals and training. Now that his master had brought him here, he was sickened and confused. All he wanted was to take part in his first quest and cut down werewolves.

The two others made a motion to take their pick, but

were stopped by Sir Vigo's raised hand. "No, Conrad has first choice. Come forward. Which of these women would you like for your time?"

His only answer was a stony expression and an impatient stare.

Frowning, Sir Vigo went to hear what the young man had to say. "What is it, Conrad?"

"I see no point in this. We are knights. We slay creatures for the order and our king. What purpose could this serve?"

The old knight was patient. "When all is said and done, we are men who accept the chance of laying down our lives. No matter how skilled, there is always the chance of no return. When a knight falls performing his duty, it is better to celebrate his sacrifice because he lived the life of a man." Glaring, he added, "What a great pity and a shame for a man to die for his people without knowing the touch of a woman. If you died without knowing that, you would be mourned by your men rather than honored." When Oryn was still uncooperative, he stated, "I shall chose then. I will know if you followed through. Until you have done this, you shall not enter any quest."

Oryn's green eyes widened and he stared back in shock.

Sir Vigo returned to the lineup. They smiled sweetly as he studied them. At last his eyes settled on a girl with dark brown hair and almond skin that smelled like honey. The old knight took her gently by the hand and brought her forward.

"What is your name?" Sir Vigo asked.

"Valencia."

Oryn could not deny that she was beautiful, but he studied her eyes and saw little intellect. Against his own wishes, he took the woman's hand and let her lead him to the hall. Before they could disappear around the corner his master called.

"Sir Oryn?" He held up a hand gesture to indicate two times and added firmly, "That is an order. See you in an hour's time, Conrad."

Many hours later, the four were on horseback. In full armor, they headed through the abandoned roads that led to the empty elf ruins north of Dargadia. They rode their horses hard and crossed the northern border by along the cliffs before nightfall. Only then did they slow for the mounts to recover, keeping the cliffs on their right flank.

"Why so put out?" one knight laughed at Oryn. "Did you have trouble impressing the woman?"

The other slapped the loud knight's shoulder. "Of course not, Polis, you dolt! Did you not see her as she chased him into the street? It looked as if she should have been paying him!" They both laughed hard.

Sir Vigo was alongside Oryn and chuckled. "Was the hour enough for you?"

Oryn was angry, but holding his temper in check. "I could have done well and died without living the hour, sir." In the twilight, he glared back at his master.

"Did you get no pleasure from her?"

There was a long pause before he answered in disgust. "Some... pleasure, but little having to do with her person. She was nothing to me."

"Good. Then you know what most men do not. A desirable woman is one who has wisdom coupled with a lovely body. Do you agree?"

Oryn glowered. "I would rather they have an ounce of honor to start with."

"Do not hate those creatures for what they are. They do not have much, and what they do to survive is all they know. Pity and forgive them. Those women are unfortunate to know only of how to pleasure a man. Some have brains and could leave, but may never because of the prosecution for their original trade. Live by the Master Knight's virtues. Compassion is all you need give them. They are only human. Save your anger for the beasts."

"Yes, sir."

The sun set and the sunlight that bathed wispy clouds faded, letting the night turn them black and blue. Already the first of the four moons was in the sky. The red moon cast the land in a foreboding glow. Slowly they made their way through the forest and along the cliffs. The night grew a little lighter as the other three moons came out.

Oryn's horse snorted and nickered as it kicked a rock, spooking itself.

His master turned to him. "Keep your animal calm. With

the moons out we need silence. Once we return from this quest you may begin training the foal you liked so much. I'll see to it that you get that wild one who bites. How did you get him to trust you, Conrad?"

"The beast shares my feelings for fools. I only have to look him in the eye and he obeys without question."

The knights chuckled quietly. "Perhaps it's that you scare him?"

"The foal likes him. I have seen the animal be affectionate to Sir Oryn." A breeze blew past and Sir Vigo became stern and wary. "We must be more watchful. This is a very dangerous quest for the undertaking of a fresh knight."

"Why did we not bring Sir Peregrine if it is so dangerous, sir?" asked Sir Nigel.

Polis grumbled. "Because he's on another quest in the far south." He turned to their captain. "What is this quest, sir?"

"This is a mission to search for survivors north of the old elf lands. A band of travelers was foolish and traveled up along the cliffs to avoid crossing Broad River. They had many goods to trade. He did not wish to pay the hefty barge toll and went north through the empty forests along the lost roads." He turned even more serious. "There was but one survivor. The man was mortally wounded. We could not get much before he passed, having gone mad with fear. He only mentioned werewolves, demons and an evil place farther north. We fear he spoke of an ancient place from long ago. It is forbidden to visit that damned plot of land."

Oryn asked darkly, "The Crescent Remains, sir?"

"Exactly, Conrad. They were said to have been emptied centuries ago, but if the dying man were right, then there may be something terrible to come. Conrad, this horse they gave you is too skittish."

Another breeze passed along the quiet cliff, rustling their capes and hair. Oryn had a strange feeling as an odd and familiar tingling ran up his spine. The last time he felt this way was while face-to-face with the alpha werewolf in the dungeons. By instinct, he gripped his sword and looked to the trees.

Sir Vigo only just noticed when a deafening roar met his ears. A large pack of werewolves raced for them in a bloodthirsty frenzy. One of the first to attack lunged for Oryn's horse, sending it into a panic. It reared back while close to the cliff. The werewolf slashed again, knocking it off balance. The steed and the young knight tipped over the edge in a freefall to the earth below.

As the horse fell, Oryn managed to grab hold of a strong tree root. He quickly put his sword back in the sheath and got a better hold of the lifeline. High up over the edge, he could hear the sounds of a bloodbath taking place without him. In a rage at being left out, he tried to climb and the next handhold gave way. After that he was not so hasty. The drop beneath him was immeasurable, while level ground was only thirty feet above. More cautiously than before, Oryn climbed.

Four times he almost fell, barely saving himself. Sweat covered every inch of him as he strained to hold on and continue. The fight had gone quiet hours ago. Dawn was on the horizon. Strong winds lashed at his back as there was not a sound besides his heavy breathing while he clung to the cliff. Eventually his persistence came through; he reached to hoist his tired form up over the brink. When he was safely on level ground again, he lay still to rest, rolling his head to one side to see the aftermath of the battle.

Red stained the ground everywhere. Most of the spills were dark as tar around the corpses of naked werewolf men. Jagged-toothed mouths were open wide to the twilight, their eyes black like the bloody grass. The remains of Polis and Nigel were near their dismembered horses. Both had been torn apart after killing many of the creatures.

Then something amid the chaotic remnants moved, surprising Oryn into leaping to his feet, ready to fight. He drew his sword and stared. Knelt in the midst of the massacre, his master, Sir Vigo stared blankly into the trees. Blood soaked his cape and white hair as he sat like a stone amongst the twenty-five dead monsters and his two closest friends. Lost in his own thoughts, he hadn't noticed Oryn until he was standing beside him, sword drawn.

Sir Vigo's look was baleful. He gingerly cradled his left hand where the pinky and third finger had been bitten off. The wound no longer bled, the same as with the mark from any werewolf. He watched his student's eyes dilate wildly and asked, "Oryn. If you would allow me, I shall take my own life, but would you let me have a little more time?"

The monsters had left Sir Vigo alive at the command of their leader. The young knight would not reach the order without help and there was no one else.

Oryn's hands shook, his mind torn in two. One side was eager to gut Sir Vigo and put him out of everyone's misery. It battled the other side, which felt a dull pain for his great master. Now that Sir Vigo's fate was sealed, he did not know what to say or do with the sword in his quivering hands. Nevertheless, Oryn kept the point at his master's neck.

Sir Vigo watched Oryn's eyes shift as he thought. "If you would allow me, I wish to see you to the order alive and unharmed. And I have one final lesson to teach. Please." He was certain that his wrathful student would strike him down.

Oryn had never seen his master this way. He had never seen him afraid, but saw it now. Without being told, he knew the trek alone would be suicide. Very hesitant, he lowered his blade.

As they walked, Oryn watched his master closely. Within a few hours he knew he would begin showing signs. First he would have angry outbursts, followed by hunger and eventually paranoia. They did not meet each other's gaze while Vigo talked.

"When I am gone, you will be your own master. Be a leader worthy of your men. A teacher and an overseer is all they need to be great, same as you. Your father would be proud to see you now." Along the way he gazed in awe at the blue sky and the green trees. Come nighttime, he would not get the chance to see them or the sun ever again.

Oryn answered respectfully, though he was disturbed by his master's behavior. "Yes, sir." Not only was Sir Vigo calling him by his first name, he was showing sentiment for flowers and birds. Not knowing what to make of it, Oryn kept his hand ready to reach his sword. There was no telling when his master would become unpredictable and aggressive.

"You were very fortunate to not join in the battle, Oryn. Their leader never saw you, thinking he had left me alone with this... injury." An even more frightened look was in his eyes as he recalled it. "Listen carefully to what I am about to tell you, lad. I have seen something diabolical. The leader of the attack showed himself. It was he who cut down our comrades. We were faring well before he arrived."

"Who came, sir?"

Sir Vigo had stopped walking. They stood side by side in the forest. Wind blew past and a chill ran through the old knight as the knowledge made his own blood run cold. He turned a stern gaze to his student. "I have seen the White-eyed Demon."

Oryn was dismayed. "Sycan? No, sir. That is not possible. The texts --"

He was cut short as his master's hand gripped his throat and lifted him up. Sir Vigo's eyes held a telltale red glint as he bellowed. "Listen to me! I've looked him in the face after watching him rip apart our brothers like flimsy toys! I know what I saw, Oryn!" Then he paused. Red light still in his eyes, Sir Vigo saw his student had the sword half-drawn.

The young knight dangled in Sir Vigo's supernatural grip, using the breathing ritual. Even though Sir Vigo had attacked, he was able to stay his own hand and waited, struggling for enough air.

Sir Vigo released him and turned away, bracing himself against a tree, fighting the anger that attempted to take hold.

Oryn landed on his feet and never let go of the sword. He watched as his master was somehow able to push back the thing that made him lash out.

The old knight's breathing became steady. Muscles re-laxed and he turned to him once more with the red light gone. "Believe me, Oryn and tell no one. The elders wrote that Sycan was destroyed by Darien and tucked away the truth. I found the text by accident not more than a week ago. It read that the White-eyed Demon, Darien's deadliest enemy, had fallen into his own shadow and vanished. No one knew where he'd gone. All wanted to believe him dead."

The look on Oryn's face showed he was beginning to be-lieve.

"If the White-eyed Demon has returned then you shall soon run across his followers, the Red Cult Witches. When you see them, then you will know the Crescent Remains are living once more. I will not be here to fight with you then. Keep a watchful eye out for Darien's heir. He could be wandering our lands even now."

They started walking again and Oryn let go of his sword. "How is it that you can fight the red rage, sir?"

For the first time that day, his master smiled. "That is the lesson I wish to teach. Your father and I made a discovery on one of our less fortunate quests. One of our number had been marked and was unaware. All of the others were slain and it was just us three, trying to do what we are doing now. Night arrived and the beasts that survived returned.

He chuckled a little. "The knight used the breathing ritual, same as we did to fight the monsters. It allowed him to resist the change! We watched as he stayed it off until his heart finally burst within. For the change to take hold, the heart must race and the blood boil. As you well know, the breathing ritual, Darien's Breath, has the opposite effect. Tell the secret to no one and do not let the council find I taught this to you. They would take your head as a penance."

After clearing his throat, he went on, "Another knight mistakenly let himself become marked and was captured by his own men. Soon after, he was taken to the dungeons. We were able to stay his execution long enough to have his cooperation and he helped us to learn more. The breathing ritual may only stay the change for a brief time. Also, it will not be able to hold off any transformations beyond the first. Once the elders became aware, they were not pleased and threatened to have us executed if we continued or told any what we knew.

"It was forbidden only because any failed attempt could allow more of the monsters to come about. I tell it to you now because I know you would not fail. Only if the need is dire, and if there is but a simple task to accomplish, then you could use this to continue without fear of being stricken from the records. This is my final lesson to you. There is nothing more I can teach."

They continued in silence. The day dragged by for Oryn, but for his master it was the shortest he ever lived. With death so near everything passed by too quickly. As the sun drifted closer to the earth, he felt a tugging at his heart, knowing it was his last sunset. Then he realized there was one last thing to tell the student he had grown to love as a son.

"Oryn?"

"Yes, sir?"

They could see the city almost ten miles out. Their walk steadily quickened and he listened to his master's final words.

"I have something of the utmost importance to tell you. Let go."

"Let go of what, sir?"

Sir Vigo took a deep breath and began the speech he had been preparing for the longest time. "Your hate; it is a tool that does no good to use. A man may fight with an even greater drive without, if he can find a purpose worth serving. Hate will only destroy you. It shall burn you from the inside out. You need the courage to let it go!"

"I have courage, sir!" Oryn snapped. "I am no coward!"

"No, indeed you are not." Vigo smiled. "But there is a difference. You are simply not afraid. For there to be courage, there must first be fear. I have that, as you can plainly see, but I have the courage to face it, lad. It is foolish to not fear these enemies, and with it comes courage. Cowards are men who flee from fear. You can have courage, if you would only let go of the hate that fuels you. That is the only wish I have for you, Oryn. Please, find a way to let it all go."

What his master said confused him, but Oryn took the words in and vowed never to forget them. He did not think his master could be entirely right in his mind. Sir Vigo was likely delusional by now, but the young knight was respectful.

"Yes, sir."

The answer pleased the older knight and he sighed. "Thank you. I may do this freely knowing you will persevere. The sun sets and the beasts shall gain. It is time to run! Now, Oryn!"

They broke into a dead sprint. All that lay between them and their destination were nine miles of forest and open plains. The dim twilight felt final, leaving an empty feeling in the heart of Sir Vigo Odette. Shadows spread like a sickness until it became night. They ran hard, leaping over small obstacles and avoiding low-hanging growth. The woods were silent as the animals knew the men were hunted by evil creatures.

Both were strong and had the endurance to run the distance without slowing. It was a death race for Sir Oryn while Sir Vigo was his insurance of survival. When three more miles lay in their way, the trees became sparse and they reached the wide open plains. Then they sensed their pursuers.

Some of the naked werewolf men snarled as they sprinted, rapidly closing the gap. They were not human anymore and their bare bodies could outrun a frightened deer. The enormous pack was hungry for human flesh. Once a full moon rose, they would catch them and gorge themselves.

It was less than a mile to go when the knights could see the torches on the high stone wall. The night watchmen paced and would see them coming. At the very least, the archers would be able to assist. That was where Oryn realized his master was no longer at his side. He skidded to an abrupt halt to search.

Sir Vigo Odette was far behind in his fighting stance, waiting for the pack to come down on him. Wearing the wolf slayer's helm with the snarling face guard lowered, he put himself into focus using Darien's Breath. When the blood-red moon shone full, the change did not come. The intense pain was dull as he let his mind sink deep into itself, allowing his body to fight of its own accord. Werewolves came and started transform while he began to mow them down in twos and threes.

Stuck standing between his master and the gates, Oryn knew the monsters were too many. He would be mutilated. His master's orders were specifically to leave him behind and get to safety. He had never disobeyed an order. This would was his first time. Without thinking further, he ran to the fight just as he saw his master falter and stagger. He drew his own sword as he got close and lowered his face guard.

Sir Vigo dropped to his knees, striking his sword into the earth before him. There he stayed, gripping the hilt with both hands and bowing his head as the monsters prowled nearer. One reached for him with lipless jaws for a taste. The monster's muzzle was quickly cut from its head. It reared back, roaring in pain, blood spewed over Oryn and his master.

The young knight stabbed its heart to finish the job, and in the blink of an eye, the pack forgot Sir Vigo. This young knight smelled so much more enticing. They came in waves while Oryn moved like a wild cat, swiftly pierced their hearts and cutting thick throats. Two came from the side and he decapitated one with a sweeping stroke before stabbing the second between the eyes. Melding compassion with wrath, he fought using everything he felt. All of his body was a fire, swaying and swinging in a deadly whirl of strikes and strokes.

The city gates released more knights to ride out to his aid. But by the time they reached the scene, there was only one werewolf left to die. It snapped at Oryn and roared when it missed completely. He brought his sword up high, cried out loud and sliced down, splitting the beast's head like a ripe melon. It gasped and quivered, collapsing among the rest.

Twenty knights stared in awe of the mess and didn't say a word. The bodies were piled upon each other in a near-perfect crescent around the two knights. Sir Oryn had fought and slaughtered nearly forty werewolves to defend the slayer who knelt behind him.

They watched from atop their horses as the knight lifted his visor and turned to his master. Slowly, he approached and stood studying him. He knew the old man no longer breathed. There was a slow trickle of blood from the mouth of his wolf-shaped visor, forming a dark puddle in the grass by the flat of his blade. A long silence prevailed as he looked down at the great slayer. Sir Vigo the master, the knight, the teacher and the man. Sir Oryn's great mentor was gone, his body knelt before the sword upon which he had made his oath to the order.

His student took a shaking breath and paid his last respects the best way he knew how. Striking his sword into the ground beside him, he took a knee to perform a flawless, kneeling bow.

The funeral was held at the first light of dawn, as was tradition. The body was burned on the white marble alter like the others before and his ashes were taken to the sea to be cast into the wind by Sir Oryn himself. The council elders saw fit to grant him the right to claim Sir Vigo's slayer's armor for his skill. He wore the shining armor of his master proudly, watching the ashes drift out on the gales and gusts. Even still, he had not and did not shed a tear.

Chapter 35
A PRICE TO PAY

Collasal moss covered trees towered over them. The forest that once belonged to the elves grew wild without their guidance. Raw magic was thick in the air. It hung in the boughs as a mist that curdled and flowed. Sunlight shone through the substance as if it was not there at all. Patches of wild ferns crowded the travelers' legs and made progress slow. At the crack of dawn, Adwen and her companions finished resting and headed west. While everyone else was happy to see the wondrous woods, Sir Oryn was wary.

If they went east along the cliffs they would have to cross Broad River. They were left with no choice but to head west. He hoped once they reached the lost roads, there would be less danger than he recalled. Riding along, he felt as if they had jumped out of the cooking pot and into the fire.

Once the day shone brighter, sunlight caught on Adwen's skin and wounds healed much faster. She sighed as the rays began to mend silver flesh, causing blood to fall away as shimmering dust. Her clothes mended as well. Once no longer distracted by the soothing sensation, she noticed the knight fondling the strange weapon.

He traced the indentation on the heavy blade thoughtfully with his thumb.

"What is it?"

"This is the Rose Thorne, a treasure of Darien's. This was the weapon he bestowed to his greatest ally and second in command." Then he shook his head. "I have no right to this. It is yours to do with as you please. Take it from me."

With a raised eyebrow, she held the heavy sword easily with one hand. Feeling the grip, she thought it was a beautiful weapon and detected power imbued into its core. Adwen smiled and playfully leaped about, testing the blade.

Oryn was content to watch the flashy attempts at swordsmanship. It was intriguing how her feminine arms supported the heavy thing as if it were a twig. She twirled, smiling as the light on the blade reflected onto the boughs. But when Adwen's eyes changed color, only the knight saw. For a split second they shined gold.

Adwen instantly lost the smile and became thoughtful. She seemed to come to a decision. Then she returned to him shaking her head and offered it. "This is definitely yours."

He was taken aback. "How are you sure of that?"

She thought for a moment and shrugged. "I don't know. It's just a feeling. This belongs to you now. Keep it."

All he could think to ask was why, but bit his tongue, knowing better than to argue with the heir.

They found a shallow river where they could drink and rest. Bright light shone off the surface like a rippling mirror. The men dismounted while Adwen wandered off, exploring and scouting for danger as they relaxed.

The knight drank his fill beside the horses and splashed handfuls onto his face.

Toth joined him, folding his arms. "Have you told her?"

He paused, splashed a bit more on himself again and wiped it away.

As Oryn stood without saying a word, the half-elf grew frustrated. "Do you even intend to?"

Oryn glowered. "I plan to when the time is right. Not before."

"Let me guess, then. You intend wait for her to confront you on the issue or until she shows more undue kindness?"

"She claims to have put what I've done in the past. And I do not wait for her kindness or revenge. Why would I wait for retribution when I already feel it upon me?" He glared and seethed. "Be angry with me if you will. The moment I saw my father's sword broken, I knew my punishment was upon me. Leave me be. I have more suffering to do."

He stalked away upstream and Toth shook his head. Going to Ulna for his bags of bread, he sensed Oryn was correct.

Ranger finished a long drink and snorted happily. It was the sweetest he had ever had. Looking up, he saw his master standing alone on the pebbled shore. His master was afraid.

Snorting again, he went to him. Gravel crunched loudly under shod hooves.

Oryn heard him coming and did not respond, staring absentmindedly at the water. Near the small island at the deep end, he could see a school of fish swimming to and fro like a flock of birds. He felt Ranger beside him, sniffing his hand in a reassuring manner. No one saw the fish suddenly scatter and the sun's reflection flicker. The knight was turning to pat his horse, but never got the chance.

A red scaly talon snatched up the warhorse. A hungry dragon swooped in. His catch was too heavy to carry far and landed on the small island. The horse screamed in horror and at the talons gouging his side.

Dashing in a vain attempt at a rescue, Oryn cried at the top of his voice.

"No!"

The dragon hissed as he saw him. A long tail whipped and caught his chest plate, knocking Oryn back into the thick ferns. Harmlessly landing among the plants, he got up and stared in disbelief. Helpless, he could only watch as the dragon took a large bite and Ranger screamed.

Ulna retreated to the thicket. Before Toth could call up the roots, Adwen leaped down from a high tree, changing into her hound self, roaring.

Swallowing the first bite, the dragon looked up at the sound as she landed on his head. Claws pierced into scaly hide. He reared and roared, spewing flames in a fit of pain and surprise. Her claws were strong enough to hold on and the dragon backed away from Ranger. Then Adwen's fangs swiftly ripped out one large reptilian eyes. Hot blood flew and the dragon roared, flailing madly until she lost her grip and landed in the shallows.

Jaws snapping, she snarled. "Get lost! The horse isn't food for you!"

Fanning vast wings, he glared through the remaining eye and hissed before taking a breath. "This deer is my kill. You cannot have it!" The beast lowered his head and released a pillar of flame. When the blast died down, the surface of the river boiled. Adwen had vanished. Thinking the white creature was burned away, the dragon moved to reclaim his feast.

Suddenly, the white hound resurfaced under the dragon's belly and slashed at tender flesh. He screeched out a horrible sound and his body quivered. Blood oozed out in buckets. The dragon screeched in agony and fear.

"Take the deer! Leave me be!"

He flew off as fast as its wings could take him and her roar echoed across the water. "That's not a deer, stupid dragon!"

Changing into her woman form, she quietly went with Toth to join the knight.

Oryn returned to the river and slowly went to the little island. Ranger lay still, breathing more slowly with every passing moment. The look on Oryn's face as he stared down at his loyal friend was of stunned remorse. He knelt down and reached to touch him.

As he did, the horse tried to right himself and stand.

He was too weak and Oryn stopped him with a gentle hand, shushing softly. "No, no, old friend. Stand down. Stand down." The knight swallowed hard, seeing more of Ranger slipping away and diluting in the river. Very gently, he laid a hand on him and watched the look of pain beginning to fade.

Ranger snorted weakly and made a soft sound.

As his eyes closed, the knight watched the breaths creating ripples on the shore. He breathed once, twice, a third time and then the surface was not disturbed again.

Adwen struggled to hold back the tears. Unlike Toth, she managed to choke them off. A few long seconds of silence passed and was broken at last by Oryn.

He spoke softly. "What did he say, Adwen?"

She and Toth stared. He had never called her by name before.

He stared unblinking at his beloved friend and asked again when she was too stunned to reply. "What did he say?"

"He said, it was an honor to run with you. And he called you Brother."

Quietly, he felt Ranger's soft nose and murmured, "Thank you. Thank you, Adwen."

He stood and backed away. There was nothing of value in the saddle he could carry. All he had left was his armor and weapons. He sighed and stated without the usual commanding tone, "We must leave this place. Other beasts will surely come. They will smell blood. We must move on."

Everyone's attention was on the fallen and no one witnessed Adwen's demeanor change. Her eyes shone gold, glancing between Oryn and his horse. She blinked and the violet color returned along with swelling tears. Something in her heart told her there was one last thing she needed to do.

She turned to Toth, wiping damp lashes. "I need you to do something, Toth."

"Anything."

"Go find four fruits and bring them here. I'm going to need your help with this."

With a little cooperation from a pear tree, Toth was able to do as asked. It bowed low for him and he soon returned.

"Here, four pears."

Together they placed the fruits around the little island. When it was done she turned to him again. "I need you to will them to grow. I'll take care of the rest."

The half-elf began a quiet chant and she changed into her hound form. Her white coat glowed until it shined on the river brighter than the sun. Then she let out a gentle tone. It was soft and grew louder into a rising voice. Her strange melody became the only sound. Light leapt from her coat in streams to the four tokens. Their combined efforts caused the fruits to erupted in an explosion of roots and branches, entwining them into a giant spiraling tree. It grew higher and higher until it stood over them as a blossoming column.

Standing back in awe, Oryn was at a loss for words. He stared at the green crown of leaves where bright sunlight shone through as a halo of the purest gold.

Adwen changed back and went with Toth to retrieve Ulna. The knight hadn't moved and she beckoned softly, "Come on. It's time to go."

The travelers carried on and covered a few more miles before the sun let out the night. No one spoke during their trek farther west. In the dusk, Adwen caught a fat rabbit for the stew but nothing for herself. She lost her appetite and disappeared into the forest alone.

Four moons shone in the sky amongst billions of tiny stars. Toth tended to Ulna while Oryn finished gutting and cleaning the hare. Still not a word was spoken between them as they went about their business. After traveling together so long, they went directly to their usual tasks. Giving the meat to the cooking pot, the knight went to gather more wood.

He returned and set them by Toth. Staring down at the pieces, the knight eventually turned away saying, "This will not be enough. I shall return with more."

There was no acknowledgement from the half-elf, who was lost in thought and still angry. As Oryn asked, Toth would let him suffer alone. When Oryn left camp, he didn't glance to watch him go. He didn't even look at the wood he had brought. There was more than plenty.

Adwen's tracks were not difficult to find. They meandered between trees and around the backside of a small mountain. From the summit was a grand view of the woods. The paw prints were deeper than a wolf's due to her size.

He followed them to the top and heard an eerie sound. The white hound sat by a ledge overlooking the camp. He moved silently closer, but stopped as she made the sound again. This time the clear note was almost human. Surprised, he listened as she started to sing.

She howled a sad, slow tune. Everything she felt was poured into the sounds. Her song rang with a mournful passion and soon her voice seemed to double on itself. With every new note, it multiplied until her voice was a choir. The knight had read of this talent Darien once possessed. Using this unique gift, he was fabled to have pacified both spirit and men or even bolster moral in battle. It even seemed to soothe his frustration toward Toth.

Adwen heard movement from behind and her song abruptly ended. Jumping up and whirling around, she snarled at the sound of rustled leaves.

Oryn had taken another step and disturbed her.

The raised hairs on her body smoothed upon recognizing him and she changed form. With a hand over her chest, she chuckled weakly. "You scared me. What are you doing here?"

He stared quietly before lowering his gaze. "I must speak with you."

She laughed wryly. "I definitely hope so."

Out of surprise, he looked up.

"Following me around in the dark, I might get the feeling you're stalking me." She sat on a log and asked, "What is it?"

"I have something to confess. I do not seek forgiveness. I do not deserve it."

As he suddenly knelt to her, she was startled. There was nothing more foreign or disturbing to her than being given this gesture. But she could feel shame emanating from the knight and knew there was no use in telling him to stop. His head hung low as he couldn't bring himself to look at her.

"I have deceived you." Oryn swallowed hard. "I intended to use you for my own ends."

Adwen frowned. "I already knew that." When he furtively glanced up, she added, "I can tell when someone is using me. So, tell me something I don't know."

"I crossed paths with an elf. Her word was: that to get my revenge, I must find a girl -- you -- and you would lead me to my chance at obtaining it. I was not simply using you to search for the princess. I intended to have you lead me to both... and then..."

"You planned to kill me."

He wouldn't dare to look at her now.

She was not surprised, but felt that he had reconsidered on the night when he saved her life. Regardless, the prospect made her feel sick.

"Please get up. Stop kneeling. Come and sit over here. I'd rather you sit next to me than kneel like that."

Oryn hesitated, but got to his feet and quietly went to sit beside her.

She softly murmured, "Go on."

"The revenge I desire is for my brother. My twin was marked by a powerful werewolf when we were young. The same night he changed and killed our parents. I felled him myself. A chance to obtain justice for the damning of my brother was my drive. The need was so great that I didn't give a care to the cost." He shook his head at the shadowy trees. "I did not think I could pay more than I was willing to spare."

She was stunned and shook her head. "Oh, Oryn. I thought you of all people would know that everything has a price. The price for revenge is high. One way or another, the cost for a life taken in vengeance is always another's, usually your own."

He thought of the elf fortuneteller's warning as she went on.

"But sometimes the price is to watch others suffer, like today. I'm guessing you wanted power for your revenge too."

The knight blinked.

Adwen became somber. "I thought so. Second to joy, power comes at the highest price of all. For strength, you pay with pain and time, but power is different. Those who want power for the sake of power are evil and selfish. The price they pay is their own soul. In turn, they become weaker than when they started. Having power to protect... there is still a price and is also high. The usual price to pay will be the things that matter most to you. Things that you treasure get taken away forever."

Staring into the night, Oryn pondered her words.

Adwen went on. "Take me, for an example: of all of this. Every day I get a little more powerful. Each time I do, the one thing I want most slips farther away." She swallowed her building emotion and whispered, "Look at me."

Oryn did as she said.

They locked eyes and she spoke, careful to not stir up her own tears. "Do you think I could ever have what I want most and go back to my family? To live a life of peace, contentment and ignorance?" She shook her head and answered her own question. "I can never have that back. All I can do is keep going and hope the work I do keeps them safe."

Watching her, he could see the great pain she had been hiding. It was in her eyes now and he felt pity. The power he had admired was costing her everything. That one dream was her price to pay for existing.

She tucked away the pain again and showed sympathy. "If you think these things are happening because of your mistakes, then I hope your sword and Ranger are all you have to pay with. No matter what you did to me, or whatever you were going to do, I still think you have a good heart. Even though you hurt me so much, I wouldn't ever want to see you hurt. I can't stand to see good people hurt."

Again, he didn't know what to say. How could she be this kind? He had been a brute. Every time he called her an animal, he had been an even more beastly thing. Yet she was kind.

A look of sudden surprise crossed her face as she sniffed then smiled.

"Toth's done cooking."

Jumping up from the log, she went to look down at the little fire among the trees. Glancing back, she grinned. "I'll see you down there! I can't say no to Rabbit stew. Hurry before it gets cold!" She crowed and leaped out into the dark, landing somewhere in the forest below.

His eyes followed her departure and he felt an odd longing. He sighed and stood to begin the hike back, thinking of how he did not deserve such kindness; least of all from her.

Chapter 36
TWISTED GARDEN

"Wake up! Adwen! Oryn!"

It was dawn. Both woke on either side of the camp with a start to find Toth standing over them in a panic.

Startled and confused, Adwen stood. "Whoa, easy! What's going on?"

Oryn had his knife out when the yelling started, but stowed it and joined them.

Toth was in an apologetic fit. "Forgive me! I didn't mean to -- I tried to stop it, but --"

"Toth! Speak slowly and clearly. Calm down. Now tell me, what is wrong?"

"I was watching over the fire. A moment ago, I heard a noise. When I looked I saw a strange kind of imp, and then..." He gulped and pointed to the satchel that carried the treaties, but there was no satchel.

Gradually her eyes grew large in horror. Her burning gaze darted back to Toth and he was ashamed. "You couldn't stop it with your powers?"

"I haven't the faintest idea what the thing was! It was so fast that it slipped past everything I sent after it! It was pitch black with red markings. I've never seen anything like it!"

"Quiet down!" she snapped. "Being sorry won't change things. Get on your horse. We have hunting to do!"

He obediently got onto Ulna and Oryn grabbed up the golden sword, setting it across his back. They swiftly followed the trail of dark magic left by the strange beast. Without the treaties they could not unite the kingdoms in time. Adwen bounded along in her true shape alongside Ulna while Oryn struggled to keep up.

The knight moved as fast as he could, but with the added weight of the blade it was difficult. He heard Adwen bark and saw her staring.

He grunted as he ran. "I'm fine! Go and leave me behind if you must!"

Her ears went back and she growled. "That's not going to happen and that's not what I'm saying!" A short howl escaped her and the blade magically vanished from his back in a flash of light, reappearing on hers.

She barked again and he understood he was not going to be left behind. With the weight gone, he was able to keep the pace. Slayer's armor was much lighter than that of most knights. The skill of a knight was indicated by how meagerly he was defended. Agility and speed were his true armor.

Soon the travelers found themselves leaving the elf wood. Though still in the forest, everything around them changed. Trees were dark and sickly, leaves shriveled, rotting on the branch.

They slowed down and the knight studied the surroundings, his stomach feeling as if it had bottomed out. This was the foul land of the north. They had run from the witches and now found themselves on their doorstep. The earth was sour. Once-clear streams were dry. Sunlight was not allowed to shine through the ever-hanging cloud of dark magic.

Atop a hill they stopped. From there they could make out a dark green labyrinth. It was the only growing thing in sight that did not look rotten. Approaching the enormous garden, an insidious mist filled leafy corridors. Fog slunk, shifted and roiled like milky snakes.

Carefully studying the opening, Adwen sniffed the air, growling as she changed to woman form. To her this work of art was like a bad liar, trying to fool them that all was safe.

Oryn caught his breath and gasped. "We must press on."

Adwen shook her head, staring raptly at the entrance. "I really don't like this. I don't know if I could protect you guys if we got separated." Her eyes glowed brighter. "I don't like what I smell in there."

"I shall enter," Toth volunteered as he dismounted. "It is my mistake and I must set it to right."

Her hand went up to stop him from going closer. "No, you're not. Knock it off. This is not your fault. We need you to keep your head on straight. Okay?"

Only just able to grasp the meaning, he nodded and brushed back some of his blond hair nervously. This place gave him the creeps like nothing else.

As she continued to delay, Oryn urged her. "There is no choice. Everything is over if the treaties are not recovered."

"I know that! But if we go in, I have a bad feeling about what will happen." Hesitating only a few seconds longer, she finally took a deep breath. "All right, we're going in, but I'm warning you all now. There are things inside that neither of you can defend yourselves from."

Toth gulped. "What are they?"

Glaring as she entered the garden, Adwen whispered darkly. "Demons."

The half-elf was startled and the knight put on his poker face. Adwen gave back the Rose Thorne while Toth led Ulna along. Upon entering the thick fog, they were blinded by rising white mist.

"Adwen!" Toth called out. "Oryn, I can't see a thing!" Their voices were distant and then the fog folded back. His heart jumped and Ulna snorted nervously beside him. "Adwen!"

They were separated by the magic of the labyrinth. Her voice was able to carry to both companions. "Just calm down! The only way out is to keep going! Keep your eyes peeled and watch your backs!"

With no alternative, each companion began their trek through the eerie place.

The knight was wary. He could sense eyes in the hedges watching his every move.

In another part of the maze, his friends shared the same experience. Ulna snorted, ears flicking as she noticed things her master could not.

The knight gripped the heavy sword tight as he rounded a corner. While he took silent steps there was the sudden feeling that someone was just behind.

Oryn whirled around. There was nothing to see, yet his instincts warned that an enemy was before him. The fog on the path swirled and something scratched his cheek. He gasped and sneered. Soon more spots of swirling fog rushing out from the hedges.

Toth saw the mist start to congeal as evil spirits moved about and circled.

The mare's eyes rolled wildly as she saw them.

The half-elf cried out, "They've found us! Adwen, what do we do?"

Oryn mustered the strength to swing his sword, but was far too slow. An invisible spirit gripped his throat and started to squeeze. The knight fought for air, clinging to the weapon as he reached to free himself. But there was nothing to fight against and the evil thing throttled harder.

Then the sound of humming filled the air. Resounding notes made the spirits pause. It grew louder.

Adwen made the spirits calm. The sound pushed back the ill feeling in the air, forcing the angry spirits to retreat. When the entities were gone and the mist with them, she smiled.

Even after the sound faded, the knight continued to be in awe. Confidence returned as he went back to traversing the wicked garden. There was determination in him as he took another step.

Toth sighed with relief and Ulna nickered with ears pinned back.

"I shall be pleased to leave this place, won't you?"

The mare snorted in agreement.

Up ahead was a fork and they stopped. He let go of the reins to approach where it parted. Neither turn seemed welcoming, but before he could come to a decision, the ground came loose. The earth gave way and he fell down a tunnel.

Ulna whinnied after him.

Adwen passed another corner to find a stone passage leading down into the earth. The smell of black magic hit her full in the face as she approached the stairs. Instincts warned that danger waited in the dark. This part of the labyrinth had few forks, assuring that this was a trap. A growl escaped her and she went defiantly inside.

The dank air smelled of mildew. A flight of stone stairs took her deeper. At the bottom she could see the flicker of torches. Red light pooled onto cool rock and cobwebs. Reaching the open door, she paused. A party in red awaited her.

Toth tumbled a long ways then slid a bit farther. Gripping his aching head, he readjusted the cloth on his eye. On the verge of complaining, the breath lodged in his throat. Toth found himself in a narrow ventilation tunnel beside a grate. Adwen was on the other side and with unpleasant company.

Witches and warlocks in red cloaks stood on either side of the chamber in military formation, observing. She glared at the lot and then at the witch who stood in the back beside a sacrificial table with candelabras. The tiny flames flickered crimson.

Adwen's eyes flashed. "I take it you're the witch, Nadeen?"

The woman smiled sickeningly. "That I am. How do you like my garden?"

"You need better gardeners. They suck."

"Yes, they do. I've seen them suck the life out of intruders."

"That wasn't a compliment. Your evil spirits are pathetic."

"Oh!" She chortled. "How silly of me to forget. Where you come from some words are used differently. How... cool."

Adwen growled and sneered. "What do you know about that?"

"Plenty. My master and lover taught me a great deal about your world. He has taught me many things, about even you." She laughed haughtily. "He never thought you could swim so well!"

She snarled and spat, "What's that supposed to mean?"

"It means I get to help him destroy you after all."

Adwen transformed and roared, leaping for the witch.

But streams of black chains flew from the ranks of the Red Cult. Enchanted, evil links held her suspended in mid air. They bound her entirely and she squirmed vainly to break free. In a rage, she barked and snapped viciously in the witch's face, saliva flying as fangs gnashed dangerously close. Try as she might to get free, it was no use. The chains sapped her strength. Eventually another small chain bound her jaws shut. Completely immobile, she growled.

The witch casually strutted around to admire the silvery fur on her neck. Adwen snarled louder while she stroked the soft fur, cooing.

"Oh, such a beautiful coat. It's so soft, so pretty. It shall make a lovely cloak for me, don't you think?"

"I can see what you really look like, Nadeen," she snarled. "It's in your eyes! You're just a hideous old hag wearing a mask."

A look that burned lit up the witch's face. Then she quickly twisted the outraged expression into a nasty smile, batting her eyes. "On second thought, this is not a high enough quality. It should make a perfect throw rug. My lover and I shall have each other upon it, over and over again."

"You're disgusting, witch."

"Really now, I understand your animal tongue fluently yet I'm beginning to tire of your banter." She snapped her fingers and a whip flicked at Adwen's exposed flank. The bladed tip made black metal cut deep, making her yelp.

Nadeen clasped both hands together, watching her writhe. "Whip her! And once she is too weak to make a sound, bring her to the horses. Take all the time you need."

She snapped her fingers again upon leaving and the lashings commenced.

Oryn grew impatient with all of the dead ends. He backtracked once again and took the next turn. There were so many twists that he was barely able to recall the routes he took. On his way he soon heard an odd noise. He sidled up to the corner and peered around the hedge.

At first he saw what appeared to be another dead end with old stone eaves and a bench. Then his heart leaped as he spotted Toth's satchel. The flap was laid open on the seat. The treaties rested just inside, but he paused. He heard the strange noise again and saw the thieving imp creature.

The small beast resembled a salamander melded with a goblin, no taller than knee high. All over the pitch-black body were red marks. It crouched under the bench, gnawing on animal bones, its tale swatting like a cat's.

Oryn stepped out to confront the little monster. It screeched at him and he watched and waited for it to come closer.

But then the imp revealed its true self. Short arms sprouted to long, slashing claws. The body became like a drake with spikes on its back with waving tendrils. Black and red swirled withing its body and the now-towering demon hissed.

When it grew to nine feet in height, the knight thought twice. Before the demon lunged, Oryn wrung the sword in his hands. If it really were a demon-killing blade, he was about to find out.

Hissing again, the Wretch rushed forward.

The swung the unwieldy weapon with all his might. His timing was right and the demon was sliced up the front, spilling purple insides over the grass. It hissed, flailed and fell as a puddle of mush.

Relieved at the good fortune, Oryn stepped around the mess and took the satchel. Everything was inside and intact, so he slung the strap over one shoulder and started for the rest of the labyrinth. He had caught a draft of fresh air amid the stale doldrums. It would surely lead to freedom.

Then he heard Adwen howling. It was not like her songs from before. She was screaming.

The realization made him all but gasp then break into an all out sprint. He could only hope to find her at the exit.

After the whippings ceased Toth climbed along the tunnel in search of an opening. He was fortunate to find an escape. With no bars blocking the way, he saw that Ulna made her own way out. The loyal mare looked down the hole and neighed, happy to see him. She lowered the reins to hoist his body up.

Oryn came bursting out from the hedges and saw the animal helping. Dashing over to assist, he gripped one of Toth's wrists, pulling him free.

"Thank you!" Toth almost retracted the thanks as the knight gripped him roughly by the front of his shirt.

"Where is she? What's happened?"

Not thrilled to be roughly handled, Toth quickly answered, "The Red Witch, Nadeen. They have her! I saw them take her away in chains."

"Why did she scream?"

With some difficulty, Toth shoved him off and protested.

"Let me go sooner and I could have the sense to tell you quicker! They whipped her with knifed lashes. Now she's been taken away by horses."

Both men dashed around the corner in time to see her white body in a metal net being dragged along a sloping road. The evil witches laughing hysterically, jeering with delight as they raced off.

The sight set a fire in the knight's stomach. They would pay for this. He would make them all pay.

Toth climbed onto Ulna. "Where will they take her?"

Before looking away, Oryn felt sicker. "Farther north."

"But to where?"

A chill crawled up the knight's spine. "The Crescent Remains."

Chapter 37
CRESCENT REMAINS

Long ago, the fortress Melanin's Eye was erected. It was as round as a moon. In the grand courtyard, many heroes were slain by the Red Cult to summon evil spirits, granting the walls eyes and many staring faces. Darien came and used his power to banish half of the damned place into a bottomless pit. Legend claimed the pit reached into the realm of the void itself.

The evil spirits were banished, rendering the structure as lifeless as a corpse. Henceforth, the half-ruined fortress was known as the Crescent Remains. It sat like a blackened scab on the earth, giving off the stench of raw corruption.

A sickly haze hung around the structure and Toth gulped. They were two miles from the wretched place on a hillside, surveying the scene. Adwen had been dragged inside.

"Is this place as evil as they've told in stories, Oryn?"

The knight took a deep breath and said nothing, preferring not to focus on that for the moment. There was only one way Adwen would be set free. He studied the many dark facets. In a few hours night would arrive. The longer he hesitated, the more time they could to do her harm.

Oryn handed the satchel over to Toth along with the Rose Thorne and pressed forward.

The half-elf was stunned. "What are you doing? It could protect you!"

"It is too heavy. I need stealth in this place if I may have it at all." He thought of the task ahead and nearly shuddered. "No matter what you may hear or think, do not enter after me. If I do not return with her before nightfall, leave and do not return. Take the treaties to the king. Do not stop or sleep until they are in his hands and his alone." Wetting his lips, he thought they seemed dry. "We cannot hope to win this without Adwen. Farewell, my friend."

"May the Spirits of Light guide your feet, friend."

He watched the knight leave for the sewer drain with nothing more than his armor, his nerve and a silver-steel dagger. Lifting his gaze to the dreary sky, Toth closed his eyes.

"Have his back. My friend has done many wrongs, but please watch over him and let him be successful. Let no demons do him harm. Please."

There was just the sound of his breath in the dark drain. Keeping footfalls soft, the knight soon came upon a small source of red light by a grate. He smelled stale air and dust. His ears were pricked, listening for the slightest sound while peering beyond the bars. Stone columns stood with many green floating lights emitting dim light, fading in and out.

When the way seemed quiet enough, he grasped the grate and removed it without a sound. He set it aside, creeping up into the sinister hall. The walls were dark and damp as if painted with fresh blood. Oryn could not tell for sure if it were blood and did not wish to know. The knight realized his hands were shaking and began the breathing ritual. They became steady as he pressed onward, sticking close to the pillars. He did not dare touch the small floating lights.

Reaching a turn, he peered around the corner. The coast was clear, but he smelled something rotten and examined the wall. A dark liquid seeped from between the stone blocks and a little had gotten onto his glove. He sniffed it, discovering it really was blood. A shiver crawled up his back and he did not touch the stones again.

Stepping out, Oryn found a pair of towering steel doors with wolf faces at the end of the hall. Blood rolled down from the eyes and out their mouths to the floor before vanishing. He continued slowly, breathing in the proper rhythm to calm himself. His stare never wavered from the steely wolf faces that wept and drooled red. Beads of sweat were on his brow as he went closer to inspect the doors. He thought he saw them blink and froze. Had it been a trick of the light? Unable to breathe, Oryn fought to get a grip.

Then he heard whispering. There was no one, but voices whispered, multiplying in number. Just as he thought he might be going mad, the voices silenced and a door back the way he came opened. Silent as a thief, the knight ducked down behind a column to hide in its shadow. He pulled his long cape with him out of the light just as a troop of witches came.

Oryn listened as the procession drew near. By far this was the most dangerous thing he had ever done. If he were discovered now, the price could be far more than his life. He observed them going through the opening wolf-head doors.

Then a voice made his blood run cold.

"Oryn."

It came from the wall before him in the shadows. He looked and blanched, resisting the need to cry out. If he made a single sound, the witches would find him. Out of the stones and blood, a demon face smiled. It began to reach for his cheek with dripping claws.

"Oryn."

The thing could almost touch his quivering face while he struggled to stay silent. His skin was pale and clammy and his eyes glistened in the dark. The knight had never known terror like this. He could not muster the focus to breathe correctly.

The witches were almost through the double doors. Oryn wished they would pass by quicker. Once the doorway finally began to close, the knight scrambled back from the shadows, away from the demon speaking his name. Once they thudded shut, he leaped to his feet and backed farther away. The thing had gone, but his breaths were labored as he tried to calm his nerves.

"Welcome to my lover's lovely home."

He whipped around to find Nadeen. All fear was gone in an instant.

In the center of the hall she stood fondling the long, bladed staff, wearing a saccharin smile.

Without a word in reply, he slowly drew the knife and stared her down.

"Oh, so you wish to play a while? Very well. I have time."

Oryn twirled the knife as the witch made the first move and lunged. The witch's strikes were swift, but weak now that she was not using magic. He blocked the repetitive blows with ease, taking time in learning her moves. Their weapons clashed again and again, the sound of ringing metal singing in the empty hall. Fighting the witch gave him a chance to regain focus.

Nadeen grew tired of being deflected and shrieked with rage, ready to strike him down. He was prepared. Blocking the blow with his blade, he struck the shaft where it was weak. The excessive force snapped the rod and he threw his weight into it, shoving her to the hard ground.

Standing over her, he felt no remorse. She was pure evil and he wondered how to kill her properly. The thought lasted long enough for him to twirl the knife once.

As Nadeen crawled away, her foot swung up and caught him in the pride. The hit stunned him momentarily, but he was in focus when the blow was dealt and he did not fall. She watched in fear as a horrible rage appeared in his eyes.

A blow from behind struck Oryn on the head and he fell unconscious at the witch's feet.

Nadeen smiled at the culprit. She stood and brushed back her hair. "You are eloquent with your timing, master."

Dressed in black with a wine-red cloak, Sycan carefully removed the enchanted mask, handing it to the witch. A long, thin scar stretched across his face diagonally from his brow and right cheek. His face was young and strong and his voice was the same.

"Nadeen, you're inviting knights into my home? I thought I told you to let that wait." He smiled and his mouth was full of pointed teeth.

She went close to play with his medium length wine-red hair. It appeared black until the light revealed a bloody shine. His bleach-white eyes looked down at the knight and the beastly pupils dilated.

"He came alone and armed with a petty knife?"

He picked up the silver-steel weapon and his glove smoked where it touched. Sycan chuckled, tossing it aside.

"I like him already. Why is he here, you silly creature? Did you coax him with a look or did you take something he wanted?"

As he moved to touch her neck, Nadeen felt fearful and closed her eyes, allowing it to fill her completely. She gasped and smiled. "I have a gift for you, master; a bit of a surprise. I think he came to take it back."

"Oh? A jewel? A treasure he finds precious? He did come in here thinking to reclaim it, after all." He licked her neck with a blue serpentine tongue. "Was it something you really meant to give to me, Nadeen?"

"Of course. I would not dare deny you the pleasure of this gift." she swallowed hard. "It is... she."

Sycan didn't understand and chuckled with a raised eyebrow. "She?"

The witch's lips were dry and she wet them. If he were angry he was liable to abuse her. "*She,* my master. She's back again."

Very slowly, he understood. The smile faded and teeth clenched. The whites around pale irises turned black as he snarled and warned, "Don't toy with me like that, my sweet. I could take back that pretty face I gave you." His other hand touched her cheek and wrinkled skin began to reappear.

She nearly jumped, taking the hand away, returning her face to a flawless state. "Not that, my master! There is no need to threaten. She is in the courtyard, bound in the chains we made."

The black left his eyes and he smirked. "You surprise me! I thought you wanted to kill her yourself, you pretty little wretch." The white-eyed young man turned to the knight again and thought he seemed familiar. Throwing the thought away, he chuckled. "Bring him to the courtyard as well. Tie him there and wait for my return tomorrow. If he wants to find her so badly, then he can watch her die. I have business at our other home. Things are going slowly now that Korig and Kotig have vanished."

"I could help, master."

He gripped her chin, making her cringe delightedly. "I need you here. I am quite capable of covering where they lack. And one more thing: if you manage to let her slip out of this noose, I will be very upset. Believe me, Nadeen. This heir is a slippery one to nail down."

The witch gulped. "Yes, master."

His hand swiftly gripped her throat. She shook with fear under his stare. "I've told you so many times: call me lover."

"Yes, lover." She smiled.

He kissed her supple lips and left without a glance.

The witch adored the monster. When Sycan exited the hall she laughed maniacally. How could the heir possibly escape?

Oryn slowly returned to consciousness. His head ached. From what he could tell, both wrists were tied at his back. He was upright with chest and legs bound to a pillar of stone. Night arrived and he looked up to see the last dying light. A moment passed until the soft glow was blocked. Focusing, he recognized the witch standing before him.

The knight scowled. As she came close he noticed the rest of the courtyard. Right away he spied Adwen in her white hound body. Her soft fur was sliced all over and the sun had not shined bright enough to heal the wounds. She lay unconscious with arms bound to her sides by a black chain, which fed from another column. He knew the heir still lived and felt his nerve and determination rise.

Nadeen's hand combed the bangs from his face while she studied his eyes. "You're so strong; so brave to come alone. Oh, why must you hate me? I didn't mean to break your sword." She let her bottom lip pout. "Can you forgive me?"

His green gaze shifted from Adwen to drill into the witch.

"Why won't you speak to me? Am I not beautiful?"

He still said nothing and glared.

She continued to play with his hair and pressed up against him. "Don't you find me beautiful, young knight?" She leaned in close enough to kiss him and whispered, "Why won't you speak to me, you handsome man?" He turned his head to shake her off and she stared in surprise.

At last he opened his mouth and spoke with a clear, ice-cold tone.

"I've known prostitutes with more depth and substance than you."

The witch's jaw dropped. She was horrified at first, but batted her eyes and smiled. "Perhaps speaking is not the best thing for you."

His expression was blank, but he breathed a deep sigh of satisfaction at being able to strike her without raising a hand.

Nadeen pursed her lips and stroked his chest plate with a

pointed nail. "No man has ever denied. It surprises me such an incredible specimen like you cannot find me appealing."

"Real men have better taste."

Her eyes flashed and she swiftly slapped him, messing his hair. The knight was unfazed. He felt more pleasure at annoying the evil woman. A moment passed and he flashed a small smile.

She stared wide-eyed with a manic smile. "You are going to pay for that."

Again he stared her down in silent defiance.

She suddenly snapped her fingers and pointed. *"Bring him!"*

Two warlocks jumped forward to cut the bonds holding him to the pillar. They hauled Oryn by the arms and Nadeen led the way toward the setting sun and the infamous chasm. They neared the abyss as she laughed. "You know, I really wanted to wait for my master's return to see you watch her die, but..." She whirled around. "I no longer have the patience to wait for your looks. I would now much rather watch you fall into forever."

The warlocks positioned him until his back was to the pit and his heels just short of the ledge. A few pebbles went over as the wicked men smiled.

Staring blankly, Oryn glanced past Nadeen's shoulder where he could see Adwen. He focused solely on her while the witch carried on ranting.

"Before you go, I'm going to tell you what shall happen after. Before your body ever reaches bottom, my master will return. Then he will tear her apart. We will paint our courtyard with her blood and desecrate her corpse. You will still be alive and falling when you hear her screams!"

Seeing a look of surprise, Nadeen thought it was about what she'd said and carried on ranting.

He wasn't listening. Adwen's head slowly rose up from the dust. Both eyes opened and glowed a brilliant gold while the mark on her head formed the Andredan emblem. She stared at him while the witch raved. Though bound by the chain, she stealthily got to her feet. Her bright eyes never left his.

Oryn watched her take a step and suppressed a smile. He was certain that she was preparing to kill the witch. Adwen would rush out, take all of the chain with her and rip the evil wench to bits.

Nadeen finished the psychotic, vile banter and grabbed his face with a hand. "You will be wishing for the bottom to come. And to think I tried to entertain you before the end."

The knight flashed a sly smile. "Glad to have been a nuisance."

Her eyes flashed and she pushed hard.

He fell. He saw Adwen lunge. His body turned away as the white hound leaped through the air. Adwen was headed straight for the wicked woman's head.

Instead, Adwen's shoulder clipped the witch, knocking her to the ground. Then the wounded creature collided with the warlocks, taking them with her over the edge. And just before her chain became taunt, her jaws snapped down onto Oryn's left armguard. Her teeth clamped tight and their full weight hit the end of the lifeline.

Oryn grunted and groaned from the shock of being caught, watching the warlocks fall screaming out of sight. His cape draped across his shoulder as he strained to look back. She had caught him from falling and her eyes still shone bright gold.

Astonished and confused, he called to her. "Adwen?"

She did not respond.

"Adwen, wake up! You must flee! Let me fall! I do not matter!" She remained unresponsive. "Adwen?"

Then he saw movement where the fortress ended before the pit. Several archers formed up on a ledge, notching dark arrows. The knight's heart leaped, and his stomach seemed to evaporate as his efforts became desperate.

"Adwen! They will kill you if you do not get yourself free! Adwen! Adwen, wake up!"

The archers fired. Oryn watch the arrows fly. One hit its mark between her ribs. Horrified, he gasped as her eyes widened and she snarled, thrashing. Regardless, she would not drop him and Adwen's eyes were still unblinking and shining pure gold.

Enraged, he bellowed at the archers, "Damn you! You'll pay for this! Do you hear me?" He turned back to Adwen and her emotionless stare. "Adwen, just let me fall. You must let me fall!"

The archers notched more arrows.

He watched them take aim and cried out, *"No!"*

The missiles seemed to drift so slowly. He could see the black crow feathers vibrating in the wind as the barbed heads came closer. Oryn wished they would hit him instead, but nothing could stop the arrows from striking her. He gasped before the four made a sickening thud into her ribcage at once. A small, heart-wrenching yelp came out of Adwen and her jaws clenched hard.

Metal screeched and Oryn cried out loud. Adwen's long, sharp fangs punched through the armguard, piercing flesh to the bone. Gasping, he clenched his teeth at the pain. But then he heard a loud cough and droplets spattered lightly on the side of his face. The knight looked back in alarm.

Silver blood dribbled from her muzzle, running down his armguard as more trickles ran from her black button nose. The gold glow faded from her eyes. The mark returned to being a golden stripe. Soft dog ears hung low and a weak whine came as she barely held on.

The five arrows protruding from her side horrified and enraged Oryn. Red in the face, he yelled and spit flew from his mouth.

"Damn you! Damn all you fools to the void!"

The archers notched more arrows.

"You'll all pay! You'll all burn alive, you soulless scum!"

And before his very eyes there was a burst of gold flames. Turning to run, the warlocks screamed as horses bathed in gold fire trampled them down. Oryn was so stunned that he hardly noticed the chain drawing them back up. Adwen's jaws remained locked as they were hoisted over the ledge and to the middle of the courtyard.

A large herd of wild roans bathed in holy flames assaulted the witches and warlocks. Their leader reared. He brayed as his flames protected and empowered the herd, leading the onslaught against the Crescent Remains. Stone structures screamed along with the burning men and women of the cult.

Toth ran to Oryn as Adwen's jaws slackened and released him at last.

The herd leader ran to their side and burned the knight's

bonds with a shot of flame. Once Oryn was free, the leader snatched up the chains binding Adwen and melted them to nothing. Finished releasing them, the stallion returned to orchestrating their escape.

The companions scrambled to Adwen and the half-elf saw the arrows.

"Stars above!"

Grabbing Toth, the knight yelled into his face. "I'll take care of her! Go to your horse and be ready to take her from this place! Go!"

Toth darted off to fetch Ulna who was assisting in the killing of evil fortress dwellers.

When Oryn turned to Adwen he saw her eyes roll back. He shook her by the thick fur on her neck. "Stay awake! Do you hear me? You must stay awake!"

He heard her whimper then turned to the five feathered shafts. After taking a few deep breaths, he gripped the first and braced her bloody side. Then he pulled hard. A high-pitched yelp came out of her and the knight moved faster. Upon each extraction her yelp grew fainter. When the last was pulled and she didn't make a sound the quiet startled him. He grabbed her by the ears, yelling into her fading eyes.

"Wake up! Listen to me! Change back! Change back or we cannot carry you out! Change back, Adwen!"

Her eyes focused momentarily, but everything was hazy. All she heard was to change. Pain erupted in her side and she coughed up even more silver. She shrank into her woman body and fur turned into garments. The gouges bled profusely as the transformation completed and Oryn scooped her up in his arms. Running past burning witches, he saw Toth on Ulna, ready to ride. Then he heard her weak voice.

"I'm cold. It hurts."

In a quick motion he handed her to Toth and watched them ride through the hole the horses burned into the structure. Another flaming horse came to collect him and he held fast to the base of its mane. Soon he was just behind Ulna and the other roans began to follow. The herd poured out through the exit, scattering into the night. Their tracks led off to all the directions of the compass. No one could hope to follow their trail out of the many leading from the wicked land of witches.

Chapter 38
LETTING GO

The flames on the horses snuffed out shortly after the escape. Toth and Oryn were taken west out of the lost roads near Dargadia's northern border. Thin clouds streaked the dawn over the woods. Droplets of dew covered greenery, making everything sparkle in the first light. Finally they stopped by a brook surrounded by trees covered in thick moss.

The knight leaped from the horse that bore him and dashed to take Adwen from his friend's arms. Feeling a cold dread, he wondered if she were still living. He gently caught her light weight and she made no sound. But the warmth of her breath touched his face and he was relieved. He laid her by a tree near the brook, letting her rest on downy moss.

The wild horse departed and Toth came to check Adwen's vitals and terrible wounds.

They glanced at each other.

"What manner of wound is this?" the knight asked. "Why is it black and green on her skin?"

Toth shook his head. "I don't know. I've never dealt with wounds on beings such as her before." He carefully inspected the punctures and touched the blackened flesh where a mixture of green and silver settled at the surface. "I think she's been poisoned. There are a few things I could try. I'll search for herbs. Watch her closely. If she wakes, make her lie still."

The knight knelt beside Adwen. Studying the rise and fall of her chest. A few misplaced strands of hair were across her eyes. With a finger, he gently brushed them aside without touching her. Though hurt, she was living. He sighed deeply at the thought and was glad. Once she awoke, he would know better if she had the strength to heal. The cuts from the lashings were shallow abrasions and her clothes began to mend around them.

The memory of the arrows flying returned, building his rage. They would have to pay, he thought. If Nadeen was alive, he would make her pay with all she had.

Oryn suddenly cringed.

Pain spiked through his forearm and he remembered his own injury. Going to kneel by the stream, he carefully flipped two clips that held the armguard closed. Then he hesitated. After bracing himself, he eased the piece open, gritting his teeth as bent metal came out of flesh. A sigh of relief escaped him when the pain eased and the armor laid open.

He was a bloody mess. Adwen's teeth marks still bled, trickling down to his fingertips. To clean the wounds, Oryn dipped his arm into the stream up to his elbow and swore at the sting.

For wrappings, he tore a strip from the hem of his cape. He finished the knot using his right hand and teeth before turning to the destroyed armguard, frowning. The armor that once belonged to his master was being destroyed by these adventures. There was no chance of repairing the part and no point in keeping it. He tossed the bloody thing into the brook, following it with his eyes as the current dragged it out of sight.

Done tending to his needs, he stood. But when he turned he saw an animal standing over Adwen. The white stallion bathed in flames had returned and gently nosed her cheek.

Oryn froze. As the beast looked up at him with erect ears, the knight knew it was Auburn, the steed of Darien Andredan.

Sniffing the air and catching his scent, the horse pinned ears back and brayed angrily. Auburn snorted as a look of shame came over the knight.

He knew why the animal was angry. He had let harm come to the girl descended from his master.

Bowing his head low, he murmured, "Forgive me."

Ears firmly set back, the fire horse crept closer. He nosed the wound on the knight's arm and looked him in the eye. Oryn stared back solemnly and watched the ears on the steed's head go slowly up.

Auburn snorted and glanced to Adwen and back again.

The knight nodded. "I'll not let any harm come to her again. I swear. I shall watch her more carefully."

Auburn seemed pleased and shook his mane lazily, turning to leave. Then he stopped to give them both a last glance. Giving the horse an assuring nod, he watched him bolt into a wreath of gold flames.

Toth returned a second later, oblivious to what had happened. Oryn didn't dare tell, not wanting to distract the half-elf from the task.

Pulling out different herbs from his satchel, he sprinkled powders and juices over Adwen's injury. Worried as he worked, hands moving quickly. The medicines collected on the piercings and he laid a few numbing leaves over the top.

"This is all I could find. These herbs only stop infection. They are not the ones she needs for a cure."

"Then what can be done?"

There was a scrap of parchment and charcoal in the satchel. He brought them out and started writing. "She needs herbs that are rare. Take this list and the last of the gold. Find the closest village with an apothecary." He gave up the rest of their coins and the list. "Hopefully, we may get the herbs soon or at least find where we are in Dargadia."

Oryn tucked the list away and nodded firmly. "I shall return by sundown." With a flip of his cape he turned to go. There were many small villages in the valleys below the mountains. If he hiked south he would surely find one soon.

It was not as easy as hoped. The knight discovered they were still just inside the northern border. He hiked along deer trails around rock outcroppings. Every so often, he searched the treetops for wisps of chimney smoke. There was nothing and the sun was directly overhead. He remained unarmed since losing his knife and left the demon-killing blade behind. Though it was his to keep, using it was awkward. His master never trained him to use such a weapon. It was more apt for experienced dragon slayers.

Sliding down another rocky slope, he noticed movement in the corner of his vision. Oryn paused to glance and what was there made him freeze.

A wild mountain cat the size of a Woar dog eyed him from upon a boulder. The beast's whiskers twitched as it licked them hungrily.

Its tail flicked and he stared the cat down, hoping to discourage it from pouncing. Without his knife and injured, he could have trouble serious trouble. As it sniffed the air, he knew it could smell blood. The knight readied himself to fight off a set of salivating jaws.

It did not pounce. After sniffing, its ears perked and its head rose up in curiosity. Then it moaned dismissively, flattening both round ears back.

Confused, he watched the cat grumble and prowl off. Oryn had seen many mountain cats and killed a few, but never seen one act that way. It kept glancing back as it left to hunt for food someplace else.

Now wary that the animals were acting strange, he kept a better watch for more.

Hours passed like minutes. He grew weary of getting no results, but the terrain began to level off. What stressed his patience now was that time before sundown was short. His thoughts wandered back to Adwen. What would become of her if he failed? The thought made him ill. Surely the first town he came across would have the herbs. The knight was determined to not fail her again. He could never forgive himself for that.

The sun drifted to hide behind the treetops when there was a glimmer of hope. He spied chimney smoke and broke into a sprint. Running a quarter of a mile he burst out of the trees into a clearing, skipping into a walk. He found a small town and the people were settling in for the night. Stretching shadows overlapped the street in the afternoon twilight. Strolling onto the dirt road, he caught his breath. Windows were starting to light with candles. Some saw him alone and quickly closed the curtains.

Paying no mind, he spotted the shop of an apothecary.

Oryn crossed the porch and opened the door to find a young woman tending the counter, cleaning with a rag. The door closed with a click and she noticed him.

"Oh! I'm sorry, Sir Knight. I didn't hear you come in. What may I do for you?"

She watched him pull the scrap of paper from his remaining armguard. "How much will you require for these?"

Accepting it, she started to read. The more she looked at it, the worse her expression became and his heart sank. Before she spoke, he knew the answer.

She shook her head and handed it back, recognizing the blend. "I'm so sorry, sir. We don't have any of these, but I know who does."

He asked right away. "Where are they?"

She frowned. "Down the road, sir. Her shop is a two-day walk south in Tanoaks." When she said the distance, he looked afraid. "I'm so sorry, sir. There is little more I can do. What poison are you looking to cure?"

He could hardly breathe and shook his head. Passing her a gold coin, he started to leave and murmured, "For your time."

The young apothecary watched him go, sad she could not do more.

When the door closed, he stalked to the end of the porch and stopped. Defeated, he stared down at his filthy boots and armor. The sun was setting and he had not gotten the herbs.

Frustration made him ball a fist with his uninjured arm. Then he punched the closest support beam, stinging his knuckles. Taking back the hand from the undamaged post, he leaned his weary head against it, closing his eyes. What was he to do? He couldn't depart for Tanoaks without telling Toth and he refused to return without something of use.

A door opened by the end of the street and he looked up at the sound of merry laughter. A busy bar was down the way and he lifted his head. Perhaps the place would have a bit of food to take back.

Oryn donned his cape hood as always in case any knights inside might recognize him. By now he would be wanted by the elders for desertion. If found, he would be dragged back by his heels. Once certain his features were concealed, he opened the door and entered the bright and prosperous bar.

A flute played merrily in the back while the long bar counter was lined with men drinking and laughing. Every table was surrounded by workers and farmers. Most carried on and paid no attention to the visitor.

Oryn approached the counter, addressing a barmaid on the other side. "Excuse me, do you serve food here?"

She saw his armor and smiled. "I'm sorry, sir. We don't, but I can offer you a drink. We have almost anything you could ask for."

He was instantly glad Toth had not come here alone. He shook his head, defeated once again. "All right. Do you serve Red Lily tea?" It was his favorite, sold and traded from the Red Lily Inn in Tanoaks to the whole of the kingdom.

"Yes, sir. I'll brew up a pot straight away!" She curtsied and went to work.

The knight gave a dry laugh. For the first time in a while there was good news. He claimed one of the remaining stools and had a seat at the counter. As the tea brewed, he rested his arms on the edge and forgot the banter around him. He concluded that he would have a little tea before leaving. When he returned and spoke with Toth, they could set out for Tanoaks. So long as she lasted long enough to reach the town from his childhood, there was hope.

An outburst of laughter at the end of the counter made him look up. The bartender seemed familiar and he instinctively averted his eyes. So much had gone wrong lately that he would hardly be surprised if someone recognized him and sold him out.

A steamy cup was set before him and he almost jumped at the suddenness. Every quick movement seemed to catch his eye. Even when he entered, he took notice that every man was armed. Not a one was without a knife and a few had crossbows slung across the backs of their seats. They must be seeing hard times, he thought as he passed a few coins to the maid along with a tip.

She thanked him and smiled.

The tea smelled sweet. Oryn stared at the steam rising around the rim. What was going to become of Adwen? Taking up the mug with his good hand, he blew on it before taking a sip. He drank. And when he took it from his lips, a throat cleared beside him.

A young man not more than fourteen stood nearby with a bold glint in his eyes.

Oryn gave a questioning look. "Is there a problem?"

Clearing his throat again, the boy spoke sternly to show he had nerve. "Yes. Your sort is not welcome here."

A few men heard and began to pay attention.

He gave a dry laugh and set the mug down. With a flick of his good arm, he brushed back the cape, displaying his armor. The young man was surprised as Oryn asked, "Since when is a Knight of the Order not welcome to drink in this kingdom's bars?"

The boy was stern. "Yes. But you are no knight... Wolf."

Everyone heard the word and hushed. The flute player hit a sour note before falling silent as all eyes turned to the bar. Suspense and suspicion thickened the air.

Raising an eyebrow, Oryn almost laughed. "What have you been drinking, lad? Find someone else to pester and let me finish mine."

A suspicious man frowned and informed the knight. "The boy hasn't had a drop."

Oryn eyed the stranger and saw he was being honest. The boy stared him down accusingly and he scowled back. "Then you must be out of your mind."

Another man retorted. "No, he's not."

"I'm the son of the town seer. I can see things for what they really are! You are no man. You are a vicious beast."

He did not think this was a very funny joke. If it were not, and he got the feeling this was serious, then this boy was making a grave mistake.

Glaring at the boy, Oryn's scowl hardened. "I am no beast, but I am considered vicious by most. You understand the penalties for falsely accusing a man of such a thing, don't you, boy?"

The young man watched as the tall knight stood over him. Gulping, he looked up into his piercing gaze. Oryn towered over him and his strong presence was enough to give the boy second thoughts. But regardless, the young man stood his ground.

Oryn's green eyes glared from beneath the hood. "Then what do you have to back yourself besides your word?"

Hands shaking, he pulled at a cord around his neck to show a long, shiny whistle.

Unimpressed, the knight stared back in silence.

"This whistle is of pure silver. The sound it makes is too high for human ears. For beasts and other creatures, it is shrill.

It has brought a werewolf to its knees more than once."

Oryn rolled his eyes. When the boy was exposed for being a foolish liar he would have the right to punish him or take his life. It would release some pent up frustration.

"Blow your whistle, boy, so I may get back to my drink."

The entire room held its breath as the boy shrugged and inhaled. Just as lips touched silver, Oryn tried to decide if he should beat the boy first or finish his tea.

An explosion of pain staggered him. A high screeching hit his ears and it felt as if spikes were driving into them. His hands went up to cover them, but it was no use. The sound got past and he cried out, falling to his knees.

Then the sound was gone. The pain stopped and an eerie, empty feeling took its place. As he gazed at the floorboards with hands over his ears, he blanched and froze. Then his recovering hearing caught the sound of drawing weapons. His pupils dilated.

In one swift motion, Oryn grabbed the closest table and threw it over to block the knives that were thrown. They hit the hard wood as he flew out the door, leaving it swinging on the hinges. Loud yelling erupted in the bar as everyone prepared to go after the unmasked creature.

Near panic, Oryn ran back the way he came as fast as his feet could carry him. His blood pumped while he fought through the dark, brushing past trees he could hardly see. When he reached the hills, he stopped and a little sense returned. Going back to Adwen and Toth would be a terrible mistake. The angry village workers were hot on his trail and would not be kind now that they saw him as a threat.

Tiny bobbing flames drifted up the hills behind. Once he heard dogs barking he swore under his breath and darted off in a new direction. It didn't matter to where so long as they were not led to his friends.

His eyes barely saw the ground dropping ahead and he slowed enough to slide down safely. The frightened knight hid in the brush, trying to catch his breath. Oryn's heart continued to race while he wondered what was going on. As he slowed his mind, he froze. The breath caught in his throat and he steadily looked to the bandage wrapped injury. Not willing to throw out the possibility, he flexed the muscles beneath the wrappings. All pain was gone.

Suspicion turned to disbelief as he fought to rip the strip of cloth. Hands shook, fumbling with the knot so he resorted to gnawing it loose. When he tore off the last of the bandages, he felt nauseous.

The wound was gone. No blemish or scar was left. In the gloom his eyes adjusted and he saw something else. He struggled to make it out as panic threatened to return. Slowly, he realized what it was. Oryn's jaw slackened.

Sharp shrieking hit his ears as the boy blew his whistle somewhere, forcing him to forget the arm and grip his aching head. Wailing cries alerted the men and once the sound was gone, the dogs were barking. They quickly found the trail.

Gritting his teeth, Oryn bolted again.

When the sun set Toth began to worry. Adwen had not awoken or moved and it worried him more than Oryn's absence. Stealing a glance at her, he shook his head and went back to building a fire. He struck flints together, again and again, clicking them.

Adwen's eyes started to move. She became restless and then gasped, sitting upright and startling Toth half to death.

He landed on his backside from the surprise and called to her. "Adwen! No, you must lie down. You'll worsen your wound!"

She cringed and grit her fangs, forcing her body to its feet. Dodging Toth's attempt to pull her back, she snatched up the Rose Thorne. "Oryn's in trouble. Get on the horse." She shuddered again and almost screamed when he ignored her. "Get on Ulna, now!"

He paused and gave a disturbed look before obeying.

While he climbed onto the mare, she slung the weapon across her back and transformed. The change made her wounds burn, but she managed. She darted off with a confounded half-elf riding in her wake.

Oryn was exhausted. The men were as tenacious as their dogs. They slowly gained as he fled farther into the woods. Coming across level ground, the trees gave way to an open field. Seeing it as a chance to put more ground between him and the men, he made straight for it. He dashed across the meadow. But a bad feeling in him worsened as he looked into the dark.

He slowed to a stop and stared raptly at the shadows. A familiar chill crawled up his spine. The knight's eyes widened in horror as he knew what was coming and turned back, desperate to warn the villagers.

"No! Go back! Stay away! They are coming! Turn back now!"

They either did not hear or thought he was a liar. All of them heard his voice and went closer with weapons ready. He watched in astonished frustration as they continued the pursuit.

"No! No! Turn away now! They are coming! They will tear you apart if you don't turn away now!" Then he heard the sounds and looked again. As expected, a pack of werewolves appeared. Resembling hairy, naked men, their eyes shined red.

Then he felt something that turned his face ghost white. A strange pressure began to build in his limbs. Oryn's veins started to throb hard under his skin. The green moon was due to come full and he spied it peering over a distant mountain.

He suddenly felt calm. While the abominations saw him and started to run, Oryn begun the breathing ritual. His pulse slowed, skin cooled and eyes became empty. The focus he found was deep. It would be enough to keep out the pain. Other sounds diminished. All he heard was his heartbeat and the sounds of the werewolves rushing forward. Behind him the villagers slowed as they noticed the massive pack.

He took a step, and through the pounding sounds, thought he heard Adwen howl. He saw the monsters hesitate and look off to the side. His empty eyes followed. The white hound leaped through the air. With one swift motion, she threw the sword into the ground by Oryn and sailed over to attack the vile beasts. Deep in a trance, he saw her bark at Toth and he turned from the battle to protect the bystanders.

Holding the change at bay, Oryn reached for the sword. The moon was about to rise and he pulled at the blade. It felt light and came loose from the soil. The moon rose full as he swung the golden sword gracefully in preparation for the first wave. The werewolves started to change everywhere and he felt his own body shudder from the tension.

There was a dull pain. Every blood vessel swelled, ready to burst as the first two werewolves leaped. He swung out like a reaping scythe. Both monsters were fully transformed as his blade struck, hewing them in half, pieces tumbling past. Supernatural strength was at his command. He breathed again and took another step. Swinging the sword in another horizontal arc, he cut down three more with a single stroke.

Again, he swung and killed two more that were pouncing. With the pounding in his ears and the deep trance, Oryn's hearing was limited. The knight did not see a stray werewolf lunging for his other arm. A sudden feeling caught his dulled senses by surprise and he looked. Clamped down on his arm were a set of werewolf jaws. Huge fangs sank in deep. For a moment he lost concentration and the trance wavered.

He felt the painful grinding of bones inside his arm and his face. A deafening roar escaped the knight and he bared his own set of fangs at the werewolf before hewing it in half.

Adwen heard the roar. She thought a new nemesis had arrived, but there was only Oryn. The severed monster fell away and she saw the knight's eyes glowing. Part of his face distorted while his left hand sprouted claws. Both eyes burned a fierce green while he displayed sharp fangs.

She could do nothing for him now. The villagers had to be protected. Helping him would have to wait.

Toth's plate was full as well. Surrounding trees roots served as weapons and defense. He used most of the strong things to form a protective fence, holding the creatures back as he tossed aside those that managed to get past his companions. He heard the roar as well, but could not turn to see from where it came.

A few werewolves remained when the knight began to stagger. Vision doubled and breathing threatened to falter. Striking the blade deep into the soil, Oryn fell to his knees, holding on tight to the sword with mismatched hands. The time to fight was over. He refocused his breathing and relaxed his straining body.

Adwen defended him from two werewolves. She slashed at their faces and snapped their necks with well-placed punches and clawed kicks. Sensing an enemy moving for the villagers, long ears twitched. Turning her streamlined head over one shoulder, bright eyes narrowed and glowed.

A werewolf bounded towards the humans.

With amazing speed, she cut the beast off and stood with her back to the root fence. Everyone cringed as the werewolf leaped and one of her clawed hands pierced the creature through the heart. It was suspended and frozen as white light shined out its throat and empty eyes. Then the body turned to ashes and fell away.

Exerting the energy caused Adwen's injury to gush silver blood and she staggered and whined.

Toth leaped from Ulna to catch her. "Adwen!"

The half-elf came just in time as she painfully changed into her woman form. He let her fall back into his arms. As he tried to speak to her, she did not listen. All attention was on the knight, kneeling to his sword. She could feel him suffering. Putting her own pain aside, she regained balance.

"I'm all right." Then she shuddered and held up a hand to stop her friend. "Keep these people back. Don't let them come any closer."

For the first time, Toth looked to his knight friend and realized something was wrong. He nodded and let her limp far across the meadow. She could see his breathing as he struggled to resist.

Buckled over, head hanging low to the sword, Oryn leaned on the physical support. It was very difficult to maintain while holding off the change. There was absolute determination in him that he would not fail. Death was the only course.

Then keen senses told Oryn something wonderful was just beside him. His numb mind flickered with curiosity. Then her voice reached past the trance and he thought his heart might skip a beat and burst.

"Oryn?"

Her voice was the only other sound he could hear aside from his pulsating body. The knight fought to maintain despite the great distraction.

"Oryn, say something. What's happening?" She couldn't tell if words reached him. There was no response so she reached to touch his arm. "Can you hear me?"

He felt contact with his skin and his heart did skip a beat. There was a wrenching inside him that twisted hard. Blood came up out of his mouth and he snapped with a gravelly voice, terrified of losing control.

"Don't touch me!"

The outburst made her quickly retract, eyes wide as a memory resurfaced. Adwen cupped hands to her mouth, horrified; she had bit through his armor. That was all she could remember after being whipped. What had she done?

Her eyes caught a glimpse of a mark on his arm where she had bitten. It was a symbol. She blinked in confusion and tried to make sense of it, but Oryn coughed up more blood.

Determind, she urged, "Please, stop this. You're killing yourself."

There was still no response.

Emotion cracked her voice as she began to plead. "Please, just stop it."

His body shuddered as he found the will to hold off the change and speak. His voice was deep and rough.

"I will not turn into a monster. I refuse to be what I have sworn to kill."

She shook her head. "You won't. I promise. I wouldn't let you be one of those things. Just please stop doing this!"

More blood dribbled from his lips to the grass. He didn't have much longer.

She tried not to cry. "Please, Oryn. Let it go."

The words were familiar and he heard them, but still refused.

"Whatever you're hanging on to, it's not worth this. Please, let go." A tear rolled down her cheek as she knelt beside him. "Please."

He still did not answer or heed the plea.

Adwen sorrowfully hung her head. After a moment of weeping passed, her head lifted. Both eyes shone gold and a look of understanding was in them. There was only one thing to say that could change the warrior's mind. She leaned in close to his ear and whispered.

"Knight... you are needed."

Her head bowed back down as the gold light left her eyes. She returned to shedding tears.

But Oryn's eyes were wide open with shock. The words rent him in two. He had no choice but to heed the call as a knight.

But if he did, he would never be able to rejoin his comrades. If he were discovered, his name would be scratched from the records and never be inscribed on a tablet in the pearly hall. He would be seen as an abomination in the eyes of the elders. Everything he ever worked for would be gone.

A shaky breath escaped him and he closed his frightened eyes tight, bracing for the consequences. After one last steady exhale, he finally let go.

The pain was immense. An unnatural wail split the silence like nothing the onlookers had ever heard. The knight's human form rapidly expanded, stretched and bulged, snapping straps that held the armor to his body. Thick, brown fur raced down the back of his neck and spread to the rest of him as the armor fell away, piece by piece. All the while, he clenched the sword and howled at the agony.

Then it was over.

Breathing came easier with every moment that slipped by. Fresh air in his chest cooled burning lungs. He heard a soft growl and felt the vibration in his throat. Both eyes were squeezed shut as he didn't dare open them, afraid of what he might see. Taking another breath, he smelled everything, but mostly Adwen. That scent was the sweetest.

Nerve and curiosity slowly got the better and he chose to face fear. He blinked and looked out of nocturnal eyes for the first time. Night looked like day. His senses were enhanced far beyond what he had known. Ears upon his long head folded back in shame and his eyes displayed the feeling even more. His deep breaths shuddered and the feeling of loss took hold.

Adwen stood by and stifled a sob as she saw him go through the change. Worst of all was knowing she was to blame. She felt his pain and wanted to ease it if she could.

Lying beside a long, silky tail was the cape from his armor. A flash of gold crossed her eyes as she picked it up and pressed the green cloth firmly to her soft lips. With all her heart she willed it to become a useful gift. As she wished, the color rippled to a deep blue and it lengthened in her grasp. She held it up and found that a larger hood and a strong clasp appeared for its owner.

Oryn felt Adwen's arms wrap around his shaggy neck and froze. The ears on his head flattened with surprise while he held still. She clasped it and set the hood up. It helped to feel concealed. He was thankful, but couldn't muster the nerve to utter a sound.

She gently beckoned. "Come on. It's time to go."

He felt numb. Taking a deep breath, he made himself stand. It was awkward with these new legs so he used the sword for stability. Cold grass tickled the spaces between padded toes. He ignored the realization of what his feet had become and refused to look at the rest. With little effort, he pulled the sword from the soil.

Adwen watched the knight-turned-hound stand at a towering height of eight feet. She dropped her gaze and headed for the trees. A moment later, she heard him following.

Toth was stunned beyond words. This was a terrible blow for Oryn. Quickly, he sent the roots into the earth and went to Ulna.

Then a man darted past, rushing after the two in the clearing. He ran hard to catch up and called out. "Wait!"

Both stopped, though only she turned to look.

The farmer stopped a short distance away and stated breathlessly, "I have something to say."

Her violet eyes studied him curiously. "Yes, what is it?"

"Come with us. I believe I speak for the rest when I say, we need to thank each of you properly." He glanced to Oryn's back and added sadly, "And to apologize for a great misunderstanding."

His sharp ears heard and he closed his eyes, hoping she would decline. The embarrassment of returning to that place as he was would be more punishment.

Adwen glanced at the others. Each nodded, putting away their weapons. She knew it was better than staying in the woods. "Thank you. We would greatly appreciate that."

Oryn's shoulders sagged as he heaved a heavy sigh.

Chapter 39
A KNIGHT'S RENEWAL

All that had unfolded was overwhelming for the three, but none so much as Oryn. The thankful villagers had fended off many werewolves over the past few weeks. The trio were more than welcome. As the men chattered with Toth on the way back to the cozy mountain town, she and their dismal friend moved in silence.

Adwen's thoughts were a whirlwind. She was certain she could not mark others. There was almost no recollection of how his arm came to be in her jaws. Even more frightening was that it wasn't the first lapse of memory. If she had done it on purpose, she would not be able to rest easy.

Oryn's own shock came with overpowering loss. It was over. He could never go back. If word of the knight-turned-beast reached the ears of the Order, he would swiftly be hunted down by those who were once his men. Finding himself on the outside looking in, he was even more ashamed. What a fitting destiny, he thought. For so long he had been like a merciless monster and now he was one.

Distracted by thoughts of disgrace, he hardly noticed they had already arrived at the tavern. Toth lead Adwen through the door and she winced as he helped her onto a stool at the counter. When the half-elf showed concern, she held up a hand to show she was well enough.

Oryn pulled his mind back to full awareness. Across the counter before his friends the big, bearded bartender studied him curiously. The vaguely familiar man was not what had Oryn's attention. A strange reflection was in the mirror over the counter covered in drinks. A tall hooded creature stared back. Soon he realized the beast was wearing a pair of black dragon skin trousers under the concealment of a blue cloak.

One familiar part of the image frightened him far more.

Brown bangs of human hair framed glowing green eyes. When he recognized them as his own, the breath caught in his throat. He swallowed hard and saw the animal in the glass do the same, eyes dilated wildly. The powerful jaws clenched, exposing sharp incisors. Having seen enough, he swiftly turned away and retreated to a table away from the rest. Moonlight shone through into the secluded corner. He took up a chair, clutching the Rose Thorne in his sharp claws.

Many villagers went home, knowing the visitors were sound protection. As they turned in for the night, many more went for a few pints to celebrate the good fortune. Adwen glanced at the lone cloaked figure.

The gruff bartender leaned on the counter and asked, "Do these men all speak the truth, miss? Did you save them from fifty werewolves?"

She studied him curiously and Toth was nonchalant, "It was nearer to forty."

Adwen shook her head at him. "Well, there wasn't much choice. Our friend was..." She glanced sadly at the corner. "...in trouble."

The bartender beamed. "That pack would have destroyed this town. Thank you. What can I serve you? All of my drinks are free of charge."

The half-elf raised a hand. "I'm not thirsty, thanks."

She smiled. "Do you have milk and tea?"

An expression of pain suddenly came over her and the bartender noticed her wicked wound. "Yes. I'll brew a cup of my best."

"Thank you." She sighed as the hurt faded enough to stop cringing.

"You'd be the Tame One, wouldn't you?" The question caught her off guard and the man smiled. When the pot was set to boil he returned and lowered his voice. "I thought so, but that wasn't my first thought when you came into my bar. If you don't mind my asking, would you be the heir of the Master Knight?"

Surprised, her eyes glowed at the smiling bartender.

"Good." He shot an envious look at the creature in the dark corner. "You've arrived just in time. Men come from Tanoaks with rumors and stories of evil happenings. Take it from me: you will have to brace yourself for what awaits down the road, in a manner of speaking."

Adwen suddenly felt uncertain.

"Don't you worry. You have two good men here. With their help I'm sure you'll succeed."

Her tan cheeks blushed. "Thank you." A moment later she was looking off into the shadows again. "Toth?"

He replied, eager to assist, "Yes, Adwen?"

She watched the cloaked figure that hardly moved. "He needs someone to talk to. You're his friend. You know him a lot better than I do."

Toth's mood quickly turned from eager to sober. "That would not be best. It would be better if you spoke with him."

Before she could object, the bartender agreed. "He would listen to you."

They both stared in surprise that he seemed so sure.

"He may be stubborn, but if the heir were to speak with him, he would surely hear the words." His smile encouraged her.

"He is right. You are the only one who comprehends what has happened."

A horrible feeling of guilt settled in the pit of her stomach.

"You went through the same. I am naïve to what else you dealt with aside from pains and changes in needs. My friend doesn't need me; he needs you."

She was unable to meet Toth's gaze. A moment passed before she slid from the stool, wincing as she limped.

His powerful form slouched in the chair, staring out the window. Glowing eyes searching for nothing. The pommel of the legendary sword rested against the table edge. Oryn's clawed thumb absentmindedly caressed the indentation of the Andredan mark. As he looked down at the emblem, a sad sigh passed through his throat as a soft growl.

His nose caught Adwen's serene scent. Then his ears twitched at the sound of a soft footfall. Only then did he realize she was so near. He almost turned to look, but refrained.

She saw his nose pick up her scent and his head moved under the cloak. Knowing he was aware of her, she observed a little longer before taking up a chair beside him.

Oryn shifted in his seat. Being in a chair was made uncomfortable by a long tail. The constant nagging discomfort on its own was demoralizing.

Their tense silence lasted longer as she could not find the right words. What could she possibly say to ease his suffering?

He heard her take a breath to speak, then sigh as she let the thought go. She was ready to try speaking again, but he let out a gentle growl.

"If you cannot find the words, then there is no use in searching for them. It would be a waste of your breath, just as I've been a waste of your time already."

Adwen frowned. "Why would you be a waste of my time? You've been too much help to be that."

"I am a wretch." He growled. "Through everything, I have managed only to get you into more danger. My presence is lethal. To keep me in your company much longer would eventually be your end."

"That is not true. Everyone dies. That's not your fault." She gave a laugh and the soft sound made his heart ache. "If you were gone, it would be just Toth and I. How far would we get without the knight?"

His claws squeezed the weapon hard and shook. He reached up and wrenched back the hood with an angry growl. Moonlight shadowed his features and powerful jaws. Both ears were pinned back while he turned his head to glare through a pained expression.

"Does this look like a knight to you?"

Then he blinked and his scowl melted into surprise.

Adwen's golden eyes were stern as her stare drilled into his. Her tone was no longer sorrowful and tender. It was a voice full of understanding and empathy.

"You look like a knight to me."

Speechless, his ears perked a little.

"You think yourself a wretch undeserving of my time? I disagree. I see into you and there would not be a moment of wasted time in your company. I see pain, shame and a misplaced sense of self-loathing." Her intense stare moved to the sword and back. "If you are so unsure, then look from a different perspective." She leaned in close and whispered softly. "Knights believe in the five virtues but do not understand what it is to stand for them. A knight becomes what he kills when he becomes a monster. A creature incapable of upholding the virtues is just that. If you still do not see yourself as a knight, look a little better at the sword you cling to so tightly. Can you or can you not follow the five virtues? Think on that. Then decide and be sure in your choice."

The moment she finished, her eyes changed to violet and her stern look softened back to sad and sympathetic. "In the end, you have to decide if you are a knight or if you are something else." She realized his hood was down when she could have sworn it was up a second ago. And he was looking at her instead of out the window. There was yet another lapse in memory.

He watched as she seemed uncertain. Then she looked disturbed and quietly left without a word. When she neared the counter, the bartender passed the steamy tea with milk. She eased painfully up onto the stool.

The man smiled at seeing her enjoy Red Lily tea and glanced at Oryn enviously.

He returned it with a calculating look before going back to being reclusive. As the golden eyed Adwen suggested, he looked at the mark on the sword. It was the symbol representing faith, courage, compassion, mercy and hope.

The ears on his head stood a little high and his eyes shifted while he thought. His miserable look lightened as he stole another glance at her. The sword he had made his original oath upon was broken and lost. The time to return to his brothers was gone, but he had a new sword and a new oath to make. He held the Rose Thorne and bowed his head.

He growled softly. "I make an oath of loyalty and honor upon this weapon of truth. By the blessing of the Light Spirits, I swear, I will aid and defend Darien's heir unto the bitter end. To protect her I would lay down all I have to give. I vow to be at her side into the end of time. Hear me, great eternal light of truth and righteousness and accept my promise to aid your warrior, tried and true, forever and on."

Day broke long before he stirred. He had fallen asleep at the table, face buried in his arms and not moved all night. Morning passed by till noon when his sensitive nose woke him. A potent odor of cologne and sweat brought him to. When he opened his eyes the light from the window was dazzlign. After adapting, he could see the room clearly.

Resting his weary head on the table, he worked a hand before him, flexing and studying bare callused skin. He could feel a difference already. That hand did not belong to a human. No matter how much he looked like it, he was not.

He groggily sat up and leaned back. When he heaved another sigh the smell was stronger so he scanned the quiet bar. He found the bartender sitting at his own empty counter, watching. Though he didn't smile, his eyes twinkled and crowfeet became more prominent.

"You know, everyone believes you're dead."

Oryn lowered his gaze to the floor. "I should like to think I've come to understand why you left, Uncle."

Malkum was curious. "How long have you been traveling with her?"

"I found her a year ago and lost her. And then found her again." Frowning, he admitted, "The first time I came across her I made a terrible mistake."

"You treated her like any other knight might have, I am sure." Oryn gaze at his aged, heavy set uncle as the bartender added, "Very poorly."

"Have they been here looking for me?"

"I've not seen the knights in a month aside from your visit. Last I saw of them, they were fighting a losing battle in the lost roads. They gave it up when too many died." Then he smiled. "She is lovely, isn't she?"

Oryn said nothing and stared at the floorboards.

Amused, Malkum stated, "Only a fool would deny that."

"I'm not denying anything, Uncle," he snapped and glowered. "She is the heir. I am a knight bound to serve her cause." Discomfort crossed his face. "For any man to take to her that way would be foul. His eyes would have to be burned from his skull for giving looks."

His uncle tried hard not to laugh. "I have a red hot poker on the coals if you wish me to fetch it for yourself."

The green eyes of his nephew flashed and glowed for a moment.

"You should be proud to be riding with her, Oryn. She

does not seem to hate you so much as you hate yourself. There is no harm in admiring something good while one has the chance. The looks I saw you giving her were none to be punished for."

Oryn looked away from his sentimental relative. "I was not giving her looks! She had offered me counsel and I was attempting to come to a decision." Fresh linens and a hooded pullover plopped onto the table along with a pair of leather boots. His eyes snapped onto them out of surprise and found Malkum beside him.

"Of course. Her willing servant wouldn't dare to find her lovely." He chuckled as he strolled to the window, looking out into the sunny street.

Oryn dressed himself, glaring at Malkum for taunting him. The dragon leather lasted through his changes well. Even though it was thin material, the soft hide was sturdy and could stretch and mold to the wearer's body.

As Oryn donned the shirts, Malkum sighed. "I believe you. I believe you understand completely why I left the life of a knight."

Finished dressing, he looked outside as well. Adwen was being helped onto Ulna. With her energy sapped, she needed assistance climbing into the saddle. A terrible look of pain was on her face as she strained.

Malkum stole a glance at Oryn. A look came over him as he wished he could end it. The last Malkum remembered seeing those eyes, they were so empty.

"Where will you go now? Not back to the order, I hope. You know what they would do to her."

Standing to go, he slung the sword across his back. Determination lit in his expression as he scowled. "They wouldn't dare. Whatever part of them touches her I will take away in the blink of an eye."

His uncle beamed. "I'm sure."

It was time and he went to the door. "It was good to see you, Uncle."

"Even though the timing and circumstance were strange, I am very glad you came." He chuckled slyly. "I knew it was you, sitting alone like that and drinking Red Lily tea. Not many knights take to it. They prefer strong ale."

A smile tugged at the corner of Oryn's mouth and he reached for the door.

Then his uncle called, "Hey, lad!" He looked back and Malkum was stern. "You watch over her. You hear? The three of you are in for a few nasty adventures."

The green in Oryn's eyes glowed fiercely in the dim light. "She is vitally important to our future. I would cut my own throat if it meant her success." With a nod he bid Malkum farewell and left his bar.

Once the door shut, the bartender smiled. He chuckled to himself and peered out to watch. Then he shook his head. "You wouldn't do those things because she is the heir. In a heartbeat you would do them out of love and adoration, you young fool."

Many townspeople came to investigate. Adwen was secure in the saddle and still in pain. Down beside her the apothecary gave Toth handfuls of helpful herbs. When she finished giving what she could, she saw Oryn approach.

Recognizing him, she smiled. "Oh! These are your friends?" She ducked her head a little, blushing sweetly. "I know these herbs aren't much, but it's all I have."

He ignored her obvious attraction. "We appreciate the gifts and we must be off."

"Wait!" A middle-aged woman with wispy hair came running with a young man in tow.

Oryn recognized the boy from the night before and glared as the woman said breathlessly, "Travelers -- my apologies, I mean, warriors. This is my son. He gave your sharp-eyed friend a bit of trouble last night. He mistook him for a werewolf. It's because of my son's haste with the seeing gift that you had such misfortune. Sir, he has something to say."

The boy looked nervous. After gulping and shifting a little, he murmured, "I'm sorry, sir. I made a mistake." His mother gave a sharp pinch, making him jump and blurt out, "Ouch! And I wish to make amends, sir."

Everyone waited with baited breath for Oryn's response.

A tense moment passed as he glared. "Remain here. Stand watch every night. Do not make the same mistake again."

"Yes, sir." As the three turned away he called out with more confidence. "I won't make the same mistake twice, sir!

Good luck to you!"

Adwen and Toth saw Oryn roll his eyes.

She giggled and stopped when it hurt, but still smiled. It was funny to see him let the boy off so easy.

Then she thought of why and the jolly mood dissipated. Within a week he lost his sword, his horse, his slayer's armor and finally his humanity. Oryn had lost everything. She had contributed and did not know what she could do to make it right. The moment she found a way to make it easier, she would do so, no matter what.

Chapter 40
HOLDING ON

While Toth led the mare, Oryn adjusted to new and very keen senses. He began to view the abilities an asset more than an affliction. With these capabilities, he could keep a highly effective watch over the others. This idea was pleasing.

Ulna snorted and stopped walking. Toth tugged the reins and she grunted, stubbornly refusing to take another step. "What is the matter? Come, girl. We must keep moving."

Oryn looked back and discovered why she wouldn't budge.

Adwen was hunched over. A silver liquid trickled from her nose as she shuddered, gritting fangs and clutching at Ulna's mane.

When she started to fall, he yelled, "Toth! Catch her!"

Together they darted over, caught her and carefully moved to a plot of ground on the roadside near a creek.

"What is hurting?" The half-elf urged.

Tears streaked her face and she gasped, "It burns. It's like I'm being stabbed." She continued to gasp and writhe.

They saw more green fluid seeping from blackened punctures.

"Hold her head up." Toth gently shifted her toward Oryn. "Stay like that." He retrieved the satchel stuffed with herbs and rigorously dug inside for the right combination.

Oryn felt her shuddering. Every time she gasped at the pain his heart leaped to his throat. What made him even sicker was knowing he could do nothing.

Toth put a variety of ingredients into the grinding cup from the apothecary. In under a minute he took the concoction and added a bit of water to make a potent tea. Bringing it to Adwen's lips, he instructed, "Drink this."

She caught a breath then drank. Swallowing hurt more, causing her to yelp.

Using the paste at the bottom, Toth liberally coated the wound. Finished, they waited. Soon her breaths were less labored. The strained expression relaxed.

Anxious, Toth asked, "How do you feel?"

Cracking her eyes open, she murmured, "A little dizzy, but it doesn't hurt. I feel pretty good."

The men's tension eased as they were relieved.

She chuckled weakly. "That did taste nasty though."

Both friends smiled and Toth replied, "That was one of the bitterest mixtures I've ever made."

Her head rested in Oryn's hands as Toth looked up at him, glared and asked in a hard voice, "Well, what should we do? Make her keep going until dawn?"

The reference to the last time she was not well caught Oryn's attention immediately. His eyes glowed back at Toth.

The powerful potion heavily dulled Adwen's perception. "We should keep going. Not until morning, because we need rest. Sundown sounds nice, though."

While the men each dared the other to make a move, the half-elf answered. "All right, Adwen. We can go until sunset. You're certain you can make it?"

An amused look played across her face as she puffed and giggled. "You kidding? This stuff is better than morphine."

Neither understood, but knew it meant she could to ride.

Once they helped her into the saddle, Toth grabbed up the reins again. This time they kept a closer watch.

The medicine seemed to do wonders for pain and a detriment to Adwen's good sense. She hummed happily while eyes became fully dilated. The drug-induced bliss made it near impossible to tell that her friends were at each other's throats.

Oryn maintained a cool composure, "We should avoid riding the whole of tomorrow. She seems to be worsening rather than healing. When dawn's first light touches her she mends quickly. If we allow her to rest through the night and --"

"No, that won't work." Toth snapped, "We tried this morning. Whatever they did with their arrows, it still harms her. The mix I gave would have put a human into a deep sleep for days. Judging from her reaction and how quickly the effects took hold, I'm sure she will need more by sundown."

Oryn glanced back, readjusting the sword strap on his

shoulder. "Could it be possible to use a little less when you tend to her? You may have used too much of something."

Anger reverberated in Toth's voice. "You saw how much pain she was in. It was luck her body took the effects at all. Besides, this dose seems to lightening her mood."

She suddenly out while her eyes threatened to cross. "Hey, are you guys fighting? Don't make me come down there and straighten you out. You guys are supposed to be friends!"

They exchanged odd looks as she sniffed the air. She smelled birds in the trees and barked. The flock squawked in answer and Adwen giggled. "Silly birds."

Toth could not help but chuckle a little. "No, Adwen. You are the silly bird."

She giggled again and swayed in the saddle. "No. You're the silly bird."

Oryn gave her a raised eyebrow and then shot his friend an astounded look.

The half-elf returned it and added, "I'll not add so many herbs."

"I believe that would be wise."

A brilliant orange and purple sunset burned bright. Small blossoms grew along the roadside. Trees stood tall and closer together. Adwen eventually passed out and taking her from the saddle was more difficult. For a bed, her blond companion willed thick moss into a cradling shape formed from the roots of an old tree. They laid her there and she didn't stir. Her face was peaceful, but pale.

Oryn leaned on the tree, watching over her while Toth rambled aloud, pacing. His expression was blank. He patiently allowed their distraught companion to babble.

"Tanoaks should be a day away. There are only enough coins for her medicine. We shall need a way to pay for a room." He clasped his hands. "My mind is weary and she is not awake yet. I'll collect firewood. If she wakes and is in pain, you may administer the mixture."

Still staring at her sleeping face, Oryn nodded.

As Toth departed into the brush.

Observing her, a tugging sensation pulled firmly within

Oryn's chest. Shaking his head, he disapproved of the feeling. The sun would set in a few minutes and be replaced by the moons. He went to sit across the small clearing, removing the shirts and boots. He felt dread for the pain, but satisfaction as well; this was a befitting punishment for his crimes.

Waiting in anticipation of the change did not frighten him. The first time had been abrupt due to holding back and letting go. Doubts crept in as to if he could tolerate the full experience. Surely he could, but would he resist and prolong the suffering? He took it as a challenge.

In the falling dark, he flexed his left hand, remembering it being one of the first parts of him to transform. The claws were black and very sharp. Stealing a glance at the tree tops, he watched the stars shine around two moons. His human eyes could not make out details in the dark. After a few days that would change.

Minutes passed before he felt a full moon rising. Blood pressure rose and he saw the backs of his hands. Veins swelled under skin like roots beneath a thin layer of soil. They pulsated while tension in his head mounted. The pressure in his skull caused the backs of his eyes to ache. Then they began to glow and he cradled his pounding head. Clutching hands shook. Each breath grew increasing ragged. Gulping, he groaned at the dull pain, beads of sweat forming across hot skin. Oryn was too overwhelmed to see Adwen had awoken.

She could see him cringing and panting. Most of the drugs effects had worn off. The wounds felt sore when she breathed. Oryn's miserable sounds alerted her to how close the moon was from rising full. Adwen gritted small fangs, hoisting herself up off the ground. It hurt to move, but could not sit back and watch. She knew there was a way to help and forced unsteady legs to walk. The effort was tiring and she swayed.

It was intense for Oryn. He could not even smell her as she came close. His whole body throbbed in time with his heart. And then the agony began.

He wailed. An explosion of ripping sensations coursed through him as bones grinded and stretched. It was impossible to keep from resisting a little and the change slowed, doubling the blinding feeling. Suddenly his whole skull crunched. Mouth and nose extended into jaws withing grasping hands.

Oryn cried out again, letting go of his shifting face, clenching sharp fangs. Struggling to turn over, he snarled, clinging onto tree roots with sprouting claws. His spine flexed, bones ground against one another and he howled.

Then the pain suddenly stopped. The changes continued, but the pain was gone. At last he smelled her and felt a hand on his back. He glanced back at her as his neck broadened and lengthened. She was taking his pain and making it her own with a simple touch. Fear struck him as he saw her wound start to pour green ooze while silver dripped from her nose. Using her power to relieve the pain was killing her.

His voice had yet to change and he struggled to speak. "No! Stop this!"

As he reached to push her, her eyes turned gold.

In an instant he was unable to move and collapsed. The mark on Oryn gave Adwen complete dominion over him. She had limited control over his body in her weakened state. It took little effort to render him limp as a doll. She gasped and her eyes rolled in anguish. He tried with all his might to stop it, but she refused to let him move. Toth's scent finally reached his lengthening muzzle and he made a desperate yelp.

"Toth!"

Toth saw her over Oryn, touching his back. Then he heard the knight yelp and saw green trickling from her wound. Kindling fell from his hands as he dashed over just when her eyes rolled back and she passed out.

Completely changed, Oryn looked in time to watch Toth catch her and drag her to the bed of moss. With ears folded back he quickly tried to stand. Near panic and still unaccustomed to this form, Oryn fell flat with a loud thud.

Right away he scrambled back up again and whined, "Is she still living? Is she --?"

Toth shouted, "You've done enough!"

Oryn was takenaback, but swiftly became angry and snarled in outrage. "I couldn't stop her!"

"Couldn't? Or wouldn't?" He took off the makeshift eye patch and used it to clean the wound.

"She had control of me!"

Ignoring the barks and snarls, Toth continued to work. Adwen was very quiet with hardly any sign of life. Breaths were frighteningly shallow.

The longer Oryn watched, the more his anger cooled and he was confused. When he couldn't look at her that way any longer, he turned and left. Oryn found balance and walked upright to stand in the trees where he didn't have to see her so near death. A strong pine caught his full weight as he slumped back against it and slid slowly to the ground. He cursed himself and feelings of despair.

There was silence until he heard a soothing female voice. "He's only afraid is all."

Turning his head, he saw Ulna beside him.

"Your friend is scared."

Surprised to be addressed by the horse he had traveled with for so long, he didn't have anything to say. Dropping his gaze, he let out a sorrowful growl.

She snorted. "You are afraid as well?"

"There is nothing I can do. What can I possibly do to help her now?" He threw his head back into the tree hard, smashing the rough bark, growling in frustration.

"Do what you may. I only have the skill to carry her and alert you when she is in need. I cannot heal her or take her to the town any faster. Worrying does no good for the heart or for her."

They glanced over to where she lay unconscious and back at each other.

Oryn shook his head and growled. "You are far too wise an animal. I wish I could have had the chance to speak with Ranger."

Ulna neighed. "Not likely. He had the foulest mouth of any stud I ever met!"

His long tail flipped in amusement.

"So, youngling. What shall you do for her?"

For a while he stared into the forest. He could not get her to Tanoaks any quicker without harming her and leaving Toth behind. Then he recalled what else needed taking care of. For the fare at the Red Lily Inn they would need something besides coins. His tail flicked again and long ears went up. The scent of their fare had already come to him on the wind.

The Red Lily Inn was a good place run by a very kind woman and her very sloppy drunk husband. For years they allowed people to stay for whatever they could offer. The last he heard, fifty pounds of meat could cover a weeklong stay. If he could bring down a big, strong buck like the one he was stalking, then there would be one less thing to sort out.

He left the sword behind. Wild animal instincts had not developed yet and his human side was dominant. He refused to let it clash with this new body. It was important that he kill the stag in his sights.

In a meadow on a hillside, moonlight shone down where the deer grazed alone. Without a sound, he stalked closer. The buck was far too busy nibbling at clover to notice him slinking through the high grass. Light shined off of his short, coarse fur while muscles worked in his back. Claws and padded feet moved stealthily.

One of his claws brushed a small rock in the grass and he froze. The buck spooked and raised its head in a flash. It saw him and stared.

As he gazed back, large doses of adrenalin flooded his veins. All at once, the deer bolted and was swiftly pounced upon by his predatory form. For a moment Oryn's animal side emerged. It brought the deer down. As his prey cried out, he silenced it.

The taste of blood brought him to. He looked down, panting and gasping at what he had done. It startled him, but the moment was over and the buck was dead. The realization that he had hunted like a wild beast was frightening. In a matter of weeks those same instincts would fully surface and he would be a real animal.

Shaking his head to stop fearful thoughts, he focused on the chore of gutting the carcass. The mare was right. Worrying about what he could not control was a waste. If Adwen could take control of his physical actions then he should have little to fear of feral outbursts.

A fire was burning at last and the glow comforted Toth. The cloth he had used was no longer suitable for an eye patch. He discarded it without a care. Adwen was not well and his personal appearance was the least of his concerns. Her wound was clean and the green liquid stopped flowing. Toth came to the conclusion that the green substance was her blood, destroyed by the poison. There was a lot on the ground and he feared she may not see morning if she did not wake soon.

As he was beginning to fear even more, her eyes eased open. At first he smiled, then joy turned to concern when tears rolled down.

"Are you hurting? I have more medicine. It won't be as strong as last time, I promise."

She let out a weak sob.

Recalling Oryn's claim, he asked, "What did you do to him, Adwen?"

"It's my fault." She murmured, "He'll hurt every night because of me."

"No. No, Adwen. You did nothing wrong. If you hadn't caught him he would not be living. You saved his life. When you bit through his armor it was an accident."

Sobbing again, she looked way and let more tears fall.

"Adwen? You did not intend to, did you?"

Refusing to look at him, she sobbed softly. "I don't know. Something happened. I can't remember and I don't know if I did it on purpose or not. I didn't want to hurt him. I just..." She sobbed harder.

Empathetic, he used his clean cloak to dry her cheeks. "Don't cry, Adwen. What do you mean you can't remember?"

Just when he asked, Oryn returned carrying the gutted buck over one shoulder. They had not seen him yet and he paused, hidden behind a broad tree. Listening in on the conversation, he kept both ears erect and caught their voices.

"I've been doing things I can hardly remember. It's like, one minute I'm doing one thing, then something's different and I don't know when it happened or how. I don't know what's wrong with me."

Toth shushed her while Oryn thought back to the times her eyes shined gold. When she had talked with him in the bar, once her eyes went from gold to violet, she looked afraid and confused.

"We have been keeping an eye on you and you haven't done anything wrong. I've been watching closely and I am not afraid."

She was baleful. "What if I hurt you, too?"

He shook his head and smiled. "No, you won't. Even if you tried, I'm sure I could stop you. Don't do anything to scare me like that again. I care about you."

Oryn's eyes dilated and his ears twitched.

"Don't go and hurt yourself on his behalf when he is in pain. I'm convinced he likes it sometimes." Toth thought about it and added, "I haven't a clue why exactly, but it makes him feel better. Oryn will be fine. He's stubborn and a bit cold, but he can get through this without too much sympathy."

Not pleased to be called cold or talked about further, Oryn stepped out into the open and acted as if he just arrived.

They saw him and Toth smiled. "Ah, good! Now I can make stew!"

Using a short piece of cord, Oryn hung the body from a branch. With incredible strength and a little experience, Oryn ripped the skin from the deer by carving with claws and tugging in swift jerks. His muzzle and claws were covered in blood and filth. He searched for a good place to begin cutting when Toth came with a knife and took a tender strip off the flank. His gaze followed the half-elf back to the fire as he went for water.

When Toth disappeared, Oryn paused to steal a sidelong glance at Adwen. She was awake and staring at the fire. Her face looked weak as the light danced in her damp lashes. There was no chance of her looking back, though he wished she would. Oryn ridiculed himself for thinking such things. He growled and started carving with beastly claws.

Hours later he finished picking meat from the bones and filled Ulna's saddle bags. He tossed the bare skeleton into the trees and was going to turn in when the horse called him over.

She shook her mane. "You're hungry, aren't you?"

It had been a couple days and he was starving. Adwen and Toth already ate their fill of stew and some was leftover. He shook his head. They should have the rest, he thought.

With a claw, he flipped open one of the bags and stared at the contents. His mind was too human to want meat raw, but he told himself it didn't matter. Taking up a hefty slab, he closed the flap and went to the fire.

Adwen was asleep again and so was Toth. He had lent her his cloak for a blanket and slept close to the fire.

Oryn settled across from them, studying the meat in his hand. It was dark and the moisture from the freshness made human tastes squeamish. He glanced around to see if his friends were looking. It felt as if he were about to do something obscene. Swallowing diminishing human pride, he took a bite. Fangs ripped a chunk away and he chewed before choking it down. To his somber surprise it was rather good. In a few minutes he devoured the entire thing.

Oryn stayed awake to keep watch and ensured no one slept too long. Oryn had watched her sleep all night. He recalled how much happier she was when they visited the strange world of cars, malls and bright lights. He wanted to see her smile like that now, but there was little chance of that. In the morning, Toth administered more herbs with the last of the stew.

Adwen's condition worsened. Her complexion became sallow and eyes dim. Bright sunlight did not help as before. She grew weaker and the medicine helped a little less. They were forced to go slowly where the earth was steep, but it hurt her despite the efforts.

Twice they stopped when the pain was too much and administered more herbs. Oryn and Toth continued not to speak, worried and aggravated by each other's company. Neither wanted to fight. Adwen needed their help.

When the sun was setting Tanoaks came into view. The town was a few miles down the mountainside. Adwen stared blankly at the vibrant horizon while the men found themselves discussing a serious issue.

Oryn nodded to the town. "Just go. I'll come from the hills at dawn and go unnoticed."

"You know that won't do. If you came alone it would be too suspicious. How would you explain it to them and avoid rumors?"

The knight glowered impatiently and restrained himself from glancing back at her. "If we halt now it may not be safe to take her along this rough path. She would be harmed more by the wait."

The half-elf frowned at the sunset. "I know, but I still cannot enter Tanoaks without your company. There's no telling what troubles we may find while attempting to buy a room."

It was the drunken husband, Mr. Mabel who had put a bounty out for Toth's head more than a year ago. Their sickly child passed away from an illness and he wanted someone to blame; he blamed Toth, convinced he could have saved the girl. Mistress Mabel knew he couldn't and urged him to flee. That was a few weeks before meeting Adwen. There could be a confrontation with the old drunk or with the other two children who were now adults.

Oryn had spent more time with Toth, but the others were once friends as well. He sincerely hoped they would not recognize him. Rumors of a strange creature with powers or that Sir Oryn was still living would not work to their benefit.

The sun was setting. Toth was worried by the decision.

"There is no time. You would not beat the full moon. It is too late." He turned to lead Ulna off of the road and set up camp. They left the horse saddled for a quick departure in the morning.

Adwen lay on another earthy bed while they went about their tasks. Oryn found the kindling and returned as Toth finished making more medicine. He tended to Adwen's wound. It had begun to bleed again and she was passed out.

Placing the wood by the fire, Oryn observed. The half-elf really did care for her, he thought.

Looking up from his work, Toth murmured, "You shall have to leave."

They locked eyes and tension swiftly rose. To avoid a pointless argument, Oryn was first to look away. He quietly removed shirts and boots, folding them in the cloak. This time he chose to take the Rose Thorne along. Before departing, he paused and carefully asked, "You know her well, don't you?"

"Yes, I'd like to think I know her quite well."

"Why would she do it? Why would she harm herself to take my pain? I don't understand."

Forgetting his work, Toth turned to give a sickened look. "You don't understand?" Shaking his head, he stormed, "How is it that you cannot understand?"

The outburst did not provoke Oryn in the slightest.

"She blames herself for what has happened to you! She believes she is responsible and wants to make it right. You saw her! She would rather die than see the pain she thinks she's caused you! How can you not see it?"

Oryn lowered his gaze to the ground in contemplation. Then he hefted the sword higher on his back and set out for a quiet place in the woods.

Toth glared after him, appalled. Oryn had caused Adwen so much pain that the half-elf could hardly stand it.

Oryn was a storm of confusion and frustration. It was not her fault, he fumed. His being marked was no more her fault than anything else. Again his anger grew and he sneered aloud.

"This was my choice."

A full moon was approaching and his blood quickened.

She could not possibly hold herself responsible. He would not allow her to take that blame.

Oryn struck the sword into the ground as the change came near. His bare feet hurt from walking across sharp rocks and fallen branches. Taking a deep breath, he waited for the real pain. Hot sweat trickled down his back. He was beginning to see clearer in the nighttime. The forest was eerie and beautiful while seeing it through nocturnal eyes.

Then the moon rose full.

Her eyes opened as the distant wailing screams echoed into camp. Adwen's eyes no longer glowed. Her skin was sallow and clammy.

Toth heard as well, frowning. "He will be fine."

A tear tumbled to her chin.

"Are you in pain?"

She shook her head while another tear fell.

He gently dabbed her dry with his cloak. "Please, don't cry. You'll be all right. You'll have a good rest when we reach the inn. They have warm beds with fluffy down pillows so soft your head sinks into them. Won't that be nice?"

Giving him a sad glance, she soon looked away. He didn't

think she was going to make it. The scent of his fear was faint while he tended to her.

"Adwen, why do you cry?"

There was a loud howl in the distance and she whispered. "That."

He scowled at the sound. "You shouldn't feel so much pity for him. Do you not recall all he did to you? Oryn never changes. He is an angry man who takes out his rage on the monsters he kills. There isn't much more than that."

She was astounded. Slowly turning to look him dead in the face, she wore an accusing expression. Tears stopped as she shook her head. "That's a lie. Can't you see it?"

Toth's anger cooled.

"He's already changed." She pleaded weakly, "Watch him. He's changed so much."

Toth found it difficult to believe. In the years he had known Oryn, not once did he show a change of heart. He was always stern, harsh and so very cold to other inhuman beings. Only Toth was lucky to have his respect. It was something he gave rarely.

He nodded. "All right. I'll try to see."

Darien's Breath was still useful for focus. He exhaled again and gracefully dropped into a fighting stance. There had only been a few difficulties while practicing footwork with the Rose Thorne. His beastly strength made the weapon feel no heavier than his father's blade.

His eyes flashed as he moved. The sword swung up and around while he performed the combat style his master taught him so well. Fighting was second nature to Oryn; it was like breathing. Once confident in his own degree of coordination, he decided to make the best of it.

Lobbing the sword up high, he listened to the sound as it went twirling. When the right sound came, he flipped backward and caught it perfectly upon landing. The feeling pleased him so much he performed it a second time. He flipped, catching the weapon then barked at the thrill of it. The feeling was incredible.

Still curious to see what else he could do, Oryn turned his

attention to the trees. Stabbing the sword into the ground, he chose to indulge in climbing.

Tail whipped as he leaped up to the closest branches. It was exhilarating. Leaping again and again, he reached the thinner branches and eventually the top of a pine. It swayed in the wind with his weight, towering high over the land. From his perch he saw many lights and smoking chimneys in Tanoaks. Even towns farther away could not escape his sight.

Wind ruffled the fur on his neck and head. He closed his eyes while smells of foods, fires and people wafted up the foothills. Adwen would survive. He knew it as he looked up at the stars. It had to be one of his favorite things about her; Adwen's nature was to care and to endure.

Chapter 41
THE RED LILY INN

At the break of dawn Oryn woke to Ulna's loud frantic sounds.

Oryn was in human form and woke with a start by the smoldering fire. Ulna pawed the ground where Adwen lay and he was at her side in an instant. The mare snorted worriedly while he knelt to touch Adwen's neck for signs of life, but hesitated. He could sense her fading. Then he saw the large pool of green she was lying in and his eyes widened in horror.

He cried out to wake his friend. "Toth! Wake up! Wake up, damn you!"

The half-elf finally snapped awake and got up, staggering from grogginess.

"Get to the horse, now! Get on the horse!" he yelled, grabbing up his blue cloak and returning to wrap her in it.

Too concerned with her condition, Toth reached to check her vitals himself.

Oryn gripped him roughly by the shirt and glared into his face, eyes glowing. "Get on the damn horse!" He let Toth go and watched him fumble onto Ulna's saddle.

Swiftly scooping Adwen's limp body in the folds of his cloak, he took her away from the sullied earth. Handing her over, Oryn bellowed, slapping the beast's flank, "Go!"

They flew down the mountainside and he was left with the challenge of catching up. Oryn donned his shirts and boots, snatching up the Rose Thorne to set it across his back on the run. Sprinting as fast as he could, he dashed through the trees and over obstacles. He avoided the meandering road, cutting through the wild terrain in a beeline for Tanoaks.

His shortcut led farther from the roadside where he glimpsed his companions. When the earth became more uneven, Oryn lost sight of them as the ground disappeared. He reached the ledge at full speed and leaped out into space. Sailing through the air, he was unafraid of the vast distance to the ground. A large boulder rushed up to meet him and he controlled the descent until his feet suddenly touched down. He grunted as he absorbed the incredible shock and sprung forward into a sprint.

He soon met back up with them on the road. They went into town and approached the large inn by the hills. The Red Lily Inn was as he remembered with cherry wood trim and red silk curtains. They reached the covered porch where Oryn leaned his weapon against the bottom steps. Then he turned to take Adwen. As he held her his senses warned she was fading faster. Dashing up to the entrance, Oryn came barging through the front door.

Her head lolled where his heart was beating madly. Behind the counter at the back sat a young man no older than Oryn or Toth.

In a moment the man was on his feet and saw the odd girl in Oryn's arms as he crossed the room. Waving a hand, he tried to dismiss him. "No! No, no, we don't accept that kind here. You'll have to go somewhere else. Take that thing out."

Then Toth came in and their gazes met.

"Oh." The man glowered, "So you chose to return and bring riffraff with you? If this is what you've reduced yourself to, then you're not welcome either. Get out!"

Toth spoke with a warning tone. "We don't want any trouble. Our friend is grievously wounded and needs a place to rest and heal. She is dying, you clout!"

He raised a skeptical eyebrow. "Well, that's not something I've heard before. How do I know she's not putting on so you may get in and leave without paying later? If that thing he's holding isn't hurt, then I'll have to call the knights on you."

Oryn was about to have words with him, but his heart somersaulted as Adwen's eyes opened. She spoke weakly.

"Let me down, please. Put me down."

He hesitated, but was stunned when she stood on her own. She was frail and very pale. At first the man was curious. With every shaky step she took, his expression became more unsettled. Adwen stood before him and swayed. He could see now that she was beautiful and stared back in stunned silence. A bit of green trickled from her nose and she shuddered. There was the sound of drops hitting the floor. He saw more dribbling from beneath the confines of the cloak. She held out a hand for the man to see and it was covered in her poisoned blood. It ran along her arm and he stared in complete shock.

"Please, can we stay... a while?"

Her eyes rolled back and she collapsed into Oryn's arms as he quickly caught her. Careful to keep her from falling, he looked up at the man and sneered, "How dare you?"

Toth spat, "Damn you, Jasper!"

Jasper was far too stunned to speak.

At that moment a woman called from atop the stairs by the counter. "What's going on down there?"

Mistress Mabel, a tall, red-haired woman appeared and gasped. Her body and face were age-worn, but she was strong and it showed in the sparkle of her eyes. "Oh my goodness, come with me! Bring her quickly! I have a place to lay her down! Quickly now!"

Oryn didn't hesitate and took Adwen back up in his arms. Halfway down the hall and across from a large mirror, she let them inside. Toth followed and closed the door as Adwen was put on the side of the bed closest to the window. The blankets were soft and cradled her.

Mistress Mabel brushed back the cloak, cupping a hand to her mouth. The wound was even blacker than before, almost the size of a splayed hand. Green oozed from all over and Toth told her, "I need your help, mistress. We must find the apothecary. We need a remedy to cure her."

"Of course, dear, come!" They went out the door in a flash.

Oryn was alone with her again. The sight frightened him as he pulled up a chair and sat, staring at the annihilated flesh. Desolation filled him. What could he possibly do? There was nothing. She was dying before his very eyes.

As the feeling grew, he reached out and laid a hand on the wound. He was about to speak, but paused. A strange sense tingled in the back of his mind. There was something inside. Quickly retracting his hand, he knew he was right. Their magical bond let him be certain of it. One of the many porous holes in her side oozed more than the rest. Reaching out again, he paused to murmur, "Forgive me."

With a finger, he felt into the wound. At first he found nothing, but then he reached his index deeper and pain suddenly shot through the digit. He gave a start and swiftly took it back. The tip of his finger was burned. Becoming determined, he glanced at her again to ask forgiveness for what he was about to do.

Oryn reached three fingers down inside and found the thing. He gasped and gritted his teeth as his fingers were seared by the hard, sharp item. When he had a good hold, he pulled and it came out. It clattered when he quickly dropped it to the floor. Examining his hand, he found the fingers were smoking, red and blistered. The object was the size of a spoon head, lying not far from his seat, still covered in green filth.

Cradling his hand, he watched her closely. Adwen's side was still black, but the flow of green ceased. Knowing the source of her poisoning was removed calmed him a little. His friend could tend to the rest.

It was a few minutes more until Toth came with Mistress Mabel and the herbal concoction. Giving up his seat, he backed out of the way.

Easing her lips apart, Toth let the herbal treatment trickle down her throat. She took it all and he gave a sigh. "Now all we can do is wait."

Miss Mable sighed as well just as Toth noticed the thing on the floor. Oryn was about to warn him, but he picked it up and was not burned. Surprised, Oryn watched as Toth cleaned it off. Then the two glared at the black, metal arrowhead. They had been in such a hurry to get out of the Crescent Remains that they failed to notice one of the arrows came out headless.

Toth turned to face him. "Was this the cause?"

Oryn lowered his eyes to the floor. If only he had paid more attention while pulling them out. Then he was surprised as his friend sighed.

"You couldn't have known. She hadn't even known. I would have made the same mistake, my friend." Turning to look at Adwen, he added, "But you've saved her. She may heal, thanks to you."

Oryn stopped chastising himself. Mistress Mabel went past to fetch warm water and a cloth and he hid his scorched fingers. Joining Toth's side, he heard his friend swear under his breath at the arrowhead.

"This is demon-steel." Casting it out the window, he fumed. "That is one of the foulest witch's creations. Metal forged with demon's blood!" He spat after the thing that caused them so much trouble. "Foul witches!"

Going to the window, Oryn looked out at the peaceful town. Everyone was beginning to stir in the streets as the sun came out from behind the mountain tops. He inspected his hand again and found the skin was still red and irritated. In an hour the burns would heal. All of him was gaining in strength, like Adwen had while under his tyrannical supervision.

Toth saw his fingers. "It burned you?"

Still studying the skin, he nodded.

Toth gave a wry laugh. "Well, since silver and pure things harm the evil, then I suppose it's only natural dark stuff would damage her and you as well. You shall need to be as cautious as she with your enemies now."

The door opened and Mistress Mabel entered with the bathing things. She set them on a table beside the bed and turned to work on her, but gasped. The men turned to look. Adwen's garments had changed and she was in a simple white nightgown. The material seemed burned away and singed at the edges around the dark wounds.

She turned to them, alarmed. "Toth, what is she? A nymph?"

"Nothing I've ever encountered before, but she is very good, mistress. She has saved our lives more than once."

Smiling sweetly, she replied, "All right, dear, I believe you." Without asking more, she gently dabbed at the wounds with the cloth.

Oryn heard Ulna whinny outside. "I'll be a moment."

On his way downstairs, he passed Mistress Mabel's daughter, Sarah. She was only a year younger than himself. Oryn paid her no mind and continued out the door.

She was surprised and stared after him with fascination.

Jasper was behind the counter and saw her watch him go. Once the door was shut, he warned, "I'd not try that one if I were you. He's in a right bad mood. Leave him be, Sarah."

She shot a questioning glance. "And I'm sure you were the

reason for his foul mood, Brother." When he shook his head and rolled his eyes, she knew the guess was correct.

Letting the door close, Oryn saw a man at the bottom of the steps. The Rose Thorne had fallen to the ground at his feet and the man's hands were seared red. The ragged thief had tried to steal the golden weapon. Gasping at his blistered hands, he hardly noticed Oryn observing. Once the vagabond looked up and saw him, his eyes bulged and he scurried off.

The Rose Thorne was glowing red hot on the dirt until Oryn picked it up. At his touch the metal became cool and he slung it onto his back, watching the man in rags run. He shook his head. Soon everyone would know of the strangers staying at the inn.

Snorting, Ulna went to him and he patted her nose. "Thank you."

As soon as the door opened behind, footsteps were coming closer. Then his nose caught Sarah's scent. Without looking, he started for the stables beside the inn.

She briskly approached and smiled. "Excuse me, sir. I can tend to your horse. She may have our best stall. Would you like me to give her grain and alfalfa, or would you rather I keep her on a stricter feeding of grass and blossoms?" As Oryn turned to her, Sarah saw his eyes and was even more captured by his presence.

The lusting look in her eye was not appealing to Oryn in the slightest. He remembered this girl. Even at a young age, she always tried to get the favor of the stronger boys in town. Now that she was giving him attention, he was not impressed, but would let her take Ulna. He gather up the two large bags of meat to carry inside. As he was about to return to the inn, Oryn struggled not to glare as she led the mare away, tossing inviting glances. She obviously wanted him to follow. Sickened by the advances, he went back inside.

At the counter, he placed the bags before Jasper.

Raising an eyebrow at the heavy load, Mistress Mabel's son asked, "What's that?"

He answered flatly. "Our payment. Almost sixty pounds of deer meat will suffice for a few days, will it not? Or have the rules for proper payment changed along with who may stay?"

Jasper grimaced apologetically. He opened the leather bags and inspected the meat. Clearing his throat, he nodded. "It will do. Sixty pounds." He counted his fingers. "That will cover five days and all meals."

Content with the trade, Oryn hefted the sword on his back and started up the stairs.

But Jasper lifted a hand and called, "I'm sorry, sir. We don't allow weapons in the rooms."

Oryn stopped to glare unblinkingly.

Jasper waved a hand to go ahead. Once he was gone, Jasper breathed a sigh of relief. He was sure his head was about to be served on a platter judging from that look. It had been a long time since he last encountered a look like that. In fact, that man seemed familiar.

Oryn watched over Adwen for the remainder of the day. She never moved. Sitting in the corner across from the bed, he allowed warm sunlight from the second window to calm him. He could feel it now. Basking in the warm rays, he understood why Adwen enjoyed it so much. The sun stroked and caressed, lending strength. Feeling the light touching the skin on his strong face and neck gave him the feeling of a caring hand, comforting lovingly.

The sun touched her too. It brought some color back to her skin and took away the deathly look. Oryn knew until she was well he would watch over her and Toth. If the Red Cult came, he would slaughter them like lambs in spring. During the previous night he learned his new body well. When the witches next showed themselves, he would make them grovel.

Hours passed and Toth knocked before entering the room. He had spent time catching up with Mistress Mabel, but Oryn earlier warned not to divulge his identity. The half-elf leaned past the threshold and announced, "We've been invited to dinner."

Thinking it over, he glanced at the waning daylight. He could afford to leave her alone for a while. He would know if danger was near.

In the dining area, everyone was present at the table.

There was Master and Mistress Mabel, Jasper and Sarah alongside him and Toth. The son gave him suspicious glances. Mistress Mabel started passing fresh buns around when he finally asked, "I'm sorry, sir, but I have yet to catch your name. As a matter of fact, none of us know who you are. What can we call you by?"

Oryn took a bun and placed it on his plate. "Call me Reynard."

Mr. Mabel raised an eyebrow and drank deeply from his cup of mead. Finished swigging, he wiped his mouth. "Do you have a surname or do you go by that animal title?" He was a complete opposite from his kind, sweet wife. Mabel was a slob. He was the town drunk and lived on his wife's excellent managing skills. She owned and ran the inn herself with a little help from the two children and a few maids. Without his wife, he would have nothing but an empty mug in his stubby, gnarled hands.

Locking eyes with him, Oryn replied, "Just Reynard."

"Well, Master Reynard," Sarah began hotly. "If you've never been to Tanoaks, I would be more than happy to show you around. I'm sure you'll find something that pleases you."

The parents were oblivious to her hinting of a venture, but Jasper rolled his eyes and took a shot at her. "I'm sure he's smart enough to find his way without getting lost, Sarah."

"I'm just trying to be helpful!"

"Stop fighting, the both of you!" Mistress Mabel commanded and they were submissive. Then she turned to Toth. "Has your friend, Mr. Reynard, heard of our tea? Pass him some, dear."

"He's heard of your famous tea, ma'am." He chuckled. "He's actually quite fond of it."

She smiled happily. "Oh! I'm sorry! I keep thinking you're foreign for some reason. You seem a bit different from the usual customer."

Oryn didn't react to the comment. He had noticed only a short while ago that some of his appearance was slightly altered. After sipping his tea, he stated, "I've not been through this place before, but the tea has reached most of where I've traveled."

For a while everyone was content to eat dinner served by

two maids. Oryn's ears caught their whispers from around the corner. Most of their banter was in regards to his appeal and a few of the comments made him choke on his food. Some of the venison was served as steaks with sauce and spices. The flavor he used to enjoy in cooked meat was nearly gone and he found himself wishing it were raw. He ate it all and complimented the whispering girls around the corner. When they realized he was aware, they fell silent and left for the kitchen.

Once he couldn't smell them any longer, he knew they had gone. At that point, Mabel downed his fifth mug and was only slightly tipsy. Meanwhile, Toth still hadn't touched a drop. Seeing the horrible man guzzling the alcohol did nothing to make the half-elf wish for drink.

Slobbering down what was left, Mabel looked over at Oryn curiously. "Where did you say you were from, Master Reynard?" He belched.

"Far from here," he answered coolly. "I've lived nowhere and everywhere in Dargadia, save for this place in the mountains."

He belched again and asked with a sideways look, "So, what kind of animal are you keeping in the room up there?"

"Melos, that's enough," Mistress Mabel snapped. "Don't insult our guests!"

"Don't be such a trusting sow, Kylie. You don't even know what that thing is and you let them bring it in! At the very least, I think we should have the right to ask what it is. So, Master Reynard, what is that thing you have using one of our beds?"

Toth watched the two closely.

Oryn chewed his food calmly and wiped his mouth with a napkin before correcting him. "She is our friend and traveling companion, Mabel."

The old slob laughed. "You mean a pet!"

The knight maintained a neutral composure. In most other circumstances he would have the man by the throat, but Adwen needed a place to stay. He sipped his tea and allowed the man to say all he wanted. Mr. Mabel reminded Oryn of how he once was before leaving the order. In a perverse way, Oryn found it entertaining.

"Tell me it's nothing like this pointy-eared half-breed."

Toth glared back as Mistress Mabel tried to tell him off. It was difficult to keep from summoning a root through the window to strangle the pig. Doing it would relieve the woman of a drain on her income, but he controlled himself and followed Oryn's lead; he let the drunk fool talk.

"This little blighter is a slippery one. I thought for sure you'd be dead by now. I guess those bounty hunters were as poor at hunting as you are at healing the sick." A maid came to fill his cup and left as he started to down it again. "So, Master Reynard, you seem like a very upstanding man. What do you say on it?"

"On what, sir?"

"These inhuman things. These people and things that can bring miracles and catastrophes. I say the lot should be either put on a leash or put down like sick animals. All of the freaks that won't follow suit should be taken to the dungeons of the order." He took another swig and continued, "Every last one of the lot that won't lend a hand or serve us. Magic shouldn't belong to them. It should belong to those who know what to do with it. So what do you think of that bit of philosophy, Master Reynard?"

All eyes fell on Oryn as he sipped the last of his tea. Setting the cup aside, he gazed at it for a few seconds before making eye contact with Mabel. "The destroying of monsters, such as werewolves and demons is for the good of the people and crucial to the survival of all." The slob smiled before Oryn continued, "As for controlling magical or inhuman beings for the better of the kingdom, the idea is asinine."

Everyone froze and stared raptly at the man with the bright green eyes. Toth was stunned.

Mabel's smile turned over on itself and he seemed caught off guard.

Oryn went on. "Inhuman beings with power and those who have magic in their blood have it only because the Light Spirits willed it so. No one can control it except the powers of that put it here. To try to force them to do our will is to strip them of their freedom. In doing so, you rob them and everyone else of the wonders that their freedom brings. A wild bird sings best in the tree, not in a man's cage. Enslaving magic brings despair, but allowing it to be will revive the land." He calmly stared at the drunk and waited.

"Asinine? Well... and I thought you were an upstanding man. My mistake." Chugging his mead, he broke eye contact.

Sunset was almost upon them. Oryn could see the darkening sky through an open window. Last he saw, two moons were due to be full before nightfall. Dinner had ended for him and he turned to his hostess, who stared back with admiration.

"Thank you for the meal, Mistress Mabel. It was delicious. Good night." He excused himself and left for the privacy of the room, astounded faces watching him go.

He reached halfway up the stairs before he felt it. The sun was setting. Ignoring the pressure and growing discomfort, he made it inside the room and closed the door tight. Adwen remained peaceful and fast asleep. He could see she still hadn't moved since he left.

Panting and unsteady, he felt more sweat gathering on his brow. His eyes glowed brighter as he staggered to the window curtains. Once the first set was drawn, he moved for the second and pain shot up his spine. He felt it shift under his skin, making him buckled over and gasp. A moment later, his back regained human shape and the agony faded. He panted from the suddenness of it, closing the second curtains.

With the view blocked, he kicked off his boots and took off his shirts, laying them on the dresser. Preparations for the evening were done so he sat gingerly in the chair to wait. Toth would come to put a privacy enchantment upon the room. His guts twisted inside and he doubled over, cradling himself. Again the pain passed and he gasped for air. The more he moved, the more his body threatened to shift. A minute went by and the door clicked open.

Toth closed it upon entering. For a while he stared at Oryn as he shook and sweated. What the knight had said at the table bothered him. Never did he think Oryn would say those things in this lifetime. He watched another wave of pain wash over him and asked, "What made you say those words? Did you mean them?"

Shuddering, he strained to speak. "I said them, so what do you think?" Pain wracked him and he shuddered harder, clenching his teeth.

"I believe you would like to think you know how to be what you are." He frowned. "But you've only just left the world of humanity behind. How could you understand the things you said?" Closing his eyes, he held a hand to the wall and performed an elf prayer. Finished, he opened them again to search him with his good eye as his blind one mimicked the movements.

Oryn cringed again and gasped for air.

"You understand how close we came to losing her. And I'm sure you still have yet to even say your apology."

Oryn turned his head and spat, *"I have."*

The swift movement made him shift and he cried out. His skull and spine crunched excruciatingly. His face distorted into a dog-like in shape. The pink flesh on his maw twisted into a pained snarl. Eyes watered as his human groans were coupled with miserable growls. Stuck in the strained limbo for a moment, he suffered even as it quickly ended and his body reverted into its human shape. He gasped and panted more, sweat running down to the end of his nose.

"When?"

Oryn tried to catch his breath and swallowed to clear his throat. Hair hung down in his face, drenched with sweat. "Hours before the treaties were taken. I went for more wood for the fire." The aching in his head was blinding.

Toth stood stunned in silence. Adwen was right. All of the while he hadn't even noticed the massive changes in Oryn. It was astonishing. The difference from who he had been only weeks ago was hardly recognizable.

Shivering and bracing his sides, Oryn glanced over at the quiet half-elf. "So, where is your pity now?"

"What?"

Resisting his body's need to cringe, he managed to say, "You said that when my judgment was upon me, you would pity me then." He swallowed and narrowed his eyes at his friend. "So where is it now?" Oryn's body was in terrible pain, but he strained to maintain his glare.

Toth said nothing. The last few days he had shown him none. Knowing what kind of creature Oryn had become, he felt guilt. Without answering, he dropped his gaze and left.

Oryn scowled at the closed door and then his eyes rolled back as more agony washed over him. Finally, he collapsed and fell forward onto the hard floor, making him moan and whine in a mixture of human and animal sounds. Outside he could feel the sun setting. Once it did, all he felt was anguish.

Claws sprouted and his head elongated. He screamed and vainly gripped his chest, feeling ribs stretching and splitting. Muscles swelled and fur rushed over him like a carpet of chocolate brown. As it finished, he cringed with every fur strand bristled. Quaking and baring his fangs, he growled and breathed, feeling the pain starting to subside. When the pain was gone his sore body slumped.

Oryn lay on the floor a while, staring at the far wall, glad it was over. His fur smoothed and ears didn't flatten to his head as tightly. He took his time, allowing his shocked body to recover.

Then Oryn abruptly froze when he heard a soft sound. The ears on his head pricked and he heard it: a light sob. Turning his muzzle to the bed, he listened. The sound came again and he knew Adwen was awake. He very much wanted to see her condition and made himself turn over. The claws on his hands and padded feet clacked on the wood. He knelt at the bedside and saw her black lips tremble as she made another weak sob.

Ears back, he whined, "Do you hurt?"

She looked at him. A few more tears fell from brilliant golden eyes. They looked like royal coins melted down. As she stared, her look became more pained and they glowed dimly in the candle light. She shook her head with what little strength she had.

"I'm so sorry. I'm so sorry."

"What for?"

"Everything. I've taken everything from you. Because of me, you know only pain. In a single night I took away any chance for you to return to the life you knew." She sobbed again. "How could you ever forgive me?"

His expression was resolute as he gave a gentle rumble. "There's nothing to forgive."

She stared in confusion.

"You are the reason I still breathe. There is nothing to forgive."

"I said the one thing that kept you from destroying yourself." She murmured through more tears, "You would have ended it and not had to endure this otherwise."

With determination, he growled. "That was my choice. Do you even know what the phrase means to a knight?"

Shaking her head, she listened.

"Those were the words Darien used to address his knights. It is a call for each knight to lay down everything in order to preserve what is greater than themselves. To refuse would have been a disgrace to all I've ever believed. It was my choice and you kept me from making a terrible mistake."

Her look became stern and questioning. "I've taken everything from you by saving your life with my fangs. You will be shunned and hunted by the men you used to call brother. Now you are an outcast, a pariah in your own land. There will be prejudice and hate for you everywhere you go. Can you forgive me even for that?" She stared, awaiting his answer.

What she said sunk in and Oryn became somber. He knew all too well it was true.

Not blinking, he growled. "Yes."

Shock widened her eyes as the answer tugged at her heart and more tears swelled. Oryn's forgiveness lifted a heavy weight.

"Thank you. Thank you, Oryn." She took a deep, shuddering sigh.

"You're not she, are you?" He stared sharply with ears raised.

A confused look came over her. Then a look of fear filled her as she stared. The gold color shined brighter as she shook her head. "Don't you breathe a word; not to anyone. Especially not to her."

"Why?" he growled, suspicious as his tail flicked.

The fear in her grew. "She's not ready yet."

They both heard the door open and he looked up in surprise. Toth returned with a cloth-covered tray and set it on the dresser by his shirts. As he went to close the door after himself, Oryn took the chance to see if the golden eyed being would answer more questions. She appeared to be asleep and he studied her closely.

Toth asked, "Is she close to waking yet?"

Oryn looked and saw her staring at Toth's back by the window. She then stared at him, worried.

After thinking it over, he growled. "No. I thought I heard her speak in her sleep. It was nothing."

She smiled thankfully before slipping away into Adwen's subconscious.

Oryn finally got up and went to his chair. Seating himself, he saw the covered platter. "What is that?"

Becoming sheepish, Toth answered. "That? Well, it's a little of the pity I owe you. You probably wanted that earlier, so I thought I'd bring it up."

Removing the cloth, there was a ten pound cut of raw venison. Giving his kind friend a questioning glance, he took up the platter and started to eat. The half-elf bid him good night and left for his old sleeping quarters down the hall.

He finished the serving and was thankful his friend had found a way to forgive him. Then his thoughts darted back to the being who had spoken so many times through Adwen. For hours he watched, hoping the Golden Eyes would return. There was more he wanted to know. For the rest of the night and unto dawn, Adwen remained still, peaceful and silent.

Chapter 42
THE GOLDEN EYES

Fog drifted into the valley overnight. A soft glow came over the mountains, reaching lazily, turning night into day. Hours ago the moons set, the air began to warm and the clouds lifted from the streets.

Oryn was wide awake. He stayed up the entire night waiting vainly for Golden Eyes to return. With the moons gone, his human body was enhanced a little further. During their travels his skin was pale. Now his complexion was brighter. No more dark circles were beneath his eyes and his musculature was more defined.

As he went out for fresh air, Sarah couldn't help but notice the strength of his walk. The door closed behind him and she sighed deeply.

The grass was moist from the mist that just departed. Many human smells wafted to him as well as those of dogs and their markings. A smile curled the side of his mouth. Hopefully he wouldn't share the same nasty habit. Oryn gave a dry laugh and watched Tanoaks come to life as first light touched the rooftops. It was beautiful and wonderfully familiar. He could pick out the old market where he and other children once begged for sweets.

Even if he wished to stay, he would not be able. It was too risky for inhuman beings to live so close to the Hall of the Master Knights. When Adwen was better, they would go far from here and seek out the king and Castle Gailarien. The treaties needed to be delivered.

The wind changed and blew at his back. Jasper's scent reached him and Oryn became tense. The man who was once a playmate came to stand just behind, watching and unaware he was expected.

Jasper cleared his throat to be sure he was noticed.

"Master Reynard, might I have a word?"

Oryn thought it over. "What do you wish to speak with me about? Business? Or something that is none of yours?"

He could tell Oryn was still very cross. Bravely joining his side, Jasper tried to look him in the eye as he gazed down the hill. "For yesterday, I want to settle things. I was a cruel-hearted fool to you and your friend. Forgive me if you can. We have had a bad streak of customers. I thought you and she could be more trouble for my mother to endure."

At last, Oryn turned to glare. "Save your apology for her when she awakes." He went back to enjoying the view.

Staring long and hard at the vaguely familiar traveler, Jasper mustered the gumption to ask a few questions. "Are you certain you were never around here as a child?"

"I'm quite sure."

Jasper watched the way he admired the town. "I'm sorry. You just remind me of an old friend I used to have."

To go along and seem inconspicuous, he asked, "Did the child have a name?"

"Yes." He observed his reactions closely. "He was called Oryn; Oryn Conrad. When he was young he was taken off to become a knight."

"I've heard the rumors along with the name."

Jasper sighed. Perhaps he was mistaken after all. "When we got word he was missing, we were very worried."

Continuing to gaze vacantly at the homes, he listened.

"He was my favorite friend, aside from his brother." Jasper chuckled at a memory. "He was such a clown that one, but Oryn was not so much the jester. He had this look. If he gave it to you, you could feel the hairs on your neck stand on end. That boy had eyes like a dragon.

Then he became somber. "But his brother is dead and everyone believes he is as well. If you could have seen the town when they got word he'd vanished. Everyone seemed to be mourning. Not a soul has spoken of his exploits in so long all the town's people and travelers lost hope."

Oryn hid his guilt.

"Do you think it's possible he could still be alive, sir?"

"How long has he been missing?"

"More than a year has passed since rumors from Deleon

reached here."

Growing stern, Oryn stated with finality, "Then your friend is dead." Turning for the inn, he gave a harsh glance. "Move on."

The spark of anger caused Oryn's eyes to flash bright at Jasper before he stalked up the hill.

It caught Jasper by surprise and he called after him. "I have one more question, sir."

Oryn ignored him and kept walking.

"My friend had a middle name; it was Reynard. Would you say it's merely a coincidence, Mr. Reynard, that you both share a name and the same sharp, green-eyed stare?"

This time he gave pause and snapped angrily, "Yes." Then he continued, leaving his boyhood friend standing alone.

Oryn did not go directly inside. Instead, he went around back to the stables. Upon entering, horses leaned out to see the visitor, sniffing as he went to visit Ulna in the far stall.

She nickered happily. "Hello and good morning, youngling!"

A little surprised to understand her without being changed, he paused before rubbing her nose. "Good morning."

"How is she? Is she faring well?"

"Better." He sighed. "She is better." He stopped stroking her coat and ran fingers through his own hair. It calmed him as he rolled his eyes. Jasper was already on to him. Then he cursed himself for not picking a less noticeable name, but there was no sense worrying. It was too late. He bid goodbye and left as the other beasts bantered about his strange scent.

Returning to the inn, he found Jasper behind the counter speaking with his mother. Oryn closed the door and they saw him headed for the stairs.

Mistress Mabel called to him. "Oh, wait, Master Reynard."

He stopped to listen after throwing a threatening glance at her son.

"Would you like some breakfast? When the maids finish tending to your friend's room they can make the most delicious eggs and lamb you've ever had."

His eyes flashed. That was the meal he used to always ask for as a boy. "No, but I appreciate the offer. I'm not hungry at the moment, Mistress Mabel."

She nodded and smiled. "As you wish, sir. Let me know when you are and there will be plenty."

When she turned to go he threw a deadly glowing glare at Jasper.

But Jasper wasn't afraid this time and smiled slyly as he continued to the second floor.

Oryn had not gotten halfway up when he detected a strong scent. He sneered when he realized it was Sarah. She was wearing perfume.

Having rummaged through the closet while he was out, she found her favorite dress. It was light blue with white bows trimming the waist and neckline. She tied back her blonde hair with a white ribbon and her soft lips were painted red. She saw him going to the room and tittered as he gripped the knob.

"Oh! Master Reynard! I --" she began, and the door closed on her in the blink of an eye as he slipped inside.

Before he entered, two maids were inspecting the odd woman with silver and gold hair. Adwen looked so strange to them. They were curious about her wound. One lifted the blankets to have a peek and both gasped at the black gouges through the burned hole in her gown.

That was when Oryn's inhuman speed let him move inside and shut the door faster than they could react. They heard the door close and one maid squeaked. The other put both hands to her mouth while her friend quickly dropped the blankets. Together they stood stark still, staring at him in surprise.

He never said a word. Hand still gripping the knob, he and the women stared for a long while. Then he scowled and gently opened the door for them to leave. The young maids tiptoed around the bed. As they passed under his deadly gaze, they ducked their heads and scurried faster to escape his sight. In the hall they heard the door close and sighed with relief.

Sarah waited with hands on her hips. "Well? Did you find out anything useful?"

The first maid giggled. "Well, we know why he's resisting your charm so easily."

"He's watching over a beautiful woman in there." The second explained. "She's horribly injured and her face is as sweet as an angel's."

The first maid scoffed. "And she apparently doesn't need

to put on a dress and so much makeup to have Master Reynard's favor." They both laughed and abruptly stopped when Sarah seethed and stormed off.

Jasper sat at the counter organizing a stack of orders for tea when she came stomping down, ranting. "You didn't tell me there was a woman with him!"

He tapped the edges on the table to even out the stack, shaking his head. "You never asked. And maybe if you paid attention last night when he said the creature in the room was a *she*, instead of trying to glance under the table to judge his boot size, you might have heard him." Again, he tapped the paper edges.

"You let me make a fool of myself!"

"No, I warned you not to try him. You made yourself look like a fool all on your own, Sister."

Even more enraged, she trudged to the other room. "Useless lout!"

When she was out of earshot he sighed. "What a tart." Finished, Jasper set the orders aside and looked up the stairs, smiling to himself. "At least you still have good sense and even better taste."

Now that the bothersome wenches were gone, Oryn sat heavily in the chair and groaned. The maids would talk. He could scare them into being quiet, but there would be even more trouble. Sunlight spilled in through the windows, casting on Adwen's face. She was safe. He would do whatever it took to keep it that way.

The door opened and the draft carried Toth's scent. Oryn relaxed, waiting for him to speak first.

His friend came to stand beside him and leaned against the dresser, sighing loudly. "It is so good to be home. Don't you think?"

An abashed expression came to Oryn's face. He looked up at Toth to see he was smiling. After giving a disgusted huff, Oryn stared out the window.

Toth chuckled. "You look stronger already. Do you think Sarah might have noticed?"

Rolling his eyes, Oryn grumbled. "I'm fairly sure she has,

Toth."

"So shall I tell her you're available?" Oryn quickly turned around in horror and he reassured him. "Don't worry. I wouldn't tell her. She's been aggressive in her advances?"

He groaned. "Excessively."

Toth laughed at his friend's expense.

"And Jasper is on to me. The maids were here a while ago having a peek at her."

"They are nosy things. If you're worried about Jasper's telling, don't be. He's not so much the fool as he seems."

"What of the maids?"

"Now, they could pose a problem. They flap their jaws about everything wherever they go."

Oryn shook his head.

"Would you like to visit the town? I'm going to market with Mistress Mabel."

"I'd rather not. Perhaps a another time, but today has been unpleasant." Then he glanced toward the bed. "She needs watching. Remaining here is more to my liking."

"Suit yourself. I'll bring up some food later, the way you prefer it lately."

Once again the door closed and he felt relief. The smells within the confines were soft and tolerable compared to other spaces. The best scent belonged to Adwen. He breathed in deeply. It was intoxicating. He took the chair closer to sit just beside her.

She was peaceful and sweet to look at. She appeared content. Toth's medicine seemed to do the trick in sparking the healing process. Of all the women he had known, she was the only one who turned his head. It was something more than her looks. She enchanted him without words. He could sit and stare all day if he wished.

And he did. Through the hours Oryn watched over her. Though her eyes never fluttered or opened, he waited. Sooner or later they would. Whether they were gold or violet, he would be glad. Sunset eventually filled the room with bright, warm sherbet shades. Toth returned with another covered platter of raw meat, setting it on the dresser before inspecting Adwen's progress.

The last of the green had gone. Silver blood started to

mend her strange flesh. Sunlight caught the shine and reflected off the watery, metallic substance.

As Toth covered her with soft blankets, he sighed, "You know, I was too harsh with you. Even when you kept your secrets, I did as well."

Oryn was caught off guard by the suddenness.

"I lied to her and to you as well." He leaned against the dresser. "I had told her the way I came by my powers was the desperation to save you." Shaking his head, he admitted, "That was the lie." He touched his blind eye, feeling the scar on the lid. "When you fell in the battle with the golem, I didn't know what to feel. But once the golem came for me, I only felt anger. I had had enough of not taking part in my own destiny. I learned in that moment simply hoping for the best isn't enough. Sometimes that means getting up and fighting back."

Toth's fists clenched at his sides. "I was helpless when Laura Mabel fell ill for the last time. It was so much like watching Adwen; it was just like when she was dying. The way I treated you in the hills was not right. I am sorry, my friend."

Oryn said nothing. He understood.

"Well," the half-elf scoffed. "My confession is done. I thank you for hearing it." Rubbing the back of his head, he gave a sidelong smile. "Sarah asked about you and seemed put out. She seems to think you are taken with Adwen."

Oryn shook his head at the floor.

"I told her she was being a loon. You, being taken with Adwen?" Toth could not restrain a chuckle. "Good night, my friend." And he went out, still chuckling at the idea of Oryn's loving the girl asleep in the bed.

When the door shut, the knight turned his attention to her. Was he really smitten with Adwen? Lacking any previous experience for comparison, he could not know for sure. The turmoil of his epiphany was interrupted by knocking. Toth's enchantment upon the room allowed the one sound to get through.

He found a maid. She curtsied, looking apprehensive with two candles in her hands. "Would you like a light for your room, sir?"

For a second he studied her. She was shy over the snooping she'd done earlier. He could smell the guilt and nodded.

"Yes, thank you."

Oryn took one and she curtsied again before scurrying away. His intense gaze still frightened her. He stole a short look up and down the hall for watchers. It was a habit that had yet to serve him wrong. Done looking, he went back into the darkening room.

Tonight there would only be one full moon. He knew for sure as he closed the curtains. It took a moment to remove his boots and shirts. He folded and set them beside the candle on the dresser. Light reflected off of the clear glass mirror, filling the room. White walls were spotless, spreading the brightness further. The flame danced on the wick like a wild child in orange and gold.

Finished staring at the candle, Oryn studied his reflection. His face was his own, but stronger. It was like looking at a very human shaped beast. As always, there was no facial hair aside from his eyebrows. Few knights had ever lost enough sense to gouge him for the fact that he could not grow any. No matter how much better at sword fighting and slaying he was, he found himself envying them sometimes. If not for his strength and skills in combat, he surely would have had a past of abuse such as Adwen described hers. He could comprehend not fitting in; Oryn never had and neither had his brother.

A grimace formed in the reflection as he thought on bittersweet memories. He opened his mouth and paused. With a finger he pulled back a lip to see better. Sure enough, his canine teeth were longer, the beginnings of carnivorous incisors. Eventually they would be as long and sharp as Adwen's. The sight unnerved him and he closed his mouth. He saw his eyes begin to glow. The pressure rose inside him and his reflection altered in the mirror. A silhouette of his beastly form appeared in the glass, yet he hadn't changed. He tried to make his eyes stop glowing, but they only flickered. As they did, his reflection flickered.

He smiled wryly at the hound face and it made a similar expression. Perhaps during the day he could play with his reflection a bit more. Then he realized his eyes could shine unintentionally. This could give him away if he was careless. After toying with the glow a little longer, he was interrupted by a full moon. Buckling over, he was careful not to overturn the candle.

He let his body drop to its knees and felt the fur spreading. Crying out, he discovered that urging it on spared him of the worst of the pain. Aggressive shouting turned to viscous snarls. Welcoming the changes lessened the time to endure as well. It was tolerable to a point and he found he could even cope with his spine growing. That had always been the worst, but now it was dulled. A minute passed and he was fully transformed. Claws gripping the dresser, he panted, feeling a sense of accomplishment.

"It's getting easier, isn't it?"

"Yes. A little." A growl escaped him as he forced his long legs to stand. Oryn went to kneel at the bedside and meet with the Golden Eyes again. She seemed stronger, but tired.

"Good. It will keep getting easier if you are willing to face it." The golden eyes smiled. "You were waiting for me all day, weren't you?"

His ears perked as he nodded and growled. "I had to guard you. There are too many fools running about. Fools can only bring trouble and I needed to deter two maids from examining you further."

"Maids? What were they doing?"

Oryn snarled viciously. "They were looking you over and poking their noses into things that don't concern them." Then he growled and his tail flicked. "But they find me frightening enough even in the day to stay out."

Her laugh made his tail stop flicking, and instead it wagged. It annoyed him, but Oryn found the will to ignore the expressive thing.

"They haven't done any harm. Let them be. I think you are afraid of their spreading word about my being here. Do not worry. This body will heal before they can cause trouble."

Oryn was glad she resurfaced. "You've been showing yourself much of the time. I've seen you as a flash in her eyes."

The golden eyes smiled. "So you've been wise to me for a while. What you've seen is my giving discreet guidance. When I do, she believes the ideas she suddenly has are her own. She never knows I am protecting and directing her actions."

He did not know if he liked the idea of a being manipulating Adwen. "If you are guiding her, then why take control like this?"

She saddened. "Sometimes there is no alternative. When she needs specific direction I cannot give it. My assistance comes as epiphanies. That takes time and is not always accurate. For the proper words at the proper time, I have no choice but to take hold. I try not to come in at a time where she would notice a lapse in her thoughts."

Oryn growled suspiciously. "She can't recall anything you do when you take control?" His tail stopped wagging.

The being explained. "She recalls my actions the same as a passing dream. Adwen could not recall how she came to be hanging from the cliff at the Crescent Remains, but eventually recalled biting through your armor before I lost my hold. Anything can trigger a recalling of my actions. When she touched you while you were in pain, it came to her and she knew she had bitten you."

He growled in frustration. "Be direct. Did she or did you mark me?"

After a moment of thinking, she answered, "We were forced. The two of us share this body while I reside in her subconscious, for now. A magic came over this body and I had the presence of mind when it occurred. I was present when these fangs took hold, but it was she after you were bitten who refused to let you fall. Because of the demon metal I was weakened and forced back. A power took control, making this body catch you before you fell too far to be saved."

Oryn huffed. "Then it was neither of you. It wasn't your fault."

She thought about it and gave a wry laugh. "I guess not. I still felt responsible." The light in her eyes dimmed. "I am still weak. I need rest."

"I have more to ask. Wait a little longer."

She shook her head as the gold color continued to fade. "I will be back tomorrow." A sweet smile curled black lips. "I wish I could stay longer, but I don't have a choice."

Adwen remained asleep and the golden eyes was gone again, but he would wait. Oryn was far too curious as to who this mysterious being was. To pass the time he would also sleep, but before he did, he would have the delicious smelling venison.

Toth shook Oryn's bare shoulder roughly. "Wake up, friend. It's nearly noon! Come down and see the town with me. There is so much more to do than just sit. Leave the sleeping to Adwen. She's much better at it than you."

As Oryn rested in the chair, arms folded over bare chest, sunlight entered by the window, making it cozy. When Toth took his hand back he finally opened one eye and warned, "If I do move, you will not be happy at the fact."

"Your look scares the girls, but it doesn't work on me. Put the glare away and get dressed. When the maids come and tend to the room, I doubt you want to give them something to talk about. They may try to compete over you with Sarah."

He opened both eyes and made his glare glow. "They wouldn't dare to come inside while I'm here. I've found a few more ways to frighten them."

Chuckling, he replied, "You might be surprised by their tenacity. I've seen them pursue wanted criminals."

At that information the glow disappeared and he was shocked. Mortified and shaking his head, he donned the shirts, but left his boots aside. "I certainly hope you're joking to make me dress myself." He glowered as his head came through the top. "Has Sarah truly sunk so low?"

"No, but she has come close. If you won't come today, then promise you will visit tomorrow. You won't regret it." Toth disappeared again.

The sleep had been good up until it was interrupted. There was a dream, but it was gone. It didn't matter. He could always have another while waiting for Golden Eyes to wake and speak again. Noon would pass into the afternoon. Then the dusk would bring night.

When the maids came, they avoided locking eyes with him and wasted no time in doing their jobs. They didn't dare inspect Adwen. He stared, invoking a feeling of unwelcome and it worked. They were glad to be clear of his sight. He smiled to himself. His way with intimidating had not dulled since leaving the order.

Afterwards, he returned to a deep sleep with a little help from the comforting sun. It felt better with the light on his bare skin, but he didn't bother to remove the shirts. Laying his head back, he let bright sunlight fall on his neck as bangs fell away from his face. For hours, his head was filled with dreams, the usual adventures filled with battles and danger. To him these were sweet dreams. As he slept, his right hand twitched whenever he thought of swinging his sword and he growled.

The next he awoke it was to a knock at the door. His head snapped back up and he blinked blearily as the wild dream faded. Getting to his feet in the dark, he saw it was sunset. When he opened the door Sarah was standing at the threshold, carrying a candle and looking reserved for a change.

Oryn stared her down. "Yes?"

Clearing her throat, she murmured, "Master Reynard."

He watched as she paused and had difficulty finding the words.

"I feel like a silly little girl. And I -- you have to be by far the most handsome man to have ever entered this inn." She blushed as Oryn looked down and shook his head. "So, if you don't have feelings for me, I want to say I'm sorry, but I have them for you."

His hand came up, instructing her to be silent and she stopped. He wore a stern expression as he looked at her. Being as clear as possible, he stated, "I am not what you are looking for."

Sarah felt a little hurt. "So, you love her then? The girl?"

Oryn's hard expression remained. Then he glanced at the mirror on the wall behind her. He grimaced as the idea came and he studied Sarah's questioning brown eyes. For as flighty as she was, when they were children she had been a kind friend. His mind was made up so he gestured to the mirror with a nod.

When she first looked and a moment passed, she was confused. Sarah stared at their reflections and saw his eyes brighten. Then his image in the glass changed and she locked eyes with the hound. Gasping, she recoiled from the mirror and turned to stare while his eyes glowed at her.

He let the light die as he continued to stare harshly.

Frightened and understanding why he felt nothing for her, she shuddered. Apologetic, Sarah gently held out the candle. Her hand shook like a leaf and she flinch when he reached to receive it. He paused and she found the nerve to put it into his grasp. Tossing another frightened look, she averted her gaze to the floor, departing for the night.

When she was gone Oryn felt a twinge of guilt and frowned at his human reflection across the hall. That wasn't his real face, he thought as he made his eyes glow. The hound guise overlapped his own. His true identity was the vengeful beast. Thoroughly disgusted, he retreated into the room.

Oryn set he candle aside, about to remove his shirts. But stopped when he heard her speak.

"There's no need. Can't you smell that?"

The air smelled different. Pulling back the curtain, the sky was starless and black while water streaked the glass.

"It is raining?"

Then there was a big sigh. "I love that smell. How did you make her leave?"

Oryn went to stand at the bedside, looking dismal. "I showed her my face."

Her voice was sympathetic. "She will be fine, but you? You were hurt by doing that, weren't you?"

His eyes locked with hers and he said with certainty, "It had to be done."

The Golden Eyes made Adwen's body sit up. It was painful, but she rested back comfortably against the pillow and headboard. Then she gestured for him to sit on the bedside.

"Do you have feelings for the girl?"

Sitting at last, Oryn gave a disgruntled look. "Not in the slightest. I have some loyalty to her as a past friend, but she has never had a concept of the term. Sarah flits from man to man like an insect among flowers."

She laughed. "A lot of girls are like that."

He quietly agreed and couldn't help but think how she was not the same.

"You were dreaming earlier. I saw your hand moving in your sleep. Were they pleasant dreams?"

He was embarrassed, realizing she had been awake for a while. "Pleasant enough for my liking."

"Can you remember the dream fully?" She watched him shake his head. "That is how Adwen knows me. There is a faint remembrance, while everything else is veiled by a curtain.

In time she will learn of me. Will you help her if she begins to notice too soon?"

It wasn't even a question. "The best that I can. What could I say if she grows anxious of not knowing her own actions?"

"Tell her enough so she knows there is no need to fear. But do not let her know too much. Do not tell her you and I have this vow of silence. If she found out she would lose all confidence in my actions as well as your loyalty."

He nodded in acceptance of the task.

"Good. Thank you."

Oryn was curious. "Why did Adwen return from the dead? How did she manage the impossible and escape the land of the passed on?"

She stared and was amused. Laughing softly, she blushed. "You flatter me. You think she came back of her own accord? It is, as you said, impossible to escape the place for the passed on. No living soul may pass go there and return without the blessing of the Light Spirits. They chose her and brought her back, but it was I who called her."

He was filled with a sense of uncertainty when his greatest question came to the tip of his tongue. Oryn had thought to ask the night before, but never got the chance.

"Who are you? Why are you here, Golden Eyes?"

The expression she wore changed gradually to one of wonder. The golden eyed being smiled sweetly and sat up to lean in close, searching his eyes. It was as if she were looking for something lost inside them.

He sat rigid as her face came up to his, feeling her gentle breaths on his skin. They bored into his and he could feel her peering into his being. As the glow intensified, she searched his soul and looked as if the things she saw were pleasing. Staring back, Oryn was paralyzed by her powers and could hardly breathe. She held him frozen like a statue. Then she cocked her head, smiling. Whatever she was looking for, she had found it. Leaning in closer to his ear, she whispered.

"You already know who I am."

And then her lips gently locked with his. His heart felt as if it might break from the feeling of longing as she kissed him. Her paralysis over him had gone, but the breath was trapped in his lungs. Oryn couldn't move as his heart pounded madly.

After a few moments that felt like a wonderful forever, she let him go. Surging emotions made his green eyes shine bright while he stared in shock. He could not deserve to touch with her this way. What had she seen?

Golden Eyes gently settled back under the covers and laid on the pillow. Her eyes flashed sweetly before turning violet and closing.

At long last Oryn let his breath go. Astonishment was replaced by disbelief. Then he saw that Adwen, who had been unconscious through each meeting with Golden Eyes, smiled in her sleep. He knew somehow she sensed what just happened. Adwen thought she was only having a strange dream.

Chapter 43
BROTHERS IN ARMS

Oryn finished the last sip at the bottom of his cup. Red Lily tea was always soothing and he turned to the man working the counter. "I'd like another. I'll take two spoons this time."

The quiet bartender of the Windy Mill Tavern was glad to oblige. He poured another, added the sugar and slid it over the polished countertop. He smiled at the stranger. "Keep your coin. That one's free to yah. The tea is cheaper here."

He borrowed a few coins from Toth. Adwen's medicine was free of charge thanks to Mistress Mabel. Blowing lightly on the hot brew, he marveled at the beauty of his old home town. Over the years Tanoaks grew in both size and vibrance.

The tavern was once such example with its clean tables, cheery maids and sharp, quick-handed bartender. While he poured drinks and took orders, he was still observant enough to know Oryn was no ordinary customer.

He was far too preoccupied with memories of the past night. The kiss she gave him haunted his every thought. As much as he had wanted to hold her, he frayed at the seams now because he could not possibly have her. She was Darien's heir. He would not allow any man to try either.

As he brooded, the bartender saw new customers coming in for drinks and turned to warn him, "Put your hood up, friend. Be invisible if you can or it might be your head."

Thinking fast, Oryn donned the hood to conceal most of his features. He did not understand why until the door opened. Four men laughed loudly as they entered and the smell of sweat and metal struck his sinuses. It was so potent Oryn wouldn't have missed it even if he were outside in pouring rain. They seated themselves by a window where the sun spilled inside.

He knew they were knights, but confirmed the theory by

furtively glanced at the mirror over the counter. Right away, Oryn ducked his head down. If he watched for too long at least one would take notice.

A knight turned and called out. "Ah, bartender! Four beers and a small snack of bread and cheese. There's a good man, thank you!"

Oryn recognized that voice. It was none other than Sir Peregrine. He was the most boisterous, outspoken knight in the Order and Oryn would have to dip his own head in boiling oil if he failed to recognize that guffaw.

The bartender left him alone to tend to the knight's order.

"Now this is a lovely place!" Sir Peregrine nodded. "Perhaps if I live to a ripe old age I'll settle down here."

Another equally recognizable voice answered. Brack's tone was sarcastic.

"I'm calling your bluff. As if Sir Peregrine would quit killing beasts to be an old codger in some cozy town, where he would waste away, wishing he could do what he's already doing now."

Oryn was further discouraged from using the glass. If Brack even got a glimpse, he was certain to be recognized.

An unfamiliar knight asked, "What about what we came to discuss?"

"In a moment, Mace. Don't be in such a rush for business when there is no urgency." Brack assured, "Our assignment isn't going anywhere."

"So the old drunk says," Sir Peregrine scoffed as the drinks and food were served by a maid. "Thank you, missy and here you go." He gave two gold coins as a patronage. "The creature has only been a rumor. It's been spread to every town since just before the princess' disappearance. There was no way to know if the Tame One even existed. Until we ran into that old man, we had no reason to suspect." He took a deep swig from a mug. "Now that we've been asked for the creature's removal and judgment, we have no choice but to look into things."

Oryn's eyes flashed with surprise.

The fourth knight sounded anxious. "I heard the Tame One is a hound with violet eyes, a great wolf creature more dangerous than a pack of werewolves on a four-full moon night."

Sir Peregrine was dismissive. "Violet eyes, blue, green, and black; no matter the color of the beast's eyes. If it exists and it is here then it shall be judged tonight."

Oryn hid clenched fists while they discussed further.

Brack sighed. "I said it once and I'll say it again: I wish we had Sir Oryn with us."

His balled fists relaxed as he listened.

Sir Peregrine slammed a hand on the table and snapped. "That's enough of that! You do this every time. He is gone, man! Let our old friend lie in peace wherever his corpse happens to be. It's been more than a year! If he were still living he would have returned long ago. Sir Oryn would never abandon his brothers in arms!"

A sick feeling started to grow in Oryn's stomach.

Mace chuckled. "Do you recall the masquerade? He ran after that girl."

Both superiors grew angry and Sir Peregrine warned the lesser knight. "Our brother wouldn't leave us for some girl. Brack and I know him better. He was dedicated to his pledge of loyalty to the order. If you had been with him for a single quest, you would know. So mind your tongue when you speak of the dead."

Then Brack shook his head. "I still cannot believe it. I would much rather think he is breathing yet. He's here in Dargadia somewhere, fighting where we cannot see his assistance."

"Brack, you dumb fool. If he were living and not hiding we would have found him by now. So I ask you this: what would he have to hide?" Glaring, he lowered his voice. "I would much rather think him dead than the alternative. And I am not referring to running off with a woman."

The feeling at the table turned dark. If their old captain had become a monster, they hoped they would never find him. If they did they would have to slay him themselves.

Oryn knew it as well. Serving the heir or not, he was no longer human.

Sir Peregrine was not one to let a table stay silent long. "Enough of this dreary mood! Everyone drink what you have and be ready to welcome our *living* brothers. They will arrive in a few hours time." He laughed out loud. "I would fancy if the beast tried to escape. It would make for a bit of sport."

With that he emptied the mug. As they all swallowed the rest, they stood to go.

Brack was last to leave, wishing his one wish. On the way to the door he noticed a man at the bar with hood drawn. For no apparent reason the figure caught his attention. Without another glance, the four left the tavern.

At the sound of the door closing, Oryn put his hood back and heaved a sigh of relief. They were coming for Adwen and he had to stop them. There would be no convincing them. She was nearly healed, but had not awoken yet.

Oryn's green eyes began to glow.

The bartender noticed along with the reflection in the mirror. Cleaning a mug with a cloth, he went to lean over the counter and whispered, "You're lucky they didn't see that."

Once Oryn saw he nearly gasped. Straight away he tried to make the light go out, but it was no use. This new shine to his eyes was permanent along with the strange reflection. Dropping his gaze, he felt overwhelmed. Then he looked up when the bartender spoke.

"You're the strange warrior who's staying at the inn, right?"

Oryn felt defeated at being found out.

"It was that old drunk, Mabel, who tipped them off. He was down here for a drink since his wife finally got the nerve to give him the boot."

There was too much on his mind to have a reply. He should have seen this coming.

"I've been tending to drinkers and travelers long enough to know that not every rumor deserves credit. I highly doubt Mistress Mabel would allow the Tame One to stay at her inn if it were a monster. Am I right?"

His mind was still tingling at the thought of facing his comrades. "She would never harm an innocent. It isn't in her to do such a thing."

The bartender smiled. "I thought so. These folk are too ready to be afraid. When something good does come their way, they try to destroy it or push it away at the least." Finished cleaning the mug, he stowed it in a cupboard. "Old man Mabel told the knights to come once the lights in the second story hall are put out. Supposedly there are going to be twenty or more. You'll either have to move her or fight them off. Just be careful. They've been losing a lot and are like wasps in a stirred hive, sending as many as it takes to avoid losing more."

A questioning look came over Oryn and he stared back. "Why do you help me? You know what I am and yet you help me?"

"I know already that you are a good... whatever you are." He gave a sidelong glance at the mirror. "I am not one to judge your nature, but I know by your eyes that you're a good one. Not all of us humans are going to fight you off with pitchforks and torches." He chuckled, folding the cloth in his hands.

The bartender had helped too much to not be thanked. Oryn slid two gold coins across the counter. "Thank you for your trouble." The man attempted to give them back, but he insisted and left for the door.

Birds outside splashed in a puddle on the cobbled stones until he came out and they took wing. Then he put his hood back up in case Brack or Sir Peregrine might be loitering where he least expected.

A stone fountain stood in the main square. When he was young he and his brother dunked each other's heads in it, roughhousing and causing trouble. Admiring it, he went closer to inspect a dark stone off to one side. There were still scratches on it forming his and his twin's initials. Oryn wondered what their life would have been like if that night never happened. Heaving a heavy sigh, he stood and saw something he only faintly recalled. As an adult he thought it was possibly the most wondrous structure he'd ever seen.

The temple was pearly white with high arches. Sunlight caught the pinnacle and fractured, giving it more of an awe-inspiring appearance. He could feel a presence as he went closer. At the steps, he stopped and had the odd sense that someone was watching.

"Beautiful, isn't it?"

His head turned abruptly to find the withered old lady with a white oak cane beside him. He hadn't even smelled her approach. She leaned heavily upon it and smiled at the temple.

"It's the last of its kind. What do you make of it?"

Oryn was still surprised by her sudden appearance, but nodded. "It is a good place. There is light inside."

Then she turned to smile up at him. "You're not a human, are you?" Shock and fear crossed his face and she chortled slyly. "Don't worry. I won't tell anyone."

"What do you know of this location?"

"This is the last of the three temples of light," she sighed sadly. "It is one of the great treasures of Dargadia, left by the warrior, Darien. The power he put inside keeps this land safe from shadows. How else would this town be so prosperous in spite of all the dark coming near?"

He nodded in agreement, admiring the inviting glow.

Then the old woman offered, "You may bring them here tonight."

Surprised again, he stared and wondered who she was.

Her wrinkled face beamed. "Bring them here to lead them away. There is only one condition. To preserve the power of the temple, not one drop of blood may be spilled and touch the ground."

Looking through the archway at the layout, he mused. It would make a perfect place for fending them off. Turning to thank her, he saw she'd vanished. She was nowhere in sight. When he tried to pick up her scent there was none. There was no point in searching so he turned his attention to the temple.

His leather boots padded on the cool marble. It was polished to a mirror-like surface. The abnormal dualistic reflection he cast walked upside-down beneath him. Broad columns decorated with scrolling gold and crimson braced overhead balconies. Sunlight shone through colored glass, spilling over railings. At the far end three doors led deeper into the temple.

His full attention settled on a stained glass window at the highest point. Darien's symbol was wreathed in sunshine, the golden hue casting onto him.

He pondered as he gazed upward. Why was he marked? Pulling back the left sleeve to look at the same shape, Oryn frowned. Did he have the right to serve Adwen and the powers of light? Letting the sleeve fall, he thought, why would she ever kiss him? He couldn't find a way to forgive himself, so how could anyone else? Finished sightseeing, he took one final look around and left the wondrous hall.

To elude suspicion, he made sure not to run. With the speed he was capable of the whole of Tanoaks would panic at seeing he was not one of the normal folk. On the casual stroll, he did not see any knights. So far he would catch them una-wares. He smiled to himself. They would not have the slightest idea what they were dealing with.

Looking to the horizon, there were three moons, each crescents or ellipses. There would be a single full moon to-night. Along the way he memorized possible obstacles or am-bush positions; everywhere they could hide with crossbows on the rooftops, or narrows where horses could be stowed. He had been a werewolf slayer longer than most; their tactics were his own. Perhaps, he thought, he could have a little fun and see if they were keeping up in their training.

He strode up the inn steps and crossed the porch.

Jasper was behind the counter working with papers and an ink stamp. Seeing him enter, he smiled broadly. "Well? Is everything as you remembered?"

Oryn paid the loaded question no mind and went up the stairs.

Stamping another document, Jasper chuckled to himself.

Once on the second story, Oryn studied the hall. There was a large window at the far end. Now all he needed was to brood over every detail. But as he reached for the door he paused. Sarah's scent was strong there and he frowned.

She was standing beside Adwen when he entered. She saw him and lowered her gaze back to the girl's sleeping form. Closing the door, he heard her murmur somberly.

"This is she? She's lovely."

"What are you doing here?"

For a while she didn't answer, admiring Adwen's face. Leaving the bedside, she approached. "I'm sorry. I've been a pest. I'm here to warn you. My father has betrayed you... and her."

"I know." When she was surprised, he added, "I learned in the tavern."

Worried, she pleaded. "I'm very sorry. Forgive my father. He is a drunk. I know he's quite cruel to inhuman beings. You won't harm him, will you, Master Reynard?"

His eyes flashed and went to the foot of the bed. Gripping one of the posts, he quietly warned, "If he dares to come near this room while she sleeps, perhaps. And if he were to enter..." He looked to Adwen and back. "There is little mercy I would grant him."

"I can keep him away. He won't even set foot up the stairs."

Oryn was content that she would keep her word. Sarah was good with these kinds of promises. "I need to ask a favor of you."

She eagerly replied, "What is it?"

"Let me douse the lights tonight. Do not come to the upstairs after dark. I mean to face the knights once they come."

Sarah smiled. "Of course. Good day to you, Master Reynard." She quickly curtsied and left as quiet as a mouse.

The plan was set. Adwen was peaceful in the covers and almost healed. Color returned to her face. She even looked like she might be dreaming, but there wasn't time to wonder about her thoughts.

Oryn sat in the chair facing the bright window. With the sword laid across his knees, he closed his eyes and began to use Darien's Breath. He began to meditate, focusing every thought into a perfect stream of imagery.

There would be at least twenty knights. Falling deeper into focus, every nook and corner of Tanoaks came to mind. They would hide two or three archers on the rooftops overlooking the main street. An armed ambush may come from any angle.

There was plenty of room to hide in the alley or in between the closed market stands. At the most, three to five would enter the inn while two more waited outside. That left the rest of the numbers to assemble anywhere.

For the last few hours, he meditated on the confrontation, imagining complications and thought of every countermeasure. It was possible for them overpower him with numbers, but it didn't matter. Death would be a sort of sweet relief. He then would have paid Adwen back in full.

At sunset, Toth paid a visit. He found his friend standing, staring out one of the windows in silence. Both hands were neatly folded behind his back. The half-elf could tell something was amiss. The air seemed tense. At last the half-elf spoke up.

"I heard from Mistress Mabel. You haven't had anything to eat and you've been up here all day since you returned. Are you all right?" Toth almost gasped.

When Oryn turned to face him, his eyes were glowing like Adwen's started to during their travels. Each day more of his human attributes disappeared. As Oryn stared back, Toth saw a faint luminous eclipse cross his eyes when the light struck them just right. They had permanent nocturnal sight.

Wearing his poker face, the knight replied, "I am not hungry."

Oryn's appearance was so feral. Toth didn't know how to feel. When he met Adwen she was partially through her transition. Seeing Oryn now and knowing more of him would vanish was like watching him die and be reborn at once. The thought was sobering, though Toth knew it was for the best.

"But is all well?"

Oryn blinked and the nocturnal flash crossed his eyes again. Turning back to the window, he answered coolly. "Well enough. I have a few things to ponder. This room has served its purpose in that."

More than ever, Toth pitied his friend. "Well, if you want anything, I'm just down the hall." Knowing Oryn wanted peace, he moved to leave. "Good night, friend." Toth closed the door and was gone.

The window was cracked to let in small smells. Already he had the scents of the knights. They were staking their positions in the shadows of Tanoaks. Night was upon them, but the dark was nothing. The sun set at last and he could still see.

Glancing sidelong at her, he hoped she wouldn't wake until later. She would probably try to stop him. More rest was what she needed and he was determined to give it to her. No one would dare deprive her of it while he had a say.

A dim gold light grew in the distance, steadily reaching over the mountains. In time with the rising of the full moon, his eyes brightened. His skin felt hot and he took off his shirts, tossing them down onto the chair. This time he wanted to see how much he could spur the transformation. Kicking off the boots, Oryn glared at the rising sphere. Oryn took a deep breath and released it slowly, flexing the muscles in his back.

Once the moon rose past the peaks, the transformation

began. A vicious snarl escaped him while he clenched sharpening teeth. He growled, clenching fists as claws and course fur rapidly sprouted. The pain intensified, but he roared and snarled, trying harder for the change.

Everything sped up. Muscles doubled and his head lengthened out into crushing jaws. Glaring down at the floor, he watched feet stretch and grind into huge padded paws, ankles serving as second knees. He hardly noticed when it was over. Rippling chest expanded as he took a deep breath, long tail flicking from side to side.

Again, he lifted his gaze to the window as the human bangs draped back. Knights were riding up the road. Oryn checked Adwen one more time. With the sword set across the glossy coat on his back, he departed.

The hall was quiet. His body was heavy, but his footfalls were light. Four candles were lit so he crept along, blowing them out one at a time. On each step he pricked his ears. Even if the men were told to stay away until the lights were doused, there was no assurance they would.

As he brought his muzzle to the last flame, his ear caught a sound at the stairs. He paused and slowly turned one eye to see someone peering at him. Gradually turning to glare, ears folded back. Oryn growled at Jasper, tale flicking warningly.

The sight of him didn't frighten the man. It didn't take much to realize who he really was. Jasper smiled and whispered, "So, this is why you've been hiding?"

Oryn ceased his growling and glared.

He gave a dry laugh. "Sarah said you would be out tonight. Good luck."

Watching him leave, Oryn didn't allow himself to be distracted. He kept his senses alert and huffed at the candle, darkening the Red Lily Inn for the night.

All was quiet. His ears already caught a light sound. It was not Jasper. A draft brought the smells of sweaty knights and armor. It was a filthy odor. Oryn could understand how most creatures disliked the scent never mind what it would mean.

There were three. The first had his sword drawn. Their visors were down, blocking most peripheral vision. As they passed the last stair, they approached Adwen's door.

As one reached for the knob, Oryn growled deeply.

"Don't you dare."

They didn't understand, but recognized the threat. Finally, the knights spied him in the corner by the hall window. Moonlight granting him a menacing silhouette. The other two drew their swords, creeping down the hall in a V formation.

His back was to the glass and they could not see the latch. When they were halfway to him, he flicked his tail up. It clicked and the men rushed forward as he put his weight into the panes, falling backward into the air.

Two more knights sat astride horses below when he landed upright between them. The animals reared and one unprepared knight fell from the saddle. By the time his backside hit the ground, Oryn was racing toward the streets. Wind whipped across his face, exhilarated him as he sprinted. Either he was very swift or the horses were quite slow.

Just as suspected, there were archers atop the shops. It was simple enough to evade the arrows as he darted past. One called to the others hiding ahead and a dozen knights came out into the town square. Their swords were drawn for a fight to the death.

The sight excited him more, but the square was their chosen battle arena. He had his own in mind. Snarling, he leaped and they thought he was attacking. Swords swung out while Oryn sailed clear overhead out of reach then tucked and rolled, darting into the temple.

They heard a loud challenging howl echo out.

Inside was lit by candle stands. The fluttery glow reached out across the marble short of the pillars. Shadows were everywhere. The knights heard their own footfalls echo with the clinking of armor. As they had trained, they stayed together, slowly stalking down the center of the hall.

Hiding in the shadow of a pillar, Oryn held his sword up, jaws bowed to it. Breathing in the steady rhythm, his focus was perfect. His ears caught the sound of their every move. He continued to bide his time and focus. A set of footsteps was steadily growing louder and he prepared to strike.

The first few knights to enter were instructed to fan out and search. They had not seen much of him yet and did not know what he was. A wary knight thought he saw something move behind a pillar past a long row of candles. He held his sword up and felt his heart flutter with a thrill. Preparing himself, the knight stepped into the gloom. There was nothing. It must have been his imagination.

Suddenly there was a sound of claws on stone. As the man looked up, the beast dropped from a stone perch. The knight hopped aside, but was immediately kicked in the chest plate. Encased in armor, his form skidded and screeched across stone till he crashed into the far wall. The others were instantly alerted and saw the beast swiftly approaching.

He snarled at the cluster of knights and let his body drop back, going into a skid. Once he bowled them over like pins on a lawn, he leaped back to his feet, roaring with the thunderous fury of a lion. The alarming sound rattled the air and his eyes flashed, pearly white fangs glistening. Then the knights began to recover and attack.

Easily as fighting a child, he batted the sword out of the first knight's hand. Then he kicked him away like a rodent, sending him skidding into another wall as two more came to take his place. Together they slashed and sliced before quickly being disarmed and kicked away like the first.

Oryn roared in outrage. "Pathetic!"

Another came to challenge him and he snarled. This knight was more skilled, evading the first two strikes, but his footing was poor. Oryn saw it right away. Barking angrily, he swept his feet out from beneath him. "Mind your footing, fool!" Quickly kicking him aside, he made way for two more.

They attacked from either side. Supernatural speed allowed him to block them without effort. Ringing steel filled the temple while they did their dance. Suddenly both slashed for his neck in unison. Oryn crouched low. Fast as lightning, he kicked one and then the other. Frustrated, they skidded a ways before getting up and charging from opposing sides.

Oryn saw their mistake long before they did. Twirling with his sword, he stepped aside. The two were about to strike each other dead and gasped, but there was a stroke to both of their weapons. Their swords deflected away from each other and their shoulders collided. Standing side by side, staring at the heavy-handed beast, they were in shock. It had saved them. For a while they were frozen and didn't know whether to continue.

Over their heads Oryn saw reinforcements forming up to enter and snarled. Setting the sword across his back, he turned and dashed for the doors masked in shadows.

The reinforcements saw him vanish. Ceasing their yelling at the threshold of the dark passage, they cautiously filed inside. Two by two, they entered. Only Oryn's eyes clearly in the gloom.

A lone knight brought up the rear. Once the others were preoccupied, claws reached down and snatched him up. The only sound was the knight's surprised, "Oof!"

Climbing quietly down from the rafters, Oryn set the unconscious knight by the door. The man would be fine. Silent as a ghost, he padded along a different passage his pursuers failed to see.

Empty torch brackets hung along the wall of the spiraling stair. It was very quiet. A single draft of air passed him from behind and the scent of a knight crossed his nose. He didn't react, choosing to wait for an open space. Up ahead his eyes caught a faint glow by a crack under a door. It was unlocked and opened.

The chamber was lined with a trove of jewel-encrusted treasures. Strong torches brightened the space and made the goblets and gaudy artifacts shine. As he passed through the collection, he paused for the sound of a swinging blade. Instead there was a loud thud and he whirled around.

Whoever had followed him was either clever or horribly overconfident. The knight brought down a board to brace the way closed and locked it shut. They were trapped and had few places to run. Oryn flicked his tail threateningly. As if he planned on running. Taking the sword from his back, he prepared as the knight drew his out and charged.

The first blow was easily blocked, but then Oryn got a surprise as the knight twirled and came in close for a deadly strike to his gut. He managed to block, but another came just as fast for his throat. He leaned away, and to force the man back, put his sword up, delivering a counter swing.

Oryn knew that whoever this knight was, he was skilled. The knight's identity was not discernable by fighting style. After striking the knight again, Oryn swept the ground to test his footing.

The knight quickly jumped to avoid losing his feet and attempted to retaliate, but failed. Though the knight was growing frustrated, he stayed in focus.

Soon Oryn's nose could smell his body drenched in sweat. Mead was on his breath. Both ears cocked on his head while he wondered whom he was fighting. It was not Sir Peregrine judging by his lesser knight's armor. The knight swung for him again, but was struck in the side by Oryn's claws, forcing him to turn away. While the man was temporarily stalled, Oryn snatched up the helm from his head, tossing it aside. The knight whirled and lunged.

Red in the face, Brack was enraged at being foiled.

Leaning to avoid the blow, and impressed by his friend's increased skill, he was beginning to enjoy the fight.

As retaliation for before, Brack swung low. He missed as the sword-wielding creature leaped overhead and was about to swing at his back. Turning to block, Brack tried to come in close, but the creature held him at bay, slowly forced him across the room. In desperation, he tried to duck under a strike, but failed and lost more ground.

Brack found himself cornered against a tall armoire, struggling to hold off his opponent. It was obvious that he was being toyed with. He could have been killed at the start, but even now the talented creature wouldn't finish him. Growing too tired to resist, he was about to lose.

Again he moved to block a blow, but it was a false strike. He watched as his blade swatted pathetically past. The beast's weapon tapped his cheek, distracting him. Then his sword was knocked up into the air by a swift kick. The hound caught it with his free hand. Its tail swung excitedly as it stepped closer, holding them both in a scissor to his bare throat.

Knowing he was as good as dead, he stared into the bright green eyes framed by very human bangs. Then he realized he had seen only one swordsman use this technique. He studied the beast's glowing gaze, heart pounding. His own stare grew wide. Could it be?

He asked weakly, "Oryn?"

Oryn's eyes widened and his pupils were pinpricks as he suddenly felt sick. Using Brack's sword, he impaled the knight by the cape, pinning him to the wardrobe.

The sound of the crunch made the knight give a start, but he turned again to see the hound dashing for another part of the temple. He was getting away.

Brack yelled as if he had been shot. *"No!"*

Then he fought to free himself and tore the cape in half. Freeing his sword, he ran after the beast down the stairway.

The dead end was full of more golden ornaments and chairs. Oryn could hear his old comrade bearing down on him. Backing away from the passage, he held his sword aggressively.

Brack arrived and stopped just after the door. His sword was in hand and he stood staring, speechless. The tall creature glared and snarled, gnashing fangs and looking very vicious.

Then he lunged, moving to slice his neck like a blade of grass. But to Oryn's great alarm, Brack wouldn't move. He abruptly stopped just short of his throat. The look in Oryn's eyes was one of terror, while his friend stared in awe. Still holding the edge at a threatening angle, he barked and snarled.

"Fight me!"

But Brack would not move to defend himself and smiled. He put his own sword back in its sheath. "It is you, isn't it?"

Deeply aggravated at being discovered, he lowered his weapon and roared. Turning and storming off to the far side of the room, he growled. Why had he been such a fool to give himself away?

His friend watched while a cloud covered the full moon outside. Seamlessly, the beast turned into his long-lost leader. Oryn faced him, wearing a stern and weary look.

"You shouldn't have followed me here."

In reply Brack almost laughed, overjoyed. "I knew it was you. Were you in the tavern? You were sitting at the bar, weren't you?"

He didn't answer and went to a chair. With the sword beside him, he sat heavily and looked back with an empty stare. If he told the others his life would truly be over. His glowing stare followed as he came a few steps closer.

Breathless, he asked, "Where have you been?"

"Everywhere," Oryn replied, still disappointed. "Under everyone's nose in nearly every corner of Dargadia."

"Why did you leave us behind? Were you going after the

princess?"

More ashamed, he replied, "Yes, but it was not my sole intent."

"Was it that girl?"

"That was no mere girl. She was the Tame One."

Then Brack became angry. "Did she do this to you? Did she mark you and make you... into this?"

Glancing at his own arm, Oryn frowned. "What has happened to me was merely a consequence. She saved my life for the umpteenth time. I serve her purpose now."

Wary, Brack asked, "What is her purpose?"

He raked a hand through his hair to brush it out of his face. "To unite the Kingdoms of Day."

"That's not possible. No one can."

Oryn dropped his gaze and thought a moment, before purposefully holding up the sword with his left arm. "The Tame One gave this weapon to me. It was shortly afterward when she gave me her mark. Do you recognize this or at the least the symbol on the blade?"

When Brack looked, the weapon seemed unremarkable aside from its size until he spotted the mark on the bracer. Only then did he notice the matching symbol on Oryn's forearm. The feelings of foreboding disappeared. His friend was no monster. A happy smile came to him.

"Has she treated you well?"

Glad that his friend understood the signs, he smiled and nodded.

"Is the Tame One really Darien's heir?"

Oryn's emerald eyes glowed brighter as the full moon was close to being revealed. He nodded once more. "She is. We brought her here to heal a wound dealt by the Red Cult Witches. I haven't much time. If there is another question, ask it before I cannot answer."

Brack sighed, shaking his head. "What shall I tell our brothers?"

Oryn's eyes flashed with surprise. Then he smiled weakly at the thought that his friend still saw him as a brother in arms. The pressure inside was building as he answered.

"Tell them... you saw my body consumed by a hound."

He had a brief moment to give a wry smile before the

moon reemerged. Crying out, he forced himself to stand. His holler turned to a blood-curdling roar as bones in his back crunched and stretched with the rest of him, but he kept most of the agony at bay. Going along with the transformation, he changed before his friend.

Brack was sympathetic yet envious. He proudly saluted his old general and captain.

Oryn took up the Rose Thorne and nodded as he left back the way they came.

He watched Oryn slip away. He would give him time to flee. The others would not be so merciful.

Stealthy as a mountain cat, the hound crept through the passage. Coming to the blocked door, he used brute force to break it open. When there were no sounds up the spiral stair, he was suspicious. He could smell them hiding. Upon reaching the main floor he stepped out and a sword met him.

Quickly dodging the hit, he grabbed the knight roughly by the front of his armor and snarled in his face. For such a petty attempt, the knight was thrown out into the open hall. Two more attacked in the dark, but he saw them coming first and disarmed them. Taking both their swords, Oryn stuck them into the overhead rafter. While he coolly stalked up a passage to the balconies they stayed behind, vainly trying to wrench the weapons loose.

Strolling up the steps, he growled. "Useless."

Oryn went to the second floor and was surprised to find the many of the knights. They all lunged as he came along the aisle. It confounded him that they would be so foolish. This place was narrow, but he had the advantage. While they crowded the balcony, Oryn saw his chance to escape. They left the main hall practically undefended.

He hopped onto the stone rail, fending off blades and kicking men back. A sword clipped one of his clawed feet and he snarled. Jumping was the only alternative so he turned and dropped through the air. Only then did he realize his grave mistake.

A vast dragnet waited with ropes tied to horses near the entrance. As he fell there was no escape and he howled.

Sir Peregrine stood by wearing his slayer's armor. He swung his sword and signaled the men. "Now!"

The net scooped him up as he barely touched the floor. The ropes snapped tight. Ensnared in the ropes and knots, Oryn lost the Rose Thorne and it landed with a clang while he was whisked away.

He roared and snarled as he collided with the side of the stone arch, but the horses did not stop. They kept dragging him farther into town until his battered body slammed into the side of the fountain. When they heard him groan, the remaining knights went closer. The creature was unconscious and deep, growling breaths were subtle.

While they worked to load the odd thing into a cart, the knights that faced him blade to blade recovered.

Brack came through the passage and saw the large sword lying in the middle of the hall. Alarmed, he dashed forward and knelt low to pick it up.

Another knight passing by rapped his shoulder. "Looks like you got a souvenir."

He didn't reply. Clenching the hilt, he was fearful for Oryn. The friend he only just found was captured. Brack knew what awaited, and at the hands of his own men, no less.

Chapter 44
WELCOME BACK

Night was dark in the shadow cast by the Hall of the Master Knights. The inside of the stone shaft was even darker. An hour had passed before they returned to the grand fortress. They worked to dump his body down the trapdoor. The knights watched him tumble out of sight and congratulated each other on a job well done. With that they closed the bars over the hole and shut the weather cover tight.

Oryn fell violently, slamming along the sides of the duct. Then he was expelled and dropped onto cold stone slabs. He had started to wake while they unloaded him, but now he was dazed. His head spun. There was a full moon somewhere, since he stood and saw he was still in hound form. When muddled vision focused at last, he saw the bars of the cell.

Wanting to know where he might be, he approached the torchlight. About to grip the unbendable steel rungs, he stopped cold. He froze and ears folded back while eyes widened in horror. Panic threatened to take hold. Desperately tackling the bars, he pulled and pried as hard as he could, but it was useless. He panted heavily, and when there was nothing else to do, he howled.

It was pointless, but he couldn't restrain himself. Some part of him found the urge undeniable. He was trapped. For a while he anxiously panted at the bars until he heard guffaws from around the bend. Knights entered the dungeon and fear was washed away by anger as he growled, slipping back into the shadows.

Several knights came to stand before his prison and Sir Peregrine was among them. The officer addressed a vaguely familiar knight. Oryn realized this was his replacement as captain. The man had a small black beard and medium length hair. His eyes were dark and he sneered at Sir Peregrine.

"So this is the Tame One? I thought it would have more of a stench and violet eyes like in the rumors. What losses have we suffered?"

Sir Peregrine was hesitant. The answer had been eating at him during the travel back. He glanced into the dark where he knew the thing was watching. "Sir, every man has returned alive and with little more than bruises and scrapes. No knight was harmed."

The captain glared. "You are surely joking."

Sir Peregrine was firm. "The creature killed no one. It fought using a large sword of some kind." He glanced through the bars again. "It toyed with us. The beast moved like a man and fought like a knight, Sir Jacques."

Now Oryn recognized him. It was the man he had put in his place for disrespecting a fellow knight and superior; himself. He scowled at the new captain from the far corner.

"No beast moves like a man and absolutely none can fight like a knight. Do not insult my intelligence." The captain backhanded Sir Peregrine with armored knuckles. Other knights caught him from falling.

Oryn's patience snapped and he rushed the bars, snatching the captain up by the front of his armor. Holding him high against his cage, he let loose a deafening roar into the foul man's frightened face.

A moment later the fearful expression melted into curious surprise. Then Sir Jacques was thrown into the far wall, bowling over the others with his weight. All of them stared and some had swords drawn. Only Sir Jacques remained calm as they got to their feet as the beast recoiled into hiding, green eyes still burning.

Smiling, the captain announced, "Gentlemen, we have ourselves a very interesting guest!"

Oryn snarled. The dishonorable man recognized him.

"Quite a few of you are acquainted with him!" He crowed, "We shall wait until full moon set to interrogate this thing, but first, I propose bets!"

Sir Peregrine was disgusted with the idea, massaging his jaw. "What would these bets be placed on, sir?"

"The true identity of our mysterious guest!"

In the armor room, knights stowed gear in assorted lockers. Brack carried the weapon of his friend now doomed in the dungeon. He made his way through the crowd and reached his own locker as a few of the new captain's companions approached.

They saw the sword and one laughed as he taunted.

"So are you going to polish that before ya' give it to me, old Brack?"

He knew they would try this. Gently propping the relic against the locker, he turned to face the four. A deadly glare lit in his eyes. "This thing is not for the likes of you. It isn't yours to take, the same as it is not mine to keep."

They chuckled. "Oh really?"

When they came closer, he quickly drew his sword and they gave pause.

"I said it's not for you! Keep your filthy hands off it or I'll take them for real souvenirs. This sword belongs to the warrior in the dungeons!"

They waited. The sound of gold coins being counted annoyed Oryn's sharp hearing. Only two knights did not take part. Sir Peregrine found some respect for the beast's dignity. It had spared his men, though they were intent on killing him.

And the captain already knew the answer. He smiled to himself as they continued to count gold. So far none of the guesses were correct. It wouldn't be much longer.

Inside the quiet cell Oryn leaned against the far corner, listening to the sound of his breath and the gold clinking. Almost a dozen knights gathered for the bets. A few merely wished to know who had beaten them to a pulp. They could barely make out the creature in the back with arms folded across his chest.

Oryn's head was empty and he refused to look at them. This was degrading and a disappointment to see them stoop so low. Under the new captain's charge things appeared to have fallen far. If he were still their commanding officer, he would have them whipped for placing such bets. He was harsh as a captain, but he at least allowed those due for execution what little dignity they had left.

Suddenly, Oryn felt a strange thing. The wall beside him was moving upward. Then he looked and saw that he was in fact shrinking down. Claws were retracting as fur was flowing away under skin.

The knights saw and fell silent as they saw him turn to cling to the stone wall. He tried to stay in hound form to avoid the embarrassment, but it was no use. In moments he took human shape, pressing his forehead against the cool rock. There was nowhere to hide.

One brought a torch to illuminate more of the cell as Sir Jacques went close. The knight held the torch high and the captain sneered, "Don't you think it's ironic?" He laughed as he saw his arms fall to his sides. "The last we met, you insulted me after I called you out as a dog. So why don't you turn and face the real knights, beast?"

Taking a breath and finding his nerve, he turned and walked into the light. As he did, he glowered, "You're the only beast in this dungeon, Jacques." At last the torch revealed his face. Oryn glared at their captain.

Half of the knights lost their hold of the gold in shock. They could hardly believe it was really him in the flesh. Sir Oryn had been found.

Smiling, the new captain replied, "You're the one who's in a cage, dog."

Oryn's eyes widened as he gazed past Sir Jacques.

When he turned, he found Sir Peregrine and four others bowing their heads and saluting. In retaliation, Sir Jacques punched Sir Peregrine and threw him into his friends.

Oryn sneered, "You should treat your men with more respect!"

In a rage, he rounded on him. "And what of you? What did you show these men when you ran away? Answer me that!" Oryn didn't reply and he snapped, "That's right! Nothing!"

The knights helped the officer back to his feet as blood ran from his nose. It wasn't broken as he wiped the fluids away, raptly watching and listening to every word of the conversation.

"Now, I'm sure everyone here wants to know why the great Sir Oryn Conrad decided to vanish. Why did you leave the ranks? Was it to find the princess or are the rumors true that you went to pursue a pretty girl?"

Looking away, he addressed those who had saluted. "I left for my chance at revenge."

Sir Peregrine and a few others knew what he was talking about and was sorely disappointed.

"That's nice. What a tidy lie." Sir Jacques scoffed. "Shall we begin your interrogation now and have it out of the way before dawn?" He glanced at the five behind him and added, "Your execution squad has already volunteered."

Sir Peregrine and the others were dismayed, but remained silent.

With a snide tone, Sir Jacques asked, "Now, dog, are you the Tame One?"

Oryn glared back defiantly.

"Answer the question, beast!"

After a moment of thinking, Oryn replied, "No, I am not." Ignoring the captain's expression, he turned to the others. "The girl who fled from the princess' celebration was the Tame One. She was tracking the princess' abductor. "

Sir Jacques' bellow echoed in the dank dungeon. "I'm the one asking you, animal! Look me in the eye when I speak to you! Your lying is incessant!" When Oryn faced him again, he cooled enough to ask calmly, "Where is the Tame One?"

A sly smile came over Oryn. "Out of your reach."

The cruel captain jeered. "So, your allegiance has faltered? I shall inform the elders of your corruption once your sentence is carried out. Did the thing mark you?"

The men waited with bated breath.

Oryn clenched his left hand, refusing to answer.

Straining to stay his own anger, the captain prompted, "Answer the question."

Glancing past, he replied, "To save my life... yes."

The onlookers were filled with a mixture of feelings. There was distain as well as pity. The overall reaction was sickened disgust. Oryn allowed himself to be marked and never came to face them on his own.

Curiosity spread across Jacques' face. "Show me the mark."

Oryn's eyes glowed bright when he replied, "After you've dragged my cold corpse from this cell, then you may see it."

Losing control, Jacques drew his sword and bellowed. "Show me the mark! Show us all the mark of the abomination that branded you!"

Oryn's eyes glowed brighter. "She is not what you think. She is not whom any one of you would expect. By serving her I continue to serve this order. After I am dead she will be sure to show you why."

"Where is she hiding? Where is this thing that has twisted your brain to her will?"

"You won't find her. She will find you. When she arrives, I warn you now: do not try to harm her. I did and came to learn I condemned myself by doing so. The Tame One is our ally."

The men were either appalled or confused while their captain seethed. "I grow tired of your deceit. After you're dead I shall carve the mark from your corpse, hang it on my wall and throw knives at it to pass the time."

Oryn scowled. His first judgment of Jacques was accurate. This was a terrible man; a beast through and through. With new insight he could clearly see Jacques as a true abomination.

The captain sighed. "Well, if you're not going to cooperate, then there's no point in continuing. We shall leave you to think on things. Enjoy your last few hours, Hot Head Conrad." Merry as could be, he strolled out of the dungeon with the others, leaving only five knights behind.

When they had gone there was silence while the remaining five stared. Sir Peregrine stepped forward and searched Oryn's eyes. He hardly recognized him. The look he had was eerie.

"Revenge? Did you truly leave us for that? Tell me it's not true."

The longer Oryn looked at the betrayed expression, the more he had a shrinking feeling.

"Did you find the princess?"

Unable to look at him any longer, he lowered his glowing eyes to the floor.

"You found your revenge at the least?"

Still not a word came from Oryn as he shook his head.

His accusing stare was intense. "Now I understand why you wouldn't return. Your fear of shame turned you into a coward. What a self-serving creature you are." With that, Sir Peregrine led the remaining four out.

Oryn sighed, sulking back into the dark corner of his cage. There he sat and brooded. Truly, he was a terrible thing.

Brack held off the brutes for a while, but became tired. The younger knights wore him down. Once he faltered, they tackled him and beat him relentlessly. Others stood by and no one helped. When they finished, they left him lying on the floor, coughing up blood.

Rolling over, he sat up and wheezed at the ring leader, "Don't touch that. You don't have the right."

Grabbing the Rose Thorne, the knight was completely ignorant of the symbol below the hilt. "All of that trouble for such a silly thing. It is heavy, but I think I could learn to use it. Gah!"

Brack felt justified as the metal glowed white hot and burned through the knight's gloves. Both hands were blistered and Brack smiled though it hurt his battered face.

"I warned you, fool."

The door burst open and Sir Peregrine stomped into view. When the crowd parted, he saw Brack and rushed to his side. He bellowed at the goons with blood on their fists.

"What is the meaning of this? You dare attack your superior officer! You'll all be whipped for this insolence!" Then he saw the man with the burned hands and the sword at his feet.

Coughing and wheezing, Brack moved for the weapon. The metal cooled with his touch as he pulled it close. Carefully, he held the hilt up. "This is his sword. The Tame One gave it to him."

Curious, Sir Peregrine looked at the indentation and almost gasped. When he turned to Brack for confirmation, he was smiling. Their brother was not a monster and most definitely no traitor. Now he could forgive him for not returning.

A jubilant jealousy filled him as he asked, "You're certain?"

"I've seen the mark myself. He showed it to me."

Gently taking the weapon, he held it up for the others to see. "Don't any of you fools recognize this?" They stared in silence. "This sword is the Rose Thorne! This is the first of the four weapons forged by the Master Knight! This was once the sword of the first and greatest dragon slayer, Keegan Jaeger Conrad!"

The end drew near and Oryn couldn't help but feel more shame. Even when he was one of them, he was feared and avoided. No one dared to cross him for fear of his wrath. Such is the life of a beast.

Glancing up through the long, narrow space to the open air, he could see dawn. A dim glow from a hidden horizon stretched across his small patch of sky. There was a little solace. Adwen was safe.

The sound of a key in the distant dungeon door caught his ear. Then he heard it open as several sets of boots came through. Sir Peregrine and four men filed into view, lining up along the wall opposite his cell. They carried bows and small quivers of execution arrows along with heartbroken looks.

At last Sir Jacques arrived and smirked.

"On your feet, dog. It's time to take your medicine. Get up."

He quietly got to his bare human feet on the cold rock. Stepping within decent range of the bows, a glimmer of hesitation was in their eyes. It was comforting, but he wanted them to do it. He wanted them to keep their ranks and their lives.

The captain spoke in a clear, loud voice. "Creature, you have been found guilty of crimes against human kind. For abandoning your post and forsaking your oath, you shall now be forgiven. Does the accused have any last words?"

Oryn reassured the men, "I do not begrudge you. You are Knights of the Order." With a nod, he added, "Perform your sworn duty as I have already performed mine. Strike true."

The men were touched while the captain was annoyed. Rolling his eyes, he turned to address the knights.

"Archers! Ready!"

Oryn watched them notch arrows and felt no fear.

"Aim!"

They hesitated and didn't lift their bows. Sir Peregrine faught back a tear as he stared solemnly into the cell. Oryn nodded and gave him the nerve he was searching for. Swift and perfect, he raised the bow level with his eye and the others gradually followed suit. They aimed at their marks. Sweat beaded on their brows. Two men's hands shook. It was what he wanted and an order they could not deny.

He watched them hone their aim. Oryn still hadn't found the will to forgive his own terrible mistakes with Adwen, but could let it go now. Yet one thing could still make Oryn's chest swell; it was knowing she was safe. Welcoming the end, he felt peaceful.

"Fire!"

Simultaneously, the arrows struck. The force lifted and propelled him across the cell into the wall. The knights watched in horror as his body slumped. Each arrow hit its mark, sticking out of him like pins in a cushion. Two in his lungs, two in his middle, and one through his sternum, piercing his heart.

Chapter 45
THE MARK

Adwen sat bolt upright as her heart raced. Outside the window was dawn's first light. She'd been having a strange dream and it was interrupted by a sudden horrible feeling. Putting a hand to her head in confusion, she looked around and saw two shirts on a chair with a pair of boots lying by the wall.

Her eyes flashed gold for a moment. A determined look came to her. Adwen's clothes changed back into battle garments and she threw back the sheets. She left for the hallway where there was a trace of his scent along with the leftover odors of knights. It only confirmed her terrible theory.

She rushed down the stairs to find Toth with a middle-aged woman, a young lady and a dark-haired young man. They stared as she approached and Toth looked relieved.

"We have to leave right now," Adwen informed. "They took Oryn."

Mistress Mabel gasped and put a hand to her mouth while Jasper grinned and became jubilant. "I knew it! I knew it was him!"

Then Sarah looked very distraught. "Oh my. Now I feel faint." She fanned her face, trying not to pass out.

Adwen raised an eyebrow, leaning in close to Toth to whisper. "Okay. What am I missing here?"

He shook his head. "Nothing really. He disappeared in the night and we haven't any idea what may have happened."

A dark tone was in her voice. "I know where he is."

In a few minutes Ulna was saddled. Toth wasted no time in climbing on. He beamed down at his adoptive family. "Thank you so much for letting us stay, Mistress Mabel."

The woman smiled and turned to Adwen. "I only wish we had more time. If you ever need a place to stay again, our doors are open."

"Just let me know if that drunk gives you any more trouble. I'll straighten him out for you." Giving a sly wink, she changed into her hound self.

They stepped back as the creature took a sweeping bow. Then the three smiled as her eyes shone brighter. Dropping to all fours, she bounded around the horse and barked as Ulna started to follow.

The family waved, watching the adventurers turn southward. They wished them well. When the rider and white creature finally disappeared over the rise in the earth, Jasper chuckled before following the women inside.

The five executioners lowered their bows. The Sir Peregrine was grave, staring mournfully at the crumpled body at the back of the cell.

Their captain smiled, soaking in the triumph over his predecessor. Sir Jacques was about to open the door and have the men drag out the body, but paused.

They heard a sound like a cough. Then Oryn moved and their jaws dropped.

It hurt horribly to breathe. Oryn could feel the arrows. With the two piercing his lungs, each breath was a short, raspy gasp. In spite of the sharp points in his flesh, another gasp escaped him while he fought for more air.

The knights were dumbstruck. Not once had they performed an execution and seen the target live. It was hard for the good knights to watch Oryn struggle to sit against the wall. And yet, they could not look away.

His eyes watered while he stared down at the shafts. Another wave of pain coursed through him, but it was nothing compared to anguishing transformations. With both hands found one arrow in his lungs. Gripping it tight, he gradually pulled it free. His face turned red from the strain. Only a little blood trickled from the puncture before it began to heal.

Again the knights were stunned. Their hopes were raised higher while the captain became terrified. His enemy was getting up.

Oryn could breathe better, but the other arrow was agony. Sitting higher, he gripped the shaft with one hand and pulled hard without snapping it. The sharp arrowhead scratched across bone and he cried out loud and gasped, throwing it aside. A moment later, he was breathing freely using the wall to get to his feet.

Once he found balance, he panted, prepared to continue the extraction. Both hands shook. Oryn clutched two shafts protruding from his abdomen. Gritting teeth and bracing himself, he pulled them out at once. There was an even louder scream and he dropped them to the ground with a clatter. The wounds bled no more than the others.

Sir Peregrine's arrow was through his sternum, scratching his heart. It should have killed him the instant it struck. Each beat of his heart came with a terrible stabbing.

The knights stood frozen, watching with rapt attention and bated breath.

The arrow was dead center and Oryn panted hard, trying to get the strength to take it out. He gripped the base in his shaky hands. Sweat ran down his red face while green eyes continued to water. Then he pulled and it struck the thin patch of bone. He screamed and fought against the pain to pull it free. A sensation of chipping came along with terrible pain while he pulled relentlessly. Then he cried out again and it came loose.

Oryn panted, leaning back against the cool stones, feeling relief. Allowing a moment to pass, the last of the pain vanished. He was able to relax. Then he stood and approached, staring into the frightened eyes of Sir Jacques.

When he was at the bars, he broke eye contact to examine the arrow. Judging the quality of the shaft, he found it was straight. Oryn tossed it back to Sir Peregrine.

"A fine shot. You've kept up in your training."

Grinning, he replied, "Thank you, sir."

The captain was still in shock when he turned to face him again.

Oryn frowned. "Do you still wish to see the mark of the Tame One?"

He put his left arm through the bars so his opponent could get a good look.

The wicked man's eyes widened in horror.

"You see?" Oryn smiled. "I'm more of a knight than you

could ever hope to be."

Jacques shuddered before dashing out of the dungeons with no intention of returning.

Oryn gave his loyal friends a somber glance, then turned back to his corner. Sunshine filtered down the stone skylight and he passed through the rays.

Sir Peregrine asked, "Is it true, sir? Is the Tame One the heir?"

Not stopping, he replied, "Yes, she is."

Coming to a decision, Sir Peregrine returned to his vivacious self. "Then I shall spread the word, sir. Not a single knight shall harm her. Any who disobey, I shall deliver their hands to your feet in a cheap sack."

One of the others quickly asked, "Sir, when will she arrive?"

"Soon enough." He sighed, slumping against the wall and sliding to the ground where he stayed.

"Sir, have you been to visit the other kingdoms? What is the heir like? Sir?"

Sir Peregrine shushed them. "If he doesn't answer when you first ask then he doesn't intend to. Let the general be." Without the permission of the captain or a higher authority, they had no choice but to leave the creature where he sat. He gave Oryn's shadowy form a sharp salute and departed with the others.

The dungeon was quiet while Oryn's mind was not. He returned to his routine self-abuse. By his own judging he was not worthy enough to see daylight. Adwen was awake. Despite the distance between them, he knew it somehow. He could sense it; she was on her way.

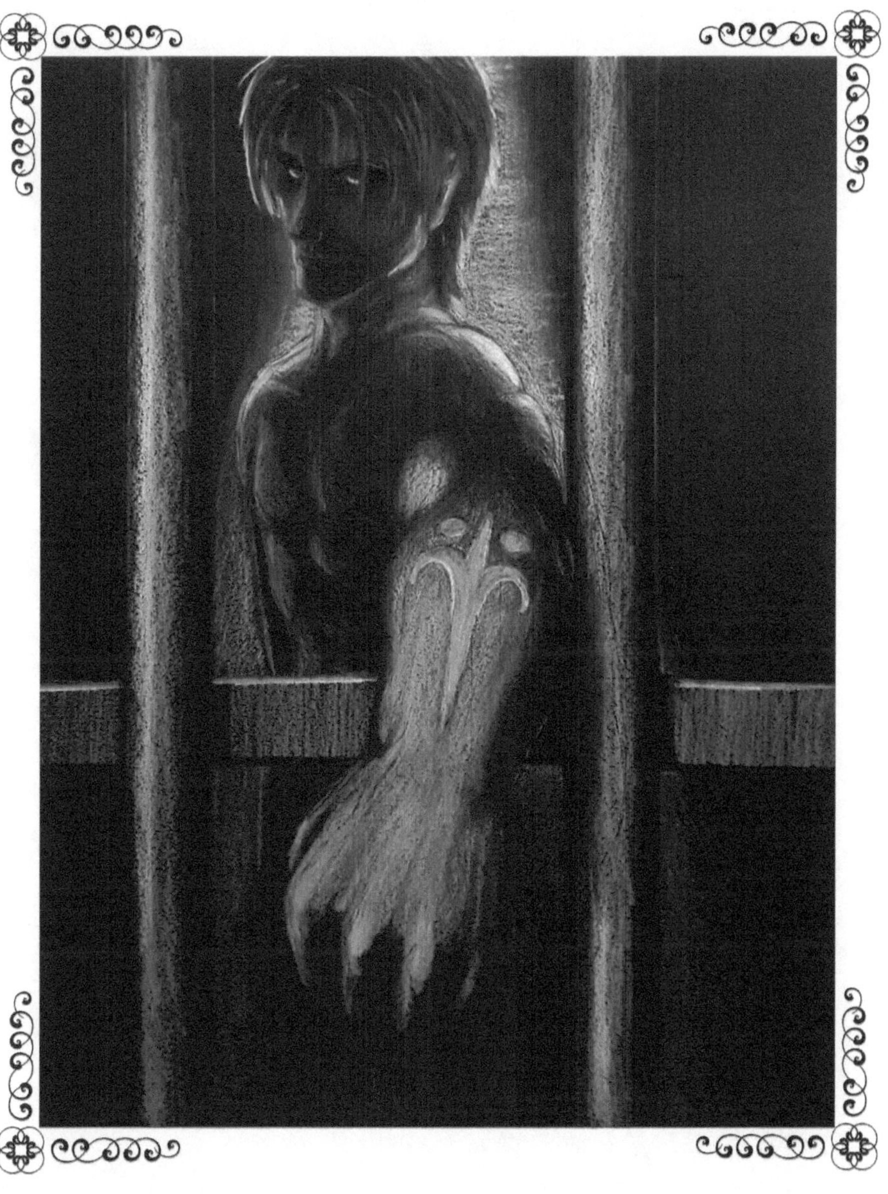

Chapter 46
HAIL TO THE KING

Toth held on while Ulna struggled to keep up. Adwen ran at the horse's fastest pace along the way to Plexus and the residence of the Master Knights. When the forest gave way to rolling open fields, they saw it at last. The fortress was twice the size of the city and the spire rose up to a staggering height. On their approach and before the guards could see them, Adwen changed into woman form, slowing to a jog.

It was noon and the way into Plexus was through an enormous doubled steel portcullis gate. Adwen went up close and peered at the grand fortress beyond the closed entrance. Her eyes flashed gold and she knew he was in there. Suddenly a voice called down from atop the wall.

"Aye, who goes there?"

Her voice reached him and his fellow watchmen. "My name is Adwen! My friend and I are here to have a word with the knights. Could you open up for a second, please?"

The two paused to look at each other before bursting out in laughter. "I'm sorry, little girl. My orders are to keep the city closed to everyone except specific traders and knights. You shall have to come another day."

She rolled her eyes. "It would be pretty hard to carry a horse and rider over the wall, so you'd be doing me a favor. Just open the gate a little for the horse to ride through and we'll be out of your way. So, please, open the gate? Don't make me open it myself."

Red in the face with laughter, they didn't have the breath to speak. The guard batted at the air to dismiss her again.

Turning to Toth, she shrugged.

He tilted his head. "These clouts are rather difficult."

"How about I go have a private word?"

"By all means." He gestured to the wall.

The guards were laughing up until the girl leapt from over the side. With a firm expression on her face, she glared at the startled men. Gasping, one drew a sword and the other quickly notched an arrow.

Not willing to wait for her to speak, the archer let it fly for her head. Their eyes bulged when she caught it and came closer, twirling it between slender fingers. They continued backing away and soon stopped as they found the wall and froze, fearing the worst.

Adwen took a seat on the wall beside them with legs crossed. Pointing the feathered end at them, she chided, "I told you I'd come up to open it myself. So I'll ask nice one more time. Please, open the gates."

With little more convincing needed, the two went to work.

Finished confronting the men, Adwen leaped and landed smartly beside Toth and Ulna. She felt a little guilty for frightening the men, but it couldn't be helped. "They actually thought I was going to kill them."

"I'm certain they did. They must be going through the shakes now from the fright you gave them."

The main street led through the heart of Plexus directly to the front gate of the fortress. Tall buildings and homes lined the cobbled roadways. All around up high, guards patrolled with archers. The city was well defended as busy people paused to stare. Others fled to hide in homes, fearing Adwen might be dangerous. They couldn't harm her so she strode casually beside the horse.

It was simple to get through the first gate onto the grounds as it was always open. The courtyard before the main entrance was filled with growing things and a few trees. Two guards holding spears stood on the other side of the arch almost failed to notice them going by. But eventually they did and did double-takes in shock and disbelief at an inhuman being striding onto the grounds.

"Hey! Hold it right there, you! I said stop!"

She didn't listen and the guards quickly cut them off, blocking the way.

Adwen remained cordial. "I'm sorry, but we have important business inside. Could you please let us through?"

The guards didn't move. "No, we shall not. Only knights

and guests are allowed to pass today. Turn back and stay out, creature."

"Please, let us go inside. We're here to find a friend of ours. Once we have him, we'll be gone and you won't have to see us again. Just let us through so we can find him and leave."

The other guard was suspicious. "Who might this friend of yours be?"

"Oryn. Oryn Conrad."

Laughing, they replied, "Where in Dargadia have you been? Sir Oryn is dead. Not a soul has seen hide nor hair of him in a year. Now leave and do not return or the knights shall deal with you."

Raising an eyebrow, she assured them. "I don't know about his hair, but his hide is in there. Can we please get by?"

The guards glanced at one another, becoming aggravated. "We would know if Sir Oryn had returned; everyone would know. He is the general."

After giving Toth a sideways glance, she replied, "Well, I can think of one reason why you wouldn't. I'll ask one more time and give you the chance to walk away. Please, let us pass."

Defiantly, they stood their ground, ready for a fight.

Adwen shrugged. "Okay. Toth? Could you do the honors?"

He smiled. "Not a problem."

Raising his hand, he summoned two strong roots. They snatched up the guards each by the arm, gently steering them out of the way.

Astonished by the one-sided situation, both sentries cried out and fought the arboreal opponents without success. They struggled to release themselves, helplessly watching the strangers approach the entrance.

Adwen and her friend were casual and unfazed by the mild excitement. "Did you ever think you might have to do that to a guard instead of a monster?"

"They can be disagreeable at times so yes."

He dismounted the mare and remembered not to leave the satchel with the treaties behind. She forced open one of the solid oak doors. And as they strolled through, Toth snapped his fingers, dismissing the tree root accomplices.

Many torches lined the passage to a grand hall filled with bright sunshine. Toth was on her heels as she took brisk strides. The knights were not likely to let Oryn go free without a fight. When they neared the end of the hall they spied a high-backed chair sitting in the open, holding a sad figure. A thin, pale man spoke with the bearded stranger and Adwen's eyes widened with surprise.

"Is that who I think it is?"

Her half-elf companion replied, "That is King Lorvan. No wonder this place is closed tighter than a vault."

Entering the grand hall, they were blocked by a pair of royal guards with razor-sharp partisans. At the sound of metal colliding, the king and his advisor looked up.

"What do you propose we do?" Toth quietly eyed the disgruntled guards.

She smiled. "We get two things for the price of one." Then she called to the king, "Your Highness! It is very important that we speak with you!"

The king quietly supported his weary head in one hand, watching with bland curiosity as the advisor raised his voice.

"Who dares disturb the king and speak to him so directly? You have no business here. Get out!"

"I have business all right. My name is Adwen and I have special documents to deliver. It's very important and I'm not leaving until he sees them."

At the name the king's curiosity grew. Putting down his hand, he sat higher in the throne to stare at the odd girl.

The advisor quickly lost patience. "I said you may not speak with the king. He is very busy and has no time for games with strange women. Guards! Show them out!"

When they made to push her back, they couldn't. Her strength confounded them.

Then she had an idea. "I was the last one to see Princess Eyrie! I was tracking her kidnapper a year ago. Not only that, but I believe I know who has her."

The advisor was about to dismiss her again, but the king raised a hand to keep him quiet, studying her intently. "You believe my daughter lives? Are you certain?"

Gold light flashed in her eyes. "I'm sure of it. She's alive somewhere and I'm going to find her, but first you need to see these papers I've brought from the other kingdoms."

Getting to his feet, he was breathless. "Are you the Tame One?"

It was Adwen's turn to be curious. "Yeah. How do you know about me?"

King Lorvan commanded his guards. "Let her pass."

The two hesitantly stepped aside and she went closer. "You know about me?"

"The day Princess Eyrie was taken, she told of a guest who might attend her celebration; an inhuman being by the name of Adwen whom she granted the title of Tame One. Please, tell me. Where would she be? Where is my daughter?"

Going to stand before him, she frowned. "The enemy has her, Your Highness and I know she is alive. All we have to do is find her."

The advisor was not convinced and spat, "How dare you tell such lies!"

"Silence!" the king snapped. Returning his attention to her, he asked, "You have brought documents from the foreign lands. Would they be treaties?"

The answer came with a clever smile. "Yes, they are."

A glimmer of happiness filled him. "I see. My being in this place is a secret. How did you know to seek me here today?"

"I didn't. I was here for other business, but once we saw you I thought we could ask for some help. I'm pretty sure he's locked up."

The king smiled. "What would the Heir of the Master Knight ask of me?"

His advisor did a frightened double-take.

"Last night our friend was taken from a town north of here. We would like him to be released as soon as possible."

"Who? I will do as you ask, but what is the name?"

She had tried to avoid telling, but it seemed like there was no alternative.

"Our friend is Oryn. He's in the dungeons right now."

The advisor blanched and the king saw. Glaring at the man, he asked warningly, "Do you know of this, Glenmore?"

Shaking his head as a bead of sweat formed on his temple, he stammered. "No. She speaks lies. That is impossible. The general is dead."

Adwen joined in glaring and her eyes glowed. "He is here. I can feel it. Oryn is here and you know it."

The adviser was frightened, unable to utter a word.

Then the king grew curious. "Why would the knights throw their own beloved general into the dungeons like the things they catch? Have you marked him?"

A sour taste was in her mouth. Adwen's black lips pursed and she swallowed. "Yes. Yes, I did. I marked him a few days ago."

The king sighed and nodded. "Good. Better for him to be marked by you than any other. Now, he is like you, is he not?"

Very confused that he understood so well, she nodded. "Yes."

The advisor was even more afraid as the king rounded on him. "You knew and kept this from me? Tell me why and chose your words carefully, Glenmore."

After gulping and tossing Adwen a disturbed look, he stammered out, "He was sentenced to be executed at dawn, my king. He is dead."

While the old man glared more dangerously, she scowled. "Looks like you need a better adviser."

Bearing over him with an intimidating stature, King Lorvan replied, "So it would seem. Glenmore, the general shall still be living. You cannot convince me against that. To have your own neck spared, take me to him. Now."

Warm light shone down and further cast Oryn in shadows. The men knew the truth, but how many would be loyal? Her greatest priority was to deliver the treaties. He was not needed to accomplish that feat. His gaze traced over the opposing wall along every crack and stone. Toth could help her in times of need and was much better suited for the job. They would do well together.

There were the sounds of unlocking and opening of the dungeon door. Soon pairs of feet came down the long curved passage. Smells from two humans reached him, but he did not recognize them. Curious as to who these visitors might be, he watched the side of the bars.

First, a very thin man with a frightened look came into

view. The robes he wore were that of a high official serving the king. Then an old man with a white beard flecked with blond appeared and neatly folded his arms. King Lorvan's stare was still striking.

Swiftly leaping from his corner, Oryn knelt a short distance from the bars. With his head bowed low, he exclaimed, "My king."

His movements were unnaturally quick and the advisor jumped back while the king was amused. He gestured for Oryn to stand. Once he was on his feet at attention, King Lorvan frowned.

"I did not think I would ever find you here of all places, General Sir Oryn."

He remained silent.

A stern and questioning tone filled the king's voice. "Did you search for my daughter? If so, then why? Why did you disobey and leave the knights behind?"

"I searched for her, my king. I evaded my own men, because they would have slain the creature who was tracking the assailant. There would have been no stopping all of them."

The king wore a suspicious look. "You mean the Tame One."

"Yes, my king."

For a while nothing was said and the king studied his appearance. What amused him most was the look in his eyes. This was not the same man who left his castle so long ago. The man was truly dead after all. He looked like a man, but the king wasn't fooled. A hint of an animal air was about him.

"How may I be your king while you serve the Tame One?"

Oryn blinked and was nervous. "I am loyal to my king and kingdom. I have not cast aside my loyalties."

Lorvan pretended to be surprised. "I see." Then he spotted the arrows scattered behind him. "Were you sentenced to execution?"

"Yes, my king."

He raised an eyebrow. "On whose command?"

Oryn didn't understand the reason for the question. "I believe it was the order of Sir Jacques, my king."

"Is that so?" Then he snapped his fingers.

To Oryn's surprise, the advisor began to open his cell. When the bars swung open wide, he didn't budge. He stood and stared in shock as the king beckoned him to join. After hesitating, he eventually stepped out.

"You look good, lad." He rapped him on the shoulder and smiled. "Walk with me."

They slowly made their way out of the dungeons and Oryn became even more confused. Watching the king's wrinkled expression, he asked, "My king, why is it that I am being released?"

He raised an eyebrow. "Would you rather go back to being caged?"

"No, my king. I simply do not understand why I would be set free."

"Oh! It was at the request of a few of your friends."

He thought the king meant the knights and smiled to himself.

"Also, I wished to see for myself that you were indeed alive and inside this dungeon. There was a very interesting rumor and I wanted to hear the answer from you. I hear you are no longer human."

Oryn abruptly halted on the stairs and dropped his gaze.

King Lorvan turned back and the advisor went on ahead to wait by the door.

"What is it?"

Shame was in his voice and he refused look up. "I am a beast, my king. I do not deserve to be in your presence or to walk with you." He heard a kind laugh and felt a hand on his shoulder. When he looked up, King Lorvan was beaming.

"That does not matter. You should be proud to be a chosen warrior for the Heir. I envy you." They continued along and the king reassured him. "No one could be more deserving or suited for the task. After all, you must live up to your family name. I'm sure your ancestor, Keegan Conrad, was no better or worse as Darien's right hand."

"What?" He had never heard this before.

"For the longest time I knew of your family ties to the Order. I commanded all within the order to withhold this truth so as to prevent your pride from swelling any further. But it seems you could use a little pride just to keep your chin up."

King Lorvan sighed ruefully. "She is a lovely creature and her eyes look sharper than daggers."

Oryn stared. While he studied the king's amused expression, the advisor opened the door. Waiting on the other side was Toth and before him stood Adwen. Arms folded at her back, she wore a curious smile.

The king approached and observed Oryn's warm reaction. "I believe I've found the parcel you were searching for, Lady Adwen. Is this the one?"

She thoughtfully cocked her head. "I don't know. It could be."

An almost betrayed look came over him.

Then she smiled. "But I guess he'll do." Quick as lightning, she tossed him his shirts and boots.

He caught them while an uncomfortable smile spread across his face.

The king chuckled and her smile widened. "Well, you better get dressed. We're going to get your sword."

She and the king led the way, chatting casually while he and Toth followed.

"I heard that we're related."

King Lorvan chuckled. "Indeed, we do share a little blood, but while I am King of Dargadia, you exist outside the laws of these lands. That is how you shall succeed: by going where no others have power or say to do what must be done. Be careful not to fall."

The warning brought Adwen a little self-doubt. "I will." Then she smiled again, quickly changing the subject. "Don't you think Oryn is funny?"

"Yes I do, but what do you mean?"

Having heard the remark, Oryn wondered why they would call him funny.

"He's so uptight! A lot of the time we are in serious situations, but he's always so...so..." But she couldn't find the word.

King Lorvan finished for her. "Stiff?"

She burst out giggling. "That's it!"

Oryn erupted behind them. "I am not stiff!"

They all paused, turning to give sideways looks. Even Toth gave him a dubious expression.

Taken aback at his own outburst in the king's presence as

well as the accusation, Oryn tried to regain some composure. "How is it that I am stiff?"

Adwen and the king smiled at each other and continued onward while Toth patted his shoulder. "You simply are."

Frustrated, he followed through the archway. And to his greater annoyance, they did not end the topic of his overdeveloped sense of professionalism. Then the Grand Hall of Knights opened around them. Adwen instantly lost focus.

All around and up the walls, marble tablets glistened with golden names of men who had fought and died with honor. Each was the size of a splayed hand. Thousands of them lined the cavernous space, reaching to the top of the domed ceiling.

"Wow."

"Here is where I leave you. Seek me in the library later. There are things we must discuss for tonight. I look forward to speaking with you further, Lady Adwen." King Lorvan bowed his head and was about to depart when Toth spoke up.

"My king? I have a request to ask."

"You may ask it."

The half-elf appeared hesitant. "May I accompany you to the library, Your Highness?"

A smile scrolled over the king's face. "Yes, you may. Come along, my pointy-eared guest."

Excited at the opportunity, Toth quickly joined his side.

Adwen laughed and watched them go. She was sure he wanted to see the rare writings in the tower. Then she returned to gazing at the multitudes of names and thought aloud, "This place is huge. Who lives here? It's bigger and more impressive than the king's castle."

Watching her turn about and soak in the scene, Oryn answered. "It was not meant for kings to reside here. Darien built it long ago for his knights and eventually for his heir."

She paused and her eyes lit up like lanterns.

He smiled and glanced around to avoid her gaze. "Everything within this fortress is your birthright. This is your home."

Overwhelming understanding left her speechless.

He was about to lead her on through the hall, but something caught her eye among the tablets. Joining the investigation, Oryn quickly realized what she was looking at. Upon the wall was a name slashed beyond recognition. It was scratched and the surface scorched to obscure the writing that had once been. She gently touched the nameless stone.

"Why would someone do this? This is terrible."

While admiring her under the torches, he explained. "It serves as a warning." Then Oryn pointed to a destroyed line below the name that not all of the plates had. "This means he was once a high-ranking officer. The only reason for the elders to scratch a name from the wall is if the knight who died was proven to be an abomination. They would have burned every record and scrap of parchment with his name. No one will ever know who he was or that he ever lived." Then he added gravely, "If you hadn't come so soon, they would have done the same to my name."

"Why? You didn't do anything wrong."

Adwen's forgiving nature nearly brought a smile to his face. "To the mind of a knight or an elder, I am a disgrace. The fact that I am no longer human draws them to the conclusion."

Sadness grew in her eyes. "All of them think that way?"

He gave a wry smile as his own eyes glowed. "Not all of them."

The armor lockers were a buzz with rumors and excited chatter. Most who knew the truth kept quiet. Regardless, it wasn't long before every knight within the fortress heard that Sir Oryn was found. The second greatest piece of gossip was that the Heir of Darien was on the way. Rumors were flying like swarms of insects over a still pond, but once the door opened the banter quieted into stunned silence. Every man fell quiet, peering around to see the cause.

Oryn stood at the threshold, examining surprised faces as men held their breath. Using new instincts along with keen intellect, he carefully appraised the suspenseful knights. Some were afraid, but most were waiting to see if their eyes were lying to their uplifted spirits. The men knew it was indeed Oryn when he entered and started for the back of the room. No one else had the same domineering presence among the ranks.

Awaiting his arrival was a proud Sir Peregrine and his four companions. They saluted and it pleased Oryn to see their acceptance. Beside them sat Brack, bruised and battered, holding the Rose Thorne. Very tired from lack of sleep, he gave a sharp salute with a happy smile.

Becoming concerned, Oryn demanded. "Who has done this?"

Everyone turned to look at the others standing in a corner. With so many threatening glances at once, the men became anxious and hoped there would be some mercy.

After throwing them a deadly scowl, Oryn turned to receive his weapon. He set it across his back by the crimson strap and helped Brack to his feet.

While the effort hurt, Brack's pained expression quickly vanished as he saw the new figure at the door.

Each knight stared dumbstruck as Adwen came inside, looking intently at the lockers and eventually their faces. No one knew what to make of her as she joined Sir Oryn and studied the eyes of his friends. They gawked and noted the wild look about her.

She couldn't help but smile. They were good men. Laughing softly, she held out a hand for Brack to shake.

He didn't know what to think of the gesture and glanced to his original captain. After receiving a nod, he nervously took her hand.

She shook with him. "Thank you for being his friend in all of this. He said your name is Brack. Is that right?"

Too stunned to meet Darien's heir, he nodded.

"You don't have to be scared of me. So long as you don't do anything dumb, I'm harmless. My name is Adwen and it's a pleasure to meet you." Then she glanced at the rotten men in the corner and added with a wry tone, "For the most part."

Sir Peregrine finally spoke up. "Adwen, the Tame One. I am Sir Peregrine. Every knight here is prepared to serve you with their lives. Ask anything of us what you will and it shall be swiftly done to the letter." He saluted. "We are at your command."

What quickly followed was the sound of each knight saluting. All around her fists were brought against strong, proud breasts. Even the sheepish ones saluted and dipped their heads. Oryn watched as she stared in shock and smelled her feelings of discomfort. He couldn't understand why she wouldn't be pleased by the offering of unending loyalty from more than fifty knights. Adwen's humility intrigued him and he restrained another smile.

Then her feelings of unease disappeared. A dangerous flash came to her eyes and she turned to face the door, sensing something foul. Turning to the doorway as well, Oryn continued to smile. She detected Jacques, glaring around from the other side of the quiet room.

The current captain wore a mortified expression as his dark eyes searched. The more he saw the knights saluting towards Oryn, the angrier he became. Once they noticed him, they parted so he could see to whom they were giving honors.

As Adwen came into view, blood boiled and his vision turned red. Drawing his sword, he bellowed, "Tame One! You dare to enter here!" He rushed at her in a blind rage and cried out. "Die, beast!"

The knights nearby drew swords to defend her, but Oryn was prepared. What was coming was the cause of his amusement. Very quickly, he pulled back the closest men and called to the others.

"Get back! Get out from behind her!"

They were obedient and stepped aside.

Adwen's eyes burned bright. The vile odor from this man was pungent and drove her sixth sense wild.

Jacques took a mad swing for her throat. To Oryn's complete satisfaction, her hand came up to block the blow. A light in her hand took the form of a bloom. And as the weapon struck the compressed energy, there was a flash and the weapon fractured. The force caught him off balance. While her free hand gripped his armor, she quickly spun and slammed him into a wall of lockers.

Her counter knocked the wind from his lungs and he wheezed. Attempting to recover, Jacques saw his sword. Even as he lifted it the metal fell to the ground in slivers and shards. Becoming more afraid than angry, he locked eyes with her for the first time.

Her gaze was intense. Adwen felt energy building in her head as she bore her eyes into his. Soon power was released and she saw into his very being.

Paralyzed, Jacques tried to blink and look away, but couldn't. While she was looking through him he was unable to move. She blinked and the power went away as the wicked captain panted and gazed in horror.

Appalled, she growled and spoke coldly. "Your heart is darker than the Blood Red Witch of the north. You have no right to be here." Near her grip on his armor, she saw a red jewel on a chain. Her eyes flashed gold at the symbol of his place as captain. Ripping the trinket away and holding it where he could see, she growled louder. "You have no right to wear this any more than a beggar in the street! Get out! Leave and never come back, or so help me, I will make you pay for everything you lack in virtues."

He was outraged. She dared to banish him?

Then she transformed into hound form and snarled.

Knights gave a start while Oryn marveled. He knew Adwen better; she would spare him. She would show Jacques a mercy he couldn't begin to understand.

She gnashed her fangs viciously. "Now, get out!"

He was thrown across the room and slid through the doorway, coming to a stop out in the hall. Staggering onto his feet, he glared back in defiance. The white creature took a few steps and he drew the knife out from his boot. Then he looked up a split second later and her jaws were inches from his nose.

Gnashing her jaws again, she roared. *"Get out!"*

Dropping the knife in fright, he gasped and scrambled to get away.

She watched the horrible man flee. With him gone, she reverted to woman form and faced the flabbergasted knights again. A little embarrassed, she blushed and came inside, thoughtfully fiddling with the pendant.

She heard one call out. "Who shall be captain?"

A few whispered that Oryn should regain the position, but she held up a finger. "Hold that thought. I'm working on it right now. It will be one of you."

The murmuring ceased as they watched her pacing. Her sharp nails played over the jewel, tapping and fiddling in contemplation. Then she clutched it tight and began studying the knights. Meticulously, she scrutinized each set of eyes. Without looking too deeply, she searched each heart.

The knights surrounding Sir Peregrine watched as she came close and smiled, holding out the pendant. He was stunned while others nodded and murmured approvingly.

As he hesitated, she wore a warm expression. "I think you would be great for the job." Then she lifted an eyebrow and smiled. "Or am I wrong?"

He wouldn't dare tell the heir she was wrong. He accepted it and replied, "I shall wear it in a way deserving of the honor, Tame One. I shall not fail you."

She blushed. "Just call me Adwen."

Sir Peregrine gave a sharp salute. "As you wish, Lady Adwen." As the newly appointed captain dropped the salute, he stole a look at Sir Oryn. The young slayer was not hiding his feelings. Then he realized it. He could see the way Oryn looked at her.

Suddenly, Sir Peregrine burst out loud in merry guffaws.

Chapter 47
ALLIES AND ENEMIES

A few offered to act as Adwen's escorts, but she insisted on exploring alone. They did not press the issue, watching her dart off. Once she was gone there was one thing Sir Oryn wanted. They left straight for the training grounds.

He instructed two knights while others observed. One thing that attracted them were rumors of his infamous rage. There was a story of a man who dared to call him a great fool in the training ring. The result was Oryn giving the man a wider smile. When his face healed, Oryn continued his training until he was one of the better dragon slayers. These two fresh knights were not experienced with his brand of training. Oryn set his own sword aside and took up common blade.

"Grip the hilt firmly. Keep your wrist from being stiff unless the opponent comes close. If your arm is relaxed it shall allow for a swifter response. Good. Now, come at me."

Without a thought, the two attacked. The first was fast, but Oryn knew the knight's grip was weak. Disarming him with a small flick, the weapon skittered away as the second advanced. Blocking the attacks, Oryn allowed the student to take more ground and gave instruction.

"Now, find the opening in my defense." To his frustration, the knight couldn't see the weakness indicated. When the pupil failed to understand, it was time to correct him. Oryn brushed the knight's sword back like nothing and put a hand to his chest, knocking the opponent to the ground. The onlookers were entertained and some clapped, but he ignored them and helped the man to his feet. Then he backed away to continue.

"This is no fencing lesson. If you deliver an attack lower than the waist you may put your opponent off balance. So many high attacks can put both fighters off guard for a low blow. Mind your feet and you may shift the battle to your favor."

"It is easy for you to claim. You are too fast! This is child's play for you because of your power." The knight saw Oryn grow frustrated and fell silent, fearful he might have made a mistake.

The onlookers held their breath.

Oryn's eyes flashed. "I am not teaching you to face an abnormally strong man. I am teaching you to fight a knight." Dropping his weapon, he added, "Yes, I am swift. I can block your every blow, but I have not shown you my fastest."

All he knew was that his instructor was in motion. Raising the blade as a startled defense, he was too slow. Oryn ducked under the swing with blinding speed, snatching the knife from the student's boot. In a split second, Oryn came up from behind and the knight froze, gasping as the cold flat of the knife lay across his neck.

From just behind the knight's shoulder, Oryn's voice was firm. "All you need to improve is skill. Learn your form until no one can touch you." To the surprise of everyone, Oryn released him and gave back the knife. "Having more accuracy and technique shall make you a force to be reckoned with. Do not allow any to tell you different."

The first knight returned to take part in the lesson. Before Oryn could continue, the words caught in his throat.

Four elder guards parted the crowd. Marching until a few paces away, the leader called, "Sir Oryn Conrad?"

Horrified, he answered. "I am."

"By order of the High Elder, we are to escort you to the council hall. You are to come quietly and meet for passing of judgment. Do not resist."

His blood ran cold. "I shall come quietly. I shall not resist."

Picking up the sword and passing it to one of the men, he allowed the four to surround and lead him away.

When the guards were out of earshot one of the knights shouted. "We must do something! Where is the heir? Spread out and track her down. The elders will condemn him!"

Like mad, the knights scattered into every door and inlet. Adwen was the only one who could override a decision made by the elder council.

Emptiness flooded Oryn. Every thought was dulled by a numbing fear. Inevitably the elders would have learned he was here. Now that they had, he could do nothing except move forward one step a time.

The sound of the guards' heavy armor was irritating chatter to his ears and the smell of their sweaty bodies curdled his stomach. He was not a human anymore. His senses served as a painful reminder. There was a small hope in the back of his mind that perhaps if he acted like a knight they might not notice the changes.

Then once the giant double doors came into view hope vanished. Elders were never forgiving or willing to show mercy for mistakes such as abandoning a post. Watching the way open, he thought it was like a set of deathly jaws spreading wide to swallow him whole. Each step past the threshold was a terrible sinking feeling in the pit of his stomach. Oryn braced himself before the many eyes of the old officials.

The council hall was vast. One side of the cavernous chamber lay open to the outside. Three colossal columns and a rail separated them from the far drop to a courtyard. As he went along with the guards, temptation tugged at him to leap out and escape. That would not do. Only in the gravest of circumstances would he take that measure. He had to have courage enough to attempt to make them see reason.

Head high and shoulders back, he marched until they halted fifteen paces from the High Elder's seat. Behind High Elder Mamalis were the rising benches for the other forty-nine elders. As they stared down, the guards saluted while Oryn held his bearing and clung to his nerve.

A guard spoke loud and clear, making his voice echo. "High Elder, presenting General Sir Oryn Reynard Conrad, as ordered."

Elder Mamalis raised a hand. "Take your leave. Return to your post and await the sentencing of the accused."

They saluted and their fists collided with armor. The sound rang in their convict's ears like the boom of a gong. His face was vacant with a thousand mile stare, as every knight was expected to have when standing before the council. There would be no room to falter. Each would look for the signs of a deserter, or worse yet, an animal. The double doors closed behind him, and as was expected from any knight, he gave a sharp and respectful salute.

Waving a hand, the wrinkled elder acknowledged the gesture.

Dropping it directly and standing with absolute distinction, Oryn waited. This was not only a judging of his crimes. For the first few minutes not a word was said to test his patience and see if he still possessed self-control. The old men analyzed his posture and even his breathing. Those who could see his face looked closely for a wavering of the mind.

Once the High Elder was content, he spoke at long last. "Sir Oryn Conrad, you are before this council for a number of crimes. The first is the charge of desertion, second is the charge of disobeying direct orders from your king, and the third is the charge of treachery."

At the last Oryn almost flinched. It was the charge used when they believed a knight was no longer human.

"Does the accused have any qualms before this council?"

"No, High Elder." The numb feeling was complete and he hardly realized he had spoken. Though he stood as still as stone, he felt as if he was shuddering like a leaf. The elders glared and scowled as if they already made a decision.

"Very well." Mamalis cleared his throat. "Then let the judgment begin."

His mouth turned dry. The pause before the first question was like standing on broken glass.

"Sir Oryn, where is the Princess Eyrie?"

He sharply responded. "The Princess Eyrie was taken by an evil creature and the trail ended in the wastes to the east. The enemy has her and she has yet to be located, High Elder."

The elder became suspicious. "Why did you not return once the trail was lost?"

Oryn paused to gather the right words. "The shame of failing to recover the princess and failing my king pressed me to not return or end the search, High Elder."

This did not please the council. "So you would rather add

the shame of failing to return to your load? Why did you desert your men knowing it is forbidden for any knight to quest alone?"

Not letting himself have the time to form a lie, he quickly answered. "I eluded the men for personal gain and to preserve the creature I used to track the enemy. She would have been destroyed by their rash actions. The quest was a near success until the creature was felled by the fiend."

A few of the council members shook their heads in disapproval.

"Was this creature the Tame One?" When the question was asked everyone hushed.

Oryn hesitated, fearful of the reaction. "The creature was the Tame One."

Small whispers hissed and the High Elder waited for quiet.

"So you traveled alone with an inhuman being and eluded this order to avoid returning to face your crimes." Mamalis studied him, beginning to glare suspiciously. "Is it true, Oryn Conrad, that you are no longer human?"

Emotions exploded inside Oryn and he could not prevent his eyes from glowing brighter. Wrinkled scowls deepened and he swallowed hard. Every one of them could see the light in his emerald eyes and there was no denying it.

"It is true."

A gasp and many whispers swept through the panel. He waited along with the High Elder for the clamor to die and they locked eyes. In that moment Oryn finally saw the lack of pity. An almost pleading look was in his own face while he searched for an ounce of understanding. There was none. Mamalis raised a hand to press for quiet and Oryn went back to maintaining his distant stare.

The High Elder's voice was as cold as mountain snow. "You allowed yourself to be marked and failed to end your life. For such a disgrace there shall be no leniency. What have you become, Oryn Conrad?"

It was all he could do to keep his voice from faltering. "I do not know, High Elder."

Uncertainty struck everyone present.

Mamalis asked with growing disgust and curiosity, "Do you know what it is that marked you?"

"She is something new, High Elder. She is no enemy to the Order. She is a great ally and it is imperative that you know who she --"

"Silence!"

He had spoken too much without being granted proper questioning.

"So many lies at once from you are an insult to this assembly. The beast is deemed a threat and it shall be dealt with. Now, to prove loyalty for a quick death, tell this council where the Tame One may be found and how it may be slain."

The demands made his expression twist into a look of horror. Oryn stared at High Elder Mamalis, silently begging him to retract the words. Oryn would rather be sent to be executed again than betray the heir.

A sudden sound distracted them, but he remained still. The giant doors cracked open to allow someone inside and the elders were outraged. They closed again, blowing a wisp of air. Oryn caught her scent and felt calm. Simply having her close brushed the fear away. Keeping silent, he watched as the High Elder was thoroughly displeased.

Her bright, searching eyes began to wander. A dry laugh escaped her and she whispered, "Wow."

Padding along, deliberately ignoring the fifty glares, she meandered, slowly turning while soaking in the sights. The hall was beautiful. The view of the rolling hills was equally stunning. Gradually continuing closer, she appeared lost in her own sightseeing.

"What are you doing here? Get out this instant! This is the Elder Hall! No women are allowed inside and certainly not during a judgment! Be gone with you!"

Still ignoring the unwelcome, Adwen's hands folded behind her and she looked away. She strolled backward until she came beside Oryn and smiled at him. At last, she turned to face the High Elder and he saw her violet eyes, pointed ears and the rest of her unusual appearance. When he visibly knew she was not normal, she shrugged.

"You wanted to know where I was, so... here I am."

Outrage melted into an abashed surprise. Mamalis' eyes widened then he cried out, "Guards!"

The four men returned and stopped a short distance behind the two oddities. They saluted and waited for further orders.

"What breed of fools are you to let this creature come walking in here? Take the thing away and lock it up! Your punishments shall come later for this stupidity!"

They didn't budge and Adwen explained. "They let me in because they know who I am." She smiled and asked in a mock-naïve tone, "Who are you?"

Red in the face with rage, Mamalis stood and puffed out his chest. "I am High Elder of the Order of the Master Knights! Who are you, woman thing, to show such incredible insolence before the Council of Elders?"

A smile tugged at the corner of her mouth. "He tried to tell you, but you wouldn't listen." Tossing her companion a sly look, she commanded, "Show him. Show all of them the mark I gave you."

Glad to obey, he rolled back the sleeve. Tilting his forearm, Oryn let the sunlight glint off the golden symbol. No sooner did the light strike the mark than the High Elder's face turned from beet red to a pale white. The elders clearly saw the mark of Andredan branded to his skin.

Adwen politely addressed Elder Mamalis. "I have met with the rulers of the five Kingdoms of Day. The treaties are to be signed tomorrow at daybreak by King Lorvan. They told me I am the descendant of Darien, the Master Knight. I am Adwen, the Tame One. It is good to meet you, High Elder."

There wasn't a single word said among the panel. A moment passed before the High Elder found his tongue after nearly swallowing it. Tucking away some pride, the elder cleared his dry throat.

"This is still a judgment. Grant me a few minutes and we may speak. The accused remains to be judged."

Adwen shook her head. "He's already been judged."

Mamalis blinked. "This council still has command over the knights. We must judge him."

Gold flashed across her eyes. Becoming stern, Adwen saw a large collection of texts enforced by the panel on his desk. She approached, and with one hand, turned the pages far back. Her pointed nail skimmed down a page until she came to a line. Leaning in close, she whispered, "Say it aloud, so that all can hear you."

Clearing his cinched throat, the High Elder read: "Knights and men may be judged by the elders, unless they should be a bearer of the golden mark of Andredan. These chosen few shall be judged by no man, but by the Andredan line and the Spirits of Light alone." Finished, he stared dumbstruck at the firm face she wore.

Again, her eyes flashed gold. Looking at them all, she called out. "You are elders. Since rising from the ranks your responsibility has not been to punish, but to direct the growth of these men. I have seen the one you chose for Sir Oryn's replacement as captain." She shook her head. "He was a poor excuse for a man, let alone a knight."

Speaking louder with disappointment, she went on, "These judgments you and your knights perform are unjust." Eyes shining, she pointed a finger and spoke with a righteous and accusing voice. "So eager to control and reach too far out of your bounds, you forget the virtues this order was founded upon in the first place! For prosecuting magical beings for their differences the same you would a murderer, how dare you!"

Angrier, she chastised the council. "Sir Oryn has already been judged! The light spirits have chosen he live! The Light Spirits took his father's sword. Next they took his horse! And then he lost his place in the order as a knight along with his humanity. You would try to take more from him? Let me worry about whether he receives further punishment. That is my responsibility now."

Then she cooled. "But you are not for me to judge. I leave that to the Light Spirits. So I find the will to forgive you."

The old men turned from shamed and threatened to being completely confused.

"I have a friend I want you to meet."

When Adwen changed into her white creature body, the panel were afraid and some tried to climb away up the stands. Facing the open veranda, she howled a soft tone, extending an open hand. A wreath of flame appeared and she shifted into woman form as the chortling phoenix entered.

The elders stared in shock, admiring the beautiful bird. Sure as the day, the legendary avian sat on the strange girl's arm, ruffling glowing plumage.

Facing the speechless High Elder, she introduced them. "This is Malik. He is a good friend of mine and he will stay to help." A few plot-filled whispers were in the stands and she gave a loud warning. "And trying to cage him for his feathers would be a very silly thing to do. This bird is not a pet. I don't need to come back and find piles of your ashes to clean up."

The old men fell quiet and she set the bird onto the table beside a disarrayed pile of papers. "Malik will help with your paperwork, and if an emergency turns up, tell him and he will find me anywhere."

As she spoke, the bird pecked at the stack and burbled, fluffing feathers out in disdain. With a flap of his wings, the papers were swept up high by a billowing flame. The pages floated and swirled around in the harmless embers until they landed in a very neat and orderly stack. They were organized, but the bird puffed up when one page was uneven and quickly aligned the edges using his sharp beak. Finished, Malik chirped at the High Elder.

Adwen smiled and relayed the message. "He says you're welcome."

The council was stunned into a lasting silence.

For a moment she was distracted by a shining spot on the floor, but regained focus and stated in a hard and final tone, "This trial is over. I will take my leave and him with me." Then she nodded. "Good day to you." Turning smartly on a heel, she passed Oryn and commanded, "Come."

There was nothing they could do as their guards also followed. The old men stared as she opened the door and took their accused. The elder guards remained at their post beside the doors while Oryn trailed just behind.

Once out of earshot, he asked, "Do you think it wise to insult the Council of Elders?"

She stopped cold and faced him, outraged. "Insult them?" Then Golden Eyes surfaced and spoke with far more anger. "They insulted me as well as the powers of light. Was it not they who chose Sir Jacques to represent the order?"

He was taken aback.

"They are an insult to this place and to the memory of Darien. They were going to condemn the best knight this order has seen since the Master Knights themselves."

The words gave him a spark of pride, but he was not about to let it grow too large. If she told him so, then it was true.

"They have all proven themselves to be fools. Insulting them was the least I could do in exchange for their disgrace." Golden Eyes disappeared to let Adwen speak on her own. She was not quite as angry and raised an eyebrow. "They're lucky that insulting them was all I did." A look of mild confusion crossed her face, but she dismissed the feeling.

Oryn knew she noticed the lapse in her thoughts. When they move on he couldn't help but think the elders might attempt to undermine her in the future. At last he realized where Adwen was headed. She opened the door to his old captain's quarters. As he joined her inside, he discovered the state of what had become of Jacques' personal space.

It was a mess. Balls of paper with random drawings of disturbing images cluttered the floor, piled high by the writing desk. A mobile hung by the open window, decorated with bird feathers and severed jay wings, turning in with the breeze. The only thing that was not in a frightful way was the bed. It was perfectly made and quite clean. Adwen didn't bother to ask why as they could smell a servant was responsible.

Oryn was disgusted, but before he could comment on the sight, she called him over to the desk. Among the dark collection were a bleached cat scull and a raven's claw.

"This guy has some serious issues. Check this out." Adwen picked up a rag doll with a green cape and someone's brown strands of hair tied around its neck. She sniffed curiously. "It has your hair on it! In my world there are superstitions with different kinds of witchcraft and one is called a voodoo doll."

He didn't bother to comment. This find spoke for itself.

She continued to study the vulgar item. "You don't know what he would do with this, do you?" Oryn shook his head. "The purpose is to make a specific person suffer. This guy actually tried to make a real one." A mischievous glint appeared in her eye. "I wonder if he really knew how to make one?"

Uncertainty came over him as he watched her take up a sharp pin. Adwen lined up the point with the doll's chest and watched Oryn's nervous expression grow. Then at last, she pricked the flimsy thing.

He flinched without realizing he expected pain, but there was nothing and she giggled. "You should have seen the look on your face! You are too funny!" Shaking her head, she left to rummage through the uniform closet.

Going to the window, he couldn't help but smile.

"I found it! Here you go!"

As he turned, she finished filling the box with her light powers and blew on the lid. Setting it on the bedside, she added, "It should fit tonight better than anything else around."

Interest piqued, he opened it to find a transformed officer's uniform. Her powers changed the colors to the same pattern of gray and gold as her enchanted garments.

"What do I need this for?"

"We've been invited to dinner by the king. You and I will sit beside him at the head of the table."

The words sunk in. His stomach clenched as he realized when the dinner would be. Staring at the sky outside, he could see the day growing short. A full moon loomed in the distant skyline, climbing higher.

Adwen's cheerful look was intended to be reassuring. "Don't worry about the clothes being destroyed. I've made them better than dragon skin. Dinner starts just before sunset so the king said you can turn up whenever is best."

Attempting to hide growing anxiety, he muttered, "I must decline."

"Why? Are you really afraid to go?"

He tossed her a look and she knew he was. Oryn sat on the bed, staring outside. "For me to go would not be wise. I would be a disruption for those attending. Remaining in here is the best course of action."

To his further embarrassment, she chortled. "You were willing to go into the Red Cult's fortress alone, but you're too scared to go to dinner with me, the king and a bunch of snobs? You're cute, but you seriously need to go."

Not a word came while he stubbornly gazed out at the forest, wishing he were there instead of in his old room. He thought there was nothing she could say to make him go.

Sitting at his side on the linens, Adwen joined in staring at the mountains. "I've had plenty of time to explore. There were some interesting things in the fortress." She became serious. "The king needs you there tonight. That's the why I'm going and why I'm not letting you hide in this room, or else I would."

Thoroughly displeased, he looked her in the eye.

"Don't worry about the rich jerks. I can protect you from them."

With a sly wink, she hopped off of the bed and willed her garments into a dress. The sweeping gown with a high collar was similar to what she wore the first night they met. The gold colors were rich while gray and white wove around the hems. She looked lovely. The sight temporarily distracted Oryn. Then to his great surprise, she found the power to disguise her pointed ears and teeth. Just before she turned and smiled, he tucked away the look in his eyes.

Smoothing the sides with normal-looking hands, she blushed. "I have no idea what would be right for a dinner with the king. Will this be okay?"

He shook his head and could not hold back the sadness in his voice. "It will do. You would not be out of place." His heart ached like he might die. She was so beautiful. He did as his uncle suggested and simply admired her. There was truly no harm in that.

Adwen thought the general was upset at the thought of showing up in his true form. She wanted to comfort him. "The king likes you a lot, and I will be right there, too. Look..."

So he looked at her again, hoping she wouldn't see too deep inside.

"I'm just as out of place at one of these dinners as you are." She put a hand on his shoulder. "Don't look at them. Go straight for the seat by the king."

His heart leaped to his throat as she touched him and he held his breath. As discreetly as possible, he ducked his head to hide the longing look from her sight.

"The things I found today are why you need to come. We have to protect the king. Do you understand?"

Too afraid his voice would crack, he nodded his hanging head. Her hand left his shoulder and she moved for the door. The sound of its opening reached his ears.

"On the bright side, at least you won't have to shave. All

you need is cloud cover. See you soon."

The instant the door closed, Oryn gasped out loud, clutching at his face roughly in emotional strain. He had wanted so badly to touch her. Then he relaxed and was glad he denied the incredible urge. She was so kind. It made him want to rip out his heart and throw it from the window. Standing up and taking out the uniform, he thought, perhaps the voodoo doll did work. There was a stabbing in his chest and it wouldn't go away.

There was plenty of time before sunset. He was not rushed and used the ample minutes to dress. Out of an ingrained knightly habit, Oryn stood before the mirror to groom his hair. The reflection was still doubled. Ignoring it the best he could, he worked to smooth back every last strand. Once content, Oryn studied himself. By the corner of his eye he could see the sun sinking as the veins on his face flared.

The familiar pressure returned with dread. He wished very much that he was still roaming the wilds in search of real danger. This kind of combat was not to his taste; he thought of how much he disliked politics. Glaring at the doubled reflection, he finally grimaced and swore under his breath.

"What am I doing?"

The sun set and he gripped the table. Snarls became louder as claws grew, driving into the furniture.

The dinner hall was home to a long table that stretched out toward a wall decorated by silk tapestries. One side of the chamber was open to the evening air. Twenty guests sat at the table covered in scarlet cloth and spread with delicacies of Dargadia. There was quiet gossip among guests, curious as to who would fill the seats beside His Highness. King Lorvan patiently waited for the final guests to arrive. When the announcer at the door stepped in, his eyes lit up excitedly.

The young man proclaimed, "Now presenting Lady Adwen."

None of the dignitaries knew the name and stopped bantering. Not knowing what to make of this interesting woman, the guests muttered as she made her way to the king.

She could hear their whispers of suspicion and scrutiny.

Many secretly scorned the king for having such a strange guest for his right hand seat.

Holding a confident appearance, Adwen felt a twinge of self-doubt. It felt like going through the high school lunch hall.

High Elder Mamalis kept quiet while his eyes followed. It was obvious she could hear every slant. There was no need to offend her more.

Before the king, she made a small curtsy and dipped her head.

King Lorvan smiled, ensuring he dip his head a little lower and gestured to the chair. When she sat, the whispers erupted and Adwen stole a glance at the elder who was watching before quickly averting his eyes. Some of the whispers were harshly scrutinizing the king for bowing lower than she.

He saw her becoming uncomfortable. Though he couldn't distinguish the conversations, he knew they were spreading vile words back and forth. "You look well tonight, Adwen. That is a wonderful gown you have."

Hearing his voice didn't make the doubt go away, but she tried to ignore it and blushed. "Thank you, Your Highness."

A long-faced old countess sitting diagonally from her grew curious. "Pardon me, Lady Adwen, but where do you hail from? Are you foreign?"

Comforted by being called into a conversation, she smiled sweetly. "Yes, I am. I'm what you might consider an emissary. I come from a very faraway place. As far apart as our homes are, it's amazing how alike everything is."

A fat baron beside her commented. "Hopefully your homeland is faring better than most of our domains." Finished with the sentence, he compulsively toyed with a thick, curly mustache beneath his cherry nose.

The countess and the man beside him both shushed, rousing Adwen's curiosity. "What's happening?"

Clearing his throat to dismiss them, he replied, "I shouldn't trouble you with the details, Lady Adwen. A lovely woman such as you shouldn't have to worry about shadows and such. The knights shall tend to those troubles soon enough."

A bright smile spread on her face as she glanced at the king. He was smiling as well and she asked the baron again, "Humor me, please."

As he did, the countess pulled out a fan to quell her own distress.

"Shadows have been appearing in the east. Already the rumor is that towns east of Broad River have fallen. My own men tell me no travelers come from there and the ever-hanging clouds of black remain. I have my own battalion of soldiers, but I fear their weapons and skill may not avail them when the cloud reaches for us."

The countess was distraught with the topic and quickly moved to change it. "Forgive my intrusion, Lady Adwen, but I have a few ears of my own running about. They tell me that you have seen the great Sir Oryn alive and well. Is he truly going to attend tonight?"

Adwen smiled and hesitated to say.

Then the sunlight finally died and a faint howl echoed into their dining place.

The baron sighed. "Sounds like the wolves are out for the night."

Others nodded while she shared a small glance with the king. They knew their friend was due to arrive shortly.

Adwen thought of something to say to set a new tone in the conversation. In an assuring tone, she stated, "Not all wolves are outside of a home and not all beasts are enemies."

Some frowned while the king and the baron nodded.

Adwen added, "I've heard a story about a pack of wolves that protected a boy from a wild mountain cat. And there have been witnesses from a hunt, who told of how a bear had them cornered and showed mercy by letting them go. Beneath the skin is where true honor or deformities can be found, meta-phorically speaking."

The countess was not as convinced, but the baron smiled. "You're speaking of things I've seen myself. I've witnessed men who turned on each other like rabid animals to escape a burning home, but a lowly hound leaped into the flames to save a boy. You speak a good truth." He smiled again. "I am Baron Bartholomew. It is good to meet you, Lady Adwen."

"It is nice to meet you, too. May I call you Bart?"

Everyone exchanged looks and the baron replied with a hearty laugh. "I suppose you could! It is a tougher sounding title! Of course you may!"

Again, the countess was eager to have her attention. "Lady Adwen. You have yet to answer my questions!"

"Sorry. Sir Oryn has been acting as escort for me through foreign lands. He's been a very diligent bodyguard." Then she thought of a way to cushion the coming shock. Oryn's empty seat was beside the snobby countess. "For the longest time everyone thought the knight was killed." She shook her head. "He was lost on a sort of inner journey. On the way... unfortunate things happened. When he arrives he's not going to be what you're expecting. He was hurt when we traveled through the north lands. Though he survived, the adventure altered his appearance. Try not to stare."

The woman was disturbed, but Bart chuckled. "I've seen my share of scarred men, Lady Adwen. He's not likely to make me flinch."

She smiled broadly and teethed on the tip of her tongue to resist a nervous laugh. "He's not scarred. He just looks a bit... different."

The announcer at the door stepped in, but appeared rather skittish. All eyes fell on him at the door as he stammered aloud, "Now p-presenting..." He glanced through and back. "Sir Oryn Conrad."

With as much pride of bearing as possible, Oryn stepped beyond the threshold. His ears were back and it was all he could do to keep the tail relaxed. It threatened to tuck and curl. The hair on his head was perfectly combed back and his nose down. He stared straight ahead, took a deep breath and moved slowly toward his seat.

The guests were dumbfounded and frightened. He was even more careful to not make a sound or show his incisors. They were very large and he had spent the last few minutes in his room attempting to hide them better. Because of their size, the tips extended just beneath his lip. It was impossible to hide any part of this form.

Everyone stared, but he spotted her at the end, making the ordeal less difficult. Oryn focused his attention solely on her and let that draw him confidently closer. When he reached his seat, he took a small bow to the head of the table.

The people were stunned by the sight of the animal's bowing and were even more alarmed as King Lorvan nodded in polite answer. Why would the king invite a creature to be at his side? No sooner did he seat himself, than everyone started to chatter again like chickens in a coop.

The king turned to him. "I'm very pleased you could come, Sir Oryn."

Knowing any words would come as snarls or a growl, he nodded.

Adwen ignored odd looks and made a soft growl that no one else could hear. "We're still alive, aren't we?"

As quiet as possible, he answered with a low growl of his own. "You are merciless with your commands of late."

Surrounding guests stared when she giggled at his upset expression. They were oblivious to their conversation.

While they exchanged discreet words, the king overheard a conversation a short distance along the table. Two guests slandered Oryn openly and he called them out.

"Speak up if you have something to say regarding my guests of honor!" Everyone fell silent as he suddenly didn't seem so old. "They have traveled far and done much on your behalf! Do not insult my guests again." They were quiet and he clapped for the feast to begin.

Then the king was about to drink from his cup, and Adwen caught his attention.

Bart and the countess watched as she took it from his hand and had a sip. Setting it aside, she began to cough. Using a napkin to cover her mouth, when she stopped coughing, there was red liquid on the cloth. She folded the napkin before offering her own goblet. "You might want my cup, Your Highness. It's not poisoned."

He accepted the wine and nodded appreciatively before taking a drink.

Those who saw were frightened. Someone tried to poison the king, but his strange guest was unfazed by the serum.

"Where did you last see Toth? Is he busy somewhere?"

King Lorvan smiled. "Last I saw he was waist-deep in a stack of scrolls."

She laughed. "He'll be at it all night!"

The vast majority of the guests were secretive with their talk. Oryn wished he couldn't hear them so easily. Bart was studying him. When their eyes met, the baron smiled and seemed to accept him as he was.

Meanwhile, the countess staved off a fainting spell. She avoided glancing at her right-side guest, fanning her face rigorously. But curiosity got the better when she saw movement. His tail flicked suddenly, startling her. In a flash, she went back to fanning her wrinkled face, struggling to stay conscious.

Oryn began to loathe the situation even more. Many were ignorant fools while the baron's type were the minority. This dinner party was a disaster waiting to happen.

Adwen growled again and the baron noticed, but didn't know what to make of her sound.

"So, do you know where they are yet?"

Confused by the question, Oryn growled. "What?"

"Can't you smell them?"

Sniffing for anything out of the ordinary, his nose was bombarded by aromas of food and human bodies. Then a hint of something else came. It was rot. He became alert.

"Once they attack, protect the king. There are only two."

He gave a nod.

The dining hall was full of anticipation for an unknown interruption. The hushed and feasting guests could feel a strain in the air. Adwen and Oryn were the only ones who refused eat. When the interruption came, they were ready.

The tapestries behind the king moved. Adwen rose from her chair, dress rippling into to battle garments while Oryn turned toward the smell of blood and decay.

Two vampires pounced from behind the tapestries. And before anyone else could react, the strange guests of honor leaped to stand between the king and the undead assailants. Adwen gripped one by the throat and Oryn snatched the other into a huge choke hold. Everyone gasped and the countess fainted. The sinister things screeched, hungry for blood, angry at being caught.

She sneered at the vampire as it shrieked. Whatever part of him touched her was burned to a crisp.

"You will die! You will die with the rest of them, Heir of the Never Born!" Then he fell silent, disintegrating into ashes within her grasp.

The other fought against Oryn. Fear drove the undead's urge to resist, but he could not escape.

The brown hound warrior's grip was too strong as he snarled at the vampire. "Hold still or there shall be more pain for you!"

The creature stopped struggling, locking eyes with Adwen.

"I have a few questions for you."

In a defiant retort, the vampire swore in a harsh, eerie language that none but Adwen understood. Her eyes flashed gold and she changed into hound form, snarling angrily at the frightened vampire.

"You dare to threaten me in the demon tongue?" Then she showed her fangs and gazed deep into his black eyes.

The human guests were even more alarmed by her than Oryn and the vampire. Only the king watched with interest. She was more powerful than imagined.

The vampire was paralyzed while she looked through him. Once her power released the undead, he gasped, terrified.

The snarl faded from Adwen, giving way to pity and she shrank into woman form.

He hissed and cried out, "You saw! You know I won't tell you anything!"

Adwen shook her head sadly. "All I want is their names. I cannot take back what's happened to you, but I can help a little." While he continued to be defiant, everyone watched her lean in close and whisper. Only Oryn heard her. "I can give death without destruction."

The creature's eyes widened. When a vampire was destroyed, their soul was obliterated; there be no afterlife. He couldn't believe her and moaned as a tear of blood ran down his face. "You lie." Another red tear fell as he watched her reassure him with a smile.

Moving closer, she listened as he shared the knowledge. "Thank you. I didn't need the names. I wanted to see if you deserved better. Are you at peace with that?"

The vampire gave a joyful sob. "Yes, I forgive your trick."

At her bidding, Oryn hesitantly released the crying vampire, watching him kneel at Adwen's feet. She held an open palm over his head. The jubilant smile he wore grew and she soothed, "This will not hurt. I promise."

The light in her palm glowed in the form of a small flower. The white blossom shined. As it bloomed, a bright burst splashed over the creature on his knees. He was finally free from the thirst. His body was instantly turned to dust and drawn out the veranda by a wisp of wind.

Adwen pondered beside the king and turned to explain the situation. "You can all relax. You're safe. While I was wandering the halls today I overheard the plans for this attack on the king. As you should know, this entire structure is protected by many kinds of magic. The vampires could not have gotten inside without help... from some of you."

The guests were outraged and a few got to their feet. "Your Highness, we've had enough trouble from these animals! Call the knights!"

The baron had Adwen's back and replied angrily, "Shut your cowardly lips! They both just saved the king's life and more than likely your own, so sit down and let them be! The knights are at Sir Oryn's beck and call so summoning them would be foolish anyhow!"

Adwen was thankful for the support. "There are only two among you responsible. These men struck a deal with the Undead King of Mortigad. When they are revealed, I will let them explain themselves. If you don't want me to expose you personally, stand up."

A few moments passed. Everyone looked to one another, waiting to see the despicable culprits. And before Adwen could call the first name, the man beside the baron got to his feet, quivering like a leaf under the king's gaze. Though Adwen and Oryn stared, it was the king's wrath he feared.

Disappointed and surprised, King Lorvan asked, "Markel? What is the meaning of this? What compelled you to strike such a deal?"

"To protect my family, my home and everything else within my lands. My end of the bargain was to see you made into an undead; your life for our families' lives. I couldn't stand the thought of my children being ripped to pieces."

When he fell silent and sat, Adwen called out again. "Will the last man have a little honor? You've been caught. You know there is no way out. Stand up." There was no answer, so she cried aloud, "Stand up, Gamelan."

A guest slowly stood near the far end of the table and everyone glared.

His face was sallow and eyes sunken in age. Angrily, he glared at King Lorvan. "Damn you, you blue-eyed fool. I did what I had to for this kingdom. You've been secretly harboring inhuman beings as servants in Castle Gailarien when they should be turned over to the order. Not only that, you show your true stupidity by siding with animals! These mongrels will only bring chaos! Look at them! They can't possibly be trusted! Our king is a fool!"

"It is you who are the fool to think they are damned," called the voice of the High Elder. He stood and looked disappointed with the man. "Lady Adwen is as far from darkness as one can get without being a Light Spirit. She is the Heir of the Master Knight. The vampire addressed her as the Heir of the Never Born. That was the title the enemies of Darien called him by. I am guilty for misgivings myself, but this truly is the heir of Darien the Master Knight."

Adwen turned to the king. "These men are under your rule. What would you like to do with them?"

King Lorvan thought deeply and stood. "You are guilty of the crime of cowardice. Both of you have betrayed everyone in this room and this kingdom." Turning to Markel, he frowned. "Your sentence is harsh, but shall fit the crime. First you are to be confined to the dungeons. After that, you shall learn courage in the face of adversity. I give you to the High Elder to put into training as a knight. Your family shall be protected while you are away."

Markel's face blanched at being left to the mercy of the Order.

Then King Lorvan rounded on Gamelan. "But you have no compassion. Bigotry shall no longer be tolerated. In this time of growing darkness we cannot afford the hunting of inhuman beings. They are kin with us because we call this land home. We must band together or fall to the tide of shadows. The only one who may give us time is Lady Adwen, the Tame One."

Heads turned at the name and one cried, "She is a wild brute! She cannot be the heir! How can the beast be trusted when she runs rampant, terrorizing farmers?"

The baron yelled back, "Those are rumors from frightened idiots, dolt!"

Then the man cried out again, "She is a monster!"

Clouds began to blot out the sky. Oryn yelled at the top of his lungs when he got his human voice and form.

"Imbeciles!"

Everyone including the king and Adwen stared.

Bangs fell into his red face as he was filled with contempt. Through trying to hide the glow of his wild eyes, he glowered.

"You pompous loons sit all day, ruffling feathers without a clue as to what a real monster is! I have faced true evil and to confuse this..." He pointed an angry finger at Adwen. "...with a monster is of the most witless thinking I have ever run across! I have seen her shed blood for your sakes. She wishes to defend you with her very existence while you sit drinking wine, mocking her, slandering her and doing all you can to drive her away! You don't even know what it is to bleed! How dare you! How dare --"

Adwen cut him off. *"Enough!"*

Oryn quickly fell silent. All sense was dashed from his mind when the man called her that word. She didn't deserve the ill treatment and they had no right to say such foul things aloud. He felt sick with rage at their incompetence.

She was patient with the seated and silent guests. In a strong, confident voice, she soothed their fear. They heard the truth within the power of her voice.

"Call me what you want. There is no way to make you accept me, but I can promise this: I will fight. Whether you call me your ally or not, I will fight with everything I have. Whether you want this to be what it is, this is the beginning of a war. Come after me with torches and spears if you think I'm your enemy, but I am the heir and I will stand between you and the shadows creeping closer. Harm me, hurt me or push me aside, but I will still be here and I will fight for you."

The people remained hushed. Each face was content, yet fearful.

The king spoke up. "Lady Adwen is right, but this dinner may continue if you are willing to feast with the heir, Sir Oryn and myself. Further business shall be continued tomorrow when everyone is rested from this night's excitement. Who is willing to share a table with the Heir of the Master Knight?"

To Adwen's complete surprise, almost the whole assembly

nodded. Then she was not surprised at all when the baron raised a glass.

"To the Tame One! Let her travels and many battles bring peace to our lands!"

With the exception of the traitors, everyone raised their glass. "The Tame One."

King Lorvan instructed the young man at the door to summon guards to take away the traitors.

Adwen found the focus to return to her seat while making her clothes change into the wonderful gown.

Oryn soon joined, watching her blush uncontrollably under the baron's beaming smile. She was still unaccustomed to such recognition.

Beside him the countess was coming to and saw him as a man. She didn't dare say a word, but returned quietly to her meal. Everyone was so calm in feasting that she thought she had only passed out and dreamed of all the strange happenings. Too embarrassed to ask such a silly question, she didn't interrupt as he was gazing at Adwen.

Adwen was going to do great things, Oryn thought. Demons were rising. They had seen the Red Cult Witches, but not tangled with their infamous founder. Eventually they would meet the white-eyed demon, Sycan.

The demon was the last of the first six werewolves; the body of a wild wolf infused with a demon. He was somewhere, plotting for whoever he was serving, if not himself. The last of the first six was waiting and Oryn smiled. He could hardly wait to see her fell the terrible demon, along with the rest of them.

Chapter 48
A NEW DAWN

Wind rolled across the high walls. It tousled Oryn's short brown hair while he stared contently at the eastern horizon. He almost forgot what the sunrise from atop the fortress looked like when everything was hushed and calm. The sky was gold. Drifting clouds were painted champagne. Leaning more heavily on the stones, he felt empty of worry. Each morning when able, he would beat the rooster's call to see the first light shine over the forests and hills. His master had shown him this place.

The wind blew in his face and he could not smell Toth coming up the passage behind. He suddenly heard the half-elf chuckle.

"They said I'd find you here." Glancing off at the picturesque view of the land, he added, "I heard of your outburst at the dinner. You were that angry when they called her a monster?"

He didn't say a word, gazing at the sun. The light washed over him, bringing a feeling of peace.

Toth looked as well. "Adwen shall want to depart in a few hours. She's meeting with the king. Once they're finished, her phoenix shall deliver the treaties. Is there anything you must do before it comes time to depart?"

At last he turned and discovered Toth was wearing a lavish set of silk robes and sporting a real eye-patch. "I have only to bid the men farewell and fetch my sword." Oryn shook his head. "Those robes shall not do well for traveling."

Amused, Toth smiled. "I'll not be joining you. The king has asked me to be his new advisor and bodyguard. You shall be traveling alone with her. The king needs better protection and the things you'll be facing are beyond me."

Oryn understood. To reassure his friend, he replied, "I

shall keep a better watch over her. You needn't fear me repeating my mistakes." Even quieter, he murmured, "And there is no need to fear my pursuing her in your absence. I would not try to take her from you."

At first Toth was abashed. "Take her from me? No, no, my friend. I do not take to Adwen that way! She is like a good sister and friend. Why would you say..." But when Oryn shot him a look Toth noticed for first time.

"You love her."

Troubled, Oryn dropped his gaze. "Do I? I haven't the experience to know." He turned away to face the sun.

"Why did I not see this sooner? You've been acting so strange since her return. Rash actions in the desert, your inability to stop staring at her. And there's how much you've been sighing. You've really fallen for the heir of Darien Andredan!"

With his back to the half-elf advisor, Oryn became disgruntled. "I am glad my foolhardy infatuation is entertainment for you."

Toth rapped a hand on his friend's shoulder. "Real love is not a foolhardy thing. I'm sure she can forgive you."

Oryn swiftly rounded on him with a dangerous gleam in his eyes. "She must not know and you shall not divulge this!"

Taking the hand back, Toth assured him, "Do not worry! I have no intention of telling. I think it is only right if you were to do the confessing. Either that or she will uncover the truth herself. There is no chance of your hiding this secret forever."

Looking over the wall and bowing his head, the knight grumbled, "I am more than aware of the fact. There is no need to remind me of the particulars." Sighing and running fingers through his hair, he asked, "Then what shall I do? Now is not the time for awkward confessions. I am but a servant to do her biding, nothing more."

Toth shook his head. "I have only one piece of advice: mind your anger. Take the dinner as an example. I have seen how far you are willing to go to defend her, but being protective has its limits. Watch your actions and your emotions closely or you're liable to make some very foolish mistakes. Do you understand what could happen if you lost your temper with an aggressive human? You could kill them with a flick of your wrist."

Alarmed by the warning, Oryn snapped back, "I am quite aware of that as well!"

"Then I am certain you shall fare well. Stop hating yourself so much. This is a fresh start! Take advantage of the freedom it brings. Let the past go."

The sun rose beyond the horizon and Oryn grew sick of allowing his own thoughts to torment him. He stood to address the king's adviser. "I thank you for your counsel, but now I must prepare. You shall do well as the king's ear."

"You shall do even better as her ear in my absence."

Oryn gave a glimmer of a smile. Nodding, he left for the passage, but the king's advisor stayed to watch the land grow brighter.

Oryn found many of his comrades waiting in the armory.

Brack smiled and greeted him by the far lockers with a pained salute.

Returning the gesture, Oryn prompted, "How are your injuries?"

Getting to his feet was far more arduous. "I shall last at the least to see you off."

"Your new captain should discipline the men better. But if he lets them falter like this, I shall have no choice but to discipline him personally. What has become of Darek? I have seen almost every face except his."

Brack turned serious. "He lives, but is no longer with the order. Darek, Sir Peregrine and I quested in the lost roads. We were cornered by werewolves. Darek was almost marked. It was the narrowest escape I've ever seen. Only Sir Peregrine was close enough and Darek did not see one coming. Just before the fangs could bite our captain severed his arm in the nick of time. We only just escaped with our lives."

Disappointed by the misfortune, Oryn asked, "Where is he now?"

"Who knows? He mentioned going home to be with family, but I haven't the faintest idea where that is. East, I think."

While they were conversing, Oryn heard a conversation between two men across the room. They sat side by side on a bench, talking about him. A sudden urge crossed his mind and he couldn't help but think a bit of Adwen had rubbed off during their travels.

Raglan scolded his sibling. "That's not the beast that fought and saved us in the temple, you dolt! It was executed at dawn and then the Tame One brought Sir Oryn a few hours later. Someone has been feeding you funny lies to show you for a fool!"

They were brothers by blood and shared the same messy black hair. Dynic had a much younger face and replied, "No, it is the truth. Why else would the elders attempt to condemn him the same day he returned?"

"Because he vanished and never returned until more than a year passed! For the sake of the white oak, he is not the sword-wielding beast. And stop glancing, Dynic! He'll know we're discussing him!"

Raglan failed to notice what his younger brother had. Oryn glanced their way and was taking up a very sharp sword from a set of training weapons. Drawing the deadly thing from the rack, he studied the weight and dynamics carefully.

Disturbed, Dynic murmured, "I think he can hear us speaking."

"He's on the far side of a room full of other jabbering mouths. His ears cannot hear our speech over theirs. For the final time, he is not an inhuman being!"

The sword came between their faces and plunged into the wooden cupboard. It stuck and stayed while the two cried out in surprise and fell over.

Most knights drew their swords in anticipation of a threat. Every eye fell on Sir Oryn as they realized he had thrown the long blade. They watched him stroll across the room to the brothers on the ground. His emerald eyes were glowing, filled with an energy they were not accustomed to seeing in him. They couldn't discern if he were angry or amused.

"Gentlemen. When danger is near knights draw swords, men stand their ground, and fools... fall on their backsides." Oryn smiled at the dumbfounded men staring up in dismay.

Everyone burst out and rolled with laughter as one cried through guffaws, "It is a miracle! Sir Oryn has made a jest!"

The merriment only increased as he helped both knights to their feet. Red in the face with embarrassment, they saluted and wondered if they might still be in danger.

He eyed them with increasing interest. "You are the two who nearly gutted each other during the attempt to slay me, are you not?"

Raglan was silent while Dynic requested with an upheld finger, "If you could excuse me a moment, sir." Then he swiftly smacked the back of his older brother's head, messing his dark hair.

Raglan took the hit and grunted at the sting.

Entertained by their bond, Oryn asked, "What are your names? You shall both be the first I take into training upon my return."

"My name is Raglan, sir," announced the messed-haired older brother.

"And I am Dynic, sir. It's an honor to meet you rather than kill you. And thank you for not letting us end ourselves before we could properly meet."

"You may retract that when your training begins. Speak with the dragon slayer Virgule if you wonder at my meaning. Perhaps he could give you safe advice for the ring. Good day to you." He bid them farewell and left to finish saying good-byes to closer fiends.

They saluted as he turned to go. But when he was far enough away, Raglan gave Dynic a vengeful slug in the arm, deadening it. Then he chuckled. "That's what you get, little brother."

"This is the only thing they requested in exchange for an alliance?"

"Yes it is. It's the only thing they want."

In a quiet study, they read over and discussed the treaties. He seemed troubled and Malik was perched on the arm of a chair, patiently waiting for his task. Reading once more to be sure he was translating correctly, the king's brow furrowed.

"Is something wrong?"

"In a manner. How am I to do this with no means with which to do it?"

Adwen shrugged. "I'm sure we can figure something out."

King Lorvan sighed and sat back in his seat. "Free trade."

"It seems like a small price to me. What do you really have to lose that's more than that?"

"Making trade with foreign peoples will eventually lead to conflicts and a loss of old traditions on all sides. I doubt any of my forefathers would have wanted to sign these."

She and Malik stared, beginning to wonder if he would agree to the terms.

"I have always been rather different from them. I see change as an opportunity. After everything is said and done, they shall have to forgive me."

While Adwen smiled the phoenix ruffled his feathers and squawked. "So indecisive!"

With a swift quill, King Lorvan drew out his rolling signature. "There you have it, Lady Adwen. The alliance is complete. And thank you, Malik, for delivering these precious documents."

The firebird chortled. "It is a small task compared to watching over fifty elders!" Malik scrunched down in displeasure at the thought. When Adwen giggled he screeched in retort. "What is so funny about nest-sitting old men?"

"Nothing." She stifled the laughter and pretended to forget about it. "So what am I supposed to do? This turned out to be pretty difficult and I was trying to do was deliver a few papers. What now, Your Highness?"

As the king rolled the scrolls tight for the firebird, he answered, "The villages to the east must be liberated. Defend all fronts until the armies can be mustered. Our peoples need you to fight on their behalf as promised."

Malik flitted to the table, fitting his talons around the scrolls. Then the bird thrust himself into the air and vanished in a ring of fire.

The flames dissipated and the king said in a much graver tone, "I have this warning, Adwen. With these silenced villages and towns, I fear the worst. If a cloud of darkness hangs over a plot of land, demons are surely present. In order to restore the sun's reach, destroy as many as possible. Beware, Adwen Andredan, for I fear you shall encounter demon commanders."

She was anxious, but put on a confident expression and bowed. "Thank you so much, Your Highness. And before I go, I'm glad I could be part of your prank."

"Prank?"

"When there was poison in your cup."

The king chuckled. "I'm glad you suggested the idea. Showing that someone like you is among us is sure to deter a few future attempts on my life. Thank you." He bowed his head and she left the study.

Once the doors closed her out, he chuckled again and shook his head. He had seen the way Oryn was watching her at the dinner. He wondered just how long she would go without noticing.

Oryn waited in the Hall of Knights wearing a stronger hooded jacket of cotton and cow hide with a tough pair of traveling boots. The Rose Thorne was across his back. When she arrived the same strange look of admiration was in his face.

She had dismissed it long ago as admiration of her identity as the heir. He looked happy so she wasn't in a hurry to tell him off for staring.

Approaching, she smiled. "Are you ready for this?"

Disguising the thrill of being near her with enthusiasm for the adventure, he nodded. "Ready enough."

Upon exiting the main gates, guards at the entrance saluted. Adwen was much more at ease to be away from the elders and knights.

As they walked the streets, Adwen mused, "Malik sure is going to have his work cut out for him."

Shrugging the weapon higher on his shoulder, he smiled. "Indeed, he will." Without thinking, he blurted out, "Was your rest well enough?" As soon as the words left his lips he quietly cursed himself.

She was not alerted. "Pretty good actually. The bed was too soft, but the window sill was cool and cozy with that breeze. I had a few dreams, but they weren't nearly as weird as the ones I back at the inn."

"What were they of, if I may ask?"

She blushed furiously. "I... don't feel like talking about it. One was really weird. Let's just leave it at that!"

A small smile came to him. He already knew what she thought she dreamt.

Word had spread to Plexus and people now showed smiles and waved. Some called good wishes down from open windows as she blushed with embarrassment. Oryn cherished her sweet modesty. Their walk to the outer wall was so uplifting that she was able to forget the elders completely.

Feeling optimistic and growing more excited, she grinned at her reserved friend.

"Race yah to the fields!" And she darted off laughing.

A wild glow lit in his eyes and he couldn't refuse her challenge. A sly expression splayed across his face as he sprinted.

Adwen knew he couldn't match her so she smiled broadly and slowed enough for him to gain. In moments, they were neck and neck, running towards the first field.

Beyond the walls of the city lay acres of rolling hills of green grass and wild star blossoms. Adwen poured on the speed to pull away. Reaching the top of the first hill, she leaped and went tumbling down the back side, laughing gleefully. All behind her flower pollen was tossed to the wind, drifting off as a sweet cloud that smelled of nectar.

Oryn skidded and hopped on his heels to the bottom where she lay still and quiet. Standing over her, he thought she might be unconscious, but she looked up and laughed. He couldn't help but shake his head. Then she flipped up onto all fours, changing into hound form, flicked her tail and barking.

She raced off, and as before, he tried to catch her. Once he had, she stayed at his pace. The wind in their faces was intoxicating; pulling them, seducing them to run. Bright sunshine cast on their backs while ahead loomed black clouds over distant trees. A storm was brewing.

The knight cast aside old worries, letting himself cherish these moments. For the first time, he felt so alive he couldn't think of a place he would rather be. As he stole another glance, for the first time in his life he felt free.